The
JULIANTHES

(The Weathered Isles)

•Pireth
Vanguard

of
Corona

ዉ⌒⌒
Pireth
Dancard

Pireth
Tulme
Tinson

Macomber

The Broken Coast

THE DEMON APOSTLE

THE
DEMON
APOSTLE

THE BALLANTINE PUBLISHING GROUP • NEW YORK

A Del Rey® Book
Published by The Ballantine Publishing Group

Copyright © 1999 by R. A. Salvatore

http://www.randomhouse.com/delrey/

LIBRARY OF CONGRESS CATALOGING-IN-PUBLICATION DATA
Salvatore, R.A., 1959–
The demon apostle / R.A. Salvatore.—1st ed.
p.   cm.
"A Del Rey book"—T.p. verso.
ISBN 0-345-39153-5 (hc : alk. paper)
I. Title.
PS3569.A462345D45   1999
813'.54—dc21   98-48574
CIP

Endpaper maps by Laura Maestro

Manufactured in the United States of America

First Edition: March 1999

10   9   8   7   6   5   4   3   2   1

This one's for Gary, the purest warrior.

CONTENTS

CONTENTS

PART ONE

▼

THE ROAD HOME

Winter is settling on the land, Uncle Mather, but somehow, fittingly, it seems quiet and soft, as if the season will be gentle this year, as if Nature herself, like all the folk of the land, is in need of respite. I do not know how I recognize that this will prove true, but I cannot deny that which my ranger instincts tell me. Perhaps it is just that I am in need of respite, Uncle Mather, and I know that Pony is, as well. Perhaps my belief that the season will be gentle is no more than hopeful thinking.

Still, Pony, Juraviel, and I heard few reports of fighting, even of any sightings of goblins, powries, or giants all during our return trip from St.-Mere-Abelle. Our journey north from Palmaris to the sister towns of Caer Tinella and Landsdown was without incident, with the only substantial garrison in the region being a contingent of Kingsmen sent from Ursal to reinforce Palmaris. They subsequently struck out north of the city to help secure the resettlement of the handful of communities in the region north of Palmaris' farms.

We have heard of few skirmishes in the weeks since our arrival; mostly it has been quiet, comfortably so. Tomas Gingerwart, who leads the three hundred daring settlers, and Shamus Kilronney, captain of the Kingsmen brigade, speak hopefully of a return to normalcy by the time winter relinquishes its grip on the land.

A return to normalcy?

They do not understand. Many have died, but many will be born to take their places; many homes have been burned to the ground, but they will be rebuilt. And so in the coming months the region may outwardly resemble what we once knew as our "normal" lives.

But I have trod this road before, Uncle Mather, after the first sacking of Dundalis—before I came to know the Touel'alfar, before I found you—and I know the scars of this war will be lasting. It is in the hearts of the survivors where the mark of the demon dactyl will remain, in the grief of those who lost friends and family, the shock of those displaced, the pain of those who return to their former villages to find a blackened field. Though they do not yet know it, the very definition of what is normal has changed. The aftermath of war may be more painful than the fighting itself.

Would I see the world the same way had the goblins not come to Dundalis those years ago? Not only was the course of my life changed by my rescue by the Touel'alfar and the training they gave me, but so were my perspectives on reality itself—my view of duty, of community, even of mortality, that greatest of human mysteries.

And so these people are changed in ways they do not yet understand.

My greatest concern is for Pony. The first destruction of Dundalis—of which she and I were the only survivors and in which her entire family was slaughtered—nearly broke her, sent her careening down a road that led her to Palmaris and a new life, one in which she could not even remember her tragic past. Only the love of her adoptive parents saw her through that dark time; and now they, too, have become victims of evil. Tragedy has visited Pony again.

When we ran out of St.-Mere-Abelle, our mission there complete, our friend Bradwarden freed, she nearly turned around and went back. Had she re-entered that structure, gemstones in hand, she would have wreaked devastation before meeting her ultimate end.

And she didn't care, Uncle Mather, for herself or for those she might have killed. So blind was her rage at the discovery of the mutilated corpses of her dead adoptive parents that she was ready to destroy St.-Mere-Abelle and all in it, to destroy all the world, I fear, in one mighty outpouring of rage.

She has been quiet since we left the abbey and crossed the Masur Delaval into lands more familiar. Setting Belster O'Comely in place as the new proprietor of Fellowship Way has helped to calm her, I believe, helped her to find a bit of "normalcy" in her life once more.

But I fear for her and must watch over her.

For myself, I know not what the lasting emotional effects of this latest struggle will be. As with all the survivors, I will grow from the losses, will find new insights as I contemplate the nearness of death. I hold few fears now. Somehow, amid all the carnage, I have found an inner peace. I know not what waits after death, Uncle Mather, and I know that I cannot know.

A simple, foolish sentence that sounds, and yet it strikes my heart and soul as a profound revelation. What I understand now is the inevitability of death, whether through battle, disease, or simply age. And because I understand and accept that, I no longer fear life. How strange that is! It seems to me now that no problem is too daunting and no obstacle too imposing, for all that I have to do is remind myself that one day I will be no more, that my body is ultimately food for the worms, and I am not afraid to try. Many times recently I have been asked to stand before hundreds of men and women and explain to them the course I think we should all follow. And while to many people—to a younger Elbryan, perhaps—that would have been uncomfortable—fearing how the audience might view my words, fearing that I would do something foolish, like trip and fall down before them all—now that nervousness seems a petty, stupid thing.

All I need do when so asked is to remind myself that one day it will not matter, that one day I will be gone from this world, that one day, centuries hence, someone might find my bones—and the embarrassing stumble, should it ever happen, seems like little to fear indeed.

So the land is at peace, and Elbryan is at peace, and greater indeed will that peace become if I can find a way to calm Pony's emotional turmoil.

—ELBRYAN WYNDON

❖ I ❖

Passion for Life

The room was dark, the curtains drawn, but the ranger could see the gray of the predawn sky around their lace-trimmed edges. Instinctively he reached behind him, seeking the comforting, warm feel of his lover's body, but she was not there.

Elbryan rolled over, surprised. Pony was not in the bed, nor even in the room, he realized as his eyes adjusted to the gloom. With a groan, for he was not accustomed to sleeping in any bed, let alone a soft one—and this one was especially pillowy, for the folk of the towns had given the ranger the finest bed in Caer Tinella—Elbryan rolled off the bed to his feet, straightened, and stretched. He went to the window, noting that Pony's fine sword was not beside his own. That did not alarm him, though; as he came more fully awake, he could guess easily enough where she was.

When he pulled aside the curtains, he found that it was later than he had believed. The sky was thick with gray clouds, but he could tell that the top half of the sun was already peeking over the horizon. And the days this time of year were shortest of all, for they were now in the month of Decambria, the twelfth and last, and the winter solstice was less than three weeks away.

A scan of the forest north of the town showed the ranger the expected firelight. He went through a series of slow, exaggerated movements then, sliding low to the floor then back up, arms wide stretching, as he limbered up his six-foot three-inch, two-hundred-and-ten-pound, muscular frame. Then he pulled on his clothes and cloak quickly, wanting to join his love, and took up the magnificent Tempest, his elven-forged sword, the sword of his uncle Mather, the emblem of his position as ranger.

His room was on the northern edge of town, as he had requested, and so he saw few of the townsfolk as he rushed away—past a corral and the skeletal remnant of the barn he and Juraviel had burned on one escape from the monsters who had previously held Caer Tinella—and out into the forest.

A blanket of snow had settled thickly about the region only a week ago, but the weather had turned warmer since then. Now a low fog clung above the ground, blurring the trails, hiding the leafless branches. But the ranger knew the small, sheltered field he and Pony had chosen for their morning ritual: the elven sword dance, *bi'nelle dasada.*

He came upon her quietly, both not wanting to disturb her and also to glimpse her at the dance in its truest form.

And then he saw her and his heart was softened, and all his body felt warm.

She was naked, her feminine frame veiled only by the morning mists, her strong muscles glistening as they moved through the perfectly balanced interplay of *bi'nelle dasada,* weaving a wondrous dance of balance and motion. Elbryan could hardly believe how much he loved her, how much the sight of her thrilled and moved him. Her thick blond hair was longer now, reaching several inches below her shoulders and trailing her with every turn, as the sparkle of her blue eyes seemed to lead her. She held Defender, a fine, slender sword, its silverel blade shining in the dull morning light or sparkling suddenly with an orange flare whenever it caught the reflection of the campfire she had lit nearby.

The ranger crouched and continued to admire her, thinking it ironic, for it used to be Pony who spied on him at *bi'nelle dasada* in the days when she desired to learn the intricacies of the dance. How well she had studied! His admiration was twofold—one part of him impressed by the beauty of her movements, the level of harmony she had achieved in so short a time, and the other based in simple lust. He and Pony had not been intimate in several weeks, not since before the end of summer on the road to St.-Mere-Abelle to rescue Bradwarden, when she had unexpectedly broken their vow of abstinence and seduced him. Elbryan had tried to repeat that passionate scene several times since, but Pony had steadfastly refused. Looking at her now, he was nearly overwhelmed. Her allure was undeniable, the smoothness of her skin, the soft curves of her honed body, the movements of her hips, her legs, so shapely and strong. Elbryan could not imagine anyone more beautiful or enticing. He realized that he was breathing more heavily, that he was suddenly very warm—and though the day was not cold for the season, the air was surely not warm!

Embarrassed, feeling then that he was invading Pony's privacy, the ranger pushed the lustful thoughts from his mind and fell fully into the meditative calm afforded him by his years of discipline with the Touel'alfar. Soon he left Elbryan Wyndon behind, taking on the calm attitude of Nightbird, the warrior title given him by the elves.

He untied his cloak and let it fall to the ground, then quietly pulled off the rest of his clothing. Taking Tempest in hand, he walked from the brush. So deep in concentration was Pony that she did not notice his approach until he was within a stride of her. She turned to face him, startled, and did not match his smile with her own.

Her expression, jaw set firm and blue eyes blazing intently, caught Nightbird off guard. He was even more surprised when Pony moved suddenly, throwing her sword into the ground near his feet so forcefully that its tip dug inches into the hardened earth.

"I—I did not mean to disturb you," the ranger stammered, at a loss, for he and Pony had shared *bi'nelle dasada* for weeks, had sword-danced together since he had taught it to her, the two working as one that they might bring their fighting styles and movements into perfect harmony. Also, both of them had come to substitute the sword dance for a different form of intimacy, the one that they had agreed they could not now share.

Pony did not reply, except to halve the distance between them, staring up at him, breathing hard, sweat glistening on her neck and shoulders.

"I will leave if you desire," the ranger started to say, but was cut short as Pony reached up suddenly, grabbing the hair on the back of his head, moving her body against his, and pulling his face down, while she came up on tiptoe, locking him in a hungry kiss.

Tempest still in hand, the ranger's arms went around her, but loosely, unsure where this might be heading.

Pony showed no signs of relenting, her kiss growing more passionate, hungrier, with each passing second. The meditative state was long gone from Elbryan; no more was he the elven warrior. Still, he kept his wits about him enough finally to push Pony back a bit, to break the kiss and stare at her questioningly. For though they had proclaimed their love for each other openly, though they were—in the eyes of all who knew them; in their hearts; and truly, they believed, in the eyes of God—husband and wife, they had vowed to abstain from marital relations for fear that Pony, whose duties were no less demanding and dangerous than Elbryan's, would become pregnant.

Elbryan started to ask Pony about that pact of abstinence, but she interrupted him with a growl. She reached over and pulled Temptest from his grasp and threw the sword to the ground, then went back at Elbryan, locking him in a deep kiss, her hands roaming about his back, and then lower.

Elbryan hadn't the strength to protest. He wanted Pony so very badly, loved Pony so very deeply. Still locked in the passionate kiss, she slid down to the ground, pulling her lover atop her. The ranger wanted this moment to last, wanted to savor the beauty of lovemaking with Pony, so he tried to slow things down.

Pony roughly pushed him over onto his back and chased him all the way, urgently, hungrily, growling with every determined movement. Then they were joined and all was motion and sound. The stunned Elbryan fought hard to remove his thoughts from the tumult, trying to make some sense of it all. Always before, their lovemaking had been gentle and warm, full of words and teasing caresses. Now, it was physical, even angry; and the grunting, growling sounds escaping Pony's lips were as filled with rage as with desire. Elbryan knew and understood that she wasn't angry with him, but rather that she was releasing her anger at all the world *through* him. This was her release from, or denial of, all the horror and pain. And so Elbryan allowed her to lead him in this most intimate of dances, tried to give her what she most needed from him, both physically and emotionally.

Even when they were done, wrapped in Pony's cloak and in each other's arms near the small fire, there was no conversation, no questions. Too overwhelmed and too consumed by the physical release to press the issue, Elbryan dozed off, and was only half aware when Pony slipped from his grasp.

He awakened barely minutes later, to see Pony sitting in the middle of the small field beside their weapons, with Elbyran's cloak pulled tightly about her. He studied the faraway look in her eyes, the glisten of a tear on her soft cheek.

Elbryan looked up at the empty grayness of the sky, as confused as he had been when Pony had locked him in that first kiss. And she was even more confused than he, he realized. He decided that he would wait patiently for his answers, would let her come to him.

When she was ready.

An hour later, when Elbryan returned to Caer Tinella, the town was bustling with activity. The ranger came back alone, for Pony had left him on the field without a word. She had kissed him tenderly though, perhaps in apology, perhaps merely to assure him that she was all right. Elbryan had accepted that kiss as explanation enough for the present, for to him no apology was needed; but no matter what Pony did or said it would not alleviate his fears for her. Their lovemaking that morning had been necessary for Pony, comforting and freeing, but the ranger knew that the demons within his lover had not been exorcised.

He was worrying about her, wondering what more he could do to help her, as he walked to his appointment with Tomas Gingerwart.

Though Elbryan arrived early, Tomas was already waiting for him in the centrally located barn that served as the town's meeting hall. Tomas was a hardy man, not very tall but stocky and hardened from years of farming. He rose and extended his hand to Elbryan; the ranger clasped it noting that Tomas' hand was rough and his grip strong. Elbryan realized that in all the weeks he had known Tomas, this was the first time they had shared a handshake. And Tomas had a wide smile—another rarity—on his dark face.

Tomas' plans were in motion, the ranger realized.

"How fares Nightbird this fine day?" Tomas asked.

Elbryan shrugged.

"Well, I would guess," Tomas said lightly. "Your beautiful companion came through town only a few minutes before you, and from the same direction—from the northern forest." Tomas offered a wink as he finished, a good-natured gesture and not lewd, but Elbryan returned it with a scowl.

"The caravan has been sponsored," Tomas declared, clearing his throat and changing the subject. "If it wasn't so late in the year, we could depart in a few weeks."

"We must be certain that winter's grip on the land is ended," Elbryan replied.

"We?" Tomas asked with a smile. Ever since Elbryan and Pony had joined him in Caer Tinella, Tomas had been trying to persuade Nightbird to join his Timberlands-bound caravan, but the ranger had been elusive and had not committed to the journey. Tomas had pressed him hard, but fairly, though some of the sponsoring merchants would not provide their money and supplies unless the ranger agreed to lead the way.

Elbryan looked at the hopeful, crooked grin on the weatherworn face of Tomas Gingerwart and recognized that the man was his friend. "I will accompany you," he confirmed. "Dundalis was my home, and Pony's as well, and I believe that we have as great a stake in its rebuilding as any."

"But what of your duties to the Kingsmen?" Tomas asked. It was no secret that Nightbird had been working with Shamus Kilronney, captain of the Kingsmen brigade, to ensure the security of the land. Shamus and the ranger had become friends, so it was rumored, and Pony was reportedly even closer to the man.

"Captain Kilronney is convinced that the region is secure," Elbryan explained. "Pony spoke with him yesterday—and might again be with him this morning, discussing his plans for returning his brigade to the south."

Tomas nodded, but he was obviously not thrilled with the news of the soldiers' impending departure.

"She is trying to convince the captain to remain a bit longer," Elbryan went on, "perhaps through the winter, and even to accompany us farther to the north in the spring. No doubt the King desires the reopening of the Timberlands as soon as possible."

"He does indeed," Tomas replied. "The merchant Comli, my chief sponsor, is a personal friend of King Danube Brock Ursal. Comli would not be so eager to press north unless he was certain of the King's desire to reopen trade with the Timberlands."

It all seemed perfectly logical to both men. During the war, many sailing ships had been lost or damaged by powrie barrelboats, and the only timber large enough to replace masts came from the appropriately named Timberlands, the land of Dundalis, Weedy Meadow, and End-o'-the-World.

"Perhaps Comli's emissary should also speak with Captain Kilronney," the ranger suggested.

Tomas nodded. "I will see to it," he promised. "Glad I am to have Nightbird and Pony along on this dangerous journey, and every sword we can enlist will be a welcome addition. I need not explain my fears to you, for we both understand that no one has yet determined the extent of the retreat of the demon dactyl's army. We might strike out to the north only to find ten thousand goblins, giants, and powries camped by the roadside, singing their songs of cruelty and torture!"

Elbryan managed to smile at that, for he did not believe the words for a moment. There might indeed be monsters up there, but not on the scale to which Tomas alluded—not with the binding force, the physical manifestation of the demon dactyl, destroyed.

"I only wish that Roger Lockless were here and could journey with us," Tomas added.

"Belster will find him if he has returned to Palmaris," Elbryan assured him. When Elbryan and Pony had passed through Palmaris on their return from St.-Mere-Abelle, they had not only established Belster as the new proprietor of Fellowship Way but also had charged him with finding Roger and telling the young man of their latest movements once he returned from his trip with Baron Rochefort Bildeborough to speak with the King. The ranger did not doubt that Roger would rush back to Caer Tinella to join him and Pony as soon as his duties to the Baron were ended.

"I hope he returns before the beginning of Bafway," Tomas said, "for the start of the third month marks the start of our journey, unless the weather turns against us. It might be that the road will stay clear enough for him to get to us, if the weather holds."

Elbryan nodded, noting the tension on the man's face. Tomas was eager to go north, as were many others, but they were all taking this unseasonable weather too much to heart. The end of Calember had brought a fall of snow, but that had been almost completely melted by many days of warmer weather. It was important—to the King of Honce-the-Bear, to the Baron of Palmaris, to the merchants, and to men like Tomas—that once the Timberlands was free of monsters, men from Honce-the-Bear be the ones to resettle it and restore the timber trade. The Timberlands was the only area that could supply the needed logs for ships' masts. By treaty, the Timberlands was not ruled by any of the three kingdoms—Honce-the-Bear, Behren, or rugged Alpinador—but it had always served the King and merchants of Honce-the-Bear well to have the region populated predominantly by their own. Rumors had come to Caer Tinella recently that the Alpinadorans meant to settle the deserted Timberlands, and while none feared that such a development would stop the trade in the large trees, all realized that it would make the merchants of Honce-the-Bear pay more dearly.

Elbryan had not been able to confirm those rumors and, in fact, believed that they might be merely a plant by Comli or some other fearful merchant to spur the caravan northward sooner. But the ranger couldn't argue against the logic of getting back to the north. And aside from the practical considerations, there were personal ones. His father, Olwan Wyndon, had gone to Dundalis to live on the frontier, to tread places where no man had been, to view sights never seen by any man. Olwan Wyndon had taken great pride in his decision to go north and had become the unofficial leader of Dundalis.

Before the darkness awakened.

It was also near Dundalis, in a sheltered grove, that Elbryan had found the grave of Mather, his long-lost uncle—the elven-trained ranger who had come before him—and where he had earned Tempest, once Mather's sword. And in the forest near Dundalis, Elbryan had met Bradwarden the centaur, a dear friend now returned to him, it seemed, from the grave itself. And in that same forest, Bradwarden had introduced Elbryan to the magnificent black stallion, Symphony, the ranger's mount, the ranger's friend.

His ties to the region were deeply rooted. Now he felt a duty to his dead father and family to go back and help rebuild Dundalis and the other two towns, then to serve as their protector, the quiet and little-seen ranger vigilantly patrolling the forest.

"Word has it that new settlers of the northern land are to be well rewarded," Tomas remarked.

Elbryan looked at him carefully, noted how he rubbed his hands together. If Tomas wanted to go to the Timberlands to make his fortune, then Elbryan knew the man was in for a great disappointment. The life there was hard. Hunting, fishing, foraging, and farming were necessary as well as the trade in wood. No, a man did not settle in the Timberlands to get wealthy; he settled there to live in a freedom that could not be found anywhere else. Tomas could speak of being "well rewarded," but Tomas would learn, if he did not already know, that those rewards came from more than the King's gold.

"We get ahead of practical thinking," Elbryan remarked. "Resettling Dundalis and the other towns depends upon whether or not the monsters have deserted the region. If they are still encamped, it will take more than the four score you mean to bring north to unseat them."

"That is why we asked Nightbird to lead us," Tomas said with a wink, "and Pony."

"And that is why Pony is trying to convince Captain Kilronney to stay in Caer Tinella through the winter and then to come with us," Elbryan replied. "Let us hope that he agrees."

"And let us hope that he and his soldiers will not be needed," Tomas added sincerely.

"Ah, Jilseponie, how sad I am to see that the light is out of your eyes."

The melodic voice from above did not startle Pony, for she had suspected that Belli'mar Juraviel was about. She had chosen to come to this forested area south of Caer Tinella because it afforded her a view of the distant Kingsmen encampment and also with some hope of finding the elf, for

Juraviel had been away for several days, scouting the southern roads. That morning, after Pony had crossed Caer Tinella, a group of Palmaris' garrison soldiers had ridden down the road past her as she moved quietly through the shadows under the trees. The riders had already come from the village, she realized, and they were headed straight for the Kingsmen camp.

"How long will clouds fill your eyes?" Juraviel asked, fluttering his nearly translucent wings to settle on a branch at her eye level. "When will you let the sun sparkle in them again, that those around you might glory in the reflections?"

"I was thinking about my family," Pony replied. "When I lost my mother and father in Dundalis, I lost all memories and thoughts of them for years. I would not have that happen to my memories of Graevis and Pettibwa."

"But you were young then," said Juraviel, to offer some hope to the beleaguered woman. "Too young to comprehend such tragedy, and so you let the tragedy pass out of your thoughts. Too young."

"Perhaps I still am."

"But . . ." the elf started to protest, but he saw that Pony didn't blink, just kept looking absently toward the Kingsmen encampment. How sad for this young woman, who had lived for only a quarter of a century, to have lost two families! Looking at her now, Juraviel feared that her beautiful face would never brighten again.

"Tell me of the soldiers who rode in this morn," Pony bade the elf suddenly.

"Palmaris garrison," Juraviel replied, "riding hard. I shadowed them and hoped to listen to their conversation, but they did not stop or slow, and I heard not a single exchange of words."

Pony chewed her lip, staring at the distant encampment, and Juraviel understood her concern. Had these soldiers come to tell the Kingsmen that she and Elbryan were outlaws?

"Baron Bildeborough is a friend," Juraviel reminded her. "Your horse and sword are proof enough of that, even if you doubt Roger's judgment."

"I do not," Pony was quick to reply. Juraviel's point hit home; Baron Bildeborough was no friend of the Abellican Church, certainly. And Bildeborough had shown great faith in Roger by giving him Greystone and Defender, the horse and sword Roger had passed on to Pony.

"These soldiers are for the Baron, not the Church," Juraviel went on. "And with Baron Bildeborough now understanding that it was a man of the Church who murdered his beloved nephew—apparently with the blessings, even orders, of the Church hierarchy—he'll not take their side against you and Elbryan. No matter the promises of the Abellican Church leaders or the pressures from the King of Honce-the-Bear."

"Agreed," said Pony, and she turned to regard the elf. "But did you get a good look at the riders? Might Roger have been with them?"

"Only soldiers," Juraviel assured her, and he did not miss the cloud that passed over her fair face. "It is possible that Roger has not yet returned to Palmaris from Ursal."

"I only hoped," Pony replied.

"You fear for him? He is in the company of a powerful man," Juraviel pointed out, for they had been informed that Roger had gone to Ursal with Baron Bildeborough to speak with King Danube Brock Ursal himself. "Few on the western side of the Masur Delaval north of Ursal wield as much power and influence as Baron Rochefort Bildeborough."

"Except perhaps for the new abbot of St. Precious."

"But his power is just that," Juraviel replied, "new. Baron Bildeborough holds the superior position, for he has been entrenched in Palmaris for many years, the heir to a long line of leaders. So Roger should be safe enough."

The argument made sense to Pony, and her expression showed some relief.

"Yet still you want Roger back with us," the elf continued.

Pony nodded.

"You wish him to accompany the caravan to Dundalis," said Juraviel, for he had some suspicions about Pony's intentions. Like all the Touel'alfar, Belli'mar Juraviel was blessed with the ability to sit back and study a situation, to observe and to listen, and then to reason things through.

"Roger is a valuable ally. I fear for his safety and prefer that he remains with Elbryan until he has learned more about the dangers of the wide world," Pony said firmly.

Her words were spoken calmly, but perceptive Juraviel did not miss that Pony's deep-seated resentment of the Church that had evolved into absolute hatred. "With Elbryan?" he pressed. "With both of you, you mean?"

Pony gave a noncommittal shrug, and that halfhearted answer only reinforced the elf's belief that she did not mean to go north with the caravan. He let the silence linger for a long while, let Pony alone with her thoughts as she stared at the distant encampment.

"I should go to Captain Kilronney," she said finally.

"Perhaps he has been recalled to Palmaris," Juraviel offered. "There are few monsters about," he added when she looked puzzled. "A force as strong as his might better serve the King in other regions."

"There is one troublesome group of powries to the west that he wishes to destroy before he turns south," said Pony. "And, for Elbryan, I will soon ask Captain Kilronney to spend the winter in Caer Tinella and then accompany the caravan to Dundalis."

"Indeed," said the elf. "And will Jilseponie also accompany the caravan?"

His blunt question hit her hard, and she did not reply for several seconds.

"Of course, Elbryan thinks you will go," Juraviel offered, "as does Tomas Gingerwart. I heard him say as much."

"Then why would you ask—"

"Because I do not believe that you intend to make the journey," Juraviel explained. "Your eyes are turned southward. Will you not return to your home?"

Pony was caught and she knew it—she even subconsciously glanced south again. "Of course I intend to return to Dundalis," she said. "If that is where Elbryan goes, then it is my place."

"And you have no say which place you two must share?"

"Do not twist my words," she warned. "If I choose to live elsewhere, then do not doubt that Elbryan will follow me."

"And what do you choose?"

Again came the shrug. "I will return to Dundalis, but not with the caravan," Pony admitted.

Even though he had suspected as much all along, the proclamation stunned Juraviel.

"I will return to Palmaris for a time," Pony went on. "I wish to look in on Belster O'Comely and see how he fares with Fellowship Way."

"But you will have the time to go to Palmaris and see Belster, and then return before the caravan departs," Juraviel reasoned.

"I have had enough of the northland and the fighting for now," came Pony's dismissive answer.

"That may be half true," the elf replied. Pony looked at him, and saw he was wearing a knowing smile. "You believe that your fight has just begun. The Father Abbot of the Abellican Church has waged war on the family of Jilseponie, and now she means to take the war to him."

"I could not begin—" she started to reply.

"No, you could not," the elf interrupted. "Do you intend to travel back to St.-Mere-Abelle to wage war against nearly a thousand battle-trained and magic-wielding monks? Or will you attack St. Precious and their new abbot, who, according to Master Jojonah, is the finest warrior ever to venture forth from St.-Mere-Abelle? And what of Elbryan?" the elf pressed, following Pony then, for she started to walk away. "How will he feel when he learns that you deserted him, that you could not trust him to join this course you have chosen for yourself?"

"Enough!" Pony snapped, spinning to face him. "I am not deserting Elbryan."

"If you go to wage war privately, then you are."

"You know nothing about it."

"Then tell me." The simple manner in which Juraviel spoke calmed Pony considerably, reminded her that the elf was a friend, a true friend, to be trusted.

"I do not go south to wage war," she explained, "though do not doubt that I intend to repay the Abellican Church for the pain it has brought me."

A shiver coursed Juraviel's spine; he had never heard Pony sound so cold before—and he did not like it, not one bit.

"But that will wait," Pony went on. "Dundalis is the primary issue for Elbryan and for Roger, if he ever returns to us. And I know that we all must wait to discover what transpired during Baron Bildeborough's meeting with the King. Perhaps my war with the Church will not be so private after all."

"Then why do you look south?" Juraviel asked quietly.

"On the road to St.-Mere-Abelle, when I thought we would meet a dark end or that this issue—all of it—would be resolved, I seduced Elbryan."

"You are husband and wife, after all," the elf replied with a grin.

"We had made a pact of abstinence," Pony explained, "for we feared—"

"You are with child," Juraviel realized, his golden eyes opening wide.

Pony, neither with words nor expression, denied it.

"But perhaps you are wrong," Juraviel offered. "That was but a few weeks ago."

"I knew the morning after we made love," Pony assured him. "I know not if it is my work with the gemstones, the soul stone in particular, or perhaps it is merely the miracle of life itself, but I knew. And all that has happened—or more pointedly, not happened—in the ensuing weeks has shown that I am with child, Belli'mar Juraviel."

Juraviel's smile widened all the more as he considered the potential for this child, born of such parents. That smile dissipated though when Juraviel looked up to consider Pony's frown.

"You should be joyous!" he said to her. "This is an occasion for celebration and not for scowls."

"The war is not nearly at its end," Pony said. "Dundalis has yet to be reclaimed."

"A minor issue," the elf replied. "And forget your wars, Jilseponie Wyndon. Consider that which is within you the most important matter for you and Elbryan."

Pony did manage a smile at the name Jilseponie Wyndon, the first time Juraviel had ever called her that. "You'll not tell Elbryan," she said, "not about my plan to go south, and not about my . . . our child."

"He has a right to know," Juraviel started to protest.

"And so he shall know—by my words and not yours."

Juraviel dipped a respectful bow.

"I will go to Captain Kilronney," Pony explained. "Let us see what these new soldiers have come about." She walked past him, and the elf fell in behind her, to shadow her movements from the forest. If they were wrong about the new soldiers, if these riders had come north in search of two outlaws, then Juraviel would stand beside his friend.

The elf spent a long time considering that notion: his *friend*. What would Lady Dasslerond—leader of the Touel'alfar—and the others of Caer'alfar think if they understood the depth of that truth within Belli'mar Juraviel's heart? Other elves had befriended Nightbird during his stay in the elven valley, and Tuntun had become close to the man, and to Jilseponie. But always before—when Juraviel decided to go to Mount Aida with the companions to battle the demon dactyl and when afterward the elf chose to lead human refugees to the elven valley; when Dasslerond allowed those pitiful humans in that secret elven place; even when Tuntun chose to follow the expedition to Aida and ultimately to sacrifice her life—the elven choices had been made out of practicality and the prospects for gain to the elves. Now, though, if Elbryan and Pony were to be engaged in a battle, it would be a fight between humans, a fight that had nothing to do with the good of the elven folk, and Juraviel's participation in the matter would not change the outcome.

Yet he would fight with his friends—and die with his friends, if that came to pass. Indeed, the elf's choice to go to St.-Mere-Abelle to help rescue Bradwarden and Jilseponie's adoptive parents had been based wholly in friendship.

Lady Dasslerond would not approve, Juraviel knew, for this conflict between his friends and the Church was one that must be decided by the humans. Juraviel's actions then and now were not in accord with the general tenets of elven society, which placed the good of the elves above all, believing the life of a single elf worth far more than those of a thousand of another race—even humans, whom the elves did not dislike.

But Juraviel would follow Pony now, and if a fight came, he would stand and die beside his friend.

As soon as Elbryan left Tomas—the discussion ended by the tumult as the Palmaris soldiers rumbled through Caer Tinella on their way to find the Kingsmen—he started straight off to find Symphony and ride for the camp. Like Pony, he feared that the arrival of these soldiers might have something to do with the gemstones and the escape of the imprisoned centaur from St.-Mere-Abelle. Also, he assumed Pony was already meeting with Captain Kilronney. The ranger breathed a bit easier as he neared the camp's perimeter and saw no scars of explosive magic: if Pony were there and the soldiers had tried to take her, her magical barrage would likely have leveled half the encampment!

"Greetings, Nightbird!" a sentry called. Another soldier moved to take Symphony's reins, but the ranger waved him away.

"New arrivals?" he asked.

"Palmaris garrison," the soldier explained. "They are in discussion with Captain Kilronney."

"And with Jilseponie?"

"To be sure, she has not yet arrived," the soldier replied.

Elbryan directed Symphony into the encampment and was greeted warmly by all he encountered, men and women whose respect he had earned in the last couple of weeks, in the few battles the group had waged against rogue bands of monsters. Captain Kilronney's soldiers had been glad to have Nightbird—and Jilseponie!—by their side when the fighting began. The ranger, in turn, had come to know and respect these soldiers; if the new arrivals had come with malicious intent in search of him and Pony, the word had not yet spread.

The ranger's relief faded when he dismounted and entered Captain Kilronney's tent. So grave were the expressions of Kilronney and the others that Elbryan's hand went to the hilt of his sword.

"What news?" the ranger asked after a tense moment.

Kilronney eyed him squarely. The captain was taller than Elbryan by two inches, and was solidly built, though nowhere near as heavily muscled as the powerful ranger. His neatly trimmed beard and mustache were strikingly red, as was his bushy hair; and all that added contrast to his intensely blue eyes—eyes that now showed a profound sadness and anger to perceptive Elbryan.

Shamus Kilronney looked to the leader of the Palmaris contingent, and the ranger tensed, almost expecting an attack. "What news?" Elbryan demanded again.

"Who is this man?" asked the leader of the Palmaris garrison, a solidly built woman, nearer to six feet in height than to five, with hair as fiery red as Kilronney's hanging in thick braids. Her eyes, like the captain's, were sparkling blue. It seemed to Elbryan that these two might even be siblings—except that her accent was closer to the rural dialect, typical of the underclass, while Shamus Kilronney's diction and enunciation were perfect.

"He is an ally," Kilronney explained, "serving as scout for my garrison."

"A mere scout?" the woman remarked, and she raised her eyebrows as she considered the powerful ranger. Elbryan saw her suspicions etched there and also a bit of curiosity.

"His accomplishments are too many for me even to begin to list them now," Kilronney said impatiently.

The woman nodded.

"Baron Rochefort Bildeborough is dead," Kilronney bluntly explained.

Elbryan's green eyes went wide. His first thought was for Roger, whom he knew was traveling with Bildeborough.

"He got murdered on the road just south o' Palmaris," the woman explained, her voice strong and determined—and hiding great pain, Elbryan realized. "They're sayin' his carriage was attacked by some beast, a great cat most likely."

"On his way back from Ursal?" the ranger asked.

"On his way *to* Ursal," the woman corrected.

"But that was months ago," the ranger protested. What he was thinking was that, if the woman's words were true, he and Pony had passed through Palmaris *after* the murder and yet had heard nothing of it.

"We didn't think to make the trip north a priority," the woman said dryly, "bigger nobles to tell than Captain Shamus Kilronney and his dirty friend."

"What of his companions?" the ranger asked, ignoring the insults and accepting the woman's explanation for the lack of communication.

"All killed," the woman replied.

Elbryan's thoughts whirled.

"They'd set their camp," another soldier offered. "Seems they were caught unawares. The Baron tried to get back into his carriage, but the cat followed him in and tore him up."

From the few words the soldier had offered, Elbryan had great doubts concerning the nature of this beast. In his years with the Touel'alfar, he had been taught the ways of animals, hunter and hunted. There were great cats about, though very few remained in the civilized lands between Palmaris and Ursal. But such creatures would not normally attack and slaughter a group of men. A hunting cat might take a lone person for food, might even stay with its victim and fight off any others who tried to take the prize from it, but the telling clue here was the pursuit of the Baron into his carriage.

"I seen it meself," another soldier offered. "All of 'em, torn up and lying in a pond o' blood."

"And who was killed first?" the ranger asked.

"Had to be one o' the guards at the fire," the man replied. "One never even got his weapon out afore the cat ripped him dead, and the others got no chance to set any defense."

"So the Baron was the last killed—in his carriage?"

The man nodded, his lips tight, as if he were choking back pain.

It made little sense to Elbryan, unless some diseased animal had attacked or unless a group of cats—an unlikely occurrence—had come in together.

"How many were eaten?" he asked the witness.

"They was all ripped," the man said. "Their guts was spillin' out. One of 'em had his heart laying open on his chest! I'm not for knowing how many bites the cat took of each."

"And ye're thinkin' this to be needed?" the woman protested to Captain Kilronney.

Kilronney turned a plaintive look upon Elbryan, but the ranger had his hand up, signaling that he would not press the issue further. He didn't need to. No hungry cat would leave as tempting a morsel as a heart uneaten, and no cat would spend the energy killing fleeing people when there was a fresh kill to be eaten. If the man's description of the scene was accurate, then the Baron had not been killed by any natural beast.

And of course that led Elbryan to even more disturbing thoughts. He had seen the gemstones at work many times, had spoken with Avelyn about them at length, and knew of one that could transform a man's arm into an animal's paw.

"The men about the Baron," the ranger began calmly, "did you know them all?"

"One was a friend," the witness replied. "And I seen the others with him before. The Baron's closest guard, they were!"

The ranger nodded. "I have heard that another—not a soldier—was traveling with Baron Bildeborough."

"The little fellow," the woman remarked. "Yeah, we heared o' him."

"And was his body at the camp?"

"Didn't see 'im," the witness replied.

That gave Elbryan a bit of relief but didn't confirm anything. The cat, if it was a cat, might have dragged Roger away to eat. Even more plausibly, the monk, if it was a monk, might have taken Roger prisoner, seeking information about Elbryan and Pony.

"What is your course?" he asked the Palmaris leader.

"We come ridin' to tell Captain Kilronney o' the Baron, as runners have been sent in every direction," she replied.

"The death of the Baron holds tremendous implications for Palmaris," Shamus Kilronney remarked, "especially following so closely on the murder of Abbot Dobrinion."

"The city's been in brew all the season," the woman added. "The new abbot's just returned from another trip to St.-Mere-Abelle—some College of Abbots, whatever that might be meanin'—and now he's taken his place, and a bit more than that, but he's not without his rivals."

The ranger nodded, hearing the words as confirmation of his worst fears. He had once met the new abbot of St. Precious—only briefly but long enough to recognize that De'Unnero was an unpleasant man, full of fire and pride. Bildeborough's death left a gaping hole in the power structure—his only heir, Connor, was dead, as was Abbot Dobrinion—that Abbot De'Unnero would hasten to fill. And the fact that De'Unnero had gone back to St.-Mere-Abelle for this college made the ranger fear the abbot might have had a prisoner, Roger Lockless, in tow.

It seemed to Elbryan then that the Abellican Church was a great black monster, rising to block out the sun. He considered his journey to Aida to battle the dactyl and his trip to St.-Mere-Abelle to steal his friends from the clutches of the Father Abbot, and he understood that those two missions had not been so very different—not at all.

"And what course for you?" Elbryan asked Kilronney.

The man blew a helpless sigh. "I should return to Palmaris," he said, "to see if I can help secure the city."

"You are needed here," the ranger reminded. "Winter may strike hard at these folk and bring in monsters that they cannot overcome without your help. And then there is the matter of the caravan north, before the start of spring."

"Ye're not for comparin' the reopenin' o' the Timberlands to the security of Palmaris?" the woman protested incredulously, moving closer to the captain and locking him with an intense gaze—one that reflected familiarity, Elbryan noted, thinking again that there might be a family relation here.

The ranger looked at Kilronney, but the captain only shrugged, defeated by the simple logic of the woman's statement.

"What of the powrie band in the west?" the ranger asked, for he and Kilronney had previously discussed their plans concerning one troublesome band of bloody cap dwarves who had not left the region, looming as a threat to any who might venture outside the secure area of Caer Tinella and Landsdown.

"We will deal with them at once," Shamus Kilronney offered.

The woman soldier began to protest.

"And then, if the weather holds and leaves the road clear, my men and I will turn to the south," Shamus said in a tone that left no room for debate.

The woman growled and turned away to stare intently at the ranger.

"I give you Nightbird," Captain Kilronney said, finally introducing him.

The ranger lifted his chin slightly but did not bow.

"Nightbird?" the woman asked, her expression sour. "A strange name."

"And this is Sergeant Colleen Kilronney of the Palmaris guard," Shamus explained.

"Your sister?" the ranger asked.

"Cousin," replied Shamus, somewhat distastefully.

"From the better part o' the family," Colleen was quick to put in, and Elbryan couldn't tell if her tone was serious or not. "Oh, me cousin's learned to speak so proper and pretty for courtin' ladies in Ursal. He's even been to the King's dinner table."

Shamus glowered at her, but she just gave a derisive laugh and turned to the ranger.

"Well, Master Nightbird—" she began.

"Just Nightbird," the ranger explained.

"Well, Master Nightbird," Colleen went on without missing a beat, "seems ye've got yer fight with the bloody caps. Me and me soldiers'll go along for the fun. We're all a bit troubled by the happenin's in Palmaris, and it might be good for us to take out our worrys on the powries."

The other two Palmaris soldiers, grim-faced, nodded.

Shamus Kilronney said, "We have not much time. The battlefield must be chosen and prepared."

"Ye make yer own battlefield when ye draw yer sword," stubborn Colleen put in.

Elbryan eyed the captain and then his cousin. There was an intense rivalry here, obviously, and the ranger understood that such feelings could lead to disaster in a fight. "I will learn where the powries have gone and choose the appropriate ground for our attack," he said, and he walked from the tent.

"Ye're a bit trustin'," he heard Colleen complain.

"None can prepare a battlefield better than Nightbird," Shamus was saying as Elbryan, shaking his head and smiling, mounted Symphony and started away. His amusement over Colleen Kilronney was short-lived, though, lasting only as long as it took him to consider again the grim news the woman had delivered.

He found Pony nearing the encampment even as he was leaving it, and he trotted Symphony over to her.

She eyed him suspiciously, and she knew even before he began to speak that something was wrong.

"Baron Bildeborough was murdered on the road, before he ever got near Ursal," Elbryan said, sliding down to stand beside his wife, "along with all his guard—though no sign of Roger was discovered among the dead."

"Powries again?" came Juraviel's voice from the trees, dripping with sarcasm. "Same clan that killed Abbot Dobrinion, no doubt."

"That thought may hold more truth than you believe," the ranger replied. "Those who found the Baron say he was killed by a great cat, but while the wounds might prove consistent with such a creature, I doubt the motive will."

"Tiger's paw," Pony spat, referring to the gemstone the monks could use to transform their limbs into those of a great cat. She closed her eyes and put her head down, sighing deeply, and Elbryan draped his arm around her shoulders, sensing that she needed the support. Every new encounter or word about the Abellican Church weighed heavily on Pony; every action these monks engaged in that was so unholy, so against the principles that had guided dear Avelyn, only reinforced her grief for her lost parents.

"Palmaris is in turmoil," Elbryan said, speaking more to Juraviel. "Our time with Captain Kilronney and his soldiers grows short. We should dispatch that powrie band before we depart."

"And what of Roger?" Pony was quick to ask. "Are we to continue our duties here, even go further away, while he might be in terrible peril?"

Elbryan held his hands out helplessly. "There was no sign of Roger, among the dead or anywhere on the road," he explained.

"He may have been taken," Juraviel offered.

"If he has been sent to St.-Mere-Abelle, I will go back," Pony declared, her tone so cold that it sent a shiver through Elbryan. He suspected that she meant to go in through the front doors this time, and leave little standing in her wake.

"And if he has been taken, then of course we will go for him," Elbryan assured her. "But we do not know that, and in the absence of evidence, we must hold our trust in Roger and continue our planned course."

"But if we continue to the north, or go against the powries, how will we discern Roger's fate?" Pony protested.

It was a dilemma, but the ranger remained unconvinced that they should drop everything and go in search of Roger Lockless. The man was a survivor. When Elbryan and Juraviel had gone into Powrie-occupied Caer Tinella to rescue him, they had found him already free. "I have no answers," the ranger admitted. "I know that I must trust Roger. If he was killed on the road, then there is nothing I can do about it."

"You would not avenge a friend?" Pony's words cut deep.

Elbryan stared at her as if she were a stranger, some different person than the one he had come to love so dearly.

Pony couldn't match that stare. She lowered her head and sighed again. "Of course you would," she admitted. "I am afraid for Roger, that is all."

"We can send word to Belster O'Comely in Palmaris," Juraviel offered. "The city is too large for us to go wandering about in an attempt to locate Roger. But Belster, so centered in the town, might be able to glean some information."

"All gossip flows through Fellowship Way," Pony added hopefully.

"I will go to Tomas Gingerwart," Elbryan offered, "and secure a trusted courier."

"None would prove more trustworthy than I," Pony said as the ranger took a step away.

Elbryan stopped in his tracks and closed his eyes; it took a long while for him to secure control of his anger. Then he turned to her slowly, astonished that she would take such a step.

"I must go and meet with Bradwarden," Juraviel remarked. "We will scout out the powries and report this evening." And the elf was gone, leaving the two, who had hardly heard his words, to their conversation.

CHAPTER

❖ 2 ❖

Jojonah's Legacy

"There are several promising brothers soon to attain the rank of immaculate," Father Abbot Dalebert Markwart said to Brother Braumin Herde when he joined the younger monk on the seawall of the great monastery of St.-Mere-Abelle, high above the cold waters of All Saints Bay.

Braumin turned to face the old man, then jumped back, startled. Markwart's hair had been thinning, but now it was gone, his head shaven clean. And that bald pate had changed Markwart's appearance considerably. His ears seemed longer and narrower, almost pointed, and his face seemed like chalky cloth laid over a skull. Braumin considered the tilt of Markwart's withered face, the hint of a sparkle—an evil glimmer?—in the man's otherwise dead eyes. And how much older the Father Abbot looked!

And yet, there was an undeniable aura of strength about the Father Abbot. He appeared taller to Braumin Herde, standing straighter than the younger monk remembered. Also, there was energy in the man's movements, and Brother Braumin knew that any thoughts he might have that the old wretch would soon die were false hopes. The shock of the Father Abbot's appearance soon wore off, but Braumin continued to study the old man closely, surprised that Markwart had ventured out in the chill wind, for Brother Braumin Herde, known as a friend of the executed heretic Jojonah, was obviously not among the Father Abbot's favorites.

"Promising," Markwart said again when his first words failed to bring any response from the younger monk. "Perhaps there are now immaculate brothers at St.-Mere-Abelle who should fear that these new peers might step ahead of them into the positions of master left vacant by the departure of Marcalo De'Unnero and the death of the heretic Jojonah."

The murder, you mean! Brother Braumin silently retorted. It had happened just three weeks before, in mid-Calember, the eleventh month, with winter beginning its icy assault on the land. A College of Abbots had been convened at St.-Mere-Abelle, and Father Abbot Markwart, as expected, had used the occasion to ask for a formal declaration that Avelyn Desbris be branded a heretic and an outlaw. Master Jojonah, Braumin's mentor and friend, had taken his stand against Markwart, arguing that Avelyn, though he defied the Church and absconded with some sacred gemstones, was a holy man and no heretic, and that Father Abbot Dalebert Markwart was in fact the true heretic, who twisted Church doctrine for evil gain.

Jojonah had been burned at the stake that same morning.

And Brother Braumin, because of his vow to his dear mentor, had watched helplessly as his beloved friend had been tortured and murdered.

"Have you seen to the preparation for the ceremony welcoming the new class?" Markwart asked. "It may seem like a long time away, but if winter comes on with a vengeance this year, you will not be able to get out into the courtyard to measure for the Gauntlet of Willing Suffering and other such necessities."

"Yes, Father Abbot," Brother Braumin mechanically replied.

"Good, my son, good," Markwart replied, his tone condescending. The old man reached up and patted Braumin's shoulder, and it took every ounce of self-control Braumin could muster not to recoil from that cold, heartless touch. "You have great potential, my son," the Father Abbot went on. "With proper guidance, you may yet replace Master De'Unnero, as Brother Francis will likely replace damned Jojonah."

Braumin Herde gritted his teeth, biting back a vicious response. The mere thought of Brother Francis Dellacourt, the spineless, plotting lackey, replacing his beloved Jojonah disgusted him.

Markwart, trying futilely to hide his grin, walked off then, leaving Braumin alone with a throat full of bile and silent screams. The monk did not doubt the Father Abbot's sincerity in hinting that Braumin might be elevated to the position of master. That coveted title would carry little practical weight under Markwart's rule, and Braumin would only be awarded the honor, if it ever happened, so that Markwart could dispel any rumbling of discontent within the Abellican Church. Master Jojonah had been highly regarded by many abbots and fellow masters, and the suddenness and brutality with which Markwart and Abbot Je'howith of St. Honce had accused, convicted, and executed him had taken all by surprise, leaving more than a few upset. Of course, any who might have protested was kept silent by terror—Markwart and Je'howith had used soldiers of the Allheart Brigade, the elite guard of the King himself, as their tools of murder, and few would dare argue against the Father Abbot of the Abellican Order in his home abbey of St.-Mere-Abelle, perhaps the greatest fortress in the world.

Now, Markwart was working to control any budding arguments based on hindsight. He had his declaration against Avelyn—that seemed secure enough—but the further declaration that had condemned Jojonah seemed open to interpretation and argument. By promoting Brother Braumin

Herde, widely known as the protégé of Jojonah, to the rank of master, Markwart would quiet such talk.

Still, even knowing that his appointment might strengthen Markwart, Braumin would have to accept, by the same vow that had kept him silent as his dearest friend had been burned alive.

The monk stared out over the seawall at the choppy water some three hundred feet below him. Small indeed did he feel physically in the face of the scope of Nature's majesty spread before him, and in every other way in the face of the plotting and power of Dalebert Markwart.

The Father Abbot rubbed his arms briskly when he entered the abbey, but even here the seawall corridor was full of open windows and offered only meager protection from the cold wind. The old man wasn't really bothered by it. He was in a generous mood this day; his words to Brother Braumin Herde were not without merit, and were not even based solely on Markwart's own conniving. For all the world seemed brighter to Markwart since the College of Abbots had rid him of troublesome Jojonah and had declared Avelyn a heretic. That declaration, along with the formal wording which hinted Avelyn and Jojonah had conspired from before Avelyn had gone to Pimaninicuit to gather the gemstones, had all but restored the Father Abbot's reputation concerning those stolen jewels. If Markwart could retrieve the stones, he would find a place of great respect in the annals of the Abellican Church; and even if he could not, the bulk of the blame had been diverted.

No, his reputation had been secured. Between the defeat of the conspiracy within the Church and the defeat of the demon dactyl, Father Abbot Dalebert Markwart's name would surely be spoken in reverence by the future generations of Abellican monks.

With a bounce in his step, the old man hurried along and pushed through a door—and nearly ran into Brother Francis Dellacourt, who was hastening the other way. The younger monk was out of breath and seemed relieved to have found the Father Abbot.

"You have news," Markwart reasoned, noting the rolled parchment Brother Francis clutched in his hand.

Francis had to catch his breath. And he, too, was startled by the change in Markwart's appearance. Francis tried to hide his discomfort, but he blinked repeatedly, his mouth partly open.

"I consider it rather becoming," Markwart said calmly, running a hand over his bald pate.

Francis stuttered through an incomprehensible reply, then merely nodded his head and began fumbling with the ribbon securing the parchment.

"Is that the list I asked you to compile?" an impatient Markwart asked.

"No, Father Abbot. It is from Abbot De'Unnero," Francis replied, regaining some composure as he handed it over. "The courier said it was of utmost importance. I suspect it might have something to do with the missing gemstones."

Markwart snatched up the parchment, flipped the ribbon from it, and unrolled it, devouring the words. At first his expression showed confusion, but it quickly began to brighten, the corners of his mouth turning up in a wicked grin.

"The gemstones?" Brother Francis asked.

"No, my son," Markwart purred. "No mention of the stones. It seems that the great city of Palmaris has fallen into a state of complete confusion, for Baron Rochefort Bildeborough has chosen a most inopportune time to leave this life."

"Pardon?" Brother Francis asked, for Markwart's words did not fit the old man's smug expression. They both knew about Rochefort's death, of course, for news had reached St.-Mere-Abelle long before the College of Abbots had been convened.

"The Baron of Palmaris died at a very inopportune time for his family, it seems," the Father Abbot said plainly. "They have concluded the search of Palmaris records, and Abbot De'Unnero's suspicions have been proven true. The Baron left no heirs. A pity, for Rochefort Bilborough, despite his oft-misguided bravado, was, by all accounts, a fine man and wise governor, as has been the tradition of the Bildeborough family for generations."

Francis sought a reply, but found none. They had received word only a few days before learning of Baron Bildeborough's demise that Connor Bildeborough, nephew of Rochefort and, it seemed, sole heir to the barony, had been killed north of the city.

"Dispatch Abbot De'Unnero's messenger with the reply that his note was received and understood," Markwart instructed, moving past Francis and motioning for him to follow. "And what of that list?"

"It is nearly complete, Father Abbot," Francis said sheepishly. "But the workers at the abbey are in a state of almost constant flux, with some leaving and others being hired every week."

"You offer excuses?"

"N-no, Father Abbot," Francis stuttered. "But it is a difficult—"

"Focus on any who might have come in after my journey to Palmaris," Markwart instructed, "including those who were hired during that time and who have already left our employ."

The Father Abbot started on his way then, with Francis falling into step behind him. "We each have work to do," Markwart said rather sternly, turning to Francis.

"I only thought that we were to speak," Francis apologized.

"And so we have." Markwart turned and walked off.

Brother Francis stood in the empty hall for a long while, wounded by the abrupt treatment and stunned by the Father Abbot's change in appearance, his harsh, almost sinister look. The Father Abbot had been in good spirits of late, but apparently that did not prevent him from cutting hard and deep. Francis considered his own failings, tried to put Markwart's ire in perspective considering that he had not completed the task. But in truth he knew he had worked diligently and without pause—except for answering Abbot De'Unnero's messenger—since Markwart had assigned him the list.

Brother Francis could accept the harsh words. What bothered him more was the news from Palmaris and the Father Abbot's reaction to it. Baron Bildeborough, the next in a growing line of adversaries to Father Abbot Markwart, was now, like all of those previous adversaries, dead. Coincidence? And how convenient it seemed that there were no other Bildeboroughs left alive to inherit the barony.

Brother Francis pushed away the thoughts, forced himself to focus on the task at hand. He had to go to the larders next, to speak with Brother Machuso, who handled all the servants for kitchen and cleaning duties. It would be a long day.

Brothers Braumin Herde, Marlboro Viscenti, Holan Dellman, Anders Castinagis, and Romeo Mullahy each made his separate way to the secret oratory prepared far below the common rooms of St.-Mere-Abelle, to a small chamber beside the old library wherein Master Jojonah had found his answers to the philosophical conflict between Father Abbot Markwart and Brother Avelyn Desbris. Since the week after the execution of Master Jojonah, the five monks had met every other night, soon after vespers, for these private prayers.

The five sat on the floor in a circle about a single tall candle and joined hands. Brother Braumin, as the ranking monk and the oldest of the group by several years, began the prayers, as usual invoking the names of Jojonah and Avelyn Desbris, asking for guidance and strength for the group from their departed mentors. Braumin noted that both Castinagis and Mullahy shifted uncomfortably at the mention of Avelyn: merely speaking the man's name in a positive manner was now considered a heinous crime by the Abellican Church—and by the state, since Avelyn had been formally declared a heretic. The same was true of Jojonah, but all five of these men had known Jojonah for a long time and not one of them accepted the verdict that had doomed the gentle master.

When the prayer was done, Braumin rose to his feet and looked down at his companions, his gaze settling on the two youngest of the group. At first their gatherings had been only three strong—Herde, Viscenti, and Dellman—but they were discovered during their fourth meeting by the other two, curious classmates of young Dellman. Neither Castinagis nor Mullahy, who had both witnessed the horrible execution of their friend

Jojonah, had been hard to convince—not only to not tell of the meeting but
also to join in future gatherings—but while both young monks seemed sincere, neither had become overly enthusiastic.

"Do you understand why we have gathered here?" Braumin asked
Mullahy.

"To pray," the man replied.

"We spend hours each day in prayer at our daily duties," Braumin
argued.

"A man can never pray too often," Brother Castinagis, a very outspoken
and forceful young monk, interjected.

"You refuse to admit the difference between our evening prayers and
our daily prayers," Braumin remarked, drawing curious looks from all the
others. Marlboro Viscenti, a skinny and nervous man with more than one
tic, began shifting uncomfortably. "That admission of philosophical difference, the open recognition that only our prayers to Master Jojonah and
Brother Avelyn are in the true spirit of the Abellican Order, is the whole
point of our gathering," Braumin went on.

"Is not the mere act of joining your private group such an admission?"
Castinagis asked.

"To the others of the group, perhaps," Braumin replied. "But such a
show of loyalty does nothing to admit the truth within your own heart."

Again the two in question looked at Brother Braumin with puzzled
expressions. Viscenti continued to twitch, but now Brother Dellman was
wearing a warm smile of understanding.

"And all that truly matters is what is in your own heart," Braumin
finished.

"If the tenets of these meetings were not in our hearts, then why would
we attend?" Castinagis asked. "Do you think us spies for the Father Abbot?
For if you mean to accuse—"

"No, Brother Castinagis," Braumin replied quietly. "And I know of your
loyalty to Master Jojonah, may his soul forever rest."

"A finer man I've never known," Brother Mullahy declared. Mullahy and
Castinagis had been quite close, even before they had taken their vows and
entered St.-Mere-Abelle; but the two were very different, as illustrated by
the sheepish manner in which Mullahy spoke, lowering his gaze to the floor
and mumbling so softly that the others could hardly hear him.

"Because you never knew Brother Avelyn," Braumin said.

Now the curious looks took on an antagonistic edge, as if the two young
brothers had considered Braumin's words as a gauntlet thrown down
against the memory of their beloved Master Jojonah.

"But they did not see the grave site," Brother Dellman interjected, somewhat relieving the tension. "They were not beside us at Mount Aida when
we viewed the extended, mummified arm of Brother Avelyn Desbris, when
we felt that aura, so powerful and beautiful."

"Nor did either of them—of you—get the opportunity to speak with Master Jojonah about Brother Avelyn Desbris," Braumin added. "If you had, then you would know that my words are no assault against the memory of Jojonah, but rather an expression of the principles that must guide us in our struggles, the principles shown to Master Jojonah, to us all, by Avelyn Desbris."

The words diffused the anger, and Castinagis, too, bowed his head reverently.

Braumin Herde moved across the small room to a chest in the corner, the same one where the secretive brothers kept pillows and the candle, and produced an old and weathered book. "The crime that split Brother Avelyn from the Abellican Order was one condemned by our Church standards," he explained.

"The murder of Master Siherton?" Brother Castinagis asked incredulously, for in the very first meeting, Brother Braumin had taken great pains to exonerate Avelyn from that alleged offense.

"No," Braumin replied sharply. "There was no murder of Master Siherton; the man was killed while trying to prevent Brother Avelyn's lawful escape."

"Brother Avelyn acted only in defense of his own life," Brother Dellman put in.

"No, I speak of the Church's actions," Brother Braumin explained, "particularly those of Master Siherton against the *Windrunner*, the ship commissioned by Father Abbot Markwart to take the four chosen brothers to the isle of Pimaninicuit in God's Year 821."

Now all three of the youngest brothers were curious, for the story of the collection of the gemstones was not a public matter in St.-Mere-Abelle. Indeed, none below the level of immaculate was formally told anything of the equatorial island where the chosen Preparers would collect the sacred gemstones—and most of the immaculate brothers didn't even know much about the place. All the Abellican monks knew that the stones fell from heaven, a gift of God, but the particulars were not a matter of open discourse in the abbey. Master Jojonah had told Braumin Herde; and he, in turn, had relayed the story to Brother Viscenti. Now, he decided, it was time to tell the others, to trust them with what was, perhaps, the deepest secret of all.

"Pimaninicuit is the name given to the island far out in the great Miri-anic, where the sacred gemstones are sent from heaven," Brother Braumin began somberly. "This most blessed event occurs only once every seven generations, one hundred and seventy-three years. We are blessed that this occurred during our lifetime, but more blessed was Brother Avelyn, for he was one of the four monks chosen to voyage to the island, one of the two Preparers allowed to go onto Pimaninicuit and witness the stone shower. His companion was Brother Thagraine, who faltered in his faith on the island and did not seek proper shelter from the glory of God. Thus, Thagraine was killed that day, by the same gemstone Brother Avelyn eventually used to destroy our greatest enemy, the demon dactyl."

Brother Braumin paused to study his companions. He was overwhelming them, he recognized. But they had to hear it, had to understand the significance and the danger. For a younger brother even to utter the name of Pimaninicuit violated Abellican rules and was cause for harsh punishment, possibly excommunication or even execution.

"What you need to understand about that mission is the truth of the voyage back to St.-Mere-Abelle," Braumin went on. "A glorious return it was, despite the death of Brother Thagraine; for Brother Avelyn, so close to God, delivered unto mankind the greatest harvest of gemstones ever taken from the island, the greatest gift of gemstones ever delivered by God.

"But then," he went on, lowering his voice ominously, "glory turned to horror, God's gift became demon sin. The *Windrunner*'s crew sailed away from St.-Mere-Abelle into All Saints Bay, their job complete, thinking their reward in hand. But that reward was false, a trick, an illusion caused by the sacred stones."

"Thieves!" Brother Dellman cried. "Thieves in our midst!"

"Murderers," Brother Braumin corrected. "For the *Windrunner* never got out of All Saints Bay. The ship was assaulted by ballistae and catapult and by magic from the walls of this very abbey, was torn asunder by the wrath of St.-Mere-Abelle, and every man aboard murdered."

Three blood-drained and wide-eyed faces stared up helplessly at Brother Braumin, as Brother Viscenti, who had heard all this before, nodded enthusiastically. Brother Castinagis shook his head, though, as if he did not believe the story, and it seemed as if Brother Mullahy could not draw breath.

"It was not always like this," Brother Braumin insisted, holding up the ancient text. He looked at the candle, which was much shorter now than when they had begun. "But our time now has run out," he offered. "Let us end with a final prayer for the souls of those lost on the *Windrunner*."

"But, Brother Braumin," Brother Castinagis protested.

"Enough," Braumin replied. "And know that if any of us is caught speaking of such things, he will surely be tortured and killed. For your proof, look only to the charred corpse of Master Jojonah, whose crimes in the eyes of Father Abbot Markwart were far less than these words." With that, Braumin knelt and began the prayer. That image of Jojonah, a sight that had burned in the hearts of all the brothers in this room, would hold them quiet, he knew; and he understood, too, that not one of them would be a moment late for their next gathering two nights hence.

A spiritual meeting of another sort was taking place that same night, at least partially at St.-Mere-Abelle. *Go to him and see what is in his mind and in his heart,* the ever-more-insistent voice inside Markwart's head had bade him. *I will show you the way.*

The voice had spoken, and Markwart listened. In the most private room of his quarters, sitting in the middle of a pentagram he had inscribed on the floor, a burning candle set at each of its five points, Father Abbot Markwart clutched tightly to a hematite, a soul stone, marveling as his magical energy connected with that of the stone, achieving new and greater levels of power.

Soon Markwart's spirit walked free of his body and hovered about the room, considering the view. He had found the pentagram in an ancient text, *The Incantations Sorcerous.* The Church had banned the book, considered unholy for centuries, burning all copies save the one kept in the cellar library of the abbey. Markwart believed that he understood the Church's reasons: this book held the key to greater power, and that, rather than any connection with the demon dactyl, had inspired fear among the Church leaders. Using the pentagram and the words of a spell within the book, combined with a hematite, Markwart had even summoned a pair of minor demons to his bidding.

With this book, the evil creatures of the underworld will be slaves to the powers of good, he thought now, his spirit looking down at his cross-legged form. He did a quick scan of his rooms and the empty hallway outside to make sure the area was secure, then set off, speeding out the main doors of the abbey and off west, flying across the miles. In mere minutes, his spirit hovered on the southern bank of the great Masur Delaval, some eighty miles from St.-Mere-Abelle.

He floated above the waters with equal ease and speed, and soon the dark structures of Palmaris came into view. Markwart's spirit rose above the city, looking down on the buildings, picking out the distinctive design of St. Precious. Down he swooped to the abbey, right through the thick stone wall. Markwart had been in St. Precious only the previous year, and he knew the layout of the place well enough to easily locate the private rooms of the new abbot.

He was not surprised to find De'Unnero pacing the floor, fists clenched with tension. The man was ready for bed, wearing only a nightshirt, but as always, he seemed too full of energy.

Get your soul stone, Markwart's spirit telepathically instructed. Monks of the Abellican Order had used hematites for rudimentary communication for centuries. One monk might even use the body of another, far away, possessing the other to speak with those nearby, as Markwart had done through Brother Francis when Francis had gone to Mount Aida. Even without possession, which was indeed a brutal step, some communication might be achieved, though it was usually crude, an imparting of feelings, perhaps. If a disaster befell the abbess of St. Gwendolyn, for instance, she might take up a soul stone and contact St. Honce or St.-Mere-Abelle to beg for help. The monks of those abbeys might understand that something was

amiss, even discern the source of the communication, might spiritually
"hear" the words of the abbess. But Markwart, with his newfound insights
and power, meant to take this practice to a higher level—and he knew he
would succeed.

Get your soul stone, he commanded De'Unnero.

The man stopped pacing and glanced around, confused. "Who is
there?" he asked.

Markwart's spirit drifted to the man, and within—not too deeply, not to
possess, but only to let De'Unnero feel his presence clearly.

The newly appointed abbot of St. Precious darted to his desk and, using
a small key hung on a chain around his neck, opened a secret compartment
within a drawer. He fumbled for a moment, before producing a hematite
and clutching it closely. Soon he, too, was out of his body, and his spirit
stood perplexed, staring at a very clear image of Markwart.

What manner of meeting is this? The spirit of an obviously flustered
De'Unnero—a rare sight indeed!—asked.

You took a great chance, Markwart coolly replied.

I fear no spirits and I knew it was you.

Not in coming to meet me, Markwart explained. *In going out to meet
Baron Bildeborough's carriage.*

Why do we speak of this now? De'Unnero questioned. *The Baron has
been dead for months, and you knew from the beginning—you had to
know!—that I was involved! Yet you spoke no word of his demise to me at
the College of Abbots.*

Perhaps I had other, more pressing duties to attend, Markwart replied.
And Rochefort Bildeborough's death has taken on a greater meaning now.

You have spoken with my messenger, then.

I have read between the plain words Marcalo De'Unnero offered, Markwart corrected. *The Baron of Palmaris was killed on the road, heirless. What
a fortunate turn for the new abbot of St. Precious.*

And for the Father Abbot, who called Rochefort Bildeborough an enemy,
De'Unnero replied.

How did he die? Markwart asked. He watched De'Unnero's spirit relax.
Even body language was clearly visible, though neither party was in his
body! A smile came over De'Unnero's spirit face, but he made no move to
answer. *You did it with the tiger's paw,* Markwart reasoned.

As you wish.

Do not play games. This matter is too important.

Like the matter of Connor Bildeborough? Or Abbot Dobrinion? De'Unnero retorted slyly.

That set Markwart back a bit, the Father Abbot surprised at De'Unnero's lack of respect. Markwart had set the young man up as abbot of St.
Precious—no easy task—because he considered De'Unnero a powerful
thorn to stick in Bildeborough's side and, more important, a loyal under-

ling. Now it seemed De'Unnero was taking his new position to mean that he was more Markwart's peer than his subject, an attitude Markwart liked not at all.

You killed them both, De'Unnero charged. *Or had them killed, by the hands of the men I trained as brothers justice.*

You presume much.

Markwart heard, or at least felt, the other spirit's sigh as clearly as if it had come from De'Unnero's body.

I am no fool, Father Abbot, and I survive through observation. No powrie killed Abbot Dobrinion. The man who brought the bodies of Connor Bildeborough and Brother Youseff back to Palmaris spouted Connor's wild claims that the Church had murdered Dobrinion. Wild claims? he scoffed, and laughed wickedly. *Wild, perhaps, to those who have not watched Father Abbot Markwart closely over the last few months.*

You tread on dangerous ground, Markwart's spirit warned. *I can destroy you as easily as I promoted you.*

A claim I do not doubt, De'Unnero answered sincerely. *And I do not desire your enmity, Father Abbot. Never that. I speak of such dark business with respect and approval.*

Markwart paused to digest the words.

During the months that Youseff and Dandelion were in training, I begged you to let me go after the stolen gemstones. I say again that, had it been De'Unnero on the trail, those stones would be back at St.-Mere-Abelle and their unlawful keepers, the friends of the heretic Avelyn, would lie dead in unconsecrated ground.

Markwart could not honestly disagree—Marcalo De'Unnero was perhaps the most competent and dangerous man he had ever known. De'Unnero was in his mid-thirties now, but carried himself with the ease and strength of a twenty-year-old, a combination of experience and power very rare in the world.

But I say this again not to criticize, De'Unnero's spirit quickly added, *only to remind you and to ask you to ask more of me.*

Like the elimination of Baron Bildeborough?

The other stopped short, caught by the blunt words.

I'll have the truth, or I shall indeed destroy you, Markwart imparted, the simple tone of his thoughts making the words a promise, not a threat. He wanted to see if De'Unnero would threaten to expose the murderer of Abbot Dobrinion and Connor Bildeborough. If he did, then Markwart would break the connection and start the process of eliminating this problem. But De'Unnero wasn't playing that game, not at all.

I am not your enemy, Father Abbot, but your subject, the spirit explained. *A loyal subject. I did venture out on the road south of Palmaris in the form of a great cat.*

Do you understand the chance you took?

No greater than the one you took, De'Unnero countered. *Less, I would say, since Abbot Dobrinion was one of our own, and his murder could turn the whole Church against you. Bildeborough's demise is not a matter for the Abellican Church.*

Only for the King, Markwart came back sarcastically, but De'Unnero's spirit seemed to shrug that away as inconsequential. In truth, Markwart agreed with the man's assessment, fearing the power of the Church far more than that of the state.

The killing was clean, De'Unnero insisted. *There is nothing to connect the death of Baron Bildeborough with me, and certainly not with you.*

A bit more than coincidence, some will whisper, Markwart replied, *especially now that there are no Bildeborough heirs to take up the barony.*

And some are already whispering, De'Unnero countered, *and were whispering before Bildeborough's demise. But lacking clear, undeniable evidence, who would dare accuse the Father Abbot of the Abellican Church? No, we should focus on the gains of our actions, not dwell on the risks.*

The gain is yet to be determined, Markwart answered. *We know not upon whom the King will confer the barony. Likely, given the whispers, Danube Brock Ursal will choose one who does not look favorably on the Church, to ensure the continuation of his own power in Palmaris.*

I do not agree, De'Unnero dared to argue. *Was it not this same King who willingly gave his elite soldiers to Abbot Je'howith for the College of Abbots?*

Over the protest of his secular advisers, no doubt, Markwart put in. *Je'howith has long battled for the King's ear at Ursal.*

A battle he must now win, De'Unnero continued flatly, *for now, with the absence of state power in Palmaris, it might be time for the Church to heighten its role in governing the masses.*

Again Markwart's spirit was set back a bit.

It is not without precedent, De'Unnero insisted. *Palmaris has no baron, and few with credentials to hold such a title would desire to leave Ursal for the less luxurious existence in Palmaris, especially considering the whispers of conspiracies and the potential danger.*

Markwart could not believe the man's nerve! De'Unnero was trying to make gains from every possible pitfall, turning the suspicions about Church involvement in the deaths into a positive thing!

Go to Je'howith as you have come to me, De'Unnero begged. *Let us force the King into an alliance that will expand Church power.*

That will expand your power, Markwart corrected.

And I serve you, Father Abbot. De'Unnero was answering before Markwart ever finished the thought. *The King will not choose to go against us now, not when the easier course is to let us help him through this chaotic aftermath of war.*

It made sense, Markwart had to admit. *I will go to Je'howith this very night,* he agreed, but then his tone changed. *You are to take no decisive actions on any matter without my permission,* he warned. *The times are too dangerous, and our positions too tentative for me to trust the judgment of one as inexperienced as Marcalo De'Unnero.*

But concerning Baron Bildeborough, De'Unnero responded, *am I to assume that you approve?*

Markwart broke the connection immediately, his spirit flying from that place. He came back into his body in a few minutes, wearing a wide smile. He should have gone to bed then, for such a long use of the soul stone was terribly draining, but strangely, the Father Abbot felt rejuvenated, hungry for more information.

Instead, he sent his spirit west and south to the one city in all Honce-the-Bear that was larger than Palmaris.

St. Honce in Ursal was the second largest Abellican abbey, smaller only than St.-Mere-Abelle. It was joined to the palace of the King by a long, narrow hall known as the bridge. The abbot of St. Honce traditionally served as spiritual adviser to the King and his court. Markwart knew the place well. Here, he had been anointed as Father Abbot of the Order by Abbot Sherman, who had been succeeded by Abbot Dellahunt, who had been succeeded by Je'howith. The ceremony had been formalized by King Danube Cole Ursal, the father of the present king. Markwart had little trouble finding the private rooms of the abbot.

Je'howith's response to the spiritual intrusion, once he had gathered up his soul stone and gone out of body, was absolute delight. *What wonders such quick communication might bring to the world!* his spirit exclaimed. *Think of the gains to warfare if captains could so communicate with their field commanders! Think of—*

Enough, Markwart's spirit interrupted, knowing the man's hopes to be nothing more than illusions. None but he could so powerfully spirit-walk— no abbot, no master, and surely no secular soldier! *I have a task for you. You have heard of the death of Baron Bildeborough, and that he was without heir?*

Word reached us just this day, Je'howith replied somberly. *Truth, Father Abbot, I have barely found a moment's rest. I only returned to Ursal this week, and now—*

Then you know of the vacancy in Palmaris, Markwart interrupted, having no time for Je'howith's blabbering.

A problem that King Danube considers wearily, Je'howith answered. *The poor man is near to breaking, I fear, though the war is finally won. He has faced so many problems these last few months, after years of peace.*

Then let us lessen his troubles, Markwart offered. *Convince him to give the barony to Abbot De'Unnero and let the Church handle the troubles of Palmaris.*

The abbot's surprise was evident in the posture of his spirit form. *King Danube does not even know this Marcalo De'Unnero. Nor do I, if the truth be told, except we met once at the College of Abbots.*

Take my word as recommendation of his character and his ability to rule Palmaris, Markwart instructed. *And understand that even in the combined position of baron and abbot, called bishop in past days, Marcalo De'Unnero will answer to me—and to you, if you do not fail me in this.*

That last thought was too much bait to be ignored.

You do remember that the Church once ruled beside the King, Markwart went on. Je'howith's spirit was nodding and smiling. *Convince the King.*

Perhaps I could go and meet Abbot De'Unnero through the soul stone, much as you— Je'howith began, but Markwart cut him short.

You could not attain this level of clarity, the Father Abbot explained honestly—and angrily—for he did not believe that Je'howith could perform this level of magic. *This is my magic, and mine alone. It is not to be discussed, nor initiated, by you, though I may come to you often in the future.*

The humility and submission that came back from Je'howith satisfied the Father Abbot, and so he soared back across the miles to St.-Mere-Abelle. There, despite his tremendous expenditure of magical energy, he was still restless. He paced for more than an hour, trying to gain perspective on the new routes of power that suddenly seemed open to him. Just that morning, Markwart had thought his reputation in Church history settled, the only possibility of elevating it being the retrieval of the stolen gemstones. But now the issue of the stones seemed almost trivial. De'Unnero's claim that the Church had once played a more active role in governing was true enough: a king of Honce-the-Bear, in ages long past, had actually been anointed as Father Abbot of the Abellican Order. But for hundreds of years, the balance of power in the kingdom had held relatively stable between Church and state: separate, but powerful, entities. The king saw to the secular activities of his subjects, managed the standing army, and handled disputes with the neighboring kingdoms of Behren and Alpinador, but claimed little lordship over the powers of the Church. In many reaches of the kingdom, particularly the smaller villages, the Church was far more influential than the distant King, whose full name many of the subjects did not even know.

But now, because of Markwart's wise and prudent actions in Palmaris, the elimination of Connor Bildeborough and Abbot Dobrinion, and because of the subsequent death of the Baron, the balance of power in the kingdom might be shifted in favor of the Church. Danube Brock Ursal was weary, by Je'howith's own words. If Je'howith managed to wrest Palmaris from him . . .

Obviously, neither Markwart nor Je'howith had many years left to live— they were both in their seventies. Suddenly the Father Abbot wasn't satisfied with that place he had secured in Church history. Suddenly his ambition went far higher—and so had Je'howith's, he believed. Together they could use men like De'Unnero to change the world.

Father Abbot Markwart was immensely pleased by such a prospect.

Not far from the quarters of the Father Abbot, Brother Francis Della-court stood in his candlelit room, staring at his reflection in a mirror. The dark shadows about him seemed a fitting frame to the beleaguered man.

For most of his life, Francis had placed himself on a secret pedestal, above the average man—above any man. He never consciously told himself that he was the chosen of God, but he had believed it, as if all the world were merely a dream played out for his personal benefit. Francis had believed himself without sin, the perfect reflection of the perfect God.

But then he had killed Grady Chilichunk on the road from Palmaris.

It had been an accident, Francis knew, for his blow to Grady's head was only supposed to stun the man and prevent him from continuing his disre-spect for the Father Abbot. But Grady had not awoken the next day, and the image of dirt falling on Grady's lifeless, bloated face as Francis had buried him had haunted the monk ever since, and had kicked the secret pedestal out from beneath his feet.

All the events of the world had swirled about Francis since that fateful day. He had watched Father Abbot Markwart order the torture and execu-tion of Master Jojonah, and while he had never actually cared for Jojonah, Francis could hardly believe the punishment fitting.

But Francis had gone along with it, had served the Father Abbot slav-ishly, for the leader of the Abellican Order had placed no blame on Francis, had insisted that Francis had acted appropriately and that the fate of Grady—and the fate of Grady's parents—had been caused by their own sacrilege. Thus Francis had become even more devoted to Markwart, had come to believe that his only chance of reclaiming his pedestal was to follow in the shadow of the great leader.

And then Markwart had ordered Jojonah dragged from the hall at the College of Abbots. The soldiers pulling the master had taken him right by Francis, and Francis had looked into Jojonah's doomed eyes.

And the doomed master, who had learned the truth about Grady's death and who understood that Francis had been responsible, had forgiven Francis.

Now the young monk could only stare at the dark shadows surrounding his mortal form like stains on his eternal soul, and battle futilely with the confusing jumble of remorse and guilt that swirled in his thoughts.

His pedestal was gone, his innocence lost.

Another man was awake in St.-Mere-Abelle at that late hour, washing the dishes, a task that he should have completed much earlier that evening. But other duties—the planning of his next, and boldest, scouting mission—had delayed Roger Lockless that night. Roger had come to this place after witnessing the murder of Baron Bildeborough on the road south of Palmaris. He had run to St.-Mere-Abelle in the hopes of finding Elbryan and Pony; and in the town of St.-Mere-Abelle, some three miles inland from the great abbey, he had witnessed yet another murder, the execution of a man named Jojonah.

Roger was a slight man, barely over five feet tall and weighing no more than the average fifteen-year-old boy. His growth had been stunted by a disease—the same illness that had taken his parents. He was quite familiar with the ways of street beggars and knew how to play the "pitiful waif" to perfection. He had found little trouble securing a job from the generous Master Machuso of St.-Mere-Abelle, and had worked in the abbey for the last three weeks. In that time, Roger had heard many rumors, garnering enough confirmation to believe that Master Jojonah had aided some intruders who rescued Bradwarden from the Father Abbot's dungeons. But then the story got confusing, full of conflicting rumors, and Roger wasn't certain if these intruders—whom he knew were Elbryan, Pony, and Belli'mar Juraviel—had gotten away, though he did know that Bradwarden was no longer in the abbey. He believed that his friends had also escaped, but before he would leave his job at the abbey, Roger had to make certain.

He thought he knew where he would find his answers, though the notion of going into the private quarters of a man as powerful as Dalebert Markwart was unnerving even to the man who had taunted powries in their encampment at Caer Tinella; defeated a brother justice of the Abellican Church; earned "Lockless" as his surname; and, most significantly of all, earned the respect of Nightbird.

❖ 3 ❖

Private Fun

"You did not tell him," Belli'mar Juraviel said to Pony.

"There is a time and place, and I do not think the eve of a battle is it," Pony replied harshly, though Juraviel had only stated a fact and there had been no hint of accusation in his tone.

Pony meant to go on, mostly to tell the elf that this issue was none of his affair, but lightning split the overcast sky, startling her. A late autumn storm churned in the dark clouds overhead.

"The child is Elbryan's as much as yours," the elf said calmly as the thunder rumbled. "He has a right to know before the battle is fought."

"I will tell him when and where I choose," Pony retorted.

"You did let him know that you mean to go to Palmaris, not to Dundalis?" Juraviel inquired.

Pony nodded and closed her eyes. When Juraviel had left her with Elbryan earlier that day, she had explained to the ranger that she needed to return to Palmaris, to try to learn of Roger's fate and to check on Belster at Fellowship Way. She had told Elbryan that she needed to put her grief to rest, and only a visit to those surroundings, she believed, could accomplish the task.

Elbryan had not responded well. Conjuring his image now—his eyes so full of confusion, hurt, and fear for her—pained her greatly.

"And you will tell him about the child before you leave?" Juraviel pressed.

"And then he will abandon the caravan to Dundalis," Pony replied sarcastically. "He will forget the task at hand and spend his days instead at my side, tending to needs I do not have."

Juraviel backed off a bit and wrapped his slender chin with delicate fingers, studying her.

"Elbryan and I will be back together soon enough," Pony explained, her voice now calm and reassuring. She understood the elf's concern for her and for her relationship with Elbryan. Juraviel was their good friend, and seeing him so troubled only reminded Pony that she must carefully examine these most important decisions.

"The child will not be born until the turn of spring to summer," Pony went on. "That will give Elbryan plenty of time—"

"More time if he was told now," Juraviel interrupted.

"I do not know if the child will survive," Pony said.

"Considering your power with the gemstones, it is unlikely that any harm will come to the babe," Juraviel replied.

"Power," Pony scoffed. "Yes, the power to keep me at the top of the ridge, watching others fight the battles."

"Do not lessen the credit deserved by a healer," Juraviel started to argue.

But Pony had turned away, hardly listening. She and Elbryan had to keep her use of the magic stones secret, especially now that Palmaris garrison soldiers had arrived. Even though the secular-serving Kingsmen were the only state force in the region, Pony had wisely limited her public use of the stones. Sooner or later, word would reach this far north that she and Elbryan were fugitives of the Church. Pony used the stones only to heal those wounded in battle; even then, she disguised her gemstone work by also applying healing salves and bandages, secretly finishing the task with hematite. Ironically, that healing proficiency had trapped Pony behind the melee during the fighting; Captain Kilronney was convinced she was too valuable to risk. Given Pony's surly mood, her almost-desperate hunger for revenge, she wasn't pleased with her role.

"Is my own role any greater?" the elf asked. "I cannot show myself before the Kingsmen, and am thus relegated to the position of private pre-battle scout for Nightbird."

"And you have been saying ever since we left the mountains around Andur'Blough Inninness that this war was not the business of the Touel'-alfar," Pony shot back angrily.

"Ah, but the little ones're always sayin' such things," came a familiar voice from the shadows. Bradwarden, the huge centaur, trotted into the small clearing beside the pair. "Never meanin' it, for the elves're really thinkin' that everythin' in all the world is their business!"

Pony couldn't help but smile back at the grinning centaur. Though Bradwarden could be a fierce foe, his face always seemed to beam within that bushy ring of curly black hair and beard.

"Ah, me little Pony," the centaur went on, "suren that I'm hearin' yer words o' frustration. I been watchin' fight after fight against the stinkin' dwarfs and goblins, and canno' even lift me club to help!"

"You wear a distinctive mantle," Juraviel said dryly.

"One ye're wishin' yerself might wear," the centaur replied.

Juraviel laughed in response, and then he bid farewell to the pair, explaining that he had to report to Elbryan on the final movements of the powrie band.

"The dwarves're makin' it easy this time," the centaur said to Pony when they were alone.

"You have seen them?"

"In a cave in a rocky dell, not two miles west o' Caer Tinella," Bradwarden explained. "I'm knowin' the place well, and knowin' that there's only one entrance to their chosen ground. I'm thinkin' that the dwarves haven't decided which way they mean to go. Some're lookin' for a fight, no doubt, since powries're almost always lookin' for a fight. But most're likely thinkin' that it's past time to go home."

"How defensible is the cave?" Pony asked, her gaze inadvertently turning west.

"Not so, if Nightbird catches 'em in there," the centaur replied. "The dwarves'd hold for some time against a siege, dependin' on how much food they brought with 'em, but they'd not be gettin' out o' there if Nightbird and the soldiers set themselves in front o' the damn hole. Me thinkin's that the dwarves're not plannin' to stay in there for long, and have no idea that they been seen. Juraviel will tell Nightbird to hit at them before dawn."

"Dawn is still many hours away," Pony remarked slyly, grinning at Bradwarden.

The centaur matched Pony's smile. "Seems the least we can do is seal the ugly dwarves up in their hole," he agreed.

The storm broke soon after dusk, a wind-driven rain lifting a swirling fog about the skeletal trees, a preternatural scene brilliantly lit by every bolt of lightning. Pony's spirit moved easily through this storm, a mere swirl in the fog, invisible to the eyes of any mortal creature. She did several circuits of the dell Bradwarden had indicated, even went inside the cave to count forty-three powries—a larger group than the scouts had indicated—and to confirm Bradwarden's claim that there was indeed only one way out of the place. That single entrance intrigued her, and she lingered beneath the arch for quite a while, studying the heavy outcropping of loose-fitting stones above. Then she went back into the forest. She found only five powries outside, but was not surprised at the meager guard. The dwarves could not have expected that any army would come against them in this wild storm.

Her spirit drifted back to her waiting body, seated in another cave some miles distant. Bradwarden stood patient sentry in the doorway, while Greystone, Pony's beautiful, well-muscled horse, stood very still inside the cave, ears flattened.

"We can get right to the cave entrance with only minimal resistance," she announced.

Bradwarden turned at the sound of her voice. A bolt of lightning hit in the distance behind him, momentarily outlining his large, powerful frame. Greystone nickered and shifted nervously.

"Ye might want to be leavin' yer horse," the centaur remarked. "He's findin' the night a bit too fitful for his likin'."

Pony rose and went to the stallion, stroking his muscled neck and trying to calm him. "Not so long a walk," she said.

"Ah, but I'll let ye ride on me back instead," the centaur offered. "Now tell me what ye seen."

"Two groups of two guards each," Pony explained, "looking more for shelter than for enemies. Both are out about a hundred yards from the cave, one to the left, one to the right. A fifth powrie is settled in the rocks above the cave entrance."

"The sound o' the storm'll cover our first attacks," Bradwarden reasoned.

"Right to the cave entrance without them even knowing," Pony said with a wicked smile. Another bolt of lightning thundered into the forest night, a fitting accentuation of her dangerous mood.

The clip-clop of hooves sounded in the ears of the tense powrie sentries. The two powries, up to now more concerned with hiding from the driving rain than with sentry duty, tightly clutched their weapons—a small crossbow and a war hammer—and came around the cluster of trees, peering through the rain. They made out the hindquarters of a large horse, and breathed a bit easier when they noted that the animal had no rider and no saddle.

"Just a wild one," one whispered.

The other raised his crossbow.

"Nah, don't ye be shootin' it!" his companion grumbled. "Ye'll just wing the thing, and then it'll give us a long chase. I'll give it a good thunk on the head, and then we's be eatin' horsie tonight!"

The two powries crept up side by side, their smiles widening as they neared the apparently unsuspecting creature. They could not make out the horse's neck and head, for it was bent forward into some brush. Another bolt of lightning split the sky in a brilliant flash, followed immediately by a ground-shaking thunderclap.

The two dwarves jumped when the centaur backed out of the brush suddenly, throwing off the blanket he had used to cover his upper torso.

With one hand Bradwarden grabbed the closest powrie, the one with the crossbow, by the top of his head and lifted the dwarf from the ground. The centaur then dropped him, batting the tumbling dwarf with his huge club, launching him a dozen feet through the air.

The second powrie reacted quickly, rushing right in and smashing at the centaur's ribs with his hammer, a blow that got through Bradwarden's defense and landed hard.

But the powerful Bradwarden, so incensed that these two had been talking about eating horse meat, ignored the blow. He pivoted, bringing his club up over his shoulder. "Ye horse-eatin' goblin kisser!" he roared. Then straight down came the club onto the powrie's bloodred cap, slamming the dwarf so hard that the creature's knees and ankles buckled outward with loud popping sounds. The war hammer fell to the ground, the powrie's arms flapping weirdly a few times. Then the dwarf's body simply folded up.

A groan from the side alerted Bradwarden that the first dwarf was not quite dead. The centaur started for him at once but had to stop and stretch; the muscles on the side of his chest where the powrie had hit him were tightening as the bruise swelled, and Bradwarden feared the blow might have broken a rib or two. Only then, looking down, did Bradwarden realize he had a rather serious gash as well, his blood dripping down his side.

The sight angered him all the more. His respect for the tough powries increased as he neared his first victim, for the little wretch had struggled to his feet and was trying hard to find some defensive posture.

Bradwarden trampled the dwarf to the ground and added a couple of solid kicks to his head as he passed.

But the powrie struggled back to his feet.

Bradwarden was more amused than concerned. He came in hard, club flying fast, and knocked the dwarf into a tumble, then followed and trampled it down for good.

Pony's approach toward the two dwarves in the forest to the right of the cave entrance was much more cautious. She used the soul stone again to walk out of her body and pinpoint their location. Each was perched on a low branch, in trees about ten yards apart, just as they had been in her first scouting mission. She let her spirit linger until she was convinced the powries would not move anytime soon and also to inspect the dwarves' weapons and possessions. Neither carried a crossbow, she was glad to see: one had a short sword sheathed on his hip, while the other cradled a club in its arms.

Pony's spirit quickly inspected the area and then went back to her corporeal form. She knew she could eliminate these two quietly and efficiently with gemstones, but decided against that course, wanting to put Defender to good use. Despite Bradwarden's suggestion, she had ridden Greystone but had left him tethered in a sheltered pine grove not far away. The night was simply too wild for her to trust her horse's responses, and so she walked now, using the wind and the almost-constant thunder to cover any noise.

After she identified the trees she knew held the powries, she stopped and crouched beside a thick elm. In a few moments, she could make out the dark forms of the huddled dwarves. Out came Defender, the magical sword which had once belonged to Connor Bildeborough. Its crosspiece was set with magnetites, lodestones, and Pony also held one in her free hand. Foot by foot, she crept nearer to the dwarf on the right, the one with the sword.

"Yach, get back to yer post!" the powrie growled at her when she was barely a yard away, obviously mistaking her for his companion.

Pony stabbed upward, Defender digging deep into the powrie's leg.

Down hopped the dwarf, sword slashing, but Pony was already backing, waving Defender and turning to the other powrie as it hopped down from its perch.

The sword-wielding powrie attacked powerfully, sword slashing in wild arcs, and Pony retreated to the left, Defender only occasionally making contact with the powrie's wildly swinging short sword. Through the lodestone, she focused her mind on a metal choker the second powrie wore, a silver skull set in the center of its neck.

Around the tree came the second powrie, roaring in glee, club up over his head. Up, too, came Pony's hand, and she opened wide her fingers and sent her magical powers flowing into the magnetite.

Suddenly there came a snapping sound, then another, and the club-wielding dwarf was staggering backward, his roars lost in gurgles, as a crimson mist erupted from his throat.

"Yach, ye witch!" the first powrie cried, charging ahead.

Now Pony turned, continuing her defense through a few twists and turns, letting the dwarf play out its anger, easily parrying or simply avoiding the swings of his shorter blade. The powrie rushed at her, his blade cutting downward diagonally.

Pony flipped Defender to her left hand and brought it up fast, stopping the dwarf's sword short. Then, with a twist of her wrist, she flicked her blade over, then under, the dwarf's. A second twist of her wrist brought her sword in line, and she lunged, stabbing the dwarf's shoulder. Pony flipped her sword back to her right hand as she spun left, Defender smacking the stubborn powrie's pursuing blade hard.

She stopped in mid-turn, stepping ahead suddenly with her right foot, sliding her sword into the dwarf's belly. She retreated as the dwarf howled and doubled up, and then came forward again, powerfully stabbing the powrie in the chest. Pony had complete control now, and she could have finished the fight quickly with a stab to the dwarf's throat or heart, but she was enjoying this moment, was playing out her rage inch by painful inch.

Again and again, the woman thrust her blade into the powrie, never wounding mortally. She had hit the dwarf nearly a dozen times by the time Bradwarden arrived, leading Greystone by the reins.

"Be done with it, then," the centaur remarked, recognizing the macabre game. "I think I'm needin' a bit o' yer magic."

Pony glanced at her friend, her anger dissipated by the wheeze in his voice, and she saw the red stain along the side of Bradwarden's humanlike torso. She drove Defender deep into the powrie's chest, slipping the tip between ribs and into the creature's heart.

She put the soul stone to its healing work on Bradwarden immediately, and found to her relief that the centaur was not badly injured.

"On we go," Bradwarden said determinedly, now taking up his huge bow and a bolt that more resembled a spear than an arrow.

Pony held up a hand and moved to the club-wielding powrie lying at the base of the nearby tree. She bent low to inspect the hole neatly blasted through the silver skull pendant and the lodestone's exit hole at the back of the creature's neck. Standing straight, she then examined the tree and found that her flying gemstone had driven itself deep into the trunk. With a sigh, Pony lifted her sword and began chipping at the hole, trying to extract the magnetite. "I will lose this one some day," she explained to the centaur.

Bradwarden nodded. "But tell me," he asked, "can ye use the stone for repellin' metal as well as ye use it for attractin'?"

Pony looked at her friend curiously and nodded. The magnetite gemstones along the hilt of Defender were enchanted, and Pony had used their magic both ways, to attract an opponent's blade that she might powerfully parry, and to repel any of her foe's defensive maneuvers.

"I might help ye in findin' a better use for the stone, then," the centaur said slyly. "But that's talk for another day."

It took Pony several minutes, but finally she dug out the stone. She flipped the blanket back over Bradwarden's broad shoulders, and the centaur dipped his telltale human torso low and led on. Pony mounted Greystone and followed, moving from tree to tree, scouting in case any powries had heard the commotion. She thought to slip back into the hematite and scout out of body again, but decided to save her remaining magical energies to use on the cave entrance with the piece of graphite she now held in hand.

When a flash of lightning lit up the area near the cave entrance Pony and Bradwarden spotted the remaining powrie sentry—and the dwarf spotted them, too. He skittered down the rocky outcropping, landing on his feet and turning to call his kin.

Bradwarden's huge arrow took the powrie in the back, lifted him off his feet, and sent him flying ten feet to slam into the stones beside the cave entrance. The centaur had his bow leveled again right away, aimed at that dark hole in the hill, waiting for any other enemies to show their ugly faces.

Pony calmly walked by him, arm extended.

"Yach, what're ye about out there?" came a call from within.

Pony thought of her parents, murdered in Dundalis; of her second family, the Chilichunks, tortured to death by the evil Church leaders. And most of all, Pony recalled the images of the demonically possessed corpses of Graevis and Pettibwa, saw again that horrible moment, felt again the sickness, the revulsion. Her rage mounted and was transformed into magical energy that flowed from her hand into the graphite, building the power within the stone to explosive levels. Pony held on until all the air around her was tingling with magical energy, until her rain-matted hair began to fly wildly from the mounting static electricity.

Then she loosed a streaking blast of white light, thundering straight through the cave entrance, exploding in the cave in a burst of blinding energy, instantaneously ricochetting from stone wall to stone wall. Powries howled and screamed in agony; and, spurred by that wonderful sound, Pony loosed another bolt, equally lethal.

The thunder echoed for several seconds within the cave, and then a powrie staggered out the entrance—only to be driven back at the end of a flying centaur arrow.

More dwarves scrambled for the exit—and Pony's next blast laid them low.

On and on, her magical assault continued, bolt after bolt smashing into the cave. The residual rumbles echoed; chunks of rock and dust fell from the overhang above the entrance.

Pony put another blast into the cave, though few cries sounded from within. Those powries still alive were hiding now, she knew, probably flat on their bellies behind stones. Her arm went higher, taking aim at the rocky outcropping, and another tremendous bolt shot forth, slamming hard into loosened stone, followed by another and then a third, bringing the entire front of the hill rolling down in front of the cave.

A few steps behind Pony, Bradwarden lowered his bow and studied his friend closely. She was on the edge of control, he realized, throwing her grief and anger into every mighty bolt as if the destructive magic was somehow purifying her from those demons that haunted her memories.

But Bradwarden had spent many hours beside Pony these last weeks. He understood the depth of those demons and knew that it would take much more than this release of energy and revenge to put the troubled woman at ease. The centaur moved a bit closer. If Pony's strength failed and her legs gave way, Bradwarden would be there to catch her.

"It is too early in the morning for such important talk," King Danube Brock Ursal remarked as he settled behind an enormous plate of toasted bread smothered in sauced beans and topped with poached eggs. Danube was a handsome man, though he had packed an extra thirty pounds onto his already stocky frame over the last three years. His hair and beard were light brown, cut short and neatly trimmed, with just a hint of gray about the sideburns, and his eyes were light gray.

"But my King," Abbot Je'howith protested, "many of the children in Palmaris will not find the luxury of a morning meal this day."

King Danube dropped his silverware roughly to the metal plate, and the others in the room, the secular advisers, shuffled nervously, some uttering words of dismay and even anger.

"The situation in Palmaris is dire, no doubt, but I fear that you exaggerate," replied Constance Pemblebury, a woman of thirty-five years, the youngest of the advisers and often the most reasonable.

"And I fear that you underestimate—" Je'howith started to respond, but he was interrupted by the sharp voice of Duke Targon Bree Kalas.

"Good Abbot, you act as if Baron Rochefort Bildeborough fed the waifs personally!" the fiery man protested. "And how many have starved in the three months since the man's death?"

Je'howith wasn't surprised in the least that Kalas had come at him so forcefully; he and the man, once the leader of the famed Allheart Brigade, were often at odds, and their shaky relationship had become even more strained since King Danube, over Kalas' vehement protests, had allowed Je'howith to take a contingent of Allheart soldiers with him to the College of Abbots at St.-Mere-Abelle. It was no secret that Je'howith had involved the soldiers in the Church's power struggle, something that Kalas, a man of the King, did not like at all.

"The city lost its baron, his nephew, and its abbot, all in the space of a few weeks," Je'howith argued, looking directly at the King as he spoke—for the opinion that would matter in the end was that of the King. "And now they have learned, or soon shall, that there is no heir to the barony, no one to carry on the name and legacy of Bildeborough—and understand that Bildeborough is a beloved name indeed in Palmaris. And all of this on the heels of a war that hit that region quite hard. By all accounts, there is great turmoil in Palmaris, which will likely worsen as winter comes on, and that may threaten the loyalty of the folk there."

"What accounts?" Kalas retorted. "Word of the Baron's death was followed by nothing other than silence. And word that there is no obvious heir arrived only a few days ago. I have heard of no subsequent messengers from Palmaris."

Je'howith looked up at the warrior, his old eyes gleaming dangerously. "The Abellican Order has its ways of communication," he said almost threateningly.

Kalas snorted derisively and narrowed his eyes.

"The city is in trouble," Je'howith went on to King Danube. "And every day we delay in setting order there, the danger of anarchy grows. Already there is talk of looting in the merchant district, and the Behrenese yatols who make their pagan temples on the docks will use this time to their advantage, do not doubt."

"So therein lies the truth of your concerns, Abbot Je'howith," Kalas interrupted. "You fear that the yatol priests of the southern religion will steal some of your flock."

"I do fear such a thing," Je'howith admitted, "and so should the King of Honce-the-Bear."

"Are not the Church and the state separate entities?" Kalas asked, before King Danube had a chance to speak.

The king eyed the man, but made no protest. He pushed his plate away, resigned that he would get no quiet morning meal, and folded his hands before him, letting the two rivals debate.

"They are brothers, hand in hand in Honce-the-Bear," Je'howith agreed, "but not so in Behren. Yatol priests rule the kingdom and dominate every aspect of the lives of the common folk. Let the yatols gain a foothold in Palmaris, Duke Kalas, and see if your king benefits," he finished, his voice dripping with sarcasm.

Duke Kalas grumbled something under his breath and turned away.

"What do you suggest we do?" King Danube asked Je'howith.

"Appoint an interim leader at once," the abbot replied. "It has been too long already, but now that the matter of blood heir is settled, you must act decisively."

King Danube glanced around at the others. "Suggestions?" he asked.

"There are many nobles here suitable for such a position," Kalas replied.

"But few, if any, who would willingly rush to Palmaris at any time of the year, and even less with the solstice fast approaching," Constance Pemblebury was quick to add. All in the room knew that her words were true. Palmaris was a rough city, with a harsher climate and many more problems than Ursal, the city of King Danube's court, where the nobles who attended the king lived in absolute luxury. Even the dukes, like Kalas, let their barons rule the distant cities, while they hunted and fished, dined fabulously, and chased the ladies here.

"There is one possible choice," Je'howith put in, "a man of great charisma already holding command over much of the city."

"Do not even speak the name!" Kalas protested, but Je'howith would not be dissuaded.

"Any semblance of order remaining in Palmaris is due to the tireless work of Marcalo De'Unnero, the new abbot of St. Precious," he said.

"You want me to bestow the title of baron on an abbot?" King Danube asked skeptically.

"The Church will give De'Unnero an equivalent title," Je'howith explained: "bishop of Palmaris."

"Bishop?" Kalas balked.

"A little-used title in these times," Je'howith explained, "but surely not without precedent. In the early days of the kingdom, bishops were as common as barons and dukes."

"And the distinction between a bishop and an abbot?" King Danube asked.

"The title of bishop confers power equal to that of a secular ruler," Je'howith explained softly.

"But with the bishop answering to the Father Abbot, and not the King," an obviously angry Kalas put in, and Danube's expression darkened at the notion. The others in the room, even cool Constance Pemblebury, bristled and whispered harshly to one another.

"No," Je'howith was quick to respond. "Bishops answer to the Father Abbot on matters of the Church, but to the King alone in matters of state. And I recommend Marcalo De'Unnero highly, King Danube. He is young and full of energy, and perhaps the finest warrior ever to come out of St.-Mere-Abelle—no small boast indeed!"

"Methinks the abbot has overstepped his bounds," Constance remarked. "With all respect, good Je'howith, you ask the King to relinquish much power to the Father Abbot, yet have offered no better reason than avoiding inconvenience to some nobleman who might be appointed to the northern city."

"I offer the King the hand of a friend in a time of desperate need," Je'howith replied.

"Ridiculous!" roared Kalas, and then to the King, he added, "I will secure for you a proper replacement for Baron Bildeborough. A man of the Allheart Brigade, perhaps, or one of the lesser, but deserving nobles. Why, we have a contingent of soldiers in the region already, led by an able-bodied warrior."

King Danube looked from Je'howith to Kalas, seeming unsure.

"And which is more dangerous, I wonder," Je'howith asked slyly, "allowing the partner to aid in a time of great need or strengthening the position of an ambitious underling? One who, perhaps, holds designs on a higher station?"

A stunned Kalas groaned and growled for lack of a reply. His face turned bright red and he clenched his jaw tight, seemingly on the verge of an explosion. Others in the room were equally distressed, but Constance grew more amused by it all.

"I ask you to consider the benefits of a single new ruler in such a time of distress," Je'howith went on, his voice calm. "If you replace Baron Bildeborough with yet another unknown leader, then the people of Palmaris shall not know what to expect from Church or state. Let them warm to De'Unnero first. They hardly know the man, for he has presided over St. Precious for but one season, and even in that time, Church duties—the College of Abbots, in which your Allheart Brigade played no minor role—" he pointedly reminded, "forced Abbot De'Unnero out of Palmaris for the better part of a month. Yet the city has remained relatively calm, considering the tragedies the folk have suffered."

"You propose the abbot of St. Precious as only an interim leader then?" King Danube asked after a long, thoughtful pause.

"After said interim—with the turn of summer, perhaps—you could decide that Palmaris, and you, would be better served by appointing another," Je'howith explained. "But I think that Marcalo De'Unnero will amaze you with his efficiency. He will put the people of Palmaris back into order and hold firm control—strengthening your position."

"What rubbish!" cried Duke Kalas, coming forward to join Je'howith at the King's side. "Surely you do not believe a word of this, my King."

"Do not presume to tell me what I believe," King Danube sternly and coldly replied, backing Kalas off a step or two.

"And you must consider the larger position," Je'howith went on, ignoring Kalas. "The Timberlands must be reopened, perhaps claimed as the domain of Honce-the-Bear."

"Good Je'howith," Constance Pemblebury intervened, "we have a treaty with both Behren and Alpinador that the Timberlands remain open to all three kingdoms."

"And yet the region has long been settled only by folk of Honce-the-Bear," Je'howith replied. "And the war has changed the situation, I believe. The Timberlands, we could argue, now belong to the powries and goblins. Since we will be the ones to drive them from the region, it will be considered conquered land, and under the domain of King Danube Brock Ursal."

"A most clever position," the King admitted, "but a dangerous one."

"All the more reason you now need the Church strong by your side," Je'howith argued, "the same Church that holds influence over many of the barbarians of southern Alpinador. Name De'Unnero as bishop and then the matter of Palmaris no longer need be of concern to you. Let the Abellican Church take responsibility should De'Unnero fail and Palmaris fall into turmoil. And if the Bishop succeeds in restoring order and prosperity, then how wise King Danube will seem to his adoring people!"

Again Duke Kalas' face brightened with rage. How dare the abbot of St. Honce so bait the King!

But Danube, never overambitious, though always willing to seize an opportunity for expansion, had already swallowed that bait. Je'howith's offer, seemingly free of risk for Danube, might well help in any expansion of the kingdom northward, and even at worst, seemed to offer Danube insulation from blame. That, above all else, proved too attractive an offer to refuse. And Danube Brock Ursal was impetuous—something Je'howith had long ago learned to exploit. "Interim leader," the King declared. "Then so be it. Let word go forth from Ursal this day that Abbot Marcalo De'Unnero has been named bishop of Palmaris."

Je'howith smiled; Kalas growled.

"And Duke Kalas," King Danube went on, "do send word to your worthy underling in command of the soldiers in the Palmaris region that he is to report to Bishop De'Unnero and to remain with the man until the situation in Palmaris is secure.

"Now leave me!" the King said suddenly, waving his hands at the advisers as if they were troublesome pigeons. "My meal is already cold, I fear."

Abbot Je'howith, still smiling, turned to come face-to-face with Constance Pemblebury, who fell into step beside him and accompanied him out of the room. "Well done," she congratulated him when they were alone.

"You speak as if I have gained something," Je'howith protested. "I only wish to serve my King."

"You only wish to serve the Father Abbot," Constance replied with a chuckle.

"Little service if King Danube decides that Marcalo De'Unnero is not the man to rule Palmaris," Je'howith reasoned.

"A difficult decision, since a bishop, by law and tradition, can only be removed by agreement of the king and the Father Abbot," Constance said slyly.

That set Je'howith back on his heels—until he considered the fact that the woman had not mentioned that little matter of law *before* King Danube's proclamation.

"Fear not, Abbot Je'howith," the woman said. "I understand that the balance of power will inevitably shift after a war, win or lose, and I am pragmatic enough to recognize the power of the Abellican Church over people battered by war. Is there a family in all the northern reaches of Honce-the-Bear which has not lost one of its own? And grieving people, alas, are more drawn toward empty promises of eternal life than to practical material gains."

"Empty promises?" the abbot remarked, his tone one of astonishment, showing that he considered the woman on the verge of heresy.

Constance let the matter pass. "St.-Mere-Abelle will dominate Palmaris and all the northland—and that will not be a bad thing for King Danube through the difficult process of reopening the Timberlands and designing a new—if there indeed is to be a new—agreement with our neighboring kingdoms."

"And after the Timberlands are secured?"

Constance shrugged. "I choose not to go against the Church," was her simple reply.

"And in return for your assistance?"

Now the woman laughed aloud. "There are enough spoils from the backs of common laborers to secure a luxurious existence for all of us," she said. "There is an old saying about the buttering of bread; I am wise enough to understand that the Father Abbot might now have a hand on that knife."

Now Abbot Je'howith was smiling widely. He didn't have an ally here, he understood, but neither did he have a foe. That was the way it would be with many of the nobles, he believed, for they were men and women who had never engaged in any serious matters before the dactyl had awakened.

He left Constance then, needing privacy while he prepared himself for the next spiritual visit of the Father Abbot. Markwart would be pleased, but Je'howith knew that the situation remained tentative, that there remained a few, like Duke Kalas, who would never accept any gains the Church made at King Danube's expense.

It would be an interesting year.

By dawn, the rain had increased again, but the wind had died. The air was unseasonably warm, and a good thing it was, for otherwise several feet of snow would have buried the area and any plans for a journey south to Palmaris would have had to be put off by several weeks.

Pony and Bradwarden were still at the powrie cave. They had no idea how many dwarves might still be alive, but every now and then a rock shifted as a dwarf tried to dig out. At first Bradwarden took care of those attempts, clubbing hard on the stone, then laughing uproariously at the stream of heavily accented curses coming back out at him.

Now it was Pony's turn to keep watch, along with Juraviel, who had joined the companions an hour earlier. Bradwarden was scouring the nearby forest, collecting broken tree limbs for kindling and larger logs for long burning.

"Got me a good one this time," the centaur announced on one return.

Pony and Juraviel chuckled, for the tree the powerful centaur was dragging behind him must have stood twenty feet tall.

"A good one if you mean to batter down a castle door," Juraviel replied.

"And I just might, but from the inside, most likely, if them soldiers catch me standin' here arguin' with the likes of a stubborn elf!" Bradwarden remarked, reminding Juraviel that they had all agreed that the elf should go out and scout for the approaching soldiers at daybreak.

"And so I go, good half a horse," Juraviel said, bowing and then skittering into the forest.

"Half a horse," Bradwarden grumbled, and he piled kindling near the cave entrance. "but if th' other part was elf, I'd have to be half a pony!"

Pony smiled widely, appreciating the good-natured game that Juraviel and Bradwarden always played.

The centaur moved a large rock aside, then jumped back as a crossbow bolt skipped through an opening deeper in the pile, narrowly missing a foreleg. "Can ye be takin' care o' that?" he asked.

Pony was already moving, graphite in hand. She loosed another streak of lightning into the opening. Cries and curses erupted within the cave, sounding more distant as Bradwarden stuffed the hole with wood. Then the centaur shifted to the side and removed some more rubble, building the cairn.

"Ye're sure ye can light the stuff?" he asked Pony for perhaps the tenth time.

Her look sent a shiver coursing through Bradwarden, and so he went back to his work.

"Nightbird approaches," came Juraviel's voice a few minutes later. "He has found two of the slain powries. The soldiers are behind him, but at a distance."

Bradwarden looked at Pony and nodded, and she came forward to the pile with serpentine and ruby in hand. She waved the centaur away, then fell into the power of the serpentine, erecting a blue-white, glowing protective shield that completely engulfed her. A subtle command to the magic moved the ruby outside that shield, to sit atop the glow, atop her open palm. Now Pony linked her thoughts, her magical center, to the swirling powers of the ruby. She took her time, sent all her remaining energy into that stone, letting the power mount until wisps of flame flickered about her.

Bradwarden and Juraviel wisely backed away even farther.

Pony looked around, chose the hollowed end of a log set low in the pile, then thrust her hand inside and loosed the magic. The sudden burst of flame engulfed her and the barricade, the concussive power shaking the stones, the fiery burst consuming every scrap of kindling Bradwarden had placed, shooting out in streaks from every crack in the pile.

Wet wood hissed in protest, but because of the intensity of the blast, most of it caught and burned. The rain joined in that hissing song, settling on the heated stones and vaporizing to rise into the heavy air.

Pony loosed another fireball, and when she stepped back, plumes of gray smoke billowed into the air. And into the cave, she knew. She dropped the serpentine shield and put the two gems away, taking out the graphite once more, for she expected that powries might be pounding at the barricade at any moment.

"The ranger approaches," Juraviel called down to them.

"I suppose that all the remaining powries are caught in that hole?" came his familiar voice from the tree line behind the friends.

"Ye think we'd sit all the night and wait for yerself and yer lazy soldier friends?" Bradwarden replied with a wink as the ranger came into view.

Nightbird looked at the smoking rubble pile, at the lightning-blasted stones, then turned to stare at Pony, who was soaking wet, her blond hair dripping. His first reaction was one of anger. How could his friends have come out here without telling him? How could Pony have put herself in danger without letting him know? But Elbryan forced himself to see this situation through Pony's eyes. She was full of rage, more so than he, and yet she could not vent that fury even in the few fights they had found over the last weeks. Since Elbryan and Pony were outlaws, she dared not use the gemstones openly in battle. Moreover, her proficiency with the healing stones, particularly hematite, demanded that she remain well away from the heart of any battle, ready to secretly heal those in need.

And when the ranger considered the situation from Bradwarden's view, he was no less sympathetic. The centaur had been treated brutally—imprisoned and tortured—since he was rescued from the bowels of destroyed Mount Aida by the Abellican monks. Yet he had been even less involved in the battles, for he was too easily identified, and Shamus Kilronney, though the man had become something of a friend, was a soldier of the King.

Elbryan focused again on Pony and recognized that, despite the drenching rain and the long, sleepless night she had obviously endured, she seemed more at peace than at any time since they had left St.-Mere-Abelle. Any anger Elbryan felt over this private war Pony and Bradwarden had waged could not measure up against that reality.

"Well, it seems that you have had all the fun," he said cheerily, "this time."

"Ah, ye'll get yer chance to stick a few afore the day's done, by me thinkin'," Bradwarden piped up. "And be sure that ye'll find more when we go to the northland."

"Soldiers approaching," Juraviel, now perched in a different nearby tree, warned. He motioned to Bradwarden, and as the centaur trotted beneath the tree, the elf dropped down atop his broad back.

"We found a bit o' the fun, though, didn't we?" Bradwarden said with a wink at Pony, and he moved off into the forest.

Pony mounted Greystone even as Elbryan slid off Symphony, the ranger drawing his elven bow, Hawkwing, and fitting an arrow as he moved to keep watch for any possible escapes through rock pile. The smoke was thicker now, billowing gray, and a fair amount of it was going into the cave.

"What got this one?" Colleen Kilronney asked incredulously as she examined the powrie lying at the base of the tree, a hole blasted right through its neck. Then she stood up to examine the hole in the tree, and shook her head in disbelief that anything could have been so deeply embedded in the hard wood of an old oak.

"A crossbow, I assume," one of her soldiers replied. "Powries oft carry them, and someone may have picked one from a body."

Colleen shrugged. Her fellow soldier had to be right, but she had never seen any crossbow that could hit this hard.

"Smoke in the forest," came the report of a scout, moving back to join the group.

Colleen was quick to her horse, kicking the mount to catch up to Shamus at the head of the column. They soon came into the clearing before the cave, and found Nightbird bending low to line up another shot through a smoking pile of wood and rock, Pony sitting calmly on her mount twenty feet to the side.

Colleen's gaze measured Pony. After Colleen had met Nightbird in her cousin's tent, she had learned that he was betrothed, or at least promised to, a woman called Pony. This had to be that woman, Colleen knew from the description the soldier had given her—a lengthy and detailed description, for the man had rambled on and on about how helpful and wonderful Pony had been after their battles.

Looking at Pony now, Colleen was hardly surprised by that soldier's attitude. Pony was undeniably beautiful, with thick hair and huge sparkling eyes. And now she was just sitting to the side, watching, like some waiting plaything for the heroic ranger. "Ornament," the warrior whispered under her breath, and she gave a snort.

"How did you ever start a fire in this rain?" Shamus asked Nightbird. The captain dropped from his saddle and moved beside the ranger.

Nightbird grinned. "I did not," he explained. "A lucky lightning strike, it would seem, took down both rock and wood from above the cave entrance, trapping most of the powries within. God is with us this day, lending us his thundering sword."

"I've seen no recent lightning strikes," Colleen interrupted doubtfully. "And did yer God then pile the brush neatly in all the cracks? Or have ye been that busy in the ten minutes ye came in ahead of us?"

"No, and no," the ranger started to answer, but Pony cut him short.

"Trapper friends," she explained. "They saw the lightning—more than an hour ago, I guess—and took the opportunity to stack the brush and feed the flames."

"And killed the bloody cap guards in the forest?" Colleen went on.

Pony gave a noncommittal shrug. "We found the trappers here and heard a quick tale. When we told them you were approaching, they bade us to keep the powries in the hole."

"Us?" Colleen asked doubtfully, looking at Nightbird, then back to the woman.

Pony let the insult pass. "Two score of the wretches, they said, though we know not how many still survive."

"And they'll not stay in the hole for long," Nightbird put in, "no matter the odds. Form your archers in a line before the rocks," he bade the captain, "and we can pick them off as they exit."

Shamus Kilronney motioned his archers to take their positions. "This is all too easy," he remarked to the ranger.

"And is that not the preferred way?" Nightbird replied. Both he and Shamus glanced at Colleen as he said it, and neither was surprised to find the angry woman frowning.

And indeed, Colleen Kilronney was not pleased by this unexpected turn of events. When at last the leaders of Palmaris had decided to send someone north with news of the Baron's death, Colleen had volunteered, had insisted, on being a part of that team. She had come out for battle, eager to avenge Abbot Dobrinion, a personal friend whom she believed had been murdered by one of the bloody-cap dwarves. She jumped down from her horse and stormed past the two men, studying the rock pile. "Might be that they've another way out," she remarked—hopefully, it seemed. "Might already be gone, circled back and lookin' at us from behind, for all we're knowin'!"

"No other way out," Nightbird said firmly. "They are trapped within the cave, where the air grows fouler by the second."

"Unless the place's vented," Colleen said. She moved a step back, looking at the hill above the fallen stone.

"Easy enough to find and plug, if that were the case," Nightbird replied without missing a beat. "Though even if there were air holes, they would not clear enough of the heavy smoke in time. The dwarves are caught and choking. Some will try to come out and we will shoot them down. The others will die in the cave."

Colleen glared at Nightbird, not liking the blunt truth one bit.

"Perhaps not," Shamus said, wearing a thoughtful expression. "One telling feature of this war is the surprising lack of prisoners taken by either side."

"And who'd be wantin' a goblin prisoner?" Colleen asked incredulously. "Or a smelly bloody cap? Just stink up the place ye put 'em in."

"Powries have shown no mercy at all to humans," Nightbird added. As he spoke the words, he glanced at Colleen and found her looking back at him, both of them wearing the same blank expression, for both were surprised to find themselves on the same side of any debate.

"I speak not of mercy," Shamus was quick to add, "but of practicality. The powries in the cave are likely battered and hopeless. As reports from all corners of the kingdom have shown, they only want to get home now, and they might divulge important information concerning their former allies in exchange for passage."

"For passage that'd let 'em turn around and kill a few more folks for fun!" Colleen vehemently protested.

And again the ranger agreed. "Could we trust powries to stay away?" he asked. "Or even if they did not strike out in our lands again, wouldn't they prowl our coastal waters, preying on helpless ships?"

"But if these powries offered information that prevented even larger groups from wreaking suffering on the kingdom, then the risk would be worth the gain," Shamus replied.

Nightbird looked at Pony. The ranger's gaze drew others, Shamus and Colleen among them, and soon Pony found many pairs of eyes staring at her.

"I care nothing for the powries in the cave," Pony said quietly but firmly.

"Kill them if you will, or take them prisoner if you will. They mean nothing to me."

"Suren there's a decisive answer," Colleen remarked sarcastically.

"I have seen too much fighting to be concerned with one small band of bloody-cap dwarves," Pony retorted.

Colleen Kilronney snorted derisively and turned away.

Pony looked at Elbryan and gave a weak but comforting smile, and he understood that she had sated her anger with this band already.

"Well, Nightbird," Captain Kilronney asked, "are we in agreement?"

"You agreed to help me rid the region of this band before you turned south," the ranger replied. "However you choose to do that is your own affair. This fight was over before you or I arrived here."

Shamus took that as the ranger's blessing. He moved to the rock pile, found what seemed to be the most open route to the darkness beyond, and called into the cave, offering to spare those dwarves that came out without a weapon.

For a while there came no answer, and Shamus set some of his men to the task of adding kindling to the smoky fire, while others stood behind the blaze, waving saddle blankets to fan the smoke more directly into the cave.

Suddenly the powries, screaming curses, charged the barricade, going at the stones furiously. Some opened passages too small for their stout bodies but perfectly suited to the archers' arrows. Others moved the wrong stone by mistake, only to start rockslides, while a couple did break clear. Arrow after arrow slammed into those freed powries, jolting them, slowing and then stopping their stubborn charge.

In a minute, the rock barricade was quiet again, save the continuing hiss and crackle of the fires, with several powries dead, and several others crawling wounded back into the cave, and with one unfortunate fellow stuck fast under some rocks, perilously close to a burning pile.

Captain Shamus Kilronney repeated his offer, identifying himself as an emissary of the King of Honce-the-Bear, with full power to bargain in the field.

This time, his offer was answered by a request for clarification, and then by a request for further assurances, before the remaining twenty-seven powries, faces blackened by smoke and many with wounds from stone and arrow and lightning bolts, crawled out of the cave, and were taken and securely bound.

Nightbird and Pony watched, the ranger leery, Pony ambivalent. Sitting not far from them astride her horse, Colleen Kilronney's feelings were more evident, her expression sour, low growls coming from her throat as each new bloody cap made its appearance at the narrow opening in the rock pile.

The group set off for Caer Tinella at once, the powries completely encir-
cled by Kilronney's wary men. The captain rode at the head of the line,
Nightbird beside him, while Pony followed behind, soon to be joined by
Colleen Kilronney.

"Seems yer healin' arts won't be needed at all," the red-haired woman
said to Pony, her tone condescending.

"I am always grateful when that is the case," Pony responded absently.

Colleen gave her horse a good kick and moved away.

Precautions

Braumin Herde moved quickly and purposefully, slipping from chamber to chamber along the top floor of the abbey's northern wing. He was collecting candlesticks, of which there were a multitude in the dark stone abbey, but specific ones, ones from a list that Master Jojonah had begun and that he had spent the weeks since Jojonah's death finishing. All the candlesticks in this wing had a single sunstone set in them, with one in thirty of the gems enchanted. This was the testing area for young students, and the masters had devised the sunstone system to prevent any cheating with clear quartz, the stone of distance sight, or even hematite.

Master Engress, a gentle and calm elderly man, had shown Brother Braumin how to determine which candlesticks were enchanted—no easy task with sunstone! Brother Braumin had gone to Engress with a story about some students swapping candlesticks. The master had not questioned him and had gladly given Braumin the task of rearranging them each night after studies.

Master Engress had no idea of the extent of Brother Braumin's shuffling. With ten candlesticks in hand, the young monk descended to the area of the next meeting of the disciples of Avelyn, strategically placing the candlesticks in adjoining rooms to discourage any spiritually prying eyes. The only hope for his group was in secrecy, Braumin knew, for if the always-suspicious Markwart ever realized how subversive their rhetoric had become, they would likely share the fiery fate of Master Jojonah.

This night, Braumin collected the candlesticks in a hurry, rearranged the others to make it less obvious that some had been taken, then rushed away.

To Brother Francis, though, the altered count of candlesticks was obvious. He crept through the study rooms even as Brother Braumin moved down the little-used back stairway and along the empty, dusty corridors four levels down.

Francis did not immediately follow but moved south along the top level to the private quarters of Father Abbot Markwart. He knocked softly, afraid to disturb the Father Abbot. Then, hearing Markwart's call, he entered to find him at his desk, a jumble of papers before him and the remnants of his dinner off to the side.

"You should take more leisure time with your evening meal, Father Abbot," Francis offered. "I worry that you—" The young monk stopped short as the old man glared up at him.

"This list is more extensive than I would have thought," Markwart replied, shoving the papers about.

"St.-Mere-Abelle requires a large staff," Francis replied. "And many of those hired are derelicts by nature, vagabonds who leave as soon as they have collected enough money to see them through a few meals."

"A few drinks, more likely," Markwart said sourly. "If that is the case, then why did you not separate the various groups represented in this list in a more orderly fashion? Those who left before the invasion and escape on one page, perhaps. Those who left soon after on another, and those who remain on the third."

"You insisted that I hurry, Father Abbot," Francis meekly protested. "And many of those who left before the intrusion, returned soon after it. I found it almost impossible to catagorize the workers unless I used many categories."

"Work on it, then!" Markwart roared, shoving the papers forward; many of them slipped off the desk and glided to the floor. "We must ensure that Jojonah and those others who invaded the abbey did not leave a spy behind. Discern likely suspects and watch them closely. If you decide that one, anyone, is possibly a spy, then arrest him secretly and bring him to me."

That you might torture him as you did the Chilichunks, Francis thought, but he wisely kept silent. Still, he realized that his sour expression betrayed his feelings when Markwart's glare intensified.

"Have you been watching Brother Braumin closely?" the Father Abbot asked.

Francis nodded.

"I do not trust him," Markwart said, rising and pacing around the corner of his desk, "though neither do I fear him. His sympathies remain with Jojonah, but that will change with time, particularly when he goes through the intensive training needed for the rank of master."

"You will promote him?" Francis blurted, eyes wide with shock—and more than a little anger, for Francis believed that he would be promoted because of loyalty to the Father Abbot. By that same reasoning, it seemed impossible that Brother Braumin Herde, friend of the heretic Jojonah, would also rate a promotion!

"It is the best course," Markwart replied without hesitation. "In De'Unnero and Je'howith I have strong allies, but many of the other abbots, and more than a few masters and immaculates, are watching closely to ensure that my actions against Jojonah were not personal."

"And were they?" Francis asked. He knew he had made a mistake as soon as the words came out of his mouth.

The Father Abbot stopped his pacing only a step from Francis, turning his wrinkled old head slowly, his eyes flaring with an intensity that frightened Francis and made him think that Markwart would strike him dead where he stood—and the old man's shaved head and pointed ears only accentuated that frightening visage. In that fleeting second while Markwart held his gaze, Francis believed that the man could do it, could simply strike him dead, and with hardly an effort!

"There are those who quietly question—*quietly* because they are cowards, you see," Markwart went on, going back to his pacing. "They wonder if the sudden turn against the heretic Jojonah was in the best interest of the Church, if the evidence of conspiracy was strong enough to so quickly convict and condemn. I have heard more than one who murmured that it would have been better if we had extracted a full confession from the man before we burned him."

Francis nodded, but he knew, as did Markwart, that Jojonah would never have confessed to anything evil. The brave man had admitted his complicity in freeing the prisoners, excusing his actions by trying to turn the accusation against Markwart. But the confession Markwart wanted—one in which Jojonah admitted that he had conspired with Brother Avelyn to steal the stones and murder Master Siherton those years ago—would never have happened. And they both knew that the conspiracy so envisioned had never actually happened.

"But enough of that," Markwart went on, waving his skinny arm briskly—and Francis understood then that something important was going on. "There has come a shift in the balance of power," Markwart explained.

"Among the Church leaders?"

"Between Church and state. King Danube needs help in restoring order to Palmaris. With the Baron and his sole heir dead, the city is in turmoil."

"And they are without their beloved Abbot Dobrinion," Francis added.

"You do test me this night, do you not?" Markwart hissed, again turning that awful glare on him. "The people of Palmaris have a stronger leader in Abbot De'Unnero than ever they realized in Dobrinion."

"They will come to love him," Francis remarked, trying hard to keep the sarcasm out of his voice.

"They will come to respect him!" Markwart corrected. "To fear him. To understand that the Church, and not the King, is the true power in their lives, their hopes beyond this mortal coil, their only chance of redemption or true joy. Marcalo De'Unnero is the perfect man to teach them, or at least to cow them until they understand the truth."

"Abbot?"

"Bishop," Markwart corrected.

He could have knocked Brother Francis over with a feather. Francis was among the finest historians at St.-Mere-Abelle, a man whose studies had long centered on the geography and politics of the various regions of the known world. He knew what the title of bishop entailed, and knew, too, that such a title had not been bestowed in more than three hundred years.

"You seem surprised, Brother Francis," Markwart remarked. "You do not believe that Marcalo De'Unnero is fit for the task?"

"N-not that, Father Abbot," the monk stammered. "I am only surprised that the King would relinquish the second city of Honce-the-Bear to the Church."

Markwart's laughter mocked that notion. "Thus I need you to be my eyes and ears in St.-Mere-Abelle," the Father Abbot said.

"You will be leaving?"

"Not yet," Markwart replied, "but I will be looking elsewhere more often than not. So keep watch over troublesome Brother Braumin and search among these new additions and subtractions to the staff." He waved his skinny hand at Francis then, turning away to resume his pacing, and the younger monk bowed and quickly left.

The news had stunned Francis, and he tried hard to sort it out as he made his way back to the study rooms, taking the same route as Brother Braumin. Francis had never been a big supporter of Marcalo De'Unnero, mostly because he, like almost everyone else, was deathly afraid of the volatile and unpredictable man. A bishop would wield great power; might De'Unnero become too strong to be controlled by Father Abbot Markwart? Francis shook his head, trying to dismiss that disturbing notion. Markwart seemed pleased by the developments—indeed, the Father Abbot had no doubt played a huge role in facilitating them.

Still, Francis remembered the image of De'Unnero after the powrie attack against St.-Mere-Abelle, the man wild-eyed and covered in blood, most from his enemies, but more than a bit from a wound he had received in the fighting—in fighting that De'Unnero had invited, for no better reason than his desire to kill powries, by opening the lower wharf gates!

The monk shuddered. Had this new development put De'Unnero in line for the position of Father Abbot? And if it had, would Francis, or any of the others so loyal to Markwart, survive?

Those were questions for another time, Francis realized as he slipped among the shadows of the lower levels, and heard the whispered prayers.

It began, as always, with a prayer to Jojonah and one to Avelyn. The group went unusually quiet after that, four monks sitting nervously, attentively, waiting for Brother Braumin to begin again his detailing of the story of *Windrunner* and the voyage to Pimaninicuit.

Braumin understood their excitement and their fear. To speak openly of Pimaninicuit, even in terms favorable to the presiding Father Abbot, was a serious crime, an often fatal error. After the voyage to the island to collect the stones, Pellimar, one of the remaining three brothers, had rambled on about his adventures.

He had not survived the winter.

And now Braumin was telling these four of the voyage—was, in effect, placing upon them a writ of execution.

Braumin thought of Jojonah, viewing his stand against Markwart in much the same light as Avelyn's stand against the demon dactyl. Braumin conjured that memory of Mount Aida, of Avelyn's arm reaching heaven-ward through the devastation as if in defiance of death itself.

Then he began his tale, recounting the story in vivid detail, as Jojonah had told it to him. He started at the beginning of the voyage, elaborating on the teasing story he had given them at their last meeting. Braumin had pre-pared himself well for this most important speech, and he spoke with pride of the battle the crew—particularly the four men of St.-Mere-Abelle—had waged against a powrie barrelboat, focusing on Avelyn's heroics in that fight.

"The man took a ruby in hand," Braumin said dramatically, holding forth his clenched fist, "empowered it and tossed it—tossed it, I say—into the open hatch of the powrie vessel, only releasing its energies within the bowels of the craft!"

A gasp came back at him. There were accounts of a stone user separating himself from the gem at the time of magical release, but it was considered an almost impossible feat, particularly with a stone as powerful and demanding as a ruby.

"It is true," Braumin insisted. "And Brother Avelyn did not even under-stand the significance of his action. When he recounted the tale to Master Jojonah upon his return to St.-Mere-Abelle, the master bade him keep it quiet; for Jojonah knew, as we do, that the usage clearly illustrates Avelyn Desbris' powers."

"And why would Master Jojonah want that to remain a secret?" Brother Dellman asked.

"Because such a variation of stone use might also be construed as heretical, a demon-inspired burst of power," Braumin replied. "Master Jojonah was wise enough to understand that inertia guides the Abellican Church, that anything beyond the ordinary might be construed as a threat to those insecure in their power." He let the words settle in their thoughts, then went on to the rest of the journey, his voice softer now, all pride gone from his almost melancholy tone. He told them of the murder of a young man—his name had been lost over the years—by Brother Thagraine, at the behest of Brother Quintal, because that young man, beyond all reason, leaped from the *Windrunner* and swam to the sacred island. He told again of Thagraine's falling from faith on the island, a disastrous lapse that left him out in the open when the stone showers commenced, to be battered, and finally killed by a blow to the head—hit by the same stone that would eventually destroy the demon dactyl.

And then, in even more somber tones, Brother Braumin recounted the journey home, the near mutiny that ended with Brother Quintal tearing apart the leader of the mutineers. Then, his voice rising in anger, he told of the phony payment to the *Windrunner*—an illusion of gold crafted through use of the sacred gemstones—and of the final insult to everything holy, detailing graphically the ultimate destruction of the *Windrunner* and her crew.

When it was over, the five men sat in stunned, exhausted silence for a long while.

In the hallway beyond the room's door, Brother Francis could hardly keep still. He wanted to kick in the door, run up to Braumin, and scream in the man's face! To shake the man and tell him that he would be tortured and executed for his foolish words, and that he would bring about the horrible deaths of the other four, as well.

And Francis wanted to argue the truth of the story, to reveal it as a complete distortion of the real events—events of which he admittedly had very little knowledge.

He did not go in, though, but stood at the door, his hands sweaty, fighting to keep his breath steady and quiet that he might hear the rest of the conversation, that he might bear witness for Father Abbot Markwart when these men were brought to trial.

"This book," Brother Braumin began again, pulling the ancient text out from a fold in his voluminous robes, "this book was found by Master Jojonah in the ancient library, not far from where we now gather. I believe that Master Jojonah knew that he had little time left in this world, and so he searched desperately among the recorded histories, seeking his answer.

"And he found it!" Braumin said dramatically. "For within this book, as detailed by Brother Francis—"

"Francis?" Brother Viscenti piped up, his voice nearly hysterical.

"A different Francis," Brother Braumin assured him, "a man who lived several centuries ago."

"I knew it could not be the same one," Brother Viscenti said with a chuckle.

"Doubtful that our dear brother Francis would write anything that Master Jojonah would find enlightening," Brother Anders Castinagis said with a laugh.

"Unless it was a suicide note," Brother Dellman added, and they all had a good laugh.

Brother Braumin calmed it quickly, though, getting back to the point and to the book, showing them that in ages past, the monks of St.-Mere-Abelle crewed their own ship to Pimaninicuit and spoke of the island openly, reverently. And there were no murders, no mutinies. The journey was an open celebration of the highest joy, not a covert mission of avarice and murder.

All four listening in the room sighed and smiled warmly, to know that the precepts on which the Abellican Church was founded were true and holy, if the modern practices were not.

Brother Francis didn't share that view or that warmth, and he could hold his peace no longer. He pushed open the door and strode into their midst. All four jumped up to surround the intruder as he stalked right up to confront Brother Braumin, their faces barely an inch apart.

"Foul words," Francis growled. "You speak heresy with the accent of reverence."

"Heresy?" Braumin echoed, his fists clenched at his sides as if he meant to strike the man. He motioned to Brother Visconti, and the nervous monk, after inspecting the corridor beyond, gently closed the door.

"Heresy," Francis said again determinedly. "Merely speaking such lies could get a man burned. Merely hearing such lies—"

"Lies?" Dellman cried, forcing his way between the principals. "Brother Braumin's tales ring of more truth than anything I have heard spoken by the Father Abbot or any of the masters!"

"Tainted words," Francis spat right back. "Half-truths, concealed in a cocoon of blessed events."

"Then you deny the truth of the *Windrunner's* fate?" Brother Braumin asked.

"I deny everything you have said," Francis retorted. "You are a fool, Brother Braumin, as are your lackeys, and you play games more dangerous than anything you could ever imagine."

"It would surprise you to learn that which we, who witnessed the execution of Master Jojonah, might imagine," said Brother Castinagis. That statement, loaded with the image of the murdered man, seemed to sting Francis profoundly.

"Why have you come here?" Brother Braumin demanded.

"To call a fool a fool," Francis replied, "and to warn the fool that his words are not as secret as he might have hoped. To warn you all," Francis said dramatically, stepping back from Braumin. "Your actions shout of heresy, and many ears are turning your way. Remember well that image of Mas—of Jojonah, Brother Anders Castinagis, and replace his defeated visage with your own." Francis turned back for the door, but he hesitated, the others freezing in place, wondering if Brother Braumin would let him leave the room.

On a nod from Braumin, the others parted, leaving the way open to the door, and Francis calmly departed.

"I would assume that our meeting is at its end," Brother Castinagis said dryly.

Brother Braumin looked at the man, then at all the others. He wanted to comfort them, to reassure them that their beliefs in him and in this cause that Master Jojonah had passed along to him were not misplaced.

He could not, though. He had nothing to tell them that would cleanse the image of Jojonah's last moments from their minds, nothing to assure them that they would not soon find a similar fate. Braumin honestly wondered then, for a moment, if he should have allowed Brother Francis to walk away. But what might they have done? Killed the man? Or captured him, and held him prisoner in the lower levels of St.-Mere-Abelle?

Brother Braumin closed his eyes and shook his head. Their secret was discovered, and the only way they might have preserved it would have been to murder Brother Francis. And that, the gentle monk knew in his heart, they could not have done.

"Brother Braumin was not in his room after vespers last night," Father Abbot Markwart stated bluntly.

Brother Francis nodded, trying to appear surprised.

"You knew this?"

"You instructed me to watch him closely," Francis replied.

The Father Abbot waited a long moment for Francis to elaborate, then blew a long, frustrated sigh and prompted, "And where did he go?"

"To the lower levels," Francis explained, and he continued when he saw that the Father Abbot's face was turning sour again. "Brother Braumin has been going down there regularly, usually to the library wherein the heretic Jojonah did his last work."

"And so he, too, is on the path of damnation," Markwart remarked.

Brother Francis almost told Markwart everything he had discovered about Braumin's little group. Let their own words damn them! But Francis had to admit to himself that he wanted to confront Markwart openly about the *Windrunner* and be reassured of the truth.

Francis held his tongue. He considered all that had happened over the last few months—the taking of the Chilichunks, the cold manner in which Markwart had dismissed Francis' killing of Grady, the execution of Jojonah—and he knew that he was not ready to learn the true story of the *Windrunner*, or of anything else for that matter. And he realized, too, that he was not ready to deal with his own conscience if he revealed all he knew of Braumin and the others, if he had to stand in the square of the village of St.-Mere-Abelle and watch Braumin and his friends be put to the flames.

"Who was with Brother Braumin?" Markwart asked suddenly.

Francis started to say that the man was alone, but he was caught too much off his guard, was too afraid that Markwart already knew the truth. "Brother Viscenti," he blurted.

"Of course, that one," Markwart mused. "A nervous little wretch. I do not know how I ever let that one into St.-Mere-Abelle. And Brother Dellman, of course. Ah, the pity there. I recognized great potential in Dellman—that is why I added his name to the list of monks who traveled to Aida."

"Perhaps that was our mistake," Francis dared to say. "Perhaps Jojonah corrupted Brother Dellman on the journey."

"Were you not along on that same journey?" Markwart asked sarcastically. Francis held up his hands helplessly.

"And who else?" Markwart went on. "Castinagis?"

"Perhaps," Francis replied. "I could not get too close, for the lower corridors echo with the slightest footsteps."

"Speaking heresy in the bowels of my abbey," Markwart remarked, moving back to sit behind his desk, shaking his head in disgust. "How deep are the roots of Jojonah's conspiracy? But no matter," he said, his tone changing from sadness to the easy voice of resolution. He pulled clean parchment from a drawer and reached for his quill. "Brother Braumin and his cohorts are a minor nuisance and nothing more. One that I might sweep away with a letter—"

"Your pardon, Father Abbot," Francis interrupted, putting a hand on the parchment.

The old monk looked up, his expression incredulous.

"I am not certain of their words or intent," Francis quickly explained.

"After all this, it is not obvious to you?" Markwart replied.

"I believe that they are simply trying to come to terms with the . . ." Francis hesitated, trying to find just the right phrase. "With the death of Jojonah," he said. "Brother Braumin and the others only knew the good side of the man. He was their mentor."

"In many things, it would seem," came the dry reply.

"Perhaps," Francis agreed. "But more likely, they are merely trying to sort through the troubles of their souls."

Father Abbot Markwart slid his chair back from the desk and leaned back, staring hard at Francis. "I find your sympathy uncharacteristic," he warned, "and misplaced."

"Not sympathy," Francis replied, "but pragmatism. Brother Braumin is well known among the other abbots and immaculates, and well liked. Everyone knows that he was close to Jojonah. Did you not admit as much in our last discussion, when you mentioned that you meant to promote him to master?"

"I cannot promote a heretic, though I can surely send one to his demon god," said Markwart.

"But perhaps Brother Braumin only needs a bit of time to recognize the truth," Francis improvised, hardly believing his own words.

Markwart laughed. "Brother Braumin needs to recognize the truth soon," the Father Abbot said, his tone deathly cold. "Very soon."

Brother Francis straightened and took a step back from the desk. "Of course, Father Abbot. And I will continue to monitor his every movement."

"From a distance," Markwart instructed, "inconspicuously. Let the heretics bring more of their own into our web. I wish to sweep this stain from St.-Mere-Abelle in one action, one display of the true power of the true God."

Francis nodded, bowed, then turned and walked from the room, thoroughly shaken. He had no idea why he had not betrayed Braumin and his conspirators. Certainly he hadn't believed a word they had said. They were on the path to heresy, as straight and damning a trail as had led Jojonah to his fiery death.

Francis held that thought solidly, repeating it over and over in his mind as a litany against one other pervasive memory.

Master Jojonah had forgiven him.

CHAPTER

❖ 5 ❖

A Proper Good-bye

lbryan and Pony helped Captain Kilronney secure his prisoners in a
barn in Caer Tinella. Though it didn't seem as if any of the powries
would try to escape, the captain set a score of guards in the place and
separated the dangerous dwarves into groups of three.

Satisfied that there would be no trouble, the ranger took Greystone and
Symphony away, while his exhausted companion went back to their lodging. Elbryan expected to find Pony asleep when he returned half an hour
later, but she was standing at a window, staring into the forest, still wearing
her drenched clothing.

"You'll rot the wood under your feet," Elbryan said with a smile.

Pony looked at him long enough to show him her own smile, then turned
back to the forest.

"We should speak about last night," Elbryan remarked. He was upset
that Pony had acted without his knowledge or help.

"Bradwarden and I eliminated a problem, nothing more," Pony replied.

"A problem that would have been eliminated anyway," the ranger said,
"with less risk."

Now Pony turned to face him, her expression severe. "To whom?" she
asked. "You could not have had a cleaner fight if all the Palmaris garrison
had come north to join you. Not a single man or woman was scratched, and
the threat is ended."

Elbryan held up his hands defensively halfway through her retort. "I only
fear—" he started to respond.

"That I might have been injured?" Pony interrupted. "Or killed? Do not
presume to protect me."

"Never that," Elbryan said, "no more than you presume to protect me.
But I fear the wisdom of your actions." He hesitated, expecting Pony to
strike back, but she stared at him, even cocked her head to the side, her
look pensive.

"Obviously it was no random lightning strike that took down the front of the cave," Elbryan said.

"You think that only because you know of my power with the gemstones."

"But still, the magical energy was considerable," Elbryan went on. "I fear that there might be monks in the area once more, searching for us and for Bradwarden. They might have detected the stone use."

Pony's admission that the reasoning might be sound came in the form of a nod.

"And what of the powrie prisoners?" the ranger asked. "What strange tales of your powers might they tell?"

"Most who saw anything worth reporting are dead," Pony replied grimly.

"But I understand," Elbryan was quick to add. "It has been difficult for you, and for Bradwarden. Both of you are full of justifiable anger, and yet you two, above all others, have been relegated to a passive role."

At that moment, Pony almost told him that she was carrying his child. She wanted to explain that this one outburst against the powries was the only revenge she would allow herself during her pregnancy, that she meant to move far from danger for the sake of the unborn babe. She hesitated, staring long and hard as Elbryan went on, talking about the trip to the Timberlands and how both Pony, should she decide to go north, and Bradwarden would have more opportunities to join in the battles when the soldiers had departed.

Pony hardly heard a word of it. Her concentration was on Elbryan, this man she loved. She moved toward him slowly, lifted her finger to her pursed lips, and then, when she got close enough, put it up to his lips, silencing him.

She moved her hand from his lips to brush his cheek, rising on tiptoe to kiss him gently.

She felt Elbryan go tense—he was remembering their frantic encounter in the woods, she realized. She held the kiss for a long while, keeping it soft and tender, then stepped back, her hand still gently brushing his cheek.

The quiet moment was stolen as a drop of water rolled from Elbryan's hair to land with a plop in the puddle at his feet. Both looked down and giggled, as much from nervousness as from amusement. Then they looked into each other's eyes, remembering the experiences they had shared, remembering why they had fallen in love. Pony kissed him again, once, twice, each one tender but more passionate.

Then she stepped back and unclasped her cloak, letting it drop to the floor. Without a word, she unlaced her tunic and pulled it over her head, and stood, bare to the waist again staring at her lover.

He wasn't sure, she realized. She had shaken him with her aggressive, even angry, approach in the forest, and now her demeanor had him off balance.

She went back to him again, smiling wistfully, then kissing him, and his arms came about her, roaming softly over her wet body.

They made love, but it was not like the frantic encounter in the forest. It was warm and gentle, full of tender words and tender caresses.

Afterward, they lay cuddled in each other's arms. Pony had made no further mention of her intentions, but they both knew that, with the morning light, they would be separated, one riding south, the other north.

Again Pony considered telling Elbryan the truth of her condition, and again she realized, for his peace of mind, that this was not the time. His road lay north, to Dundalis, which would one day be their home. If he was to make that journey safely and help secure that region, his concentration would have to be complete.

They spent the rest of that day and all night alone together in the small house, speaking little, just enjoying each other's presence.

The morning dawned bright and clear, and the pair went out together, sharing one last sword dance. All too soon after that, Pony had Greystone saddled and packed with supplies.

"We will meet back here at the spring equinox," Elbryan said to her.

"Just over three months," Pony remarked. "Will that be enough time?"

"I will not be able to hold Shamus back much longer than that," the ranger explained. "He is eager for the Timberlands, and, if the weather stays mild, he'll likely want to set out before then."

"Then go," Pony replied, thinking that her lover had meant to go north all along. "Leave as early as the weather allows, and return as early as you can. I will be here waiting for you."

The ranger sighed.

"Mid-spring's day, then," Pony said. "That should give you near to eight weeks to go and secure the Timberlands."

"Too much time away from you," said the ranger, flashing his boyish smile, his green eyes sparkling in the morning light.

"Caer Tinella on mid-spring's day," Pony agreed. "And I will come back to you with my grief put to rest, ready to look to the road ahead."

"A quiet road," Elbryan said.

Pony chuckled. She knew, and so did Elbryan, that no road would be quiet for an elven-trained ranger. They would live on the edge of the Wilderlands, protecting three towns from goblins and powries, giants and wild animals. They would work with Bradwarden to protect the animals and the forest from careless and callous humans.

No, the road ahead would not be quiet, she knew. If nothing else, it would be filled with the sounds of a baby's cry and the laughter and joy of proud parents. Again she almost told him. She gave Elbryan a long, tender kiss, whispered another promise to meet him on mid-spring's day, then climbed upon Greystone's strong back and kicked the horse into a quick trot down the road to the south.

She didn't look back.

*   *   *

"She is gone," Elbryan said quietly when the image of his uncle Mather appeared in the mirror at Oracle. "I miss her dearly already, though the morning is but half through!"

The ranger sat back against the cool wall of the small cave and gave a self-deprecating chuckle. He did indeed miss Pony, and he was pained by the thought that she would not be with him for several long months. Sitting there, in the dark and quiet, Elbryan could hardly believe how much he had come to depend on her. Besides the obvious benefit of Pony's skill in battle, she was Elbryan's emotional support, his best friend, the only one of his closest companions who could see the world through the eyes of a human and the only one with whom he chose to share so much of his thoughts and feelings.

Elbryan gave a great sigh, then another chuckle, thinking how empty the road north to his home would seem without Pony and Greystone trotting along beside him and Symphony.

"I understand why she had to go, Uncle Mather," he went on. "And though I still do not agree with her choice, I admit that it was hers to make. And I am not nearly as worried as I was just a few days ago. Pony has found a better and more secure attitude—I saw that clearly when Shamus Kilronney decided to capture, and not kill, the trapped powries. A week ago, Pony would never have agreed to that, or more likely, would have killed all the powries before we arrived. Perhaps she has put enough of her grief behind her now. Or if not, then perhaps this trip back to Palmaris, to see Fellowship Way—which I am confident Belster O'Comely has brought back to its previous reputation—will grant her peace of mind.

"I miss her, and it will be a long few months waiting to see her again," he admitted. "But this may be for the better. Pony should be removed from battle for now, should be in a quiet place where she can properly remember the Chilichunks, and properly grieve for them. I do not believe that the road north will be such a place. We'll find many powries and goblins, and even giants, before Dundalis and the other two towns are rebuilt, I do not doubt."

Elbryan closed his eyes and ran a hand through his thick mop of brown hair. "The soldiers have left, as well," he told the silent ghost, "soon after Pony, though they did not know that she had gone out before them. I will miss Shamus Kilronney—he is a good man—but I am glad that he and the other soldiers are not making the trip north. The folk kept the secret of Bradwarden and Juraviel, and those who knew said nothing of Pony's proficiency with the gemstone magic. I am sure of this, for Tomas Gingerwart kept a close eye on his fellows and understood the urgency of the situation. Pony and I can remain obscure to all but the most knowledgeable and prying eyes, I am sure, but Bradwarden's distinct heritage would mark him clearly to any who knew the recent histories of St. Precious or St.-Mere-

Abelle. Better that Shamus turned south; Bradwarden, Juraviel, and I will clear the way to the north."

The ranger nodded as he finished, believing the logic of his words. He was glad Pony had gone to Palmaris, if that was what she needed, and he did believe that Dundalis would be easily reclaimed. He thought again of his last intimate encounter with Pony, the tenderness, the sharing, and contrasted that with their almost angry encounter in the forest. This last encounter was sincere, he knew; the truth of his love for Pony, and hers for him, and the simple fact that she had been able to put aside her anger so completely gave him hope.

And so it was with complete trust in his wife that Elbryan came out of that small cave to see the bright morning, the clouds finally giving way. He found an extra blessing awaiting him: a rainbow, stretching from horizon to horizon. That brought a smile to Elbryan's handsome face, a sparkle in his olive-green eyes, and a strange feeling that the rainbow was for him and Pony, that they would be joined, despite the miles, by its bands.

The thought settled and Elbryan put it, and all of his other feelings for Pony, into a warm place in his heart. He could not afford any distractions now. This was the life the elves had given to him: the ranger, the protector. Nightbird.

The task of reclaiming the Timberlands fell squarely upon his strong shoulders, and woe to any powrie, goblin, or giant that stood before him.

Sitting astride Greystone in a copse of trees off the side of the road just south of Landsdown, Pony, too, saw the rainbow. She hardly stopped to appreciate the beauty, though, nor did she hold any romantic notions of a rainbow bridge connecting her to Elbryan.

Her focus was pragmatic, and her gaze now had settled on a rising cloud of dust coming from the north, the telltale approach of Captain Kilronney and his soldiers.

Pony eased Greystone a bit farther back into the wooded cover when the group came into sight.

A point rider led the way, trotting his mount swiftly some fifty yards ahead of the main group. He went past Pony's position, head turning as he scanned for potential enemies, but she was well concealed.

Shamus Kilronney and his strong-willed cousin led the main host, arguing as they rode. They always seemed to be arguing, Pony noted. She realized that she would miss Shamus Kilronney, and her gaze lingered on him as he moved past her. She respected this man, and liked him and thought that if they had met under different, less trying circumstances, they might be great friends. Her feelings toward Colleen were more ambiguous; she certainly wasn't enamored of Colleen's condescending attitude. But Pony would not allow herself to be too judgmental. Above all else, Colleen Kilronney possessed an aura of competence. The warrior woman had likely been through many trying experiences during the war, Pony realized, and if she wasn't trusting, it was understandable.

Four ranks of five soldiers each, including most of Colleen Kilronney's warriors, came next, all alert and looking for signs of danger. It struck Pony that none of them, not even the two leaders, seemed splendid in the morning light. They didn't resemble the knights of the famed Allheart Brigade, whom Pony had seen thundering about in their shining armor during her time in the King's army; rather, they were capable, battle-hardened warriors, a bit weary but ready for any foe.

Behind them, tied together waist to waist and each laden with a huge pack of supplies or a tied stack of firewood, came the score and seven powrie prisoners. Despite the load, the powries, prodded by soldiers, rolled along at a tremendous pace. Powries were legendary for their endurance—the dangerous powrie barrelboats had no sail and were propelled by pedaling dwarves, yet these ships traveled the rough waters of the open Mirianic and had been known to overtake sailing ships in a stiff wind! And now the powries lived up to that reputation, stepping to keep pace with the trotting horses without a grumble or complaint.

The whole group moved down the road, around a bend, and out of sight, save the telltale cloud rising up above the trees. Familiar with Captain Kilronney's tactics, Pony knew to wait a bit longer, and sure enough, the trailing pair of scouts came by.

The woman jiggled Greystone's reins and the horse started out of the copse.

"And still you did not tell him," came a familiar voice.

Pony turned the horse to the side and scanned the trees, finally picking out Juraviel sitting calmly on a branch some ten feet from the ground.

"Are we to have this fight again?" she asked indignantly.

"I only fear—"

"I know what you fear," Pony interrupted. "And I fear it as well. If Elbryan is killed up north, then he will die without ever knowing that he has fathered a child."

Juraviel, obviously agitated, hopped down to a lower branch. "How cold are your words," he remarked.

"How true are my words," she corrected. "Both Elbryan and I have been living with the shadow of death looming over us since before we journeyed to Aida."

"Thus I would think that you would wish to tell him."

Pony shrugged. "I do wish to tell him," she said, "but I know that to be the wrong course. If he knew, then he would not go north—or not without me, at least. And I am not going to Dundalis."

"Never?"

"Of course I will return to my home, and Dundalis is my home," she was quick to reply. "But not now. And Elbryan would not go without me if he knew that I was with child."

She paused. "And that would be to the detriment of us all," Pony went on. "The Timberlands must be reclaimed, and none will do that better than Nightbird."

Juraviel nodded.

"So, no, Belli'mar Juraviel, I did not tell Elbryan," she said bluntly. "But I will promise you this: I plan to raise my child in Dundalis, and will rejoin Elbryan before the babe is born."

"If we get into a situation from which I can see no escape," Juraviel said quietly, "or if Elbryan is grievously wounded and near death, I will tell him the truth."

Pony smiled and nodded. "I would expect nothing less from you, my friend," she said.

"One more promise and I shall be satisfied," Juraviel said after another pause. "I will have your word that you will always remember the life that is within your womb," he said firmly. "Promise me that you will keep safe, and that you will not go in search of a fight and will avoid any which find you."

Pony eyed him sternly, indignantly.

"The child within you is the child of Nightbird," the elf said, not backing down. "Thus, the safety of the babe is of great interest to the Touel'alfar."

"Of course my concern is for my child," Pony retorted. "Need you ask—"

"Need I remind you of the powries in the cave?" Juraviel interrupted just as forcefully. Then he did back down, though, offering a disarming, sincere smile. "The child within you is more than the child of Nightbird," he explained. "It is the child of Elbryan and Jilseponie. Thus, the safety of the babe is of great interest to Belli'mar Juraviel."

Pony could take no more. The elf had her trapped by the honest concern of friendship. "I surrender," she said with a laugh. "And I promise."

"Farewell then," Juraviel said somberly. "And hold to that promise. You cannot begin to understand the importance of the life that grows within you."

"What do you know?" Pony asked with concern, for Juraviel's words and tone hinted at something larger.

"I know the beauty of a child," the elf replied.

It seemed to Pony that he was being evasive, but she knew the ways of the Touel'alfar well enough to understand that she could not coerce anything from one of them.

"I am to meet Elbryan and mid-spring's day in Caer Tinella," she explained. "I expect that Belli'mar Juraviel will see him there safely."

Juraviel did a silent count of the months. He knew from Pony's words that the child had been conceived on the road to St-Mere-Abelle in late summer. Juraviel thought to comment that Pony would meet Elbryan only if she was still fit to travel then, but he kept quiet. She knew the timing better than he, he assured himself.

Pony paused and reached into her pouch, producing a smooth gray stone, the soul stone. "Perhaps you should take this," she offered. "It is the stone of healing and you may well find use for it."

Juraviel shook his head. "We have the magical armband Bradwarden wears," he said. "You keep the gemstone." His gaze drifted down to her belly and she understood that he feared she might need it even more.

Pony pocketed the gem. "Mid-spring's day," she said.

"Fare you well, Jilseponie Wyndon," Juraviel replied.

The elf nodded. Pony offered a last smile, kicked Greystone into a brisk walk out of the copse, then trotted off down the south road.

Juraviel watched her ride out of sight, honestly wondering if he would ever see her again. He hoped that she would hold to that last, all-important promise to keep out of harm's way, but he recognized the pain and rage within her and understood her need for action. The powrie fight had sated that need, had brought a measure of calm, but only temporarily, Juraviel knew.

Like the smiles Pony had shown him in this meeting. They were not lasting things, not signals of true contentment. Pony's mood had shifted dramatically in the course of seconds, at the prompting of only a few words. Watching her go, Juraviel could only hope that no trouble found her among the dangerous streets of Palmaris.

And even if Pony did get to Caer Tinella for mid-spring's day, Juraviel doubted that he would be there to greet her. It was nearing time for him to go home, back to Andur'Blough Inninness. Lady Dasslerond needed to know about the babe, the child of Nightbird, who was, in effect, the child of Caer'alfar.

Pony soon had the trailing riders in sight. She took care to stay back, but the group was focused on the road ahead so she had little trouble shadowing them all day.

They set camp among a group of deserted farmhouses, one of many such settlements that had not yet been reclaimed.

Pony set her small camp in sight of the soldiers, taking comfort in the warm lights that shone through the windows and in the silhouetted forms of men walking about the blazing fire set on the common ground between the houses. They were confident, obviously so, that there were no sizable groups of monsters in the area—none that would challenge them, at least—and Pony knew that their confidence was well placed. Still, she thought it foolish for Captain Kilronney to advertise his position, especially with more than a score of dangerous powrie prisoners in tow.

So Pony did more than rest that night; she went out with her soul stone, keeping a silent and vigilant watch over the troop.

As much a ranger as her husband.

At the same time, Elbryan, Juraviel, and Bradwarden reclined comfortably on a bare hillock some distance north of Caer Tinella. The ranger lay on his back, hands folded behind his head, eyes staring up at the starry sky. Bradwarden was similarly at ease, plopped on the ground, his front horse legs crossed before him. Even in his reclining posture, his human torso remained upright. "Hard on the breathin' if I lay on me side," he explained to his friends.

Juraviel was the most agitated of the three, looking as much at Elbyran as at the skies above, though any elf would surely enjoy the quiet splendor of the sky this clear, crisp evening. Juraviel's concern was for Elbryan, for the ranger was obviously sad, and his posture spoke more of resignation than of serenity.

Bradwarden saw it, too. "She'll be back," the centaur offered. "Ye know she's not to leave ye for long, and know, too, that there's no other man for her heart."

"Of course," Elbryan replied with a chuckle that turned into a sigh.

"Ah, but for the ladies," Bradwarden lamented dramatically. "Oft times I'm glad indeed that I've seen none o' me own kind o' the fair sex."

"Sounds a bit lonely," said Elbryan. He managed a wry smile and looked at Juraviel. "And frustrating."

"Ah, but there's the beauty in being a centaur," Bradwarden interjected with a mischievous wink. "I'll be takin' a ride on a dumb horse, with no questions to be answered and no explanations to be given!"

Elbryan pulled his hands out from behind his head and covered his face, groaning, left speechless by the crude centaur and not wanting to conjure such a picture in his mind.

"Just be glad that Symphony is a stallion," Juraviel put in, and the ranger groaned again.

Bradwarden only laughed harder.

Then it went quiet on the hillock, the three friends each alone and yet sharing the splendor of night sky. Some time later, Bradwarden took up his bagpipes and started playing a haunting melody that drifted through the trees like an evening mist, unobtrusive and adding to the mystical qualities of the night.

❖ 6 ❖

Sitting on the Fence

Roger Lockless thought himself foolish. He scolded himself that his judgment was distorted by desperation and loneliness. But stubbornly he kept moving along the corridor outside Father Abbot Markwart's quarters, broom in hand, trying very hard—too hard?—to look as if he was on some cleaning duty.

He paused outside the Father Abbot's door, looking both ways along the quiet corridor, even sweeping a bit.

"An hour," he whispered to himself to bolster his confidence. The monks were gathering for vespers, and none would likely come this way for at least an hour. Roger had studied the routine carefully, night after night, for he knew that one mistake now would get him tortured to death. He thought of Elbryan and Pony and the heroic centaur he had never met, and found his resolve. With a final glance each way, he went right to the door, falling to one knee.

True to his surname, Roger had the simple lock opened in a matter of seconds. Surprised by how easy it had been to break into the quarters of the highest-ranking Abellican monk in the world, he paused, fearing suddenly that there might be some magical or mechanical trap set about the door. He gave a thorough inspection of the seams on the jamb, but found nothing; then he hesitated again, looked both ways, and took a deep breath, reminding himself that a magical trap would likely offer no physical signs.

Except for the ashes—his ashes—left behind after it was sprung.

With a growl, the stubborn young man pushed open the door.

Nothing happened, and then he was inside, falling to one knee again to relock the door. Leaning against it, catching his breath and his resolve, Roger scanned the suite. Markwart's quarters consisted of four rooms. This office, the largest, was the hub, with a door—closed—to the left, another across the room behind the great desk partly open to reveal a corner of the Father Abbot's bed. A third door, to the right, was open wide, revealing a group of four comfortable chairs set on a rug before a smoldering hearth.

Roger went through that open door first, into the study, but returned to the office in a short while, having found nothing of any importance, not a single clue concerning his missing friends. He moved into the bedroom next, and found Markwart's journal on a night table. Roger wasn't much of a reader, though a kindly woman in Caer Tinella, Mrs. Kelso, had taken him in and taught him. Markwart's writing was stylish and quite legible; Roger could understand quite a bit of the script—an amazing feat for one who had lived the life of a common peasant in Honce-the-Bear. The monks could read and write, as could the majority of the nobility, the elven-trained Nightbird, Pony, and other exceptional individuals. But less than two in thirty of those who called themselves subjects of King Danube Brock Ursal could understand simple letters.

By that standard, Roger Lockless was an amazing reader. Still, he found many words that he did not know, and sometimes he could not discern the logical connection between the sentences. A quick perusal of the journal showed him nothing of value. Self-serving philosophical musings mostly, the Father Abbot writing his thoughts about the importance of the Church above the importance of the common folk, and above the secular leaders, even the King. Roger winced at the words, recalling all too clearly the murder of one of those secular leaders, Baron Bildeborough, the man who had taken him in and joined in his cause against the Church.

Roger continued to scan the book, and though he had little luck with its finer points, he did come to believe that it had been penned by two different men—one hand, perhaps, had done the actual writing, but a large part of it must have been dictated, Roger believed. It wasn't so much the wording of the text but rather a difference in tone.

Either two men had done the writing, or Father Abbot Markwart was a man in serious emotional turmoil!

Now Roger wondered if he might find some way to use this journal against Markwart. Perhaps he could go to the King and present this book, along with his claims that a monk, and no powrie, had murdered Abbot Dobrinion of St. Precious, and that an agent of the Church, and not a wild animal, had killed Baron Bildeborough.

He would be treated like a blithering idiot, Roger realized, even with the journal as evidence. He read again all the entries he could find about the King and recognized that the author, Father Abbot Markwart, had been quite careful not to cross over the line into treason, spouting merely about philosophical differences, but writing of no actions against the Crown. This was gossip, not evidence.

One other thing caught Roger's attention: Markwart's repeated references to a new insight, a voice inside his head, guiding his hand. The Father Abbot clearly thought himself speaking directly to God, acting as the single agent of the Supreme Being.

Roger shuddered at that thought, seeing the split personality within the writing in a new light and understanding that no man was more dangerous than one believing himself to be the agent of God.

He put the book back on the table and left the room.

Thinking to leave the office for the last and most thorough inspection, Roger went to the closed door next. His suspicions heightened when he found it secured with not one, but three separate locks. Even more intriguing, the young thief found an even greater protection, a needle-and-spring trap, on two of the locks.

Roger spent a long time studying those traps, then went to work with nimble fingers and delicate picks, disabling them but in a manner that would allow him to easily rearm them upon his exit. Roger groaned as minutes slipped by and he realized how much time he was losing at this door, but still he took the time to inspect it once more for further traps before going at the locks, popping all three open, considering again the possibility of a deadly magical trap before pushing open the heavy door.

The room was empty except for a few candlesticks, a large book lying open, and a curious design cut into the floor, but Roger's heart started beating quickly, his blood racing, his breath coming in gasps. A tangible aura, a coldness that seeped right into his spine, assailed him, a darkness of spirit, a sense of profound hopelessness. He stayed only long enough to glance at the title of the great tome, *The Incantations Sorcerous,* and then he left the room in a hurry, leaning again against the closed door for several long minutes while he steadied his trembling hands enough to reset the locks and traps.

All that remained was the office and the great desk, with many drawers showing, and, likely, many more concealed.

"He should be here, brother," Master Machuso, a round little man with red cheeks that seemed to envelop his tiny nose, said apologetically when he led Brother Francis into the larders only to find that the young man in question was nowhere to be seen. The master had been on his way to vespers when Francis had intercepted him, claiming a most urgent necessity. "Roger Billingsbury has been assigned to the larders all the week."

"Your pardon, Master Machuso," Francis said with a polite bow and smile, "but it seems that he is not here."

"Obviously!" Machuso agreed with an embarrassed burst of laughter. "Oh, I do try to keep them in line, you see," he explained, "but most of those who come here for work will not stay long. Only long enough to earn a bit for the drink or pipe weed, I'm afraid to say. All the villagers know our generous nature and know that no harm will come to them if they run off. I will even hire them back, if they come 'round in a few weeks begging again for work." The cheery master laughed again. "If men of God cannot forgive human foibles, then who can?"

Francis managed a strained smile. "Villagers, you said," he remarked. "This Roger Billingsbury is of St.-Mere-Abelle village, then? Are you familiar with his family?"

"No to the second question," replied Machuso. "And likely no to the first. I know most of the townsfolk—certainly every leading family—and know no Billingsburys. Well, none but the young Roger, of course. A fine lad. Good worker and quick with his hands—and with his wits, so they say."

"Did he claim that he was from the village?" Francis pressed.

Machuso gave a noncommittal shrug. "He might have," he replied. "In honesty, I pay little attention to such details. Many have been displaced by the war. Entire villages that once were, simply are no more. So if our young Roger claimed that he was of St.-Mere-Abelle, why would I question him?"

"You would not, of course," Brother Francis answered, bowing once more. "And I do not question your procedure, Master Machuso. If all of us at St.-Mere-Abelle could attend our duties as well as Master Golvae Machuso, then surely the Father Abbot's life would be much easier."

That brought another laugh bubbling from the jovial Machuso.

"Is there anywhere else that the young Billingsbury might have gone?" Francis asked.

Machuso's face scrunched up in thought, but he was soon shaking his head and holding his hands up helplessly. "If he has not left the abbey, then I am sure he will return to the larders," he offered. "A good worker, that young man."

Francis worked hard to hide his frustration. He hoped that Roger had not left St.-Mere-Abelle, for if his suspicions about the young hireling were correct, then Roger could help rid him of some very troubling issues. He said a quick farewell to Machuso and rushed away, back to his private quarters, back to the soul stone the Father Abbot had allowed him to procure from the private collection. He had to do his own searching, and fast.

The hints were sparse: a crumpled piece of paper, apparently a first draft of the edict that had condemned Master Jojonah, which spoke of some mysterious "intrusion and escape" at St.-Mere-Abelle, and another paper concerning a continuing conspiracy at the abbey. To add to Roger's frustration, he had not found a single secret compartment in the great desk, though he was certain that there had to be many. Still, he had counted carefully the minutes and knew that he was fast running out of time. He went back to the door, glanced about the room one last time to make sure that all was as he had found it, then quietly went back out into the hall.

"You should reset the lock," came a voice from the shadows, even as Roger turned to do just that.

The young man froze in place as if turned to stone. Only his eyes moved, darting to and fro, looking for some way out. Waves of panic rushed through him, and he tried to concoct some believable story. He caught a movement out of the corner of his eye, turned, and straightened suddenly to face the man, broomstick in hand.

"An odd tool for the larders, Roger Billingsbury," Brother Francis said calmly.

Roger recognized from the white rope binding the dark robes that this was a higher-ranking monk, an immaculate brother, perhaps. "I was told to come up here and clean—"

"You were told to work in the larders," Brother Francis interrupted, having no time or patience for such foolishness. With his soul stone, Francis' spirit had soared about the corridors of the abbey, and chance alone had brought him to the office of his superior, only to find, to his absolute amazement, the young kitchen helper bending over the great desk.

"Ah, y-yes," Roger stuttered, "but Brother Jhimelde—"

"Enough!" Francis growled, silencing the man. "You are Roger Billingsbury?"

Roger nodded slightly as he considered his options. He might strike the monk with his broom and dart away, he thought, for though the monk was larger than he, the man did not appear strong.

"And where are you from?" Francis asked.

"St.-Mere-Abelle," Roger replied without hesitation.

"You are not from St.-Mere-Abelle," Francis stated coldly.

"The v-village, not the abbey," Roger stuttered.

"No!"

Roger stood straight and gripped the broom all the tighter. He had killed a monk before, a brother justice. It was an experience he'd hoped he would never have to repeat.

"There are no Billingsburys in St.-Mere-Abelle village," Brother Francis insisted.

"New to the region," Roger replied. "Our homes were burned—"

"And where were those homes?" Francis asked.

"A small village—"

"Where?" Francis demanded, and added in rapid succession, his voice wickedly sharp and intimidating. "What was its name? How many people lived there? What other family names?"

"To the south," Roger started, but his mind was whirling.

"You are from a village somewhere north of Palmaris," Brother Francis put in, "unless I miss my guess—and that is not likely, I assure you. I recognize your accent."

Roger straightened and stared hard at the man, but Francis' next words nearly knocked him over.

"You are a friend of those who knew Avelyn Desbris," the monk announced. "Perhaps a friend of the heretic yourself."

Roger's jaw hung slack.

"But no matter," Brother Francis went on. "You are a friend of the woman, Pony by name, and of her companion, the one called Nightbird."

Roger's knuckles whitened, so tight was his grip on the broom. Desperate, he started to move to strike, but Francis came against him hard, grabbing the broom handle with one hand, slapping Roger back with the other. "Fool," the monk said, pulling the broom free with a subtle twisting maneuver. "I am not your enemy. If I were, you would be in chains already, on your knees before the Father Abbot."

"Then what?" Roger dared to ask, rubbing his sore cheek, surprised that this man, seeming so average, could have so easily disarmed and struck him.

"Come along, and quickly," Francis instructed, turning and starting away. "Vespers is at its end and you would not be wise to let the Father Abbot find you loitering here.

"What are we to do?" Brother Viscenti asked for perhaps the twentieth time, and, like all the other times before this, Brother Braumin offered no direct response.

"When will Dellman join us?" the older monk asked.

Viscenti glanced at the door of Braumin's room as if he expected Dellman to burst through it at any second. Then he twitched and turned his head quickly, eyes darting. "He will be here—he said he would," Viscenti insisted, his voice rising with his anxiety.

Braumin patted a hand in the air to try to calm the man. In truth, though, Braumin understood the gravity of their situation. Brother Francis, perhaps the closest counsel of Father Abbot Markwart, had walked right in on their meeting!

"We should go and beg the Father Abbot for forgiveness!" Viscenti said suddenly, frantically.

Braumin turned a cold stare on the nervous man, angered that Viscenti would consider such a notion. Even if he was tied to the stake, the fires burning beneath his feet, Brother Braumin Herde would not beg for Markwart's forgiveness. And how, if he truly believed in the holiness of Avelyn and Jojonah, could Viscenti say such a thing?

But Braumin calmed quickly, sympathizing with the man's fear. Viscenti was scared, and with good reason.

"Better that we admit to wrongdoing against the Abellican Church," Braumin said in as calm a tone as he could manage. "We met for prayer, nothing more. Better that we craft our story—"

He stopped as a quiet knock sounded; both men froze.

"Brother Dellman?" Braumin whispered to Viscenti.

"Or Brother Castinagis," the skinny man replied, his voice nasal even in a whisper.

Braumin moved slowly and silently to the door, putting his ear up close, trying to get some hint of who it might be.

Another knock sounded.

Braumin looked back at Viscenti; the man was nearly chewing his bottom lip off. With a helpless shrug, Braumin gingerly grasped the handle and took a deep breath, his imagination conjuring images of Father Abbot Markwart and a host of angry, armed executioners come to cart him away. Finally he mustered the nerve and opened the door a crack, and though it was not Markwart and a mob, Brother Braumin's heart sank.

"Let me in," Brother Francis said quietly.

"I am busy," Braumin replied.

Francis snorted. "And whatever you might be doing, I assure you that this takes precedence," he declared, putting a hand on the door and pushing.

Braumin braced his shoulder against the wood and held the door steady. "I assure you that we have nothing to discuss, good brother," he said. He started to close the door, but Francis stuck his foot in the opening.

"Good brother, I am terribly busy," Braumin said more insistently.

"Preparing your next meeting?" Francis asked.

"A prayer meeting, yes," Braumin replied.

"Blasphemy, you mean," Francis said sternly. "If you prefer to air this argument with me in the corridor," he went on, raising his voice, "then so be it. You are the one in need of secrecy, not I."

Braumin swung wide the door and stepped aside, and Brother Francis promptly entered the room. Braumin poked his head out into the corridor behind the man, then closed the door. He turned his attention back to the room to find Francis and Viscenti staring hard at each other. A wild look was in Viscenti's eye, the look of a timid animal caught in a corner; for a moment, Braumin thought the skinny man might pounce upon Francis. Viscenti couldn't hold the stare, though, and he turned away, hands twitching at his side.

"You seem to be walking in on my every conversation," Brother Braumin said dryly, purposefully diverting Francis' attention from Viscenti. "Someone less trusting than I might believe that you were watching me."

"Someone wiser than you would understand that you need watching," Brother Francis replied.

"And you are that wiser man?"

"I am wiser than to speak heresy in the cellars of St.-Mere-Abelle."

"Only truth," Braumin said, and his lip turned up in a snarl and he advanced a step.

"Only lies," Francis retorted, not backing away an inch.

Brother Viscenti scrambled suddenly to stand right beside Francis, very close, so that he and Braumin had the man between them, the two conspirators holding a threatening posture.

Still, Francis seemed totally unconcerned. "I did not come here to argue theology," he explained.

"Then why did you come here?" Braumin demanded.

"To warn you," Francis said bluntly. "I know of your group, dedicated to the memory of the heretic Jojonah and to Avelyn Desbris."

"No heretic!" Viscenti squealed.

Francis paid him no heed. "And the Father Abbot knows of you, too, and soon enough he will turn his attention to you and destroy you as he destroyed Jojonah."

"No doubt using information that Brother Francis dutifully supplied," Braumin replied.

Francis blew an exasperated sigh. "You cannot begin to understand his power," he said. "Do you really believe that Father Abbot Markwart needs anything at all from me?"

"Why are you telling us this?" Braumin asked. "Why not just accompany the Father Abbot's guards when they take me? Perhaps Markwart will allow you to add the first flaming brand to the pyre beneath my feet."

A strange expression came over Francis, one that gave Braumin pause. The man seemed wounded almost, or perplexed, a faraway look in his eyes.

After some time, Francis focused again on Brother Braumin, his look deadly serious. "The Father Abbot is closing in on you," he said earnestly. "Do not doubt this. He will prepare heresy hearings, and since none of you have attained the rank of master, they will be convened here at St.-Mere-Abelle with or without the blessings of the other abbots. You cannot hope to win."

"We are not heretics," Braumin replied through gritted teeth.

"That matters not at all," Francis replied. "The Father Abbot has all the evidence he will need against you. If he deems it necessary, he can manufacture any other crimes easily enough."

"Do you hear your own words?" Braumin cried. "Is there no true justice in our Order?"

Francis stared straight ahead, giving no signals.

"Then we are doomed," Brother Viscenti wailed a moment later. He looked to Braumin for comfort, for some denial, but the man had nothing to offer.

"Perhaps there is another way," Francis remarked.

Brother Braumin's face went tight. He expected Francis to advise him to openly disavow the heretics Jojonah and Avelyn, to genuflect before the all-powerful Markwart and beg forgiveness. Viscenti might choose that course, Braumin realized, as might one or two of the others.

Brother Braumin closed his eyes and pushed past the one moment of anger he held for his fellow conspirators. If they chose to beg for mercy, whatever they might say or do, even if their actions weighed heavily against him, he would not judge them.

Nor would he join them. Brother Braumin determined then and there, with certain doom staring him right in the eye, that he would accept the punishment, the flames—but that he would not divorce himself from the tenets of Avelyn Desbris and would speak no ill of his mentor Jojonah.

But then Francis caught him off guard.

"I can get you out of St.-Mere-Abelle," the monk offered, "and you might fly away and hide."

"You would help us?" Viscenti cried doubtfully. "Have you found truth at last, Brother Francis?"

"No," Braumin answered before Francis could respond. Braumin studied him curiously. "No, he does not agree with our beliefs."

"I called you a heretic," Francis confirmed. "My word for you, and not the Father Abbot's."

"Then why would you help us?" Braumin asked. "Why would you see us out of St.-Mere-Abelle when you know that we present no threat to you or your beloved Father Abbot?" Even as he spoke the words, Brother Braumin wondered if the Father Abbot might know of Francis' visit, might have sent Francis here in an attempt to quietly rid himself of the problem monks. "Or do you see a threat?" Braumin asked slyly. "Perhaps you fear the reaction, from within the Church and without, when we five, like Jojonah before us, are tied to poles and publicly burned. Perhaps you wonder how solid the Father Abbot's hold over the Church truly is."

Francis was shaking his head slowly and somberly, but Braumin pressed on. "Thus, you convince us to leave, and by that overt action, we have severed our position in the Church."

"Your reasoning is not sound, brother," Francis replied. "You overestimate the negative reaction of the populace to a gruesome execution. Many of the villagers still speak in excited, even thrilled, tones about the burning of the heretic Jojonah."

"Do not call him that!" Brother Viscenti demanded.

"They were not terribly upset by the spectacle, as you well know," Francis went on. "And indeed, they would welcome another bit of excitement in their mundane existence. And as to the other Church leaders, they are back at their own abbeys now, recovering from a war. They will not raise more than an eyebrow, I assure you. The Father Abbot will name you as heretics and be done with you before any can protest; and then, the deed done—one less problem before any of them—they will let the matter fade."

The answer set Braumin back on his heels and killed his previous suspicions about Francis' motives. Markwart, who dared to usurp the power of Abbot Dobrinion while he was in Palmaris, who took citizens of another town captive and let them die in his care, who burned Jojonah publicly before the Church leaders, would not fear any retaliation if he chose to get rid of a handful of minor conspirators. But why, then, was Francis here?

"You haven't the belly for it!" Marlboro Viscenti said suddenly, hopping back and pointing at Francis. "Even Brother Francis, the Father Abbot's avowed lackey, was sickened by the treatment of good Jojonah."

Francis didn't immediately respond, and Braumin looked from him to Viscenti, who wore a confident expression. Marlboro Viscenti was not considered a great thinker by either his peers or his instructors, but Braumin knew that he was possessed of certain insights. Perhaps it was his perpetual nervousness that kept him keenly aware of his surroundings; but whatever the reason, Viscenti many times found answers to puzzles that had seemed quite beyond Brother Braumin.

"You believed Jojonah a heretic," Braumin said to Francis.

"His actions doomed him," Francis said firmly. "You heard him admit that he helped the intruders steal our prisoner."

Braumin waved his hand as if that mattered not at all. "I'll not argue the virtue of his actions with you," he explained. "We can agree that you considered him a traitor to the Church, and yet my good brother Viscenti has spoken truthfully. Why then, Brother Francis, do you fear to see us burned? Why did the spectacle of Jojonah's fate so unnerve you?"

Francis was fighting hard to hold his cool, determined demeanor, but he was losing the battle now, Braumin could see. He was trembling, sweat on his forehead.

"Master Jojonah forgave me," Francis at last blurted. "He forgave me my sins, against him and against others."

Braumin eyed him incredulously, then looked at Viscenti, trying to make some sense of it, but found his friend staring at Francis, equally at a loss.

"Do not confuse my coming to you with compassion or any agreement with your beliefs," Francis added. "I offer you a chance to save your miserable lives, to get out of St.-Mere-Abelle, out of my life and the life of the Father Abbot. To go hide in a hole and bury your foolish beliefs with you."

"How do you plan to do that?" asked Viscenti.

"And where are we to go?" Braumin added.

"You know that Jojonah aided the escape of the centaur Bradwarden," Francis explained. "And with him, we believe, were two former friends of Avelyn Desbris."

Again Braumin painted that suspicious look on his face. Were he and his companions to become the signal beacon to the lair of a larger conspiracy?

"Yet there remains at St.-Mere-Abelle another of those conspirators, a man who came in afterward and only recently learned that the centaur and his other friends had escaped. He will be returning to them, I believe, and I believe also that you might persuade him to take you along."

"How convenient for you and the Father Abbot," Braumin remarked.

"I'll not guarantee your safety," said Francis. "Once you are out of the abbey, you must fend for yourselves—and do not doubt that powerful foes may come against you. Do not doubt that the Father Abbot will recapture the centaur and take the other conspirators as well. No, your fate beyond St.-Mere-Abelle is your own to decide. I only do this one thing alone to repay Jojonah. I'll not spend the rest of my life in the debt of a heretic."

"If he was a heretic—" Viscenti started to protest, but Brother Braumin held up his hand, indicating that the man should be quiet. Braumin understood, if Viscenti did not—if even Francis did not.

"All that I ask in return is that you do not name me if you are captured," Brother Francis went on. "And . . . the book."

"What book?" Braumin asked.

Francis turned a stern stare on the man. "The book you read from at your ridiculous meeting," he explained, "the book of lies about our past, by which you measure the rumors about our present."

Braumin scoffed at the notion.

"You will not leave St.-Mere-Abelle unless I have that book," Francis said calmly.

"Why?" Braumin retorted. "So that you might put it on a shelf of forbidden tomes? So that you might bury it away with all the other truths that would tumble down the walls of your sacred institution?"

"There is no compromise here, brother," Francis stated. "I will have the book, or I will take it from your room while you are burning."

"Jojonah gave me that book," Braumin said. "He bade me to keep it safe."

"It will be safe," Francis replied. "And back where it rightfully belongs."

Brother Braumin closed his eyes, understanding that Francis would hold fast. He prayed to Master Jojonah for guidance then, to help him through this dilemma. Was it now his time to stand up for the truth? Was his fight to end so soon? Jojonah had wanted him to ascend the ranks of the Abellican Order, but if he left now, that would be impossible. Even if he managed to elude Markwart's executioners, he and his friends would be outside the Church, unable to bring about any positive change.

But if they stayed, Braumin believed, they would die, and soon.

His answer came in the form of an image, a memory of a faraway place, once the home of evil incarnate but now the tomb of a true saint. Braumin saw again the arm of Avelyn, sticking from the ground, uplifted, the final act of defiance against the demon dactyl, the final act of reaching for God.

Brother Braumin had his answer. Whatever God had in mind for him, he wanted to see that place again before he died. He moved to the side of his bed, bent down to the floor, and reached under it, then moved back to stand in front of Francis, locking the man's gaze with his own. Braumin gave a slight nod and turned over the book. "Read it," he said. "Read the words of another Brother Francis of St.-Mere-Abelle. Learn what once was, and know the truth of the man you serve."

Brother Francis didn't say a word, just moved past Braumin for the door, then out of the room.

"You gave it to him," Marlboro Viscenti said incredulously and fearfully. "Now he will surely betray us."

"If he meant to betray us, then Markwart would already have us," Braumin insisted.

"Then what are we to do?"

"Wait," Braumin answered, laying a comforting hand on Viscenti's shoulder. "Let Francis do as he promised. He will return to us."

Brother Viscenti wiped his hand across his lips and shuddered. He didn't question Braumin further, though, just stood with him, staring at the door, wondering.

In truth, if the door hadn't been there to block their vision, the two men would have still seen Brother Francis in the empty and dimly lit corridor, staring down at the tome Brother Braumin had given him. In one unacknowledged corner of his brain, Brother Francis understood that there might well be a measure of truth in Braumin's claims. Surely Francis had seen enough brutality perpetrated by his beloved Church to give some credence to the pessimistic man's arguments.

And now Francis held this ancient book, which could shatter the foundations of his beliefs, which could make a lie of his life and a devil of his master. If he opened the pages and read it, would he, too, be brought into the depths of heresy, as had Jojonah, and now these disciples of the man?

Brother Francis tucked the book under his arm and started briskly for the stairwells that would take him to the lower library, where he might rid himself of the dangerous tome. He had to pay another visit to Roger Billingsbury and had many other preparations to make, but they would wait, he decided. Burying this book in a dark corner of a dark place was far more important.

PART TWO

▼

CHURCH AND STATE

For centuries, the kingdom of Honce-the-Bear has been divided between the secular powers of the state and the spiritual powers of the Church, and this balance, I have come to believe, is essential to the long-term life of any country. This is not the case in Corona, as I learned during my time with the Touel'alfar—how wise are the elves about so many subjects! In Alpinador, religion is a day-to-day practice, an important aspect of every man's every action. This, I believe, is because of the rigors of the Alpinadoran environment, where the possibility of death is ever present. A barbarian slays a deer, then prays over its carcass, giving thanks that he and his family will not starve. He finds himself far from home and prays to the god of storms, and then, if the weather grows more ominous, to the god of home to help him quickly find his way. Few matters of such a man's daily routine do not involve spirituality, but to the barbarians, religion is a private matter, for there is no organized church in Alpinador, other than the small missions set up by the Abellicans. That is true, too, of the state, for the villages of Alpinador are, in effect, independent states, too isolated by landscape and climate to hear the edicts of any central government. My homeland, the towns of the Timberlands, were much like that, except that we acknowledged the King of Honce-the-Bear.

Still, we did not hear much from the man, or from any of his emissaries.

In the southern kingdom of Behren, church and state are much the same. The Chezru chieftain of Behren is also the highest-ranking yatol priest, a dangerous situation lacking the balance of power necessary to hold tyrants in check. The Chezru chieftain is all-powerful, and can, and often does, kill at a whim without fear of consequence. Could King Ursal of Honce-the-Bear make the same claim? I think not, for in Honce-the-Bear the actions of the King are monitored by the abbots of the Church—if only for selfish reasons, so they could expose any crimes of the state and weaken the King considerably in the eyes of his subjects.

But what of the crimes of the Church, Uncle Mather? Logically, the King should be their counterweight, yet I have heard of no complaints from King Danube about the treatment of the Chilichunks by the Church. Perhaps it is a matter of practicality, with King Danube and his nobles weighing the value of the Chilichunks' lives against the trouble that exposing the Church might bring. For that matter, would King Danube strike hard against the Father Abbot if he knew the actual cause of Baron Bildeborough's death?

Or, perhaps, has the balance of power dangerously shifted?

This is my fear, Uncle Mather, and I do not think I am simply overreacting to personal loss. I believe the Abellican Church has always held the upper hand in this struggle. The daily routines of the subjects of Honce-the-Bear are no doubt more greatly influenced by the state than the Church. Taxes, the military, construction of roads and tolls to pay for them are all the domain of King Danube.

But in the end, the Abellican Church holds the power. In the end, on one's death bed, it is faith and not material wealth that matters. In the end, it is not the edicts of King Danube or any other secular leader, but the words—calming or threatening—of the local abbot or friar that ring true. King Danube holds the purse strings, but Father Abbot Markwart holds the soul; and that is by far the greater treasure, and the greater power. The King may hold power over people's lives and livelihoods, but the Church can promise far worse than death. The Church can threaten eternal damnation, and no pain in this life can compare to that.

The Church holds the true power, Uncle Mather, and if, as I have seen over the last few months, the Church chooses to twist that power into something malicious, then the darkest days are yet ahead—even if all the powries, goblins, and giants have been banished, even if the demon dactyl has been destroyed.

Destroyed?

Or maybe not, Uncle Mather. Perhaps the dactyl's spirit is alive and well and living in an even more dangerous host.

—ELBRYAN WYNDON

❖ *7* ❖

Shifting Winds

The fire burned low. They were fugitives now and had to take precautions, but the night was cold. Brother Braumin had allowed Dellman to light the small fire.

Braumin took some comfort as he considered his four companions. It was no small matter that they had all agreed to flee St.-Mere Abelle and thus leave the Abellican Order. Even the youngest of them had been a member of the Order for a decade, not to mention the eight years of preparation required to be allowed entry into St.-Mere-Abelle, and now to throw all of that work away. . . .

And it was not just fear of Markwart's temper that had inspired the desertion, Brother Braumin realized, and he was warmed by that knowledge. He chuckled as he considered Marlboro Viscenti, the nervous man now crouching by the fire, his head darting from side to side as he scanned the darkness beyond the fire. Perhaps for Viscenti, fear of Markwart was enough of an inspiration.

Braumin recalled the reactions of the others when he'd told them that they were to run away from St.-Mere-Abelle with this kitchen hand who had some unknown tie to those who had once befriended Avelyn Desbris and Master Jojonah. His four friends were even more incredulous when Braumin had disclosed the source of his contact with the man. To think that Brother Francis had put them on this course! And yet, in trusting in Braumin's decision, in leaving St.-Mere-Abelle with him, these four young monks had passed the most important and difficult test thus far. Long before this last crisis, they had joined Braumin to carry on the work of Avelyn and Jojonah, but until this morning, the work had been naught but talk, secret meetings full of complaints, even hiding the feelings they'd had as they'd watched Jojonah burn. Now Markwart was apparently about to make his move against them. Each of them had been faced with a desperate choice: to hold fast beside Braumin and be executed or to betray the words and spirit of Jojonah.

Braumin wasn't sure which course his friends might have chosen had that critical moment come. He wanted to believe the others would have stood beside him, accepting Markwart's immoral judgment, as had Jojonah. He wanted to believe that he, too, would have held true. But fortunately, Brother Francis had offered them a third option, and at least postponed that supreme test of faith.

For Markwart would come after them, Braumin Herde did not doubt, and if the Father Abbot caught them, their lives would surely be forfeit.

Now, Braumin decided, his thoughts had to turn instead to the road ahead, to hopes of meeting the mysterious friends of Avelyn Desbris and finding confirmation of all he held dear.

He sought out Roger Billingsbury, who was sitting alone on the other side of the camp, drawing in the dirt with a stick. He was not surprised to find that Roger had drawn a rough map of the region, with pebbles representing St.-Mere-Abelle, the Masur Delaval, Palmaris, and some points far to the north.

"Your home?" Braumin asked, indicating those.

"Caer Tinella," Roger replied, "and Landsdown. Two towns on the northern edge of Honce-the-Bear. It was in Caer Tinella that I first met Elbryan, the one known as Nightbird."

"Friend to Bradwarden," Braumin said.

"I never met the centaur," Roger admitted, "though I saw him once, tied up at the back of a fast-traveling caravan, heading south for Palmaris."

Braumin Herde nodded. He had been part of that caravan, making the return trip from Mount Aida. "And is this Nightbird a disciple of Avelyn Desbris?" he asked.

"He was a friend of Avelyn's," Roger replied. "But in truth, his companion, Jilseponie—he calls her Pony—is the true disciple of the monk. No one in all the world can bring forth more powerful magics."

Braumin looked at him skeptically.

"I understand the doubts of one who has spent the bulk of his life in an abbey," Roger replied calmly, "but you will learn better."

Braumin was eager for that. He could hardly wait to meet this woman, Avelyn's student.

Brother Dellman, looking relaxed compared to the others, wandered over then and crouched low to examine Roger's map.

"How far from Palmaris are these towns?" Braumin asked.

"A week of hard marching," Roger replied.

"Is this where we will find the friends of Jojonah?" Dellman put in.

Roger shrugged and shook his head. "With the weather holding mild, they may have already left for their original home of Dundalis in the Timberlands." He pointed to the map as he spoke at a spot north of Caer Tinella.

"Another week, then?" Dellman asked.

"At least," Roger replied. "Dundalis is about the same distance north of

Caer Tinella as Palmaris is south. There is only one road north from Caer Tinella—not a very good road—and I do not know if it is clear. Even before the monsters and the dactyl, the road to Timberland was considered dangerous."

"If that is where Nightbird and Jilseponie are to be found, then that is where we shall go," Braumin declared.

"I want to find them as much as you do," Roger assured him, "but we can only guess where they are. They are fugitives of the Abellican Church, and that is no small matter. They might be in the northland or they might be in Palmaris. I could make a reasonable guess that Bradwarden, at least, did return to the north, for a centaur wouldn't be easy to hide on city streets!"

That brought a smile to Braumin's face, but Dellman glanced all around. "Should we be speaking openly of this?" he asked nervously.

"You fear that we might have spiritual visitors?" Braumin asked.

"It is possible that Brother Francis put us together with Roger and then let us out of St.-Mere-Abelle that he might follow our movements and find these two friends of Avelyn," Dellman explained.

That brought a frown to Roger's face, but Braumin remained calm. "I trust Francis—on this matter," he replied. "I do not know why. Surely he has given me no previous reasons to trust him, but this time, he seemed sincere."

"As he would feign if he was working as Markwart's agent," said Dellman.

Braumin Herde shook his head. "The Father Abbot could have accomplished what you fear using Roger alone. In fact, that course would have been easier, for Roger, no master of the gemstones, would never have suspected that the monks might be following him spiritually."

Dellman smiled, accepting that.

"As to Francis," Braumin went on, "I believe his tale of Master Jojonah's forgiveness was true, for Master Jojonah was dragged past him out of the College of Abbots, and certainly kindly Master Jojonah would have forgiven him."

"Is that not the whole point of who we are?" Brother Dellman interjected.

Braumin nodded. "And thus," he added, "it pained Brother Francis to watch Master Jojonah die so horribly. Perhaps it shook the foundations of his world."

"Your premise is correct, brother, but your conclusions . . ." Dellman replied, shaking his head, not convinced. "Francis hated Master Jojonah. That much was obvious to us on our journey to Mount Aida. And he hates you even more, I believe."

"Perhaps he hates himself most of all," Braumin answered, staring out into the empty night—and he was confident that it was empty.

Brother Dellman followed that gaze into the darkness. He wasn't as confident as Braumin, but, in truth, it really didn't matter. The Father Abbot would have executed them had they stayed, they all knew, or he would have forced them into terrible confessions and retractions—the price of their souls for the sake of their bodies. Whether Markwart caught them on the road or descended upon them in St.-Mere-Abelle, the end would be the same.

Dellman and the others could only hope that Braumin's assessment of Francis was correct.

Master Theorelle Engress was probably the most benign and gentle monk Brother Francis had ever known. Completely unassuming, Engress was as old as Markwart and had been a fixture at St.-Mere-Abelle for more than five decades. He was not an ambitious man, having attained his rank merely as a matter of longevity rather than any great deeds. Humble and generous, much respected by all the monks of St.-Mere-Abelle and all the Abellican Order, Engress went about his daily routines quietly, never speaking out of turn. He had been quite distressed, whispers said, about the trial and execution of Jojonah, but, as in all other matters, he kept his opinions to himself, arguing only when he deemed it necessary—as he had in the matter of Brother Francis' premature promotion to the rank of immaculate.

Maybe that was why Brother Francis found himself outside the gentle master's door late that same night he had ushered the conspirators out of St.-Mere-Abelle.

Master Engress, dressed in a nightshirt, showed no real surprise when he opened the door and found Francis standing in the hall. "Yes, brother?" he asked politely, managing a calm smile though it was obvious that Francis had disturbed his sleep.

Francis looked at the man numbly.

"Is there trouble afoot?" the master prodded. "The Father Abbot, perhaps? Does he wish to see me?"

"Not him, master," Francis said and swallowed hard. "Me."

Engress spent a long moment studying Francis. It was no secret that he had quietly opposed Francis' promotion to immaculate and had recently also spoken to the Father Abbot, arguing against Markwart's obvious plans to elevate the young monk to the rank of master. Then Engress stepped back and invited Francis into his chamber.

Francis sat down in a chair beside the small night table, sighed deeply, and put his chin in his hand.

"It has nothing to do with your qualifications, you understand," Master Engress said to him, "or with your character."

Francis looked at the old man, his gentle eyes, deep with wisdom, his soft mane of thick white hair—so different from Markwart's newly shaved head!—with a puzzled expression, "No," he explained. "This is not about my rank or any promotion I have been given or am soon to receive. It has nothing to do with the hierarchy or politics of St.-Mere-Abelle. It is about . . . me."

At first, Engress regarded the surprising young man suspiciously. But, apparently coming to the conclusion that this was no trick by Francis to assure promotion, the gentle master sat down on the chair opposite the troubled monk, even placed one of his leathery old hands on Francis'.

"You are distressed, brother," Engress said. "Pray alleviate your burden."

Francis looked up at him, stared deeply into those wise dark eyes. "I ask for Penitence," he said.

Engress's surprise was obvious. "Would not the Father Abbot better suit such a blessing upon you?" he asked calmly. "He is your mentor, after all—"

"In some matters, yes," Francis interrupted, "but not in this."

"Then speak, brother," Engress said kindly. "Of course I am willing to bestow the blessing, if you are truly repentant."

Francis nodded, then again fumbled, searching for the right words—and quickly discovered that there were no right words for this. "I killed a man," he blurted. It took every bit of strength within him to sit straight and square his shoulders as he made the admission.

Engress's eyes widened, but he, too, kept his emotions under control. "You mean that your actions contributed to the death of a man."

"I mean that I struck the man, and as a result of that blow, he died," Francis said. A tremor coursed through him; he bit his lip to keep it from quivering. "On the road," he explained, "coming back from St. Precious. It was I who struck the younger Chilichunk—Grady."

"I have heard of this," Engress replied, "though I was told that Grady Chilichunk died merely as a result of the rigors of the journey."

"He died because I hit him . . . hard," Francis said. "I did not mean to do it—at least not to kill him." Francis then poured out the whole story, a great cleansing. He told Engress of how Grady was spitting on the Father Abbot and that he, Francis, had only wanted to protect the Father Abbot, had only demanded respect from Grady.

Engress remained calm, even reassured Francis at several points that crimes against God are made with the heart and not the body, and thus, if it was truly an accident, then Francis could put his conscience at rest.

But the troubled Francis did not stop there. He told of Jojonah and the College of Abbots, of how Jojonah had forgiven him before being dragged to his death. Again, Master Engress was calm and forgiving, but still Francis was not finished. He told Engress of Braumin Herde and the other heretics.

"I let them go, master," Francis admitted. "I have gone against the wishes of Father Abbot Markwart and showed Brother Braumin the way out."

"And why would you do such a thing?" Engress asked, obviously stunned as well as intrigued.

Francis shook his head, for he had not answered that question, even to himself. "I did not want them killed," he admitted. "It seems so brutal— too brutal!—a punishment for their errors of judgment."

"The Father Abbot will tolerate no heresy," Master Engress reasoned.

"There is a long tradition of tolerance in the Abellican Order, but rarely does it extend to those who threaten the very fabric of the Order."

"And that is my pain," Francis explained, "for I understand the importance of keeping the Order secure and united. I agree with the Father Abbot—and even if I did not, I would not oppose him! Never that."

"But you could not bear to watch any more executions of your fellow monks," Engress stated.

Francis had no response to that.

"Do you believe what you have done is evil?"

"Which act do you mean?" Francis asked.

"That is for you to decide," Master Engress replied. "You came here asking for the blessing of Penitence, and perhaps I can bestow that upon you, but only if you tell me that for which you are asking Penitence."

Francis held up his hands, completely at a loss. "I have told my tale in full," he said.

"Indeed you have," Engress agreed, "but your tale shows a pendulum's swing of actions. For the Father Abbot, against the Father Abbot."

"And is he to be the measure of Godly crime?"

"Again, my brother, that is for you to decide. If you came here asking for forgiveness of your actions against Father Abbot Markwart, then I am afraid you are speaking to the wrong man. Unless those actions, in your heart, are also crimes against God, you will have to plead with the Father Abbot for his forgiveness, for I cannot speak for him. If you came seeking forgiveness of your actions on the road, then I, like Jojonah, will bestow the blessing, because it is obvious that you are truly sorry for those actions and because you are not wholly to blame.

"If you came seeking Penitence for your actions concerning Brother Braumin, then I must ask you to return when you have decided if those actions were indeed a crime against God, and if so, were they malicious or wrought of cowardice?"

Brother Francis sat quietly for a long while, trying to take in what Engress had said, and trying to decide what his reasons for each really were. Finally, too confused to work it out here, he looked helplessly at Master Engress. "For the attack against Grady Chilichunk," he said quietly, the only one of those questions he could honestly answer.

"Penitence was already given," Master Engress replied, rising from his seat and helping Francis to his feet as well. "So let your heart be free of that burden. If you decide there are any other burdens that need lifting, then do return to speak with me. But be quick to find your heart, young brother," he said with a smile, "I am an old, old man, and I might be gone from this world before you ever sort things out!"

He gave Francis a pat on the back as he ushered him to the corridor, then moved to close his door.

"I trust that this will remain confidential?" Francis asked, turning back to face Engress.

Engress reassured him. "It is a sacred blessing, a pact between you and God. I cannot speak of it because I, the mortal Master Engress, was not even present at your confession."

Francis nodded and walked away.

Engress stood in the doorway and watched him until he turned a bend in the corridor. The old man stood there, overwhelmed by the information Francis had given him. He had played his part in the blessing perfectly, detached and calm, the eyes and ears of God.

Almost perfectly, Engress had to admit after a few moments. He thought that Acts of Amends, a method of contrition and repayment to society, were needed for the death of Grady Chilichunk. Engress had to scold himself now—and promise his own Acts of Amends—because the reason he had not ordered any from Brother Francis was the practical matter of not wanting to draw attention to this meeting. If Father Abbot Markwart, who always kept Francis at his elbow, saw the monk performing Acts of Amends, then many dangerous questions might be asked. Engress had not acted exactly as his religion demanded, and that troubled him, as it always did when matters of practicality took precedence over the pure practice of his religion.

And now he had another problem, for though Engress the monk would not divulge to anyone what Francis had told him, Engress the man was shocked. To think that such a conspiracy had begun in St.-Mere-Abelle! To think that young brothers of the Abellican Order, good men every one, had met in private to question the decisions of the Father Abbot, perhaps even to plot against him!

And yet, considering the war, the events at St. Precious and in the dungeons of St.-Mere-Abelle, and most of all, the horrible execution of Master Jojonah, Engress could understand that men of good conscience would band together to oppose the very Order itself. Engress had been a friend of Jojonah's, and though he had no evidence to refute the charges Markwart had leveled against him, he could not, in his heart, reconcile the Jojonah he had known with the heretic Markwart claimed he was.

"You grab your power too tightly, Dalebert Markwart," the old monk whispered. "And thus do many followers squeeze through your fingers."

Feeling very weary and very old indeed, Master Theorelle Engress closed his door. He knelt beside the bed and said a prayer for guidance.

Then he added one for Brother Francis.

Then he added one for Brother Braumin and his companions.

"The departure of Jilseponie weighs heavily on us all," Tomas said somberly, "as does the departure of Shamus Kilronney and his worthy soldiers. But neither event has changed our destination, of course, especially since you have declared that you still intend to accompany us."

"I will indeed," the ranger replied with an exasperated sigh, growing close to frustration, for Tomas had been dancing around his main point for many minutes now, carefully feeling Elbryan out.

"And the weather has been favorable," Tomas went on, "save the one storm. And even those snows were quick to melt away."

Elbryan shook his head and stared at Tomas, his expression speaking clearly that Tomas should get on with it!

"Some folk have been whispering that we should begin our journey," the big man finally admitted—no surprise to the ranger. "They are saying that we could have made Dundalis already and had more than a fair share of shelters constructed, if we had left soon after the supplies had been offered by Comli and the others."

The ranger chuckled at the predictable hindsight. Indeed, they could have long ago reached Dundalis, and, unless they found many monsters blocking their path, could have put up enough shelters and stored enough firewood to survive the harshest of winters. But they could not have known that the mild weather would hold. Winter storms often rolled up the coast, settling for a long stay in the Gulf of Corona, dumping many inches of sleet and rain on the coastal regions and many feet of snow inland. If a storm had caught Tomas' caravan on the road, Elbryan, who had lived most of his life in this region, knew that the few who survived would have been forced to turn back for Caer Tinella.

"The ground is nearly frozen," Tomas reasoned, "and it remains clear of snow."

"Down here, at least," said the ranger. "We do not know what we might find a hundred miles to the north."

"Likely the same," Tomas replied without hesitation. "You admitted as much yourself."

Elbryan nodded, conceding the point. He and Juraviel and Bradwarden had found no signs of inclement weather farther north.

"And if we wait until Bafway, we'll likely find our wagon wheels sinking deep into the spring mud," Tomas went on.

"And if we leave now and a great storm rises against us?" Elbryan asked bluntly.

"And who is to argue that such a storm could not find us even in the spring?" Tomas countered.

Elbryan wanted to argue, wanted to remind the man that spring storms, however deep the snow, were rarely as dangerous as winter storms, since the weather soon after a spring storm almost always turned warm, melting a foot of snow in a few hours. And it wasn't just the snow that Tomas and the other should fear, the ranger realized, for the temperature could plummet in the winter, leaving a man frozen on the ground—even if that ground was not covered in snow.

"If we had left after the first storm of the season—the only storm of the season," Tomas went on, "we would be settled now, cozy in Dundalis. I am thinking, and so are many others, that it is worth the try now. The weather holds and shows no sign of changing. With the ground hard and Nightbird to guide us, we can be in Dundalis in a week, bringing enough wood with us to build a few shelters, and with plenty left to burn against winter's bite, should it ever come."

Elbryan stared hard at the man. He had plenty of practical arguments against Tomas. But they would fall on deaf ears, he knew, and, in truth, he wasn't sure that he wanted to dissuade Tomas.

Not this time.

Pony was gone, and all he wanted was to be back in her arms. Perhaps if he gave Tomas his wish and led them to Dundalis now, before Decambria had ended and the year had turned to the month of Progos, he would have discharged his responsibility to the caravan long before the end of winter. The ranger smiled as he fantasized about surprising Pony in Palmaris before the turn of spring.

That smile disappeared when he looked at Tomas, fearing that he was agreeing only for selfish reasons, perhaps to the detriment of those hardy souls who would make the journey north.

In truth, though, that very morning both Bradwarden and Juraviel had made similar arguments to Elbryan for setting off at once for the north-land, all realizing that Tomas had asked to speak with him precisely for that purpose.

"You understand that I can guarantee nothing?" the ranger asked.

Tomas smiled widely.

"If a storm catches us—"

"We're tougher than you are supposing," Tomas replied.

The ranger gave a great, defeated sigh, and Tomas followed the cue with a heartfelt belly laugh.

"I can guarantee nothing," Elbryan repeated somberly. "We can find and destroy, or avoid, any monsters, I believe, but I cannot make the same claims concerning the whims of nature."

"She'll stay calm and inviting," Tomas assured him. "I feel it in my old bones."

Elbryan nodded, and then he said the words that Tomas Gingerwart and so many others had been aching to hear for so many days. "Pack up."

❖ **8** ❖

The Bishop's Initiatives

Pony crouched at the corner of the gatehouse, watching the spectacle at the Palmaris docks. The ferry had just come in, crowded with folk from the town of Amvoy across the Masur Delaval, and now the Palmaris city soldiers and a pair of monks from St. Precious jostled the newcomers, inspecting their goods, barking questions at them. Every day it got worse.

Pony had been in the city for more than a week. After she'd seen similar problems at the north gate when she'd arrived, she entered the city secretly at night, using malachite to boost her and Greystone right over a little-guarded position along the city wall. What a thrilling ride that had been, cantering Greystone into a great leap and using the levitational powers of the gemstone to let them soar far above and beyond the ten-foot wall!

After arranging board for Greystone at a stable on the city's north end, Pony had gone straight to the thriving Fellowship Way, finding Belster O'Comely along with a woman, Dainsey Aucomb, who had come on to help the Chilichunks years before, when Pony had been indentured in the army. Several others from up north were at the Way as well, some working, others patrons; and at first Pony was afraid that being recognized by so many could lead to serious trouble. Belster had taken care of that, though, calling a quick meeting and helping Pony to change her identity. Now she was Carralee dan Aubrey, a combination of the names of a friend and her infant niece, both of whom had been killed during the original goblin raid on Dundalis many years before.

Only then did Pony appreciate how organized Belster and his friends were. Such an underground brotherhood had become necessary, he explained, because of the policies of the new head of the abbey of St. Precious, Abbot De'Unnero. Some were already whispering that he was not merely the abbot of St. Precious but also bishop of Palmaris, a title that conferred the powers of both abbot and baron. That notion terrified Pony, for in a world where edicts from King and Father Abbot could take weeks to arrive, such a position gave De'Unnero, in effect, the powers of a dictator.

Now that she had settled into the routines of Fellowship Way, Pony had been going out each day to witness the events about the town, particularly near the gates and the docks, where the changes seemed most acute.

Palmaris was a fortified city, but primarily it was a trading city, a port at the mouth of the great river, the hub for any merchants operating in the northwest of Honce-the-Bear. As such, the city gates had always been only lightly guarded, but now . . .

The reason given for the increase in security was the deaths of both Abbot Dobrinion and Baron Bildeborough. But from what Elbryan had told her, and everything she had witnessed of De'Unnero, and everything Jojonah had told her, she knew De'Unnero knew the Church had been intimately involved as well in the murder of Baron Bildeborough. This made it clear to Pony that De'Unnero was using the fear of the Palmaris populace only to increase his power. He was using the murders as an excuse to solidify his own position.

Pony thought about the implications of De'Unnero's new title for a long while. Church and state power united in one man. Seeing the soldiers working with the monks now at the ferry sent a shiver along her spine.

When about half the travelers were allowed to enter Palmaris but the other half put back on the boat to return to Amvoy, the soldiers and monks turned their attention elsewhere. On their way off the docks, they paused long enough to taunt and heckle, even spit at, a group of Behrenese youngsters who were playing a game on a street. The southern dock section of Palmaris had been an enclave for the Behrenese for many decades. In all the years Pony had lived in Palmaris, the Behrenese, even the yatol priests, had been viewed with compassion and brotherhood by the city's folk, particularly by the monks of St. Precious, who would often be seen down by the docks with armloads of food and clothing, helping any new Behrenese arrivals settle comfortably in the strange city.

How the times had changed! But it wasn't just the poor folk living by the docks, or the less-connected travelers trying to get into the city who were having trouble with the new policies.

Pony made her way quickly across Palmaris, into the hilly section on the city's west side where the wealthier citizens resided. In the Way the night before, one of Belster's contacts had mentioned some strange happenings in this area, something Pony had just confirmed when she'd overheard a man at the ferry dock.

It didn't take Pony long to see what Belster's informant and the man at the docks were talking about. She saw a group of about a dozen city soldiers and three Abellican monks walking boldly down the middle of Bildeborough Way, the main avenue in this section of Palmaris. Fortunately, Pony saw them before they spotted her, and ducked behind a hedgerow—

which were quite common in this wealthy part of the city. Hardly daring to breathe, Pony berated herself for coming here physically instead of simply using her soul stone and spiritually spying on the region.

Then as the group neared, she realized one of the monks was using a red gemstone.

"Garnet," she whispered under her breath. Garnet, the Dragon Sight, the stone used to detect the emanations of magic. This group was out in search of magic stones!

Pony watched as they stopped at a gate, one of the soldiers slapping his metal gauntlet against the large entry bell. A pair of house guards appeared almost immediately. Within seconds, the sound of the exchange became loud enough that Pony, though she was several doors away, could make out the words.

"We'll not stand here and argue with mere merchant bodyguards," the soldier who had slapped the bell declared. "Open wide the gate, by order of the bishop of Palmaris, or we shall trample it down, and trample, too, any who stand before us."

"And do not think that your master will protect you with his tricks of magic," another soldier interjected. "We have brothers of St. Precious with us who are more than able to defeat any such attacks."

A bit more prodding, a bit more yelling, and finally the house guards opened the gate. They asked that only one or two men enter to speak with their master, but the whole group shoved past them. They emerged a few minutes later, a middle-aged man in a rich robe in their midst. One of the monks caught Pony's attention, for he was holding a large headdress—a crown of sorts—set with many glittering gemstones.

She realized that some of those stones must have magical properties, for she had heard that merchants often bought stones from the Church and, using alchemists and other stones, converted them into magical items. This merchant's crown no doubt carried strong magical energy, and that, she believed, was what had led the group to his door. Glad indeed was Pony that she had not come out here spiritually!

The group went past—and Pony breathed easier—heading west down the wide street in the direction of Chasewind Manor, formerly the home of the ruling Bildeborough family but now, by all accounts, the residence of Abbot—Bishop De'Unnero.

"So strange," Pony whispered to herself as she made her way back to the more crowded central areas of the city. She told herself that there might be many reasons De'Unnero would seek out magic use in this dangerous time so soon after the end of the war and so soon after the deaths of the two former city leaders. But she suspected the search through the city had another quarry.

The Bishop was looking for her.

*   *   *

"Cousin, if you are wise—though I know that you are not—you will dismiss your anger before we arrive at Chasewind Manor," Shamus Kilronney said to Colleen. The two hadn't even passed through the northern gate of Palmaris when some of the sentries had begun blabbering about the many changes that had taken place in the city. Shamus and Colleen had gone straight off to St. Precious to speak with the new abbot, but they had been turned away and pointedly told to return to their assigned quarters and await a summons.

Then came the long wait, and it was all that Shamus could handle merely keeping Colleen in check. As each rumor filtered out to them—the abbot had been appointed Bishop, which gave him all the powers of abbot and baron; the man had taken up residence at Chasewind Manor; Colleen's soldiers were being used as escorts for missions of the Church—both Shamus and Colleen became more and more uneasy. For Colleen in particular, still upset by the death of her beloved Baron, this new turn of events was almost more than she could take.

Finally, more than a week after their return to Palmaris, the pair was summoned to Chasewind Manor, to report to Bishop Marcalo De'Unnero. They were met in the courtyard by a host of monks. There they waited for more than an hour. Other prominent soldiers filtered in, and then came a great carriage, which Shamus recognized as one of the King's own. The captain didn't know the names of the two men who stepped out, but he did know that they were from the court of King Danube, important emissaries indeed.

They strode past the group outside without a word, not even a nod to the Kingsmen captain.

"And how long do ye mean to keep us waitin'?" Colleen asked loudly before the men had entered the house. They simply ignored her, and so did the monks. In fact, the only response she received came from her nervous cousin.

"They will keep us waiting as long as it suits the noblemen," Shamus scolded. "You do not understand our place in this or the potential punishments if we do not hold to that place."

"Bah." Colleen snorted. "Ye'd have me bowin' and beggin'. Yes sir and no sir, and might I wipe the spit from yer chin, sir?"

"You do not understand the nobility."

"Been servin' the Baron for ten years," Colleen argued.

"But Rochefort Bildeborough was a man of Palmaris, not of the court of Danube Brock Ursal," Shamus warned. "These nobles will have your respect, or they will have your tongue—or worse!"

Colleen spat on the ground, very near the foot of the closest monk. She looked around at her fellow soldiers, many of whom had been house guards for the Bildeborough family, and took comfort in their grim expressions, understanding that they, too, were not pleased. All of them had served

Rochefort Bildeborough for years; all of them had come to respect and even love the man as their leader.

A monk came out the front doors of the manor house, a scroll in hand. "Shamus Kilronney," he called. "Captain of the Kingsmen. And Colleen Kilronney of the city guard."

"Beware your treasonous temper," Shamus whispered as he and Colleen strode toward the man.

"And if I cannot control it, cousin, I'm sure ye'll cut me down," she replied with a snarl. "I'm just hopin' that I can get the imposter's head afore ye do!"

Shamus glared angrily at her.

"Ye just watch me do it," she said stubbornly, as if daring him to betray her.

The point proved moot, and Shamus breathed a bit easier, because inside the house, they were accosted by a group of armed soldiers—who were not known to Colleen—and many grim-faced Abellican monks who demanded their weapons. Shamus readily complied, for he knew only specially assigned guards were allowed any weapons at the King's court. Colleen slapped away one monk's hand as he reached for her weapon, then she drew out her sword threateningly. The monk jumped back into a fighting stance and several soldiers put their hands to sword hilts.

But Colleen only smiled and laughed, and flipped her weapon over, catching it at mid-blade and handing it over.

"I'll not fight on your side," Shamus warned quietly as they were escorted to the audience room.

"And ye're thinkin' that I'm not already knowin' as much?" Colleen replied dryly.

The audience room was large, but it did not seem so to the two, for many monks and soldiers and visiting nobles and merchants all clustered about, eyes aimed at the young, strong Bishop. Many heads did turn to glance without interest at the two soldiers, Shamus in his splendid Kingsmen dress and Colleen in her weathered traveling outfit.

"I do say, it is not difficult to discern which of these two comes from the court of the King," said one of the visiting Ursal nobles with a sniff.

The Bishop waved at the man to be quiet, locking stares with Shamus and then with Colleen.

The man was impressive, Colleen had to admit, his stare strong and intense. This first meeting quickly became a contest of wills, the two staring, unblinking, as many moments slipped past.

Finally, Bishop De'Unnero dropped his eyes to regard the Kingsman. "You are Shamus Kilronney?" he asked. "Captain Kilronney?"

The man straightened his shoulders. "I am, sir."

"Very good," said De'Unnero. "You have been told of my appointed position?"

Shamus nodded.

"And do you, both of you," he added quickly, glancing back at Colleen, "understand the meaning of my title?"

"I'm thinkin' that it means there be no more Bildeboroughs," Colleen remarked, drawing an elbow in the ribs from Shamus. But De'Unnero only laughed.

"Indeed there are not," he said with a chuckle. "Nor were any others deemed worthy of the position. Thus, I serve both the King and Father Abbot now, as baron and abbot—bishop, by title."

"We have been informed, Bishop De'Unnero," Shamus said quickly, before Colleen could offer any more sarcasm.

"And since the city is in such disarray, King Danube has deemed it necessary to lend me a contingent of his soldiers," the Bishop explained.

"I understand," Shamus replied, then followed with the standard, accepted line of obedience. "And, of course, my men and I are at your complete disposal."

"Of course," the Bishop echoed. "And what of you, Colleen Kilronney? I have heard many of the guards here at Chasewind Manor speak highly of you. Of course, I have also heard many whisper that Colleen Kilronney would not be in good spirits when she returned from the north to discover the changes in her city."

Colleen's eyes widened, surprised that the new bishop had so bluntly put that out on the table. She started to answer, but De'Unnero stopped her.

"I understand your anger," he said. "I have been told that none were more loyal to Baron Rochefort Bildeborough. Of course that sentiment will carry over for some time after his death. I applaud such loyalty." He leaned forward in his chair, so that only she, and perhaps Shamus, could hear. "But I will not tolerate any disloyalty to your beloved Baron's successor."

Colleen's eyes narrowed dangerously as De'Unnero eased back. Again the two locked stares—and this time, it was Colleen who finally backed down.

"I will require a full accounting of your travels up north," De'Unnero went on, never taking his imposing stare from the warrior woman. "Unfortunately, at this time, I have other matters to attend."

"We will return when you summon us," Shamus replied and started to bow, thinking it was time to take their leave.

"No, you will stay and you will wait," De'Unnero corrected. He motioned to one of the monks. "Find them a place, a side room somewhere," the Bishop instructed absently.

"Ye sure 'twas on that eye?" Dainsey Aucomb asked for the third time, reaching out again to adjust Pony's eyepatch.

"The right eye," Pony replied with a sigh, growing impatient. Pony worked hard to hide that frustration. Dainsey wasn't the brightest-burning torch in the room, but the disguise had been her idea and her doing, and it alone allowed Pony free run of Fellowship Way. Besides, Dainsey had been a loyal worker for Graevis and Pettibwa, a daughter of sorts, filling the void that had been left in their lives when Pony had been sent into the army by Abbot Dobrinion as punishment for her attack against her husband, Connor Bildeborough. And, more recently, Dainsey had proven to be a great help to Belster, had willingly given him control of the tavern—left in her care when the Chilichunks had been abducted by the Church—and had stayed on without complaint to help Belster operate the business.

So Pony, for all her frustration and fear, took extra care not to let any hint of her anger out.

"The right one, ye say?" Dainsey asked, honestly perplexed.

"Thought it was the left eye," came Belster's voice, as the portly inn-keeper entered the room.

Pony turned a one-eyed glare his way, and saw the jovial man smiling wider than usual—and that became a belly chuckle when Dainsey stub-bornly reached for the eye patch.

"Right eye," Pony said firmly, pushing Dainsey's hand away. She was more frustrated with Belster than with the woman, for she knew the inn-keeper was only teasing her. She turned her gaze from Belster, for her obvious distress was only making him smile all the wider, and looked directly at Dainsey, pointedly grabbing the woman's wrist and pulling her arm down.

"Right eye, then," Dainsey at last agreed. "Yer own skinny neck, it is. Ye let me get ye some more powder, though. Can't be havin' any o' that golden hair o' yers shinin' through!"

The mere mention of the gray powder sent Pony's hand up to scratch at her temple, then to run her hand back through her thick mane. She knew that Dainsey was right. With Dainsey's help, she went into the Way each night as Belster's wife, Caralee dan Aubrey O'Comely, padded and frumpy, and fully twenty years older than Jilseponie Ault.

"Any information?" Pony asked.

"Nothing important," Belster replied. "It is as if our friend Roger Lock-less walked into the damned Masur Delaval." The innkeeper gave a frus-trated shake of his head, then paused, waiting until Dainsey left. "And what of these soldiers?" Belster asked quietly. "You are certain that they were looking for the gemstones?"

"If not, then why have monks accompanying them?" Pony replied. "And the monks were using garnet, the stone also known as Dragon Sight because it bestows on its user the power to detect magic."

"But the gemstones have to be in use for such detection?" Belster asked nervously.

Pony nodded and the portly innkeeper breathed a sigh of relief. "And I've not used any since my return," she added. "Brother Avelyn once told me that many merchants have purchased gemstones from the Church."

"And now the Bishop's taking them back," Belster reasoned.

"That may be part of it," Pony agreed. "But he is looking for the gemstones, mostly because finding them may lead him to the friends of Avelyn Desbris."

"That I do not doubt," said Belster, "though it may be more than an extension of the search for you and Nightbird. I am not liking much the rumbling I am hearing from St. Precious—or from Chasewind Manor, since that is where the new bishop has taken up residence."

Dainsey returned then, singing a happy tune—and Pony wished that she still had such melodies within her—and the two went quiet. A bit of powder, a bit of grayish paste on Pony's fair face, and the woman stepped back to admire her work.

"Belster's wife?" Pony asked, hopping from the stool and turning slowly, arms out that they might regard her fully.

"Ho, but I like you better the other way!" Belster said with a wry laugh—a laugh that was cut short by a knock on the door.

"Soldiers in the Way," came the hushed call of Heathcomb Mallory, another friend from the northland who worked in the Way on those few nights he was not drinking there.

"You are certain that you did *not* use the stones?" Belster asked again, moving toward the door. Dainsey joined him, and the two left the room, but Pony only peeked out.

The Way bustled with a large crowd this night, as it did almost every night, but the innkeeper had no trouble in picking out the soldiers. Not only were they in their full military dress, he noted, but they carried swords at their hips. Belster immediately moved to the corner of the long bar closest to the three and started wiping it down, painting a wide smile on his face. "Gentlemen!" he called. "Rare it is that we see our protectors in here. Too rare, I say! Name your pleasure; the treat is the Way's to give!"

One of the soldiers smacked his lips and leaned on the bar. He started to speak, but another man dropped an arm across his chest to cut him short. "No pleasure," the second soldier said, "not this night."

If the first man had any intention of arguing, he dropped it when a monk of St. Precious pushed through the crowd, coming between the three soldiers to stand facing Belster.

"You are O'Comely?" the monk asked bluntly.

"Belster O'Comely," the innkeeper replied, sounding cheerful as usual, though the lack of respect from this man barely half his age made Belster grit his teeth.

"And how did you acquire this tavern?" the monk asked. "Were you acquainted with the previous owners?"

Before Belster could respond, Dainsey came strutting by. "I give it to 'im," she declared. "And it was mine for givin', since all accounts say that the Chilichunks won't be comin' back anytime soon."

The monk studied Dainsey carefully, then turned to glance at the three soldiers.

"Oh, don't ye go thinkin' that way!" Dainsey protested. "I already been taked to yer jail three times. How many times ye got to hear that I'm not the woman what stole the stinkin' stones?"

The monk studied her once more, then looked back at his companions.

"She has been there," one of the soldiers admitted, and his blush showed that he had been one of the many to "interrogate" Dainsey.

"Some of the precious gemstones have been stolen?" Belster asked innocently, looking at Dainsey as if he had no idea what she was talking about.

The monk eyed him intently.

"There was a man and a woman up north said to have some magic about them," Belster admitted, for he knew that the tales of Nightbird and Pony and their exploits were common Palmaris stories by now, certainly accounts that the Bishop and his minions would have heard.

"You are from the northland, then?" the monk asked.

"Caer Tinella," Belster lied, thinking that tying himself to Dundalis might be too close for comfort. "Thought to go back there, too, until Miss Dainsey here offered me and my wife a new life here at Fellowship Way."

"And what do you know of this man and woman up north?" the monk asked.

Belster shrugged. "Not much. We were running south and heard that our escape from the monsters was helped by them, that is all. Never did actually see them—or I might have seen the man, though from a long distance, sitting splendid atop a great black horse."

"Splendid?" the monk echoed sarcastically. "He is a thief, Master O'Comely. You should take better note of your companions."

"No companion," Belster insisted. "Just someone who helped me and many others get away from the monsters." He noted the expressions of the four men as he spoke reverently of this supposed outlaw, looks ranging from disdain to intrigue. The innkeeper took more than a little pleasure in promoting the reputation of his friend Elbryan and in sowing the seeds of doubt among the Bishop's faithful pawns.

Pony came out of the back room then, boldly walking to stand beside Belster. "Did ye offer any drinks, then?" she asked the big man, hooking his arm.

"My wife, Carralee," Belster explained.

"Ah, Father," Pony said to the monk. "Have ye any o' them wonderful stones about ye? Do ye think ye might fix me eye then? Got it all torn on the end of a goblin spear, ye know."

A sour look crossed the monk's face. "Come to the abbey," he said insincerely. "Perhaps one of the elders . . ." He ended by waving his hand and turning away, motioning for the soldiers to follow.

"More than a bit of a chance you just took, by my measure," Belster said quietly to Pony when they had turned to go.

"Not so much of a chance," Pony replied unemotionally, as she watched the men leave. "If they had recognized me, then I would have had to kill them."

Dainsey gasped.

"And if they had invited you to go with them to St. Precious?" Belster calmly asked.

"To heal my eye?" Pony scoffed. "Not the Church that Avelyn ran away from. Not the Church that murdered my family and tortured Bradwarden. The Abellicans help when they need to help, and aid only those who might return the favor with gold or power."

The coldness in her voice sent a chill through Belster, who tried to change the subject. "And once again, we have Dainsey to thank," he remarked, turning to the smallish woman, who curtsied rather clumsily.

"It is true, Dainsey," Pony said sincerely. "You have helped me so much since I arrived. I understand why Pettibwa and Graevis loved you."

Dainsey blushed deeply and giggled, spinning away to gather up a tray and skip to some beckoning patrons at a nearby table.

"A good girl, she is," Belster remarked.

"And that, unfortunately, will probably get her killed," said Pony.

Belster wanted to yell at the woman for her pessimism, but he could not. In the last few days, the men of the new bishop, soldiers and monks alike, seemed to be everywhere, seemed to be closing a noose about Pony, and indeed, about all of Palmaris.

The monk left Colleen and Shamus in a side room furnished only with three small chairs and a tiny hearth. No fire was lit and the cool wind moaned down the chimney.

Shamus slid into a chair, put his hands behind his head, and leaned back against the wall, closing his eyes. Familiar with the ways of nobles, the captain knew that this could be a long wait.

Colleen, predictably, was much more agitated, pacing back and forth, sitting down, then jumping back up. No matter how much noise she made, no matter how hard she stomped her heavy boots against the wooden floor, she could not get any reaction from her cousin, which, of course, only made her all the more angry and impatient.

Finally, after more than an hour, she settled down, pulling a chair against the wall, and sat staring intently at the door.

Another hour passed. Colleen began to complain, but Shamus opened one sleepy eye and reminded her that Bishop De'Unnero was now the ruler of both the secular and spiritual aspects of the city, and certainly the two of them were not his highest priority.

Colleen grumbled again and leaned back, arms crossed over her chest, jaw set firmly.

Another hour, and then another. Colleen went from sitting to pacing and back again several times. She stopped her grumbling out loud, though, for there seemed no point—Shamus was fast asleep.

Finally the door handle began to move, and Colleen sprang up, moving quickly to give Shamus a kick. He opened his eyes as the door swung in, and to their mutual surprise, it was no messenger come to fetch them but Bishop De'Unnero himself.

"Stay seated," he bade Shamus, and he motioned Colleen into her chair. The Bishop didn't sit but stood towering over them.

"You will detail for me your time in the northland," De'Unnero explained. "I need not know about the monsters you have battled, nor any specifics of the environment. I am more concerned with those you might have allied with up there, particularly any warriors who might aid us should the darkness befall us once again."

"Easy question," Shamus obediently replied. "Nightbird and Pony dominated the forest battles."

De'Unnero laughed suddenly, amused at how easily he had uncovered the coveted information. One simple question had shown him the whereabouts of the two most wanted by the Abellican Church. "Yes, Nightbird and Pony," he purred. Now he did claim the other chair, sliding it up close. "Do tell me of those two. All about them."

Shamus looked sidelong at Colleen, his expression curious and concerned, as was hers, for both detected something strange in the Bishop's tone. To Colleen, it seemed almost as if the man was hungry for the information, too eager to want to know about the two heroes, given his stated reason.

"Were the two in Caer Tinella when you arrived?" De'Unnero pressed Shamus. "Or did they arrive subsequent?"

"Both," the soldier answered honestly. "The two were in the northland long before us, but they were not actually in Caer Tinella when my soldiers arrived."

"Until . . ." the anxious Bishop pressed.

Shamus brought his hand to his chin, trying to remember his first encounter with Nightbird and his beautiful companion. He couldn't remember the exact date but knew that it was sometime around the turn of Calember.

De'Unnero pressed him repeatedly, and now it was obvious to the perceptive soldiers that the man had more interest in these two than as possible future allies.

Finally, the Bishop had heard enough of the timing of the first meeting and began pressing Shamus, and then Colleen, more pointedly about the demeanor of the pair. He even asked about a centaur—had one been seen?—and when Shamus replied that he had heard rumors of such a creature but had not seen it himself, De'Unnero was positively gleeful.

"Wait, but wasn't it a man-horse that yer monk fellows, the trouble-makin' caravan from St.-Mere-Abelle, dragged through Palmaris?" Colleen asked.

"You would be wise to take care how you refer to my holy brethren," De'Unnero warned, but he brightened quickly as he turned the subject back to the fugitives. "And these two, Nightbird and Pony, are in Caer Tinella still?"

"There or just north of the place," Shamus admitted. "They were to lead a caravan to the Timberlands, though that was scheduled to go near the turn of spring."

"Interesting," De'Unnero mused, stroking his chin, his eyes taking on a distant look. He got up from his chair then, holding his hand out to keep the two from doing likewise, and started for the door. "You are dismissed," he explained. "Go back to your quarters and tell no one—no one, do you hear?—of this discussion."

And then he was gone, leaving a very perplexed Shamus and Colleen sitting in the chairs.

"So yer friend an' his girl are outlaws o' the Church," Colleen remarked after a lengthy pause. "There's a kick in the gut for ye!"

Shamus didn't reply, just kept looking nervously in the direction of the door.

"And what're ye to do?" Colleen asked him, standing up and practically pulling him out of the chair.

Regaining his composure, Shamus straightened his jacket and squared his shoulders. "We do not know anything of the sort," he said firmly. "Not once did the Bishop indicate that Nightbird and Pony were outlaws."

"Ah, but there's the little matter of the centaur," Colleen remarked, obviously enjoying her smug cousin's distress. "The centaur labeled as outlaw by the Church, taken by the Church, and then taken back from the Church. Seems yer friends might be a part o' all that. So what's Captain Shamus o' the Kingsmen to do?"

"I will serve my King," he answered coolly, starting for the door, "and you shall do the same."

"Yer King—or the Bishop?" Colleen asked, falling in step beside him.

"The Bishop speaks for the King," was his curt reply.

Colleen slowed down and let him move away from her, studying him carefully. She recognized the clear distress in his every move and thought that Shamus, with his blind devotion, deserved a bit of discomfort. He had developed an honest liking and deep respect for both Nightbird and Pony, she knew, and was now having a hard time swallowing the notion that the two were not all that they had seemed—or, perhaps, that the two were much more than they had seemed.

For Colleen, the feelings came more from the gut. It did not bother her at all that Nightbird was an outlaw in the eyes of Bishop De'Unnero. In fact, her respect for the man and for Pony as well was increased. She was a soldier of the Baron, not the King, and since her beloved Baron had been at odds with the Church right before his death, the startling changes in Palmaris were not at all to her liking.

Any trouble that Nightbird and his friend might cause would please her greatly, she thought with a smirk.

For Shamus, the meeting with De'Unnero had left thoughts much more troubling. In the stories the folk of Caer Tinella had told him about the ranger, and in the time he had spent beside Nightbird, he had seen only good in the man, a true hero to the beleaguered folk of the northland. Surely there was some mistake here; surely the man could be no outlaw!

Trailblazing

Nightbird had not named his horse. The name had come to him magically, an extension, a gift, the only mantle that would fit the magnificent black stallion. And now Symphony lived up to that name fully, navigating the fog-shrouded forest as easily as most horses could run through an open field. The horse cut fast and thundered ahead, leaping trees downed by the heavy snow of the early winter and swerving safely wide of low-hanging branches. Nightbird did not guide him; rather, he let his wishes be known to Symphony, then put his complete faith in the horse.

And they were gaining on the goblin ahead.

They cut around a small line of thick spruces, Symphony's hooves digging hard against the turf.

Ahead in the fog, Nightbird saw a movement: the goblin on the small horse, galloping flat out.

Symphony leaped in pursuit, closing still more ground, and soon the goblin was in range and the ranger lifted Hawkwing.

Frantic, the goblin kicked harder at the small horse's flanks, and the horse put its head down and sprinted ahead. But the goblin, knowing that it was being chased, knowing that its enemy was closing fast, was looking back and only glanced ahead in time to see the thick limb close the last few inches to its face.

The riderless horse continued on, but slowed with each stride.

Nightbird and Symphony trotted up to the squirming, squealing goblin, the creature rolling about on the ground, clutching its broken face. The ranger had Tempest out and struck down hard and true, and the wretched creature lay still.

Nightbird wiped the sword on the goblin's cloak, then slipped it back into its sheath on the side of Symphony's saddle. He glanced about the misty forest, then clamped his legs tight about the horse, and Symphony turned and thundered off the other way. Within seconds, the pair had spotted another fleeing goblin, and Symphony pursued.

This one was running, ducking from tree to tree, but it made the mistake of crossing the ranger's path only a dozen yards ahead of the running horse. Nightbird recognized the small, hunched silhouette; and Hawkwing hummed, the arrow catching the wretched creature in the side, boring through both lungs and throwing it, dying, to the ground.

A noise from behind had the ranger glancing back, to spot another goblin bursting from the brush and running wildly the other way. Nightbird didn't even think to turn Symphony, but rather turned himself by throwing one leg over the saddle, facing backward, and loosing an arrow.

For the third time in a matter of half a minute, a goblin fell dead.

Perched in a tree not far away, Belli'mar Juraviel considered the ranger's shot with something more than respect, something bordering on awe. The elves had trained Nightbird, but to say that they had taught him everything he knew, Juraviel realized, would have been a tremendous falsehood. What the elves had taught Nightbird was quick thinking and how to bring his body in line with his plans, but the human's creative use of that knowledge was stunning.

As was the ranger's technique, Juraviel thought, looking at the goblin shot through the head, a perfect hit by the ranger while his horse was in full gallop the other way!

Juraviel's keen eyes continued to scan through the fog as he shook his head. There, he saw suddenly, in the same brush from which the last goblin had bolted, hid yet another creature, curled and cowering. Up came the elf's bow. He wanted a clean kill, but could hardly make out any critical points on the diminutive creature through the branches and the fog. He shot at center mass instead, his small arrow disappearing into the black figure.

With a scream of pain, the goblin leaped out, and Juraviel promptly shot it again, then a third time before it got fully onto the path, and then a fourth time as it took its first running steps. He raised his bow for the fifth shot, but saw the creature staggering, and knew that his task was done.

Callously, Juraviel turned his attention away, scanning the rest of the area and lamenting that it had cost him nearly a fifth of his arrows to kill a single goblin. Still, there were other ways, Juraviel knew, and so he started back on his original course, fluttering from branch to branch until he found a perch on a low, thick limb that crossed the path just above the height of a rider's head. Laying his bow to the side, arrow ready across bowstring, the elf took out his slender, strong silverel cord.

The centaur, too, was running through the forest, screaming taunt after taunt at the terrified goblins. When he discovered that several of the goblins were riding horses—something very unusual—Bradwarden took up his bagpipes and played a different tune, one of quiet, calming music and not screaming insults. Bradwarden had to work hard to concentrate on the melody; for decades, he had run the forests of the Timberlands as protector of the wild horses, and now the mere thought of a smelly goblin atop so graceful and beautiful a creature outraged him.

Hardly caring for the goblins scrambling about on foot, the centaur picked out his next target and took up the chase. He knew how to talk to a horse, any horse, with his pipes; and instead of arrows, he sent music in pursuit. A grin turned up the corners of Bradwarden's mouth—he had to resist the urge to burst out in laughter so that he might keep filling his pipes with air—when he ducked under a branch and plowed through some brush, breaking out onto a small dirt clearing. There, some ten feet ahead of him, sat the frantic goblin, kicking desperately at the horse's flanks and wildly jostling the impromptu rope bridle.

But the horse had heard the call of the centaur and would not move.

It took some fancy finger work, but Bradwarden held the tune, playing with one hand while he took up his heavy cudgel in the other and quietly and methodically advanced. The goblin looked back at him briefly, but then only kicked and pulled more desperately, hopping up and down in its stationary seat.

The horse nickered softly, but did not move.

Now the centaur did laugh aloud, tucking his pipes away under his arm. "Ye about done there?" he asked matter-of-factly.

The goblin stopped its jostling and slowly turned its ugly head to regard the powerful centaur, who was standing right beside. It started to scream then, but the cry was cut short by the cudgel crushing skull and shattering neck bone. The goblin bounced from its perch and dropped heavily to the ground, twitching in the last moments of its life.

Bradwarden paid it no heed. "Now ye go and hide yerself in the woods," he said to the horse, pulling off its bridle, then sending it away with a solid slap on the rump. "I'll be callin' for ye when it's time for leavin'."

Now Bradwarden did look down at the goblin, still twitching, and he shook his head in disbelief. This was the second goblin he had caught as it tried to ride away, but at least the first had found the sense to get down off the damned stopped horse!

This one was a strong rider, for a goblin, Nightbird realized as Symphony worked hard to close ground. The goblin knew the area fairly well, the ranger also surmised, for it moved off the trails only at brief intervals and then only to get onto yet another narrow path. And even running its horse full out, the goblin knew when to duck and when to swerve.

Symphony was more than prepared to meet the challenge, and the great stallion pounded on gracefully, closing.

Now the goblin was a ghostly gray form in the fog ahead. Nightbird tightened his legs about Symphony and raised Hawkwing. He pulled back and fired, but the goblin's horse turned, and the arrow flew harmlessly past.

Nightbird worked hard to get down low as Symphony thundered around that same bend. As the path straightened, up came Hawkwing again, but right before the ranger let fly, the goblin ducked under a low branch that crossed the path and the shot was lost.

Growling with frustration, the ranger, too, went under the branch. He feared that this would prove to be a long chase, though, for the path ahead was anything but straight. He did catch sight of the goblin at last, riding hard. It sat up straight for just a moment, glancing back.

And then, suddenly, it was jerked free of its seat, sent flying back through the air as the horse galloped on.

The creature's arms and legs flailed wildly for just a second, and then it hung limp in midair, twisting slowly. Nightbird understood as he neared and saw Belli'mar Juraviel perched on a branch above the goblin's head, one end of his elven cord fastened to the branch, the other around the goblin's skinny neck.

"Saving your arrows?" the ranger asked sarcastically.

Before Juraviel could answer, a commotion in the forest sent the elf fluttering higher up the tree. Even from the higher vantage point, he couldn't see much through the fog, but his keen ears brought him all the information he needed. "It would seem as if our moment of surprise is ended," he called down. "The goblins are regrouping."

No sooner had the words left his mouth than another voice rang out strong and clear in the morning air. "So nice for ye to oblige," came Bradwarden's roar. "Gettin' yerselves all in one place for me!"

And that, predictably, was soon followed by sounds of renewed fighting.

"Bradwarden decided to regroup with them," Juraviel said dryly, and off the elf went, hopping and flying from branch to branch.

Symphony leaped away at Nightbird's bidding, off the path, cutting a straight line through the brush, following the centaur's voice. Pressing for speed, neither rider nor mount could avoid much of the underbrush, and both got scratched by sharp branches and bushes. Turning one bend around a thick tree a bit too tightly, the horse crunched Nightbird's leg. The ranger didn't complain, though, just threw his arm up in front of his face to protect his eyes, held on more tightly, squeezed his legs in as close as possible to Symphony's sides, and lay low across the horse's neck.

Sensing the urgency, intelligent enough to understand that a friend was in peril, Symphony, too, accepted the minor cuts and did not slow. In a few moments, they broke through the last of the underbrush, onto the rim of a bowl-shaped depression.

One goblin was down, its head split wide. Another rolled about, howling in pain and clutching its smashed shoulder. But eight more of the creatures remained, surrounding Bradwarden, prodding at him with spears and swords, forcing the centaur to work furiously to keep the goblins at bay so that they couldn't follow through and stick him deep. Bradwarden kicked and spun, and swished his great club with mighty swings, roaring threats. He couldn't hope to maintain that frantic pace, though, and as each turn came a bit slower, the goblins managed to move a bit closer and stick him a bit deeper.

On one such turn, the centaur spotted Nightbird and Symphony leaping down to join the fray. "Taked ye long enough!" Bradwarden roared; and with new hope came new energy. He spun back the other way and charged ahead, driving the goblins back and luring those behind, thus distracting them from the charge of the ranger.

Nightbird threw his left leg over the saddle, pulled his right foot from the stirrup, and replaced it with the left, leaving him standing atop the running horse. As they neared the closest goblins, the creatures finally turning to meet the charge, the ranger dropped from the horse and Symphony dug in his hooves and veered hard to the left.

His forward momentum unbroken, the ranger rushed ahead suddenly, stabbing Tempest out straight. The goblin made a fair attempt to block the thrust, but it couldn't comprehend how fast the weapon closed the space.

Nightbird ran right by, tearing Tempest free of the goblin's chest. He dove into a roll to help slow his progress, and came up on one knee with a mighty slashing parry of the next goblin's thrusting spear.

Overbalanced as the front half of its weapon got sheared away, the goblin stumbled toward the ranger, who stabbed straight out, sticking the goblin deep in the chest. With a powerful heave, Nightbird lifted the impaled creature and tossed it to the ground behind him, then rose quickly, slapping his blade against the sword of the next goblin as it came in at him. Deftly—this one was a fine warrior by goblin standards—the goblin sent its sword in repeatedly, once, twice, thrice, but each attack was neatly parried by the ranger's flashing sword. Its momentum lost, the goblin tried to retreat, but that gave the ranger the opportunity to attack.

Now Tempest came in, once, twice, thrice. To the goblin's credit, it managed to parry the first two blows.

Spurred by the appearance of his ally, Bradwarden had not been idle, though he hadn't scored any definitive blows. But neither had the goblins, obviously distracted by the appearance of the ranger, of Nightbird, whose name they had heard whispered in their worst nightmares. When the third fell to the slashing Tempest, the other five had seen enough, and they turned and scattered for the cover of the trees.

Nightbird started to follow, but he pulled up short, startled, as something zipped past his face. He understood when the object—one of Juraviel's small arrows—buried itself deep into the hamstring of a goblin, turning its retreat into a slow stagger. Another arrow came flying past, catching the next goblin in line, but the elf's aim was a bit too high, and the creature only ran off all the faster with the arrow stuck into its buttocks.

"Oh, don't ye be runnin', I'm tired o' runnin'!" Bradwarden wailed, and in frustration, the centaur threw his club at the closest fleeing creature. The weapon skipped past harmlessly, but the goblin did stop to notice, and then glanced back—noting that Nightbird had disappeared into the brush at the side, following the one Juraviel had crippled. Behind the goblin, Bradwarden's club settled into the brush.

An evil grin spread across the goblin's ugly face. "Now yous got no weapon," it reasoned, lifting its sword and charging back at Bradwarden.

"Dumb," the centaur mumbled. "Was that yer brother sittin' stupid on the horse?" With a great spinning leap, Bradwarden pivoted about, throwing his rump in line with the charging goblin. His hind legs touched down. Then he hopped and kicked, muscled legs shooting past the goblin's puny arm and puny weapon, one hoof catching the goblin's shoulder, the other its chest. Muscles extending, the centaur's kick hurled the goblin twenty feet backward, its arms and legs flailing wildly, to crash hard into the brush.

The centaur calmly walked past the broken, dazed creature, to retrieve his club. Then he came back, towering over the goblin. "Got no weapon, eh?" he taunted, and the cudgel came crashing down.

Back in the center of the bowl, Juraviel finished off those squirming on the ground, then moved out into the brush, to find the one he had hamstrung. It lay dead in a pool of blood, the result of a single, efficient sword thrust under the back of its skull.

"Where's the ranger?" the centaur asked when Juraviel emerged. Symphony, standing beside the centaur, stamped the ground hard.

"Hunting, I would guess," the elf replied casually.

Bradwarden looked at the misty forest and smiled.

The goblin leaned against a tree, slapping the side of its rump in a futile attempt to alleviate the pain, not daring to touch the arrow Juraviel had put into its butt. Then the creature froze at a nearby sound, eyes wide with terror, but it relaxed as two of its companions came skittering over.

One grasped the arrow shaft and started to extract the bolt, but the goblin cried out in pain, and the other stopped and slapped a hand over its mouth.

"Quiet!" said the third in a harsh whisper. "Yous wants to bring the Nightbird and the horse-man on us? Yous already left a line of blood. . . ."

The goblin's voice trailed off, and all three looked down at the unmistakably clear trail of the wounded goblin's passage.

Three sets of eyes came up, the terrified goblins staring at each other, none daring to speak.

Nightbird dropped from a branch to land right in the midst of them. Out went his fist to strike one goblin, out went the pommel of his sword, then ahead came the flashing blade. A backhand strike took down the second goblin, slashing diagonally from shoulder to hip as it staggered from the force of the pommel, and then the ranger spun around, landing a powerful overhead chop on the first goblin as it tried to recover from the punch in the face and tried to bring its unwieldly spear to bear.

It took the ranger longer to extract Tempest from the goblin's split head than it had to kill all three.

Elbryan found his friends waiting for him back on the road a short while later, the two resting comfortably in the unseasonably warm sun, passing Bradwarden's heavy wineskin—which Elbryan knew to be filled with *Questel ni'touel*, the fine elvish wine more commonly known as boggle— back and forth.

"Am I to hunt alone then?" the ranger said with feigned anger. "Three escape us, with three of us to give chase, and yet I find myself out alone in the forest."

"And just how many did ye get, ranger?" the centaur asked.

"They were all together," Elbryan explained.

"Easy enough, then," reasoned Juraviel.

"And still ye're whinin'," Bradwarden remarked, taking another swig of the potent liquor, then lifting it toward the ranger.

Elbryan declined with a smile. "I do not drink much boggle," he said. "Every time I try to lift a flask of it to my lips, my arms ache with pain," he explained, an obvious reference to his early days of training with the Touel'alfar, when he had gone out to the bog every morning to collect the milk stones, then take them to the gathering trough where he had to squeeze the flavored juice out of them until his arms had ached.

It was said as a joke, of course, but Bradwarden was ever the master at turning a joke back on the speaker. "Whinin' again," he moaned. "Ye know, elf, yerself and yer kin'd be better takin' in me own folk for yer ranger trainin'."

"We have tried, good Bradwarden," said Juraviel, pulling back the wineskin. "And a fierce fighter indeed is an elven-trained centaur, though short on cunning, I fear."

Bradwarden gave a low growl. "Insultin' me even as he steals me boggle," he said to Elbryan as the ranger moved to slide his sword back into its sheath on Symphony's saddle. That done, Elbryan checked the horse carefully, noting one especially painful-looking scratch along the side of Symphony's strong neck. The wound had already been tended, he was glad to see, by gentle elven hands. "Is this how I am to spend the rest of my life?" he asked suddenly, his serious tone drawing the complete attention of both centaur and elf. "Traveling forest paths, hunting down rogue monsters?"

"At your present pace, you will clear all the region soon enough," Juraviel said with a smile, but those words brought a look of horror to the faces of the other two.

"I certainly hope not!" Elbryan replied with a laugh, walking over and pulling the wineskin from Juraviel's grasp.

The other two laughed as well, for when they thought about it, they understood the ranger's reasoning. The presence of goblins and giants and powries had certainly been a terrible thing for the folk of the region, a bitter war that had shattered homes and families, that had left many innocents dead. But there was something else that had come with the darkness and the tragedy, a sense of purpose and of comradery, a necessary joining of folk who might not even have been friends in peaceful circumstances. And also, undeniably, this phase of the war, the last hunting, the reclaiming of lands when all of the helpless, innocent folk were out of harm's way, proved truly exhilarating. Just as it had on that very morning, when riding point for Tomas Gingerwart's caravan, the three friends had spotted the encampment of a dozen or so goblins. They formed quick plans and the fight, and then the chase, was on.

Elbryan, by far the youngest of the three, felt the excitement most keenly. At those times when he could put his elven training to use and become this other persona, Nightbird, he was most alive.

"Gingerwart," Bradwarden remarked, seeing smoke rising down the road to the south. At last the fog was beginning to clear.

Elbryan regarded the distant sign of approach. The way was clear for another day's travel; they would be in Dundalis, or in what remained of the place, in a matter of two or three days.

❖ 10 ❖

The Humanist

"I will bring the city in line," the new bishop determinedly said—with his mouth and not through the telepathic communication of spirit! And Markwart heard him, and clearly, though the Father Abbot's corporeal form was resting a hundred miles away in his private quarters in St.-Mere-Abelle.

"I have already begun taking action in that very direction," De'Unnero went on, regaining the composure that had been shattered by the unexpected appearance of this so-solid apparition of the Father Abbot.

Markwart nodded—and how strange it seemed to him that even such nonverbal language was crystal clear through this spiritual communication. The last time he had come to De'Unnero by means of the soul stone, he had only been able to manage rudimentary communication, imparting to the abbot of St. Precious that he should go get his soul stone that they might meet more fully in the spiritual state. This time, though, that extra step had proven unnecessary, for Markwart had so fully transported his spirit to Chasewind Manor that he could speak directly to the physical De'Unnero, a level of communication far beyond what they had achieved before, even though De'Unnero now held no complementing soul stone. It almost felt to Markwart as if he could simply step his own physical form through the connection, could fully transport himself to this distant place!

And clearly De'Unnero, too, was impressed.

Markwart watched him closely, noting the hunger on his face. Always had Marcalo De'Unnero been an intense man, especially when some measure of power was at stake. Always, though, he had maintained self-control. Even when jumping into the middle of a group of goblins, he had always kept his head clear, had always let his mind guide his body.

"You must be careful not to overstep your bounds," Markwart explained. "The King will be watching closely, to see how well having a bishop replace one of his barons suits his needs."

"Then I am to pay special care to any emissaries from Ursal," De'Unnero replied. "And I assure you that the King's soldiers, led by Captain Kilronney, shall be excluded from many of the more distasteful duties I must carry out to meet my ends. The city guard will suffice.

"I intend to retrieve all the gemstones in the city," the Bishop explained, "and thus, if the friends of the heretic are about, I will have them."

"The merchants will complain to the King," Markwart warned. But the Father Abbot was thinking of something else—was concentrating on De'Unnero's last statement and the man's nonverbal cues as he had spoken. Markwart had gotten the impression that the Bishop was playing him for the fool now, for he perceived De'Unnero did not really believe that confiscating the gemstones in the city would lead to the capture of Avelyn's former companions. No, Markwart realized, De'Unnero had only said this to placate him. However, the deception pleased Markwart, for if De'Unnero knew better than his false claim, he likely had a good idea where the fugitives might be.

De'Unnero smiled widely, drawing the Father Abbot back into the present conversation. "The merchants will do as they are told," the Bishop explained. "They fear me too much already to plead to King Danube."

Markwart knew De'Unnero was playing a dangerous game. He could not keep track of all the merchants and the many guards and scouts they employed. News of the Bishop's actions against the merchant class would surely be open gossip in Ursal before much time had passed, if it wasn't already. But still, the Father Abbot hesitated in demanding that his pawn cease. The possibilities here intrigued him. Suppose the Church reclaimed all the sacred gemstones, claiming it to be the divine order of God himself? As long as the King didn't oppose the move, the merchants would be powerless to resist.

"And even if they do inform the King," De'Unnero went on, his smile wider than ever, "we have an excuse for the action. King Danube knows of the stolen stones—was it not his own troops who took the traitor Jojonah to the pyre? So if we present the missing gems as a threat to him and his kingdom . . ." The Bishop stopped and let the enticing thought hang in the air.

And, indeed, it was enticing to Father Abbot Markwart. Perhaps it was time for the Abellican Church to repossess the gemstones, *all* the gemstones. Those taken back from the merchants would more than make up for the ones lost to the thief Avelyn. Perhaps it was time for the Church to assert itself, to follow the wake of war by again becoming the dominant force in the life of every person in the civilized world.

What legacy would Dalebert Markwart then leave behind?

"The Behrenese enclave in Palmaris is considerable," Markwart said on sudden inspiration.

"Down by the river," De'Unnero confirmed.

"Make life particularly difficult for them," Markwart instructed. "Let us create as many common enemies between Church and state as possible."

De'Unnero's smile showed that the prospect did not displease him at all. "And what of the gemstones?" he asked. "May I continue?"

Now it was Markwart's turn to smile, for he understood that the upstart Bishop would continue with or without his permission. "Yes, do," Markwart said. "But do not overstep. We can keep King Danube on our side, I am confident, but only if we do not anger the entire merchant class."

Markwart let the connection lapse then, his spirit flying fast from Chasewind Manor back to his waiting body in St.-Mere-Abelle. In truth, he wasn't too worried about angering the merchants, or even the King. Markwart was beginning to gain a sense of his true power now. The war had changed the balance within the kingdom, he believed, in favor of the Church. This appointment of De'Unnero as bishop had opened so many intriguing corridors for the Father Abbot.

Possibilities . . . possibilities. How far might he reach?

Back in his private room at St.-Mere-Abelle, the Father Abbot looked down at the hematite resting in his hand. He thought again of how complete this last spiritual journey had been, of how he felt as if he could actually pull his corporeal form along with him instead of sending his spirit back to it. What power that might bring! To be in any place at any time, and without leaving any hint of a trail.

Possibilities . . . possibilities. Perhaps he could reach all the way to Ursal, all the way to King Danube's court, all the way to the King himself.

Brother Francis had found the Father Abbot in fine spirits that day, and it had given him hope that his news concerning Braumin and the others would be received with some measure of tranquillity. And after a brief moment when Markwart's face had gone bright red and he'd seemed on the verge of an explosion, the Father Abbot had calmed considerably, had even managed a crooked grin.

"And they, all five, have run off?" Markwart asked calmly.

Francis nodded.

"You are certain of this—Braumin Herde and the other conspirators have left St.-Mere-Abelle?"

"They are gone, Father Abbot," Francis dutifully answered, lowering his gaze.

"St.-Mere-Abelle is a large place," Markwart remarked. "There are many shadows."

"I believe that they are gone," Francis replied, "out of the abbey altogether, and I doubt they mean to return."

"And what did they take with them?" Markwart asked, his voice a growl of rising rage.

Francis shrugged, surprised by the question.

"The gemstones," Markwart clarified, barking out the words. "Did they take any of the sacred stones?"

"No, Father Abbot," Francis blurted. "No, I am certain they did not."

"The words of a fool," Markwart retorted sharply. "Have a dozen brothers inventory the sacred stones at once."

"Yes, Father Abbot," Francis replied, turning to go, and thinking himself foolish for not anticipating that Markwart would fear another theft. Certainly news of more heretics fleeing the abbey would cause the Father Abbot to wonder if the curse of Avelyn Desbris had visited him again.

"Where are you going?" Markwart yelled as Francis took a step away.

"You said to see to the inventory," the flustered brother protested.

"When we are done!"

Francis rushed back to the desk, standing straight as if waiting for a judgment to be passed upon him.

Markwart paused for a long while, rubbing his wrinkled old face many times. As the seconds passed, and as he considered all the ramifications, his face seemed to brighten.

"And, Father Abbot, I fear that the kitchen boy, Roger Billingsbury by name," Francis went on, "has also fled the abbey."

"And I should care about this because . . ." Markwart prompted.

Brother Francis stared long and hard at the surprising man. Was it not Markwart who had asked him to compile a list of workers at the abbey? And was it not Markwart who had told Francis that he believed there might be a spy working within the abbey? Suddenly Francis wondered if he had been wise to mention Roger. He had assumed that the Father Abbot had scrutinized his list, been led to the same conclusions that Francis had drawn; for, given the lack of other potential enemies, it had not been difficult for Francis to discern that Roger was the most likely prospect.

"The hired peasants often leave," Markwart reminded him, "by your own words. A complaint you had concerning compiling the list, if I recall."

Francis considered these words carefully, surprised that the Father Abbot was attempting to dispel the notion of a conspiracy between Braumin's group and the suspicious kitchen boy. Up to now, Markwart's suspicions had bordered on paranoia—or at least had seemed the result of a carefully constructed plan to divert all blame for everything that had happened at St.-Mere-Abelle over the last few years to Avelyn, Jojonah, and their followers.

"I do not understand, Father Abbot," Francis replied.

Markwart looked at him quizzically.

"Your present demeanor," Francis explained. "I had thought that you would be outraged by this desertion."

"Outraged?" Markwart echoed incredulously. "Outraged that our enemies would take an action so helpful to our cause? Do you not understand, young brother? Braumin Herde's desertion of the abbey spells the end of Jojonah's little conspiracy, as sure an admission of guilt as I have ever seen."

"Or an admission of fear, Father Abbot," Francis dared to say.

He backed off a step from Markwart's great desk as the Father Abbot stared at him. "They would have had nothing to fear if they had followed the rules of the Order," Markwart stated with a wry smile. "It brings me great pleasure to know that I inspire fear among heretics. Perhaps when they are caught—and they will be caught, do not doubt—we might study them closely, that we can measure and record their level of terror."

Francis shifted uncomfortably from foot to foot as he thought of the punishments Markwart might exact, as he considered the fate to which he might have inadvertently led Braumin and the others.

"You seem distressed, brother," Markwart remarked.

Francis felt as if he were withering under the old Father Abbot's scrutiny. "I only fear . . ." he started to say but then paused, seeking a different, and better, direction for his argument. "That Brother Braumin has strayed, I do not doubt," he said at length, "as well as the others."

"But . . ." Markwart prompted.

"But there was once a true calling in their hearts—in Brother Braumin's, at least," said Francis.

"And you believe that we might help them to find their way back to the proper road?"

Francis nodded. "Perhaps with leniency," he said, "perhaps with generosity. Would it not be better for the Church, and for your legacy, if you could take the protégés of Jojonah and bring them back into the flock? Would it not serve our God better if someone of Brother Braumin's talent was brought back to the proper road? And then, in all likelihood, he would become a credible and fanatic critic of Jojonah and Avelyn, a prime example of one who had sunk to the darkness, but was climbing again into the light." Francis was desperately improvising here, for he did not want to see any more executions of brothers of the Order. But while he liked the simple logic and the sound of his words, the monk understood that he was chasing a shooting star. Even if Markwart agreed, would Braumin Herde? Francis doubted it. More likely, the stubbornly principled fool would denounce Markwart all the way to the stake. Still, Francis, more desperate about this matter than he would have previously guessed, pressed on. "I only wonder if we might not turn this situation into an even greater gain."

"No, Brother Francis, that is not what you wonder," Father Abbot Markwart said solemnly, standing up and walking around the desk. "No, what I recognize here is not pragmatism but compassion."

"And compassion is a virtue," Francis said quietly.

"True," Markwart agreed, draping his arm about Francis' shoulders, an unusual gesture for the normally detached man and one that made Francis more than a little uncomfortable.

"But true only if the empathy is placed upon one deserving," Markwart went on. "Would you offer leniency to a goblin? To a powrie?"

"But they are not human," Francis started to argue, his voice rising at first, but falling off weakly as Markwart began to laugh at him.

"Nor are heretics human," Markwart retorted suddenly, angrily, but again he calmed quickly and continued in a cool, controlled manner. "Indeed, heretics are less than goblins and powries because they, formerly being human and thus possessed of a soul, have thrown aside the gift of God, have insulted the One who created them. Pity the powries before the heretics, I say, for powries are devoid of this gift, are wretched creatures indeed. Powries and goblins are evil, because evil is their nature; but the true heretic, the one who turns his back on God, is evil by choice. That, my brother, is the epitome of sin."

"But if one is lost, Father Abbot, can we not rescue that soul?" Francis reasoned.

This time, the Father Abbot didn't mock the notion with laughter but rather silenced Francis with a stern and uncompromising glare. "Take care, Brother Francis," he warned gravely. "You are bordering on the very tenets that brought about the downfall of Jojonah, and of Avelyn before him, the very idealistic and foolish notions that forced Braumin Herde and his fellow conspirators out of St.-Mere-Abelle."

"By the words of St. Gwendolyn, does not love beget love?" Francis replied, taking great care to control his tone so that he sounded as if he was merely asking for clarification and guidance, not disagreeing with the Father Abbot.

"St. Gwendolyn was a fool," Markwart said casually.

Francis fought hard to control his expression, but his eyes did widen and he had to bite his lower lip to keep from gasping. No words of insult were permitted against saints—that much Francis knew clearly from his years of study, a tenet that was spelled out again and again in Church canon.

"Do not seem so surprised," Markwart said. "You are soon to be a master . . . perhaps," he added slyly, casting a sidelong glance at him. "And as a master, you must understand and admit the truth. Gwendolyn was a fool; most of my colleagues know that beyond doubt."

"The process of her canonization was without protest," Francis argued.

"Again, out of pragmatism," Markwart explained. "Gwendolyn was the only potential candidate among the women of the Church, and if you carefully read the history of that troubled time, you will understand that it was necessary to placate the women. Thus, a saint was born. Do not misunderstand me, my young student, Gwendolyn was possessed of a generous heart and a warm nature. But she never—as Jojonah never—appreciated the larger truth of our purpose.

"Take care," Markwart said again. "Fear that you might become a humanist."

"I do not know the term," Francis admitted.

"Fear that you might place the rights of the individual above the greater good," Markwart explained. "I thought that I had dispelled this weakness in you during our dealings with the Chilichunks, but apparently it is rooted deep. And so I make it clear to you now, the last warning I shall ever offer you. There are those, Avelyn and Jojonah among them—and this was their biggest sin—who believe the Abellican Church should be the caretaker of the flock, the healer of all wounds, spiritual and physical. They would have us live as paupers, and walk among the peasants with the sacred stones, bettering the lives of all."

Francis cocked his head curiously, for that did not sound very much like sin.

"Fools!" Markwart snapped sharply. "It is not the place of the Church to cure the ills of the world; it is the responsibility of the Church to offer a greater hope of a world beyond this world. Would St.-Mere-Abelle inspire anyone if it became nothing more than a collection of hovels? Of course not! It is our splendor, our glory, our power that offers hope to the rabble. It is the simple fear of us, the emissaries of a vengeful God, that keeps them walking the true path of enlightenment. I cannot stress this truth to you enough, and I warn you never to let it out of your thoughts. Are we to open the doors of our abbey? Are we to hand out gemstones to peasants? Where, then, will be the mystery, young brother? And without the mystery, where, then, will be the hope?"

Francis was trying desperately to digest this surprising speech; and surely some of Markwart's argument resonated profoundly. But Francis could not help but see some inconsistencies. "But we *do* hand out gemstones, Father Abbot," he dared to remind him, "to merchants and nobles."

"It is a balance," Markwart admitted. "We do sell, and even give away, some of the stones, but only in exchange for greater wealth and power. Again, we have a standing to support that the peasants might look to us for hope. It is our solemn duty to maintain the Church above the common rabble, and sometimes, sadly, that forces us to work beside the secular powers of state and the merchant class." Markwart chuckled ironically then, but he sounded somewhat sinister to Brother Francis.

"But fear not, young brother," the Father Abbot finished, leading Francis to the door, "for now the Abellican Order is blessed with a leader who has both will and way to correct some of the more distasteful necessities of the past."

Overwhelmed, Brother Francis bowed to his superior and walked off in a stupor. He was honestly afraid for Brother Braumin and the others, but he was more afraid that he would have to witness their eventual punishment— was even more afraid that Braumin, or more likely one of his weaker cohorts, would be brought back to St.-Mere-Abelle and would break under the inevitable torture and name Francis as the one who had ushered them out of the abbey.

Would Father Abbot Markwart consider the loyalty Francis had always shown him and be lenient, or would the "greater good" dictate a very different course of action?

❖ 11 ❖

Friends in the Forest

The Masur Delaval was exceptionally bright this day under a gentle sun. Whenever a puffy cloud covered that sun, Roger and his five companions were reminded that winter had just begun. The air was not warm—and neither was the spray kicked up by the huge ferry, its square front slapping hard against the waves.

The group had taken a roundabout route to get to this point, fearing pursuit from St.-Mere-Abelle, and also wanting to change their appearances— grow some facial hair and acquire clothes other than their telltale brown robes. Now, finally, they had Palmaris in sight, and it was with more than a little trepidation that they approached the city of Marcalo De'Unnero. No doubt the abbot of St. Precious had been informed of their desertion by now, and despite their best efforts at disguise, Braumin and the others did not doubt that the dangerous man would recognize them if he saw them.

So, despite Roger's desire to look in on some of the companions he had known in the northland who were still, presumably, in Palmaris, the group came off the ferry on the Palmaris wharf intent on moving straight out to the north. They found little trouble navigating the quiet streets, having only occasionally to turn down an alleyway to avoid some marching soldiers.

After less than half an hour, in sight of one of the northern gates, they found another problem, though, for no one was getting in or out of the city without a complete inspection by the grim-faced city guard.

"Perhaps we should have taken a stone or two," Brother Castinagis offered, "amber, at least, that we might have walked across the river north of the city."

A couple of the others—most vigorously, Brother Viscenti—nodded their heads in agreement.

"Any theft of stones would have ensured that Markwart would have hunted us relentlessly," Brother Braumin reminded them. Viscenti's bobbing head immediately started shaking side to side.

"Then how are we to get out of here?" Castinagis asked.

Braumin had no answer, and so he looked at Roger.

Roger accepted the responsibility without complaint; in fact, he took it as a great compliment. Now that his reputation had been put on the line, the young man began to assess the problem. In the end, his plan was really very simple. Since the weather had held fairly mild, many wagons were rolling out of the gates. Farmers from south of the city were rushing through Palmaris northward, bearing hay and other supplies to farmers who had recently reclaimed their lands from the monsters.

Roger guided the five monks along to a street lined with taverns—and filled with the wagons of farmers who were inside, getting one last drink before heading north.

Into the hay they went, two men to a wagon. It was stuffy, damp, and uncomfortable; but soon enough the wagons were rolling along, and they were safe from any casual inspection. They heard the guards at the gate questioning the farmers, but they were interrogated perfunctorily.

The first wagon out on the road north of the city held Brothers Castinagis and Mullahy. They crawled from under the hay as the oblivious farmer drove along, and they dropped out of the wagon and trotted behind it for some distance, then moved to the side of the road and waited.

Several wagons rolled by, some going north, some back to the city. Then the pair spotted Brothers Dellman and Viscenti walking quickly down the road, and soon after, the four met with Roger and Braumin Herde.

"Once again you have proven your resourcefulness," Brother Dellman congratulated Roger.

"Not so much, really," Roger replied, though he was thrilled by the compliment. "The road should be easier the rest of the way. The first few miles will have the eyes of many farmers upon us, I am sure, but after that, the houses are sparse and widely spaced, and we should be able to get all the way to Caer Tinella without answering too many questions."

"And there we will find the friends of Avelyn?" Braumin asked.

It was a question Roger had heard a hundred times since their departure from St.-Mere-Abelle, and one that he had not been able to answer. He could guess that Pony and Elbryan had gone back to Caer Tinella, especially since they had Bradwarden in tow, but he couldn't be certain. He looked around at the five monks, every one of them hanging hopefully on his answer, as they always were when this question was posed. Their expressions reminded Roger of just how desperate these men had become. They were intelligent, and every one of them had lived for at least twenty years, Braumin Herde for more than thirty. Yet on this issue, they seemed almost like children, needing the guidance of a parent—in this case, Roger.

"We will find them, or we will find the way to them," Roger offered. The monks' smiles widened. Brother Viscenti immediately began spouting hopeful possibilities, surmising how the friends of Avelyn might help put the world in order.

Roger allowed him his ridiculous fantasies without question. He pitied this man, and all of them, or at least sympathized with them. They had thrown away everything, had branded themselves heretics—and they all knew the punishment for that! All they had now were their principles. No small thing, Roger knew.

But you couldn't eat principles.

And principles wouldn't stop the thrust of a sword. Or cool the heat of a burning pyre.

They walked until late that night, putting as much ground between them and Palmaris as possible. Still, when they set their camp on a quiet and lonely hillock, the lights of Palmaris remained in sight, across the miles.

Roger stood looking southward at the last few of those lights, late in the night, when Braumin Herde joined him. The two stood silently for some time, two lonely figures in a world gone crazy.

"Perhaps we should have chanced a stay in Palmaris," Braumin offered. "You might have found some of your friends."

Roger was shaking his head before the man even finished. "It would have been a pleasure to see some of them again," he said, "but I approve of the decision to strike out of the city immediately. I do not trust that place."

"You mean that you do not trust those who rule that place," Braumin said with a chuckle. "Yet they are the same as those who rule St.-Mere-Abelle."

"I was with Baron Bildeborough when he was murdered," Roger admitted, staring at the distant lights, not even turning to face Braumin when he heard the monk gasp.

"We were going south to Ursal to speak with King Danube about the murder of Abbot Dobrinion," Roger explained.

"Murdered by a powrie," Braumin said, repeating the commonly accepted story.

"Murdered by a monk," Roger retorted gravely. Now he did turn to face Braumin. "It was no powrie, but a monk—a pair of monks, actually, men your Church name brothers justice—who murdered Dobrinion." Roger watched Braumin's expression shift from bewilderment to denial to something bordering on anger.

"You cannot be certain of this," Braumin said, obviously fighting hard to sound as if he was speaking with conviction.

"Connor Bildeborough, nephew of the Baron, discovered the truth," Roger replied, turning back to the distant lights.

"But young Bildeborough was taken and questioned by Father Abbot Markwart," Braumin reasoned. "He had reason to hate the Church."

"His evidence was firm," Roger answered calmly. "And to lend it credence, those same two brothers justice chased him out of Palmaris, intent on murdering him. That was where they met me and Nightbird and Pony, and that was where they both met their end, though not before one managed to murder Connor."

"Describe them," Braumin Herde bade him, a distinct tremor in his voice.

"One was a huge and strong man," Roger replied, "and the other, by far the more dangerous, by my estimation, was small of frame but quick and deadly."

Braumin Herde rocked back on his heels at this confirmation, for he had been with the caravan when it had met Markwart in Palmaris, when Connor had been taken prisoner, and then subsequently released. Along with Markwart were two very dangerous men, Brothers Youseff and Dandelion, and those two had left the caravan on the road east of Palmaris and had not been seen since.

"Connor's evidence was enough to convince the Baron," Roger went on, "and when Rochefort Bildeborough could not gain any satisfaction from the new leader of St. Precious, he decided to take his case, with me as his witness, to the court of King Danube Brock Ursal. On our first night out, the carriage was attacked, and all were killed except for me."

"And how were you so fortunate?"

"I was out in the woods at the time the great cat attacked," Roger explained. "I saw only the end of the fight—more a slaughter than a fight, actually."

"Describe the cat," Braumin prompted, a sinking feeling washing over him.

"Not so large," Roger replied, "but fast and vicious. And moving with a purpose—of that I am sure."

"You do not believe it to be the random attack of a wild animal?"

Roger shrugged, having no practical response. "It seemed more than that," he tried to explain, "and I am familiar with the great cats of this region—tawny panthers mostly. But this cat was orange with black stripes. A tiger, I believe, though I have never seen such a cat, and have only heard of it from travelers who dared the western Wilderlands." Roger stopped abruptly as he looked over at Braumin, for the man stood with eyes closed and fists balled by his side, trembling.

For it all made sense to Braumin Herde now: terrible, brutal sense. He knew well the new abbot of St. Precious, the new bishop of Palmaris, and knew the man's favored stone, the tiger's paw, with which he could transform parts of his body into those of the great cat.

"There is a great darkness settling on the world," Braumin remarked finally.

"I had thought one just lifted," Roger replied.

"This one may be darker yet."

Roger, who had witnessed the murders of Connor Bildeborough, Baron Bildeborough, and Jojonah, could not find any logical argument against the reasoning.

The fire had burned to embers. The wind blew cold, and the four sleeping monks were huddled close to the fire, wrapped tightly in blankets. Brother Dellman sat a short distance away, quiet and calm, with Roger, for it was their turn on watch.

Several times, Roger tried to strike up a conversation with the earnest, sensible young monk, but it was obvious that Dellman wasn't in the mood for talking. Roger understood the man's turbulent feelings, and so did not press him. But sitting there quietly as the minutes turned into an hour, and that to two, had Roger fighting to keep his eyes open.

"I'll not last the watch," he announced, pulling himself to his feet and briskly rubbing his arms and legs. "The fire invites me to sleep. A walk will help."

"In the forest?" Dellman asked skeptically.

Roger waved the monk's concern away. "I spent months in these forests," he boasted. "And at that time they were thick with powries and goblins, and huge giants." He was hoping to see some hint that his words had impressed the young monk, but Dellman only nodded.

"Do not go too far," he bade Roger. "We share the watch, and thus, share responsibility."

"I will find no trouble in the open forest," Roger replied.

"I do not doubt your abilities, Master Billingsbury," Dellman answered. "I only fear that I might fall asleep, and that Brother Braumin will waken and find me such." He ended with a smile, and Roger returned it.

"Not far," Roger promised as he moved down the side of the hill, pausing as soon as he was out of the direct light of the low fire to let his eyes adjust to the darkness. Then he pressed down into the shadows, for Roger did indeed feel safe out here. He trusted his senses, and he was confident that he could blend into the shadows and avoid any enemies.

Except Craggoth hounds, he quietly reminded himself, remembering the huge, terrible dogs the powries sometimes kept, the wicked creatures that had tracked him on one excursion through powrie-occupied Caer Tinella. Roger still carried many scars from that capture and imprisonment, mostly from the bites of the savage hounds.

Still, he felt safe as he made his way from the hillock into the forest. He was in his element out here, a part of the landscape. Within a matter of a few minutes, the distant campfire seemed but a spot of light. Roger finally settled on a large boulder, staring up at the stars. He wondered about Elbryan and Juraviel, and mostly about Pony. How he missed those special friends, the first real friends he had ever known. Not only did they support him when he needed them but also they were not afraid to point out his faults and to help him learn to overcome them. Because of those three, Roger had learned to truly survive, had learned to temper his anger and his pride, to keep a clear head no matter how desperate the situation seemed.

A shudder coursed through him as he considered how he might have acted when Bildeborough was being murdered if he had not learned so much from Nightbird and his friends. His pride might have drawn him in, and then the cat would surely have killed him. Or, if he had run away, he would have likely gone to Palmaris, screaming his wild tale, making enemies far too powerful for him to defeat. Yes, because of the work of his dear friends, Roger had learned to consider the greater good before acting.

And now he wanted to see those friends again, wanted to tell the ranger all that he knew and show Nightbird the man he had become. He wanted to see Juraviel again, for he knew that the elf, too, would approve of him, and Roger desperately wanted that approval.

But most of all, Roger wanted to see Pony again, the flash of her blue eyes, the flash of her beautiful smile. He wanted to watch the hair bounce about her shoulders and to bask in the flowery smell of that lustrous mane. Roger knew that he could not have her as his own. Her love was for Elbryan, and for Roger she held only true friendship. But that didn't matter to Roger somehow. He wasn't jealous—not anymore—of Elbryan, and took deep pleasure merely in being around Pony, in speaking to her or watching her graceful movements.

He lay on that boulder for a long time, staring absently up at the stars, but seeing only beautiful Pony. Yes, Pony and the others would help Roger put the world, or at least their little corner of it, aright.

He took comfort in that notion, in the belief that he would be among powerful friends soon enough, but then he remembered his present responsibilities. He sat up on the boulder and looked back to the distant hillock. All seemed quiet and calm, so Roger started off at a casual pace.

Just a few steps along the path back, though, Roger stopped and glanced all around, an uneasy feeling creeping over him. Perfectly still, perfectly quiet, the alert man shifted his eyes slowly, moving from shadow to shadow, trying to pick up some sign of movement.

Somehow he knew that something was out there, watching him.

Roger could feel his muscles tightening, could feel his heart beating faster suddenly. He couldn't shake the image of Baron Bildeborough's slaughter, and feared that the same great tiger was watching him now, poised behind a bush or up in a tree.

It took Roger a long time to take another step. He eased his toe down and gently shifted his weight, trying to make not a whisper of noise. Satisfied, he took another step.

A movement at the side caught his attention, some creature swift and stealthy.

Despite his intentions, Roger let out a cry and sprinted away.

Something shot past him, startling him, making him stumble. He didn't fall, though, for a slender but strong, sticky line held taut before him, supporting him. Another dart shot past, then one across his back. Roger was spun around frantically, trying to make some sense of it as more and more filaments crossed him from every conceivable angle. His movements only tangled him all the more, and soon he was hopelessly stuck.

Now Roger's training came into play, that cool and clear thinking in an apparently desperate situation. He righted himself and set his feet firmly, then sorted out one filament and started to tug.

Even as he began, there came a movement from the side and above. Roger froze, expecting an enemy to jump down. After a few seconds passed, the young man dared to look back over his shoulder, and he nearly slumped with relief to see—not a tiger or some giant spider—but a familiar form, sitting on a branch, looking down at him.

"Juraviel," he breathed.

"Where is he?" asked the elf. From the voice—a female voice—Roger realized that this was not his elven friend but another of the Touel'alfar.

"W-where is who?" he stammered. Then he turned and stumbled as more elves appeared all around him, some on the ground, some on branches.

"You just named him," the elf said impatiently. "Belli'mar Juraviel."

"I—I do not know," Roger stammered, overwhelmed and more than a bit fearful, for these elves did not seem friendly, and every one of them held a small bow. Roger knew better than to take any comfort in the size of those bows, for he had many times seen Juraviel put one to deadly use.

"You are Roger Billingsbury," another elf stated. "Roger Lockless."

The young man started to respond, but was cut short by another elf. "And you search for your friends, our brethren Juraviel and Nightbird the ranger."

Again Roger started to reply, but another of the elves interrupted. "And the woman Jilseponie Ault."

"Yes, yes, and yes!" Roger cried. "Why do you ask if you do not want—"

"We do not ask," the first elf remarked. "We state what we know."

Roger didn't try to respond, expecting that the elf, or another, would interrupt him.

"We suspect that Belli'mar Juraviel went to the east," the elf on the branch added, her voice the most melodic of all, "to the great monastery."

"To St.-Mere-Abelle," Roger agreed. "I mean, I do not know if Juraviel was there, but Nightbird and Pony—"

"Tell us all of it," another elf said curtly.

"Everything you know," another chirped in.

"I am trying to do just that!" Roger cried in exasperation.

The elf on the branch called for quiet, from him and from all the other elves. "Pray tell us the complete tale, Roger Lockless," she bade calmly. "It is very important."

Roger looked down skeptically at the practically invisible strands, then held up his hands helplessly.

On a nod from the elf on the branch, apparently the leader, several others scrambled to Roger's side and helped free him.

Then Roger was more than happy to comply with the request for the story. He knew from his dealings with Juraviel that the Touel'alfar were not his enemies, and could certainly be powerful allies. He relayed everything he had learned during his time in the abbey: how Bradwarden the centaur had apparently been rescued in the bowels of the blasted mountain home of the dactyl demon and then taken prisoner; how the ranger and Pony, and possibly Juraviel, had later slipped into the great abbey and rescued the centaur. Then he told of Jojonah, a monk who had helped the rescuers, and the grim fate his actions had brought upon him.

"Who are your companions?" the elf asked him. "They are also of St.-Mere-Abelle, are they not?"

"Disciples of Jojonah," Roger explained, "and of another monk, a Brother Avelyn, before him. Avelyn was a great hero, a friend of Nightbird and Jura—"

"We know of Brother Avelyn Desbris," the elf assured him. "Another of our brethren journeyed with him to Aida and willingly sacrificed her life that Nightbird and Avelyn and the others might destroy the demon dactyl."

"Tuntun," Roger exclaimed, for Pony had told him the entire tale. His smile went away at once, though, seeing the grim expressions of the elves.

"Your friend's assessment may prove painfully accurate," the elf went on gravely.

Roger looked at him curiously.

"The monk," the elf explained, "Brother Dellman—his assessment of the dark road may prove prophetic, for the events in Palmaris are unsettling."

"How do you know about Dellman?" Roger asked, but when he thought about it, when he considered the scouting prowess of the Touel'alfar, as exemplified by Belli'mar Juraviel, he realized that he should not have been surprised to learn that the elves had been watching him. "You know of the changes in Palmaris?" Roger asked.

"We know much, Roger Lockless," the elf explained. "We know of your fateful ride south with Baron Bildeborough, and we know of De'Unnero, who is now bishop of Palmaris. The Touel'alfar do not often concern themselves with the affairs of humans; but when we do, I assure you, we have the means to learn what we desire."

Roger didn't doubt that for a minute.

"Go back to your friends," the elf instructed. "You are heading north to find Nightbird?"

"I believe that he will be somewhere around Caer Tinella," Roger replied.

"And what of our brethren Juraviel?"

"As far as I know, he is with Nightbird," Roger answered.

The elf looked around at his companions, all of them responding with an assenting nod.

"Travel with the knowledge that the Touel'alfar are not far away, Roger Lockless," the female elf on the branch finished.

Roger watched as several of the elves silently faded into the shadows. One by one, they simply disappeared, and then Roger was alone. He went back to the encampment, to find Brother Dellman sitting in the same position as when Roger had left, except that his eyes were closed.

Roger moved to wake him, but then changed his mind. He had felt secure before, enough so to wander out into the forest. Now, knowing that the Touel'alfar were near, Roger understood that there was no need for any watch. He moved to an empty spot near to the fire, lay down with his hands behind his head, stared up at the stars, and did not try to resist when sleep beckoned.

❖ 12 ❖

In Motion

"'ll not tolerate your lies," the spirit of Markwart stated bluntly, his expression menacing. Both Markwart and De'Unnero were amazed by the completeness of the communication. No telepathic messages this time, not even in the initial greeting. Markwart's spirit, seeming tangible, almost physical, had merely walked into De'Unnero's private room and struck up a conversation with the Bishop!

Despite the imposing presence, the confident Marcalo De'Unnero only smiled and rested back calmly in his comfortable chair.

"Do not doubt that I can reach you," Markwart warned.

"Oh, but I do not, Father Abbot," the Bishop replied. "I only doubt that you would desire to strike out against me, since our goals are the same and I am no threat to you. Perhaps it is merely my methods that anger you."

"It is your lies," Markwart growled.

De'Unnero held up his hands innocently, as if he didn't understand what Markwart was talking about.

"The gemstone confiscation," Markwart clarified, "the pretense of it. I do not disapprove of your handling of the merchants—they are not men of the Church and thus should not be in possession of the sacred stones. We agree on this point."

De'Unnero studied the man closely. He knew they were both pleased by the prospect of strengthening the Church's hold and power over the kingdom, but he thought and was keen enough to understand that the Father Abbot shared this view—that his and Markwart's motives might not be similar.

"Do not pretend that your work in Palmaris is directly related to the friends of Avelyn Debris," Markwart went on. "You are well aware that they are not in your city."

De'Unnero conceded the point with a nod. "My focus will change as I learn more about their whereabouts," he promised.

"Your focus will remain on Palmaris," Markwart instructed. "Your work here is even more important than capture of the fugitives."

De'Unnero's expression went suddenly grim; Markwart's last edict had obviously caught him off guard. "Father Abbot," he said deliberately, "even while I strengthen my—our—hold over Palmaris, I have been collecting information concerning the fugitives. They are north of the city but not beyond my reach."

"*Your* reach?" Markwart echoed. "Are we back to that, Master De'Unnero?"

De'Unnero lowered his eyes, not wanting the man to see the boiling rage reflected there. *Master* De'Unnero? The word simmered in the bile at the back of his throat. How crude a reminder of who was the leader here and who the servant. In the Abellican Order, referring to a man by his previous title was considered among the most pointed of insults.

"How many times must we wage this battle?" Markwart asked. "How many times must I tell you that others will manage the business of the legacy of Avelyn Desbris and that the business of Marcalo De'Unnero is of a higher matter?"

"And how many others must fail before you allow me to finish this business of Avelyn's legacy?" De'Unnero dared to reply. "First Quintal, then the fools Youseff and Dandelion."

"Fools trained by De'Unnero," Markwart reminded.

"And De'Unnero told you that they would fail," the Bishop retorted. "These friends of Avelyn have proven themselves resourceful and dangerous foes. They have survived, not merely by running and hiding, but by confronting and defeating everything we have sent their way. And let us not forget our strong belief that these fugitives journeyed to Mount Aida, confronted Bestesbulzibar, and won!"

Markwart emitted a low, feral growl.

"We cannot underestimate them," De'Unnero countered. "By all accounts, the woman is proficient with the gemstones, hugely powerful, and the man—"

Markwart's sudden laugh stopped the Bishop short, and De'Unnero realized he was being mocked.

"I do so enjoy the hunger in your eyes as you speak of worthy opponents," Markwart explained, finally catching on to the Bishop's real meaning.

"They command our respect," De'Unnero insisted.

"They intrigue you," Markwart corrected. "You have come to view this man Nightbird as a personal challenge. Is it possible that Marcalo De'Unnero is not the greatest warrior in the world?"

"Are we not to retrieve the stolen gemstones?" De'Unnero said dryly, trying to change the focus, which of course only confirmed Markwart's suspicions.

"Of course, Bishop," the Father Abbot purred. "Yet it seems to me as if the stolen gemstones are not your primary motivation where the one called Nightbird is concerned.

"Be assured that I am not chastising you," Markwart added as De'Unnero leaned forward to protest. "Indeed, I admire your aspiration. Ever since you first came to St.-Mere-Abelle, you have been determined to prove your supremacy in the fighting skills. You heard the whispers that you are the finest warrior ever to come forth from the Abellican Order, and those whispers bother you profoundly."

"How so?" De'Unnero asked. "If I am as full of vanity as you seem to believe, then should not those whispers thrill me?"

"No," Markwart answered bluntly, "because they are just whispers, and because not everyone agrees. And because, most of all, they speak of you as the greatest of the *Abellican* warriors. You would not limit your reputation so."

"Pride," De'Unnero replied. "The deadliest sin of all."

Again Markwart laughed. "The man who is without pride is without ambition, and the man who is without ambition is no better than a beast of burden. No, Marcalo De'Unnero, bishop of Palmaris, the world holds greater conquests for you. Perhaps Nightbird is among those challenges. But only—" the Father Abbot paused, holding a skinny finger out threateningly "—only if your contest is waged in the natural course of other, more important events. The world is changing, and we are the harbingers of that change. I'll not risk my legacy and the potential dominance of the Abellican Church for the sake of my underling's pride."

"But how much stronger will we be when Nightbird is no more?" De'Unnero protested loudly. "I know where to find the thieves; destroying them and retrieving that which was stolen will prove but a minor task."

"No!" Markwart retorted sharply, and there was power in his voice that put De'Unnero back in his seat, silent, staring at the specter.

"No," Markwart said again. "There is no need to take such a chance now. Your focus must remain the vital work in Palmaris."

"But—"

"Plot carefully, my friend," Markwart continued. "There are better ways to proceed. Gain the trust of Nightbird and the woman that we might catch them off their guard."

"I doubt the disciples of Avelyn Desbris would ever trust the Abellican Church of Dalebert Markwart," De'Unnero replied bluntly.

"You are fortunate, my servant," Markwart answered, "for I know that you are wiser than your words would indicate. There are better ways for you to encompass the demise of Avelyn's followers. You will discover them, if only you care to look." With those teasing words echoing in the darkened room, the spirit of Markwart faded.

De'Unnero sat in his chair, his hands up before him, fingers tapping

together as he considered his options. The meeting hadn't gone as he had
hoped, for Markwart was proving himself far more astute than the Bishop
would ever have believed. De'Unnero had thought that his assignment to
Palmaris, and particularly his elevation to bishop, would bring him some
autonomy, but Markwart's newfound tricks with the soul stone had put
him more under the thumb of the Father Abbot than he had been at St.-
Mere-Abelle.

That truth only made him angrier, and he leaped up from his chair and
stormed about the room. He almost took up his tiger's paw and fell into its
magic, fantasizing about running hard to the north as a great cat. If he
killed the two prime enemies of the Church, could Markwart remain angry
with him?

But if he failed, if his attempt only warned Nightbird that the Church
was still watching—only forced him into deeper hiding—then, De'Unnero
realized, he would be better off if the dangerous warrior slew him in the
forest.

Better that than face the wrath of Markwart.

And who was this man? the Bishop wondered, and he wasn't thinking
about Nightbird. De'Unnero had known Dalebert Markwart for more than
a decade and had been one of his advisers for several years, ever since he
had trained the first brother justice, Quintal, to go after Avelyn Desbris.
Yet now, speaking with this spirit, feeling the deeper power within the will
of the Father Abbot, De'Unnero felt as if he didn't know the man at all . . .
or at least, as if he had underestimated him all these years.

That alone made him consider carefully the advice Markwart had given
to him, and led him, after a sleepless night of pacing his room, to an alternative plan.

Markwart soared back to his waiting corporeal form, lying on his bed in
St.-Mere-Abelle. He was pleased as he crossed through his outer room,
noting that no one had disturbed the place.

His body shuddered as his spirit entered, and then the Father Abbot,
though it was very late, climbed out of bed. Yes, it was good that St.-Mere-
Abelle was now free of Brother Braumin and his followers, he mused, for so
many pressing issues beckoned, from both Ursal and Palmaris.

Without even noticing, the Father Abbot went to his desk and took out a
small ruby and hematite, then wandered into the summoning chamber with
its pentagram. He walked around the pentagram, bending at each point
and, with a thought sent into the ruby, produced a small flame to light each
candle. Then he moved to the very middle of the pentagram and sat on the
floor cross-legged, his usual place and position for deep meditation.

The voice in his head had taught him this. At first Markwart had resisted.
Nothing he had ever read, even in *The Incantations Sorcerous*, had men-

tioned sitting *within* the pentagram. Such a design was normally scribed for the purpose of summoning and confining extraplanar creatures—indeed, Markwart had used it for just that purpose, bringing up a pair of minor demons to inhabit the corpses of the Chilichunks.

But now, with his new insight, Markwart had found a second, and perhaps even more important use for the pentagram. He used the soul stone to fall within himself, into the deepest recesses of his own mind, the highest level of contemplation.

For with this combination of stones and position Father Abbot Markwart could find answers to the greatest mysteries of the universe, to personal dilemmas and grand events that would shake the foundation of both Church and kingdom. Deep within the gemstones, he found such a level of solitude that all the distractions of the material world were left far behind, and within that solitude Markwart found God.

The voice tonight was stronger than before, even as his connection to De'Unnero had tonight achieved a new level of completeness. Markwart pondered the questions that disturbed him, and the voice, as always, gave him the answers. He must get Brother Francis to work even harder now. He must solidify his base of power at St.-Mere-Abelle, bring all the monks into a tight line behind him, so that when he stretched out his arms to engulf the rest of the kingdom, he need not worry about treachery from within. The other abbeys, though they might question or even verbally oppose his policies, would not openly go against him without some hint that there might be allies within St.-Mere-Abelle—greatest of all the abbeys, greater than all the other abbeys combined—to lend them support.

And his principal opponent would no doubt be St. Honce, the abbey most tied to the secular powers of the kingdom.

Yes, now that he and De'Unnero had come to a proper understanding, now that Palmaris was coming under Church control, Markwart would have to be ready to meet the predictable outrage from Ursal—if not from the King, then surely from Danube's advisers.

One step at a time, he reminded himself. Trust De'Unnero, for the man spoke truthfully when he had declared that his goals and Markwart's were one and the same. And get Brother Francis working hard to uncover any dissent, any complaining at all, from those here.

Markwart's eyes closed and he swayed softly, deep in meditation. His thoughts kept drifting back to De'Unnero, the eager warrior. He began to understand then that perhaps the man was in the wrong position. A bishop had to be a subtle, cunning politician, not a straightforward warrior. But Markwart was far from discouraged by this realization, and he began to shape a new role for his appointed bishop.

Does not the sun shine brighter after the darkest night? came the voice from within his head.

Might De'Unnero, so imposing, so brutal, prove to be that night?

And does not the warrior hunger for battle all the more when his enemies stand facing him, yet out of reach? the voice asked.

He could hold De'Unnero back, like drawing back on a Y-bow, the deadly weapon employed by the To-gai nomads of western Behren. Dangling Nightbird before him would draw those bands all the farther, Markwart knew, and when at last he released the Bishop, the man would shoot out swift as an arrow.

And the Bishop's absence would allow Markwart to shine as the morning sun.

All the answers seemed before him, and the now-contented Father Abbot opened his eyes and stretched. He was pleased, and so was the voice within his head, the voice he thought to be the insights of God.

After Avelyn had loosed the godly magic of the amethyst and destroyed Mount Aida, the demon dactyl Bestesbulzibar had lost its foothold on Corona, had lost its physical form. Only the desperation of the terrified Father Abbot Dalebert Markwart, inadvertently reaching out through a chance usage of *The Incantations Sorcerous*, had allowed the demon spirit to retain any hope that its latest opportunity to shape the world had not been completely lost.

Markwart was the Father Abbot of the Abellican Church; he should have been the demon dactyl's most hated foe.

That made these advisory sessions all the more enjoyable.

Captain Shamus Kilronney was summoned to Chasewind Manor early the next morning. He found Bishop De'Unnero in an excited, almost frantic state, despite his admission that he had not slept at all the previous night.

"This is too important a time for such trivial matters as sleep," the Bishop explained, motioning to a chair opposite him at his delicate garden table, where two morning meals had been set.

Shamus bowed and took his seat.

"You have concluded, no doubt, that our discussion about your friends in the North was of great importance to me," De'Unnero began before Shamus even got his fork into the thick omelette.

"It is not my place to make conclusions concerning the affairs of my superiors," the captain replied.

De'Unnero smiled; he liked such blind obedience. "These two, Nightbird and Pony, they were your friends?"

"Allies," Shamus corrected. "I fought beside them, and, as we indicated to you, we were glad for their help."

"And you never saw the centaur?"

Shamus shook his head and held up his hands.

"Indeed, your cousin remembered correctly," De'Unnero explained.

"There was a centaur with the caravan that came through Palmaris—Bradwarden, by name. He is considered among the most dangerous fugitives in the world, a conspirator in a plan to steal the sacred gemstones from St.-Mere-Abelle. We had him, and were preparing to crush the conspiracy, when your friends—your *friends*, Captain Kilronney—stole him from the jail of St.-Mere-Abelle."

Shamus sighed. So it was true: as Colleen had surmised, Nightbird and Pony were outlaws of the Church. "I did not name them friends," he explained to the Bishop. "I did not know them well enough to bestow such a title upon them."

"Apparently, you did not know them at all," De'Unnero said sarcastically. "But you did name them allies, and that will not mark your record well. The Father Abbot, should he learn of your complicity, will most certainly speak with the King about your commission and continuing career."

Shamus had no answer. He got the distinct feeling that De'Unnero wanted him to deny all association with the outlaws, but his honor would not allow such a lie. No, he had fought beside these two, and would suffer whatever consequences awaited him.

"You should consider yourself quite fortunate," the Bishop went on, "for you are an officer of the King's court, a representative of the law in Honce-the-Bear."

Shamus looked at him curiously, not understanding.

"The centaur is dangerous, no doubt," said De'Unnero, "but the other two, Nightbird and Pony, are perhaps the most dangerous criminals in the world. So, yes, you are fortunate, Captain Kilronney, for you have met them and lived. Either of them could have killed you, caught off your guard as you were."

"Why would they?" Shamus dared to ask. He had no useful response to De'Unnero's claims, for he had no knowledge of this supposed conspiracy or of Pony and Nightbird's breaking into St.-Mere-Abelle. Shamus did have more than a little trouble reconciling De'Unnero's claims with the two companions he had known in the northland.

De'Unnero only laughed at the question. "When we find more time," he said, "you and I will speak of the nature of evil."

"I am a soldier in the King's army, and have seen battle for many months," Shamus replied.

De'Unnero snorted derisively. "You fought powries and goblins, perhaps a giant or two," he said, "but what are they when measured against the true evil of Nightbird and Pony? No, my friend, you cannot begin to imagine the good fortune that allows you now to draw breath. But no matter. Now you are forewarned, and so when you return to the North, this very day, you and your men will take all proper precautions."

"Return to the North?" the captain echoed skeptically.

"Take a dozen—no, a score, even two score—of your finest soldiers," the Bishop instructed. "Ride hard back to Caer Tinella—or beyond, if, as we fear, Nightbird and the woman have already departed for the Timberlands."

"And am I to take them prisoner?" Shamus asked, forcing the words from his mouth.

"On no account!" De'Unnero roared, horrified at the thought of yet another attempt at the ranger bungled by inferiors. "No! You are to aid them in the reclamation of the Timberlands. I want you standing by Nightbird's side when I arrive. *Then* justice will be done."

A very shaken Shamus Kilronney left Chasewind Manor soon after. He thought to go to Colleen, but realized before he had taken his first step toward her barracks that he would find nothing there but grief. And trouble, for Colleen would only laugh and might speak out publicly against De'Unnero. Shamus was having a difficult time believing that Nightbird and Pony were as evil as the Bishop had claimed, but he must look past his personal feelings, he determinedly reminded himself, and serve his King.

He was not looking forward to the meeting when Bishop De'Unnero joined him in the North.

Partings and Greetings

Elbryan breathed a deep sigh, not pleased at all by what he was hearing yet unable to dispute the elf's reasoning. He had suspected that Juraviel meant to depart soon after Dundalis was reclaimed, but for the elf to leave now, when they were but halfway from Caer Tinella to the Timberlands, was a surprise.

"I long for my home," Juraviel explained. "This is the longest time I have been away from Andur'Blough Inninness in all the centuries of my life."

"You were back there not so long ago," Elbryan reminded him, "when you escorted the folk we found in the Wilderlands. It was at the doorstep of Andur'Blough Inninness that Pony and I found you."

"A short stay," replied Juraviel, "and a short reprieve from the longing in my heart. It is the way of my people, Nightbird. You above all other humans should understand this. We live for the valley, for the nights of dancing under the clearest of skies and for the company of one another."

"I do understand," the ranger admitted, "and I do not disagree with you. Tomas brought able-bodied warriors, one and all, and as Bradwarden is soon to be scouting his familiar haunts in the forest around the three Timberlands towns, we'll not be taken by surprise. Allow me my selfishness, my friend, for I will miss you terribly. As I miss Pony."

"We hardly share the same place in your heart," Juraviel said dryly.

"A different place," Elbryan agreed, "but no less of one. You are as a brother to me, Belli'mar Juraviel. You know that. And when Tuntun went into the molten stone, I lost a sister."

"As did I."

"And surely my world will not be as bright without Belli'mar Juraviel beside me."

"I'll not be gone forever—not even forever in the accounting of a human," Juraviel promised. "Allow me my time with my kin, and then I will return to the Timberlands for a visit to my adopted brother."

"I will hold you to that promise," Elbryan said. "And if I do not see you before the next spring is in full bloom, then expect that I will be on my way to Andur'Blough Inninness! And with Pony beside me—and do not doubt that she will be even less forgiving than I toward the elf who forgot us!"

It was said in jest, of course, and Juraviel smiled back at Elbryan. He knew better, though. Elbryan, and especially Pony, would not be making the difficult and dangerous journey to the elven homeland the following spring, not with a baby to look after. Juraviel almost told the ranger then, but he fought the impulse.

"When are you leaving?" Elbryan asked.

"Tomas plans to break camp at dawn," Juraviel replied. "I will be gone before that."

"Have you told Bradwarden?"

The elf nodded. "Not so difficult a task," he explained. "The centaur has lived for a long time, my friend, and will outlive you and your children's children unless an enemy's weapon cuts him low. He has long dealt with the Touel'alfar and knows our ways. He admitted that he was surprised that I stayed with you this long—and was even more surprised that I went with you to the great abbey."

"Bradwarden would not expect his friend to come rescue him?"

"Bradwarden learned long ago not to expect too much from the Touel'alfar," Juraviel said seriously. "We have our own ways and our own reasons. You should take a lesson from him."

"I expect nothing from the elves," Elbryan replied, "except for Belli'mar Juraviel, my friend, my brother."

Again Juraviel, though not entirely agreeing, smiled back at the ranger.

"Farewell," the elf said. "Remember all we have taught you, and understand the responsibility of your position. You carry Tempest, forged by the elves, and Hawkwing, a gift from my own father. Your actions, good or ill, reflect upon us, Nightbird; you will be held accountable for those actions by Lady Dasslerond and all the elves and, most of all, by me."

The ranger, understanding that Juraviel was not speaking in jest, squared his shoulders and set his face determinedly, more than willing to accept the burden. Elbryan knew what it meant to be a ranger, had learned those lessons all too clearly over the last year, and was confident that he would not disappoint those who trained him, those who had given him these wonderful gifts, the name of Nightbird most special of all.

"Farewell," Juraviel said again. He moved away, blending into the deepening shadows of dusk.

"There," Elbryan said, pointing down the slope and through the brush.

Tomas Gingerwart stooped low and peered intently. He could hear fighting down below, and the thick brogue of a hearty warrior obviously enjoying the battle, but he couldn't make out anything distinctly. Something flashed across his limited field of vision; it might have been a rider.

"Come along," the ranger instructed, taking Tomas by the arm and leading him quickly along the ridgeline, to a more open area. He didn't want to miss the spectacle of the fight, and thought it would be better if Tomas didn't miss it either. A few steps brought them the scene: Bradwarden running circles around a battered and obviously dazed giant.

Tomas' eyes were wide, his mouth gaping, though not at the sight of the giant, Elbryan knew, for Tomas had seen many fomorians. No, it was Bradwarden, the huge powerful centaur, that had stunned him.

"Ha-ha! Ye're not seein' much, now are ye, ye great fat cow!" Bradwarden roared. He reared up on his hind legs as he taunted the giant, his forelegs kicking wildly at the huge creature's belly and chest. And when the fomorian brought its huge arms down to block the barrage, Bradwarden smacked the giant on the top of the head with his cudgel.

The brute staggered backward and Bradwarden rushed in pursuit, then stopped short and swung around to kick out with both hind hooves, smashing into the giant's midsection, doubling the creature over. Around came a laughing Bradwarden, club flying.

Tomas winced as he saw that heavy cudgel bash the side of the giant's face, wrenching its head violently to the side, teeth falling with a gush of blood from its mouth.

"Bradwarden," Elbryan explained, "a powerful ally."

"And not so weak a foe," Tomas remarked. He winced again as Bradwarden smashed the other side of the giant's face, then hit the brute with another overhead chop, this one dropping the giant to its knees.

"Cut 'em down and finish the job, I'm always sayin'!" the centaur howled, and he spun and kicked again, each hoof taking the giant in an eye. Head snapping, the fomorian reeled backward so far that its shoulders almost touched the ground, and then it stupidly struggled back to a kneeling position.

Bradwarden kicked it in the face again.

This time the giant stayed down. Bradwarden, club swishing casually back and forth, moved around the great body and stood staring down at the dazed giant's torn face.

Up on the ridge, Elbryan nodded to Tomas and the two turned and started away. They had taken only a couple of steps when the first sharp crack of Bradwarden's club sounded against the giant's skull.

They didn't look back, nor did either of them speak until they neared the encampment of those brave folks following Tomas back to the Timberlands.

"He is no enemy, I assure you," Elbryan said, noting the look of concern on Tomas' face.

"Never doubted that," the big man replied. "I have learned to trust the word and judgment of Nightbird. Still . . ." The man paused, obviously uncomfortable. "When we were in Caer Tinella, some of the latter folk to arrive—those that came right before or after you and Pony—brought much talk from the southland. Of course, in the aftermath of a war, rumors abound. . . ."

"And are there any particular rumors that trouble you, my friend?" the ranger prompted.

"Not until a few minutes ago," Tomas admitted. "One rumor named a centaur as an outlaw. Knowing how rare such creatures be, I'm fearing that your friend Bradwarden might be the one."

"And did the rumors name any other outlaws?" he asked.

"No," Tomas replied, "none that I have heard tell of."

"The bearers of such rumors did not tell you that the Abellican Church searches for a woman as well?" Elbryan pressed. "And that their search for her is even more desperate than the search for the centaur? She is powerful with the sacred gemstones, you see, and has quite a hoard in her possession."

Tomas' eyes widened with recognition. He had known for some time that Elbryan and Pony feared that they might be in trouble with the Church, but what the ranger was hinting at now was far beyond anything Tomas had ever imagined.

"It is true," Elbryan went on. "They search for her and for her companion, a warrior from the Timberlands, one known to ride a black stallion with a diamond-shaped white patch above its eyes. It would seem these two went into the heart of the Church's power, into mighty St.-Mere-Abelle itself, and freed the wrongfully imprisoned centaur. Tomas Gingerwart, might that be a description of anybody you know?"

Tomas gave a wide smile and laughed despite his very real fears. "No," he answered innocently. "Not a man I ever met from the Timberlands would fit that description, and even if one did, no doubt he'd be too damned ugly for the likes of the woman the Church seeks."

Elbryan smiled at him, then clapped Tomas on the shoulder. Together they started again for the encampment. As they neared the perimeter, Tomas pulled up short and looked seriously at the ranger. "What about Bradwarden?" he asked. "A secret between me and you?"

"And Belli'mar Juraviel," Elbryan corrected. "Though I fear that our little friend will not remain with us much longer, as his road has turned to the west. And without him, Bradwarden becomes all the more important, for the centaur has friends in the forest and is as fine a scout as ever there was."

"Good scout, good fighter," Tomas remarked good-naturedly. "I believe that I will hire him!" The man's smile faded. "And what of it, then? Am I to keep the truth of the half-horse a secret, just giving Nightbird all the credit Bradwarden's due?"

Elbryan looked at the camp. There were more than four score people there, all able-bodied adults, all risking everything to reclaim the Timberlands. "The centaur is not a secret," he decided, "but neither is Brad-warden a topic of open discussion. Use your judgment, Tomas."

The big man mulled it over for a few moments. "They all deserve our trust," he said. "They came north trusting us, and so we should do the same."

"Still, I think it better if Bradwarden remains outside the camp," the ranger replied. "The sight of him might unnerve more than a few, and the less chatter about him the better."

"You fear the Church will come looking for him again," Tomas reasoned.

"They never did come looking for him," Elbryan explained. "His only crime was to be found in the bowels of Aida by the monks who went north to investigate."

"Crime?" Tomas echoed incredulously. "Considering the glorious events at Mount Aida, it sounds as if finding him there should have made him a hero, not a criminal."

"I agree," said the ranger. "I cannot understand the Church's actions, and stopped trying to a long time ago. They called Avelyn an outlaw, and yet, on my word, he was among the finest and holiest men I have ever known. They arrested Bradwarden and threw him in a dark dungeon simply because they believed that he could give them information about Avelyn—and now, about me and Pony. And so we, all three, are outlaws—and Juraviel would be as well, if the Church knew of him, for he, too, jour-neyed to St.-Mere-Abelle to rescue our friend."

Tomas nodded and sighed. "And what of Pony?" he asked. "You just named her as an outlaw, and yet she walked back into Palmaris, where the Church is stronger still, no doubt, since Baron Bildeborough is no more."

"Pony is resourceful," Elbryan said firmly, though it was obvious to Tomas that he was more than a little worried. "She will not be caught unaware, and thus, she will not be caught."

They let it drop there. They had to look ahead, not back, for they still had a few more days of hard travel before them; and though the war was won, there remained dangerous monsters in the area, like the rogue giant Bradwarden had just defeated.

Perched in the sheltering boughs of a tall, thick pine, Juraviel watched Nightbird and Tomas walk into the encampment. The elf noted the admir-ing stares from every man and woman the ranger passed, and he took com-fort in watching the hands go quickly to work when Nightbird or Tomas gave a command. This was an efficient crew, hardy, strong, and well-picked; Juraviel had no doubt that the Timberlands would soon be back in the control of the humans.

That was no small matter to the Touel'alfar. The elves had a design for the human kingdoms; they liked to keep the world beyond Andur'Blough

Inninness orderly. That was the real reason they trained the rangers, though they didn't tell that to the humans they trained. The rangers acted unwittingly as elven agents, patrolling the borders of the three human kingdoms and protecting human settlements in the Timberlands and the Wilderlands. The elves thus not only helped secure the region against invading monsters—Nightbird's magnificent work in the last war was proof of that—but also had windows through which they could glimpse all the major areas of potential human advancement.

Therefore, all events on the heels of the war were the concern of the Touel'alfar, and Juraviel was confident that he could return now to his home with news that the reclamation of the Timberlands was imminent— by men of Honce-the-Bear, including Nightbird. Juraviel knew Lady Dasslerond worried that the Alpinadorans would seize this opportunity to encroach upon the valuable forested region. Juraviel had gone far ahead of Tomas' caravan, had already been in the area of the three towns, and was satisfied that the barbarian folk under the watchful eye of Andacanavar were nowhere about.

The shortest route back home for Juraviel was almost due west, but when he left his vantage point overlooking the human encampment, the elf went south. He had heard something the night before, some distant melody carried on the wind, and he suspected it to be *tiest-tiel*, the star song of his brethren. There hadn't been an audible song, of course, but the Touel'alfar had magic of their own, magic independent of the gemstones. The elves could soothe with their melodies, could even lull unsuspecting enemies to sleep. They could speak to animals and read the signs of nature clearly, usually well enough to discern the recent history of any area.

But the greatest innate magic of the Touel'alfar was their empathetic, almost telepathic, bond. When Tuntun had died in the remote bowels of Mount Aida, the elves in Andur'Blough Inninness had felt her demise. They were a small group, highly intimate, and they could sense one another's movements. An elf coming upon a place where one of his brethren had recently passed would know it.

Juraviel felt something to the south, and so he went toward the distant star song.

❖ 14 ❖

Grabbing at the Soul

"I have been told some very disturbing stories by merchants traveling from the North," King Danube Brock Ursal stated bluntly as soon as the abbot of St. Honce arrived. Uncharacteristically, this conversation between the two leaders was private; only three other men were in the room—a bodyguard and a recorder for King Danube and a single monk who stood beside Je'howith.

"No doubt, the transition will be difficult," Je'howith replied. "The Church asks for your patience."

"There are rumors that your Bishop has decreed that all gemstones are to be returned to the Church," Danube pressed, pulling no punches. The ruling family of Honce-the-Bear possessed quite a collection of such stones, gifts from abbots dating back centuries and even several "gifts of office" from the periods when the King also held the title father abbot.

"I cannot speak for the Father Abbot," Je'howith admitted, "for truly your words have caught me unprepared. I would assume the situation in Palmaris is unique, for that is the region where the followers of the thief and heretic Avelyn Desbris are said to be."

King Danube nodded and uttered a few uh-hums, obviously far from convinced.

"I intend no such decree in Ursal," Je'howith flatly stated.

"Nor would one be advised," Danube remarked, his tone showing the words to be an open threat. "And how far do you expect your Church to reach in this time of uncertainty? I do not doubt that the Abellican Order can be comforting and helpful to people, especially following the devastation to our northern reaches during the war, but I warn you now that there is only so much I shall tolerate."

"You have charged us with a most vital mission," Je'howith replied. "The calming and reordering of Palmaris is no small matter. But I beg you to have patience. Let our results be the determining factor, not the messy details of this transition period."

"Am I to ignore the pleas of some of my favored merchant families?" the King asked skeptically, "men whose fathers served my father, whose grandfathers served my grandfather?"

"Delay the answers," Je'howith suggested. "Explain that this is a critical time and that all will be put aright soon enough."

King Danube stared at the old abbot doubtfully for a long while. "You understand that even Constance Pemblebury would be hard-pressed to support your Order on this matter." He chuckled and looked around at the empty room. "And you know, of course, the likely reaction of Duke Targon Bree Kalas. I granted your Church the rulership of Palmaris but only for a trial period. I bestowed the title of bishop, and I can revoke it"—he snapped his fingers—"just like that. And further understand, and do inform your Father Abbot, that if I am forced to revoke the title and privilege, your Church's standing will be greatly diminished within my kingdom. Do we understand each other, Abbot Je'howith? It would displease me greatly to think that you left here now not recognizing the gravity of this situation. You asked for patience, and so I shall be patient, but for a short while only."

The abbot thought of several responses, but none seemed fitting or useful. The King had caught him off guard; Je'howith had no idea that ambitious De'Unnero had moved so quickly and so forcefully to solidify his base in Palmaris. Did Father Abbot Markwart even know of these developments?

Je'howith smiled slightly as he mulled over that question. He remembered his frightening spiritual communication with Markwart, and did not doubt that he kept in similar regular contact with De'Unnero. No, this situation might prove to be a true crisis between Church and state, he realized, for if the Father Abbot himself had formulated the Palmaris policy, then Markwart and King Danube were surely riding right at each other on a narrow trail.

The abbot wondered then if he should begin his own campaign. Might now be the time to begin distancing himself from the Church hierarchy? If he whispered to King Danube a subtle denouncement of the Father Abbot in general and of this policy in particular, might he be laying the foundation for an even stronger position for himself should King and Father Abbot come to open conflict?

But memory of the unpleasant spiritual contact with Markwart stood out in Je'howith's mind, the sensation of power he had felt in Markwart. He would have to be careful, he realized, for if the situation deteriorated between the King and the Father Abbot, Je'howith was far from certain which one would win. And to be on the wrong side of that conflict, he knew, would be dangerous.

"I will learn what I can and report fully to you, my King," the Abbot said with a bow.

"No doubt," Danube replied dryly.

* * *

Pony was bent over a basin, throwing up. She tried to keep the telltale sign secret, though Dainsey Aucomb had been giving her suspicious looks lately.

Pony took a sip from a cup of water, swished it around in her mouth, then bent over to spit it out.

She heard the footstep behind her, heard the creak of the opening door. "Dainsey," she began, standing and turning, but she stopped short, surprised to see Belster O'Comely in the doorway.

"You are sick every morning," the innkeeper remarked.

Pony stared at him hard. "I've not been feeling well," she lied. "Not so bad that I cannot do my work."

"As long as you loosen your apron strings to make room for the belly," Belster replied slyly.

Pony looked down automatically, a bit confused, for her stomach was just beginning to bulge.

"Well, not yet, perhaps," Belster said.

"You make many assumptions," Pony said, a hint of anger in her voice. She walked to the door and pushed past Belster. He caught her by the shoulder and turned her so that she was facing him squarely.

"Had three of my own," he said.

"You speak in riddles."

"I solve riddles," the innkeeper corrected, a wide smile on his face. "I know that you had time with your lover. I know that the demands of the war had lessened, and I know what young people in love do. And, my secretive friend, I know what morning sickness signals.

"You are with child," Belster said bluntly.

The edge of defiance faded from Pony's bright blue eyes. She gave a slight nod.

Belster's smile nearly took in his ears. "Then why are you apart from Nightbird?" he asked, and then he frowned suddenly. "He is the father, of course."

Now it was Pony's turn to smile and to laugh aloud.

"Then why are you here, girl, while Nightbird's up north?" Belster asked. "He should be beside you, taking care of your every need and desire."

"He does not even know," Pony admitted, but then she told a little lie. "For I did not know when I left him in Caer Tinella."

"Then you must go to him."

"To be caught in a blizzard?" Pony asked skeptically. "And you are assuming that Elbryan is in Caer Tinella. Since the weather has been so mild, he might already be on his way to the Timberlands." She held up her hand to calm Belster, who was growing visibly agitated. "We will meet again soon after the turn of spring, soon enough to tell him," Pony explained. "Fear not, my good friend. Our roads have separated, but not forever, not even for long."

Belster considered the words for a moment, then burst out in laughter and wrapped Pony in a great hug. "Ah, but we should be celebrating!" He roared, lifting her from the ground and spinning her around. "We'll have a great party in the Way tonight!"

For Pony, it was a bittersweet moment, and not just because she knew that a party, or any other open proclamation, was out of the question. Mostly it was Belster's reaction that stung her heart. It should have been Elbryan lifting her and spinning her, Elbryan sharing in her joy. Not for the first time, the woman regretted her decision not to tell her husband.

"No party," Pony said firmly when Belster put her down. "It would only draw unwanted questions. No one knows but you, and that is the way I prefer it."

"Not even Dainsey?" Belster asked. "But you should tell her. She is a good friend and loyal. And though she might not be so quick about some things, in others—and likely this is one of them—she is wise indeed."

"Maybe Dainsey," Pony agreed. "But in my own time and way."

Belster smiled and nodded, satisfied. Then suddenly, he burst out in laughter and wrapped Pony up again, twirling her about.

"Time for going!" came a call from back in the main room.

"Ah, yes," Belster remarked, lowering Pony gently and putting on a serious expression. "In all the excitement of your throwing up, I almost forgot. A crier, a monk from St. Precious, just walked down the street, calling all good Abellicans to gather at the town square before the doors of St. Precious. It seems that our new Bishop has a speech to make."

"I'm not certain that I would be considered a good Abellican," Pony said, "but I would not miss this gathering."

"A chance to learn more about your enemies?" Belster asked sarcastically.

Pony nodded, taking the question seriously. "And to learn more about the disturbing events in Palmaris," she said.

"Leave your gemstones," Belster advised.

Pony agreed wholeheartedly; after all she had witnessed these last few days, a person-to-person search in the town square would not surprise her in the least. The new leader of Palmaris did not seem interested in the rights of his citizens.

"Dainsey will see to your face," Belster remarked, "unless you dare to walk undisguised among the crowds."

Pony considered it for a moment. "A bit of a disguise, perhaps," she decided, for she did not want to go through the ordeal of the full transformation into Belster's older wife, nor did she believe that she would have trouble blending in with the masses.

Pony, Belster, and Dainsey left the Way soon after, joining the hundreds of people moving down the streets toward the great square. As Belster had suggested, Pony carried no gemstones with her—a decision that gave her quite a bit of comfort as she moved into the crowded square and saw the whole place was surrounded by armed soldiers, with monks mixed among them, all studying the crowd intently.

The new bishop stood on a platform erected before the abbey's great doors. Pony had seen the man once before, within a ring of defensively circled merchant caravans that had been assaulted by raiding goblins. Pony and Elbryan had helped the merchants survive. This man and his fellow monks, who had been not that far back down the road when the goblins attacked, showed up only after the battle had ended. Even then, the only monk who had helped tend the wounds of the injured was the kindly Jojonah, and it had been obvious to Elbryan and Pony that Bishop De'Unnero was no friend to Jojonah.

As she worked her way to the front of the crowd in the square, Pony realized that her first impressions of De'Unnero agreed with what she saw now. He stood with his arms crossed over his chest, surveying the crowd like some god-empowered conqueror. Pony was a perceptive woman; she could read De'Unnero now, quite easily. His arrogance surrounded him like a shroud; his stern gaze was all the more dangerous because this prideful man held himself above all others and could therefore justify practically anything.

The closer she got to the platform, the more keenly Pony believed her initial perceptions. De'Unnero's physical posture—his taut muscles, crossed arms with robe sleeves pulled back enough to show his powerful forearms, his predatory eyes and closely cropped black hair—screamed at her to beware. As his gaze scanned the area where she was standing, she was certain that he was looking directly at her, only at her.

The moment of panic passed, for Pony soon realized that everyone in the area, indeed everyone who fell for only a brief instant under that penetrating gaze, shared her reaction.

The crowd continued to grow, whispering this or that rumor. "I'm hearin' that he's payin' back the filthy merchants for all the years they robbed us," one old woman said. "And the yatol priests," said another. "Dirty scum from Behren. Put 'em all on a boat and send 'em south, I say!"

Listening, Pony grew concerned. De'Unnero was furthering his ambitions and hunting for Avelyn's followers, and he was creating scapegoats for any dissatisfaction in the general populace. He had treated the merchants horrendously, and the Behrenese even worse, but if he could portray them as enemies of the common people, then might not those people rally behind him? Pony shuddered.

The Bishop stepped forward and held his arms out wide. Then, in a powerful, resonating voice, he called for prayer.

Thousands of heads bowed—Pony's included.

"Praise God that the war is ended," De'Unnero began. "Praise God that

Palmaris has survived and has found its way back into the arms of the Church."

He went on from there with the standard speech of all Abellican ministers at large gatherings: calling for good crops and no diseases, for prosperity and fertility. He cued the crowd to chant at appropriate places, timed perfectly to hold and heighten their attention. Then De'Unnero began improvising. He made no mention of Baron Bildeborough, Pony noted, nor of King Danube, though he reverently invoked Father Abbot Markwart's name repeatedly.

When he finished and called for a final arm-uplifting, all hands reached skyward.

And then the crowd began to whisper once more, and many made as if to wander away.

"You are not dismissed!" De'Unnero cried sharply. Every head turned to the man, and every whisper halted.

"There is another issue for discussion," the Bishop explained, "one not for prayer but for pragmatism. You citizens of Palmaris, perhaps more than any others in Honce-the-Bear, have borne witness to the horrors of the demon dactyl. Is this true?"

A murmur of "Yes, my lord," rumbled through the crowd.

"Is this true?" De'Unnero roared, so suddenly, so frightfully, that Pony jumped.

Now the response was tremendous, an agreement yelled in fear.

"Blame naught but yourselves for the rise of Bestesbulzibar!" De'Unnero screamed at them. "For the blackness in your hearts spawned the demon dactyl; the weakness of your flesh gave flesh to the diabolical creature. You cannot avoid the blame! Not you, nor you, nor you!" he yelled, running across the front of the platform, pointing at various terrified individuals. "How great have been your tithes to the Church? And what tolerance have you shown for pagans? Your docks are littered with the unwashed unbelievers.

"And who has been your leader these past years?" he cried. "Abbot Dobrinion? Hardly, for you, like so many others, have heeded the words of a secular leader."

He calmed and stood still. The whispers began again despite the fear, for he had just spoken ill of Baron Bildeborough, who had been so beloved by the folk of Palmaris.

"Do not misunderstand me," De'Unnero went on. "Your Baron Bildeborough was a fine man, a humble man who did not place himself above God. But now, my friends," he said, raising his fist in the air before him, the muscles on his forearm tightening like iron bands, his face brightening with sheer intensity, "now we have the chance before us to lay Bestesbulzibar and all its evil demon kindred to eternal sleep. Now, because of the wisdom of King Danube, Palmaris shall shine as never before. We are the borderland, the sentries of the kingdom. King Danube knows this, and knows, too, that if Palmaris finds its soul, Bestesbulzibar cannot pass through our gates!"

The flourish as he ended the statement brought a great cheer from the crowd. Not from Pony, though. She looked around at the faces of the common folk, many wet with tears. He was good, she had to admit. This new bishop understood his flock. First he took action against the two classes that the Palmaris commoners were more than willing to consider enemies: the merchants and the foreigners. And now he was calling them to spiritual arms. So many of them had lost loved ones in the fighting—and even before the war, so many of them had faced death daily—that De'Unnero's hint now that they might somehow transcend their meager existence was obviously appealing.

"You must come back to God!" De'Unnero cried. "I will look for every one of you—for you and you and you," he said, again pointing and rushing across the platform. "No longer will the monks of St. Precious minister to a paltry few. No, I say, because God has shown me the truth. And God has spoken to your King, has inspired him to give the city into the care of the Abellican Church. Thus, we will be the guardians of the soul. We will defeat the seeds of Bestesbulzibar. I will show you how."

The cheering grew with each proclamation, and Pony studied those around her, looking carefully for signs that this public accord might not be as deeply rooted as she feared. She did see many people holding their hands out to the Bishop, desperate to believe in something; but she saw many others going along with the cheering simply out of fear of the ever-present monks and soldiers.

It wasn't until De'Unnero finished that Pony looked back at the platform and saw him standing with his arms crossed again. He was an inspiring orator, a man who stirred the soul. But Pony knew the truth and knew that his actions in the name of God were designed, in fact, to serve a mortal being.

But the people didn't know it, she reminded herself, scanning the crowd; and their ignorance could allow De'Unnero to exact a brutal toll on anyone who did not agree with the Church. Still, Pony was convinced that there was skepticism here, waiting to embrace the truth.

Now all she had to do was figure out how to get her message to the common folk.

While presiding over the morning prayers of the younger students, Father Abbot Markwart recognized the tingle of spiritual communication. Someone was trying to contact him using a soul stone, but the telepathic intrusion was so slight that Markwart couldn't recognize the soul.

The Father Abbot abruptly excused himself, turning the duties over to Brother Francis, and hurried back to his private quarters. He started for that most private room of all, but hesitated, remembering that a spirit-walking monk could see his physical surroundings. Even if he went out spiritually to intercept the monk, might the man slip past him and view that room?

Markwart laughed aloud. No, this monk, whoever he might be, was a puny thing, a mere child. Holding the calling spirit at bay, Markwart collected his soul stone and, with hardly a thought, he fell into the smooth grayness of the hematite, his spirit walking free of his body.

He saw that Je'howith had come a-calling, and he saw, too, that the spirit of the other man already showed signs of magical weariness. Markwart's spirit waved the abbot away, making clear that they would communicate in St. Honce and not here. Then he went back into his body, moving into the room with the pentagram, where he felt his power most keenly.

In moments, the specter of the Father Abbot appeared in Je'howith's quarters to face the physical man. It was obvious to Markwart that Je'howith's spiritual excursion to St.-Mere-Abelle had exhausted him. After Markwart calmed Je'howith, the Father Abbot ordered him to speak plainly and quickly.

"The King is not pleased with Bishop De'Unnero's actions in Palmaris," Je'howith explained. "He is taking gemstones from merchants—stones they bought from us. It is incredible that De'Unnero would show such nerve, and so soon after taking—"

"Bishop De'Unnero acts with my blessing," Markwart replied bluntly.

"B-but, Father Abbot," Je'howith stuttered, "we cannot anger the entire merchant class. Surely the King will not allow—"

"This is not a matter for King Danube," Markwart explained. "The gemstones are the gifts of God, and thus, the sole domain of the Abellican Order."

"But you yourself have sold them to merchants and nobles," Je'howith dared to reply. A cold feeling washed over him even as the words left his mouth, bringing a sensation of dread beyond anything he had ever before known.

"Perhaps I was not as wise in my younger days," Markwart replied, seeming calm—and that only unnerved the abbot even more. "Or perhaps I was too bound by tradition."

Je'howith looked at him curiously. Markwart had always prided himself on tradition; in fact, whenever the College of Abbots had objected to his decisions, he had nearly always used past practices as justification.

"You have learned a better way now?" the abbot asked cautiously.

"Witness my growing power with the stones and understand that to be a manifestation of a greater insight to God's desires," Markwart replied. "I have come to see that our selling of the sacred stones was wrong." The Father Abbot paused, for his own words had struck him as curious. After all, had not Avelyn Desbris espoused the very same argument? Was not the abbey's selling many of the stones Avelyn had collected on Pimaninicuit one of the primary causes of his desertion?

Markwart was amused at the irony, for, yes, the actions had indeed been the same, but the reasons were very different.

"Father Abbot?" Je'howith asked curiously after several long moments had slipped past.

"Bishop De'Unnero acts in accordance with my new insights," Markwart stated firmly. "He will continue."

"But he angers the King," Je'howith protested. "And do not doubt that King Danube considers the appointment of bishop a trial only, and will revoke the title and place a baron—and likely one not so favorably inclined toward the Church—to oversee Palmaris."

"King Danube will find it is more difficult to revoke a title than to grant one," Markwart replied.

"Many believe the Church and the state are separate entities."

"And they are fools," said Markwart. "We cannot claim rulership all at once," he explained, "for that would surely incite the frightened rabble to act on King Danube's side. No, our domination will be a step-by-step acquisition of Church control over one city, one region at a time."

Je'howith's eyes widened and he looked away, staring at the corner of his room. He had not heard of this plan before and had no idea that Markwart's ambitions ran so high. Nor was he comfortable with the thought. Abbot Je'howith had a secure and comfortable life in the King's court at Ursal, and he wasn't thrilled with the idea of anything disrupting that luxurious existence. And he could not dismiss the thought that he could even end up on the losing side of a titanic battle.

The abbot looked back at Markwart's spirit and tried hard not to show his fears, for he understood there was hope of a compromise with the Father Abbot on this matter.

"King Danube will understand my view," the Father Abbot assured him.

"And what am I to do?" the dutiful abbot asked.

Markwart chuckled. "You will discover that you have less to do than you believe," he said mysteriously. Then he faded from the room.

A moment later Markwart blinked open his physical eyes. His room was as he had left it; even the candles had not burned down noticeably. But before Markwart could ponder the miracle of this spiritual communication, he had the feeling something was out of place. Slowly he scanned the room. Nothing seemed different, but Markwart sensed something had changed, that someone, perhaps, had entered the room.

Yes, that was it. Someone had entered the room, had witnessed him at his work. Markwart leaped to his feet and rushed into his office.

This room, too, seemed unchanged, but Markwart again sensed that another person had recently been here, as if the intruder had left behind some detectable aura.

Markwart went into his bedroom next, and in the doorway he felt it again. Even more astounding, the Father Abbot realized he could trace the intruder's very steps. The man had come through the office and to the bedroom door but then had turned and gone into the summoning room. It all seemed remarkably clear to him. . . . Perhaps his work with the hematite had allowed him to leave behind enough of his awareness that he could register the events about his corporeal form.

Markwart nodded, thinking he had the puzzle figured out . . . and he also had a fairly good idea of who the intruder was.

Back at the Fellowship Way, Belster remarked to Pony and Dainsey, "He had them on their knees. They're needing something to believe in. Our new Bishop knows that."

"And will try to take advantage of the situation," Pony added.

"Pity the Behrenese then," Dainsey said with a snort. "If the Behrenese are deservin' of any pity!" The woman started to laugh, but she saw that her attempt at humor wasn't appreciated.

"That is exactly the attitude Bishop De'Unnero hopes for," Pony said to Belster, "and the attitude we must fear."

"Few of the Behrenese are well regarded in the city," Belster admitted. "They've got their own ways—strange ways, that make folk uncomfortable."

"Easy targets for a tyrant," Pony reasoned.

"What're ye sayin' then?" Dainsey wanted to know. "Now I've never been fond o' churchmen, especially since they been takin' me in for their questions of late, but the man's the Bishop, put there by the King and the Church."

"Two marks against him," Pony said dryly.

"And what're ye thinkin' ye might do?" Dainsey asked. When Pony looked at Belster, it was obvious to her that he was thinking much the same as Dainsey.

"We have to use De'Unnero's own actions against him," Pony explained, improvising as she went along. Her mind was whirling—she knew she had to take some action against the Bishop, had to try something to stop him from securing his hold over Palmaris. But what? "We have to let the people of Palmaris know, Belster," she decided.

"Know what?" the innkeeper asked skeptically. "The Bishop explained everything he means to do."

"We have to make them know the reasons for these acts," Pony declared. "De'Unnero is not concerned for the people—not in this life or in any that might follow. His goal, the goal of his Church, is power, and nothing more."

"Strong words," Belster replied. "And I am not disagreeing with you."

"You have an extensive web of informants already in place," Pony reasoned. "We can use them to keep people together . . . and keep them informed about the actions of Bishop De'Unnero."

"Are you looking for a fight, then?" Belster asked bluntly. "Do you think that you might create a riot in Palmaris that will sweep away De'Unnero and all the Church—and all the soldiers?"

The question set Pony back. That was exactly the thing she was now fantasizing about, but when it was spoken so openly, she realized just how desperate, even ridiculous, it sounded.

"I've a network, indeed," Belster went on, "for protection—hiding folks who have fallen into trouble—for helping to keep your own identity secret. Not one for fighting a war!"

"Ye'll not do that," Dainsey added. "Oh, I've wanted to kick them damned monks all the way across the Masur Delaval, but if ye raise an army o' peasants, ye'll soon enough have an army o' dead peasants."

Belster put his hand on Dainsey's shoulder and nodded grimly. "A tall order, going against St. Precious and Chasewind Manor," he said.

"Not taller than the odds we faced in Caer Tinella," Pony replied, and a grin spread over Belster's face.

"We can at least act as a voice for the common folk," Pony went on. "We can whisper the truth, and if they hear it often enough, and measure our words against De'Unnero's actions, perhaps they will come to understand."

"And then they'll be as miserable as ye make yerself," Dainsey argued, "and with nothin' they can do about it."

Pony looked at her long and hard, then stared at Belster.

"I have some friends," the innkeeper explained, "and they have many more friends. Perhaps we might arrange a meeting or two and voice our concerns."

Pony nodded. She was hoping for a bit more fire from her two closest companions in Palmaris, but she realized she would have to be satisfied with that.

She went back to her own room to rest before the evening crowd began to gather.

Dainsey's words followed her to her bed. The woman's attitude might be more pragmatic than pessimistic, Pony had to admit, and that thought distressed her greatly. She wanted to fight De'Unnero, wanted to expose the Church for the evil institution it had become, but she could not deny the danger to herself and to any who allied themselves with her. Suppose she did raise the common folk, had them shaking their fists in the air defiantly and marching boldly against the abbey and the manor house . . .

That stirring image was erased when she envisioned the trained, well-equipped army that would confront them, an army reinforced by magical gemstones—and St. Precious, no doubt, had a fair supply of those.

How many thousands would die in the streets before the first morning of the insurrection was at its end?

Pony slumped in her bed, overwhelmed, and she reminded herself she had to move slowly. Whatever happened, she decided, she would find a way to do battle against wicked De'Unnero.

Brother Francis knelt on the floor in the corner of his room, facing the wall. His face was in his hands, a sign of humble submission to God—one not often used in the modern-day Abellican Church. But now the brother felt every gesture was important, as if somehow giving himself fully to his prayers would bring an end to the confusion that tore at him.

Of late, Francis had almost managed to forget the death of Grady Chilichunk. Francis believed his helping Braumin Herde and the others escape from St.-Mere-Abelle somehow made up for that—at least in part. Now, though, the image of Grady, lying lifeless in the grave Francis had dug, was haunting him. He remembered Grady. He saw again blasted Mount Aida, Avelyn's arm protruding from the ground. And most vivid of all, he couldn't stop seeing Father Abbot Markwart sitting cross-legged beside a pentagram—a pentagram!—candles burning at every point and a wicked book, *The Incantations Sorcerous,* lying *open* on the floor beside him.

But as horrifying as that image was, Francis tried to hold on to it—both to try to make sense of it and to block the more frightening image of Grady, dead in the hole.

But Grady's lifeless face would not go away.

Francis's shoulders shuddered as he sobbed—more from the fear he was losing his mind than from guilt. Everything seemed wrong, upside down. Another image—Jojonah's torso bursting open from the heat of the pyre— flitted through his mind. The memories mixed together into a great jumble of agony.

Soon the image of Markwart sitting cross-legged drifted to one side and the other three to another: Avelyn and his friends against the Father Abbot. Francis now saw there could be no peace, no reconciliation, between the two.

He sighed, then froze. He'd heard a slight rustle behind him. He held still concentrating, listening intently, terrified, for he knew who had entered.

A long moment passed. Francis suddenly feared he would be brutally slain.

"You are not at your appointed duties," came Markwart's voice, calm and pleasant.

Francis dared to turn and lift his face from his hands to regard the man.

"Your duties?" Markwart reminded.

"I . . ." Francis started, but he surrendered at once, unable even to remember where he was supposed to be.

"You are troubled obviously," Markwart remarked, walking into the room and closing the door. He sat on Francis' bed and stared at Francis, his face a mask of peace.

"I . . . I only felt the need to pray, Father Abbot," Francis lied, pulling himself up from the floor.

Markwart, calm and serene, continued to stare at him, hardly blinking— too much at peace. The hairs on the back of Francis' neck stood up. "My duties are covered by others," Francis assured the Father Abbot and started for the door. "But I will return to them at once."

"Be calm, brother," said Markwart, reaching out to grab his arm as he passed. Francis instinctively started to jerk away, but Markwart's grip was like iron and held him fast.

"Be calm," the Father Abbot said again. "Of course you are fearful, as am I, as should be any good Abellican in these troubling times." Markwart smiled and guided Francis to the bed, forcing him to sit down. "Troubling, yes," Markwart went on. He stood up, moving between Francis and the door. "But with a promise not seen by our Order in centuries."

"You speak of Palmaris," Francis said, trying to remain calm though he wanted to run out of the room screaming—maybe all the way to the sea wall, maybe over the sea wall!

"Palmaris is but an experiment," Markwart replied, "a beginning. I was just conversing with Abbot Je'howith . . ." His tone was leading, as was his gesture—his arm pointing toward the hallways and especially to his room.

Francis thought he had not changed his expression, but he saw from Markwart's eyes that he had betrayed himself. "I did not mean to enter your chambers unbidden," Francis admitted, lowering his gaze. "I knew that you were there, and yet you did not answer my call. I feared for you."

"Your concern is touching, my young friend, my protégé," Markwart said. Francis looked up at him curiously.

"Ah, you fear De'Unnero has replaced you as my closest adviser," Markwart said.

Francis knew the Father Abbot was diverting the conversation, knew that the words were ridiculous. Still, he found that he could not ignore them, and he hung on the Father Abbot's every word as Markwart continued.

"De'Unnero—Bishop De'Unnero—is a useful tool," Markwart admitted. "And with his energy and dominating spirit, he is the right man for the experiment in Palmaris. But he is limited by ambition, for all of his goals are personal. You and I think differently, my friend. We see the larger picture of the world and the greater glories in store for our Church."

"It was I who told Brother Braumin and the others to leave," Francis blurted out.

"I know," Markwart replied.

"I only feared . . ." Francis began.

"I know," Markwart said again with conviction.

"Another execution would have left a foul taste with many in the Order," Francis tried to explain.

"Brother Francis included," said Markwart, stopping the younger monk cold. Francis slumped, unable to deny the charge.

"And with Father Abbot Markwart as well," the old man said, taking a seat next to Francis. "I do not enjoy that which fate has thrust upon me."

Francis looked up suddenly, surprised.

"Because of the times, the awakening of the demon, the great war, and now the opportunity that has been laid before us, I am forced to explore everything about our Order, the very meaning of the Church. Even the dark side, my young friend," he added, shivering. "I have brought minor demons into my chambers to learn from them, to be certain that Bestesbulzibar is truly banished."

"I—I saw the book," Francis admitted.

"The book Jojonah meant to use for ill," Markwart went on, seemingly unconcerned that Francis had seen him. "Yes, a most wicked tome, and happy I will be on the day that I can once more relegate it to the darkest corner of our lowest library. Better for all if I just destroyed it outright."

"Then why not?"

"You know the precepts of our Order," Markwart reminded him. "All but a single copy of a book may be destroyed, but it is our duty, as protectors of knowledge, to keep one copy. Fear not, for soon enough the wicked tome will be back in its place, to remain unused for centuries to come."

"I do not understand, Father Abbot," Francis dared to say. "Why must you keep it? What might you possibly learn?"

"More than you would believe," Markwart replied with a great sigh. "I have come to suspect that the awakening demon was no accident of fate, but an event brought about by one within St.-Mere-Abelle. Jojonah, possibly with Avelyn, tampered with this tome secretly. He—or they—may have gone places, perhaps accidentally, where they should not have ventured, and may have awakened a creature better left dormant."

The words hit Francis hard, left him gasping. The dactyl demon awakened by the actions of a monk in St.-Mere-Abelle?

"It is possible that Avelyn and Jojonah were not as evil as I believed," Markwart went on. "It is possible that they began with good intentions—as we earlier discussed, the basis of humanism is good intent—but that they were corrupted, or at the very least, horribly fooled, by that which they encountered.

"No matter," the Father Abbot added, patting Francis on the leg and standing. "Whatever the cause, they are responsible for their actions, and both met an appropriate end. Do not misunderstand me. I may feel compassion for our lost brothers, but I do not grieve over their deaths, nor do I forgive their foolish pride."

"And what of Brother Braumin and the others?"

Markwart snorted. "All the kingdom is ours to take," he said. "I care nothing for them. They are lost lambs, wandering until they meet a hungry wolf. Perhaps I will be that wolf, perhaps Bishop De'Unnero, or, more likely, perhaps another unrelated to the Church. I care not. My eyes are toward Palmaris. And so should be yours, Brother Francis. I expect that I will be journeying there, and you will accompany me." He went to the door, but before he left he threw out one last tantalizing tidbit. "My entourage will be small, including but one master, and that man will be you." Markwart left.

Francis spent a long time sitting on the bed, trying to digest all he had heard. He replayed Markwart's words, seeing them as an explanation for the evil tome and the pentagram. Those horrid images swirled about him, but now the one of Markwart did not seem so troubling. It struck Francis that the Father Abbot was incredibly brave and stoic, accepting these burdens for the greater good of the Church, and, thus, of all the world. Yes, this battle was a wretched thing—and put in that context, Francis found it much easier to forgive himself for Grady. The fight was a necessary one, and when theologians and historians looked back at this pivotal time, they would recognize that, for all the painful personal tragedies, the world emerged a better and holier place.

Francis found his perspective again.

"Master Francis?" he asked aloud, hardly daring to speak it openly.

Father Abbot Markwart was pleased with himself when he returned to his room. The truth of real power, he understood, was not a measure of destruction, but of control.

And how easy it had been for him to play on Francis' weakness. On the guilt and the fears, on the flickering speck of compassion and the desperate ambition.

So easy.

CHAPTER

❖ 15 ❖

The Elven View of the World

The night air was crisp, the sky bore only a few dark clouds, soaring high on the wind. A million stars were sparkling despite the brightness of the full moon rising in the east. It was a night sky suitable for the Halo, Juraviel thought, but alas, that colorful belt was not to be seen.

The elf was farther south now, in the region where dells, clustered thick with trees, were scattered among cultivated fields, divided from one another by drystone walls. He made his way among the shadows, running and dancing, for though he felt he must hurry, he could not resist the pleasure of a leaping twirl that brought him to the side of his intended path. And even though he often saw candles burning in the window of a newly reclaimed farmhouse, Juraviel did sing a quiet, haunting melody that reminded him of Andur'Blough Inninness.

So caught up was he that many moments passed before he noticed other voices singing, their harmony wafting through the quiet air.

The song did not put the elf on his guard, but it did calm him and sent him running straight. He realized his instincts, his sense of star song, had guided him true. His heart soared, for he dearly wanted to see his brethren again. He found them gathered in a grove of oak and scattered pines. Smiles broadened on a dozen elven faces. The presence of some of the Touel'alfar—like Tallareyish Issinshine, who, despite his great age, loved to wander out of the elven valley—didn't surprise Juraviel. But the appearance of one elf in particular stunned him. At first he hardly noticed her, for she wore the hood of her cloak up, only her sparkling eyes showing.

"You have been missed, Belli'mar Juraviel," she said. Her voice—that special voice, powerful and melodic all at once, even by elven standards—halted the dancing Juraviel.

"My lady," he said breathlessly, surprised, even stunned, to discover that Lady Dasslerond herself had come forth from the valley. Juraviel rushed to her and fell to his knees, accepting her hand and kissing it gently.

"The song of Caer'alfar is diminished without your voice," Lady Dasslerond replied, one of the highest compliments one elf could pay to another.

"Forgive me, lady, but I do not understand," Juraviel said. "You have come forth, and yet I know that you are needed in Andur'Blough Inninness. The dactyl's scar . . ."

"Remains," Lady Dasslerond replied. "Deep is the mark of Bestesbulzibar upon our valley, I fear; and so the rot has begun, a rot that may force us from our homes, from the world itself. But that is a matter for decades, perhaps centuries, to come, and now I fear that there may be more pressing needs."

"The war went well. Take heart that Nightbird is back in his place—or shall be soon," Juraviel told her. "The land will know peace once more, though it came at a great cost."

"No," Lady Dasslerond replied. "Not yet, I fear. Ever in the history of humans, it has been the aftermath of war that brings the most unrest. Their hierarchies and institutions are shaken. Inevitably, one will arise to claim leadership, and often it is one undeserving."

"You have heard of the death of the baron of Palmaris?" Tallareyish remarked, "and of Abbot Dobrinion, who led the Church in Palmaris?"

Juraviel nodded. "Word came to us before Nightbird went north to the Timberlands," he explained.

"Both were good, and safe, as humans go," Lady Dasslerond explained. "Palmaris is an important site for us, since it is the primary city and garrison between our home and the more populated human lands."

Juraviel knew Palmaris was an important city to the elves, and yet they could not go into the place openly. Few humans knew of them—in fact, because of Juraviel's efforts in the war beside Nightbird, the number of humans who could honestly claim they had seen an elf had probably at least doubled over the last few months. But the doings of the humans were of concern to the elves, and Lady Dasslerond had sent elves into Palmaris every so often over the last decades.

"We are not pleased by the rumors coming out of the city," Tallareyish remarked. "There is a fight within the Church, one in which we—you— have inadvertently played a role."

"Not so inadvertent," Juraviel replied. He was surprised by the somewhat accusatory looks coming his way and he held up his hands. "Was it not Lady Dasslerond herself who instructed me to go to Mount Aida?" he asked. "And did not Lady Dasslerond herself come out of Caer'alfar to my aid when Bestesbulzibar descended upon me and the human refugees?"

"You speak truly," Lady Dasslerond agreed. "And it was Tuntun, not Juraviel, who fulfilled our rightful place on the journey to Mount Aida."

"You even brought the demon to our home," Juraviel replied. "And I do not disagree with your choice," he quickly added, seeing her scowl. "Indeed, were it not for that choice, I would have been destroyed north of our valley."

"And that is where it should have ended," Lady Dasslerond explained, "in Andur'Blough Inninness for us, and in Mount Aida for Tuntun. Our part in this conflict was played out when the demon dactyl was destroyed."

The weight of her words hit Juraviel. Indeed, it had seemed that the elves were done with the conflict, until Nightbird and Pony had arrived on the mountain slopes above the elven valley. An enchantment forbade their entrance, so Juraviel had gone to them. Then, with Lady Dasslerond's reluctant blessing, Juraviel had departed with the pair to take up the fight against the scattered remnants of the demon dactyl's army.

"Had you ordered me to stay in Andur'Blough Inninness, I would have offered no complaint," Juraviel said softly to the lady of the valley. "I have only followed that course which seemed truest to me."

"All the way to St.-Mere-Abelle?" Tallareyish remarked, his tone not complimentary.

That was it, Juraviel recognized: the breaking point of elven tolerance. Lady Dasslerond had sent him with Nightbird and Pony to watch the progress of the war against the goblins, giants, and powries, but he had followed the ranger and interfered in the heart of the affairs of humans.

Juraviel lowered his gaze to the ground before the great elven lady. "My journey to St.-Mere-Abelle was to rescue Bradwarden the centaur, who has been an elven friend for many, many years," he said humbly.

"We know," Lady Dasslerond replied.

A long moment passed, and then all the elves around him began talking at once, whispering the name of the centaur. Juraviel heard the word "justified" spoken several times, and at last found the courage to look up into his lady's eyes.

Lady Dasslerond studied him intently for a few moments, then nodded slowly. "I cannot, in good conscience, dispute your decision," she admitted, "for you did not understand fully the implications of involving yourself in such matters. What news of Bradwarden, then?"

"He is in the north with Nightbird," Juraviel replied. Before he could elaborate, one of the elves in the branches of a nearby tree signaled that someone was closing on their position, and in a moment all the elves disappeared into the underbrush.

A short while later, the light of a torch could be seen, winding through the trees, and then Juraviel smiled as two humans, one of whom he recognized, walked into view.

"You know that one," Lady Dasslerond stated, indicating Roger. As she spoke, several of the other elves began to sing softly, their voices blending with the normal sounds of the forest night. Using their star song, they wove a sound wall, a magical barrier through which elven voices would not carry, that they might continue their conversation without fear that the approaching humans would hear.

"Roger Billingsbury," Juraviel confirmed, "though more commonly known as Roger Lockless—a title he has well earned."

Dasslerond's nod showed that she, too, had learned the truth of Roger Lockless. "And the other?" she asked. "Is he known to you?"

Juraviel studied the man closely, trying to recall if he had seen him on those few occasions when he and his two companions had passed monks on their way to St.-Mere-Abelle. "No," he replied. "I do not believe that I have ever seen him."

"His name is Braumin Herde," Dasslerond explained, "a disciple of Brother Avelyn."

"Disciple?" Juraviel echoed skeptically.

"There are five of them with Roger," the lady explained, "all brothers of the Abellican Order and all dedicated to your old companion Avelyn. Roger is leading them north to find Nightbird, for they are now outlaws of the Church, men without a home."

Juraviel's expression showed his doubts. "Or are they brothers justice," he asked, "wearing the guise of friends that they might find Jilseponie and the gemstones Avelyn took from St.-Mere-Abelle?"

"They are sincere," Lady Dasslerond assured him. "We have watched them carefully these last days, hearing their every conversation."

"And do they know of you?"

"Roger alone," the lady said. "He has told the others about us, but they do not believe him." She glanced at Juraviel, then looked back at the two approaching men. "Perhaps it is time we were formally introduced." She moved boldly out into the torchlit path of the two men. How Braumin Herde's eyes widened at the sight of Dasslerond, and how Roger's eyes and smile widened when Belli'mar Juraviel stepped up beside the lady of Andur'Blough Inninness!

"Juraviel!" Roger exclaimed, coming forward to greet his friend. "It has been far too long." Roger's excitement waned when he glanced at his companion and saw Braumin Herde backing up, trembling with every step, his face white in the torchlight.

"Calm, Brother Braumin!" Lady Dasslerond commanded, and in her voice was a quality of command beyond anything the monk had ever encountered—even beyond the power of Markwart's stern tone at recent abbey gatherings. He stopped short.

"Did not Roger Lockless tell you of us?" Lady Dasslerond asked bluntly. "Did he not tell you that you would likely find the man you seek in the company of Belli'mar Juraviel of the Touel'alfar?"

"I—I had thought—" Braumin stuttered.

"We are exactly as Roger Lockless described," Lady Dasslerond went on.

"Lockless?" Braumin echoed, looking at his friend.

"A title more than a name," Roger replied.

"This we know because even as he was telling you of us, we were in the trees above you, listening," Lady Dasslerond went on. "So be surprised that his tales ring so true, but let that surprise pass quickly, for we have much to discuss."

Brother Braumin took a deep breath and composed himself as much as possible.

Roger looked questioningly at Juraviel, caught off guard. He started forward tentatively once more, but his friend, wary of Lady Dasslerond's temper, held him at bay.

"Take us back to your encampment to meet your companions," Lady Dasslerond ordered. "I do not wish to answer the same questions twice."

The reception at the camp was predictable, the four other monks obviously shocked to find Roger's outlandish tales were true. Brother Castinagis did a fair job of restraining himself, as did Dellman; but Mullahy sat down in the dirt, staring mutely, and Viscenti fell all over himself with excitement, tripping several times—once nearly pitching headlong into the fire.

"Belli'mar Juraviel brings good word," Lady Dasslerond began when at last the monks calmed. "For Nightbird is not so far ahead, though his road, like our own, heads north. We will find him in Dundalis, in the Timberlands."

"And the centaur," Roger remarked. "You will be amazed at how powerful he is, if his wounds have fully healed."

"They have," Juraviel assured him, smiling at Braumin and Dellman, both of whom had met Bradwarden before.

"And Pony," Roger remarked, obviously enchanted by the mere mention of the name. "Jilseponie Ault," he explained, "Brother Avelyn's dearest friend and principal student."

Juraviel said nothing, but observant Lady Dasslerond caught the look that momentarily came over the elf's face and recognized that he had some information contrary to Roger's claim.

"She is the one with your gemstones," Roger went on, and the startling admission caught Lady Dasslerond's attention and forced her to focus on the five monks, carefully measuring their reactions. She saw no hint of any underlying intentions, and since she usually found it easy to read the hearts of humans, she took comfort in that.

"Perhaps if we form a Church of our own, Jilseponie Ault will see fit to return the stones," Brother Castinagis remarked.

Roger laughed at the thought. "If you form a Church of your own, one based on the life of Avelyn Desbris, you should beg Pony to serve as your Mother Abbess," he said.

"A request that she would no doubt find most flattering," Lady Dasslerond said. "But let us consider the road before us and not the meetings we may find at the end of that road."

"That road seems less dark indeed, now that we have found such allies," Braumin Herde said with a low bow.

"Traveling companions," Lady Dasslerond corrected sternly. "Do not misunderstand our relationship," the lady of Andur'Blough Inninness continued, her voice sharp and clear. "Our road follows the same path as your own, it would seem, for the present, thus it is to our mutual benefit to travel side by side. We can serve as your eyes in the forest, and you can gather information from any humans we might meet along the way. But convenience does not necessarily constitute an alliance. However, if we happen upon a mutual foe—goblin or powrie or giant—my kin and I will destroy it, and thus, in that limited situation, you may consider us as allies."

Roger stared at Juraviel as she spoke, taken aback by her detached, even callous, tone. Juraviel's expression offered little information. The elf understood Roger's surprise: up until then, the only elf Roger had met was Juraviel. But Lady Dasslerond spoke with the responsibility for the fate of the Touel'alfar upon her. Juraviel knew her attitude toward the humans was not unusual.

"However," Lady Dasslerond continued, looking at each of the six men, "should we happen upon enemies of your own making—King's soldiers, perhaps, or men of your Church—then any battle is your own to wage. The Touel'alfar shall not concern themselves with the affairs of humans."

Juraviel felt that last statement keenly, knew that Lady Dasslerond had put it that way to aim it directly at him.

"I only meant—" poor Braumin Herde tried to explain.

"I know what you meant," Lady Dasslerond assured him. "And I know what you assumed."

"I did not mean to anger you."

Lady Dasslerond laughed at the thought, and there was no mistaking her condescension. "I am merely showing you the truth of the matter," she said in a matter-of-fact tone. "For to misunderstand our relationship could prove fatal." She motioned to the trees about them, and branches rustled as the other elves skittered away into the dark forest night. "You should set watch this night and all others," Lady Dasslerond explained to the men. "We will be about to call an alert should a monster wander near you, but if the intruder is human, your vigilance alone will protect you."

With that, she turned, Juraviel in tow, and walked slowly away, not fading into the shadows quickly, as the elves often did, but letting the men watch her for as long as possible, letting them take her measure.

Juraviel, too, marked well his lady's attitude, a fitting reminder to him of the relationship between the two races. Juraviel had made great friends of several humans, but that was not the norm, he was pointedly reminded.

Back in the forest, Lady Dasslerond bade Tallareyish to set the other elves in sentry positions, a perimeter that would include a watch over the human encampment. Juraviel moved to volunteer for one position, but Lady Dasslerond excluded him from the duties.

"You believe that we will have little trouble in finding Nightbird?" Lady Dasslerond asked him when Tallareyish and the others had moved away.

"He will not be hiding," Juraviel replied. "And even if he was, his favored place to hide is the forest."

"The ranger is important to us now," Lady Dasslerond said. "I have had kin, Tallareyish among them, in Palmaris since you went on your journey to the east. We have been watching the Church mostly, and I am not encouraged by all that we have seen."

Juraviel nodded.

"Nightbird may play an important role in all this," Lady Dasslerond explained, "to secure the outcome that we most desire."

"As may Jilseponie," Juraviel remarked.

"Yes, the woman," said Lady Dasslerond. "Tell me about her. She is not with Nightbird—that much was obvious from your reaction to Roger Lockless' claims."

"She is in Palmaris," Juraviel explained, "or should be."

"You fear for her?"

"The Church seeks her desperately," Juraviel replied. "But Jilseponie is an experienced warrior, and her power with the gemstones is considerable indeed."

"But she is not our concern," Lady Dasslerond prompted.

"Nightbird taught her *bi'nelle dasada*," Juraviel admitted. "And she is wonderful."

Lady Dasslerond's jaw tightened and she stood very straight. In the trees about them several elves gasped and whispered, obviously affronted. Juraviel was not surprised by the reaction, for he, too, had been angry when he had first learned that Nightbird had shared such a gift—a gift that was the Touel'alfar's alone to give. But then he had witnessed Pony's weaving a pattern of beauty with Nightbird as they fought side by side against many goblins, and he could not deny that she was worthy of the gift, nor that Nightbird had taught her well.

"I ask, my lady, that you withhold judgment until you can watch Jilseponie at the dance," he begged. "Or better still, watch her at the dance beside Nightbird. The harmony of their steps is—"

"Enough, Belli'mar Juraviel," Lady Dasslerond interrupted coldly. "This is a concern for another day. Our focus must be the ranger now, that he uses the gifts we gave to him to the best advantage for the Touel'alfar."

"Our concern must also be with Jilseponie," Juraviel dared to disagree.

"Because of the gemstones?" asked the lady. "Because she has learned *bi'nelle dasada*? That alone does not qualify her as friend of the Touel—"

"Because she is with child," Juraviel cut in. "Nightbird's child."

Lady Dasslerond was intrigued. The child of a ranger! This was not without precedent, but it was rare.

"The bloodline of Mather will continue, then," came Tallareyish's voice from the canopy. "That is good."

"Good if Jilseponie proves worthy," Lady Dasslerond replied. She looked hard at Juraviel.

"She will exceed your every hope," the elf told her. "Rarely have two so worthy humans brought forth a child." He couldn't tell if the lady of Andur'Blough Inninness was pleased.

"Were you going to Palmaris to watch over her?" she asked.

"I had thought to take that course," Juraviel admitted. "But, no, I was coming home to Caer'alfar, for I longed for the company of kin and kind."

"You have found that company," said Lady Dasslerond. "Are you satisfied?"

Juraviel understood the honor Lady Dasslerond had just conferred by offering him a choice. "I am satisfied," he said. "And so, with your permission, I choose to remain with you, on the road back to the north to find Nightbird."

"No," Lady Dasslerond replied, surprising him. "Two will continue to the north to escort the humans, but my course, and yours now, is south."

"To Jilseponie?" Juraviel asked.

"I wish to take a measure of this woman who will bear the child of Nightbird," Lady Dasslerond explained, "of this woman who has learned *bi'nelle dasada*, though it was not the Touel'alfar who taught her."

Juraviel smiled, for he was confident that the lady would be pleased.

Only a pair of elves continued shadowing the movements of Roger and the monks in the morning, all of the others running and dancing quickly south.

"We build it, they tear it down. So we build it again, and they tear it down again," Tomas Gingerwart lamented, staring at the burned-out ruins of Dundalis. The place had been completely flattened, not a single board left unburned or unbroken. "And now here we are, stubborn fools, ready to build the place again." Tomas started to chuckle, but looked at Elbryan, seeing the profound pain there.

"I was a boy when the first Dundalis was sacked," the ranger explained. He pointed to the charred remains of one building near the center. "That was Belster O'Comely's tavern," he explained, "the Howling Sheila. But before that, long before Belster and the others you met even came to the northland, it was my home."

"Ah, and a fine town it was in those first days," remarked Bradwarden, surprising Tomas and Elbryan by stepping out of the brush, showing himself to the people. Tomas had told them of the centaur, and many had caught fleeting glimpses of him, but, the gasp from the group was fairly general.

"I preferred that first town to the second," Bradwarden said. "More filled with the songs o' children. Like yer own, Nightbird, and those of Pony."

"Pony, too, was from that first Dundalis?" Tomas asked. "I do not know the tale."

"And we've not the time for it now," Elbryan replied. "Tonight, perhaps, when our work is done and we have gathered about a fire."

"But why was the first town full of children, and not the second?" one man pressed.

"The second group, Belster's companions, came north to a town that had been destroyed," Elbryan explained. "As with our caravan, they knew the recent history of Dundalis, and brought no children with them. They were a hardier folk than those who lived in the first town."

"And yet, they, too, would've been killed to the man if they'd not had a ranger lookin' over them," the centaur remarked.

Elbryan took the compliment in stride, but, in truth, it was his greatest pride that he had helped to save the majority of the folk of Dundalis before Bestesbulzibar's army had arrived. He had found people in the exact situation that had taken the lives of his own family and friends, and, using the gifts of the Touel'alfar, he had made a substantial difference.

"And here we are, thinking of building the place again," Tomas remarked.

"Ah, but ye'll be gettin' yer ranger," said the centaur.

Tomas looked long and hard at Elbryan, and saw that the cloud of pain had not gone from his olive-green eyes. "We came to rebuild," he offered, laying his hand on the ranger's shoulder. "But it does not have to be here. There are other fitting locations."

Elbryan looked at the man, sincerely touched by his concern and his offer. "Here," he replied. "Dundalis will rise again, in defiance of the goblins and the demon and any others who would try to stop us. Right here, a town again as it was before; and when the region is secure, we shall bring others—folk with children—to fill the air with song."

Murmurs of assent came from every member of the group. "But where to start?" one woman asked.

"Up that hill," Elbryan answered without hesitation, pointing up the north slope. "A tower up there will command a view of all the northern trails. And down here, we will start with a strong meetinghouse, a place of drink and song in times of peace, a shelter should winter at last descend, and a fortress should war find its way here again."

"You sound as if you've planned it all," Tomas remarked.

"A thousand times," Elbryan replied, "every day from the day I was forced to run and hide in the forest. Dundalis will rise from the ashes again—this time to stay."

That brought smiles, encouraging whispers, and even cheers.

"And the other towns?" Tomas asked.

"We have not the manpower to reclaim Weedy Meadow and End-o'-the-World at present," Elbryan explained. "Bradwarden and I will scout them out, but for now, let them lie. Once Dundalis is alive and thriving again, more settlers will come north, and we will aid them in the reclamation of the other two towns."

"Each with a meetinghouse fortress?" Tomas asked with a wide grin.

"And a tower," Elbryan replied.

"And a ranger," said Bradwarden with a laugh. "Ah, but ye'll be runnin' all about, Nightbird."

And so they began that very day, clearing debris and staking out lines for some of the new structures. The foundation of the central building was cleared, the walls outlined, and first poles—the bottom rigging of the tower Elbryan wanted placed overlooking the valley of caribou moss—were placed later that same afternoon.

Up there, on the ridge of that northern slope, the ranger relived some of the most vivid and powerful memories of his youth: his father leading the hunters back with the dead goblin, the first sign of trouble; his many days spent up here with Pony, looking down at the beautiful white brush blanketing the ground about the rows of fir trees; the night he and Pony started up here, only to be stopped by the spectacular sight of Corona's many-colored Halo glowing across the southern sky like a heavenly rainbow.

And, perhaps the most vivid memory of all and the most painful, he remembered his first kiss with Pony, the delicious and warm feeling that was shattered by the screams as the goblins sacked the town.

He told all that to Tomas and the others that night around the campfire. They all were weary from a hard day of work, and all knew that they would have another equally grueling schedule the next day. Yet not a person fell asleep, entranced by the tale the ranger wove for them. The moon had already set by the time he finished, and every one of them went to sleep with even more determination that Dundalis would rise again.

PART THREE

▼

POLITIC

There is something freeing about this existence, Uncle Mather,
something true and without hypocrisy in living among the ever-present
dangers on the borderlands of so-called civilized lands. I have been
watching Tomas and his friends, many of whom have lived most of
their lives in Palmaris, and have witnessed a change: gradual, but not
so subtle if I measure their present state against the attitudes I saw in
them when first I came to Caer Tinella. Their façades and pretensions
have gradually slipped away, I think, to allow the real faces of these
men and women to shine through. And I, who was raised in Dundalis
and then among the blunt—often brutally blunt!—Touel'alfar, greatly
prefer these true faces.

Simple survival out here requires trust, and trust requires honesty.
Without it, all is in jeopardy, for when danger descends, cooperation
holds the key to survival. I know my friends, Uncle Mather, and my
enemies, and I would willingly take a spear aimed at a friend, as any of
them would for me. That notion of mutual benefit, of true community,
has been buried in the lands where the thrill of life on the edge of
peril has been replaced by the competition of intrigue, the building of
secret alliances. A secure, comfortable life, it seems, allows the darker
aspect of human nature to emerge.

I have spent many hours thinking on this since my journey through
the populated lands, through Palmaris and to St.-Mere-Abelle. It might
be that the people there are bored, for much of life's risk and adventure
have been removed; and thus, the folk have added their own
adventures, false adventures. The levels of intrigue that I found in the
populated South, particularly in the Church, have overwhelmed me. It
almost seems to me as if these people have too much time to think,
and they sit around weaving improbable conclusions to misguided
beliefs.

I could not survive in that world, and would not deign to try. I shall
let the rise and set of the sun and the moon guide my hours, and let the
weather and seasons guide my actions. I shall eat enough to sustain life
and never descend to gluttony, and always shall I remember to
appreciate the animal, or plant, that provided me with food. I shall
hold nature in a place of godliness and stand humbly beneath her,
remembering always that she could destroy me in the flicker of an
instant. I shall tolerate weaknesses in others, for in them, I see my
own. And I shall raise my sword or bow in defense only, never for
personal gain.

These are the vows that have come to me in my reflections, Uncle
Mather, and I know them to be the ways of the ranger. I choose to live

simply, and honestly, as did my father, as did you, Uncle Mather, and as the Touel'alfar showed me. As those in the cultured and civilized kingdoms have seemingly forgotten.

I shudder at the concept of a world tamed.

—Elbryan Wyndon

❖ 16 ❖

Lessons

In the two weeks following the speech of the new bishop, Palmaris had changed considerably. Every fourth day, St. Precious was filled to overflowing, more than two thousand people at a time celebrating the holy rituals. Few dared question why those rituals involved several collections of the silver and gold bear-stamped coins of the kingdom, or even, if the person had no money, a piece of jewelry or clothing.

Outwardly, there were few signs of discontent. The Bishop's show of power—monks and soldiers parading the streets daily—kept the peace, kept a smile, however strained, on the face of every member of the congregation. In the words of Pony, it was "faith by intimidation."

For the Behrenese in the dockside neighborhood, the situation worsened. Since De'Unnero had taken charge, the soldiers and monks had been given free rein to harass them, but now even the common Palmaris citizen thought nothing of hurling an insult, a ball of spit, even a rock, at the "foreigners." The Behrenese, with their dark skin and different mannerisms, were easily identifiable. Convenient targets for De'Unnero's scapegoating, Pony noted. She spent many days by the docks now, watching and studying; and it seemed obvious to her that the Behrenese, though they showed no outward signs, had begun to put together an organized plan of common safety. Before the soldiers and monks arrived on any given day, though they followed no schedule, most of the weaker Behrenese—the elderly, the infirm, a woman great with child—seemed to have disappeared.

And always, Pony noted, the same handful of men and a pair of women were about, accepting the insults to pride and to body.

Another fellow caught her attention, and Pony watched him more closely. He was a tall, dark-skinned sailor, commanding a ship called the *Saudi Jacintha*—a man of some renown, apparently, one even the monks did not bother. Pony knew Captain Al'u'met by name, for he had been the one to ferry her and Elbryan, Bradwarden, and Juraviel across the Masur Delaval on their return from St.-Mere-Abelle. They had gone to him on

Master Jojonah's recommendation; and with that monk's writ in hand, had secured transport with no questions asked.

Al'u'met was much more than a pirate, Pony and the others had realized, and much more than captain of a ferry for hire. He was Jojonah's friend; the Master's recommendation had been of the highest order, words based more on principle than on pragmatism. Now, it appeared, the captain was again showing courage. Outwardly he appeared removed from all the turmoil, walking the decks of his ship, but Pony saw him exchanging knowing nods with the leader of the Behrenese on several occasions.

Pony's work with Belster was going fairly well—most of his substantial network were, to Pony's relief, not enamored of the new bishop—not at all. Now she dreamed of linking her group to the Behrenese, but that, she knew, would prove a far more difficult task.

That captain of the *Saudi Jacintha* might prove to be the key.

"I shall accompany you personally this day," an agitated De'Unnero explained to Brother Jollenue and several soldiers as they prepared to leave the abbey on their daily rounds of the merchant quarter in the relentless search for gemstones. The night before, the Bishop, with his garnet, had detected some fairly powerful stone usage from a particular mansion, a house the monks had visited before. The merchant there had sworn he had no magic stones.

Brother Jollenue eyed De'Unnero suspiciously and fearfully. Jollenue had been Bishop De'Unnero's leading collector of stones. There had been whispers in the abbey—though mostly from brothers jealous of the attention Jollenue was receiving from the new bishop—that Jollenue had been making deals with the merchants, allowing them to keep their more precious stones, surrendering only those of lesser power.

"I shall not fail, my lord," the monk, a fifth-year brother, remarked. "I have been most thorough."

De'Unnero's look was incredulous.

"It d-does not please me to bother a man as important and busy as you," Brother Jollenue stammered, melting under that gaze. "I endeavor to fulfill my duty."

De'Unnero continued to stare at the man, enjoying watching this underling squirm. His decision to accompany the monk had had nothing to do with distrusting him but was more a matter of his own boredom—the chance to make an example of this lying merchant.

"If you have heard something less than exemplary concerning my performance in this most vital mission you have assigned—" a nervous Jollenue started.

"Should I have heard such?" De'Unnero interrupted, unable to resist. The young brother was trembling now, beads of sweat appearing on his forehead.

"No, no, my lord," the man replied immediately. "I mean . . . they are just the false accusations of jealous brothers."

De'Unnero was enjoying this; in truth, he hadn't heard a single complaint against Jollenue.

"Every stone collected," Jollenue went on, a hint of desperation in his voice. He grew more animated with every word, waving his hands. "Never would I allow a man not of the Church to keep even a tiny diamond, even if his house was bereft of candles," Jollenue declared. "Pray in the darkness, I would tell him. Reveal your sins to yourself. Let God—"

The man's words turned into a groan as De'Unnero caught one of his swinging hands and bent his thumb back. Faster than the brother could react, the Bishop stepped beside Jollenue's shoulder and drove his index finger up under poor Jollenue's ear on the pressure point.

Paralyzed with agony, poor Jollenue could only whimper and beg for mercy.

"Why, dear Brother Jollenue," Bishop De'Unnero remarked, "it never occurred to me that you might be cheating me and cheating the Church."

"Please, my lord," Jollenue gasped. "I have not."

"Are you lying?" De'Unnero casually asked, pushing so hard with his finger that Jollenue's legs buckled.

"No, my lord!"

"I know the truth," De'Unnero declared. "I give you one last chance to speak that truth. If you lie, I shall push my finger right into your brain, a most painful death, I assure you." Jollenue started to answer, but De'Unnero pushed harder. "One last chance," De'Unnero repeated. "Have you cheated me?"

"No," Jollenue managed to say, and De'Unnero released him. He fell over, curling up on the floor, groaning and clutching the side of his head.

De'Unnero raked his eyes over the soldiers, and each of them backed away respectfully.

That reaction pleased the new bishop immensely.

After Jollenue recovered, they set off—a half dozen soldiers and the two monks. At first, Brother Jollenue remained a respectful stride behind De'Unnero, but the Bishop beckoned the man to his side.

"You have been to this house before—or perhaps it was one of the other groups," De'Unnero explained. "It does not matter," he quickly added, seeing the man grow nervous, probably formulating some excuse for his failure. "This merchant is cunning, it would seem. I am not certain if he surrendered some stones, keeping his most prized, or if he somehow managed to elude us altogether."

"But only for a short while, it would seem," Jollenue said hopefully.

De'Unnero's lip curled, as much a snarl as a smile, and he glanced at Jollenue. He picked up the pace, walking determinedly. Soon they were in the merchant quarter, walking along a cobblestone road, neatly trimmed hedgerows to either side and great stone houses set far apart, each a fortress of its own, complete with a surrounding wall.

"That one," De'Unnero explained, pointing to a rather plain brownstone dwelling.

Brother Jollenue nodded and lowered his gaze.

"One of your inspections?" De'Unnero asked.

"Alloysius Crump," the monk replied. "A boisterous man, strong of body and of spirit. A trader of fine cloths and furs."

"He refused your right of inspection?"

"He allowed us entry," one of the soldiers explained. "The man cooperated fully, my lord, as much as a proud man like Master Crump can cooperate for such an indignity as an inspection."

"You speak as if you know the man," he accused.

"I guarded a caravan on which he was a principal," the soldier admitted. "A journey to the Timberlands."

"Indeed," said the Bishop. "And tell me of Master Crump."

"A warrior," the soldier said, obviously impressed by the merchant. "He has seen many battles and never shies from a fight, no matter the odds. Twice he was left for dead on a field, only to walk back in hours later, very much alive and seeking revenge. They call him Crump the Badger, and it is a name, I assure you, that is well earned."

"Indeed," the Bishop said again, obviously not impressed. "You trust and respect this man?"

"I do," the soldier admitted.

"And so, perhaps your judgment of the man hindered Brother Jollenue's inspection," the Bishop surmised, putting the man on the defensive. The soldier started to protest, but De'Unnero held up his hand. "Our discussion of this matter will wait until a more convenient time," he said. "But I warn you, do not hinder my inspection. Indeed, you shall wait out here in the middle of the street."

The man bristled and squared his shoulders, puffing out his chest. De'Unnero marked his defiant attitude and realized he could enjoyably put that pride to the test later.

"Come along, and quickly," the Bishop ordered the others. "Let us pay the merchant a visit before he has the time to hide his precious gemstones."

"Master Crump has dogs," Brother Jollenue warned, but that hardly slowed De'Unnero. He rushed to the gate, leaped and grabbed its top, then pulled himself over in one fluid motion. A few seconds later the baying of hounds began, and the gate swung open wide. Jollenue and the soldiers ran to join the Bishop, but De'Unnero didn't wait for them, rushing into the open yard, in defiance of a shouting guard and the two barking dogs, their short black coats shining, their white teeth gleaming.

The lead dog sprinted for the Bishop and, barely ten feet away, leaped high for his throat.

De'Unnero quickly dropped into a sudden squat. Over his head went the the dog, and up snapped De'Unnero's hand to grab its hind leg. Up went the bishop and out snapped his other hand, catching the dog's other hind leg. His hands were crossed, left holding the dog's right leg, right holding the left. He lowered the dog down to its front paws, the beast trying to turn and bite him.

De'Unnero pulled his arms back, forcing the dog's legs wide, beyond the tolerance of its pelvic bones. Hearing the crack, De'Unnero dropped the howling, crippled dog to the ground and spun in time to react to the second dog, flying like an arrow for his throat.

Up snapped the Bishop's forearm, under the dog's snapping jaw, turning the dog in the air. The beast slammed into him and managed to nip his forearm, but De'Unnero's free hand shot out to clasp the dog's throat.

With a feral growl, the Bishop held the hundred-pound dog out straight with seemingly little effort.

Behind him, Brother Jollenue and the guards gasped in amazement; before him, the lone guard slowed his charge to a walk, mouth open.

De'Unnero held the pose for just a moment, then crushed the animal's windpipe. He tossed the dying creature to the ground at the feet of Crump's guard.

The man uttered some low threat and advanced a cautious step, sword extended.

"Stop!" Brother Jollenue yelled at him. "This is Marcalo De'Unnero, the bishop of Palmaris."

The guard stared hard at the man, obviously unsure how to proceed. De'Unnero made the decision for him, walking boldly to the man and slowly pushing him aside. "There is no need to introduce me to Master Crump," the Bishop explained. "He will know of me soon enough."

Up to the door he went, Brother Jollenue and the soldiers falling into line behind him, the guard still standing in the courtyard, staring blankly at the intruders. A kick had the door swinging wide, and the Bishop walked right in.

Servants, who had come into the foyer to see what the disturbance was about, scrambled to get out of the dangerous man's way. Then another man, a huge, ruddy-looking fellow with thick curly black hair sprinkled with gray, entered from a door across the way, his face a mask of outrage.

"What is the meaning of this?" he demanded.

De'Unnero glanced back at Brother Jollenue.

"Aloysius Crump," the younger monk confirmed.

De'Unnero turned slowly, a smile spreading over his face, to regard the man, who was now approaching as if he meant to lift the Bishop and throw him out into the street. Certainly this Crump was an impressive specimen, closer to three hundred pounds than to two, De'Unnero estimated, and the lines of several garish scars were clearly visible, including a scab on the side of the man's neck, a very recent wound.

"Meaning?" De'Unnero echoed softly, with a chuckle. "There is a word heavy with connotation. *Meaning.* The meaning of this, the meaning of life. Perhaps the word *purpose* would have better suited your intent."

"What nonsense do you spout?" Crump retorted.

"Does not true meaning come from that which is holy?" De'Unnero asked.

The guard from the courtyard rushed in then, and ran right by De'Unnero and his entourage, up to his master, whispering—the identity of the intruder, the Bishop knew.

"My lord," Crump said a moment later, offering a bow. "You should have warned me of your visit, that I might have properly—"

"Hidden your gemstones?" De'Unnero finished.

Aloysius Crump nearly choked on that choice of words. He was a strong man, a fighter who had forged his business in the toughest regions of the Timberlands and the Wilderlands. Once he had been a trapper, but then he learned how much more money he could make as a middleman for the other trappers and the markets in Palmaris and the more civilized lands.

"I have already answered the questions of your Church," Crump insisted.

"Words," De'Unnero said quietly, waving his arm. "What useful tools these words be. Words for meaning, words for lies."

Crump's face screwed up at this confusing response. He was not the most articulate man, but it was clear to him that he was being mocked. His huge fists balled up at his sides.

But then, without warning, De'Unnero closed the five feet between them in the blink of an eye and drove the point of his index finger under the man's jaw. "I was here last night, fool Crump," he snarled into the man's face.

Crump reached up and grabbed De'Unnero's wrist, but found that moving the stabbing finger was no easy task.

"Words," the Bishop said again. " 'Prithee know that these stones, fallen to the ground of sacred Pimaninicuit, be the gifts of the one true God for those of his chosen flock.' Do you know those words, merchant Crump?" He gave a shove with his finger, and Crump staggered back a couple of steps.

"They are from the Book of Abelle, the Psalm of Gems," De'Unnero explained. " 'And God thus did give knowledge to his chosen, that the stones be used to advantage, and all the world rejoiced, for they saw that this was good.' " The Bishop paused long enough to take note that the man's fists were now unclenched.

"Do you know those words?" he asked Crump.

The man shook his head.

"Brother Jollenue?" De'Unnero asked.

"The Book of Deeds," the young monk said, "penned by Brother Yensis in the fifth year of the Church."

"Words!" De'Unnero yelled into Crump's hairy face. "The words of the Church . . . of *your* Church! Yet you believe that you understand them better than those who administer the word of God."

Crump was shaking his head now, obviously confused and intimidated.

"My edict was clear," De'Unnero explained. "No, not mine, but in fact the words of Father Abbot Markwart himself. Ownership of the enchanted gemstones by anyone outside the Church is forbidden by Church doctrine."

"Even if it was the Church who sold—"

"Forbidden!" De'Unnero roared. "Without exception. You were told this, Master Crump, and yet you did not turn over those stones you possess."

"I have no—"

"Those stones you possess," De'Unnero cut back in with that feral growl behind every word. "I was here last night," he said. "I felt the magic in use. Your denial means nothing to me, because I saw the magic."

For a long moment, the two teetered on the edge of disaster; no one there could decide if Crump would attack the Bishop. The big, proud man didn't blink, but neither did De'Unnero, his steely gaze inviting a fight.

"I could burn your house to the ground and sift through the ashes," De'Unnero promised.

Aloysius Crump licked his lips.

"If you do not cooperate, you will be branded a heretic," De'Unnero promised.

"You have no right to come into my house," the man said deliberately. "I was a personal friend of Baron Rochefort Bildeborough."

"Who is dead," De'Unnero said with a chuckle—one not appreciated by the soldiers standing behind him.

Again the two stood staring hard at each other. Then the tension broke, as Crump turned and nodded to his personal guard. The man looked at him skeptically.

"Go!" Crump yelled, and the man ran off.

"A wise choice, Master Crump," Brother Jollenue started to say, but the Bishop silenced him with a stern glare.

The guard returned a few moments later, bearing a small silk purse. He handed it to Crump, who tossed it at De'Unnero. The Bishop's hand snapped up to pull it from the air, and without taking his stare from Crump, he handed it to Jollenue. "I trust that you would not be so foolish as to make me or one of my emissaries take a third trip out here," he said.

Crump glared at him.

"Do tell me, good merchant," De'Unnero went on, his entire demeanor changing abruptly, "what stone did you use last night?"

The man shrugged impatiently. "No stone," he said gruffly. "I do not know."

"Ah, but it seems as if you found a bit of fighting last night," De'Unnero remarked, pointing to the man's scab.

"I find fighting many nights," Crump replied, trying hard to keep his voice level as De'Unnero reached back and motioned for the purse. "Keeps me strong for the journeys north."

De'Unnero opened the purse and emptied the gems—an amber, a diamond, a cat's-eye agate, and a pair of tiny celestites—into his hand. He looked at them curiously for a moment, then looked again, suspiciously, at Crump's neck. "If there are any others, your life is forfeit," he stated clearly, drawing a gasp from the soldiers behind him and from Crump's guard, as well.

"You asked for my gemstones—stones I bought fairly—and so I gave them to you," Crump replied. "Do you imply that I am not an honorable man?"

"I imply nothing," the Bishop answered without hesitation. "I call you a liar openly."

Predictably, Crump came forward in a rush, but De'Unnero spun around and kicked the man, sending him staggering backward into the arms of his surprised guard.

De'Unnero stuffed the purse and gems into a pocket of his robe, then turned on his heel and stormed out of the house, his men following closely. They got to the street, but there the Bishop stopped suddenly.

"Have we more business in this district this day?" Brother Jollenue dared to ask after several long minutes slipped by.

"Do you not understand?" De'Unnero replied. "Master Crump has lied to us."

"And are we to search his house?" asked one soldier.

"The ruins of it," De'Unnero retorted, and every one of them knew he was not joking. "But perhaps it will not come to that." De'Unnero honestly believed that statement, for the perceptive man had learned much more than Aloysius Crump had intended to tell him. The man had been in a fight that previous night—that much was obvious from the wound on his neck. And it was equally obvious to De'Unnero that the wound had been treated with either powerful herbs or with magic. A soul stone would have left no sign of a wound, for it would not have taken much magical energy to heal such a minor cut as that.

So perhaps it was an herbal concoction. Perhaps.

"Follow," De'Unnero instructed, starting back for the house and producing a garnet from another pocket in his robe. "And learn." The Bishop stopped in front of the gate—which a servant had closed once more—pausing just long enough to concentrate on the garnet and to let a smile spread across his face. Before his companions had even caught up to him, De'Unnero was over the wall, and this time, he did not bother to throw open the gate behind him.

He sprinted across the courtyard, ignoring the cries from the guard, who was back outside. Right up to the doors and through them went the Bishop, and there, in the foyer, stood a very surprised Aloysius Crump, flanked by several female house servants, all fretting over the wound De'Unnero had given him—a wound already on the mend, the Bishop noted.

De'Unnero stood perfectly still and took a deep draft of air. No scent, no indication of any herbs. The Bishop did not need to go back to his garnet to figure out his riddle, for he was no novice to the games merchants often played with the sacred stones.

"Remove your boots," he ordered Crump.

The man furrowed his brow. "In the company of ladies?" he asked sarcastically. He raised one eyebrow slightly as he glanced over De'Unnero's shoulder.

Few would have caught the clue, but for De'Unnero, it sounded as clearly as one of St. Precious' massive bells. He spun around, registering the movement of the approaching guard's extended sword, and slashed his arm against the side of the blade. The edge cut the sleeve of his robe and drew a line of blood on De'Unnero's forearm. Now he had the guard off guard. De'Unnero's hand snapped out, wrapping the guard's sword hand. The Bishop jerked his arm back, then drove his shoulder into the man's chest.

He could have rained blows upon the guard's face and chest then, but De'Unnero's focus remained on that sword hand. He grabbed the guard by the wrist with his other hand, then bent the guard's hand, overextending his wrist. De'Unnero felt the man's grip weaken and timed his release perfectly so that he caught the weapon by the hilt. A deft twist of his wrist, a step away, then a lunge, drove the guard's sword deep into his belly.

A shove sent the dying man sprawling to the floor, and the Bishop let go of the sword hilt and turned back to face Crump, who had barely moved.

De'Unnero was laughing now. He heard his companions bumble into the foyer behind him, but he held up his hand to keep them at bay.

"But, my lord," Brother Jollenue protested. More than one of the soldiers gasped at the sight of the groaning man on the floor, his blood pooling out around him.

"This lesson is mine to teach!" De'Unnero growled, his tone, as cold as death, silencing the younger monk.

"I will ask you again," De'Unnero said to Crump, "in deference to your position. Remove your boots."

"Murdering dog!" the merchant replied, rushing to the wall behind him and pulling free an old boar spear mounted there. " 'Tis your own boots they'll be pulling from your stinking feet, so as not to waste so fine a pair on a worthless corpse!"

"Bishop De'Unnero," one of the city guardsmen said.

"Hold your ground!" De'Unnero shouted at his companions. "I am the teacher, and Crump the student."

"Go and take back his sword," Crump offered, pointing his spear—a nasty, black metal affair with a second hooked blade just below the head to prevent an impaled animal from sliding down the shaft. "Never let it be said that Aloysius Crump killed an unarmed man."

De'Unnero laughed. "Unarmed?" he echoed. "It would seem that your soldier made the same mistake."

Crump lowered the spear and came forward a cautious step, showing the dangerous bishop due respect. He waved the spear slowly back and forth, showing complete control of its movements, as if to prove that the Bishop could not slip by its deadly point as he had the guard's sword.

De'Unnero started forward suddenly, then retreated quickly two steps as Crump let out a howl and stabbed hard. His spear fell short, and the angry merchant charged ahead, stabbing again for De'Unnero's head.

Down squatted the Bishop, turning and rolling to get far from the blade. Thinking the advantage his, Crump pursued, thrusting again.

De'Unnero twisted fast to the side, slapping his forearm against the spear, half deflecting the blow. Crump was fast, though, and strong enough to reverse the momentum in the blink of an astonished eye. He let the spear fly out.

De'Unnero hardly seemed to move from the waist up; his legs bent under him so efficiently that the swishing blade passed beneath his feet before Crump or any of the onlookers realized that he had dodged. When he finally did understand his obvious vulnerability, Crump gave a yell and backpedaled desperately. To the merchant's surprise, the Bishop did not leap inside the reach of his weapon but rather stood gingerly on one leg, wincing as if he had injured himself.

Another yell, this one of victory and not of fear, and Crump skidded to a stop and leaped ahead once more, his spear driving fast for the apparently vulnerable Bishop.

De'Unnero doubled over as the spear came in; behind him, Brother Jollenue screamed, thinking him impaled.

But the tip never dug in. De'Unnero somersaulted right over the thrusting weapon. He drove his hand down, pushing the spear lower and clasping the haft. Then he used Crump's forward momentum, kicking both feet out, one of his heels smashing the merchant in the face, the other hammering into Crump's chest.

Crump simply stopped cold, and his arms fell to his sides. The spear would have fallen to the floor, except that De'Unnero now held it fast. Agile and acrobatic, the Bishop came off Crump as cleanly as if he had leaped against a wall, turning and twisting to land gracefully on his feet at the same time that the dazed Crump crashed to his knees.

De'Unnero tossed the spear aside. He grabbed Crump's hair, jerking his head back, exposing his neck, stiffened fingers of his other hand ready to strike. He could have put his fingers right through that neck, but his better judgment made him merely leave Crump gasping for air but very much alive.

De'Unnero looked around at the spectators, savoring the victory. Then he placed his foot on Crump's shoulder and unceremoniously kicked the man to the floor. He went and knelt over the man.

"I told you not to make me return," he said to the still-gasping merchant. "What clearer warning might I have given? Ah yes, but they are just *words.*"

De'Unnero moved down and reached for Crump's boot, but the ever-stubborn merchant kicked at him. Up went the Bishop to his feet, slamming his foot right into the merchant's groin.

Crump howled and doubled up in agony.

"If you kick at me again, I will castrate you, here and now," De'Unnero calmly promised. Crump offered no resistance as the Bishop pulled off his boots. There, on the second toe of Crump's left foot, was the item the Bishop had suspected, a gold ring set with a small hematite.

"Witness the resilience and innovation of merchants," De'Unnero told Jollenue, reaching down and yanking the ring from Crump's toe. "Once a simple soul stone, of which there are dozens at St. Precious alone, but through the cleverness of an alchemist and a powerful monk of some long-past century comes this: a ring that will begin a slow but steady healing process on the wounds of its wearer. A magnificent little item, one that has allowed our Master Crump here to build an impressive reputation of walking off battlefields on which he was left to die, seemingly mortally wounded.

"So ends the legend, the mystery explained," the Bishop said to the soldier who had first told him of Crump's exploits, the man having followed the others into the house this time.

The soldier glanced at his companions, obviously nervous, as was everyone in the foyer, not knowing what the volatile Bishop would do next.

De'Unnero let them linger in that uncertainty for a few long moments, then said suddenly, "Take him to St. Precious! To the same dungeon that held the outlaw centaur!"

Two soldiers jumped at the order, rushing to Crump, hooking their arms under his broad shoulders and hoisting him to his feet. De'Unnero was right there. "One bit of resistance," he warned . . . and he held up his hand, now the limb of a tiger, claws extended. "Castration."

Crump nearly swooned, then moved along limply as the guards pulled him away.

De'Unnero looked at the guard on the floor. "Bury your dead," he instructed the servants, "facedown and in unconsecrated ground."

One woman cried out. By the measure of the Church, De'Unnero had just ordered the greatest affront that could be offered to this man and to any surviving family he had.

"Cover his grave with a blocking stone," the merciless Bishop went on, taking the insult even farther, "that his demon-filled spirit cannot escape the realm of the underworld."

De'Unnero's eyes narrowed as he considered each of the servants, letting them know that their fate would be equally grim if they failed.

Then the Bishop swept out of the house, taking up brother Jollenue and the remaining soldiers in his wake.

It was a lesson, he knew, that none in attendance would soon forget.

❖ 17 ❖

A Measure of Trust

"You are certain they are out there?" Brother Viscenti asked for the third time. The nervous monk peered into the darkness beyond the campfire's glow and shivered, for the night wind, sweeping down from the north, blew cold.

"Have faith," Roger replied. "The Touel'alfar said that they would accompany us to the north, and so they have."

"We've not seen them since we passed through Caer Tinella," Brother Castinagis remarked. "Perhaps that was as far as they intended to go in their search for Nightbird."

"It was the Touel'alfar who told us that we would find him in Dundalis, even as they said they would accompany us," Roger was quick to remind them. "And so we shall, perhaps as early as tomorrow."

"We are close?" asked Braumin Herde. "You see familiar landmarks?"

"I have never been to Dundalis," Roger admitted. "But there is only one road heading north to the Timberlands, and as the trees have grown taller about us, it seems obvious that we are nearing our goal."

The five monks looked at one another doubtfully; more than one rolled his eyes in dismay.

"The trail is easy enough," Roger said firmly. "And the Touel'alfar are out there, do not fear. That we do not see them means nothing—we would never see any sign of them if there were a hundred of them shadowing our every move, unless they chose to let us see.

"And even if they were not with us, I would not be worried," Roger added. "For as long as we move near Dundalis—even if we miss the place by several miles—Nightbird will find us. Or Bradwarden will. This is their forest, and nothing moves through it without their knowledge."

"Except the Touel'alfar," Brother Braumin said lightly with a wide grin, and the other monks brightened as well.

"Not even the Touel'alfar," Roger said grimly, wanting to show his rightfully nervous companions the true depth of his respect for the ranger.

"The sooner we sleep, the sooner we will be able to break camp," Brother Braumin remarked. He motioned to Dellman, who typically took the first watch with Roger—watching for humans and not monsters, as Lady Dasslerond had explained to them.

Four of the monks settled down, moving their bedrolls as near the fire as possible, for the air was growing colder with every passing minute, it seemed. Roger and Dellman settled near the fire, and remained quiet for a long while, until Roger realized that the rhythmic breathing of his sleeping companions was beginning to settle him into a dangerously deep relaxation.

He rose abruptly and began pacing, rubbing his arms briskly against the cold.

"Do you plan another venture into the forest?" Brother Dellman asked through a yawn.

Roger looked at him, smiled, and shook his head, as though the whole idea of venturing into the forest this far north was preposterous.

"Then you are more concerned than you admitted," the perceptive Dellman remarked.

"Concerned?" Roger echoed, his tone light. "Or merely cold? Surely I could freeze dead in the dark forest away from the fire."

"Concerned," Dellman said in all seriousness. "The night is cold, but with this wind, even the fire offers little protection. Yet you will not venture alone into these woods at night, nor have you done so since we left Caer Tinella more than a week ago."

Roger looked away, into the blackness of the forest. For many months after the powrie invasion, the young man had called the forest his home and had wandered through it alone on the darkest of nights without fear. But Dellman was perceptive, he had to admit. He did fear these woods. Roger could hardly believe how much darker they seemed than those just a couple score miles to the south. How much taller and thicker, and so filled with strange sounds! No, it wasn't fear, Roger decided, but respect, a healthy respect for a forest most deserving of it. Even if all the powries and giants and goblins were banished to the far ends of the world, the Timberlands was not a place to be taken lightly.

With that understanding, Roger's respect for Elbryan and Pony increased. Compared to the forests near Caer Tinella this place was untamed.

"Do you really believe that we are close?" Dellman asked.

"I do," Roger replied. "I know that the distance from Caer Tinella to Dundalis is roughly the same as the distance from Caer Tinella to Palmaris, and we have nearly covered that ground. And we cannot have strayed, for the road is too well marked. Indeed, we have even seen signs of the caravan's passage—deep ruts that can only have been made by the laden wagons Nightbird was to accompany."

"Well reasoned, Roger Lockless," came a voice from the side, a voice Roger recognized.

"Nightbird!" the young man cried, rushing to the edge of the firelight. He paused there to let his eyes adjust, and gradually he made out the shape of the large man, sitting comfortably on the lowest branch of a wide tree, barely fifteen feet from their encampment. It seemed apparent to Roger that he had been there for some time.

Behind Roger, Brother Dellman scrambled up, waking his brothers, whispering that Nightbird had come. Soon the five wide-eyed monks moved cautiously to stand beside Roger.

"He told you that I and Bradwarden would find you," the ranger explained. As he spoke, the centaur emerged from the darkness to stand beside the tree. The monks had seen Bradwarden before, of course, when he was taken to St.-Mere-Abelle, but that creature seemed a mere shell of the formidable centaur now before them, a thousand pounds of muscle and with fiery and intense eyes.

And of course Roger, who had only glimpsed Bradwarden before, was stunned. In boastful style, he had remarked to the monks that they would be amazed at the power of the centaur when he was fully healed, but Roger's words had been based on the stories told to him by Elbryan, Pony, and Juraviel. Now he looked upon Bradwarden—an obviously healthy Bradwarden—for the first time, and those stories, however dramatic they had been, seemed to pale in comparison to the truth of the magnificent creature.

Nightbird jumped to the ground. He extended his hand to Roger, but the younger man leaped upon him, wrapping him in a hug. The ranger returned the hug, but he looked over Roger's shoulder and smiled at Braumin Herde.

Finally, Roger let go, jumping back a step and holding out his hand to Bradwarden.

"Excitable fellow," the centaur said to Elbryan.

"My road has been long and filled with tragedy," Roger said seriously. "We came north to find you, and so we have, and now, only now, might I breathe more easily."

"We have been watching you for two days," the ranger explained.

Roger's eyes widened. "Two days?" he echoed, as if insulted. "Then why have you come to me only now?"

"Because yer companions are monks, whatever clothes they might now wear," the centaur remarked. "And me and them monks ain't been known to be the best o' friends."

"How could you know the truth of us?" Brother Braumin put in, glancing down at his ordinary peasant clothing, with certainly no telltale markings to distinguish him or his four companions as members of the Church. He and his fellows were growing tired of these meetings—first the elves and now these two—where the visitors apparently knew everything about them before the introductions had even begun!

"We said we been watchin' ye," Bradwarden replied, "and that means listenin' to ye, don't ye doubt, Brother Braumin Herde."

The monk's expression was incredulous.

"Oh, I heard yer name, and I know ye from the road out of Aida," the centaur remarked.

Suddenly Braumin seemed embarrassed, remembering the horrid treatment the centaur had received from his brethren on that march.

"But I travel with them openly," Roger protested. "Would I lead enemies to you?"

"We had to be certain," Elbryan explained. "We trust you; doubt that not at all! And yet, we have been dealing with the Abellican Church long enough to understand that they have ways of coercing allies from the ranks of enemies."

"I assure you—" Brother Castinagis started to protest.

"None needed," the ranger replied. "Bradwarden has spoken highly of Brother Braumin, remembering him well from that journey. He has named Braumin as friend of Jojonah, who was friend of Avelyn, who was friend of Elbryan and Bradwarden. And we know that you come in disguise, hiding from your Abellican brothers."

"A situation you have known before," Brother Braumin remarked, "with Avelyn Desbris, I mean."

"Ho, ho, what!" Bradwarden roared, imitating Avelyn's voice perfectly in his annoying trademark expression.

Elbryan glanced at him sidelong, seeming less than pleased.

"Had to be done," the centaur said dryly.

The ranger just sighed, praying that it wouldn't become a habit. Then he nodded back at Braumin. "Except that Avelyn never stopped wearing his robes," he replied, "even when all your Church was hunting for him."

Braumin smiled, but Castinagis puffed out his chest and squared his shoulders as if he considered the ranger's statement an insult. Overproud, Elbryan noted—a very dangerous trait. He walked up to the monk, extending his hand in formal introduction.

Remembering his manners then, Roger went around to the other four monks with the ranger and the centaur, introducing each.

"Another friend to Jojonah," Bradwarden remarked when they came to Dellman, for Dellman, too, was known to the centaur from their time together on the road. "And not a friend to the one called Francis, the lackey of Markwart."

"And yet it was Brother Francis who smuggled us out of St.-Mere-Abelle," Brother Braumin remarked, drawing curious stares from Elbryan and Bradwarden.

"I'm thinkin' it's past time we heard yer tale in full," the centaur said. He glanced at the campsite, more particularly at the remains of the food the monks had left out near the fire. "After we take a bit o' supper, of course," he added and trotted to the fire.

The others were quick to join him there—if they hadn't been, the centaur wouldn't have left a scrap for them—and when they were finished eating, they all sat back and let Brother Braumin and Roger tell their tale. Roger began, detailing the murder of Baron Bildeborough; Brother Viscenti, finally finding his voice above his nervousness, explained their suspicions that Marcalo De'Unnero might have been involved.

Then Roger solemnly told of the end of Master Jojonah; both the centaur and Elbryan were as touched as the monks by that sobering story. When they had left St.-Mere-Abelle after rescuing Bradwarden, Elbryan had considered Jojonah as perhaps the greatest hope for justice within the Church. He wasn't surprised by the news of the execution, not at all, but he was profoundly saddened.

Then came the more immediate story—and the more relevant one—as Brother Braumin explained the events at the abbey that had led to the self-imposed exile of the five. He told again of how it was Francis who had smuggled them through Markwart's tightening fist, but he could not explain the man's motives, only his actions.

The other monks took turns telling of their adventures on the road, and the ranger and the centaur feigned interest in the unremarkable journey—though they were both more than a little concerned to learn of the continuing tightening of Church control in Palmaris, and were both surprised to hear that the Touel'alfar, including Lady Dasslerond herself, had been shadowing the band. Elbryan and Bradwarden exchanged confused stares; they found it strange that so large a contingent of elves would come into the region without contacting either of them. More than a dozen elves traveling together out of Andur'Blough Inninness was an exceptional tale indeed!

"And so we have come to your land, Nightbird," Brother Braumin finished, "in hopes that you will offer us sanctuary and friendship, as you once offered to our lost brother Avelyn in his time of need."

Elbryan sat back and considered the words carefully. "These are the Timberlands," he said at length, "a wild land, where men must band together to survive. All men of kindly disposition are welcomed."

"And more than a few not so kindly inclined," the centaur added with a burst of laughter that broke all tension.

"I will take you into Dundalis in the morning," Elbryan assured the group. "Tomas Gingerwart, who leads the settlers, will gladly accept six pairs of strong hands to aid in the rebuilding."

"Five builders," Roger corrected with a smile, "and a new scout to help Nightbird and Bradwarden."

"And then, perhaps, you and I can speak privately," Brother Braumin said to the ranger, ignoring Roger and drawing curious stares from all his companions, Roger most of all.

Elbryan recognized the intensity in the man's eyes and voice, and readily agreed.

Like the workings of a finely crafted Ursulan clock. Or so it seemed to Pony as she watched and marveled at the movements of the Behrenese as soon as their scouts spotted city guards turning down the main avenue that led to their enclave. Pony had been watching the southern folk very carefully over the last days. The Behrenese were no strangers to oppression in Honce-the-Bear, but now, under the added weight of Bishop De'Unnero's reign of terror, it seemed they had elevated their skill at quiet resistance to an art form.

Pony watched in awe as the word passed from mouth to mouth, as signals were knocked against walls, even the subtle drop of a flag on one of the nearby ships. Her respect for these people continued to grow with each observation.

Now a group went out to the south—the oldest and the youngest, a woman great with child and one man who had lost both arms.

Pony had seen this departure many times but had never been able to follow them to learn where they went. Every time the soldiers came to the Behrenese enclave near the docks, they found few targets for their abuse. Once a larger search had been organized, soldiers even inspecting every ship in the port, but they had found nothing.

Now, at last, after hours of searching, Pony thought she had the riddle solved. She made her way carefully along the alleys and rooftops, moving slowly south, letting the trailing line of Behrenese get ahead of her. Quietly, in the shadows of buildings, the procession moved past the docks; along the riverbank past long, low warehouses; around a bend in the Masur Delaval just north of the city's southernmost wall. There the riverbank was a bluff of white limestone. There were a few buildings overlooking the river; but they were invisible, Pony discovered, to anyone at the water's edge right below—a view further hindered by a long wooden fence constructed near the edge, most likely, to keep children from tumbling down to the river. Pony moved along that fence now, crawling between it and the cliff. Peering down, her suspicions were confirmed.

This near the Gulf of Corona, the Masur Delaval was strongly affected by the tides, with the water's depth varying as much as ten feet. At the lowest tides, dark cracks could be seen in the limestone just above the water: the mostly submerged entrances to caves.

Pony nodded as the Behrenese group went down to the water's edge and one by one, holding a guide rope, plunged into the frigid water, disappearing from sight.

Apparently those caves behind the entrances were not under water.

"Beautiful," she remarked, her voice full of respect. She was amazed by their resourcefulness; they had found a way to escape the persecution quietly and safely, and all at the cost of a cold dunking and a few hours in an uncomfortable cave.

Or was it even uncomfortable? Pony wondered. How well had the Behrenese outfitted their secret homes?

She wanted to go down there, then, to leap into the cold water and swim into the Behrenese private neighborhood. The thought of what these people had accomplished warmed her and gave her hope that the whole city would find a way to resist the wickedness of Bishop De'Unnero and his Church. The notion that the Behrenese—only one or two hundred strong and so clearly marked by their skin color—could so easily evade the persecution made Pony wonder what five thousand might do, standing behind her against De'Unnero. Yes, looking down the hundred feet to the water's edge, where the last of the group was even then disappearing, deeply inspired her.

The rustle of grass behind her warned her. She glanced back to see the approach of a Behrenese warrior: a small, wiry man armed with a scimitar, favored by the southern people. He came in without a word, without a hint of compromise on his dark face, his blade aimed straight at Pony.

Pony grabbed the hilt of her sword and, tucking her chin against her chest, launched into a forward roll, just ahead of the approaching warrior. She drew Defender, stabbing the sword above her as she landed on her back. The crosspiece of Defender's hilt was set with enchanted magnetites, and Pony called on their power fast, attracting her attacker's blade to her own as he rushed in.

Surprise showed clearly on the man's face as his blade inexplicably swerved down to slap Pony's; and that moment of confusion bought Pony all the time she needed to roll over, hop to her knees, then stand, evenly faced now against the attacker.

The Behrenese warrior tore his blade free and leaped back into a defensive crouch. When Pony didn't press the attack, he gradually stood, a bright smile widening across his black face. He began to swish his curved blade in balanced and harmonious circular movements, the movement of his arms perfectly complementing the graceful line of the scimitar.

On he came in a sudden rush—no novice, this one—his scimitar low, then high, then diagonally aimed at the side of Pony's neck.

He was clever, she realized, noting the angle of attack, recognizing that the usual parry to that maneuver—sword moving from across her chest to over her left shoulder—would not work. The curving blade would slide around the flat of her sword, driving it back over her shoulder, leaving the scimitar in line for a strike.

Instead, Pony thrust Defender up diagonally to meet the diving scimitar, pressing on so quickly that before the curved blade could expel her sword, it was against Defender's hilt. A sudden twist of Pony's wrist deflected the scimitar over her, the blade swooshing harmlessly short of the mark.

The Behrenese warrior tossed the scimitar to his left hand, turning it over, and cutting it back at Pony's midsection.

The woman sucked in her belly—she nearly swooned with terror for her child!—and leaped back, then slapped Defender behind the back curve of the passing blade and pushed it the other way. She quickly retreated a step, her mind whirling, sorting out her opponent's style, seeking its weaknesses. The Behrenese warrior whipped his blade across, then up high and down low, even behind him, to be caught by his right hand and come slashing out again from the opposite direction. The display was meant to impress, to demoralize his opponent, but for seasoned Pony, it served only to inform.

Now she understood. The man's style would prove undeniably effective against the typical sword-and-shield stance common in this country. But Pony didn't fight that way.

She fought the way Elbryan fought, the way the elves fought, and her confidence mounted as she considered that her style, *bi'nelle dasada,* would prove even more effective against a curved blade. She found her fighting stance, her center of balance, her left foot back, right foot forward, her knees bent, weight perfectly distributed over both feet. Elbow bent, wrist turned, she kept Defender pointed at the man, her back arm raised behind her as a counterbalance.

Now her biggest problem was figuring out how to win the fight without killing him, no easy task given the precarious perch they both held on the edge of the cliff.

On came the dark-skinned warrior, scimitar slashing furiously.

Pony kept Defender rolling over the swishing blade while she executed a perfect hopping retreat. That was the difference between them: the fighting style of the land, as well as that of the Behrenese, was one of side-to-side cuts and flowing movements, but *bi'nelle dasada* was far more efficient, a style of front-to-back attack and retreat.

The Behrenese man stepped back, lifting his blade up beside his face, peering at Pony from around it, as if with new respect, as if trying to take her measure.

She didn't give him the chance. She stepped forward and leaped up; out went the scimitar for a slashing defense. But Pony's feet were already moving into position. To the stunned Behrenese, it seemed as if she had hardly even touched the ground, but already she was advancing suddenly, too fast to comprehend, and his blade was still out far too wide.

She could have taken him anywhere: in the throat, the heart, or even the eye. Instead, she stabbed the man in the shoulder, stealing the strength from his sword arm. She didn't drive Defender right through his arm, though she could have, but rather found her balance at once and retreated two steps. The scimitar continued its stroke, but with no energy or strength behind it, and Pony rolled Defender over and under the blade, taking the weapon cleanly from the warrior.

He stood staring at her incredulously, clutching his bleeding shoulder.

Pony offered a quick salute, turned, and ran.

But not very far, for coming at her the other way was another Behrenese warrior. Pony skidded to a stop and glanced side to side, then nervously back at the first attacker, who was stubbornly retrieving his scimitar with his left hand. She wasn't worried about whether she could defeat this new foe or finish the one behind her, but settling any fight without sending one of them to his death over the cliff would not be easy. And whatever else might happen up here, she had no intention of killing either of these men—men, she knew, who were merely trying to defend their families.

She leaped to the side, grabbing the top of the fence—which groaned precariously and seemed as if it would tumble over the cliff with her—and scrambling fast to pull herself to the other side, before the second attacker's scimitar caught up to her. Now she was in the open. She thought that alone might provide her protection from the Behrenese, but this was a little-inhabited section of Palmaris, filled mostly with empty buildings. The south-erners were intent, it seemed, on protecting their secrecy and security. A third warrior came into view, darting behind a nearby building, and then she spotted another, coming from the other direction, the south, mov-ing cautiously but determinedly through the shadows at the base of the city wall.

Pony muttered a curse under her breath, her free hand going for her hidden pocket filled with the gemstones. She could get out of this predica-ment using those stones, she believed. She could call upon the hematite to possess one of the attackers, perhaps, and use the man as her mouthpiece to distract the others. Or she could take a more straightforward approach and use her graphite to issue a stunning lightning blast at the group closing around her, leaving her free to run away. Or malachite, perhaps, to levitate out of reach, to find the top of a building and run along the rooftops.

But using the stones carried its own risk, Pony knew, and she reminded herself that these men were not her enemies and that those she might attract by using the gemstones were.

She came to an alley a moment later, glancing back just long enough to see both attackers climbing over the fence. She muttered another curse and moved along cautiously, but she sensed that her flight was at its end, that still more warriors were all around her.

Two Behrenese stepped across the far exit of the alley; another pair blocked the one side exit. She heard a shuffle above her and yet another group, three this time, peered at her from the roof. Without a word, the four on the ground approached; one from the roof dropped lightly to the ground, barely ten feet behind her.

Pony's hand clutched the graphite. It would be so easy, she knew, and yet she understood, too, that she would be walking a fine line, that she would have to release enough energy to stun the men but not enough to kill them. She couldn't be sure.

"I am not your enemy," she started to say, but was cut short as the man behind her charged in suddenly, curved blade slashing.

Pony stepped outside the reach of the cut, then parried the blow downward banging the man's blade against the building wall. Then she turned and stepped forward, lifting her elbow to smack the man in the face twice. As he staggered back, Pony drove her knee against his elbow, pinning it and his weapon against the wall. A downward punch with Defender's pommel broke the man's grasp on his scimitar, the blade falling to the ground.

Still moving fluidly, Pony cupped the man's chin with her free hand and pulled his head back, sliding Defender into a killing position across his throat. She pulled the man so that his back was against the wall, his predicament clear to his companions. Pony eyed the approaching warriors, hoping, that the sight of their helpless companion would keep them at bay.

They did slow, for a moment, then began calling to one another in their own language. Then, obviously willing to let this comrade be sacrificed, they came on once more.

A thousand fears whirled through Pony's mind. Fears that she would have to kill these men. Fears for her unborn child—could she allow these warriors to kill her when Elbryan's child's life was also at stake? Fears that her only option seemed to be the gemstones, and that could bring a deeper darkness down upon them all—upon her and her innocent child and upon the innocent Behrenese, people simply trying to survive.

A long and confusing, horrible moment. In the end, with the approaching soldiers showing no signs of hesitating, Pony had to remind herself that these were not evil men.

She jumped back from her prisoner, glanced both ways, and threw her sword to the ground. "I am not your enemy," she stated firmly.

The man she had wounded on the cliff face called out something, and then Pony was tackled from above, taken down by a second soldier leaping from the rooftop. She hit the ground hard, all the breath blasting from her body, and managed to roll over just in time to see a scimitar descending toward her face.

Her last thoughts were for her unborn child.

❖ 18 ❖

Queen Vivian's Garden

The tall black-skinned man yelled angrily at King Danube as they came into view around the corner of a great flowering bush in the magnificent garden behind Ursal castle.

Not a good sign, Abbot Je'howith knew. The Behrenese ambassador must be outraged, and that outrage had to be justified for King Danube to accept such treatment.

"I will find a baron who despises your Church as much as I do," Duke Targon Bree Kalas promised, leaning over to whisper in the abbot's ear.

"And I will show you a God who will remind you of those words when your feeble mortal coil rots in the ground," the old abbot replied quietly.

Duke Kalas, so young and strong and full of life, only laughed at that notion, but if Je'howith's threats did little to unnerve young Kalas, the Duke's mocking did not ruffle the aged priest in the least. Je'howith looked at him with absolute calm, offering silent assurances to the man that he would learn better as the years passed by, as his bones began to ache with every coming storm and he found his breath harder to catch after a lawn game, a ride, or even a walk in the garden.

Kalas read the smug abbot's thoughts clearly, and his laughter abruptly stopped, smile turning into a frown. "Yes, a God," he said, "your God— the all-powerful being who could not save Queen Vivian. Or was it, perhaps, the failure of the frail vessel your God chose to utilize in that pitiful attempt?"

Now it was Je'howith's turn to frown, for Kalas' remarks cut quite deep, especially here in the garden Queen Vivian had designed, the garden that King Danube walked every morning in tribute to his lost wife. They had been so young and full of life then, the King and Queen of Honce-the-Bear. Danube had been barely into his twenties, dashing and strong, and Vivian but seventeen, a sweet and beautiful flower, with raven hair that hung to her waist, mysterious gray eyes that called to the souls of all who gazed into them, and skin as bright as the petals of the white roses climbing around the castle's garden door. All the kingdom loved them, and all the world seemed theirs.

But then Vivian had been touched by the sweating sickness, a swift, rare killer. On the morning of that fateful day nearly twenty years before, walking in this garden, she had complained of a headache. By noon, she had taken to her bed with a slight fever. And by supper, when Je'howith had at last arrived to relieve her discomfort, she was delirious, her pale body lathered in sweat. The abbot worked furiously at her bedside and called for the most powerful stone users of St. Honce to join him.

Queen Vivian had died before the other monks arrived.

King Danube had not blamed Je'howith; indeed he had thanked the old abbot repeatedly for his heroic efforts. In fact, many of the court advisers had remarked often about how gracious King Danube had been in those days following Vivian's death. But Je'howith, who had spent many hours with the couple and who had performed the ceremony of their marriage, had never been convinced that Danube's love for Vivian had run deep, despite these daily walks in the garden. More likely, the abbot thought, the walks were more for Danube's own pleasure than out of respect for the memory of his dead wife. The King and Queen had been happy together— outwardly blissful—but it was no secret that Danube had taken many lovers during their three years of marriage, which explained to many people how Constance Pemblebury, not of noble lineage, had risen to a position of official court adviser, and was rumored to be in line for the duchy of Entel when Duke Prescott, who had the profound misfortune of marrying six barren women—to hear him tell it—finally died.

It was rumored, and Je'howith knew that it was more than rumor, that Vivian, too, had found a bedside companion.

That man, Duke Targon Bree Kalas, had never been fond of the Abellican Church, but his sarcastic dismissals of anything Abellican had turned to open hatred toward the Church and particularly toward Je'howith the night Queen Vivian died.

"Enough of your personal feud," Constance Pemblebury commanded both of them, coming to stand between them. "Yatol Rahib Daibe himself has come to call on King Danube this morning, and his behavior this day is most disrespectful."

"A result of Palmaris," Targon Bree Kalas said, then pointedly added, "of the Church's mishandling of Palmaris."

"Enough!" Constance demanded. "You do not know that. And even if your suspicions prove true, your duty is to King Danube, to stand strong and united behind him against the Behrenese ambassador."

"Yes," Kalas agreed, eyes narrowing as he looked over at Je'howith. "One problem at a time."

The group quieted then, as Yatol Rahib Daibe stalked past, tossing them all a nasty glance, with a particularly vicious scowl aimed at the old abbot in his Abellican robes.

"Suspicions confirmed," Targon Bree Kalas muttered under his breath, and he turned to greet King Danube, who was walking toward them, shaking his head.

"Our friends of the southern kingdom are not pleased," the King informed the trio, "not at all."

"Because of the Church's actions in Palmaris," Kalas was happy to say.

"What is this persecution of the Behrenese?" King Danube asked Je'howith. "Are we at war with Behren, and if so, why was I not informed?"

"I know of no persecution," Je'howith replied, lowering his gaze respectfully.

"Now you do," King Danube loudly retorted. "It would seem that your new bishop is not fond of our dark-skinned southern neighbors and has begun a systematic persecution of them in Palmaris."

"They are not Abellican," Je'howith said, as if that was some excuse.

King Danube groaned. "But they are powerful," he replied. "Would you start a war with Behren because they are not Abellican?"

"Of course we desire no war with Behren," Je'howith said.

"Perhaps you are too stupid to understand that one action might lead to another," Targon Bree Kalas put in. "Perhaps—"

Constance Pemblebury grabbed the volatile Duke by the forearm and glowered at him so fiercely that he growled and then quieted, waving his arm dismissively at Je'howith, then stalking away.

"Behren would not go to war with us no matter the situation in Palmaris," Je'howith stated flatly. This was not the line of reasoning he wanted to take; he had no desire even to discuss the possibility that De'Unnero's rash actions might cause further trouble for the King. Even if the problems in Palmaris wouldn't lead to war, they could complicate other delicate matters.

King Danube had confided in Je'howith that he had issued a command to Duke Tetrafel, the duke of the Wilderlands. Normally, that was merely a decorative title, one of the many empty titles given to keep wealthy families happy and supportive of the Crown. But now King Danube had a plan. The King favored the strong pinto ponies of the To-gai tribesmen of western Behren. Once an independent kingdom, To-gai-ru had been conquered by the yatols a century before, and now all trade for the shaggy To-gai pintos had to go through the Chezru chieftain's court in Jacintha. Danube figured that if Tetrafel could somehow find a pass through the towering peaks of the western Belt-and-Buckle to the To-gai steppes, they could secretly work far better deals for the coveted horses.

Of course, such deals would involve substantial bribes to the ever-observant Yatol Rahib Daibe.

Still, Je'howith had to defend his Church, and remind the King that the Behrenese did not follow the same God. And he had to reassure the King that the Bishop's actions in Palmaris would lead to nothing serious, for a war with the fierce people of Behren could prove disastrous for Honce-the-Bear, especially coming so soon after the conflict with the minions of the demon dactyl.

"No, but they will likely make travel for our merchant ships difficult," King Danube replied.

"Yatol Daibe hinted at just that, wondering how our ships will fare against the numerous pirates running the coast of Behren without the Chezru chieftain's fleet protecting them. He also spoke of tariffs and other unpleasantness, including a moratorium on the trade in To-gai pintos. Has your Church gone to war against Honce-the-Bear's merchants, Abbot Je'howith? First the demands that the merchants return their gemstones— gemstones they paid your own Church dearly to acquire—and now this."

"What of the gemstones?" Targon Bree Kalas asked, returning, obviously concerned.

King Danube waved him away. "I fear that the trial has proven disastrous, Abbot Je'howith," he said.

"More time, my King," Je'howith replied, but his words seemed more like a courtesy than a heartfelt plea, as if Je'howith were speaking merely in his role in the Church and not from his true feelings. "The city is being brought under control, a necessary first step after so difficult a war."

King Danube shook his head. "Honce-the-Bear cannot afford to give more time to Bishop De'Unnero," he said.

Je'howith started to protest, but the King held up his hand and started back toward the rose-ringed door, Constance Pemblebury and Targon Bree Kalas falling in place behind him.

"A baron who despises the Church," the Duke whispered to Je'howith as he passed. "I promise." And it was no idle threat, Je'howith knew, for Palmaris fell within the boundaries of Kalas' duchy.

The sight of the old abbot sitting on the edge of the bed, his face drained of blood, his hands trembling, reassured Father Abbot Markwart, reminded him of the power of his aura. He was only a spiritual entity here in Ursal, and yet the insubstantial mist that was his spirit could evoke primal terror in one as aged and experienced as Abbot Je'howith.

What might the aura of the specter evoke in one who had not studied the history of the gemstones, one who could not bring forth the magic to any great effect? It was time for the King of Honce-the-Bear to learn the truth of power.

Through the walls went Markwart, following the directions Je'howith had given him. He passed unsuspecting soldiers with hardly a thought, then moved through the grand private chambers of the King, through the great audience hall and the private meeting rooms, through the private dining chamber and into King Danube's bedroom.

There lay the great man, fast asleep, alone in a bed that could have held five men comfortably. Such opulence did not offend Markwart; it only whetted his taste for greater riches. And they were within his reach now, he realized, as he moved a cold spectral hand to Danube's face and called softly to the King. The man stirred, grumbled something unintelligible, and tried to roll over.

But then, suddenly, the drawn face of Markwart was there, invading Danube's dreams, forcing its way into his consciousness. He came awake with a start, sitting up quickly, glancing all around, cold sweat beading his forehead.

"Who is there?" he asked.

Markwart concentrated, strengthened the magic to make his form clearer in the darkened room. "You do not know me, King Danube Brock Ursal," the Father Abbot said, his voice as solid and strong as if his corporeal form had been in the room. "But you know of me. I am Father Abbot Markwart of the Abellican Order."

"H-how can this be?" the King stammered. "How did you get past my guards?"

Markwart was laughing before the King finished the question. As he came more awake and more aware of the truth of this specter, King Danube, too, understood the absurdity of his words. He fell back then, sliding down, grabbing the thick comforter and pulling it up higher about him.

But this was not the kind of coldness a thick comforter could defeat.

"Why are you so surprised, my King?" Markwart asked calmly. "You have witnessed the miracles of the gemstones. You are aware of their potential. Does it surprise you that I, the leader of the Church, can make such contact?"

"I have not heard of such a thing," the shaken King replied. "If you wished an audience, Abbot Je'howith could have arranged—"

"I have no time for such useless propriety," Markwart interrupted. "I wished an audience, and so I am here."

The King started to protest, speaking of protocol and courtesy, and when the spirit of Markwart remained unimpressed, he tried a different tack, threatening to call the guards.

Markwart laughed at him. "But I am not here, my King," he said. "Only in spirit have I come to you, and all the weapons of Ursal could not harm that which you see before you."

The King mustered his nerve then, and snarled at Markwart, throwing off the comforter, getting out of bed, and moving determinedly for the door. "Let us see," he stated firmly.

Out reached the specter's arm, and out went Markwart's thoughts, a barrage of commands insinuating themselves into Danube Brock Ursal's mind, compelling him to return to the bed. The man struggled, trembling as he determinedly took another step toward the door.

Markwart's spectral hand reached out for him more powerfully and clenched in the empty air. The command "Return!" pounded in Danube's head. Now his progress stopped, though he continued struggling against the tangible will of the Father Abbot. And then he took a step back and then another, and he turned and staggered to the side of the bed, falling over it.

"I warn you," he gasped.

"No, my King, I am the one who issues a warning," Markwart explained, his tone deadly calm and even. "The arrangement in Palmaris goes quite well. Bishop De'Unnero's work has been wondrous and the city is functioning more efficiently than even before the war. Whatever threats the Behrenese might spout, whatever the complaints of foolish merchants, the course of Palmaris has been determined. You will do nothing now to jeopardize that.

"And indeed, my King," Markwart went on, changing his tone again to one of quiet obedience, "I beg you to meet me in Palmaris that you might learn the truth of the place, rather than listen to the ridiculous rumors uttered by those seeking to gain favor."

King Danube stubbornly rolled back off the bed, to his feet, and turned to face the Father Abbot, determined to assert his rulership here. But when he turned, he found the room empty, the specter of Markwart gone. He glanced all around, even ran about the room in a frantic search, but could find no trace that the Father Abbot had ever been there. Had the Father Abbot really been there?

He tried to tell himself it had all been a dream. After all, the situation in Palmaris had been troubling him deeply when he had gone to sleep that night.

The King slid back onto his bed and eased himself under the thick comforter. But the ghastly feeling of Markwart invading his thoughts was impossible to ascribe to a dream, and it was a long time before King Danube dared to close his eyes and let sleep take him.

Markwart walked out of his summoning room, exhausted but satisfied. He had planned to go next to De'Unnero, to warn the man again to slow down. He would go to Palmaris, as would the King, and it was important that Danube saw the city in good spirits.

Or was it? Recalling the words of that inner voice, that the sun shone all the brighter after the dark of night, Markwart was no longer certain of that. Perhaps he should goad De'Unnero to an even darker place, let the man clench his fist tight, and then let him have his desire to go rushing out after Nightbird and Pony.

Then he, the shining sun, would have so much more to rescue!

Markwart climbed slowly into his own bed and rolled over with a groan. His journey to contact so fully a man not possessing a soul stone, and thus not reciprocating the contact, and one who was not even well-trained in any use of stone magic or mental meditation, had cost him great amounts of energy. He realized that he could not go to De'Unnero now even if he so desired. But no matter, the Father Abbot decided. Given the measure of terror he had exacted upon King Danube, such a step was no longer necessary. The King would not dare oppose him, no matter the situation in Palmaris.

King Danube held his daily audience with his three primary advisers, secular and religious, in the small east garden of Castle Ursal that next sunny morning. This garden was sited below the castle on the high cliff wall overlooking the great city and was backed by the castle wall and surrounded by its own lower wall, secure because it had been built at the steepest face of the two-hundred-foot cliff.

Abbot Je'howith shifted uneasily from foot to foot, swaying as he stared at the impressive city below, and carefully did not glance at Targon Bree Kalas. The Duke appeared very smug this morning, convinced that he had at last settled the fight with Je'howith, and despite the visit the previous night from the Father Abbot, Je'howith wasn't sure that the Duke's confidence was misplaced. Danube hadn't yet arrived, and Je'howith feared what might happen when he did.

"So the war continued a bit longer than we had anticipated," Kalas was saying to Constance Pemblebury. "How were we to know that our enemies would come from within?"

"You exaggerate, my friend," the calm woman replied. "No war, but merely a dispute between great leaders."

Kalas snorted at the thought. "If we let the fool De'Unnero continue his policies in Palmaris, then we will know real war again, and soon, do not doubt," he declared. "By Yatol Rahib Daibe's own words."

"Words you interpret to suit your own needs, Duke Kalas," Je'howith dared to say, had to say, turning to look directly at the man.

"I foresee the logical implications," Kalas started to protest, but his ire washed away as the castle door creaked open and King Danube strode out into the garden, accompanied by a pair of soldiers. He took his seat at the shaded garden table and waited for the other three to join him.

"We must consider carefully the works of Bishop De'Unnero," he said bluntly, getting right to the point. "The transition in Palmaris is not without pitfalls."

"I have a list of candidates drawn for you, my King," Duke Kalas said, "each with his own strengths and advantages."

"A list?" King Danube seemed genuinely surprised.

"Candidates to assume the barony," Kalas explained.

King Danube seemed more annoyed than intrigued, something that confused Kalas and Constance but not Je'howith, who began wondering just what might have occurred after Markwart had left his chambers.

"Premature," King Danube decreed, waving his hand, ending any debate before stubborn Kalas could even begin. "No, we must first more honestly assess the work that Bishop De'Unnero has done."

"Y-you have heard the reports," Kalas stammered.

"I have heard what others have been saying," Danube replied coldly. "Others who no doubt have their own agendas concerning Palmaris. No, this matter is too important. I will go to Palmaris personally to assess the situation.

"And only then," the King said sharply, cutting off Kalas' forthcoming protest, "and only if I am not satisfied, will I consider any talk of potential replacements."

Kalas sputtered and simply turned away; the King's decision went completely against what Danube had decreed only the morning before.

But he was the king, after all, and he could change his mind on a whim, if the fate of the whole kingdom weighed in the balance.

Or, Je'howith understood, though the other two advisers did not, Father Abbot Markwart could change his mind for him.

❖ 19 ❖

Allies of Choice and Necessity

Elbryan sat astride Symphony at the edge of a tree line at the top slope of a wide field. He shaded his eyes from the grayish glare. A severe winter storm had hit the night before, blowing winds drifting the snow in places so that it stood higher than a tall man. The folk of Dundalis had fared well, though, since they had constructed an appropriate shelter; thankfully, the place had stood under the tremendous weight of the snow and the power of the wind.

But now they had another problem, as Elbryan and Bradwarden had discovered the day before, right before the storm had broken. Many goblins were in the area, living in the ruins of Weedy Meadow, only a day's march to the west.

"Glad I will be when Lady Dasslerond and the elves make their appearance," the ranger remarked. He could still hardly believe that a troop of so many elves—Roger had put their number at more than a dozen—would be operating in the area without contacting him.

"Ye never can tell about them little folk," Bradwarden replied. "Could be in a tree right above us, and the best-trained human'd never know it."

The ranger turned a sidelong glance at the centaur, recognizing a strange expression there, and then, at last picking up the cue, he did look up. There, perched upon a branch some twenty feet above his head, was the unmistakable winged form of an elf.

"Greetings, ranger. Far too long has it been since we have shared a song," the elf called down.

"Ni'estiel!" Elbryan called back up, recognizing the voice, though he could still make out little more than a silhouette against the somewhat brighter gray sky, and through the flakes that still drifted down. "Where is your lady, and Juraviel, and all the rest?"

"About," Ni'estiel lied. "I have come to tell you that the goblins are on the move."

"Which way?" the ranger asked. "Further west, to End-o'-the-World, perhaps? Or to the east?"

The elf shrugged. "They are not where they were, that is all I—we, have been able to discern thus far."

"Roger's out scoutin'," Bradwarden reminded, sounding somewhat concerned for their friend.

The ranger shared that concern; Roger was a cunning scout, adept at hiding, adept at running. But a deep snow could neutralize many of those abilities, could make him much easier to spot and much easier to catch.

"And another force is on the move," Ni'estiel called from above, "closing on this very position from the south."

The ranger started to ask the elf to elaborate, but the elf skittered off, rushing along the branches, then fluttering to another tree and running on.

"Now who are ye supposin' that might be?" Bradwarden asked.

It was all too much to digest for them both. Elbryan kicked Symphony into a trot along the wind-cleared ridgeline, then plowed down through the snow, working the horse hard to get to another ridge not far away that commanded a better view of the southern trails. As soon as he and Bradwarden arrived up there, they spotted the force, a group of soldiers, their glittering helms and spear tips marking them obviously as Kingsmen. They moved slowly through the snow, an obviously weary and battered group.

"Out in the storm last night," Bradwarden remarked. "Oh, but I'm bettin' they're in a fine mood this day!"

The ranger smiled and chuckled, but then his grin went away, replaced by intrigue as the band moved closer. "Shamus Kilronney!" Elbryan said happily. "I recognize the posture of the rider and the gait of his horse. It is Shamus at the head of the soldiers."

"Oh, but blessed by the gods must we be," Bradwarden mumbled sarcastically under his breath, though certainly loud enough for Elbryan to hear.

"A good man," the ranger replied.

"And a man who might be lookin' for yer new monk friends," Bradwarden reminded.

That took the smile from Elbryan's face, but for just a minute. Shamus and his soldiers would certainly prove to be of great assistance fighting the large goblin band they had found at Weedy Meadow.

"He would not come hunting them," Elbryan said at length. "Or even if he has, we will discover that truth soon enough and easily slip the monks away into the forest."

"I'll be lookin' forward to their company," Bradwarden said dryly, and then Elbryan understood that the centaur's dour mood had little to do with the plight of the five monks. Bradwarden had come into plain view of late, and was known and accepted without question by all the folk following Tomas Gingerwart. It would be harder, much harder, to explain the centaur to the King's soldiers, men who were probably, at least peripherally, allied with the Abellican Church. It wasn't that Bradwarden cared much for the company of humans anyway, with the possible exceptions of Elbryan and Pony, but he had long ago grown tired of having to hide from them.

"They'll be seein' us soon," the centaur remarked, "so I'll be takin' me leave." He kicked the ground and swung his great body toward the deeper woods.

"Shamus is a good man," Elbryan said before he had taken a single step away.

Bradwarden stopped and looked back over his broad shoulder at his friend, looked into those honest green eyes.

"He will accept you and not judge you," the ranger declared.

"Ye'd be a fool to tell him," replied the centaur, "for then ye'd mark yerself as me rescuer. Pick yer own fights with the Church, boy, but I've no desire to see the inside o' St.-Mere-Abelle again."

Elbryan had no practical response to that.

"So go and make yer plans for the goblins," Bradwarden continued, "but be quick if ye're lookin' to kill any yerself. I'm on me own huntin' again, and got a bellyache for goblin meat." He gave a hearty laugh then and walked away into the shadows.

Most of all, Elbryan heard the hollow resonance of that laugh. Bradwarden had aptly been named the forest ghost by the original settlers of Dundalis; and until Nightbird had returned, elven trained, to the region, the centaur had been a solitary figure. But Bradwarden had come to enjoy the company of Elbryan and the others over the past months; that much was obvious to the ranger more from the sound of that laugh than from the centaur's original dour mood at the sight of Shamus and the soldiers.

Elbryan sighed and urged Symphony into a trot along the ridge, moving to intercept his Kingsman friend. It would be good fighting beside Shamus and the well-trained soldiers again, though better still would it be if the situation was not so complicated.

Pony awoke in darkness and started to rise, only to slam her head against unyielding wood barely two inches above. In the stifling darkness, a surprised and panicked Pony reached up, hands striking wood, hard and solid, and finding no handle.

A scream welled in her throat; she kicked up and bruised both knee and toe.

And the wood seemed to close down on her.

She was shut in, locked, buried alive. Desperately she reached for her pouch, but the gemstones had been taken from her, and her weapon was gone. Just this, in a coffin, in the darkness.

Pony punched hard against the wood and yelled out as loudly as she could. Ignoring the pain, she punched again and again, and kicked and clawed. Maybe she would break through and the dirt would pour in on her, suffocating her, crushing her, but better that attempt at freedom, over a slow, lingering death. She screamed again, though she realized that she could hardly expect to be heard.

But then . . . a reply. And not from above, but from the side. And suddenly she was not in darkness anymore but bathed in the soft glow of a lantern—a lantern held in the doorway of the cabin. A cabin! And she lay not in a coffin, but in a bunk bed, in the top berth with her face close to the ceiling.

Pony closed her eyes and breathed deeply, relief flooding through her. She recognized then that she was in the hold of a ship, could tell from the slight swaying movement that the river, and not hard earth, was below.

Pony turned her attention to the man, a man she knew, a man who had once given her, Elbryan, Bradwarden, and Juraviel passage across the river with no questions asked.

"Captain Al'u'met," she remarked. "It seems that fate has brought us together once more."

Al'u'met looked at her curiously for just a moment, then recognition sparked in his dark eyes. "The friend of Jojonah," he said quietly, calmly. "Ah, but that alone explains so much."

"I am no enemy of the Behrenese," Pony stated bluntly, "nor any friend of the Abellican Church."

"Or of the city, then, since they, Church and city, are now one and the same."

Pony nodded carefully—for her body ached from the beating she had received—slid her feet to the side, and extricated herself from the bunk, coming down shakily to the floor. Al'u'met was by her side in an instant, supporting her with his strong arm.

"You speak ill of the union," Pony noted, "yet you are a friend of Master Jojonah of the Abellican Order."

Al'u'met's smile only somewhat hid a wince, and Pony figured that he had seen her ruse for what it was. Only as Al'u'met replied did she realize that there was something much more terrible than that bothering the man.

"Jojonah did not approve of this Church," he said confidently.

Pony started to nod, but Al'u'met's use of tense suddenly intrigued her. Had Jojonah changed heart?

"I met him only once," Al'u'met explained, moving to the side and hooking the lantern on a peg, "on a passage up the Masur Delaval to Amvoy, his return to St.-Mere-Abelle. He told me then to remember the name of Avelyn Desbris, and so I have, and now that I have heard that name openly blasphemed in the Church of Palmaris, I have come to understand Jojonah's concern. He cared for Avelyn deeply, I understand, and fears for the man's legacy."

Again the past tense with reference to Jojonah, and Pony's expression reflected her growing fear.

"Master Jojonah was executed as a heretic," Al'u'met explained, "for conspiring with intruders who stole away the Father Abbot's most precious prisoner, a centaur said to have witnessed the destruction of Mount Aida and the demon dactyl."

Two steps back and Pony sat on the edge of the lower bunk.

"Might you know anything of such a conspiracy?" Al'u'met asked coyly.

A glare came back at him, Pony not appreciating the sentiment.

Al'u'met offered a bow in return. "You confuse guilt with grief," he observed.

"You saw my companions when we crossed the river."

"I did indeed," said the captain, "and I hold no doubt that the conspiracy claim against Jojonah was true enough. As for the charge of heresy . . ."

"Jojonah was more attuned to the truth and goodness of the Church than any man I ever knew," Pony asserted, "except for Brother Avelyn Desbris."

A second bow from Al'u'met came back to her in response. "What, then, of the centaur?"

Pony studied him carefully for a moment, trying to gauge his sincerity. Was he, perhaps, an agent of the Church? As soon as she remembered the circumstances of her capture, she recognized that as improbable. Al'u'met and his dark-skinned southern brethren were obviously not her enemies.

"Bradwarden runs free in the northland," she said frankly, showing her confidence in the man in offering both the information and the centaur's name, "a fitting reward for a hero."

"And he was at Mount Aida, at the reputed end of the dactyl?"

"More than reputed," Pony replied with a chuckle. She ran one hand through her thick blond mane, shaking away the last of her grogginess. "I was there when Brother Avelyn destroyed the demon and its home, as was my human companion on the journey with you across the Masur Delaval." She hesitated as she spoke, wondering if she might be giving too much away, but then decided, on pure instinct, that too much was at stake and that time was of the essence. If she was to take any stand against Bishop De'Unnero, then this man would have to be involved, she realized. "We thought Bradwarden had given his life to save us, and yet, by a stroke of good fortune and elvish magic, he did survive, only to be brought to the dungeons of St.-Mere-Abelle as a prisoner."

"Because the Father Abbot did not believe his story of the demon dactyl?"

"Because the Father Abbot fears the truth of Avelyn Desbris," Pony corrected.

Al'u'met pondered the profound words and their implications for a moment, then moved to sit beside Pony on the bed. "Thus was poor Jojonah convicted and removed," he remarked.

"And thus was De'Unnero inserted as bishop of Palmaris," Pony replied. She stared intently at him as she added, "And what are we two to do about that?"

Al'u'met's determined smile told her that he was thinking along the same lines as she.

He handed over her pouch of sacred gemstones.

From the gloom under thick boughs, Bradwarden watched Elbryan guide Symphony down to the group. The soldiers were well trained, the centaur saw, for at the sound of an approaching horse, they moved immediately into a defensive position. That formation fell apart when they recognized the rider, and the centaur watched as Elbryan moved right up beside the leader—Shamus Kilronney indeed—and exchanged a warm handshake and a pat on the shoulder.

The centaur narrowed his eyes and grumbled out a few quiet curses. He had a bad feeling about this soldier's return, but was willing to tell himself that it was just his own anger at being once more relegated to the shadows.

Thus, with a frustrated grumble, the centaur turned to go.

He was not alone; he knew that immediately. Something crept at him through the brush, deep down, brushing through the snow. Bradwarden quickly assessed the direction of the approach and the distance, and measured that against the visibility in the gloomy forest.

He turned back then, and moved his telltale humanlike torso behind a tree, so that the part left visible to the newcomer would seem only the hindquarters of a horse.

"Ack, ye little horsie," came a grating goblin's voice. "Get me some food afore we're pickin' at the bones o' the men."

Bradwarden restrained the urge to turn and run the thing down, waited patiently, and let the goblin come to him.

"Now don't be movin' so I kills ye quick," the goblin said quietly, standing right beside the centaur.

How its eyes widened when Bradwarden stepped back, revealing the truth! So frightened, so caught off guard, was the creature, that it threw its spear—just a sharpened stick, really—to the ground. How it scrambled and tried to run away, but the centaur caught it by the throat and held it fast while his other hand came up with his heavy cudgel.

Up, up, and then down right on top of the squirming goblin's head. Only Bradwarden's strong grasp held the dead thing upright.

"So ye came outta yer holes," the centaur said quietly, surprised, for, since the war had become a rout, few monsters had shown any initiative toward starting any fights, with most looking only to run as far away as fast as possible. Ni'estiel's warning that the goblins were on the move only made him think that they had heard of the human settlement and had decided to run the other way, to the west and the farthest of the towns. When he thought it over for a few moments, Bradwarden saw that the eastward march made sense. This goblin and its kin had become entrenched in Weedy Meadow enough to recover their wits. The powries and giants were probably long gone, so the goblins had likely consolidated their ranks around a single leader, or a couple of strong figures.

And now winter had come on, and the goblins thought to sneak in on the unsuspecting humans and hit at them hard, perhaps to steal some needed supplies.

The centaur stood very still, all his senses tuning to the forest about him. Gradually, he made out the telltale sounds of the monsters on the move: a soft rustle here, the snap of a twig there. Yes, they had come from Weedy Meadow, heading east, back toward Dundalis, obviously spoiling for a fight with the new settlers.

And now, like the elves, like Elbryan and him, they had spotted the approaching soldiers.

The centaur glanced back over his shoulder; if his guess concerning goblin numbers in Weedy Meadow was correct, then Elbryan and the soldiers were in for an unpleasant morning.

"Dundalis has been reclaimed," Elbryan said to Shamus Kilronney as soon as they had completed the pleasantries. The ranger recognized all of Shamus' soldiers, as they recognized him, so no introductions were necessary. "You can soon report to your king that the Timberlands are secured."

"My king?" Shamus replied, his tone light but with a hint of something deeper behind the question. "Is Danube Brock Ursal not Nightbird's king as well?"

It was the first time that question had ever been put to the ranger, and frankly, he had no idea how to respond. "My roots trace to Honce-the-Bear," he admitted, carefully weighing the reactions of Shamus' men to his every word. "Yet I was born and have lived all my life outside of King Danube's domain."

He paused then, considering carefully how he felt about the issue. Was he indeed a citizen of Honce-the-Bear, or . . . or what? he mused. A homeless rogue? Hardly. But he had never considered Danube his king, nor, for that matter, Lady Dasslerond his queen. He gave a helpless shrug then, his expression perplexed. "However you may define the matter, it would seem that King Danube and I are on the same side in this conflict," he added with a chuckle, and Shamus joined in, though the ranger did not miss the fact that the man's laugh seemed a bit strained.

"And what of the present?" the captain asked a moment later. "Dundalis has been reclaimed, but there is another town, is there not?"

"Two others," Elbryan corrected. "Weedy Meadow, at present, is in the hands of a goblin band, a fairly strong contingent, we believe, but End-o'-the-World, the third and westernmost town, as far as we know, remains deserted."

As if on cue, a huge arrow thudded into the ground between the two riders, and both horses twitched and nickered. The soldiers went into a frenzy, calling "To arms!" and "Draw blades!" repeatedly and fighting to turn their horses into a defensive line.

And not a moment too soon, for before the formation was even properly prepared, the goblin charge came on, dozens of the wicked creatures appearing as if from out of the insubstantial mist, screaming and cursing and throwing their spears, running headlong at the group with an aggressiveness Elbryan had not witnessed since he and Pony, on their way to St.-Mere-Abelle, had happened upon a seemingly helpless merchant caravan east of the Masur Delaval.

Before Kilronney's soldiers were even set, one man went down under the weight of two spears, and another lost his horse, the poor creature hit several times. Another soldier took a grazing hit, and Nightbird missed catching a spear in the face only because he managed to get Tempest at a perfect angle to deflect the missile—at the very last moment!

Shamus Kilronney recognized that his most advantageous move would have been a thunderous charge, rolling over the weakest section of the goblin circle. But they had not the time to gain any momentum through the deep snow, for the goblins were among their ranks almost before they had recovered from the unexpected volley.

Nightbird urged Symphony into a short burst, the powerful stallion burying the closest goblin under pounding hooves, the ranger slashing down another as he rushed past. Shamus almost cried out in protest, fearing that the ranger was fleeing the fight, but as soon as he cleared that initial line, Nightbird turned Symphony around, scanning to see where he would best fit in.

Shamus was relieved and admitted to himself that his fear was more the result of De'Unnero's warnings about the ranger than any actions Nightbird had ever personally shown to him. No time to analyze now, the captain reminded himself—and a prodding goblin spear pointedly reminded him! He batted the spear aside and leaned to strike, but he had to retract his sword to parry the swing of a spiked club. Catching it successfully between two of the spikes, Shamus turned it aside, but then realized he had a problem: the goblin's subsequent pivot prevented him from easily extracting his blade and left him open to the returning thrust of the first monster's spear.

Shamus yelled aloud and closed his eyes, and . . .

Nothing.

Shamus' eyes popped open to see the goblin crumble down under the blow of another soldier's sword, the shining blade creasing the goblin's head and spraying crimson blood all over the snow. For that soldier, though, the move proved disastrous, as a pair of goblins leaped from the side, catching him in their grabbing hands and pulling him from his saddle.

Shamus pulled free his sword and leaped his horse past the club-wielding goblin. The creature smacked the horse hard on the rump as it passed, drawing a deep gash, but the wounded animal responded with a solid kick to the goblin's chest that sent it flying to the ground.

Shamus tried desperately to get to his rescuer, but the goblin horde was thick about them then and the captain had all he could do to keep the grabbing hands and swinging weapons at bay.

Symphony's hooves dug deep ruts in the snow as the ranger masterfully turned the horse. He spotted one soldier in trouble immediately and started that way, but pulled up before Symphony had taken a single stride, and wincing, turned to find another.

The soldier, skewered through the chest by a goblin spear, tumbled to the ground.

Another man was on the ground, having lost his mount in the initial spear volley. In rushed the ranger, Tempest slashing, driving back the goblins with mighty strokes. He threw his leg over Symphony's back and leaped to the ground in a run, using the turquoise gemstone set in Symphony's chest, the telepathic link to the magnificent stallion, to guide the horse.

A goblin tried to whip its club across, but Nightbird was already too close. He jammed his forearm into the goblin's arms, holding them at bay before the swing had truly begun, then bowled the creature over, stabbing once, to keep it down.

Then he was standing over the soldier, Tempest working in a blur to fend off the attacks of three goblins. Left and right went the blade, picking off a thrusting spear and a slashing sword. The ranger dug in one foot and wheeled about, Tempest coming across just in time to deflect the sharp tip from yet another stabbing spear.

Nightbird thought to go forward, to finish the suddenly unarmed goblin, and he even started that way—but only as a ruse to the two behind.

He spun back and sidestepped, free hand grabbing the shaft of the spear as it stabbed past, turning the weapon harmlessly outward as he stepped forward. Tempest circled, tip down, before the ranger, catching the goblin's sword slash under the blade, lifting it high over the goblin's head, and then sliding behind it to push it away. A deft twist of the ranger's wrist brought Tempest's tip down and in line, and he advanced; the sudden thrust of *bi'nelle dasada*, and the goblin fell back with a shriek, clutching its torn chest.

On came Nightbird, pulling the spear, goblin still attached. The stubborn goblin wouldn't let go, still had both hands tugging at it, when Tempest came slashing across its face.

The ranger turned fast and breathed a bit easier to find the soldier standing once more, finishing off the goblin with the broken spear.

But other monsters were all around and came happily at the two humans who were not on horseback.

Symphony rushed in to help Nightbird, who caught the saddle and pulled himself astride in one fluid move, then reached down and caught the hand of the soldier, pulling him up right behind.

The goblins, surprised, skidded to a stop, but Nightbird paid them no heed. They went by fast, and the soldier leaped from Symphony's back onto his own horse, struggling into the saddle while Nightbird kept the goblins busy.

Then the ranger turned back to the general melee and saw that Shamus' men were gaining even footing against the ambushers. Hope soared, and then died as the ranger spotted a pair of goblins standing at the side, spears in hand and with several more lying on the ground at their feet. Symphony leaped toward them, but one goblin lifted its arm to throw at a soldier battling furiously, his back to the creature, and Nightbird realized he couldn't get there in time!

He shouted, trying to draw the goblin's throw his way.

The goblin went flying away suddenly. The ranger nearly broke Symphony's stride, pulling up in his stirrups in startlement, but he was back low again in an instant, head down and yelling, forcing the remaining goblin to concentrate on him.

The creature turned, trying desperately to flee, even as it tried to throw. The spear flew far wide of the mark, not even slowing the ranger, who dispatched the vulnerable creature with a brutal slash as Symphony ran by.

Only then did he notice that the goblin had been wounded, a small arrow protruding from its lower back. Now his hopes soared; if Lady Dasslerond and the elves had arrived, the fight would soon be a rout!

Again the horse's hooves dug in deeply, Symphony pivoting back toward the battle. Nightbird smiled as he passed the first dead spear thrower, a very large arrow driven through its side.

With only a glance up at the tree line, one that didn't show him Bradwarden or any of the elves, Nightbird focused on Shamus Kilronney, guiding Symphony through the thickest tangle of goblins to get to his friend's side.

Blood covered the captain, but to Nightbird's relief it was much more the blood of his enemies than his own.

"The day is ours!" Shamus cried, urging his horse ahead, bowling down one goblin and knocking another off balance.

Tempest took that stunned creature on the side of the head, flipping it head over heels to the now-bloody snow.

"The day is ours!" Shamus cried again, more loudly, lifting his sword so that his men would rally about him.

And, indeed, the tide had turned against the goblins, the better-armed, better-trained horsemen gaining a stronger advantage with each passing second.

Another goblin went down under a flurry of swords and trampling hooves, and another ran off, screaming, their cries of terror helping drain even more of the morale of the faltering goblin horde. To the ranger's delight, that running creature staggered once, then again, then yet again, as three elvish arrows laid it low.

Nightbird charged back into the fray, Symphony bowling a goblin to the ground, the ranger working Tempest furiously, batting aside a weak club attack, then slashing down a second time to crease the goblin's face. Then over the other way went the blade, slashing down at a goblin battling another rider. The blade missed as the goblin shrieked and dodged, but its desperate move left the monster off balance, a situation Nightbird was quick to exploit as Symphony continued past, stabbing straight and sure through the goblin's shoulder, dropping it writhing to the ground, an easy finish for the other mounted soldier.

The fight ended as abruptly as it had begun. The remaining goblins broke ranks and scattered back into the mist and the forest. Several soldiers briefly gave chase, ensuring that the creatures would not come back, but most, including the ranger, dismounted quietly and ran to their fallen companions.

Nightbird figured that the goblins would all be dead in a matter of moments anyway; Bradwarden and more than a dozen elves were nearby in the forest.

Shamus Kilronney sat astride his horse, fixated by the image of Jierdan and Tymoth Thayer, brothers who had served with him through all the war. Jierdan, covered in blood, much of it his own, knelt beside his prostrate brother, working furiously to hold a wound closed. But the tear across half the man's belly was too big, and blood and guts and gore spilled out around Jierdan's hands. He cried out for his brother repeatedly, fought with the wound a bit longer, then threw his head back and screamed helplessly. Gasping for air, Jierdan fell back over Tymoth, cradling his head, putting his face close to his brother's as if to breathe life back into him. "Don't ye die," he said over and over, rocking back and forth. "Don't ye die!"

Rage boiled through Shamus. He glanced all about, seeking some outlet.

"Ride to town and find a man named Braumin Herde," he heard Nightbird say, and only after the ranger repeated himself did Shamus realize that he was speaking to him. By that point, the captain had found a focus for his rage, a pair of goblins scrambling up the ridgeline and into the trees. Shamus dug his heels in hard and his horse leaped away.

"Shamus!" Nightbird called after him, but it was obviously futile, for the captain didn't even look back. The ranger instructed another man to go and find Braumin, then he ran back to Symphony and took up pursuit of his friend.

Shamus crashed into the treeline, shoving away branches, ignoring the scratches and prodding his horse forward. He couldn't see the goblins any longer, but knew they were still running—in a straight line away from the fight. The brush thickened about his mount; the horse resisted a push through a tangle of pine branches, so Shamus jumped down and, sword leading, charged on. He came to the edge of a narrow ravine, ten feet down—unless the snow was deeper than it appeared—and perhaps twice that across, with sides so steep that they did not hold much snow.

A single, new trail led down through the snow, so down the captain charged, stumbling, falling, but scrambling back to all fours and scaling the other side. He tripped over a stump just past the far lip of the ravine, but continued his wild scramble on hands and knees, hands and feet, then up again in a run, ignoring the bloody cuts on the knuckles of his sword hand and the cold numbness of his fingers. Another pine grove loomed before him. He put his head down and charged, meaning to go right through.

But then he heard a groan and the sharp crack of bone, and he went ahead cautiously, pulling the branches aside, peering into the gloom.

A goblin flew through the air and smashed into a tree. Shamus' eyes widened when he looked back the other way and made out the huge form of a centaur, one hand clasped tightly around a goblin's throat, bending the creature backward, while the other hand, holding a huge cudgel, was raised above the centaur's head.

Shamus winced as that club descended in a sudden, savage attack, and the goblin's skull shattered. With what seemed to be no more than the flick of his wrist, the centaur sent this monster, too, flying away. The centaur then picked up a huge bow—the largest bow Shamus had ever seen, and one that explained the enormous arrow that had come as a prelude to the goblin attack—and trotted off into the forest the opposite way, never looking back.

A hand grasped Shamus' shoulder and he, so unnerved by the sight of the centaur, nearly jumped out of his boots. He spun to find Nightbird standing beside him, Hawkwing in hand.

"There is another enemy in the forest," Shamus declared.

"Many, likely," replied the ranger, "for the goblins have scattered. Let them run, my friend. If they remain in the area, we will find them soon enough, though it seems far more likely to me that those who survive will run all the way back to their dark holes in the mountains."

"Another enemy," the captain said more forcefully, drawing a curious look from Elbryan, "a larger foe, and one more dangerous by far."

"Giant?"

"Centaur," said Shamus, his eyes narrowing.

That set the ranger back on his heels. He looked past the captain and noted the closest dead goblin. Shamus had seen Bradwarden, and the secret hadn't even lasted until the soldiers had entered Dundalis.

"No enemy," Elbryan corrected, his voice firm.

"There is talk of a centaur outlaw," Shamus said, "one who is reported to have come to this region. Few centaurs, I would guess, survive in this age."

Elbryan and Shamus stared hard at each other for a long time. The ranger understood that he was making a stand here that could destroy his friendship with the captain, that indeed could bring the two to blows, and mark him more clearly as an outlaw. But he also understood that he was standing up for Bradwarden, so unjustly accused, Bradwarden, whom he numbered among his most trusted, dearest friends.

"One and the same," he said, jaw set firm, growling the words. "The centaur you have seen is Bradwarden, who was taken to St.-Mere-Abelle unjustly. The centaur who fired the arrow into our midst to warn us of the attack was that same Bradwarden who is rumored to be an enemy of the Abellican Church."

"His actions against a goblin band, a common enemy, do not excuse—" Shamus began.

"I have wounded to tend," Elbryan interrupted, and he turned and walked away.

Shamus Kilronney stood among the trees for a long while, considering all that he had seen. He was an officer of the King, and an officer of the Bishop, and certainly not empowered to judge the justice or injustice afforded this centaur.

The captain closed his eyes and remembered De'Unnero's instructions and warning. Certainly the mere presence of Bradwarden in this region, and the fact that he was obviously a friend of Elbryan, gave credence to the Bishop's words.

This warrior, Nightbird, this man he had known as ally and friend, was indeed the outlaw who had invaded St.-Mere-Abelle.

By the time Elbryan came back over the ridge, the fighting was finished, and all wounded goblins had been put to the sword. Now the soldiers were tending their own wounds, and the ranger had to pause and draw a deep breath when he saw three bodies covered by cloaks.

Many more goblin dead littered the field, he realized. Though this was not the first time Elbryan had seen men fighting beside him die, the cost of this battle had been too high, by his estimate, and would have likely been far higher had not Bradwarden given them a few extra seconds of warning.

But where were the elves? Elbryan wondered. In searching the battle-field, he found only a couple of goblins who had been wounded by elvish arrows. More than a score of monsters had ambushed them, but Dasslerond's band, if it was as large as Roger had insisted, could have cut that number down before the first of the goblins got near the riders.

It made no sense, nor did Elbryan understand why the elves—the finest scouts in the world, creatures who knew the ways and sounds of the forest better than any, centaur and ranger included—had not given more of a warning.

Still, Elbryan blamed himself; he had known about the goblin encamp-ment, but had not believed these creatures would attack them, even after Ni'estiel's warning that the goblins were on the move. Thus, he and the newly arrived soldiers had been taken by surprise.

And they had paid a heavy price.

A short while later, Roger Lockless, Braumin Herde, and the other monks came running down the road with the rider the ranger had dispatched.

A fourth man had died by then.

❖ 20 ❖

Regrets

"**B**ut you are not thinking clearly, girl," Belster said, more loudly than he had intended. He put his finger over his pursed lips and glanced all around nervously. The Way was crowded and noisy this night, and apparently no one had heard.

Pony leaned heavily on the bar, twiddling her thumbs impatiently.

"How many of these folks do you think will join with the dark skins?" Belster asked earnestly, using the common synonym for the Behrenese.

"Of course," Pony replied sarcastically, "we are in a secure enough position to ignore possible allies. The odds are so overwhelmingly in our favor already, after all."

"You know what I am saying," Belster grumbled back. "The Behrenese are not—have never been—loved by the folk of Palmaris. In that above all else, Bishop De'Unnero has plotted well. Not hard to make of them an enemy, and now you are coming along and saying that we might fight beside them. No, a mistake, I say. We shall lose more allies than we gain if you follow this path beside this Captain Almet."

"Al'u'met," Pony corrected. "As honorable a man as I've ever met."

"His skin color alone will stop many folk from seeing that."

"Then they are misguided," Pony insisted, and then she looked questioningly at Belster. "Is this what you truly fear, or are you also unreasonably prejudiced against the Behrenese?"

"Well . . ." Belster mumbled, caught off guard by the blunt accusation. "Well, I've not known enough of them to make a judgment. I met one once, but only for a short—"

"Enough said," Pony said dryly.

"Oh, but you are twisting my words and my thoughts!" the innkeeper wailed.

"Only because you know that those thoughts are without merit," Pony retorted. "Al'u'met will stand with us, if it comes to that, and so will the Behrenese. They are allies we cannot ignore."

"You believe in this man?" Belster asked for the fourth time since they had begun this conversation.

"He could have killed me," Pony replied.

"And so he chose right in letting you go," Belster agreed, "but to his own gain, by my thinking."

"He gave me back the magical gemstones," Pony added, "every one."

Belster gave a great sigh and threw up his hands in defeat. He shook his head, but his smile widened, until at last he looked at Pony helplessly.

Only to find that she wasn't even looking at him, but rather past him, her expression worried. Belster turned back toward the door and saw a pair of soldiers entering—town guard and not the King's warriors who had been common, too common, in Palmaris of late. Belster noticed that one of them—a woman, an officer with fiery red hair—held Pony's attention.

"You know her?"

"We fought together in the northland," Pony replied softly. "Colleen Kilronney by name. I know her and she knows me."

"Your disguise is well done this night," Belster replied, trying to allay some of the panic he saw creeping over her. Both he and Pony knew his words for a lie, though, as Pony had come in only recently and, since Dainsey Aucomb was not in, it had been up to Belster to help with the finishing touches.

Pony silently cursed her foolishness; she knew this predicament was no bit of bad luck but rather the result of a dangerous trend. As the situation had grown more critical in Palmaris, as Pony had become more and more involved in organizing resistance to De'Unnero, her attention to her own security had lessened. She had gotten careless and understood now, quite clearly, that such inattention could ruin everything.

She turned back to the bar and lowered her head as Colleen Kilronney and her companion approached and passed right by her, the woman warrior pausing a moment to take a closer look, but then moving on.

"It might be better if you went out and took in a bit of the night air," Belster whispered.

Pony glanced around doubtfully at the crowded room.

"I'll get Prim O'Bryen to help me," Belster said, referring to a regular customer, a money counter employed at Chasewind Manor. "He's run up a bill of near to forty gol' bears and will be happy for the chance to bring it down since De'Unnero has not been as generous as Baron Bildeborough. And Mallory's about, or soon to be."

His attempt at levity brought only a hint of a smile to Pony. She glanced around again, head low, then stood and turned abruptly toward the door—away from Colleen—and started off at a quick pace.

Her departure was not unnoticed, Belster realized as the red-haired woman got up from her chair and started off in Pony's wake. The innkeeper stood up to intercept her, smiling widely. "Good soldier, are you leaving already?" he asked, then turned to the bar. "Prim O'Bryen," he called, "you go back there and get a drink for the woman soldier, one of Palmaris' heroes!"

That brought a couple of cheers and lifted glasses from some folk nearby, but as Belster reached to put his arm around the woman, he saw that his diversion would not work. She slapped him away forcefully and pushed past him, her eyes on the door and the departing Pony.

Belster gave a sheepish grin at the woman soldier's companion. He thought briefly of going after the woman but realized that he would only be causing a disturbance that would bring even more unwanted attention. No, he decided, Pony was on her own. "Well go on back, Prim," he instructed loudly. "Certainly there is another in the Way this night deserving our drink."

"And too many for Belster to handle hisself," Prim O'Bryen commented, grudgingly crawling over the bar. "I'll be looking for some gol' bears off me tab."

Belster waved him the rest of the way over the bar, again trying hard to make as little commotion as possible. Despite his determination, he glanced toward the door more than once.

It was no accident or coincidence that brought Colleen Kilronney to the Way that night. The woman was no fool by anyone's measure, and she had always been among the most attentive of Baron Bildeborough's house guards. While Colleen had not been good friends with the Baron's nephew, Connor, she had seen him many times, including on his wedding day.

And she had seen his bride.

Something had struck Colleen as familiar when she had met the woman companion of the one called Nightbird, though Connor's wedding had been years before. At first Colleen had assumed Pony merely resembled Connor's bride, Jill, daughter of the former proprietors of the Fellowship Way.

As time passed, other clues had begun to fall into place for Colleen, particularly the familiar-looking hilt of the sword Pony had carried belted at her hip. Colleen had hardly noticed it up north, but as she considered the meeting, replaying it in her keen mind, that sword hilt had become more and more tantalizing.

It resembled, to no small degree, the sword of Connor Bildeborough, a celebrated family weapon, Defender by name.

Now, in the Way, the resemblance between Belster's wife and the woman Pony was harder to dismiss. Though Belster's wife appeared older, the way she had moved belied that. She moved like a warrior, like the woman who had accompanied Nightbird, the woman who had resembled the wife of Connor Bildeborough.

Colleen stood in the street outside the Fellowship Way collecting her thoughts, putting all the clues together. All the area was quiet and dark, save one burning streetlamp and a pair of men sitting against the wall of the next building.

"A woman," Colleen asked of them, "a woman who came out of the Way—did ye see her?"

The two men shrugged and went on with their conversation.

It made no sense to Colleen; there was no way Belster's wife could have gotten that far ahead of her. She turned back toward the tavern door, wondering if, perhaps, the woman had not really left the place. She even started that way but stopped then, remembering something else about Connor's wife, something she had once overheard. Connor had been talking to a friend, another of the Baron's house guards, when he had mentioned a special place that he had shared with his Jill, a quiet place within the city, yet removed from the city. . . .

Pony sat on the back roof of the Fellowship Way, staring up at the stars and wondering if Elbryan was looking at the same night sky. She missed her lover dearly, and had been looking forward to seeing him at their appointed rendezvous in early spring. Her belly would be thicker then—it already was starting to show, and so she would have to share her secret with him. The thought pleased her immensely, for she so wanted to share this with Elbryan. As she sat and watched the night sky, her fingers gently swirled about the sides of her belly, a truly comforting feeling, and she wanted Elbryan's hands there, too, wanted him touching their child, perhaps to feel its first movements.

But Pony knew in her heart that it would not be. The events in Palmaris had changed her plans, for she could not think of leaving the city at this critical time. Her duty was clear to her: to somehow bring together all the factions, even the Behrenese, who would oppose De'Unnero and the Church. Simply thinking of that duty replaced her feelings of contentment with rage. Images of her dead—her murdered!—parents, their bloated bodies lifting up in demonic inspiration, assaulted her, pulled her hands up to cover her face. She would pay back the demons parading about as leaders of the Abellican Church, every one! She would take her vengeance all the way to the Father Abbot himself and make him answer for his crimes against Graevis and Pettibwa, against Grady and Connor. She would . . .

A great sadness washed over her then, an overwhelming despair, and she could not hold back the sobs.

Thus, she did not hear the approach as someone climbed up the gutter to the roof behind her.

The sadness passed quickly—Dainsey had warned her of these abrupt changes of mood in pregnancy—stolen by a renewed determination that she would find her revenge. She leaned back against the warm bricks of the chimney and studied the night sky once more, hoping to catch a glimpse of the Halo, hoping that its beauty alone would bring her back to a place of peace.

"A bit of a climb for the wife of Belster," came a voice behind her, freezing her, thought and body. She knew the voice all too well—and Pony was growing more than a little tired of people sneaking up on her!

"Not so much a lift," she replied, laying on a thick Palmaris street accent, a fair imitation of Pettibwa Chilichunk, she thought.

"Not for the companion o' Nightbird, no," said Colleen, "one who's somehow hurt her eye since I saw her last in the north."

Pony's heart sank. She slipped a hand into a pocket, where she held several gemstones, the deadly lodestone and graphite among them. Mustering her nerve, she turned and saw Colleen standing three feet away, hand resting on her sword hilt. Pony eyed her cautiously. She thought to stand up. If she could get on even footing with the soldier, she had little doubt that she could take her down, despite the fact that the larger woman had a weapon.

But as Pony moved as if to rise, Colleen edged closer, and her hand tightened about her sword.

Pony slipped back to an unthreatening posture. "No nightbirds about, by me own seein'," she replied, "but if ye've seen a few, might be that I've a bit of crumb for the tweeters."

"No nightbirds," Colleen replied firmly. "They'd be farther north, I'm thinkin', runnin', and not flyin', about the forest."

A long, uncomfortable moment slipped past.

"Ah, but I left me Belster all alone in the Way," Pony said. "He'll be a screamin' fool when I get back."

"Belster has help," Colleen replied, "as you arranged."

Pony painted a puzzled expression on her face, but she was beginning to understand from the woman's ready posture that the masquerade was at its end. She clenched the magnetite, knowing that with a thought she could drive it through the woman's metal breastplate, but then she moved her fingers to the graphite instead, settling on the notion of a stunning, hopefully nonfatal, lightning blast.

"Enough useless banter," Colleen declared. "I know who ye are, Pony friend o' Nightbird, Jill wife o' Connor. I'm not a fool, and I have heard enough and seen enough to know ye."

Pony started to protest but stopped short, pulling her hand from her pocket and holding it extended in Colleen's direction. "Have you, then?" she asked, dropping the put-on accent. "And do you know enough of me to understand that I can take your life with but a thought?"

That set Colleen back on her heels, but only for a moment. She was a warrior, battle hardened, and with a well-earned reputation for fearlessness. "Truly ye're the rogue that De'Unnero painted ye to be," she spat back.

But Pony caught an inflection in Colleen's voice, less than complimentary, as she pronounced the name of the bishop.

"You mean Bishop De'Unnero," Pony goaded, "the rightful, lawful ruler of Palmaris."

Colleen did not reply, but her sour expression spoke volumes.

"Are we to fight, then?" Pony asked bluntly. "And am I to use magic and destroy you, or would you prefer it, would you think it more fair, if I went and retrieved my sword?"

"Connor's sword, ye mean."

Her perceptiveness surprised Pony, but it did not put her off her guard. " 'Twas Connor's," she admitted, "until emissaries of the Church murdered him and his uncle."

Colleen's eyes widened.

"And the abbot," Pony pressed, spitting every word. "Do you believe that a powrie did it? A wretched little dwarf walked into Palmaris, into St. Precious itself, and killed the great man?"

"Ye're knowin' this to be true?"

"As Connor told it to me, when he came north to find me, when he learned that I was next targeted by the Abellican Church."

Colleen stood very still, and it seemed to Pony that she was not even breathing.

Pony lowered her hand, dropping the gemstone into her pocket. "Not a fair fight if I use the magic that was taught to me by a true man of God," she said. "Let me get my sword then, Colleen Kilronney, and I will happily give you a lesson you shall not soon forget!"

Colleen's pride alone forced her to square her shoulders at the open, brazen challenge. She did not hold the pose for long, though, too curious about this woman's surprising words and nerve.

"Though I wish you'd stand down," Pony conceded, "for I am not convinced that we two are on opposing sides."

"Then what're we to be doin' about it?" Colleen asked.

Pony considered the words for a long while. What indeed? The outline of a plan was taking shape in her mind, a coalition involving Belster's underground network, the persecuted Behrenese, and now Colleen and whatever other soldiers—and Pony guessed that there might be more than a few—they might find who would stand, at least quietly, against the wicked Bishop. But she wasn't ready to share that plan, wasn't ready to trust in this soldier with information concerning her comrades just yet.

"You come back to the Way in three days' time," she offered. "We shall speak again."

"Where's yer Nightbird friend?" Colleen asked abruptly.

Pony eyed her curiously, suspecting a trap.

"Don't ye answer, then," Colleen offered. "If he's come to Palmaris with ye, then keep him low and safe, because De'Unnero's onto his game. And if he's in the north, still, as we've heard, then ye get a runner to him, for Shamus is back out on the northern road. And though he's sayin' that he's comin' to help, he's really going to put a watch on yer friend, to ready Nightbird for De'Unnero's takin'."

The blunt offer of such valuable information put Pony back a step, and she merely nodded dumbly as she tried to digest it all.

"I'll get me friend and be on me way," Colleen said, turning for the gutter and going over the edge of the roof without hesitation. "Three days," she confirmed, looking up only once at Pony and then moving swiftly down to the alley.

Pony held her ground and her pose for a moment longer, then turned back toward the night sky, seeking that elusive glimpse of Corona's heavenly ring.

She gave up at once, though, for she knew that she would find no peace this night.

The fires in the Way had burned to embers, the orange-glowing eyes the only watchful patrons as the hours of darkness turned toward dawn. On the street outside, three drunken men, including a satisfied Prim O'Bryen and Heathcomb Mallory, slept soundly, and a dozen more occupied the inn rooms upstairs, while Dainsey and a suitor had at last settled down in one quiet room in the proprietor's wing, Belster snoring contentedly in another. And in the third bedroom of that first-level wing, sat Pony, comfortable on her bed, wearing a soft nightshirt, a soul stone in hand.

Shamus Kilronney was on his way to find Elbryan, and her lover would not suspect that the man was an agent of Bishop De'Unnero.

Pony trusted Elbryan and reminded herself repeatedly that he had powerful allies, Bradwarden and Juraviel, by his side. Still, if he was caught unaware . . .

Pony sighed deeply and looked down at the gray stone, a darker spot on her pale hand in the moonlight shining through her window. She had chosen to come to Palmaris, had followed the course determined by her need for vengeance, and now she was not so certain that she had chosen rightly. She had known that her road would be dangerous—that Elbryan's would be, as well—but suddenly that danger seemed closer and more threatening. Suddenly Elbryan seemed to be in trouble, and she was too far away to do anything about it.

Or was she?

She continued to stare at the soul stone, wondering what help it might offer. She didn't need to remind herself of the danger of using the stone, any stone, in this city, with De'Unnero's magic-sniffing hounds patrolling the streets. But still, after her conversation with Colleen, after learning the truth, could she possibly sit quietly and hope that Elbryan would survive?

But there was something else, some fear buried deep in Pony's mind.

What other wonders might a journey to the realm of the spirit show her? What other truths to shatter denial? She couldn't think about that now, not with danger closing in on her friends in the north.

She fell into the stone, heart and soul, her spirit sinking deep into its inviting depths. She felt a strange energy in that spiritual state, separate, yet joined. Pony understood, but abruptly turned away from it, and focused outward. In a moment, she was walking free of her corporeal form, sliding quickly through the outer wall of the inn and off into the night along the quiet streets of Palmaris, through the city's northern gate, where the guards gamed with bones, keeping only a halfhearted watch to the empty north road. Then past the darkened farmhouses she went, and along the road. With a thought, she outpaced the swiftest bird, the strongest wind. She passed through Caer Tinella at a dizzying pace, slowing only to seek any signs of Elbryan or Shamus. But no, they were not there—too many were missing, including the wagons that had been procured for the Timberlands caravan. They had already set off, heading farther north. North, too, went Pony, soaring down the road, hardly registering the blurred landscape until she came into regions more familiar, into the land of her birth.

Then her spirit was walking more slowly once more, for though she understood the importance of finding Elbryan quickly and ceasing to use the telltale gems, she could not resist the images of her home: the north slope leading out of Dundalis, the pine and caribou-moss valley beyond.

Shamus Kilronney and his soldiers were in town, she observed at once, noting the military-style encampment at the western edge of the main group. Pony went to the soldiers and through their barracks, and was relieved to find that Elbryan was not in their midst. Relief quickly turned to desperation as she searched the rest of the town and found no sign of her lover, leaving her spirit standing alone, pondering the enormity of her task, in the middle of the village square. He could be anywhere, she understood, and though she could move with the speed of a moonbeam, Elbryan—Nightbird—in the forest would not be easy to find.

Pony forced herself to remain calm, cleared her thoughts of all distractions, and turned her senses to the quiet night.

And there, drifting on the breeze, came her answer, a familiar piping melody, the song of Bradwarden.

She found the centaur moments later, standing solitary on a round-topped bluff, piping his mournful song. She thought to go to him, to try somehow to communicate with him, that he might guide her to Elbryan, but then she spotted Symphony at the bottom of that hillock, standing quietly as if mesmerized by the centaur's song. On a low branch near the magnificent horse rested a familiar saddle.

She heard the great horse nicker softly as she glided past, but her senses caught something else, something even more familiar, something warm and wonderful.

She felt her lover keenly, as if she and Elbryan were somehow spiritually joined. She knew exactly where he was as surely as if he were standing and calling her.

Secure, no doubt, in the knowledge that Symphony and Bradwarden were nearby, the ranger lay deep in peaceful sleep on a raised bed of hay and blankets, heated stones underneath him. He had both of his weapons, Tempest and Hawkwing, lying beside him, ready to grab.

Despite her urgency, Pony paused to soak in that sight and again doubted her choices. How could she have kept the child secret from this man? And how could she have left him?

Because her outrage had gotten the better of her, she had to admit; and truly, she felt as if she had failed at that moment. A desire to rush back to Palmaris, to run to the stables and retrieve Greystone, then ride as fast and hard to the north as possible, nearly overwhelmed her, nearly launched her spirit on its way. But she could not do that, not now. She had chosen, perhaps badly, but that choice had led to new circumstances and responsibilities. She could not abandon Palmaris now any more than Elbryan could go there.

But what of the child? Oh, but she wanted to tell him then! And oh, how she wanted to feel his gentle fingers massaging her swelling belly!

Pony spent a long moment composing herself, finding her center of reason and duty. She stared long and hard at Elbryan for a moment longer, not quite understanding what she should do—or even what she could do. But then the magic of the soul stone came clearer to her; and with a thought, she soared down at her lover, *into* her lover, joining him in his dreams.

Elbryan awoke in a cold sweat, sitting bolt upright, alert that something might be lurking nearby.

The moon, Shelia, was low in the western sky. Bradwarden had stopped his piping, but Symphony stood nearby, calm; that alone told the ranger that no enemies were near.

But something, someone, had been there, he knew, though it was all a mix of dream and consciousness. Several deep breaths steadied him, and he put his head down in his hands and thought hard.

And then he knew. Somehow, through some magic, Pony had come to him.

Pony! The mere thought of her sent shivers along his spine and pangs of emptiness through his heart. But it had been Pony, of that he was suddenly sure; and she was all right. She was safe in Palmaris.

But there she had to stay, and there, he could not go; that, too, came clear and unmistakable. Their planned early spring meeting was no more, for Palmaris was in turmoil and Pony could not abandon the folk in need. Nor could he go there, nor should he go there, for . . .

Something else tugged at the ranger's consciousness, some warning that he felt he should heed. But he could not, not then, for the thought of Pony, the image of Pony, the regret at being away from Pony, was too consuming, too engulfing. So he sat in the quiet, dark forest as the minutes turned to an hour, thinking of her, remembering her embrace and her kiss, the taste of her neck, the depth of her eyes.

He could only hope that their paths would soon cross, that duty, painful duty, would not keep them apart for long.

Those same regrets followed Pony as her spirit swept back into Palmaris, as she moved down the still-quiet streets and back into the dark common room of the Fellowship Way. She went straight for her door, thinking that it was long past time she reentered her corporeal form and dismissed the magical energies, but as she glided along the hallway, she paused, hearing, sensing, some tumult beyond another door. Hardly thinking, Pony slipped through that wall into Dainsey's room.

The woman and her companion twined and groaned, caught in the passion of lovemaking.

An embarrassed Pony retreated at once, but stopped, mesmerized, because the energy, the heat, of Dainsey and the man, brought back to her memories of Elbryan's embrace, when they broke their vow of celibacy when they thought the world was safe once more.

To the conception of their child.

It had been such a beautiful thing, a moment of purest ecstasy, of completeness and security.

But maybe it had been no more than this. Maybe it had been the fulfillment of something more base, a physical need. And succumbing to that need had led to . . .

To what? Pony had to ask herself honestly; and the answer that screamed back at her caught her completely off guard.

It had led to a complication. A dangerous complication.

Pony's spirit soared from the room and back toward her waiting form. She approached with all speed, thinking to fall into the material world and out of the gemstone magic abruptly, without time to think or to see.

But she sensed that other presence, that spirit within her physical being.

She tried to hurry, but she could not avoid a brush with that life!

Barely a second passed before her body shuddered back to consciousness, but it was a second too long for Pony. She knew now, beyond all doubt. She had a child within her, a living creature, forming, growing, and growing strong. Of course she had known for some time that she was pregnant, but the word had meant little to her. When she had told Juraviel that perhaps she would not be able to see the child through to term, she had been serious. Somewhere deep in her mind, she had figured that the child would be stillborn or miscarried, for the notion that this was real, that she was to be a mother, seemed unlikely, even seemed impossible.

But now she knew. This was real; the child—her child, Elbryan's child—was alive.

Tears soaked her cheeks and streamed from her eyes. She felt all alone and out of control. Her hand went to her belly, but found no comfort there, found only vulnerability.

"Damn you," Pony growled into the darkness, cursing herself. Without even consciously registering the move, she got up and started pacing the floor. "Damn you!" she said again, fists clenched at her sides.

Why hadn't she waited? Why had she seduced Elbryan, practically forcing him to make love to her, with such potential for disaster?

Pony growled and slapped a plate from her night table, hardly noticing that it crashed to the floor.

"What fool am I to have done this?" she asked aloud. Again her hand was on her belly, but it wasn't massaging gently, but rather clenching the skin. "All the world is in peril, and in the name and memory of Avelyn, I am charged with the fight. And yet, how can I? What warrior am I with this in my belly?"

Again she reached toward the table, this time to seize its top, thinking to pick it up and hurl it at the wall through the window. But she stopped, for she realized only then how loud she had been. And then she heard the shuffling footsteps coming down the hall, then a soft knock, and the door creaked open. A frightened Dainsey Aucomb stood in her doorway, staring wide-eyed at her.

"Are ye feeling ill, Miss Pony?" the woman asked sheepishly.

Pony relaxed her grip, too embarrassed to continue her tantrum, but still deep in the throes of anger and regret. She straightened and turned, facing Dainsey.

"Can I be getting ye something to calm ye?" Dainsey offered.

"I am with child," Pony stated flatly.

"Well, that much I been knowin' for some time," replied Dainsey.

Pony snorted derisively. "Have you?" she asked with open sarcasm. "You have known the simple truth, that Pony is pregnant, but do you have any idea of what that really means?"

"I'm thinkin' that it means ye'll be hatchin' a baby in a few months' time," Dainsey said with a hopeful chuckle. "The sixth month o' the year, by me guess, or it might be the end o' the fifth."

A flick of Pony's arm sent the table toppling to the floor and Dainsey jumped back.

"It means that you have lost an important ally in this critical war," Pony growled at her. "It means that when all Palmaris roils with revolution, should it come to pass, Pony will roil with the pangs of childbirth."

Pony's visage softened, and she looked down and added quietly, "It means that I have failed."

"Miss Pony!" Dainsey said, stamping her bare foot on the wooden floor.

"How foolish I have been," said Pony.

"How foolish ye're bein', ye mean!" Dainsey snapped. "Are ye regrettin' the child in yer belly, then?"

Pony didn't answer, but her expression was all the confirmation Dainsey needed.

"But ye're makin' a mistake," Dainsey dared to say, advancing a cautious step. "Ye must not be thinkin' ill o' the child in yer belly. No, never that, for he knows, Miss Pony. He'll hear yer thoughts, don't ye doubt, and then—"

"Shut your mouth!" Pony snapped at her, coming forward a step.

Dainsey started to retreat, but she stopped abruptly and straightened defiantly. "But I'll not," she stated firmly. "Ye're missin' yer lover, and scared for him and for yer child, but ye're bein' the fool, and no friend am I if I'm not tellin' ye so!"

Even as she finished, Pony was on her, pushing her toward the door. Dainsey tried to resist, but Pony soon had her out in the hallway. Dainsey recovered quickly and tried to go back, but Pony slammed the door in her face.

Stubborn Dainsey banged on the wood. "Ye hear me, Miss Pony!" she said. "Ye hear me well. Ye feel that life inside ye and know that it, and not this stupid fight, is where's yer most important duty. Ye find yer heart . . ." With one last frustrated knock on the door, she retreated down the hall.

Pony was back on her bed, wet face buried in her hands. All her life seemed confusion and tumult. She wanted Elbryan to be there, to hold her. And she wanted to not be pregnant.

The realization of that last thought, hearing the actual words in her mind, brought her up straight, eyes wide, hardly realizing that she was gasping for breath.

"By God," she muttered, and her hands went frantically to her belly, stroking emphatically, trying to take it back, all of it, trying to assure this living child inside her that she did not mean such a thing.

The door to her room pushed open and Dainsey stood there, looking at her.

"Miss Pony?" the woman asked gently.

Pony swooned and nearly toppled, but Dainsey had her, hugging her close, whispering in her ear that everything would be all right.

Pony only wished that she could believe those words.

CHAPTER

❖ 21 ❖

Destiny

"You are certain that we are alone?" Brother Braumin asked as he and Elbryan walked through the afternoon shadows of the forest outside of Dundalis. A myriad of patterns speckled the ground before them as sunlight snaked its way through the bare branches. The snow had melted a few inches in the week since the storm, but the pair still had to slog through some uncomfortably deep drifts.

The ranger shrugged. "Who can know?" he admitted. "Bradwarden is not about—of that I am fairly certain. And no men are nearby, unless they are men of the forest, walking silently, without disturbing even the most skittish of birds. Roger Lockless, perhaps—he is known for hearing what he should not, and seeing what he should not."

"And of course, the elves," Brother Braumin added. "They could be but a body's length away and not even Nightbird would know it, I guess, if they did not want him to."

Elbryan conceded the point with a nod. Indeed, he had seen little sign of Ni'estiel and the others since the fight, though he had heard a couple of elven voices lifted in song one quiet night. They were still about, but what that meant, the ranger was no longer sure. Why hadn't they warned them, and why hadn't they been more involved in the fight that had cost four men their lives? And, perhaps most perplexing of all, why hadn't they come to Nightbird afterward, at least to explain? The ranger eagerly looked forward to that meeting, if it ever came, for even if Lady Dasslerond was among their ranks, he meant to speak loudly and not favorably.

"But we are as secure as we can hope to be, it seems," said Brother Braumin. He slowed and looked long and hard at Elbryan, drawing the ranger's gaze. "I have a request," he said solemnly.

Elbryan continued to stare, not knowing what to expect. He feared that Braumin would ask about the stolen gemstones, Pony's gemstones—and rightfully so, by Elbryan's thinking!—and then he would calmly have to put the man off.

"My friends and I are out here alone," Braumin stated. "By deserting St.-Mere-Abelle, we have severed our ties to the Abellican Church."

"That much seems obvious," Elbryan replied. "Though, given your Father Abbot's thirst for vengeance, I would say that you must hope and pray that those ties are truly severed."

Braumin managed to grin briefly at the ranger's sarcasm. "Severed on our part, at least," he clarified. "And thus we have become men without a home—and worse, Nightbird, we have become men without a purpose."

"You have found friends here in Dundalis and anonymity in the vastness of the Timberland forests," the ranger replied. "I do not believe that Shamus and the soldiers knew who you were, had any idea at all that you were of the Church. And so, perhaps you have found a quiet existence. There are worse fates."

"True, but do not forget that we are men of purpose, men who have devoted all our lives, from the last days of childhood, to the study of God," Braumin explained. "This was our calling, a divine calling, we all believe, for only such deep-rooted convictions will allow one to attain the levels of piety necessary even to enter St.-Mere-Abelle."

The ranger's eyes widened at that prideful declaration.

"I speak humbly," Braumin quickly added, "and speak only the truth. Absolute dedication is required of any would-be student of the Abellican Order."

"And yet you deserted that Order."

"Because we learned the truth of Father Abbot Dalebert Markwart's interpretation of the Abellican Order," Braumin said, his voice rising. He glanced around nervously and quickly lowered his voice to a harsh whisper. "Because Master Jojonah taught us that, as your friend Avelyn Desbris taught it to him."

The ranger had no argument; he felt Avelyn had also taught him much about the truth of God.

"We did not desert the Order," Brother Braumin asserted. "We followed the true spirit of the Abellicans, a journey that forced us from St.-Mere-Abelle."

"And so you have come all the way to Dundalis," Elbryan reasoned, "and yet you feel that your journey is not complete, that the simple life of this region will not fulfill your spiritual needs."

Now it was Braumin's turn to stop and stare, for the ranger's blunt assertion had taken him by surprise.

"Could you not build a church here and teach the song of God as you hear it?" the ranger asked.

"And how long would such a church be allowed to survive, so close to Honce-the-Bear and the Abellican Order?" Braumin asked skeptically.

"Then it is fear and not purpose that will push you further."

The monk's face screwed up with confusion, and then, as he figured out that the ranger was teasing him, he suddenly laughed. "It was fear that drove us from St.-Mere-Abelle," he admitted after a moment, "and yet, in a way, we were all more afraid of leaving than staying."

Elbryan nodded. "You said you had a request," the ranger said. "What would you have me do?"

Braumin took a deep breath, yet another hint to Elbryan that this request was no small thing.

"I would have you lead my friends and me to the Barbacan," he said quickly. Elbryan wondered which frightened Braumin more—asking for help or stating his intentions out loud.

"The Barbacan?" the ranger echoed incredulously.

"I have seen the glory of Avelyn's tomb," Brother Braumin said sincerely. "I know I must go there now; Brother Dellman, feels he, too, must return there. The others must see it; it is a pilgrimage necessary if we five are truly to become of one mind and one purpose."

"And that purpose is . . . ?"

"I hope the pilgrimage will show me," Braumin admitted.

"The Barbacan is still a hostile land," Elbryan pointed out. "The destruction of the dactyl and the defeat of the monstrous army has done little to tame the northland. Perhaps I could get you there, but then what? That you might stay only a matter of days, or even hours, then take the road back to Dundalis again?"

"Perhaps," Braumin said honestly, "perhaps not. I believe in my heart that Avelyn will show us our true course. He gave his life for the good of the world and in death he reached for the heavens. There is something magical about that place, something healing and godly. I felt that keenly when I viewed the tomb."

"More than three hundred miles of wild land is a long way to travel in hopes of inspiration," the ranger said dryly.

"Yet it is the only road before us," Braumin replied. "I know that I am asking much of you, but I do so in the name of Avelyn, and in the hope that he, and Jojonah, have not died in vain."

That set the ranger back. He wasn't sure that this journey to the Barbacan would accomplish anything more than getting them all killed or sending them all running back to Dundalis battered and humbled. Still, there seemed a greater measure of sincerity in the man, and a huge determination. Braumin had lived as a monk for years and understood the inner working of the Abellican Church far better than Elbryan ever could. Could Elbryan deny the possibility that such inspiration might come to a man who had willingly given his life to the search for God and good? Besides, the ranger, too, had seen where Avelyn was buried shortly after the explosion. Though he understood that Avelyn had extended his arm upward hoping to keep the pouch of sacred gemstones and Tempest safe, there was something mystical—or at least a very fortunate coincidence—that Avelyn's extended arm had somehow reached above the destruction.

"You understand the dangers?" the ranger asked.

"I understand the futility of not going," Braumin replied, "for then we are dead, all five of us, spiritually if not physically. And perhaps worse than physical death is the notion of spiritual impotence, of our voices silenced under the smothering blanket of Father Abbot Markwart."

"And the Barbacan will change this?"

Braumin gave a shrug. "I know that I must journey to the grave of Avelyn, and so must my companions, and we shall go, with or without Nightbird."

The ranger didn't doubt him. "Progos is but half gone," Elbryan reasoned. "Winter is here—you have seen her fury, and I assure you that the snow which fell the night before Shamus Kilronney arrived was no unusual storm for this part of the world. I do not know when the trails north will be clear. And even if they are clear, know that the wind among the mountains ringing Aida and Avelyn's grave could freeze the blood in your body quickly."

"The dangers are not ignored," Braumin assured him, "nor will they stop us."

Elbryan looked hard at the man, at his determination in the face of potential disaster, and he was impressed. "I will speak with Bradwarden," he offered. "The centaur knows the northern terrain better than I and has animal friends who might better give us some idea of what we will encounter."

"We?" Braumin noted hopefully.

"No promise, Brother Braumin," the ranger responded, but it seemed clear to both of them that Nightbird would guide the group. That notion struck the ranger, for he had no intention or desire to ever return to the forlorn remnants of Aida—indeed, a little over a week before, until his strange dream about Pony, he had thought his road was in the opposite direction! No, he could not call it a dream. Pony had come to him in his sleep—he knew that without doubt—and their roads could not cross again just yet.

Was he now thinking of going so far north out of spite, out of some anger at Pony? He did not have the answer, but he realized that he needed to sit down and figure it out before committing to the journey.

"You should go," Roger asserted, walking at the ranger's side through the dark forest. "These are good men, every one."

Elbryan gave no reply. He had already explained to Roger all the problems of such a journey—not the least was that if he left he would be abdicating his responsibilities to Tomas Gingerwart for a month or more.

"I worked in St.-Mere-Abelle," Roger went on, "and I can attest to the courage Brother Braumin and his companions showed in leaving the place. What they did to Jojonah—"

Elbryan held up his hand; he had heard it all before—in the last few minutes actually. "Let us learn what Bradwarden thinks of such a journey," he said. "I do not doubt Brother Braumin's sincerity, or even his judgment in claiming that he and his friends should go to Mount Aida. If I did, I would not even be talking with Bradwarden this night. But there are larger issues to be considered."

"Pony," Roger remarked.

"That is one," the ranger admitted, and he ducked under a branch and around a chestnut tree, to the edge of a clearing opposite the centaur. "And the season is another."

"Ye're late," Bradwarden said, his tone grim.

A moment later, catching a rustle in the tree above, the ranger understood the source of his friend's discontent. As he focused his gaze on the shadows above, a pair of elves moved down and into view, dropping to the lowest branch. The ranger's eyes widened.

"Why do you seem so surprised, Nightbird?" said the female of the pair, Tiel'marawee by name—or nickname, for the ranger did not know her real name. Indeed, that true name had been lost to the ages, Juraviel had told a younger Elbryan during his days in Andur'Blough Inninness. To all the Touel'alfar, she was Tiel'marawee, "songbird," a title most fitting for one whose melodious voice was legendary even among the beautiful voices of the elves.

"I had thought our alliance ended," the ranger replied grimly, "with the Touel'alfar turned down other roads. It has been many days."

"A long while only to the impatience of a human," said Ni'estiel, assuming a more defiant posture on the branch. After an uncomfortable moment in which the elf and ranger locked simmering stares, Ni'estiel stood on the branch and gave a sweeping bow, smiling from ear to ear.

The ranger didn't smile in return. "As you say," Elbryan conceded. "And yet, the children of Caer'alfar did not see their way to warn Nightbird of the impending goblin attack, and did little to fend off those monsters, though their bows would have proven invaluable."

"Or they did not know that Nightbird would be among the soldiers," Tiel'marawee replied.

"And that excuses . . ." Elbryan started to ask, but he stopped, reminding himself of the true nature of these creatures. Elves were not humans, however Elbryan might wish to pretend otherwise. Their view of the world did not correspond to those attributes—compassion and community—that Elbryan would seek in humans. Still, the ranger could not completely excuse the lack of warning and aid, for the choice of allies among humans and goblins should not be a difficult one, from any point of view. "Four men died," he said grimly, "and another three were grievously . . ." He let it drop again as he considered his audience, as he realized that the expressions of both elves had not changed, would not change. The life of a human was not important to a being that would likely outlive twenty generations of men.

And these two, Tiel'marawee and Ni'estiel, if Elbryan remembered them correctly from his time in Andur'Blough Inninness, were among the most dispassionate of the elven people with regard to *n'Touel'alfar*, anyone who was not elven. That thought struck him profoundly then, for, that being the case, why were these two the ones to come forward and speak with him? Where was Juraviel? And where Lady Dasslerond?

The ranger didn't like the implications.

"Well, Nightbird was among the soldiers, and he, too, might have been slain," the ranger said at last, thinking to end that part of the discussion.

Ni'estiel wouldn't let him be done with it so easily. "And if he had been slain by mere goblins, then perhaps he would have shown that he was not worthy of the name Tai'marawee, the name the Touel'alfar gave to him with confidence," the elf said with a sarcastic laugh, and Tiel'marawee joined in the mirth; but it seemed to Elbryan as if the pair were only half kidding.

"But that is past now, and we need look to the road ahead," Tiel'-marawee remarked in a leading manner.

Elbryan turned a surprised look on Bradwarden. "They know?"

"Elfy ears," the centaur replied.

"You consider a journey to the Barbacan," Ni'estiel stated flatly, "to the place of the dactyl demon's destruction."

"To the tomb of Brother Avelyn Desbris," Roger said solemnly.

The elves didn't seem much impressed.

"And how do the Touel'alfar view such a journey?" Elbryan asked.

"Why would the Touel'alfar care?" asked Ni'estiel.

"Your road is your own to choose, Nightbird," Tiel'marawee added. "We will help where we may."

"And if ye so choose," Bradwarden added dryly.

"There is always that," admitted Ni'estiel.

"Have you been able to determine the security of the region?" the ranger asked Bradwarden. He had spoken with the centaur earlier that day, explaining Brother Braumin's request and also reminding Bradwarden of his duty to Tomas Gingerwart and his promise to help with the rebuilding of the Timberland towns.

"No sign o' the goblins, or any other monster scum in the area," said the centaur. "Them that got free o' the battle kept on runnin', by me own thinkin'."

"Not a sign of potential trouble anywhere in the region," Tiel'marawee added.

"And we're to be believin' yerself?" the centaur asked.

But it was Elbryan who answered, stating firmly that he did believe the elves. He understood them, and so did Bradwarden, if the centaur could only look past his present anger at this pair. While the Touel'alfar might on occasion stand by and allow humans to be slaughtered—they had done so, for example, during the destruction of the original Dundalis, when Elbryan's own family had been killed—but they would never favor goblins and other monsters over humans. If these two said now that they saw no signs of monsters in the area, then Elbryan believed them completely—and so did Bradwarden, as the centaur admitted with a derisive snort and a wave of his huge arms.

"Then what am I to do?" Elbryan asked. "Truly I do not desire to journey to the Barbacan—not ever again—but these men have placed a great trust in me by simply coming to the northland in search of me. And they are disciples of Avelyn, heart and soul. Of that I have no doubt."

"Then you owe your dead friend this favor, at least," Roger said hopefully.

"I been thinkin' that a journey to the north might not be a bad thing," Bradwarden offered. "Besides, I ain't seen this grave everyone's been talkin' of."

"Nor have I," said Roger.

Elbryan nodded as each of them was speaking, his road coming clearer before him.

The centaur looked up at the elves. "And what o' ye two?" he asked.

"We may go," said Ticl'marawee.

"Or we may not," Ni'estiel quickly added.

They had a private agenda here, Elbryan understood, one given them by Lady Dasslerond and one, he believed, that concerned him. He still couldn't understand why Lady Dasslerond hadn't come out to speak with him personally on so important a matter. Or Juraviel. . . . Where was his dearest friend among the Touel'alfar at this critical time? A disturbing thought crossed his mind then: perhaps Lady Dasslerond, Juraviel, and the others hadn't followed the monks to the north—perhaps these two elves alone had come to the Timberlands.

"All we're needin' to do now is wait for the weather to allow it," Bradwarden remarked. "And I'm thinkin' that to be a long and frustratin' wait!"

The ranger didn't disagree in the least. He knew what winter could mean in the Timberlands: days, weeks of sitting in the dim light of a low-burning fire, using only the wood needed to keep the room warm enough for survival, staring at the bare walls and at the companions who had long begun to grate on one's nerves.

The ranger and Roger turned back for the town then, moving to a heavy tent pegged to the southern wall of the large meetinghouse. Braumin and the other five monks were already inside, some sitting on their hands, all looking very nervous.

"If we can get the agreement of Tomas Gingerwart and the soldiers that the area is secure, I will lead you to the Barbacan," Elbryan announced at once, dispelling the tension. There came a chorus of quiet cheers and excited whispers.

"Three hundred miles and more," the ranger warned them, his tone grim, "a longer and more difficult trek than the one that brought you from Palmaris to this place."

"Not so difficult," remarked the quiet Brother Mullahy, his voice barely audible.

"Nor so long," added an almost giddy Brother Viscenti.

"We should know more of the disposition of the immediate area by midday tomorrow," Elbryan assured Brother Braumin, "that we might begin our preparations."

"And when shall we leave?" asked an impatient Brother Castinagis.

"When the wind will not kill us and the snow will not bury us," the ranger replied firmly. "The beginning of Bafway, perhaps, or the end of it."

All the eager monks looked disappointed by that proclamation, but the ranger would not be swayed by their foolish hopes. "To leave prematurely would bring only disaster," he said. "You have seen the snow and heard and felt the bite of the wind. Yet we are south here, far south, of Avelyn's grave, and at a much lower elevation. Up there, in the north among the mountains, the snow lies deeper, and the bite of the wind will kill the strongest of men. Do not doubt my words. The season has been mild thus far, and if that continues, we may begin our trek shortly before the turn of Bafway. But no sooner—even if the sun came out tomorrow with such strength that we stripped off our clothes and basked in its warmth!"

With that, the ranger bowed and left the tent; but Roger did not follow, preferring to stay and share the occasion with his newfound friends, a moment of happiness that could not be dulled too much by the ranger's last grim warning.

Elbryan started for Tomas Gingerwart's tent, but changed his mind. Tomas wouldn't be difficult to persuade; the more important ally in this matter was the man who would likely replace him as primary guardian of the new settlers.

He found Shamus awake, strolling about the perimeter of the Kingsmen's camp, his eyes raised to the stars, his hands clasped behind his back, his face a mask of concern. That mask changed, but far from convincingly, when he noted Elbryan's approach.

"When winter breaks, my road will take me from this place for some weeks," the ranger said bluntly. "I will travel to the north with some men."

"North?" asked a surprised Shamus. "But our duty is here, rebuilding the Timberlands."

"I will not go until I have been assured that the region is secured," the ranger replied. "And I will not be gone for long—a month at the most. Also, I leave Tomas Gingerwart and his fellows in the capable hands of

Captain Shamus Kilronney and a contingent of the King's own soldiers. What role can I fill with such capable companions all about?"

"You flatter me, ranger," Shamus said with a disarming grin. "But if the region is secure, as you state, then perhaps I can accompany you."

"Not necessary," Elbryan replied, his tone showing Shamus that there was no room for debate.

"What business could these men possibly have in the northlands?" Shamus inquired. "This is the land rich in valued timber, and surely there are ample trees here to supply the masts of a thousand thousand great sailing ships."

"They will go north in search of riches of a different sort," Elbryan replied cryptically, "and I believe they might just find what they are seeking."

"So Nightbird plans to get rich?" Shamus asked with a chuckle.

"Perhaps," the ranger replied in all seriousness, his tone taking the mirth from the other man.

"Your road is your own to choose," the captain said somberly, sounding very much like the detached Tiel'marawee at that moment. "I only hope that you will not be gone from us for long—and that you will reconsider my offer to journey along with you."

"I will, to both," said Elbryan and he bid the captain a good night and moved back into the forest.

Shamus stayed outside for a long while after Elbryan had departed, considering carefully the words and their implications. The captain was more than a little unsettled by the sight of Bradwarden the fugitive, and by his realization that Nightbird meant to accompany the six men who had recently joined the settlers. More than a few hints had indicated to Shamus that these men were, or had been, Abellican monks, including one quiet, and quickly corrected, reference one had made to another as "brother."

Had Nightbird perhaps figured out that Shamus was acting as an agent of De'Unnero?

As he stood musing over that possibility and coming to the conclusion that such could not be the case, Shamus heard the approach of the little man, smallest of the group of six.

Roger walked by swiftly, nodding only slightly to acknowledge the captain.

"Nightbird told me that he will accompany your group to the north," Shamus said behind him, stopping him in his tracks. Roger swung about, eyeing the captain—surprised but not suspicious, for by Roger's understanding, the soldiers of the Baron, and thus the soldiers of the King, were on his side against the Church.

"And so he will," Roger replied. "And glad are we six for the company."

"A valuable ally on so dangerous a journey," Shamus said.

"The first part will likely be the worst," said Roger. "If the rumors of the extent of the catastrophe at Mount Aida prove true, it is doubtful that any monsters have returned to that blasted place."

Shamus did well to hide his surprise. They were going to the Barbacan!

"Still, I do not understand," he said. "Why would you venture to such a forlorn place as that?"

Now Roger went on the alert. He didn't mistrust the captain, but he understood the monks' need for secrecy and feared that he might already have said too much—though he assumed Elbryan had already told Shamus at least as much. "Who can rightly say?" Roger replied. "There are many places in the world that I have not seen and that I wish to see. Some are merely more convenient than others." Hoping he had covered his tracks, Roger gave a great yawn and explained that it was past time for him to retire.

Shortly thereafter, Shamus Kilronney handed a rolled parchment to his most trusted rider and ordered the man to ride south, braving the weather and snow-blocked road, to get to Palmaris and Bishop De'Unnero. Shamus understood that he was only doing his duty as a sworn officer of the King—and he told himself that repeatedly—but he felt uneasy about betraying Nightbird, even if the man was in the presence of a known criminal.

PART FOUR

THE HEART AND SOUL OF CORONA

I never thought of it before, Uncle Mather, because it never seemed an issue and, truly, never seemed to matter. And, perhaps more to the point, because no one had ever before asked. Is Danube Brock Ursal not Nightbird's king? is what Shamus inquired of me, a simple question to the ears, but one that caught me so off guard that I knew not what to answer. I offered some words in response, but I still have not sorted out the answer that is in my heart.

Am I a homeless rogue? I spent my childhood in Dundalis, but that place is no more, even if new buildings are constructed on its ruins. I grew to manhood in Andur'Blough Inninness, among the elves, whom I consider the dearest of friends.

But family?

No, I cannot rightly call Belli'mar Juraviel my brother, nor Lady Dasslerond my queen. I love Juraviel as I would a sibling, to be sure, and would heed the commands of Lady Dasslerond, but it is a simple fact of our physical beings that we cannot view the world in the same manner. Elven eyes perceive a different hue of truth and meaning than those of humans.

So Andur'Blough Inninness is not, cannot be, my home, however I might wish it to be. Upon my return to the elven valley, I was not even allowed entrance. Juraviel once labeled me as n'Touel'alfar, and though I argued it with him, even convinced him of my way of thinking, we both understand the truth of those words: Elbryan— Nightbird—for all his training and all the love, is not of the people of Caer'alfar.

Lady Dasslerond is not my queen; does that, by default, leave Danube as my king?

No, Uncle Mather, and I understand now that his father before him was no king to you. Homeless rogues, we two? Hardly. For my home is here, in the forests of the Timberlands, in the Wilderlands, in the fields of northern Honce-the-Bear, or in the steep and rocky slopes of southern Alpinador, if I so choose. This is yet another aspect of the life of a ranger that has only recently come clear to me. Home is a feeling, not a place; and that feeling, for a ranger, is a portable thing, a matter of terrain, perhaps, but never of walls. I am home here in the forests of the Timberlands because of the feeling in my heart whenever I return to this place.

So speak not to me of kings and queens, tell me not of empires and kingdoms. Whichever ruler extends his boundaries to cross over this land is unimportant and irrelevant, for boundaries are an invisible thing, a mark on a map and not on the land. They are an extension of ego, a claim to power, a means to wealth. Yet that ego is a lie, that power more a trap than a freedom, and that wealth a façade.

A façade, yes, Uncle Mather, and nothing more valuable than a way for one man to feel superior to another. Avelyn once told me a tale of a tower on the outskirts of Ursal. The place served as a prison for those who spoke ill of the King, and, usually, the door would open for such a pitiful man in only one direction. Decades after this place was built, another prison was constructed, and thus this tower had no more official use. The King, in a generous gesture, awarded the structure to an enterprising Duke. For many years, the man knew not what to do with the structure, for though it was comfortable enough, now that it had been cleaned of all implements of torture and all shackles, it was too far from the grounds of Ursal Castle, where the Duke liked to court the ladies.

But he was an enterprising man, Uncle Mather, and so, when among the nobles of Ursal, he spoke often of the "grand views" afforded him in his country estate. Such beauty, this Duke claimed, must remain the province of the wealthy, and, since he could not spend enough time at his tower to see to its upkeep, he would offer a lease, and at the enormous, even outrageous, price of five hundred gol' bears a season. The price alone brought many curious nobles out to see the tower, and whenever they gathered the Duke was crafty in keeping the conversation about the views.

The views! He played on their vanity, and the expense itself became a reason for purchase. To hear Avelyn speak of it, the argument over who would lease the tower flowered into bloody duels—and nearly into a minor war between three separate provinces. Ladies begged their noble husbands for residence in the tower; single courtiers desired the place that they might entice desirable ladies to come and experience the view.

In the end, the Queen of Honce-the-Bear demanded of her husband that he take back the tower; but the King, being a man of honor, would not go back on his word to the Duke. Instead, the King rented the tower for a mere one thousand gol' bears a season.

And thus the Queen got her desired view, the same view that had been, for decades, afforded enemies of the crown for free.

What is wealth, Uncle Mather, but a matter of perception? And the burning need to be better than others is nothing more than a weakness in one's self. And the King is trapped, I say, in the formalities of his office, by the dangers of the envy of his inferiors, and by the very real possibility of attempted revenge by his enemies.

I will keep my freedom, Uncle Mather, and my love, Jilseponie, and we will carry our home with us, wherever we choose to go and be wealthier by far in matters of the heart and the spirit.

And those two treasures, in the greatest measure, are all that truly matter.

—ELBRYAN WYNDON

CHAPTER

❖ *22* ❖

Seeds

They called it the "Progos thaw," and though it seemed to occur at the turn of each year, it always had the folk out and about, shaking their heads and mumbling about the strange weather. And this year, for the first time in many years, the folk did have something to mumble about. Spring weather came on suddenly in Palmaris, with several storms in succession starting out with threatening heavy snow but producing only cold rain before the second month had even begun.

The winter, among the mildest that even the oldest folk could remember, was fast ending, and Pony's belly was becoming noticeable. Thus, she made it a point to keep her bar apron around her waist even when she was not working in the Way, even when she was going out at night, as she was this evening, to meet with one or another of her fellow conspirators.

The base of resistance was solidifying, she reminded herself hopefully as she brushed past Belster and out of the inn. Between Belster's many friends, Colleen's information from inside the enemy camp, and Al'u'met's Behrenese and sailor comrades, those opposed to Bishop De'Unnero controlled much of the street and dock talk in the city. Not that they were open in their complaints and resistance; it had not come to that.

Not yet. No, they were planting the seeds of rebellion, fostering a different viewpoint concerning the manner in which the Church was ruling the city. If it came to a fight—and a large part of Pony dearly hoped that it would—the Bishop and his minions would be surprised indeed at the scope of the resistance.

That notion of an open battle against the Church prodded Pony to step more quickly as she headed for her appointed meeting with Colleen Kilronney. The fires of vengeance had not cooled within Pony, and if it came to blows, she remained determined that she would use her magic, Avelyn's magic, to wreak devastation on the leaders of that accursed Church that had murdered her parents and her friends.

She was surprised indeed when she turned into the alley and saw that

Colleen was not alone, and her surprise became amazement at the sight of
Colleen's companion. A monk! A monk wearing the robes of St. Precious!

She came forward cautiously.

He leaped at her, hands grasping for her throat. Like all Abellicans,
the man had been trained in the fighting arts, and so his attack came swift
and sure.

Pony fell back under his weight. Her hands grabbed at his wrists, trying
to pull his fingers from her throat. She fell quickly into the trained warrior
mode, and even as a stunned Colleen rushed in from behind, Pony hooked
her thumbs under the monk's, then bent her legs and fell to her knees,
bringing the man down with her. Now leverage became Pony's ally, and a
simple twist broke the monk's hold—and she could have twisted farther
and shattered his thumb bones altogether.

But she did not—in deference to Colleen, who had brought this monk to
her. She stood up quickly, sweeping her hands under the monk's forearms,
then yanking his arms out wide. Using her momentum, she turned one
palm out, curled her fingers tightly in, and drove the heel of her hand under
the monk's chin. The blow lifted him from his feet and shoved him several
inches back.

Up came his arms in desperate defense, but Pony was already moving
like a striking serpent straight ahead. She connected again, this time with a
stunning blow to the bridge of his nose, and then again as blood began
pouring from both his nostrils.

Colleen caught the monk as he fell and offered him support, but also
neatly immobilized him, slipping one arm under his shoulder, then around
the back of his neck, and hooking her other hand, pulling the monk's other
arm back at the elbow.

"I see you have brought your friends," Pony remarked sarcastically,
straightening her clothes and eyeing the man dangerously. She had done well
to control her mounting, boiling anger—anytime a man wearing the robes
of that Church offered her an excuse, she meant to punish him terribly—
but resolved that if he came at her again, he would not leave this alley alive.

"She is the one," the monk tried to explain to Colleen, spitting blood
with every word.

"The one who'll be breakin' yer stupid neck?" Colleen retorted.

"T-the companion of N-Nightbird," the monk stammered.

"I told ye that much," said Colleen.

"The friend of Avelyn the heretic, the thief of the sacred stones, the ally
of the demon dactyl," said the monk.

"Seems like every time I'm hearin' it, yer reputation for troublemakin'
grows," Colleen said to Pony. "I'm likin' ye all the better, girl!"

"You do not understand," the monk cried.

"I understand that I could be lettin' ye go now, and lettin' ye get yerself
killed," Colleen shot back; as she said it, she did release the man. "Go on

then, I'll be enjoyin' the sight o' me friend kickin' the life from yer robed body."

The man hesitated, glancing nervously from Colleen to Pony. He reached up to wipe the blood from his nose with his sleeve.

"A friend of Avelyn, yes," Pony admitted. She reached into her apron and tossed the man a rag. "A friend of Avelyn, the same Avelyn who destroyed the demon dactyl, despite what your masters have told you."

The man continued to stand his ground, continued to look all about.

"Why did you bring him?" Pony asked.

"He's no friend to De'Unnero," said Colleen. "I was thinkin' that a common enemy might be a good place for startin' an alliance. And can ye doubt how valuable a man inside St. Precious might prove to be?

"And I didn't know," Colleen added, giving the monk a kick as she spoke the words. "I told him about ye and he seemed friendly enough."

"A ruse so he could get at me," Pony remarked.

"We could just kill 'im," Colleen replied, and as she did, she slid a dagger from the back of her belt and put it firmly against the monk's back, forcing him to arch his shoulders.

"I am no friend of Bishop De'Unnero," the man said.

"Thought ye'd be seein' it that way," said Colleen, but she didn't remove the dagger.

"Then you are no friend of Father Abbot Markwart and no friend of the Abellican Church," Pony replied. "And closer in mind to Avelyn Desbris than you believe."

"The college branded him heretic and murderer."

"To the dactyl's own home with your college!" Pony retorted. "I've not the time to teach you the truth, Brother—"

"Brother Talumus," Colleen explained, "one I thought a friend."

The monk half turned and glowered at her. "That was before I knew you conspired with outlaws."

"One who came out here to plot against De'Unnero has a strange way of defining that term," Pony remarked.

"Are we to convince him or kill him?" asked the brutal Colleen. Both Pony and Brother Talumus understood that she was not kidding.

"Not kill him," Pony replied immediately.

"Are ye ready to be convinced, then?" Colleen asked him in his ear.

Talumus did not reply, but neither did he turn away or give any clue that he would not be receptive.

"Did you revere your former abbot?" Pony asked.

"Speak no ill of Abbot Dobrinion!" Talumus replied, his tone more forceful even than when he had attacked Pony.

"Never that," said Pony, "for Dobrinion was a good man, a great man, and more akin to Avelyn Desbris than you know. That is why Father Abbot Markwart had him murdered."

The monk stammered a syllable, then chewed his lip.

"Colleen brought you here, and so I assume she has judged your character correctly," said Pony. "Though she has erred before on such measures," she added, tossing a disarming smile at the woman soldier. "I will tell you the truth, plainly, and then let you judge my veracity. Be convinced or not, as you judge."

"But if ye're not . . ." Colleen said, prodding him with the dagger.

"If you are not, then we have a place to put you until this distasteful business is complete," Pony put in. "And you shall not be mistreated, in any case."

"Abbot Dobrinion was slain by a powrie," Talumus said. "We found the wretched creature dead on the abbot's bedroom floor. And I know of no powries in St. Precious."

"Slain by the same powrie that did not take the time to open a cut on Keleigh Leigh and dip its beret in her blood?" Pony asked. That had caught Talumus by surprise, she realized by his expression.

The monk thought to respond that perhaps the creature had not the time, but changed his mind and asked bluntly, "How do you know this?"

"Because Connor Bildeborough told it to me."

"Connor, who annulled your marriage," said the unconvinced monk.

"And who came north to warn me that the same men who murdered Abbot Dobrinion were after me, and after him," Pony corrected. "Connor, who was also killed by one of those men, by a brother justice, trained and loosed by the Father Abbot of St.-Mere-Abelle."

"Connor, whose uncle was murdered by the man ye now call bishop," Colleen added.

Talumus' shoulders sagged under the weight of these accusations—ones he had obviously heard before.

Pony recognized the posture. The monk did not believe the words, of course, but neither could he dismiss them. And any hint of their truth could send his entire world crashing down around him.

"The Behrenese are being persecuted," Pony stated flatly.

Talumus, seeming thoroughly defeated, nodded.

"And you do not agree with this policy."

Again, a nod.

"Then stand with us if you will, or at least do not stand against us," said Pony. She motioned to Colleen, who at last put away her dagger.

"I will not stand against my Order," Brother Talumus said boldly.

"Then stand back and watch with an open mind," Pony explained. "And bid your fellows of St. Precious to do so as well. Bishop De'Unnero is not a good man, and not truly an Abellican at heart. We will prove that to you."

"I been a friend o' yers for years," Colleen reminded him. "Ye don't betray me on this."

"I will watch," Brother Talumus agreed after a long moment. "And I will view, and review, things in light of the revelations you have offered. But when I am done, if I am convinced that you are wrong and that your claims against the Church are unfounded, I will go against you."

Colleen's hand slid back toward the dagger, but Pony cut her action short. "That is all that we can rightfully ask," she replied, "and generous and wise of you, by any measure."

Talumus backed away from the pair, eyeing Pony nervously as he moved cautiously down the alley. When he judged that he was far enough away, he turned and ran off.

"You should not have brought him here," Pony scolded Colleen, "not yet."

"When then?" asked the other woman. "Are ye thinkin' we can stand long against the likes o' Bishop De'Unnero without any help from the monks? Bah!" She snorted. "They'll find ye and kill ye to death, don't ye doubt. I only bringed Talumus because he confided to me that another of his brothers sensed magic coming from the general area o' Fellowship Way the very last night, and he's knowin' that I been going there."

Pony's shoulders slumped at this news. She had used the hematite again last night, to visit the child that was growing within her, the child who had become such a pleasurable focus of her life of late. She could hardly comprehend that her spiritual bonding with her unborn child might have ruined everything. Were De'Unnero and his minions that efficient?

"Warned me to keep clear o' the place," Colleen went on.

"Then De'Unnero is coming," Pony reasoned.

"No," Colleen replied. "The monk that saw yer magic use told none but Talumus, who told only meself. And then I bade Talumus to tell t'other monk that it was him using the stones, and no enemies o' the Church. And so he did, and so he'll continue to say now, for I think ye handled that one well."

Pony paused to consider the words, to consider whether or not she and Belster and Dainsey should abandon the Fellowship Way altogether, though such a move would surely destroy much of the progress they had made in beginning an underground alliance over the last few weeks.

"Brother Talumus is sincere," she decided. "He will not betray us. Not now."

"Then we got some provin' to do," Colleen remarked.

True to his word, Brother Talumus was already mulling over recent events in light of Pony's words as he made his way back toward St. Precious. One meeting was particularly significant: Baron Bildeborough and another man had come to see Talumus shortly before Bishop De'Unnero had arrived in Palmaris, and shortly before Bildeborough had gone off to the south and been killed on the road to Ursal. Both Bildeborough and his unknown companion that day had spoken to Talumus about the murder of

Abbot Dobrinion and had quietly mentioned that same fact: the powrie had not cut Keleigh Leigh and dipped its beret in her blood. This now seemed meaningful indeed to the young but experienced monk.

Not knowing too much about powries, Talumus couldn't give that the same weight as had Baron Bildeborough, his companion, and now the woman, Pony. But could it be evidence of so heinous a betrayal as the Abellican Church going against one of its most respected abbots? Brother Talumus wasn't yet ready to make that jump.

In the foyer of St. Precious, Talumus was met by a friend, Brother Giulious, the one who had detected the magic use near the Fellowship Way.

"Brother!" Giulious exclaimed, gesturing at Talumus' bloodstained nose. "Pray, what has happened?"

"The issue of stone use near the Fellowship Way is settled," Talumus told him.

Giulious backed off and stared at him skeptically. "Did you not tell me that it was you with the stones?"

"Half truth," Talumus admitted, and Giulious' eyes widened with shock.

"I sought the services of a woman down there," Talumus lied. "Yes, brother, I was weak of the flesh, as are we all."

Pious Giulious nodded and lifted his hand in a customary, though little used, Church sign: raising his hand perpendicular to his chest, lifting it to his brow, then sweeping it down and to one side, back again, and down and out to the other—the sign of the living tree.

"This woman was ill," Talumus went on, "a sickness of the loins, it seems. And so I allowed her to borrow a soul stone that she might heal—"

"A street whore who knows how to use the sacred gemstones?" Giulious asked incredulously.

Talumus only smiled. "Street whores know how to do many things," he replied with a mischievous grin; and simple embarrassment provided ample deflection of any suspicion. "I went back to retrieve my stone this night, but the woman had decided that it was too useful an item for her to relinquish."

"Brother Talumus!"

"She hit me," the monk explained.

"But you retrieved the stone?"

"Of course," Talumus lied, and he hoped that Giulious would not ask to see it!

But Giulious, whom the others at St. Precious often called "Giulious the innocent" was a trusting soul, and he only made the sign of the living tree again.

"I trust that you will hold confidence about this matter," Talumus bade him, "and say nothing at all about the detection of magic use near the Fellowship Way. Bishop De'Unnero is not enamored of me, and I need no more grief from him!"

Giulious smiled warmly at his friend. "You should repent," he scolded sincerely, "and should be more careful of the company you keep."

Talumus smiled at this man, whom he considered a dear friend.

Satisfied, Brother Giulious went to the task of helping Talumus clean up his face, chattering about how the whore did indeed seem possessed of other talents—particularly in the area of striking a man.

Talumus grunted now and then to make Giulious think he was actually listening, but in truth, his thoughts were far from that room, were back in the alley near the Fellowship Way. So very much to consider, and all of it more than a little unsettling.

"Yo, ye boy, bring the cup over!" the drunk yelled, and he lurched so forcefully in the direction of the battered cup lying on its side in the alley that he overbalanced, even from his sitting position, and tumbled down against the base of the wall.

Belli'mar Juraviel, looking very much a street waif, his face darkened with soot to disguise the distinctive angular elven features, his wings folded under a cloak—uncomfortably so!—glanced at the wanted item, but made no move to retrieve it.

"Ye hearin' me, b-boy?" the drunk stuttered, pulling himself to a sitting position again, and then—with great difficulty and using the wall as support every inch of the way—moving up to stand. "Ye get me the cup or I'll give ye a beatin'!"

Juraviel shook his head in disgust. This man represented the worst example of humanity the elf had ever seen—worse even than the three trappers he had met during his travels with Nightbird. And he knew that his elven kindred, scattered all about in strategic locations, were equally unimpressed, and probably growing much more impatient than he with this drunk's tiresome and troublesome rambling.

"Ye hear me, boy?" the drunk yelled more loudly, too loudly. He took a step forward.

Juraviel exploded into motion, spinning a kick that landed solidly against the man's loins, then jumping up—and inadvertently and instinctively trying to beat his wings for support—and how that hurt!—and landing a pair of solid punches on the man's face, sending him back hard against the building.

"Oh, but ye're up for some sport," sputtered the drunk, and he tried to push himself off the building.

But then he jerked weirdly—and Juraviel did, too—as a brick bounced off the side of the man's head and fell to the gutter. The drunk went down, out cold.

The elf looked up to see one of his kin standing on the edge of the roof.

"You may have killed him," Juraviel whispered harshly.

"And if not, and if he awakens and begins that unwelcome noise again, then surely I shall!" said the other elf. Juraviel recognized the voice to be that of Lady Dasslerond herself, and knew from her tone that she was hardly speaking idly.

With agility beyond that of the most dexterous human, the elven lady spun over the edge and slipped down the building's side, coming lightly to her feet beside Juraviel, who was bent over, checking the man to make sure he was still breathing.

"Has she returned?" Lady Dasslerond asked.

"She is inside, tending tables," Juraviel replied, "as Belster's wife."

"Belster's pregnant wife," Dasslerond remarked, "for any who would care to look closely enough."

Belli'mar Juraviel didn't disagree; Pony's condition was becoming more evident with each passing day.

"She dispatched that monk with ease and grace," Lady Dasslerond said cheerfully. Juraviel knew that she was offering this only for his benefit, only to make him understand that she was not truly angry with Jilseponie.

"Yet you fear the consequences of her having met with a man of the Abellican Church at this unsettled time," Juraviel replied.

"It was a dangerous ploy for the soldier woman to bring him," Lady Dasslerond explained.

"Do you fear the Abellican Church that much?" Juraviel asked.

"Not I, but your friend certainly should."

"Lady Dasslerond, too, by my guess," the observant Juraviel dared to reply.

To his relief, the lady of Andur'Blough Inninness did not argue. "I fear any humans who believe that their god sanctions their actions," she admitted. "And this Church has shown a propensity for making enemies of those who are different. Witness the plight of the Behrenese at the docks. Could the Touel'alfar expect any better treatment?"

"Would the Touel'alfar care?" Juraviel asked.

"We are more tied to the humans than we like to admit," Lady Dasslerond replied grimly.

Juraviel didn't understand; the only ties that he knew of, other than those with the rangers, were dealings with a few selected merchants, trading boggle for those goods the elves could not get in their valley. And all that was done in secrecy: anonymous drops of goods, without even most of the merchants understanding the true source of the wine.

"The war is ended," Lady Dasslerond explained. "And after every war, the humans inevitably expand their borders. They'll not go south, for the folk of Honce-the-Bear have no stomach for a war with the kingdom of Behren, despite the Bishop's actions against the dark-skinned humans here. Nor will they go north, where they would inevitably face the undesired prospect of angering the fierce Alpinado-rans. And east lies the great sea."

"And west lies Andur'Blough Inninness," Juraviel reasoned.

"They are already too close, by my estimation, especially if their leadership becomes entrenched in the fanaticism and self-righteousness of the Abellican Church," Lady Dasslerond explained.

"But how to stop them, short of war?" asked Juraviel. "And we could not hope to win such a struggle against the human masses."

"It may be time to speak openly with the King of Honce-the-Bear," Lady Dasslerond said simply, the stunning declaration making Juraviel's knees go weak, "as it was in centuries past."

"Would the present human king even remember the Touel'alfar?" Juraviel asked. "Are we not merely fireside tales to him or songs for children?"

"If he does not remember, then he will learn the truth," Lady Dasslerond replied. "Or perhaps it will not come to that. Palmaris may prove to be the keystone to the Church's aspirations."

"And the King is on his way here, or soon will be, by all reports," Juraviel put in.

"And so is the Father Abbot," Lady Dasslerond reminded.

Juraviel knew that already, of course, but he winced anyway at hearing the words spoken.

"We came here to gather information," the lady said firmly. "The opportunity to do such will be greater when the powers of the kingdom gather before us. So fear not, Belli'mar Juraviel. These events are to the benefit of the Touel'alfar.

"And that," she added pointedly, staring hard at him, "is all that should matter to you."

Belli'mar Juraviel gave a low whistle and stared hard at the wall of the Fellowship Way. The road was about to get darker for his human friend Jilseponie, he knew, and it seemed as if there was little that he could do about it.

As soon as she donned her disguise and entered the common room of the Fellowship Way, Pony knew there had been some trouble. One of Belster's primary informants glanced her way, offered a slight nod, and then headed for the door, leaving a sour-looking Belster leaning on the bar. The place was not so crowded at this late hour, and so Pony went to her duties efficiently, thinking she would be able to speak privately with her co-conspirator soon enough.

It didn't happen that way, as more and more people filtered into the Fellowship Way, many of them part of the underground network, seeking information, Pony realized. That only confirmed for her that something troubling had indeed occurred.

Finally, at halfway between midnight and dawn, the last of the patrons staggered out of the tavern, leaving Pony alone with Belster and Dainsey.

"A fight at the docks," Belster offered before the obviously curious

Pony even had the chance to ask. "A band of soldiers, drunk by all reports, wandered down to the docks in search of some fun at the expense of the Behrenese."

"Beatin' a child!" an outraged Dainsey interjected. "Ye're callin' that fun?"

"I'm calling it nothing but trouble," Belster corrected angrily. "And they weren't beating the lad—a young man more than a child—but just pushing him about."

"And askin' for what they got, by me own measure," said an obstinate Dainsey.

"The other Behrenese came to the boy's aid?" Pony asked.

"A dozen o' them," Belster confirmed, "matching the soldier's fists with clubs."

"Beat 'em good," Dainsey muttered. "And left 'em on the docks, one near to dyin', though we've heard that the monks saved him. Pity."

"Blessing, ye mean," Belster shot back. "As it's standing, there's a thousand soldiers moving near to the docks, or meaning to with the morning light."

"They'll not likely find a single Behrenese waiting for them," Pony reasoned.

"That'd be a wise choice," Belster grimly replied.

"Ah, but it'll blow past like a summer storm, and no damage done," Dainsey said hopefully, slapping a rag against a tabletop, wiping it briskly. "Short memories, and shorter still when men been takin' o' the bottle."

"More likely, the Bishop will find a scapegoat or two and hang them in the public square," Belster reasoned. "How is your Captain Al'u'met to like that? If the man is still about, I mean."

That caught Pony as more than a little curious. "Still about?" she echoed.

"Al'u'met's boat put out to the water and put up sail," Belster explained, "heading south down the river, so it's said."

Pony mulled that over for a moment. It seemed strange to her that Al'u'met would leave without informing her, so what had sent him on his way? To beg audience in the court at Ursal, perhaps, or to find allies along the towns south of Palmaris? There were rumors floating about town that the King planned to visit. Did Al'u'met plan to intercept him?

"Al'u'met will return soon enough," she decided, for she knew that the man would never desert his kin. "And as to this supposed hanging, he'll not stand for it. The Behrenese would likely choose an open battle before allowing one of theirs to be unjustly hanged."

"Then the Behrenese are stupid," Belster replied, his blunt and somewhat callous attitude catching Pony off guard. "If they give the Bishop the excuse he needs, they will be killed to the man, woman, and child."

"And how are we to like that?" Pony asked suspiciously. "Where do we stand?"

"In the gallery," Belster replied firmly, "watching."

"Acting?"

"Watching," the innkeeper said again. "We are not ready for any war," he added with a snort. "And likely, we'll never be ready for such a war. If you are thinking that you shall find many who will join you as you try to help the black-skins, then understand that you are wrong."

Pony forced several steadying breaths into her lungs to calm herself and give her a moment before responding. "And where does Belster stand?" she asked, though the answer was becoming painfully obvious.

"I told you a long time ago that I am no friend to the black-skin Behrenese," Belster admitted. "I have never pretended otherwise. I do not like the way they smell and do not like the god they pray to."

Pony looked to Dainsey for support, but the woman just kept wiping the same table, harder and harder.

"The god they worship is their own to choose," Pony said to Belster. "And for their smell—well, I'd guess that few would care for the smell of Belster O'Comely, with beer spilled all over him."

"Their choice, and mine, too."

"And what if I stand with them," Pony asked. "Will Belster then stand in the gallery of the curious cowards?"

"I am not going to fight you on this, girl," Belster replied so calmly that Pony understood her appeals would have little effect. "You knew how I felt about the black-skins all along. I never made it a secret. And I am not the only one feeling such. If the Behrenese mean to stand with us against the Bishop, then so be it, but—"

"But we are not to stand with them," Pony finished for him, her hands clenched at her side, her voice trembling with mounting rage. "Which group, then, shows the stronger character, Belster O'Comely? Which shows itself worthy of alliance and friendship, and which shows cowardice?"

"Not going to fight you on this, girl," Belster said again. "I feel as I feel, and you are not about to change that. Do not for a moment think that you can."

Pony winced and grimaced repeatedly, chewed her bottom lip, and finally just headed for some privacy in her room. Anger burned in her— indeed it did—but more profoundly came the feeling of disappointment. With more the weakness of resignation than the fiery posture of rage, she fell to the edge of her bed, sitting, her shoulders slumped.

It was a side of Belster that she had suspected since her first mention of the Behrenese and Captain Al'u'met, but one that she had chosen not to probe more deeply. For she liked this man honestly, and he had treated her as a daughter—and indeed, he did remind her of her adoptive parents, though his temperament leaned more toward Pettibwa's than toward Graevis'. Yes, she liked him, indeed she loved him, but how could she see past this obvious flaw?

Pony looked up to find Dainsey standing in her doorway. Dainsey always seemed to be standing in her doorway!

"Don't ye judge him too harsh," the woman said quietly. "Belster's a good man—just a bit blind on the black-skins. He's not knowin' many, and none well."

"And that excuses his attitude?" Pony shot back, throwing up a wall of anger in self-defense.

"Not meanin' to," Dainsey replied. "But it's just words, and words from a scared man. He's not thinkin' that we can win, with the black-skins or not. Don't ye judge him till the fightin' starts, if it starts. Belster O'Comely's not to stand and watch while an innocent man gets his neck stretched, whatever the color o' that man's skin."

Pony's wall of anger tumbled down. She believed Dainsey; she had to believe that about a man she so loved. Though she still feared that Belster's warning about the others would prove true, Dainsey's words had at least brought a temporary comfort.

"Would ye really fight with the black-skins?" Dainsey asked. "I mean, if ye knew ye'd be standin' alone?"

Pony nodded, and started to explain that she'd get her fight with De'Unnero, at least, and then, even if the rest of the Palmaris army and clergy fell over her, she would have the satisfaction of knowing that she took the evil Bishop down with her. She wanted to say all that, wanted to proclaim that principle would guide her more than any odds or hopes of ultimate victory, but she stopped short, a puzzled expression on her face, her hand going to her belly.

Dainsey was beside her in an instant. "What is it, Miss Pony?" she asked in alarm, but that faded as Pony turned to her, a smile, a contented glow, spreading across her face.

"He moved," Pony explained.

Dainsey clapped her hands together, then slipped one to Pony's belly. Sure enough, there came another kick of a little foot—or a brush of a little hand.

Pony didn't even try to hold back the tears, though she knew that their source was much more than the simple joy at the first obvious movement of her unborn child.

How could she, in good conscience, go to war with a life growing in her belly?

CHAPTER

❖ 23 ❖

Unleashed

"From Captain Kilronney," the soldier explained, handing the parchment over to the Bishop.

De'Unnero took it with a look of surprise etched upon his face. "The man can write?" he asked incredulously. "A mere soldier?"

The other man bristled, but that only made the Bishop snort all the louder. De'Unnero had made no secret of his feelings that the soldiers, city's and King's, were inferior when measured against the Abellican brothers. Whenever his patrols went out onto the streets, whether their mission was to find gemstones or simply to enforce the laws of the Bishop, the accompanying monks, whatever their rank and experience, always held jurisdiction over the highest ranking soldiers. Obviously, the soldiers weren't enamored of this fact, but De'Unnero, so entrenched in power, with both King and Father Abbot standing behind him, hardly cared. In fact, he made it a point to enjoy the situation. He did now, with his messenger.

"And did you read it?" he asked the man.

"Of course not, me lord."

"Could you have read it?" De'Unnero asked slyly.

"I was told to deliver it to yerself with all speed," the soldier replied, and he shuffled his feet uncomfortably, a motion De'Unnero noticed and enjoyed. "And so I rode hard to Caer Tinella, so hard that me poor horse had to be put down. They give me another, and just as hard, I rode to yer court. Three hunnerd miles, me lord, though I left the side o' Captain Kilronney barely a week ago."

"And you are to be commended," the Bishop assured the soldier, then held up the rolled parchment before the man's eyes and said more forcefully, "but did you read it?"

"No, me lord."

"Could you have read it?"

The soldier did not immediately answer, and so the Bishop, smiling wickedly, pulled the ribbon from the parchment and unrolled it so that the penned side was exposed to the soldier's eyes.

The man winced, but dutifully held his ground.

"What does it say?" the Bishop demanded.

The soldier gnashed his teeth, but did not answer.

"Tell me!"

"I canno', me lord!"

De'Unnero backed off at once, walked over to his desk, and slid comfortably to sit on the edge, turning the parchment around carefully. "Your captain writes well," he started to say, noting the smooth and steady sweep of Kilronney's lettering, but he stopped short, his eyes widening as the meaning of the words began to come clear to him, as he began to realize that the outlaw Nightbird was apparently slipping through his fingers again.

With a growl, the Bishop tossed the parchment across the desk, his angry gaze falling over the messenger, who, he noted, had backed a couple of steps closer to the door.

"Leave me!" the Bishop barked. The man was more than ready to comply, turning quickly and, without consciously considering the act, stepping before he could even reach for the door, and banging into it, hard, before finally managing to stagger around it and out of the room.

De'Unnero grabbed the tiger's paw from his pocket and nearly fell into its magic, running out full for the northland. He put the stone back, though, reminding himself of his duties—duties the Father Abbot would view as more important, even if De'Unnero disagreed with that estimate—and produced instead his soul stone.

Markwart should hear of this, he decided. He would make the Father Abbot see things his way.

Markwart tried to concentrate on his prayers, but every other line came to him, in that strengthening voice within his mind, as "Let him go."

I pray thee, Lord, that the sacred stones forever hold thy power.
Let him go.
I pray thee, Lord, that you guide my hand through thine eternal plan.
Let him go.
Show to me wickedness, that I might dispatch.
Let him go.
Show to me goodness, that I might revel in thy glory.
Let him go!

And so it went throughout those evening prayers immediately following Markwart's latest talk with Bishop De'Unnero, the talk in which De'Unnero had begged to be sent after the man called Nightbird, in which the

Bishop's spirit had screamed at Markwart that not only Nightbird but also the five conspirator heretics might slip away, beyond their grasp forever.

Let him go!

The Father Abbot leaned back from the kneeling stool, giving up all attempts at prayer. "Why the Barbacan?" he asked aloud. Whatever could Nightbird and the five rogue monks want in that forlorn and blasted place? Markwart had seen the Barbacan, had gone there spiritually, inhabiting the body of Brother Francis when the expedition had reached its destination, and he saw nothing practical to gain from a journey to a place that had been utterly destroyed in the collision between Avelyn and the demon dactyl.

"Do they plan to build a shrine?" the Father Abbot asked, and he chuckled at the thought, for how long could such a structure, could any human-built structure, survive in the wilds of the monster-infested northland? But perhaps that was their plan, he mused. To build a shrine and organize pilgrimages, as had been done in the past for other saintly heroes. The mere thought of that brought another smile to the Father Abbot's withered old lips. He pictured hundreds of eager, misguided fools, on the road to pay homage to a murdering heretic, only to be slaughtered on their way by marauding monsters.

What perfect justice.

But the voice in his head did not agree, and showed him a different scene, one where the outpouring for Avelyn—or at least, against the present incarnation of the Abellican Church—proved so great that the road was tamed, and pilgrimages common and successful.

And then came another teaser: *Perhaps they do not have all the stones.*

Markwart was nodding his head before the refrain began again. *Let him go.*

Indeed, it was time, the Father Abbot realized, to unleash De'Unnero, to give the Bishop his greatest reward and let him settle this issue of Nightbird.

And time to alter the course of Palmaris, to show a gentler side of the Abellican Church before the King's visit, before his own visit.

A few moments later, the Father Abbot knocked on the door of Brother Francis Dellacourt's room.

The man, who had obviously been asleep, opened the door a crack, then threw it wide when he recognized the caller. Markwart swept into the room, motioning for Francis to close the door.

Francis complied, and then rushed back to stand before Markwart.

"Bishop D'Unnero has found a road he must travel," the Father Abbot explained, "a real one, and not a spiritual path," he added, seeing the confusion on Francis' sleepy face.

"But the city—" Francis began, but Markwart cut him short.

"Go quickly to Palmaris," he ordered. "Use whatever magics might help you, take a solid supply of gemstones—whatever you deem necessary."

"Necessary?" Francis echoed, but his question was, in truth, more a reflection of his general confusion, and that Markwart would allow him to take any gemstones at all.

"You are to serve as headmaster of St. Precious and as interim bishop of Palmaris while Bishop De'Unnero is away," Markwart explained.

Francis swayed and seemed as if he was about to faint.

"I will soon journey to your side, to meet with King Danube as he, too, comes to the critical city," Markwart went on. "You are not to change any of Bishop De'Unnero's policies, but do loosen the grip. By comparison to Marcalo De'Unnero, the folk of the city should speak favorably of Brother Francis Dellacourt." Markwart paused to listen to the voice in his head, then repeated, "They should speak favorably of *Master* Francis Dellacourt."

Again the sway, and this time, Francis had to sit on the edge of his bed or fall over onto the floor. "But the procedures to elevate me to master are lengthy," he reasoned.

"We have discussed this before," Markwart said sternly. "Why are you so surprised?"

"To master and then to interim bishop?" Francis asked incredulously. "It is so fast, and at a time of such crisis."

"A crisis is the only time such a thing could be done," Markwart explained. "The other abbots will not question me, not when they understand you are simply a pawn for the betterment of our grasp of Palmaris."

Francis blinked repeatedly, trying to digest the words.

"Of course, I will portray you as such," Markwart said with a laugh, and he dropped a comforting hand on Francis' shoulder. "A mere pawn, though we two both know the truth of it."

Francis nodded numbly. "I fear that I am not worthy of your expectations," he admitted, lowering his head.

Markwart laughed at him. "I have no expectations," he said, his voice changing, growing suddenly grave, bordering on ominous. "Little will be required from you in this matter. You are to go to Palmaris and allow things to play out as Bishop De'Unnero has begun them. The less the people—even your fellows at St. Precious—see of you and hear of you, the better. Just loosen the grip. Cut back the patrols and tax demands and instruct the preachers to temper their rhetoric."

"Am I to lead in any rituals?" Francis asked.

"No!" came the sharp retort. "To do so could only invite criticism, and that you cannot afford if I am to further solidify your position—as master or as bishop."

Francis let his gaze fall to the floor.

"Fear not, for you will have your day, and sooner than you believe," Markwart promised him. "Headmaster will lead, very swiftly, to abbot of St. Precious, do not doubt; and it might be that the time will soon come for

Bishop De'Unnero to be replaced permanently. The King might well demand that of me, at least. How convenient for me to have Headmaster Francis already in place as logical successor."

The overwhelmed Francis nodded and asked nothing more, and so Markwart left him alone with his thoughts. The last statement, along with Markwart's pointedly telling him that he should compare favorably *to De'Unnero*, led him to believe that the Bishop had fallen far from Markwart's graces, or would be on the road out of Palmaris for a very long time. In any case, the other thing that Brother—soon-to-be-Master—Francis understood was that Markwart's description to the other abbots of him as a pawn would prove to be a lot closer to the truth than the Father Abbot wanted him to believe.

But Francis was soon able to dismiss all of those unsettling notions. The important thing was that he, despite his helping the five renegade monks, was still playing a vital role in the direction of the Order, even if that role would be only as Markwart's pawn. Jojonah and Braumin had forgiven him his crime against Grady Chilichunk, that was true, but Father Abbot Markwart had never blamed him in the first place. To Francis now that lack of guilt to absolve was preferable.

"I have considered your information most carefully," the spirit of the Father Abbot said to De'Unnero in the Bishop's private quarters at Chasewind Manor later that same night. "You are certain that Nightbird means to go north?"

"By the words of Shamus Kilronney," De'Unnero replied. "I see no reason for the soldier to lie to me."

"There are resentments in Palmaris," Markwart warned.

"Shamus Kilronney is a man of the King, and never the Baron," De'Unnero was quick to answer. "I chose him as my spy because I trust his loyalty to King and Crown, and therefore, to me, as bishop and King's voice in Palmaris."

"That is good," said Markwart. "And what of these other men, the six you spoke of? Can we be certain that they are our missing brethren?"

"It is likely that Brother Braumin and the other four heretics are among them," De'Unnero said. "As to the identity of the sixth man, I cannot attest."

"You will find out," Markwart instructed.

"I have spies—"

"No spies!" the Father Abbot roared. "De'Unnero alone will find out."

A look of anger and confusion came over the startled Bishop's face, but then his eyes widened as the meaning of the Father Abbot's words came clear to him. "Am I to go?" he dared to ask.

"For years you have asked for the chance to fight the one named Nightbird," Markwart explained. "Your arguments have at last convinced me that Marcalo De'Unnero alone might bring this one to justice. Do not fail me in this! The return of the stolen gemstones and the death of Avelyn's protégés will strengthen our position within the Church, and thus, the position of the Church will be strengthened within the state."

"And what am I to do with Braumin and the heretics, if it is indeed them?" De'Unnero asked breathlessly, practically panting at the possibilities looming before him.

"It would be preferable if we have one or more of them," Markwart reasoned, "that we might extract a confession before putting them all to the stake. When you slay Nightbird, his woman companion, and that filthy centaur beast, use Kilronney to help capture the rogues. If they resist, then kill them as well. All I charge you with is the return of the heads of the two closest to Avelyn and the gemstones. We can always go back for Braumin and his stooges.

"What a glorious victory lies before us, my friend," Markwart continued, "one that will play the King's hand for him. He will not dare speak against us when we walk down the streets of Palmaris with our gruesome trophies, proclaiming that the evil is purged to the cheers of thousands!"

"I have told you all along that the one called Nightbird is mine for the taking," De'Unnero replied with confidence. "I understand my role now, the calling that God brought to me when he led me to St.-Mere-Abelle and drove my body through hours of training. This hunt is the task for which Marcalo De'Unnero was born, and in it I shall not fail!"

Markwart didn't doubt him for a minute, as was reflected by the wicked laughter of his spirit. De'Unnero, so intense, rubbing his fingers together eagerly, did not join in.

"When may I go?"

"As soon as you are prepared for the road," Markwart replied.

"Prepared?" De'Unnero scoffed. "What preparations must I make?"

"A little matter of food and transport," the spirit of the Father Abbot replied sarcastically. "Are you to ride horseback or in a wagon?"

"Ride?" the Bishop echoed. "I will run, will find my food as I go."

"Pray tell me," Markwart prompted.

The Bishop grew more animated. He moved around the edge of his bed, extending his hand toward the Father Abbot, showing the spirit his tiger's paw gemstone. "It is incredible," he admitted. "Like you with the soul stone, I have found a new level with the tiger's paw. When I fell into the magic in pursuit of Baron Bildeborough, it affected more than my limb. I *was* the tiger, Father Abbot, in body and in heart; surely such a creature will have little trouble with the winter terrain."

Markwart, caught by surprise, paused to digest the startling information. He wondered if De'Unnero, too, had found this inner voice, the voice of God; his pride made him hope that the man had not!

But then he understood, for the voice told him the truth of the matter:

De'Unnero had found the higher level of stone use because of his intense emotional state when he had set out after the Baron. That intense level would be useful now, Markwart thought; again the voice showed him the way.

"Still, you have preparations to make," he said to De'Unnero. "Who is your second?"

"A pitiful sort named Brother Talumus."

"Do you trust him?"

"No."

"Tell him that you are leaving, but that he is to take no action nor inform anyone," Markwart instructed. "Tell him to deflect any questions concerning your whereabouts."

De'Unnero shook his head. "Questions and issues will be raised daily," he explained. "The road is long before me."

"And Brother Francis will leave this very morning for St. Precious to serve in your stead," Markwart explained. "That one is trustworthy, and too insignificant to cause any problems for either of us."

Now De'Unnero was smiling.

"One last issue," Markwart went on, listening again to that voice in his head. "What has happened to the merchant Crump?"

"He remains in the dungeons of St. Precious."

"Repentant?" Markwart asked.

"Hardly," replied the Bishop. "That one is far too proud and stubborn to admit the error of his actions."

"Then parade him out publicly tomorrow morning," the Father Abbot instructed. "Accuse him loudly of treason, and let the fool speak."

"He will deny it to the word."

"Then execute him in the name of the King," Markwart said callously.

Even brutal De'Unnero was taken aback by that command. But only for a moment, and then a grim smile made its way across his face.

"Now open your mind to me," Markwart instructed. "I will show you the manner in which you might best use your favored gemstone, in which you might easily attain again that highest level of magic."

They joined then, spirit to spirit, and Markwart gave the Bishop the needed information. When they were done, De'Unnero could readily bring forth the tremendous level of power—the one he had found when in pursuit of Baron Bildeborough.

"May the speed of God's own legs carry you swiftly," Markwart said, a traditional parting when haste was needed.

In answer, De'Unnero held up the tiger's paw for Markwart's spirit to see. "Indeed they shall," he said. "Indeed they shall."

❖ 24 ❖

The Light of Perspective

Proud and stubborn Aloysius Crump played his role perfectly in the public square the next morning. Standing with his hands behind his back lashed through a loop in a heavy pole, he answered De'Unnero's accusations of treason and murderous intent by spitting in the Bishop's face.

That only made it all the more delicious for De'Unnero. Proclaiming the glory of God, he brought forth a gemstone, a serpentine, and summoned its bluish-white protective shield—not around himself—around the surprised Crump.

The crowd, several hundred strong, mostly street vendors and fishmongers out early, gasped at the display, though they knew not what it might be.

One woman at the back of the crowd, standing more in an alley than in the square, recognized the glow, though she couldn't fathom the reasoning behind putting it around the accused merchant. Pony watched quietly and so did Dainsey, standing beside her, asking her question after question without waiting for answers.

Bishop De'Unnero brought up a second protective shield, this one around himself, and then held forth another stone, glittering red.

"Ruby, for fire," Pony explained, "though no fire will have much effect on either of the men with the serpentine shields about them."

"Then why?" Dainsey asked.

Pony shook her head, but then her eyes widened and her mouth gaped as she watched De'Unnero plunge his ruby-holding hand through Crump's serpentine shield, holding the red gem against the man's shoulder.

"In God's name," she gasped.

"What does it mean?" Dainsey asked.

"I give you one final chance to denounce your actions, Aloysius Crump," Bishop De'Unnero cried loudly, "one last chance to admit your treason against the King of Honce-the-Bear and live."

Crump spat on him again, and moved to spit yet a third time. But his eyes widened and he gasped repeatedly, the saliva bubbling in his mouth as De'Unnero began bringing forth the fires of the ruby, fires contained by the unrelenting serpentine shield and within the body of Aloysius Crump. Smoke streamed from his shoulder; his eyes fluttered and rolled up.

"In the name of the King, then, let the fires of God cleanse you!" De'Unnero proclaimed. "And may he have mercy on your tainted soul!" And with that, the Bishop loosed the full power of the ruby.

Its energy bulged and shook the serpentine shield, but no flames could pass through that barrier, nor could Crump.

"He's alive with fire!" Dainsey cried. Everyone else in the square cried out, as well, for the man within the serpentine shield seemed an orange ball of flame, a living creature of fire.

Crump was consumed suddenly, brutally, the energy of the fiery burst incinerating his clothing, his skin, evaporating his bodily fluids.

De'Unnero pulled his hand back and dropped the serpentine shields, and the blackened, tattered remains of Aloysius Crump tumbled to the platform.

"God be praised," the Bishop said. He walked away, his last duty done, eager for the road that would bring him to Nightbird.

By the time Brother Francis set out on the road from St.-Mere-Abelle, before the midpoint that same morning, the city of Palmaris was without its leader, as eager De'Unnero had already begun his swift flight to the north.

Francis' movements were less eager and far less swift. He and five bodyguards rode in a wagon drawn by two strong horses, moving steadily along the road to the west. They carried a valuable load: several chests of gol' bears to be used by Francis to endear himself to the Palmaris populace.

Normally the seventy-mile journey to the Masur Delaval would take three full days, but Markwart had charged him to take no more than two. To that end, one of the other brothers carried a hematite and a turquoise; he would use them to bring in animals and steal the life force from them, lending it to the horses.

And so at the end of that first day, Francis and his fellows had put more than forty miles behind them. When night descended, their team fresh from the life force of some white-tailed deer, they continued on.

Francis preferred the frenetic pace. Since they didn't stop for the night, there was no time for any of them to relax; and he did not have to face the inevitable introspection, the thousand questions and thousand doubts that surrounded him. He drove the team until exhaustion overwhelmed him, and then he slept, but only for a brief period. His second nap came shortly after the dawn of the second day, and Francis quickly fell into a deep slumber, one that might have lasted well past noon. However, he was roused with still two hours to go before midday, and notified that they had reached the great river.

A fog was thick on the Masur Delaval, so Francis could not yet see the outline of the city that would serve as his new home. By the time the slow-moving ferry had crossed half the river, though, that fog was gone; there, before Francis, loomed all his doubts.

King Danube's journey to Palmaris was not nearly as swift, though certainly more comfortable. Danube, Duke Targon Bree Kalas, and Constance Pemblebury, along with several other nobles, sailed on the royal ship, *River Palace,* a large caravel crewed by the most experienced sailors and oarsmen in the King's military, staffed by beautiful women, and stocked with the finest foods and finest drinks.

Surrounding the ship sailed half of Ursal's fleet, ten warships loaded with weapons and soldiers. The miniature fleet sailed in the defensive formation called the lance-left—two ships behind *River Palace*, two to the port, one directly ahead of her, and the remaining five strung westward from *River Palace*'s starboard bow. The lead ship was some six to eight hundred feet ahead of the King's caravel; lookouts watched for danger both along the riverbank and in the waters ahead.

Not that the King and his escort were expecting any trouble; riders had been sent ahead along both riverbanks, warning the local inhabitants to stay away from the water and to have no boats out when the red sail emblazoned with the black bear rampant of King Danube—the mainsail of every warship of Ursal—came into view.

As they were in no hurry, they meant to put in at nearly every port; the King had allowed for three full weeks of travel at a leisurely pace. And so it was, the days drifting lazily and uneventfully past them, the on-board party nearly constant and growing bawdier by the day.

They were at just such revelry late one afternoon when the ship lurched unexpectedly, throwing more than a few to the deck.

"Captain, do warn us!" the King cried to the man standing on the bridge.

"Battle mast!" Targon Bree Kalas interrupted, running forward past the King. Danube turned to see the man leap to the rail, grab a line, and then lean out so he could get an unobstructed view of the river ahead.

"The lead ship has dropped its mainsail!" Kalas explained. "As has the second!"

"What is it?" King Danube asked his captain.

"A ship in the river ahead," Kalas answered before the captain had a chance to respond, "a common trader, by the looks of her sails."

"I thought we instructed all vessels to keep off the water," King Danube replied.

"As you ordered, my King," the captain replied.

"But this one either did not hear or chose to ignore," Kalas added.

"Order it to move aside, then," said the King, "or sink it!"

"We are positioning to act accordingly," the captain assured him.

Duke Kalas looked at his King and smiled at the captain's false bravado. Danube, a man of action, was likely as enthralled as Kalas over the sudden excitement, the first excitement other than carnal since the journey had begun. But Danube had to keep up appearances, and thus his seemingly aggravated call for sinking the trader. The ship would move aside, they both knew, for it stood no chance of winning a battle with the warships in Danube's fleet.

The *River Palace* and her escorts dropped sail and were propelled ahead by their oarsmen. The trader had lifted a white flag and had dropped anchor, a sign of parlay. The warships had formed a triangle around her, their catapults, ballistae, and archers at the ready.

"Nothing in the water ahead of her," Kalas observed.

They all watched, intrigued, as a small boat was lowered from the trader, then rowed out to the nearest Ursal ship.

"Saudi Jacintha!" came a shout through a horn from that ship, a call echoed down the line until it came to the ears of Danube and the others.

"Saudi Jacintha?" Constance Pemblebury echoed, a puzzled look on her face; the words meant nothing to her.

"The vessel's name," Kalas explained. Then he tapped his finger against his chin, considering the name, one he thought he had heard before.

A second message was passed down the line, this one naming Captain Al'u'met, who had sailed all the way from Palmaris in hopes of speaking with King Danube.

"I know no such man," an exasperated Danube said. "Captain, call back for the ship to move aside or be sent to the depths. I have no time—"

"Al'u'met!" Kalas said with sudden recognition. "Of course."

"You know the man?" Danube asked.

"Behrenese," Kalas replied. "A fine sailor by all reports."

"Behrenese?" Danube echoed incredulously. "This ship, this *Saudi Jacintha*, from Behren?"

"Sails from Ursal and Palmaris," Kalas clarified. "Al'u'met is Behrenese, but his crew is not, nor is his ship. He claims to be a subject of the King of Honce-the-Bear, I believe." There was another little fact about Al'u'met, concerning the man's religious convictions, that Kalas knew as well, but he thought it better to keep that private for the time being.

"You know him?"

"I have heard his name, that is all," Kalas admitted. "Surely a Behrenese ship's captain on the Masur Delaval is a rarity, and thus Al'u'met has gained some measure of fame."

"And he has come from Palmaris in hopes of speaking to me," King Danube mumbled. "Cheeky, I would say."

"Perhaps," Kalas said in a leading tone. Then he and Danube locked gazes, and both understood the potential significance of a Behrenese sailor coming from Palmaris. What news might this Al'u'met bring King Danube? What stories of the terrors of Bishop De'Unnero?"

Off to the side, Abbot Je'howith shuffled his feet uneasily, and that only made Kalas press on more firmly.

"Hear him," the duke begged the King. "We know not the true situation in Palmaris, only what aggrieved merchants and churchmen have told us; and obviously both are prejudiced on this issue."

"As is a Behrenese sailor," Je'howith pointedly reminded them.

"But at least it may provide a third perspective," Kalas shot back, and the two eyed each other dangerously.

King Danube glanced around, trying to measure the level of intrigue among his entourage. He didn't want to interrupt the party and certainly didn't want to turn the rest of the voyage glum for the sake of a mere sailor—and especially one of Behrenese descent. But such a meeting might actually serve to make the voyage more tolerable.

"You cannot grant audience to every commoner who comes begging," Je'howith remarked, but the abbot's opposition only strengthened Danube's resolve.

"Send a messenger to him to see what he desires," the King said to Duke Kalas. "If his subject is worthy of my attention, arrange for the merchant boat to lead us back to Palmaris, where I will find a moment's time to speak with the man."

"Drop a boat and two to row!" Duke Kalas ordered, taking command of the situation. The crew, not daring to question his authority, immediately complied. To everyone's surprise, and to the delight of many ladies, the Duke then swung over the rail and dropped nimbly into the small craft, standing in the prow as the two men began to row.

"Such a man of action," Constance Pemblebury muttered, but her sarcasm was lost on the swooning ladies all about her.

Targon Bree Kalas loved the water, loved the lurching motion of a boat and the feel of damp wind on his face. He would gladly give up his land holdings for the title of Duke of the Mirianic, but that title belonged to Duke Bretherford of Entel, who showed no signs of dying anytime soon, and who had several heirs. So Kalas took his waterborne pleasures where he could find them—and he found one now, the men behind him propelling the craft past the four warships ahead.

The sight of the three Ursal warships filled him with pride as they came into view. One ship had its two heavy ballistae tilted slightly upward. Kalas understood that these weapons shot circular bands wrapped in chains. When flung out, the spinning motion of the bands caused the jagged chains to spread wide, shredding the enemy's sails.

A second ship carried two small catapults that shot burning pitch; and the third fired metal-capped ballistae spears that could drive fatal holes through the hulls of any but the most heavily armored ships. Add to those heavy weapons the rows of skilled archers—their great yew bows bent back, their many arrows wrapped with rags, ready to be lit—and Kalas knew without question that the *Saudi Jacintha* had no options; any show of resistance would result in the swift destruction of that vessel and all aboard.

Kalas ordered his oarsmen to bring him right up alongside the *Jacintha* to a jack ladder that had been dropped. He recognized the man standing at the rail as Captain Al'u'met.

"You have requested an audience with the King?" the Duke asked, accepting Al'u'met's extended hand to help him to the deck of the *Saudi Jacintha*.

"Indeed, that was my sole purpose in sailing south," Al'u'met replied. "The rumors in Palmaris said that King Danube was on his way, and I know that it is not customary in this difficult season for the King to travel. I hoped he would choose the more comfortable way of the river over the roads."

Kalas glanced around at the warships. "You view this as a favorable situation?" he asked with obvious sarcasm.

"I could have asked for nothing less," Al'u'met replied. "And, truthfully, if I did not find my King so well guarded, it would have been cause for concern."

Kalas smiled at the fine answer, particularly at Al'u'met's reference to Danube as "my King."

"I pray that King Danube will hear me," Al'u'met went on. "Again, that is all that I could rightly ask, and more than I, a humble sailor, deserve. But there are problems in Palmaris that he must know of, and I, perhaps better than anyone, am in a position to explain them."

"From your own perspective," Kalas reasoned.

"An honest perspective," the tall black-skinned man replied, squaring his shoulders.

"And these problems concern the Behrenese of Palmaris?"

Al'u'met nodded. "They are being unfairly persecuted by a bishop out of control—" Kalas' smile and upraised hand stopped him.

"This is known to the King," the Duke explained. His mind was whirling at the possibilities here, for it was obvious that Al'u'met would prove to be another witness against the Bishop, and thus, against Church control. King Danube had set the terms of any meeting with the sailor—a meeting that would occur in Palmaris. But Kalas feared that Je'howith would find a way to deflect the situation by then; also, the Father Abbot might already be in Palmaris by the time the King arrived. "But perhaps it would be better if he heard them again, from a true witness," the Duke decided, and he turned aside. Al'u'met, after a cautionary glance around, led the way back into the rowboat.

Again Duke Kalas took the position in the prow, so he was the first to witness the incredulous look on the face of King Danube when they neared the *River Palace* and the King noted the new passenger.

"Pray you listen to this man here and now, my King," the Duke said, climbing over the rail and onto the deck of the ship before Danube, Constance Pemblebury, and the other nobles, including an obviously distressed Abbot Je'howith. "He has come from Palmaris with news of the most recent actions of our Bishop." He turned and grabbed Al'u'met's hand then, and hoisted the man up beside him.

King Danube spent a long and uncomfortable moment staring at the impertinent Duke; but at the same time, he would hear nothing of Je'howith's complaints, holding up his hand whenever the abbot of St. Honce started to speak.

"You have come to plead the cause of your people," the King said to Al'u'met.

"I have come to speak for citizens of Palmaris who are being treated badly in the name of their King," Al'u'met corrected.

"Behrenese citizens," one of the ladies at the side muttered distastefully, but then she looked away when all eyes turned toward her.

"Of Behrenese descent," Al'u'met conceded, "many whose families have resided in Palmaris for nearly a century. And, yes, some who have recently arrived from the southern kingdom. We look different, and so you are uncomfortable," he stated bluntly, "and our customs to you seem strange, as yours do to us. But we are not criminals, and we have settled in the city honestly. We do not deserve such treatment."

"Is this what your god teaches you?" Abbot Je'howith said sarcastically.

Duke Kalas bit his lip so as not to chuckle, for he knew that the abbot was treading on dangerous ground here—with Al'u'met the Abellican.

"My god is your god," the captain calmly explained. "And, yes, he does instruct us to treat each other with decency and respect, whatever the color of our skin. Abbot Dobrinion of Palmaris knew this."

"Abbot Dobrinion is dead," Je'howith said sharply, his tone giving away his frustration with this meeting.

"The city mourns," Al'u'met replied.

"Not so," said Je'howith. "Was not Dobrinion Abbot of St. Precious when the demon dactyl came awake, when war was brought to our land?"

"You imply that Abbot Dobrinion played a role—" Al'u'met started to vehemently protest, but Danube had heard enough.

"I do not mean to start a war here on the deck of my ship," the King said. "If you insist on arguing with this man, Abbot Je'howith, pray wait until we get to Palmaris, or take your fight back to his ship with him when we are finished here. Now," he said, turning to Al'u'met, "you came here to tell me a story, and I am ready to listen."

Duke Kalas wore a smug smile. Abbot Je'howith's embittered attitude was playing favorably for him, he knew, as would the story Al'u'met was about to tell. His hopes were high, then, that the Church rule in Palmaris would be short-lived.

Of course, Duke Kalas had no way of knowing of the private meeting between the King and the imposing specter of the Father Abbot.

Captain Al'u'met's long and detailed account of the events in Palmaris not only backed up the complaints the many merchants' representatives had been moaning to King Danube, and the protests of Ambassador Rahib Daibe, but took those problems to a new level and a new urgency. The captain's accounts of women and children and the elderly having to plunge into cold waters to avoid what could only be described as torture by the city soldiers had the ladies gasping, the nobles groaning and shaking their heads, and even the King casting angry sidelong glances at an increasingly frustrated Abbot Je'howith. It wasn't that any of the gentlefolk on the *River Palace* really cared about the commoners—except perhaps for Constance Pemblebury—especially the black-skinned Behrenese, but the personal accounts did strike a chord and somewhat shamed King Danube that some of his subjects were being so badly treated.

Certainly by the time Al'u'met finished, Abbot Je'howith was rightfully uncomfortable.

"I have heard these rumors," King Danube replied to the captain. "They, in fact, have precipitated my voyage to your city."

"And you plan to correct the injustice?" Al'u'met asked.

The King, not accustomed to such talk from commoners—Al'u'met had been given permission to tell his story, but that did not extend permission for him to question the King—turned a narrow gaze on the man. "I plan to view the situation," he responded somewhat coldly.

"I only hope that you will view Palmaris with the perspective of those who have felt the uninvited wrath of Bishop De'Unnero," Al'u'met replied. "If my accounting brings that result alone, I shall consider my journey down the river worthwhile."

Duke Kalas took his arm then, for both men understood that Al'u'met was wearing thin his welcome. "I thank you for hearing me, my King," he said, dipping a low bow. "Truly your repute as a great and honest man is not unearned." He bowed again and followed Duke Kalas back to the waiting rowboat.

"You did well for your people," the Duke whispered to him as they parted at the rail.

Back on the main deck, an uncomfortable silence surrounded the gathering, with many stares continuing to fall on Abbot Je'howith. No one spoke any complaints or angry words, though, all waiting for the King to take the lead.

But Danube Brock Ursal, remembering his nighttime encounter with Father Abbot Markwart, had little to say, though much to think about.

* * *

"As you wish, Master Francis," the brother said yet again. Though he liked hearing his name prefaced by that title, Francis was growing quite perturbed by this one's overeager attention.

"Abbot Dobrinion's old quarters will more than suit my needs," Francis explained.

"But Chasewind Manor—" Brother Talumus tried to argue again.

"Chasewind Manor is to be prepared for the visit of men greater than Master Francis," Francis replied.

"Headmaster Francis," the nervous Brother Talumus corrected.

"Headmaster of St. Precious, and so at St. Precious he should stay," Francis declared in no uncertain terms. "As Bishop De'Unnero will remain at St. Precious should he return before the Father Abbot and the King have left the city."

Brother Talumus' eyes widened in horror.

"Bishop De'Unnero will defer to the King and to the Father Abbot, certainly," Francis stated, understanding the source of that terror. Francis, too, would not wish to be the one telling De'Unnero that he had been removed from his palatial home!

"The issue is settled, brother," he said. "We have more important matters to discuss."

Talumus seemed to calm down at last. The man had been in a tizzy since that morning, when the wagon from St.-Mere-Abelle had arrived at the abbey bearing both the new headmaster and, according to the whispers, a king's treasure.

"I will begin meeting with the merchants this very day," Francis explained. "You have a list, of course."

"Detailing every gemstone surrendered, and by whom," Talumus assured him.

"I will see that at once," said Francis, "and then begin with the procession of merchants."

"One will not be able to attend," Brother Talumus remarked, lowering his voice. "He did not survive his disagreement with Bishop De'Unnero, and was executed in the public square the morning the Bishop departed."

Francis gasped; but when he thought about it, when he considered De'Unnero's vicious temperament, he was not surprised. "Invite the survivors of his house, then," he instructed.

"None, I fear," Talumus replied. "Aloysius Crump had no family. Many of the servants have stayed on at his house, I have heard."

Francis struck a pensive pose. His first instinct was to wait until Father Abbot Markwart arrived and then let the older and wiser man decide what to do about the house of Crump. But Francis overruled that instinct. He was a master now, he reminded himself, the headmaster of St. Precious, and soon, possibly, to be the bishop of Palmaris. He must be decisive and assertive, must act within the desires of Father Abbot Markwart and for the good of the Church in Palmaris. "Take his house for the Church," Francis said.

Brother Talumus' eyes widened. "T-the people are already angry about the fate of Master Crump," he stammered. "Are we to insult them?"

"Take his house for the Church," Francis said again, more determinedly. "Keep the staff, all of them, and pay them well."

"And what are we to use the house for?" Talumus asked. "Will you live there?"

"Did I not already instruct you that I will remain here?" Francis shot back, feigning anger. "No, we shall find a use for the house, one that will benefit the people of Palmaris. Perhaps we will distribute food from there, or dispense healing from gemstones."

Brother Talumus' defensive frown began, slightly, to turn up into a smile, and Francis knew that he had chosen correctly, that his action, while bene-fitting the Church with a valuable piece of property, would also aid the common folk.

"The list, brother," Francis instructed, motioning at the door. "And send our messengers out to the effected merchants. Tell them that they are to be compensated this very day."

The monk nearly tripped as he spun and rushed for the door.

"And Brother Talumus," Francis called, stopping him short just before he exited the room, "do instruct our messengers that they are not to be secretive about their message."

Talumus smiled and was gone, leaving a contented Francis alone. He could get used to this position of authority, the new master decided. The constant game of politics intrigued him.

CHAPTER

❖ 25 ❖

To the North

He found Caer Tinella to be at peace. Fields were beginning to be plowed, and homes rebuilt and repaired, and new ones added. Though it had only been a matter of months since the town had been occupied by smelly goblins and powries, the stench of the creatures was gone now, De'Unnero knew, and all the folk had settled back into seemingly normal and peaceful routines.

And the Bishop meant to keep things that way. On the outskirts of the village, looking down from a hillock, he dismissed the magic of his tiger's paw, but with great reluctance. For the better part of five days, using his own inner hunger and what the spirit of Markwart had shown him, De'Unnero had been immersed in the gemstone, had been as much great cat as human being; and he liked the feeling, the power, and the freedom.

Too much, perhaps, the Bishop mused. He knew that traveling on the powerful legs of a tiger he could have covered the hundred and fifty miles from Palmaris to Caer Tinella in three days, perhaps two, since he had learned that he could use the soul stone of Aloysious Crump's ring on other animals nearby and literally feast on their life forces, a refined version of the life-stealing that monks had used on deer and the like to rejuvenate horses. Now, as a tiger, De'Unnero could go directly to the source, linking life forces with his intended prey using the soul stone and then literally eating the energies out of the creature. It was perfect, he believed: the ultimate transfer of energy; and after such a meal, De'Unnero the tiger was ready to run once more.

And yet, that beauty and strength had actually slowed him despite his urgency in dealing with the one called Nightbird. For in his travels, he had strayed from the path, and often, merely to partake of his feasts.

No matter, he believed, for he could move with all the swiftness he would need, and all the world wasn't large enough to keep Nightbird from his claws.

He went down into Caer Tinella in the simple robes of a monk, with a serene, disarming expression on his face.

"Good day, good father!" came the enthusiastic greetings from one farmer after another, the men and women hard at work repairing homes and—amazingly, for the turn of spring was still two weeks away—readying fields surprisingly free of snow. The last storm, a rainy washout, had melted all the snow along the level ground, and now the farmers were piling up stones, marking the new property lines drawn in the resettlement.

"And to you, my child," he always answered politely. "Pray tell me where I might speak with the governor of this village." The cooperative villagers spoke the name and pointed across the way to the northern reaches, fields bordered by the thick woods, where white traces of winter could still be seen, lining the edges, in the shadows of the trees.

The leader was not hard to find: a stocky woman of about forty winters, hard at work in her own field. She put up her hoe when De'Unnero approached, leaning on it with both hands atop its end and her chin on her hands.

"You are Janine o' the Lake?" De'Unnero asked cheerily, repeating the name the farmers had told him.

"That I be," she answered. "And yerself? A preacher come to start a church here in Caer Tinella, perhaps?"

"I am Brother Simple," De'Unnero lied, "passing through your humble community and nothing more. Though I do believe that the Church will send a minister as soon as the world is set aright."

"Well, we've got our Friar Pembleton," Janine o' the Lake replied, "not more than a day's ride to the east. 'Tis about all the preachin' the folk got belly for, by me own guess."

De'Unnero resisted the urge to punch her face.

"But ye're lookin' like yer own belly could use a bit of feedin'," the woman went on.

"Indeed," the monk replied, lowering his gaze humbly. "A bit of a meal and news of the road north, for I am bound for the Timberlands, where the folk have found no preaching of late."

"Nor ever, from what I heared o' that wild place," Janine said with a laugh. "Well, find a dark place and take some rest. I'll be done me work soon enough and then I'll fatten ye up for the road."

"Oh, but please, good lady," the charming monk replied, reaching for the hoe. "Do let me earn my food."

Janine seemed honestly surprised, but she did let go of the hoe. "I'm not for expectin' a monk o' St. Precious to be lookin' for work," she explained, "but I'll take the help, and be grateful for it!"

And De'Unnero did work in the field tirelessly: an effort, he presumed, that would never be expected from the Bishop of Palmaris, one that would be a stretch of expectation from the simplest of Abellican monks. Afterward, Janine o' the Lake treated him, and a select few others of the townsfolk, to a wonderful hot dinner, though De'Unnero found the food strangely dissatisfying after his wild meals.

The conversation was polite enough, and informative enough, with the Bishop being assured that the road north was safe, by all accounts, and that his journey to the Timberlands would be no more difficult than his journey from Palmaris had been thus far—unless, of course, winter made another appearance. The snow remained thicker up there, he was told.

After the meal, Brother Simple excused himself, accepting an invitation to sleep in Janine's barn and explaining that she would not likely see him in the morning, as he meant to get as early a start as possible.

In truth, the man was out of the barn and out of Caer Tinella within the hour, making his way north across the moonlit fields and falling deeper and deeper into the magic of his tiger's paw with every step. So complete was the process that his robes blended into skin, that the ring upon his finger became a band about one digit of a tiger's paw. By the time he had crossed the northernmost field, De'Unnero walked not with the comparatively clumsy stride of a man but on the padded feet of the tiger, and saw not through the daylight-attuned eyes of a human but through the keen night-senses of the great cat.

Now he was loping, front paws hitting the ground every so often for better balance or for quicker direction changes; and now, already, he smelled the presence of another animal. De'Unnero quickened his pace, following that scent, basking in it, for it wasn't the stool of an animal, wasn't even the musk of a wet pelt. It was fear, fear of him, and it came to him as something delicious, as something pure and natural.

And it was all around him. The tiger slowed, picking a careful, silent path, blending perfectly into the nighttime forest. Unseen and unheard, but his prey knew that he was coming.

That made it all the sweeter.

Keen ears caught a rustle to the side, and then he saw them: a pair of white-tailed deer, a buck and a doe, the male's antlers many pointed.

Softly the tiger moved in, one paw touching down, feeling the ground, smoothly settling.

The buck pawed the ground; the doe hopped as if to leap away.

But she didn't know which way to run, De'Unnero realized. He was close, very close, within range of a single tremendous spring. He'd go for the buck, the more difficult kill.

He leapt out with a startling, horrifying roar, claws extended, paws out wide, but the buck did not fly away and did not freeze. It came around to face the predator, head down, formidable antlers leading an answering charge. De'Unnero felt one prong sink into his chest as they crashed together, but he hardly cared, caught up in the sudden and desperate frenzy. With a second roar, the tiger's arm slashed down, slamming the buck on the head, hooking on an antler and turning the head to the side—a sudden violent jerk, the crack of bone, and then the buck was falling.

De'Unnero went right for the neck, tearing open the great veins, washing in the spouting blood. His thoughts went instinctively to the soul stone, capturing the buck's life force, feeding on every aspect of this creature.

And when he was done, he did not seek a quiet and dark place to retire, for all of the buck's energy had joined with his own. Now he was restless. He knew that he should go straight off to the north, toward Dundalis, running full speed, but the scent remained, the smell of fear.

Off he went in search of the doe; and when he found her, and caught her from behind, he feasted again.

"The road ahead is clear," Roger announced, coming back to Elbryan and Bradwarden, who had been searching east and west. Behind them in a clearing off to the side of the road—in truth no more than a path worn by the march of the demon dactyl's army—the five monks sat in a circle, huddled close to a blazing fire and eating the stew Viscenti had made from assorted roots.

"How far have they run?" the ranger asked, shaking his head incredulously. The group had traveled more than halfway to the Barbacan from Dundalis and had not encountered a single monster, nor any sign that giants, goblins, or powries were anywhere about.

"The Wilderlands 're a bigger place than ye know," Bradwarden explained, "bigger than all the kingdoms o' men put together. Far went the cry o' the demon dactyl, out to goblin holes and the shelf roosts o' giants in mountains unnamed by men. Out to powries, though them wicked creatures be living on lumps o' rock far out to sea."

"And so they have returned to their rocks and holes, it would seem," said the ranger. "And yet, I do not feel that the world is a safer place."

"Funny how men keep doin' that to themselves," Bradwarden said dryly.

Again the ranger shook his head, looking all around, seeking some sign.

"We should not complain, I would say," Roger cut in, misunderstanding the ranger's curiosity for a strange disappointment. "Better to find no enemies than too many."

"One would be too many," Elbryan replied.

"Unless ye're lookin' for somethin' better eatin' than stew." The centaur laughed. "Ho, ho, what!"

The Avelyn impression brought a wide grin to Elbryan's face. "Had to be done?" he asked.

The centaur nodded.

"Are we to go out scouting again?" Roger asked. The other two didn't miss that he was looking longingly at the warm fire as he spoke.

"No scouting," Elbryan decided, though he knew that he would be out late into the night, and that Bradwarden would pick up the patrol when he left off. "Go and join the brothers and sleep warm by the fire."

Roger nodded and rushed away, calling to Castinagis to leave him some of the stew.

When Elbryan looked at the centaur, he saw Bradwarden's expression had turned grim.

"He's not lyin' about the fire," the centaur said.

"A chill on the breeze," the ranger agreed.

"More than that, I'm fearin'," Bradwarden explained. "We been lucky, ranger. This far north, the wind can still freeze yer bones, and we could wake one morn to find snow piled deeper than a deer's antlers."

"We have come far to the north."

Bradwarden nodded. "And earlier than we should've, by me own figurin'. We're fast on to spring, to be sure, but spring at the Barbacan's not the same as spring in Dundalis. I'm thinkin', and hopin', that the blown mountain's mixed it all up, and dulled the winter. Might be that enough of it went into the sky to serve as a blanket. Ye seen the colors o' the sun settin' and risin'. The dust'd do that, and it might be that the dust'll keep the weather more to the middle, winter and summer, if ye get me guess."

Indeed, as Bradwarden spoke, the western sky began to turn a glowing shade of red, almost as if the clouds had been set on fire. The reasoning made sense to the ranger, and even if it didn't, he would have taken Bradwarden's word for it. The centaur was old, three times the age of the oldest man; and no creature, not even Lady Dasslerond of the Touel'alfar, was more attuned to the workings of nature. What the centaur had left unspoken, and what Elbryan could figure out for himself, was that if the air was cold now, it would only get worse as they continued north, and worse still as they climbed into the mountains ringing blasted Mount Aida. Had they been lulled by the unusual mildness of the Timberland winter? Might they find the high passes of the more northern stretches blocked by snow?

"Come," he bade the centaur. "Let us go and take our meal with our friends."

Bradwarden shook his head. "Ain't got the belly for it," he said. "Saw no monsters in me scoutin', but more than a few runnin' meals!" With another laugh, the centaur bounded away, pulling his great bow from his shoulder as he went.

"Stay close!" Elbryan called.

"Ye fearin' unseen monsters?" Bradwarden called back.

"Not at all," replied the ranger. "I am just of the mind to hear the piping of Bradwarden this cold night!"

"Oh, ye'll hear it," the centaur roared from the edge of some brush, and then he waded into the foliage, disappearing from sight so that only his thunderous voice remained. "Unless I get me lips frozen stuck to the damned pipes!"

From his perch in a branch overlooking the small community, De'Unnero noticed immediately that this place, Dundalis, differed greatly from Caer Tinella. It wasn't so much the size, though Dundalis in its present state was less than half the size of Caer Tinella, but more the attitude surrounding the towns. There were no large fields outlined here, no farmers working at ordinary tasks, preparing for spring planting. Dundalis had never been a farming community; but even the activities more typical of the place, tree-cutting and the like, were not evident now.

Life had not yet returned to normal this far north. Indeed, Dundalis seemed more a fort than a settlement, an image only heightened by the presence of Shamus Kilronney and his men. De'Unnero noted the beginnings of a dozen structures, and several already completed, but more prominent and important loomed the wall connecting them all, taller than a tall man and patrolled by many soldiers. Up on the rise to the north, a tower had been erected, and the Bishop could see the forms of two men up there, silhouetted against the twilight sky.

There were sentries in the woods, as well, though De'Unnero had seen none of the trained soldiers outside the settlement and had found little trouble in slipping through the barely organized ranks to find this viewing perch.

He thought to bypass the town altogether, and would have, except that he wanted to speak with Shamus, and perhaps would even instruct the captain and his soldiers to accompany him to the north. He slipped down from the tree and moved back into the forest away from the town, trying to figure out how he might get to Shamus without alerting any of the possible allies of Nightbird that the Bishop of Palmaris had come out so far alone.

He found his answer soon after, while eavesdropping on a pair of scouts: a man of medium build and unremarkable appearance, and another of considerable size and rugged. It became obvious from the way the smaller man was addressing the larger—one called Tomas—that this man held some high rank within the town hierarchy; and to De'Unnero's delight, they mentioned Shamus Kilronney by name.

He took the cue to walk into their midst.

Both men jumped, the larger producing a sword in the blink of an eye and leveling it the monk's way.

"Pray calm, brother," De'Unnero said, holding his empty hands up before him in submission. "I am a humble man of God and no enemy to you."

Tomas lowered the sword. "How did you get up here?" he asked. "And who are you with?"

"By my own feet and with only myself for company," De'Unnero answered, smiling.

The two men exchanged skeptical looks.

"The Bishop of Palmaris is concerned that the Timberlands will be reclaimed without any Church participation," said De'Unnero.

"The Church never was concerned with the Timberlands," the smaller man replied.

De'Unnero noted some movement in the forest behind him—the footfalls of two men, no doubt coming to investigate the source of agitated voices. "The old Church," the Bishop corrected. "We are much more concerned with the goings-on of the kingdom now, much more tied to the affairs of state." He made no defensive movement as the two men stalked in behind him, taking positions behind and to either side.

"The Timberlands are not part of King Danube's state," the smaller man said with prideful contempt.

Tomas shuffled uncomfortably at the blunt words.

"Again you speak of the past, my friend," De'Unnero explained. "The war has changed much."

"Ye're saying that Dundalis belongs to the King o' Honce-the-Bear?" the volatile man retorted, his voice rising in anger.

"I am saying that we do not know the disposition of Dundalis or all the Timberlands," De'Unnero replied, reminding himself that these men, and their opinions, were not important to him. "And I am saying that all of you would do well to understand that, especially with a contingent of King's soldiers in your midst."

That backed the man off a step, and again the larger man shuffled.

"I am Tomas Gingerwart," he said loudly, but in a friendly tone, and he extended his hand. De'Unnero was glad that he held his tiger's paw in his left hand as he reached out to shake.

"And are there not monks of the Abellican Church also within the walls of Dundalis?" the Bishop asked, catching them off guard. Again the uneasy shuffles, and De'Unnero delighted in knowing that these were caused both by his knowledge that Dundalis was now walled and by the fact that he knew of Braumin and the others, who had come up here in disguise.

"No monks," Tomas replied too quickly and decisively.

"A pity, then, that they have already left," said the Bishop.

"No monks," Tomas insisted. "Never any."

De'Unnero struck a pensive pose. "They never made it here?" he asked with concern, throwing the men further off balance. Now they didn't know for sure if he was talking about Braumin and the others, he understood, and that was exactly what he had hoped for. Tomas' simple reaction to his inquiry had given him all the information he needed about this man's allegiance—he was a friend of Nightbird, no doubt.

They all were.

"I fear for my brethren," the Bishop said, "but the road was clear, all the way from Palmaris and through Caer Tinella. What might have delayed them?"

"Plenty of monsters still to be found," Tomas said unconvincingly.

De'Unnero almost smiled at the irony of that statement, for even as Tomas spoke the words, the Bishop was falling into the power of his gemstone. He slipped his left hand, fast becoming a great paw, up into the generous folds of his long sleeve.

"Come along into the village," Tomas instructed. "We will talk more there."

The big man turned to leave, but stopped, for the Bishop held his ground, shaking his head.

"Tomas Gingerwart leads in Dundalis," the smaller man explained.

"Tomas Gingerwart leads those who will be led by Tomas Gingerwart," De'Unnero replied. "What claim might he make over a captain of the King's army? Or over an emissary of the Abellican Church?"

"In the village," Tomas said, motioning in the direction of Dundalis.

"Pray you go to town, brother Tomas," said De'Unnero, taking the upper hand. "Go along and quickly. Fetch me Captain Shamus Kilronney."

The demeaning manner of his speech brought Tomas back around to face him squarely, and made the other three men bristle and grumble.

"Consider yourself fortunate that I have not the time to argue with you," De'Unnero said. He realized that he would find little gain in agitating this group, but he was simply enjoying it too much to stop now. "I will speak with Captain Kilronney, but out here. I have no desire to enter the dirty hovels you call a village."

Again the men behind him bristled.

"Then turn your back and walk south," Tomas said defiantly, "where you came from, and where you belong."

"So it is true," said De'Unnero. "You are a friend of the one called Nightbird."

Tomas' eyes widened in shock, but before he or his friends could react, in the blink of an eye, De'Unnero spun to the right and brought his left hand, his tiger paw, raking down across the chest of the stunned scout standing there. He could have killed the man—indeed he wanted to do just that—but he wisely pulled the attack, claws latching onto the man's leather tunic and slicing it to tatters in a single, brutal swipe.

The man fell back, crying out in horror, and his companion moved toward De'Unnero. But the Bishop moved first, stepping away from Tomas and swinging right at the advancing scout. Again before any had made a definitive move to stop him, De'Unnero had the man defenseless; the Bishop's human hand held the scout's hair, tugging his head back, and the tiger paw was clamped over his face, claws extended so that they prodded the tender skin, but not hard enough to draw blood.

Tomas and his companion and the guard's partner all fell back a step, holding their hands up, trying to bring a level of calm.

De'Unnero surprised them by releasing his prisoner, shoving the man forward to the grasp of Tomas' companion. "Men in your position should be careful of the enemies they make," the Bishop explained. "Do not underestimate the Church's intentions here, or the lengths to which we shall go to get that which we desire. Now go and fetch me Shamus Kilronney. I have not the time nor the patience for your foolish games."

The four men held their ground for a moment, but then Tomas' companion looked to his leader, and the big man nodded to him to be away.

"When did they leave for the Barbacan?" the Bishop asked bluntly.

Tomas and the other did not answer.

"As you will," the Bishop conceded with a bow. "Your choice of alliance is confirmed, but be warned: a man might well be judged by those he names as allies."

"You are assuming a bit," Tomas said. "You keep mentioning Nightbird, as if you believe that we know the man, or woman, or whatever else it might be. But—"

De'Unnero held up his human hand and looked away. "As you will," he conceded, and he pointed to a cluster of thick pines. "Tell Captain Kilronney that I will await him there, that we two might speak privately." Without even bothering to keep a wary eye on the men he had just all but named as enemies, the Bishop walked away, confident that they would not attack. De'Unnero had an uncanny ability to measure potential enemies accurately—that was perhaps his greatest strength as a warrior—and he understood that his confidence only added to the intimidation, and that such intimidation would stay any action from the likes of Tomas Gingerwart and his peasant companions.

Shamus Kilronney joined De'Unnero soon after, as dusk settled thickly about the forest. The captain had been told only that an Abellican monk wished to speak with him; and he was amazed to find the Bishop himself waiting.

"Why did you allow Nightbird to wander away?" De'Unnero asked before the man could even offer a proper greeting.

"W-what choice lay before me?" Shamus stammered in reply. "I would either let him go or fight him then and there, something which you explicitly forbade."

His voice had risen considerably, and De'Unnero motioned for him to be quiet, pointing out that many curious ears were tilted their way.

"You were to watch him," De'Unnero said quietly. "And yet I find you here, sitting in this miserable village, while Nightbird wanders far to the north." Now the Bishop's voice rose along with his frustration.

"I asked him to allow me to go along," Shamus Kilronney argued loudly. "He would not have me."

"You *asked* him?" De'Unnero echoed incredulously. "You are a captain in the King's army. Does that rank count for nothing?"

Shamus merely laughed and shook his head. "You do not understand the man called Nightbird," he tried to explain, "nor his relationship to these people. I doubt that the King himself would outrank Nightbird in the wilds of the northland."

"A dangerous presumption," the Bishop replied in a low and grim tone. "You should have gone along with him, or at least you should have shadowed his movements. Gather your men this very night and set out, double-step, in pursuit."

"And you will accompany us?"

De'Unnero gave him a disgusted look. "I will precede you," he explained. "By the time you catch up to me, my business with Nightbird should be at its end. You and your soldiers will help me escort the survivors, if there are any, back to Palmaris."

Shamus started to respond, but the Bishop cut him short. "It is time to go," De'Unnero explained, stepping out of the grove.

There stood Tomas and several other men, all pretending to be occupied with other small matters.

"They know that you hunt Nightbird," Shamus whispered in De'Unnero's ear.

The Bishop snorted as if that hardly mattered. "That we hunt him, you mean," he whispered back. "Tell them not who I am."

Shamus only nodded, for he would not question the Bishop, who served as the voice of his King. Not now.

Tomas and the other men stiffened at the approach of the monk and the soldier, and more than one of them clutched his weapon tightly.

But they wouldn't strike, De'Unnero knew. They hadn't the courage; and so the Bishop took the tension that lay so thick in the air and heightened it, twisting it to his greater enjoyment. "If any deign to follow me, or perhaps to precede me on my way to find the one called Nightbird, then let him know that he is acting against the Abellican Church and that punishment shall be swift and sure," he said calmly.

Shamus hesitated and sucked in his breath, thinking that De'Unnero might have pushed too far.

But the Bishop was in control here, and Tomas and the others moved aside to let him pass.

More angered than impressed, Shamus Kilronney hesitated and studied his companion as they moved off alone into the forest. Only then did he notice the Bishop's feline limb, the mighty claws protruding from under the folds of his large sleeve. A shudder coursed through the captain, but he said no more all the way to Dundalis. There De'Unnero again instructed him to be on the move that very night, then took his leave, heading out to the north.

Back in the forest, Tomas Gingerwart and his companions inspected the torn tunic, the leather ripped apart as if it were some flimsy material.

"Nightbird'll be having his way with that one," one of the men proclaimed, to the assenting grunts and nods of the others. Tomas, too, joined in that chorus, though the big man wasn't so sure that he agreed with the assessment. He had to go along, though, had to help them all find some comfort in their less-than-sincere confidence in their friend Nightbird. This strange and deadly monk had unnerved them all, particularly Tomas, who had looked the man in the eye, had come up against willpower and an inner strength and serenity based on supreme confidence—beyond anything he had ever imagined.

He prayed that this monk would not find his friend.

It wasn't really a cave—more a deep overhang of stone, a natural alcove formed on the rocky side of a bluff—but Elbryan, who had been using nothing more convenient than an abandoned bear's den or the natural tent formed by the lowest branches of a large pine, considered himself lucky to find so readily available a place for Oracle. He went into the deeper shadows as the bottom of the sun dipped below the western horizon, the sky still a brilliant explosion of red, pink, and violet, and set his mirror on a stone, then hung his blanket over the opening, dimming the place even more. He took one last peek out, one last look at the beautiful sky.

Then Nightbird sat, his back against the cool stone, staring at the barely seen mirror, letting his gaze focus completely within the depths of the glass. In moments, the inner reaches of the mirror fogged over and the specter appeared.

"Uncle Mather," the ranger greeted, though of course, the specter did not reply.

The ranger put his chin in his hands and tried to sort through his thoughts. He had felt compelled to come to Oracle this night, to speak with his uncle Mather, for he felt uneasy and out of sorts. Elbryan had not yet discerned the source of that discomfort, though, only knew that he did not want to be on this road at this time.

"Have I lost the desire?" he asked honestly. "Was my training by the Touel'alfar longer lived than my calling to the duty of that training? In the fights, when the goblins ambushed us and those soldiers were slain . . . I did not want to be there. I was not afraid, and certainly had no reluctance to kill goblins, but that edge, that eager spirit, was not with me, Uncle Mather, nor has it followed my trail to the north. I understand that the journey to the Barbacan is important to Brother Braumin and his fellows, and that they pay great tribute to my friend by going to his grave, and yet . . ."

The ranger paused and lowered his head with a great sigh. For so long, the entire time since he had left the elves, Elbryan had known a purpose, a clear sense of duty. He had spent the months of the war seeking battles, not avoiding them. Then, when the monsters had been driven off, the ranger had found a new purpose and direction and a new enemy—the jailors of Bradwarden—to defeat. He could tell himself that this journey was just an extension of that battle, a furthering of Avelyn's war against his wicked brethren.

But somehow the ranger didn't feel that sense of purpose and urgency. Somehow, something was missing.

"Pony," he whispered, hardly even aware that he had spoken her name. He looked up and stared back into the mirror, the source of his anguish coming painfully clear.

"It is Pony, Uncle Mather," he stated more firmly. But what was it about Pony? Surely he missed her, had missed her ever since she had left him in Caer Tinella, from the very moment she had gone out of sight down the southern road. But he always missed Pony when she was not with him, even if it was only for a day of scouting in the forest. Elbryan didn't understand it, but neither did he fight against these feelings. He loved her, with all his heart and soul, and couldn't imagine his life without her. She made him better; certainly she had helped him take *bi'nelle dasada* to a higher level of mastery. But it was more than physical. Pony elevated Elbryan emotionally, gave him a more honest perspective on the world around and his place in it, and brought joy to him, every day. She completed him, and certainly he was not surprised to discover that he missed her now.

But it was more than that, he knew.

"I am afraid, Uncle Mather," he said quietly. "Pony is in a dangerous place, more dangerous than my own, though I have walked into the Wilderlands, on a course toward the home of the creature that darkened the whole world. I cannot help her if she needs me; I cannot hear her if she calls my name."

He finished with another sigh and sat staring at the specter, the impassive figure, as if waiting for Uncle Mather to confirm his distress, to show him a sign that he was wrong, perhaps, or to tell him to turn and rush to Pony's side in the south.

The image in the mirror did not move.

Elbryan searched deeper into his mind, and then, when that failed, into his heart. "I am afraid for her because of the way we parted," he heard himself say, and then he considered the words honestly. Then he admitted to himself that he was angry at Pony for leaving him, and that he didn't really understand why she had to go, what good it would accomplish for her to run back to Palmaris. He wasn't really afraid for Pony—she could take care of herself, and any around her, better than almost anyone else in the entire world! No, he was afraid that if something did happen to keep them apart, he had left her on terrible terms, with anger in his heart where there should have been only love and trust.

The ranger sat back against the wall and chuckled at his own stupidity. "I should have listened to her more carefully," he explained to the specter, but more to himself. "Perhaps my road, too, should have been to the south. Perhaps I should have gone with her." He gave another self-deprecating chuckle. "Or at least, I should have learned better why she had to go, and should have come to a point of acceptance before we parted.

"And now even more miles separate us, Uncle Mather," he lamented. "Pony is in Palmaris, where she said she had to be, and I am walking further from that place."

As he finished, the specter began to fade away, a fog filling the glass. At first, Elbryan thought that Oracle was at its end, that the meditation spell had slipped away. Perhaps he had found his resolution. Before he began to rise, the fog cleared in the center of the mirror, replaced by a glow that could not be a reflection.

Out rolled the fog, leaving an image for a startled Elbryan, a crystal-clear image, though the rocky alcove had darkened almost to black. An image he knew.

There was the flat top of Mount Aida; there was Avelyn's up-reaching arm, protruding from the stone.

A sense of warmth rushed over Elbryan, a sense of love and magic as intense as anything he had ever felt.

And then it was gone, but it took the ranger a long while to emerge from the alcove. He nearly slipped on a thin patch of ice when he came out.

That ice had been but a slick of water when he had entered the alcove. Ice—and they were not even in the mountains yet.

The ranger shook the warnings away. Oracle had shown him the way, and he knew now that he had to go to Avelyn as surely as Braumin and the others needed to make the pilgrimage: knew now that he, too, would find some answers in that special place.

The deepest snow would not deter him.

He wrapped his blanket tightly about him, and only then did he realize that the song of Bradwarden, the piping music of the Forest Ghost, drifted on the evening breeze. He didn't follow that tune, though, but went to the fire, to check on the monks and Roger, who was supposed to be on watch but who had succumbed to the haunting melody of Bradwarden's distant piping.

No matter, the ranger decided, for he knew that there were no goblins or other monsters in the area. He traded his blanket for his traveling cloak, checked on Symphony to ensure that the horse was comfortable for the night, then went out from the camp, following the tune as only one trained by the Touel'alfar could.

He found the centaur on a bare-topped hillock—ever Bradwarden's favorite stage—and approached quietly, not wanting to disturb the centaur's magical, musical trance. Indeed, Bradwarden played on for a long, long while.

When at last the centaur stopped and opened his eyes, he was not surprised to find Nightbird sitting beside him.

"Been talkin' to ghosts?" the centaur asked.

"To myself, mostly," the ranger corrected.

"And just what did ye tell yerself?" asked Bradwarden.

"That I did not want to be here, on this road, moving away from Pony," Elbryan replied. "I agreed to accompany the monks because I was angry. Did I tell you that? I was mad at Pony."

"Good a reason as any," Bradwarden said sarcastically.

"She came to me in a dream, back in Dundalis," Elbryan explained. "She told me that we could not meet, as we had agreed, soon after the turn of spring. And so I decided to accompany Brother Braumin, though I had no desire to go back to Aida."

"Dundalis is no further from us than Aida, boy," the centaur remarked. "And ye trust me when I'm tellin' ye that I've got less o' love for the dactyl-smellin' place than yerself!"

Elbryan shook his head. "I said that I *had* no desire." He explained, emphasizing the past tense. "I have seen better now, and know that I must go to Mount Aida, with or without Brother Braumin. Bad intentions put me on this road, but good fortune alone made it the correct road for Elbryan."

"Seems ye're gettin' all yer thoughts from dreams and ghosts," the centaur said with a snort. "I'm worryin' for ye, boy, and worryin' for meself for followin' ye!"

That brought a smile to Elbryan's face, and so did Bradwarden's following notes, these coming not from his booming voice but from his melodic bagpipes. The music started abruptly, but melted quickly into a sweet, graceful melody, the music of the night, the music of the Forest Ghost.

❖ 26 ❖

The Assassin

"Brother Pantelemone," announced Headmaster Francis' attendant, one of the five who had accompanied him from St.-Mere-Abelle.

Francis nodded; this visit was not unexpected. Brother Pantelemone had recently come from St.-Mere-Abelle to announce the impending arrival of Father Abbot Markwart.

The monk entered and went straight to the headmaster, handing him a rolled parchment tied with a blue ribbon bearing the insignia of the Father Abbot. Francis unrolled it quickly, just scanning it, not too surprised by the instructions penned there. The Father Abbot wanted a huge welcome, all the city out and cheering his arrival.

"The celebration must be monumental," Francis explained to the two. "The Father Abbot will arrive in three days. By that time, we must have all the city prepared for his visit."

A fourth monk joined the group then, Brother Talumus, hustling to Francis' quarters upon hearing the news that a monk from St.-Mere-Abelle had arrived.

"Go to the merchants we have . . ." Francis started to say, but he stopped and chuckled. What exactly had they done to the merchants? Repaid them for their lost stones? No, in truth, Francis knew, the merchants had been bribed, plain and simple. But most of them had accepted the gold with a smile, a hopeful smile, for they knew that they could not afford to have the Church as an enemy. Not now.

Of course, Francis had to be more politic when speaking openly. "Go to the merchants whom we have compensated," he explained. "Tell them that the source of their new wealth, the Father Abbot himself, is coming to Palmaris and that we require their assistance to properly welcome him."

"Is not King Danube also nearing our city?" Brother Talumus asked.

"He is a week away, at least, by all reports," Francis replied. "The Father Abbot will arrive first."

"And so we will likely organize this celebration all over again within the week," Talumus reasoned. "For it is to be as grand a parade for King Danube as for the Father Abbot, is it not?"

Francis didn't like his almost accusing tone. It had become increasingly evident to Francis over the last couple of weeks that there might be a problem growing with Talumus. The monk was out often and, according to the whispers Francis had overheard, he had even lent a soul stone to a street whore.

"Surely the King has spies within the city who will report to him immediately if his entry parade is not as grand as that of the Father Abbot," Talumus said.

"That will be for the Father Abbot to decide, and to organize," Francis replied. "Our duty is to prepare the celebration for the Father Abbot alone."

Talumus started to protest, despite the grimaces on the faces of the two monks flanking him, but Francis would hear no more.

"Father Abbot Markwart is better suited for such a task," the headmaster explained. "No one in all the world is better versed in protocol, I assure you. Or more experienced. Father Abbot Markwart has hosted royalty on many occasions, and organized a successful College of Abbots just a few short months ago."

"But . . ." Talumus started to say, but, glancing around, noting that he had absolutely no support, he threw up his hands. "What else would you have us do, headmaster?" he asked.

"Start with the merchants, then send the soldiers out to the streets to the open markets and the taverns," Francis explained. "We will prepare a greeting at the ferry, then rouse all the folk of Palmaris along the route that will bring the Father Abbot to St. Precious."

Francis waved them away then, figuring they had enough to do. Two of the monks scurried out of the room, though Brother Talumus walked more slowly, looking back several times at the new headmaster.

Francis was relieved, for his time of trial, this most urgent trial, was nearing its end. And he had done well, he believed. Most of the merchants were satisfied, and even those who had left his office grumbling would not speak ill of him to the Father Abbot—they were certainly more enamored of Headmaster Francis than of Bishop De'Unnero. As were the common folk, Francis knew. The sermons had been gentler of late, and the taxes less demanding.

Markwart had given Francis explicit instructions for the handling of Palmaris, and there could be no doubt that the headmaster had performed to perfection. All that remained was the celebration, the welcoming parade, and that, Francis believed, would prove to be the easiest task of all.

The Fellowship Way bustled that night with news of the coming visit, and of the role the people were being told they would play in welcoming the Father Abbot. More and more people kept filtering in, and those who arrived did not quickly leave, getting caught up in the exciting and somewhat confusing talk of the events of the last few weeks. When De'Unnero had been in command of the city, there was a general consensus that the strict Bishop—and thus, by extension, the Abellican Church—might not prove well suited over the long term to lead Palmaris, but now . . .

Now, the people did not know what to think.

The confusion proved troubling for Pony, waiting tables and listening in on practically every conversation. She winced as if she had been hit every time someone spoke favorably about this man Francis, for she remembered Francis—indeed she did!—from her journey to St.-Mere-Abelle. The lackey of Markwart, Bradwarden had labeled him. And indeed, when Elbryan had encountered the man, he was in the process of beating the chained centaur.

And now here he was, all smiles and give-away gold, the interim bishop, fast becoming a hero to the beleaguered folk of Palmaris. De'Unnero had clearly shown the power of the Church, had played the tyrant's role. Now Francis could build on that, showing the merciful, beneficent side of the Church. As the many conversations wound along, the threads began to shift favorably toward Francis, and in a hopeful direction at the mention of the Father Abbot's impending visit. "Mayhaps the Church'll come showin' us the true way, with the war done and all," one man remarked. That prompted a series of toasts to the Abellican Church, the new Bishop—may he remain in place even if De'Unnero returned!—and the Father Abbot— may he hear the calls of the peasant folk!

By the time they got around to that last toast, Pony had already left the tavern, walking out into the night air and the chill breeze blowing from the north. When several deep breaths did not calm her, she started around the building, moving to the rainspout that would lead her to the roof and her private place.

"You are not to be climbing in your condition, now are you?" came a voice behind her, Belster's voice.

"And aren't you leaving Dainsey alone with quite a crowd?" Pony remarked, though she could not easily dismiss Belster's words, not with her belly sticking out so far now, the child within hardly ever still.

"Mallory will help her," Belster replied with a dismissive wave. "And Prim O'Bryen has come in. And most have had too much already and will not be drinking much more."

"If only I could blame their stupid words on drink," said Pony.

Belster gave a great sigh. "Still you have that anger, girl," he said.

Pony stared at him incredulously; did he believe that her anger was misplaced?

"Even you, so full of hate for the Church, recognize that this Bishop is better than the last," said Belster. "For some of the folk, that's enough."

Pony shook her head and leaned heavily against the pipe.

"You have got your own anger," Belster said calmly, approaching and putting a comforting hand about her shoulders. "No one will deny you that, or even that it is justified. But most of the folk are trying hard to look ahead, not back. They just want to be left in peace to go about their work and their fun, and they ask no more from a leader than to keep them safe should the goblins return."

"And the Church is that leader?" Pony asked skeptically. "Bishop Francis is that leader?"

Belster shrugged, and Pony almost—almost—slapped him.

"And will Belster go out and cheer at the arrival of the Father Abbot?" Pony asked, her voice dripping venom.

"That is what we have been told to do, and so we should," the innkeeper declared. "If that will make the Father Abbot happy, and him being happy will make our lives a bit easier, then it seems a small price—"

"Prettyface!" Pony yelled, a common name used by children to describe someone who says one thing but then does something completely different. She pulled away from him, and saw that she had wounded him with her insult. But she didn't stop. "You know what they are! You know what they have done!"

"Indeed, my friend," Belster said somberly, quietly, "I know. I hold no foolish ideas or hopes that these men—the new Bishop and the Father Abbot—are good men. But they might just be doing good for the folk of Palmaris if doing good for us suits their purposes. What more might common folk ask for?"

Pony's anger changed to confusion. "Are you speaking of a fight between the Church and state?" she asked. "Are you thinking that the Father Abbot is trying to use the city against the King?"

"It might be that it is not so much a fight," Belster explained, "but it does seem, from what I have heard from my friends who know the merchants well, as if both sides plan to make a claim for Palmaris, though I expect that the Church wants the city more."

"Wants the city enough to murder Abbot Dobrinion and Baron Bildeborough," Pony pointedly reminded.

Belster patted the air now, trying to keep her calm. "And are you planning to stop them?" he asked quietly, though the incredulity was clear in his voice. "We have been going around on this talk for weeks now, and surely you have come to see that you cannot fight them. Perhaps, if luck is with us, you will not have to, and that will be a good thing, girl. Good for Palmaris and good for yourself—and good, most of all, for the baby you are carrying in your belly."

Pony's hand went to her bulging belly. Always it came down to that for Belster; every time Pony started talking of action, he would gently remind her of the baby.

And she did calm down somewhat; she always did when feeling that life inside her. She recognized Belster's stand for what it was—not cowardice but pragmatism. The innkeeper had already carved out a comfortable existence in the city, as had most folk; and he, like the others, preferred simply not to care about what their leaders might have done in the past as long as their present actions were helpful, or at least benign.

Pony could accept that from Belster and the others. Rationally, she tried hard not to judge them. But at the same time, Pony could not accept such an attitude from herself. Not at all. This was Francis, who had beaten Bradwarden; and the Father Abbot was responsible for the murder of her adoptive parents and brother. No, Pony could not forgive, and could not forget; the talk in the Way, from men and women she had come to think of as friends, hurt her. But there was little point in arguing it with Belster, here in the alley in the cold of a late winter's night.

"Go and help Dainsey," Pony said to him. "I wish to remain out here alone." Belster started to respond, but Pony kept on talking. "I shall consider your words," she promised. "Perhaps we can avoid a war, after all."

Belster held his ground for a moment longer, but he realized that he had gotten as much of a concession as would be coming from one as stubborn as Pony. He came forward again and gave her a hug—one she returned—and then he headed back out of the alley, saying only, "You be careful with that belly before you even think about going up that pipe!"

The woman only smiled, and that was enough to allow Belster to return to his duties in the Way.

As soon as he had gone, Pony made it to the roof without a problem, quietly and quickly using a malachite to aid her. She slipped into her customary spot, leaning against the back of a dormer. She did indeed want to consider Belster's words, but she could not give the reasoning any credence. Every time she tried to think of the possible gain to Palmaris in letting go of the past, in judging the new leaders by their present actions, she thought of Graevis and Pettibwa, dear and innocent Graevis and Pettibwa. No, this new Bishop was no better than the last, she realized, and the Father Abbot was the worst and most dangerous of the lot.

They had done nothing to improve life in Palmaris, not if one considered where the city had been before the deaths of Bildeborough and Abbot Dobrinion. Yet no one seemed to remember that! All they could chatter about in the Fellowship Way was that this Bishop treated them better than the last, and that the monies demanded by the Church had lessened, and the sermons sounded less judgmental. And that, to Pony's distress, seemed to be enough for them.

It was all too pat for Pony, and she even looked beyond that and wondered just how much of this present situation had been carefully orchestrated.

*   *   *

A grand caravan made its way to the banks of the Masur Delaval. Twenty wagons strong, armed monks riding all around, the procession of Father Abbot Markwart came to the riverbank with the intent of using the magical powers of the amber to walk across. But when Markwart saw the splendor of the ferries and the accompanying fleet awaiting him, he instructed his monks to put their amber away.

More than a score of ships bobbed in the waters just beyond the docks at Amvoy, and several barges were tied to the wharves, awaiting the wagons. On one of these sat the new carriage for the Father Abbot, a magnificent gilt affair, with a team of four perfectly groomed, shining white horses pawing the planks, eager to pull. The driver, a city guardsman, wore a splendid uniform, the full regalia of Baron Bildeborough's personal guard.

As the flotilla started across the wide river, trumpeters on flanking ships took up the welcoming call, a song that was repeated by every ship in the line, trumpets answering trumpets, the blaring call telling of the impending arrival. So impressive was Francis' plans that the call reached all the way across the miles of water to the docks at Palmaris, where answering horns echoed the notes.

One thing that Francis could not avoid was the slow progress across the water of the bulky, square boats; the minutes became an hour, and then two. Finally the docks of Palmaris came into sight, and the noise of trumpets reached the Father Abbot's ears, along with cheering.

Cheering!

"How different this is from my last visit," the old man said to the two masters, Theorelle Engress and a much younger man, flanking him. "Perhaps they have come to appreciate the glory of the Church at long last."

"A testament to the work of Bishop De'Unnero," the younger master replied.

Markwart nodded, for he had no desire to explain, but he knew the truth, knew that any sincere applause he might receive in Palmaris would be the work of Headmaster Francis. Beyond that, of course, it was truly the work, the master planning, of himself.

The crowds reached down to the docks, lining the way. Markwart noted that many Behrenese were there as well, gathered all over the docks, and though their cheering was not nearly as exuberant as that of the white-skinned Palmaris folk, many of them were clapping their hands and calling out the name of Father Abbot Markwart.

"Oh, Francis," the old man muttered under his breath, "truly you have made my task here easier."

Pleased, Markwart took his seat in the gilded carriage and bade those monks who had been chosen as personal bodyguards to step onto the running boards at either side. The masters organized many other monks to flank the magnificent coach, including one skilled with horses to take a seat up beside the soldier driver.

And then the parade began, the song of trumpets calling from every section of the city, the yells and cheers drowning even those. Entertainers of
every persuasion—jugglers, sleight-of-hand magicians, and many bards—
filtered behind the crowds, singing and laughing. And there, as well, were
the soldiers, trying to keep out of the Father Abbot's sight as they prodded
the crowd to be more enthusiastic.

Markwart basked in it all, reveled in the glory he believed that he
deserved. Had he not brought Honce-the-Bear through the war, including
personally leading the victory over the main powrie flotilla at St.-Mere-
Abelle itself? Had he not restored order to the beleaguered city of Palmaris
while the inept King remained in Ursal, no doubt riding his private stock of
horses and women?

Of course, the Father Abbot did not consider the more covert and less
glorious actions that had led him to this point, any more than to remind
himself that Dobrinion and Bildeborough had proven ineffectual and could
not see the broader and more important possibilities in the wake of the war.
Yes, that was dark business to consider on another day; for now, Markwart
merely sat back, waving occasionally, and then even smiling when his wave
brought more enthusiastic cheers.

Francis would become the bishop, he decided then and there. If De'Unnero returned a hero, with the head of Nightbird and the stolen stones—
and perhaps even with the five heretics in tow—he would find another use
for the man, a duty more suited to one who was more a creature of action
than of politics. Yes, it was all falling neatly into place, the completion of
the puzzle that would allow the Abellican Church to steal more and more of
King Danube's domain, a completed picture that would return Honce-the-
Bear to the theocracy it had been in more glorious days.

It all started here, in Palmaris, and the dream resounded in Markwart's
ear with every cheer and trumpet blast.

And nearly everyone in the crowd was cheering, and those cheers were
sincere, a prayer from the common folk that their lives could now return to
normal and the dismal days of the war and its immediate aftermath would
be put behind them. The Father Abbot saw it all very clearly and basked in
the glory of this, his greatest moment.

Several hundred feet away, leaning against the slanted roof of a taller
building, watching the procession, Pony, too, recognized the cheering for
what it was: a desperate plea for leniency. They would forget the past—not
all the folk, but a significant number, certainly too many for her to find continuing support for any major resistance against the Church rule. They
would turn a blind eye to the murders and the injustices, would lament the
name of Chilichunk whenever they came into the Fellowship Way, but
would call it "a pity," or an "unfortunate consequence," rather than "an
atrocity," a crime that needed to be avenged. The beleaguered people had
seen too much of war, had found their world turned upside down several

times over the last few months after years of constant and stable rule. How many years had Abbot Dobrinion overseen St. Precious and the spiritual needs of Palmaris? How many decades—centuries even!—had the family Bildeborough ruled rather benignly from their seat in Chasewind Manor? It had all come undone in a matter of weeks, and now the common people wanted only a return to that safe existence.

And to their thinking, Father Abbot Dalebert Markwart was the only one who could give it to them.

The thought brought bile into Pony's throat, made her hands tremble with outrage. She chewed her lip and tried to think of something she could scream, that she didn't have to hear the cheering.

The cheering! The cheering! It went on and on and on—and for Markwart, for the man who had persecuted Avelyn, who had tortured Graevis and Pettibwa and Grady to death! The man who had ordered heroic Bradwarden dragged from the bowels of Mount Aida, locked in chains, and slung into the dungeons of St.-Mere-Abelle. The man who had ordered the assassinations of Abbot Dobrinion and Baron Bildeborough!

And now they were cheering, and it went on and on, hammering at Pony's heart and soul, pushing her further and further from her desire to strike back at this man and the corrupt institution he represented. It would all die here, she realized. Any hopes that she might have allowed to flicker about a potential revolution against the Church would all die here on the streets of Palmaris, buried beneath a chorus of "prettyface" cheers.

Pony clenched her hand tightly, and only then realized that she had fished one of the gemstones from her pouch. She looked down at it, but knew what it was before she did. Magnetite, the lodestone, and it was no accident that she had plucked this particular stone.

She looked from the stone back to the man in the gilded carriage. He was closer now, and rolling along a course that would bring him barely a hundred paces from her.

Pony could focus and loose a lodestone over a hundred paces.

"Come on, ye rotten waifs!" the soldier prompted, giving a shove to what he thought was a young boy.

Belli'mar Juraviel accepted the treatment stoically, for he, like all the other elves in the area, understood that they were observers who were to take no action to cause any disturbance whatsoever. He glanced over at Lady Dasslerond, apparently next in line for the pushy soldier's abuse, and the lady winked at him to indicate that he should play along.

She started cheering for the Father Abbot before the soldier reached her, and her companions all joined in.

For Lady Dasslerond, though, this sight was particularly unnerving. She wanted to deal with the King, if she had to deal with any human at all to ensure the security of her people, but this reception for the Father Abbot, so completely and professionally orchestrated, made her understand that this dangerous man would play a much larger role in determining the fate of Palmaris, and any potential expansion of the human kingdom, than she had believed.

She cheered, and her kin cheered, and the soldier moved along to the next less-than-enthusiastic onlookers in the seemingly endless line.

"Am I an assassin?" Pony asked aloud, and her face crinkled in disgust at the thought. She was a warrior, trained in *bi'nelle dasada* and in the use of gemstones, a warrior who could meet her enemy on an open field, sword against sword or magic against magic. So she had hoped ultimately to meet Markwart.

But it would not come to that, she realized painfully. There would be no rebellion, no open fight.

She held her arm extended over the roof ridge now, looking down it as if it were a drawn arrow at the rolling carriage. More out of curiosity than intent, the woman slipped into the magic of the stone, looked through it toward her intended target. Every metallic item along the route shone clearly to her: the swords of the soldiers behind the crowd, the shoes of the horses, even the jewelry and coins of the onlookers.

Pony narrowed her focus, eliminating all but the metal on the carriage, and then even narrower, seeing clearly only the metallic items worn by Father Abbot Markwart. She noted the three rings on his hands, the brooch clasping the top of his brown robes. Yes, that brooch. It was off center, and too high above his heart, but a strike through it would surely cause a grievous wound, probably a fatal one to a man as old as Markwart.

Pony's arm gradually slipped lower. Could she murder a man, any man, like this? Was she an assassin? The man was defenseless. . . .

Pony noted something, then, a strange feeling in the lodestone, almost a repulsion. She brought her arm back up and looked through the magic again; and then, as she focused more closely on the ring on the index finger of Markwart's left hand, she had her answer. The ring was set with magnetite. Of course, Pony realized, the Father Abbot was protected from metal-tipped missiles, his magical ring sending off a defensive deflection shield. Likely he wore other shielding items—an emerald, perhaps, to bring a defensive shield against wood as the magnetite protected him from metal.

Pony clenched her stone more tightly. He wasn't defenseless, and somehow that challenge pushed her past her emotional barrier.

"Do you think you've the power to stop this?" she whispered grimly, focusing on that brooch, thinking to blow a hole through the man's chest and shoulder. She sent her energy into the lodestone, let it build and build an attraction to that one item. In mere seconds, the stone was pulling against her grip, but Pony held on, sending even more energy into the stone, charging it to tremendous levels.

She noted something else then, a sudden impulse as the Father Abbot flashed a wide grin to the cheering crowd.

The man had a metal tooth, likely a golden one.

She shifted her angle only slightly and blocked out the brooch as she had blocked out all other metal in the area; and now her focus was on that one tooth halfway down the Father Abbot's jaw on the right side of his face.

The lodestone was humming now, vibrating with power, begging Pony for release. Still she held, throwing all of her strength into that stone. "Do you think you've the power to stop this?" she asked again, and she un-clenched her hand.

It flew with the speed many times that of a diving falcon, had reached its target before Pony had even finished opening her hand, and yet she saw it as if it were moving slowly, as if all the world were moving very slowly. It soared past the rooftops, nearly clipping an eave, diving in a straight line. She saw one woman turning her head right into its path, but too slowly, and the stone zipped past, startling the woman.

And then the way was clear to the Father Abbot, to his gold tooth. On the stone tore, blasting into the side of the old monk's face, explod-ing bone, tearing flesh, and then ripping on, through the man's tongue, smashing bone and teeth on the other side of his jaw, driving up and out through the side of his skull and then burrowing into the side of the carriage.

Pony watched Markwart's head snap violently to the side, watched the man jump out of his seat, then fall back limply, blood spraying all over his robes and the carriage, all over the attendant monks rushing to the Father Abbot's side, and all over the back of the soldier driving the carriage, the man still oblivious of the disaster behind him.

Absolute chaos exploded around Lady Dasslerond and her companions, for the carriage was almost directly in front of them when the Father Abbot got hit. Elves scrambled to get some sense of what had happened, but Dasslerond and Juraviel had already figured it out.

"Gemstone," Juraviel said grimly.

"It would seem that your friend is ambitious," Lady Dasslerond replied in less than complimentary tones. Dasslerond shook her head in disgust and turned her attention back to the chaos at the carriage. Soldiers and monks closed ranks about the stricken man, yelling for the driver to race to St. Precious.

Dasslerond could only watch as her scouts fanned out, trying to give her the most complete and accurate information possible. The situation had just become even more complicated, she knew. And so did Juraviel, who hoped that their suspicions about the method and source of the attack would be proven wrong.

* * *

Pony rolled to her back and slid down the sloping roof so that she was below the crest. And so she was an assassin—at least, if the old wretch died before the monks could get to him with any soul stones. "No," she said aloud, shaking that thought away. She had seen the impact and knew the power of the gemstone. Markwart had died the instant it hit him.

A strange emptiness washed over Pony, a hollow feeling that was not the sweet taste of revenge she had expected. That man, that dangerous wretch, had killed her parents and her brother; he was an evil man in a position to continue hurting people, so many people, and the world was a better place without him. Pony knew all that, but it mattered little at that horrible moment.

She heard the commotion behind her, the screams.

Pony blanked it out, couldn't bear it at that time. She felt unclean and tainted. She moved lower on the roof and vomited until her sides ached.

CHAPTER

✦ 27 ✦

Looking Death in the Eye

They watched him climb the stony cliff with some amusement, but also with a fair amount of pride, for Elbryan moved with a grace and agility beyond that of most humans, especially one his size. For the Touel'alfar, those movements, so natural and animallike, served as a testament to their training and their way of life. To their thinking, Nightbird's achievements were their achievements; but by their estimation, he still could not match the agility of even the most clumsy elf.

Far down below, across the rocky remnants of an old riverbed and under the canopy of a large cluster of pines, Bradwarden, Roger, and the monks busied themselves setting up camp. The two elves had watched them start unseen and unnoticed, as they had been for almost all this journey, and then they had followed Nightbird so inconspicuously that even the elven-trained ranger had taken no note of them.

The ranger inched his hand above him, fingers walking up the stone, seeking a crack. He closed his eyes, focusing on his sense of touch, letting his fingertips "see" for him. He found, so high above him that he had to rise on tiptoe, a crack barely deep enough to admit his fingertips and only wide enough for one hand. The ranger fell into a state of absolute calm, allowing the muscles in his hand to go rigid. He inched up, up, barely noting the move, deep in thought, all his willpower focused squarely on that hand.

His shoulder at last rose higher than his elbow. He inched his other hand up, walking it up the stone, hunting the next hold. This time he found a deeper crack, and he managed to wedge his fingers in, then swing one foot out and placed his toes in the crack. The next move was easy: the muscles of his arm and leg worked to bring him closer, then angle him upward. The next hold was in a wider gap, and from there, the ranger found a grip for both hands above him, a narrow ledge, a place to rest.

Elbryan pulled himself up—and he nearly toppled in surprise, for there, waiting for him, sat Ni'estiel, a pipe in his mouth, blowing smoke rings into the air.

"Too slow," the elf criticized.

The ranger pulled himself over into a sitting position and took a welcome deep breath. "I would have come up faster if I, too, wore a pair of wings," he replied dryly.

"Faster still if you were not trapped in so large and unwieldy a body," Ni'estiel said. "And why have you decided to make so arduous a climb with the sun already low in the western sky? The season's cold will be unforgiving so high up after the sun is gone. How well will your fat human fingers grasp a ledge of icy-cold stone?"

"I wanted a look ahead," the ranger explained. "Roger found some goblin sign, a small lean-to."

"You could have simply asked," answered Tiel'marawee, fluttering up to land beside her kin.

"Asked? I did not know if the Touel'alfar had come along for the journey," the ranger admitted. "Nor did you seem eager to help me, whatever course lay before me."

The elves glanced at each other, Ni'estiel shook his head, and then they turned back to face the ranger, neither of them looking particularly pleased.

"What have I done?" Elbryan asked bluntly. "Surely your attitude toward me has not been that of friend to friend, and yet I cannot understand what has so changed our friendship."

"Friendship?" Tiel'marawee echoed skeptically. "I spoke to you not at all during your years in Andur'Blough Inninness, Nightbird. Why would you assume that we two are, or ever were, friends?"

The words stung the ranger, and he had to admit their truth. "But I am elf-friend," he reasoned. "Is not a friend of Lady Dasslerond a friend to all the Touel'alfar?"

"It is a friendship that you have strained," Ni'estiel said plainly.

"What have I done?" the ranger replied, his voice rising. "When Belli'mar Juraviel left—"

"You taught her," Ni'estiel said.

"Taught?" Elbryan echoed, caught by surprise, but as soon as he paused to consider the word, he understood.

"*Bi'nelle dasada* was our gift to you," Tiel'marawee explained. "It was not yours to offer another."

"Juraviel and I already had this conversation," the ranger tried to explain.

"Belli'mar Juraviel's word on this is far from final," Ni'estiel retorted. "Lady Dasslerond will decide if you are to be punished for your foolish action. But understand this, Nightbird: even if the lady chooses to ignore your error, we of the Touel'alfar know what you did and are not pleased."

"Not at all," Tiel'marawee added.

"Pony is of my own heart and soul," Elbryan answered. "Even Belli'mar was amazed when he saw the harmony of our dance. And am I *n'Touel'alfar* or of the people? Which is it, I ask, because surely, for all the words of friendship and kinship—"

"And how many years has Jilseponie spent in Andur'Blough Inninness?" Ni'estiel interrupted sarcastically. "How many hours speaking wisdom with one of the Touel'alfar, learning the emotional strength to go with the formidable weapon of *bi'nelle dasada*?"

"Our dance—" the ranger began.

"Is a matter of the physical," Ni'estiel cut him short. "But the truth of *bi'nelle dasada* transcends the physical and goes to the spiritual. Any person might learn the physical movements, but what a dangerous and terrible thing *bi'nelle dasada* would become if it were merely that."

"The warrior is a blend of heart and body," Tiel'marawee added. "It is the injection of the soul into the movements of the body that brings heart and compassion, that tells when the blade should be used in addition to how to use it."

"And this is what you have violated, Nightbird," Ni'estiel went on. "So you have taught the woman, and who will she choose to teach? And they, in turn, will pass it along to others; and what is left, then, of our gift?"

Elbryan was shaking his head, for he knew Pony better than that, knew she would keep the secret between them; he knew her heart, and knew, beyond the comprehension of his elven detractors, that there was no one else with whom she, or he, could possibly share so intimate an experience. But the ranger didn't voice those thoughts, and understood the fears of his elven friends. Despite the differences in size and strength—in fact, partly because of those differences—the average elf could easily defeat even skilled human soldiers in combat. *Bi'nelle dasada* was their edge, a fighting style that the slashing styles of heavier humans could not match.

Despite his empathy, the ranger felt he had not violated the elven trust, that Pony was an extension of his very soul and that she was every bit as worthy as he to know the dance.

"Lady Dasslerond will go to her," he reasoned.

"Lady Dasslerond, and Belli'mar Juraviel and many others, are already in Palmaris," Ni'estiel admitted.

For a moment, the ranger feared that Dasslerond and the others might harm Pony to protect their secret, but that dark thought passed. The elves could be dangerous; their way of looking at the world and concepts of good and evil were very different from the ways of humans. But they would not harm Pony.

"I apologize to you for my transgression," Elbryan said. "No, I apologize for the discomfort my choice has brought to you. But I assure you that once

Lady Dasslerond has had the opportunity to meet and know Pony, and once she has witnessed the beauty of Pony's sword dance—a beauty of the spirit as well as the body—she will understand and will be at peace."

By their expressions, the ranger could see that his words satisfied the two elves—as much as they could be satisfied now.

"Lady Dasslerond did not go to Palmaris to measure your lover's ability in the sword dance," Ni'estiel said, and he looked at his elven companion as if seeking approval, something the ranger did not miss. He stared at Ni'estiel hard, prompting the elf to continue.

"She went to see Jilseponie, the lover of Nightbird, soon to be the mother of Nightbird's child," Ni'estiel remarked.

"Pony and I have decided that we will not bear any chil—" the ranger started to reply.

The slightest breeze could have blown Elbryan from the ledge at that awful and wonderful moment, the most confusing and dizzying array of feelings washing over him.

"How do you know this?" Elbryan asked breathlessly.

"Belli'mar Juraviel knew. He told us on the road in the southland, when he came upon our band as we shadowed Roger Lockless and the five monks," Tiel'marawee admitted. "Thus did Lady Dasslerond decide to go south, with the majority of our kin, while we two alone continued north."

Elbryan could hardly breathe. It all made perfect sense to him, seemed to explain so many things, such as the absence of warning and aid from the elves during the goblin attack, and yet it made no sense at all. How could Juraviel have known that Pony was pregnant? The elf had been with Elbryan since Pony had gone to Palmaris.

And then the awful truth hit Elbryan. Pony had known. And she had left him. She had run to Palmaris out of fear that continuing north might cause injury to the unborn baby. And she had not told him!

"You judge her, ranger," Ni'estiel observed.

Elbryan turned a blank stare over him.

"And yet you do not know the truth," Ni'estiel went on.

"How did Juraviel know?" the ranger asked. "Did Pony tell him? And if she did, then why did she not tell me?"

"You know only what your fears tell you," Tiel'marawee added. "You are thinking the worst, and yet should you not be full of joy?"

Elbryan held up his hands helplessly, for he did not know what to think or to feel. "I have to go to her," he said.

"Spoken like a human," Ni'estiel remarked dryly.

"Perhaps, if your assumptions are correct, you have just answered the question," Tiel'marawee added. "Abandon all and rush to her side, but you will do no practical good there."

"You doubt that I should be with Pony at this time?"

"If the situation allowed for it, then of course you should," Ni'estiel replied sternly. "But that is a matter of the joy you deserve, and not of any practical purpose. Pragmatism demands that you finish your task here, and then go to your lover."

"Now go back down and take your sleep," Tiel'marawee said to him. "We shall scout the road ahead and speak with you in the morning."

The ranger nodded, and gradually, as he dismissed the negative assumptions and began basking in the reality of the situation, a smile widened across his handsome face. Surely he wanted Pony to have his child—a hundred children! Surely this was a blessed thing, the result of a true union of love.

"The bottom of the sun finds the horizon," Ni'estiel warned.

Elbryan's smile faded when he looked down at the formidable descent. "A long climb," he said with a groan, stretching his tired muscles.

"Did you not just insist that you were not *n'Touel'alfar?*" Tiel'marawee said to him in a lighter, teasing tone. "Flap your wings, then, elf."

With a groan, the ranger began to climb down.

Ni'estiel and Tiel'marawee, true to their word, set out immediately to the north. They found the lean-to Roger had discovered and more goblin signs beyond that, including a camp only recently abandoned. They weren't particularly surprised, or alarmed, by the discoveries, since they were far into the Wilderlands and definitely in goblin-infested territory. To find no goblin sign would have been more surprising, and more alarmed would they have been had any of their findings indicated that powries, a far more cunning foe, were in the area. That wasn't the case, the two elves were fairly certain, for powries built different and stronger structures, even for temporary camps, than goblins.

"Only goblins," Ni'estiel said to Tiel'marawee as Sheila began her ascent over the eastern horizon, lighting the encampment enough for Ni'estiel to point out one particularly rickety structure. Now all they had to do was find the somewhat dim-witted creatures, and instruct Nightbird and his friends on how they might simply avoid them.

Another set of eyes also viewed that structure. The eyes of a cat, scanning the dark forest as clearly as a man might see it in the light of day. Keen eyes saw the elves, keen ears heard their words, and a keen nose smelled the blood within their tiny and tender bodies.

The tiger De'Unnero crept closer. He was not knowledgeable of the Touel'alfar, but he knew these two for what they were, and by what he had overheard he knew they were friends of Nightbird. And De'Unnero did know the legends of the elves, mostly that they were powerful and deceptive enemies.

Better to deal with them efficiently, he decided; better to take the ring of defense away from his primary prey.

The tiger came a stride closer on quiet, padded feet.

Ni'estiel froze, as did Tiel'marawee; the elves, attuned to their environment, sensed his presence, the sudden hush that preceded the charge of the predator.

Out came slender swords, and on came De'Unnero, a great pounce that sent him flying to land on Ni'estiel.

The elvish blade stabbed repeatedly, sinking into muscle and flesh, but so, too, raked the great claws, tearing deep lines, severing the tendons controlling that arm.

Tiel'marawee was there in an instant, her sword flashing, and De'Unnero had to leap away. But now they lined up one against one, for Ni'estiel could do little more than roll about in agony and cry out for Tiel'marawee to flee.

"Yes, do try," the tiger said, and both elves stopped short, eyes widening in shock.

Then the tiger began to transform, first its head and then its torso, though the limbs, except for one arm, remained feline.

"What manner of demon is this?" Tiel'marawee said, and on she came, thinking to catch the creature in mid-change and score a deadly strike.

Too quick for the obvious move, De'Unnero sent his still-feline arm swinging across to intercept the sword, accepting the pain of the solid hit. Then out snapped his human arm, just missing a solid and devastating connection on Tiel'marawee's face as the elf spun away.

"Very impressive," the monk's now-human face said. "All that I would expect from the legends of the Touel'alfar."

"Who are you?" Tiel'marawee asked, her tone indicating that she was in control now. "What dactyl demon has arisen this time to bring grief to the world?"

"Demon?" the Bishop echoed with a chuckle. "Why, my dear, tender little elf, you could not be further from the truth. Do you not recognize Marcalo De'Unnero, the Bishop of Palmaris?"

Tiel'marawee blanched. It seemed impossible, ridiculous, and yet she found that she did not disbelieve him. "And thus your Church names the Touel'alfar as enemies?" she asked bluntly, trying to remain calm, though her composure frayed as she glanced over at Ni'estiel, who was now lying still, obviously near death.

"I name anyone who befriends the outlaw Nightbird as an enemy of the Church!" De'Unnero growled at her.

That set Tiel'marawee back on her heels once more. "And so you convict and execute without trial," she replied.

"That is my prerogative," the Bishop answered, and his powerful tiger legs sent him soaring forward.

She was ready for him and leaped straight up, flapping her wings to bring her above the Bishop. Then she dropped, like a bird of prey, sword stabbing like a talon.

De'Unnero hit the ground and rolled, swinging his arm frantically to intercept her blade. These elves did live up to their legend! He batted the sword and tried to grab it, but Tiel'marawee was already moving to the side, landing a dozen feet away and coming around in perfect balance to meet any forthcoming attacks.

"Well done," the Bishop congratulated, standing straight as a man once again, his legs reverting to human form. He dismissed the gem magic altogether then, and showed Tiel'marawee that he was completely human now.

"You err, Bishop of Palmaris," Tiel'marawee said. "Do you mean to start a war with the Touel'alfar? We are enemies beyond your comprehension, do not doubt."

"I tremble, good elf," De'Unnero replied. "And in truth, I might heed your words and see if a bargain could now be struck, except ..." He paused and laughed aloud.

"Except that I am intrigued by your mastery of the sword, and your movements so lithe and balanced," he finished. "And now I must learn the extent of that skill." With that, he fell into a fighting crouch, legs apart and balanced, arms swaying and crossing defensively in front of him. He carried many wounds already—blood shone in the moonlight against his bare skin—but though her enemy was merely human, Tiel'marawee understood that she had to be cautious. This one was quick and balanced, and too strong. She would wait him out, let him tire, let his blood continue to flow from those wounds she and Ni'estiel had given him.

A gasp for breath from Ni'estiel reminded her that she did not have the time, though, and so she came on in sudden fury, sword stabbing straight ahead.

Tiel'marawee miscalculated.

The elvish fighting style featured straight-ahead thrusts, sudden bursts that moved the tip of a slender elvish sword many feet forward in the blink of an eye. But De'Unnero's style, the open-handed maneuvers of the Brothers of the Abellican Order, was also a straight-line form, and so he crossed his forearms before him and brought them up in a gentle, but perfectly timed manner, lifting Tiel'marawee's sword high with only minimal damage to himself.

That left her open to a counter; she knew it and tried another lightning-fast defensive dodge.

De'Unnero's open palm crashed against the side of her cheek, stunning her, stealing her strength so completely for that instant that her sword fell from her grasp.

"Flee!" Ni'estiel cried in a voice filled with blood.

The word caught in Tiel'marawee's mind and stuck there, her legs and wings pumping hard to get her away. She hated the thought of leaving her companion, but understood, as elves always understood, her duty to the greater cause of the Touel'alfar, a demand now that she survive to bear witness, to tell Lady Dasslerond of the Bishop and his Church.

Her speed amazed De'Unnero. Moving away and up into the air, she would have gotten away cleanly except that the Bishop called upon his gemstone again and leaped at her with the power of a tiger's legs, grabbing her with an arm that once again bore the paw and claws of the great cat.

He caught her on the side, just below a wing—and only good fortune kept those claws from tearing the wing in half and dropping Tiel'marawee back to the ground. Tiel'marawee cried out in agony, but kept flying upward, knowing that to be dragged down was to be killed. A great patch of her skin from hip to knee tore away, but then she was free to fly, higher and higher, going to a tree branch, but then pushing on without hesitation, forcing herself to focus on the one mission before her: to get back alive to Nightbird.

Deeper into the stone went De'Unnero, thinking that as the tiger he would pace her and catch her and devour her.

She fluttered through the trees; he raced along the ground, leaping up whenever she swooped lower to dodge a branch or to find a foothold. Tiel'marawee tried a different tack, landing on a high branch and pulling her bow around, then launching a stream of small arrows at the tiger. She scored hit after hit, even as the tiger scrambled away, but though more than half her quiver was empty, she realized that she had done little real damage to the creature, that its wounds seemed to be healing almost as fast as she was inflicting them!

This was not a mystery to Tiel'marawee, who knew of the gemstones and understood that this man had used one to transform himself into the cat and was using another one to heal.

The one thing her volley had done was buy her some space. She put another arrow into the bushes where the tiger had disappeared, then rushed away, hoping that the cat would stay hidden long enough for her to get far, far from the spot.

And Tiel'marawee needed that, she realized, for her torn leg had gone numb, and the blood flowed freely. She felt cold at the edges of her small body, and her peripheral vision showed only darkness as death crept closer and closer.

She stumbled and toppled, tried to catch herself by willing her wings to beat furiously. But then she was down on the ground in a heap, trying to orient herself enough to get back up in the tree. But it was over, she realized, when she saw the tiger steadily approaching. Even if she managed to right herself and leap high, the cat would spring and catch her in mid-flight. Now she was to die, and a great sadness washed over her for the centuries she would not see, and even more for her failure to warn her lady, for the coming tragedy might well overwhelm the fragile world of the Touel'alfar.

The cat charged. Tiel'marawee closed her golden eyes.

She heard a last growl, then felt a rush from the side—powerful, thunderous. She opened her eyes to see the tiger spinning away. Powerful legs, equine legs, tore the earth next to her; Symphony neighed loudly, urging her up. When she could not find the strength to mount, the horse came down low.

The tiger leaped ahead, and so did Symphony, taking a vicious swipe on the flank. The chase was on. Tiel'marawee held on for all her life as Symphony thundered through the trees, cutting close corners.

De'Unnero gave good chase, but only for a short distance, for the cat could not match the pace of the great stallion. So the Bishop tried a different tack. He came out of his tiger form and sent his thoughts to the stallion through the hematite—and found an easy connection through the turquoise that was set in Symphony's breast.

He thought he had them both—and what a sweet meal they would make!—but Symphony was no ordinary horse, was possessed of an intelligence beyond his equine form. All De'Unnero received as a response to his call was a wall of anger.

Frustrated, the Bishop turned and ran for Ni'estiel, hoping that the fleeing elf might be foolish enough to turn the stallion around and try to rescue him.

Tiel'marawee knew her duty and, besides, she wasn't even in control of the horse; Symphony moved of his own will.

The sight of Ni'estiel, still alive but delirious from pain and weakness, brought a wicked smile to the Bishop. He shifted back into his tiger form, smelled the blood, and fell over the semiconscious elf in a tearing and biting frenzy.

Bradwarden found the stallion, sweating and exhausted, but still moving purposefully toward the encampment some time later. Tiel'marawee lay unconscious across Symphony's back, the horse working hard to keep her there.

"By the god Dinoniel," the centaur muttered, seeing the garish wound. He immediately pulled the magical red band from his arm, the elven healing band that had kept him alive for weeks when he was trapped beneath the rubble of Mount Aida, and tied it tightly about Tiel'marawee's arm, though he had no idea if the magic would work on wounds inflicted before the armband was placed on the victim.

He was relieved to see the blood flow slow a bit, but he seriously doubted that any healing had come in time to save the poor creature. He lifted her from Symphony's back, cradling her in his strong arms, and headed for the camp, the stallion at his side.

Elbryan's feelings upon seeing her came as a mix of agony and amazement. What creature could have done this to a Touel'alfar? And even more disturbing, where was Ni'estiel?

"She's said not a word since I came upon her and yer horse," Brad-warden explained. "Me thinkin's that Symphony pulled her from whatever enemy found her."

The ranger looked to his horse, found that connection through the magi-cal turquoise set in Symphony's breast, and nodded his head. And then his fears grew as Symphony imparted the image of a great and powerful cat, one that matched perfectly the description Roger had given him of the cat that had murdered Baron Bildeborough.

"Oh, if only I had stolen a soul stone from the abbey!" Brother Viscenti lamented as he and the others came upon the scene.

Elbryan, too—and not for the first time—regretted that he had not ac-cepted that one stone from Pony when she had turned her road to the south.

"Will she live?" Roger asked, as Brother Braumin, skilled in healing arts even without gemstone aid, moved over the elf, trying to make her more comfortable. Not understanding the nature of the armband, he started to untie it, but Bradwarden and Elbryan quickly corrected him.

"She's looking a bit better," Bradwarden offered hopefully.

"But her wounds are from the claws of a cat," the ranger explained. "Dirty wounds."

"A cat?" Roger asked, eyes widening.

Elbryan looked at him hard and nodded. "A great orange cat, striped in black," the ranger explained. Roger's knees weakened and he nearly top-pled, except that Brother Castinagis was at his side, supporting him.

"Like the one that killed Baron Bildeborough," the ranger confirmed.

"Bishop," came a weak voice from below, as Tiel'marawee tried to ex-plain. "Bishop . . . tiger."

Elbryan bent low. "Bishop?" he asked, but Tiel'marawee's eyes had closed once more and she lay very still.

"De'Unnero," Brother Braumin explained. "The Bishop of Palmaris. He is known for the use of the tiger's paw, a potent gem that can transform an arm into the powerful paw of the great cat."

"More than the arm," Roger insisted.

"He is here?" the ranger said incredulously, looking up to scan the forest as if he expected the tiger to leap out at them at that very moment.

"And we canno' be doubtin' his reason for comin'," Bradwarden remarked.

"He's searching for us," Brother Braumin reasoned. "We have brought danger to you by asking for your help."

The ranger shook his head. "I suspect that I am more his target than you and your friends," he stated.

"Any Pony more than yerself," Bradwarden added, a particularly unset-tling thought for Elbryan. If De'Unnero had come out here looking for him, did that mean that the man had found Pony in Palmaris, had perhaps tortured her into revealing his whereabouts?

"I must find him," Elbryan said suddenly, still staring into the forest, his fears for Pony and his unborn child growing.

"I'm thinkin' that he's to find yerself soon enough," Bradwarden said dryly.

"What do we do?" asked Brother Braumin.

"We keep goin' the way we're goin'," Bradwarden answered before the ranger could interject his thoughts. The centaur was wise enough to understand that Elbryan was thinking of his lover then, and was likely thinking of turning back for Palmaris. And that, to Bradwarden's thinking, would be a tremendous mistake.

"Ye told me yerself just this night that the elves're with her in Palmaris," he said to calm the ranger. "Suren they're to protect her as well as ye could."

The ranger wasn't so sure of that, wasn't sure that the elves, given their obvious negative feelings about Pony's learning *bi'nelle dasada*, would even want to protect her. He shook that thought away, though, and reminded himself that the Touel'alfar, however different their viewpoint might be, were not enemies but allies.

"Or have ye gotten so full o' yerself that ye think yerself better than the likes o' Lady Dasslerond and Belli'mar Juraviel, and all th' others put together?" Bradwarden pressed, a ridiculous notion but one that made Elbryan remember the truth of the power of the Touel'alfar.

"We go on," the ranger agreed, "but we keep a tighter scouting pattern."

"And what of the little one?" Bradwarden asked, looking down at poor Tiel'marawee. "I'm not thinkin' she's ready for travel right now."

"I am not even certain that she will live out the day," Brother Braumin admitted.

"We will wait for her," the loyal ranger said without hesitation.

"One way or another," Brother Castinagis quietly remarked.

"And I will go out with Symphony to find Ni'estiel," the ranger added, ignoring the harsh comment, though he knew that it hadn't been said with any malice.

"Not alone, ye won't," the centaur replied.

"I can move faster alone on the horse."

"And I can pace ye," the centaur insisted.

Elbryan looked around at his friends. He didn't like the idea of taking Bradwarden with him, thus leaving the others, though there were six of them, unprotected.

"Take the centaur," Brother Castinagis insisted. "To go out alone against De'Unnero would be foolhardy."

"The Bishop is a formidable enemy," Brother Mullahy added.

The ranger didn't need their confirmation; anyone who could bring down two of the Touel'alfar was obviously formidable. "I am more concerned with those I leave behind," he said plainly.

"There are six of us," Roger answered.

"And we five of St.-Mere-Abelle are trained in the fighting arts," Brother Castinagis insisted in a confident tone.

The ranger motioned to Bradwarden, then moved to saddle Symphony. One look at the horse, though, lathered in sweat and with a fairly serious cut on his flank, told him that he would do better walking the animal for a bit, so he plopped blanket and saddle over Bradwarden instead, bridled Symphony, and led the stallion into the forest, the centaur at his side.

They found the tattered remains of Ni'estiel two hours later, the tiger nowhere in sight.

"Ye'll pay that one back for doin' this," the centaur said.

Elbryan stared at the torn form, then looked at the forest and nodded.

Tiel'marawee was not ready for travel the next morning, though she looked somewhat stronger and even managed to open her eyes and tell more of the story, confirming that the creature that had attacked the elves had been sometimes human, sometimes tiger, and sometimes something in between. She also managed to confirm that the Bishop was hunting for Nightbird and was more than happy to kill anyone who called herself a friend of the ranger. And then Tiel'marawee closed her delicate golden eyes once more and settled quietly in her place, seeming so fragile, so on the very doorstep of death.

Stubbornly, the ranger went out for *bi'nelle dasada*, stripping off his clothes and finding a clearing on the edge of a small lake. He fell into the sword dance with furor, using it to confirm his dedication to the elves and his determination to avenge this outrage, and also as a challenge to De'Unnero, hoping the Bishop would find him and come at him, in either form, that he might end this there and then.

And indeed, from a place not too far away, De'Unnero watched the ranger's powerful yet graceful movements, and he came closer, trying to decide whether to go at the man as tiger or human. He settled on human, for he wanted to prove that he was the better fighter without the use of magic, wanted to confirm his own place in the world.

But then De'Unnero discovered that the powerful centaur also watched the ranger, and as confident as he was, he did not desire to battle the two of them. He would bide his time, he decided, slipping back into the dark cover of the forest, though remaining close enough to watch the entire spectacle of the dance. Shamus Kilronney was on his way, with soldiers who would neutralize the ranger's friends.

Then De'Unnero could prove himself.

CHAPTER

❖ 28 ❖

Consequences

"**B**e off the street!" the soldier shouted at a surprised Belster O'Comely, who had come out of the Way to dump a bucket of garbage. The soldier approached, weapon drawn, but the innkeeper faded back to his door and through it, hands up defensively, not bothering to retrieve the bucket.

"And don't ye come out again!" Belster heard the man yell as he closed his door. With a great sigh, the innkeeper moved back to the common room, where Dainsey and Mallory sat quietly sharing a drink. Just that morning, anticipating an upsurge in business with patrons coming in to gossip about the arrival of the Father Abbot and the impending arrival of the King, Belster had formally hired Mallory and Prim O'Bryen.

How ironic that seemed now, with the Way deserted save for three fellows who had rented rooms a day before, with none of those gossip-hungry patrons able to come to the place even if they were so inclined.

"Where'd she go?" Belster asked, and Dainsey motioned at the door to the private quarters.

He found Pony in her room, sitting quietly in the dark, staring out the lone window. Every so often there came the bark of a soldier or monk, warning people off the streets. After the attack on the Father Abbot, St. Precious had all but shut the city down.

"Oh, what have you done, girl?" Belster asked, moving to tower over Pony. "And it was you—don't you lie to me! Last man coming into the Way told me a gemstone hit the Father Abbot and that all the monks were amazed that someone had struck so hard and from so far away. They had wards in place against such attacks, so it's said—so they, and I, know the assassin was a person of great power with the stones. Only one person I know could have done that."

"Avelyn Desbris could have torn his head from his shoulders," Pony stated matter-of-factly, not taking her gaze from the scene beyond the window.

That callous attitude sent Belster into a sudden rage. He grabbed her by
the shoulders and turned her forcefully to face him. "And Avelyn is dead,"
he replied. "We both know that, and we know, too, who it is that has his
gemstones. And one of those stones was lodestone, was it not? And it was a
lodestone that hit the Father Abbot. So where is your lodestone, girl?"

Pony's big blue eyes narrowed. boring into him, her gaze so forceful and
determined that Belster backed away half a step.

"It was Pony who attacked the Father Abbot," Belster said quietly.

"I would no more apologize for slaying the Father Abbot than I would
for playing a role in the defeat of Bestesbulzibar," she said firmly, though
she didn't understand the irony of such a statement.

"Oh, but what have you done?" Belster lamented, throwing up his hands
and spinning away, pacing nervously. "You believe that you have done a
favor to our friends? To your own? Look outside, girl! Do you see anyone
walking in the street, anyone coming into the Way this night?"

"They will loosen their grip after a short enough while," Pony insisted.
"They are afraid now, and so the soldiers and the monks sweep the streets
to prevent any larger uprising; but that, too, will pass."

"And what about your Behrense friends?" Belster asked. "Will the retri-
bution from the Church that your actions bring upon the black-skins soon
pass? Will those who survive the coming onslaught soon forget those who
will be executed?"

"The Behrense?"

"Do you doubt that many are blaming *them* for the attack?" Belster
asked incredulously.

Pony scoffed at the absurd idea. "The Behrense have never been known
as stone users," she reasoned. "Their religion does not even acknowledge
the gemstones as the gift of God, but maintains they are a temptation from
Ouwillar, their recognized incarnation of the demon dactyl. Yatol priests
view the stones as a means to avoid hard and honest labor and as dangerous
because they offer power to people whom they consider undeserving of
that power. The thought that a Behrense executed a gemstone attack on the
Father Abbot is purely—"

"Convenient," Belster interrupted. "So you had your fun. Are you feeling
the better for it?"

Pony shook her head in frustration. How could he not understand?
Feeling better? Hardly! She had done only what needed to be done, had
done what was demanded of her out of loyalty to the Chilichunks and to
Connor, and out of her hopes for a better future for the kingdom.

"You have put us all in a pretty fix, now haven't you?" Belster went on
sarcastically. "It might be that they will name the dog De'Unnero as next
Father Abbot, and then all the kingdom will feel the pain he has already
inflicted on Palmaris."

Pony continued to shake her head. "Markwart was the force behind the rise of the Abellican Church," she said. "It was he who gained control of Palmaris for his Order and without him—"

"It was he who killed your parents," Belster said bluntly. "And that is all you understand and all you considered. And it might be that Markwart deserved what you gave him, but don't you think for a moment that you did any favors to the rest of us. Not a one, I say! We'll all be living in the hell Pony made for us now."

Pony looked back out the window, and nearly jumped out of her chair at the sudden sound of Belster slamming the door behind him. He was wrong, she told herself repeatedly. Times would be difficult for a while, perhaps, but it would pass; by her estimation, the city would more likely revert to state control now, and the people would more likely be able to find a calm and peaceful existence.

She had to believe that, for her actions had brought her little other comfort. She had sated her thirst for vengeance, perhaps, but that had done little—nothing at all!—to fill the hole in her heart left by the deaths of Graevis, Pettibwa, and Grady. And Connor. At the most, she now hoped that with her revenge exacted, she could get on with, and get over, the terrible process of grieving.

"It was the woman," Tallareyish Issinshine informed Belli'mar Juraviel and Lady Dasslerond that night of the attack on the Father Abbot. "She struck from a rooftop, some distance away."

"It would seem you have not exaggerated her power with the gemstones," Lady Dasslerond said to Juraviel, though it was painfully obvious from her tone that she was neither impressed nor pleased with Jilseponie Wyndon at that moment.

"Jilseponie has suffered greatly at the hands of Father Abbot Markwart," Juraviel tried to explain, but he, too, heard his words as hollow. Because of her position, because she carried the child of Nightbird and knowledge of *bi'nelle dasada*, Pony should have acted more wisely than that; she had the responsibility to look at the overall picture of the good of the world, not act out some personal vendetta.

"She acted rashly," Dasslerond said with her typical bluntness, "and without regard for greater events about her."

"Events that she could not know of, since we have not contacted her," Juraviel pointed out.

"Events that include the child in her womb," Dasslerond was quick to retort. "That fact alone should have stayed her hand."

Juraviel wanted to reply that Pony obviously decided she could make the strike and get away with it without any greater loss than the single stone. But he held his tongue, for his excuses were a defense—precisely because Pony's actions needed defending. In truth Belli'mar Juraviel, too, was far from pleased with the woman and saw her latest action as merely another in a series of blunders that had begun when she had left Nightbird, particularly without telling him of the child. For Juraviel, too, was Touel'alfar, and, despite his frequent contact with humans, he could not see the world through their eyes.

"The Abellican Church will realize almost absolute control over the city now," Dasslerond went on. "And they will orchestrate every movement of King Danube, using security as an excuse. Your friend has cost us much. How am I to arrange a meeting with Danube Brock Ursal? And certainly we cannot reveal ourselves to the Church. It was a foolish choice she made, Belli'mar Juraviel, the choice of a human, of *n'Touel'alfar*, which Jilseponie surely is."

In her frustrated sigh, Juraviel heard clearly Dasslerond's further dismay that this same woman was also a keeper of the secret of *bi'nelle dasada*. It would take Pony a long string of good decisions to make up the lost ground in Dasslerond's eyes, and the lady's feelings toward Pony would go far in determining her patience with Nightbird.

But Juraviel could do nothing about it all—not now. Pony was a pawn in the great game being played out in Corona, and pawns were often sacrificed.

The three patrons staying at the Way joined Belster and his four helpers—for Pony had come out of the back room and Prim O'Bryen had managed to slip into the Way—but other than that, only two brave patrons dared the patrols to come into the tavern. All ten looked up with startlement and concern when the door to the common room burst open and a host of soldiers strode in.

Pony's hand went to her pouch of gemstones, while her other moved near Defender, lying on a shelf behind the bar. She relaxed, though, and so did Belster and Dainsey, when they took note of the woman leading the soldiers: Colleen Kilronney.

"Master O'Comely," she said, motioning her dozen companions—some town guard, some King's soldiers—to a pair of nearby tables. "Mugs o' ale for all me friends."

"At your command, good soldier," the innkeeper replied, hustling to the bar and filling mug after mug, then handing each tray to Dainsey and Mallory.

Colleen wandered over while Belster was at his work, calling back to her companions that she would see to it that the innkeeper was properly paid—though more than one of the other soldiers, Kingsmen, called out that he should not be compensated, that he should be thrilled at the chance to serve soldiers of the crown.

Colleen waved their words away and came up to the bar, producing a purse fat with coins. Belster started to tell her not to bother, but her look explained to the man, and to Pony standing next to him, that Colleen had used this as a pretense to speak with them away from her fellows.

"They said it was magic that felled the Father Abbot," she whispered, "magic more powerful than any o' them ever seen."

Belster glanced at Pony, a look Colleen did not miss.

"So it *was* ye," she said with a grin. "Well, a fine shot, by me thinkin'."

"And one that made the world a better place," Pony replied determinedly. "Better are all the folk of Honce-the-Bear, of all Corona, without Father Abbot Markwart."

"Without?" Colleen asked skeptically.

That took the smile from Pony's face.

"He's living?" Belster asked.

"Fine and well," Colleen replied. "The monks with him when he got hit thought he'd die, thought he *had* died; but the stubborn old dog held on, somehow, and when them monks at St. Precious got at him with their healing stones, they took fine care o' him. Still, they're callin' it a miracle, ye know, and some're even sayin' that God would not let the Father Abbot die at this critical time."

Belster groaned and slumped. Though he was angry with Pony, he, too, had hoped that her rash action had at least rid the world of Markwart.

Pony was devastated. "I hit him too hard," she said, her voice barely a whisper, as if she could not draw breath. "I saw his head explode, and no soul stone could put that back together. I killed him. The power of that gemstone would have killed a king of giants."

"Ye didn't kill him, though I wish ye had," Colleen replied. She gave Pony a bright smile then, and an affirming nod. "Ye got the belly for it, girl," she said with obvious respect.

"Belly of stone," Belster complained, "and a head to match."

Colleen's smile disappeared as another soldier, a Kingsman, walked over to join her. "Haggling the price?" he asked.

"The good Belster's givin' it to us for free," Colleen replied. "And he's askin' when folks'll be able to walk on the streets again, when they might wander into his tavern."

"That will be for Father Abbot Markwart to determine," the Kingsman replied, "or for King Danube, if the ban has not been lifted before his arrival." The man offered a stern look at Belster and Pony; Pony held her breath, for she knew this one from the campaign at Caer Tinella and could only hope that he wouldn't recognize her through her disguise. She wondered if her eyepatch was on the appropriate eye, if her hair was well powdered.

He started away—but he kept glancing back suspiciously.

"He's always like that," Colleen explained.

"You are certain that the Father Abbot is alive?" Pony asked quietly.

Colleen nodded. "Seen him meself, orderin' monks around at St. Precious," she said. "His talkin's a bit crooked, if ye get me understandin', but he's up and about, and brimmin' mad, don't ye doubt!"

"Damn him," Pony muttered, and she looked down at the floor, full of rage, full of frustration. How could it be? How could any man, any giant even, have survived the strike of that lodestone with the amount of energy she had put into it? Pony knew then that this man was an even more formidable enemy than she had believed. But still, she meant to kill him.

Indeed she did.

"The gemstone was found deep into the metal side of the carriage," Tallareyish explained when he returned again to Dasslerond. The lady was alone this time, for Juraviel was out among the shadows of the streets, watching the soldiers and monks on their rounds, taking a measure of the security curtain that had been dropped over Palmaris. He also meant to speak with Pony, if he found the chance, and with Dasslerond's blessings, though the lady had limited what Juraviel might tell his human friend.

"In the carriage after blasting through his hard head," the lady said. "And yet he lives?"

"He does," Tallareyish confirmed. "And those monks who attended him are now pacing the corridors of St. Precious, loudly praying to their God, speaking of miracles and of the glory revealed in their Father Abbot."

"His wounds were grievous then?"

"Our scouts insist that none of the monks thought he had a chance of living, even when they began their work with the soul stones," Tallareyish explained. "Some even called for funeral preparations. The lower half of his face was torn away and smashed apart. But now, mere hours later, the man is up and about, seeming strong and angry, with no more than a lisp and a swollen bottom jaw to show for the attack."

Lady Dasslerond kept those words, that description of the recovered Markwart, in her thoughts as she finished with Tallareyish, dismissing him to his scouting duties, asking him to keep watch over Juraviel. Then she went alone to a quiet corner of the roof that was serving as her temporary base.

Though her people did not use many gemstones, Lady Dasslerond, above all others of the Touel'alfar, understood the power of the gems and she could hardly believe that Markwart—that any man, let alone an old one—could have survived that attack. And yet he had, and had thrived!

Dasslerond, knowledgeable in the ways of the world, in the legends of all the races and all the dactyl demons, feared the implications.

❖ 29 ❖

The Guest of Bi'nelle Dasada

"Are ye to go out again, then, ye stubborn boy?" Bradwarden asked before the dawn of the second day of their forced halt. Elbryan had awakened a short time before and, after a check on Tiel'-marawee—who was resting more comfortably but did not yet seem ready to be moved—the young man began stripping off his clothing.

"Every day," the ranger replied. "The sword dance is where I find my center of balance, where I clear my thoughts in preparation for the trials of the day."

"More likely that ye'll find a trial at the damned dance, if the Bishop's anywhere about," said the centaur.

Elbryan's answer came in the form of a grin and an eager stride as he moved out of the camp. "You keep a watch over our friends," he called back from forest's edge; and then he was gone, leaving Bradwarden alone with the seven sleeping forms.

He went to the same clearing beside the small lake, stripped off the remainder of his clothing, and came out to the center with a deep and steadying breath, clearing his thoughts, dismissing his fears for Tiel'marawee, for his other companions, for himself, and for Pony—who was more and more in his thoughts. With all the tumult moved aside, he became Nightbird, the elven-trained ranger, attuned to his surroundings. He felt the ice-crusted grass beneath his feet, saw the shimmer of the morning sun on the thinly glazed surface of the pond. Despite his concentration, Nightbird couldn't help considering the strangeness of the scene. In a normal year at this season, he might have found several feet of snow beneath his feet, and the pond would have been white with drifting snow and thick with gray ice instead of this meager coating. Now only part of the lake was iced over; the rest, near where the stream exited on the far bank, remained open water.

It was indeed a strange winter, but that, Nightbird pointedly reminded himself, was something to ponder at another time, in another place. He had to get moving, had to get the blood flowing, for the icy grass was beginning to numb his feet.

And so he fell into *bi'nelle dasada*, the movements perfect in harmony and perfect in balance. He flowed with grace and precision, muscles interacting through balanced turns and balanced cuts of mighty Tempest. He did not think of the coming movement—did not have to, for *bi'nelle dasada* was so familiar to his body, so embedded in his muscles and nerves, that every following movement came naturally and easily, twist and thrust following rolling parry, leaps ending in sudden rushes, his legs and feet in the exact position to launch him forward as his feet gently touched the ground. The dance was not the same each day, far from it, for at Nightbird's level of mastery, he constantly improvised.

Truly he was a beautiful sight, and to Bishop De'Unnero, watching from the bushes and knowing this time that Nightbird had no allies in the immediate area, the ranger's dance only heightened his intrigue. This one would be a challenge, the monk knew, perhaps the greatest challenge he could possibly find.

"Without any armor, I see," De'Unnero remarked, striding out into the open field. The Bishop wore only the simple brown robes of his Order, a white rope belt interwoven with strands of gold, and plain soft boots. A ring adorned one finger, but he showed no other jewelry, no gemstones.

"As are you," the ranger said calmly, not surprised at all, for the forest had told him of the man's presence; in truth, he had come here specifically hoping that De'Unnero would show up.

"Yet I never fight in armor," De'Unnero remarked, circling to the right. And the ranger, too, slowly took up a circular walk. "Not even the leather jerkin worn by Nightbird, nor the heavy boots. It hardly seems fair."

"Fully clothed, I wear nothing that would stop the thrust of even a goblin's crude spear," Nightbird replied.

"So you do not admit disadvantage?" De'Unnero asked, for he wanted there to be no excuses later on. For the challenge to be proper, and the victory to be savored, the fight had to be on even terms.

"Fair enough," the ranger replied with a wry smile, "though you seem to have forgotten your weapon."

De'Unnero laughed, and as he did, he lifted his arm, his hand emerging from his voluminous sleeve and transforming into the tiger's paw. "I carry my weapons closer to the skin, that is all," the Bishop explained. He gave a chuckle, not at the expression Nightbird then wore, but because of the ease with which he had enacted the transformation—the gemstone in his pouch and not even in his hand! Father Abbot Markwart had shown him something wonderful, a newer and greater level of power.

"Continue," Nightbird bade him, "all the way, into the form you used when you murdered the elf, when you murdered Baron Bildeborough and his entourage."

Now De'Unnero laughed louder. He considered the offer for just a moment, but shook his head. He wanted to beat Nightbird on even terms; by his estimation, his tiger arm was the equivalent of the beautiful sword the man carried.

"You know why I have come?" he asked.

"I know that your Church can invent whatever excuse is convenient," the ranger replied.

De'Unnero was shaking his head. "Not the Church, Nightbird," he explained. "I come to you as Marcalo De'Unnero, not as Bishop De'Unnero. Were you to offer your surrender now, Marcalo De'Unnero would not want it, though Bishop De'Unnero would have no choice but to accept it."

The ranger cocked his head, not really understanding.

"I have come for you, De'Unnero against Nightbird," the monk went on, "as it has to be."

Now the ranger laughed, catching onto the absurdity of it all. "This is about pride, then, and not your twisted vision of justice," he reasoned. "This is about who is the finer warrior."

"The finest warrior," De'Unnero corrected. "I have come to settle the issue."

"And then?"

"And then, when I have torn out your heart and eaten it, I will settle with your friends," the Bishop promised, for he guessed correctly that the ranger would never allow him his pleasure for the sake of a mere challenge. "I will kill the centaur first, and then the small, sneaky man. And then I will see to the monks. Perhaps I will offer them the chance to surrender, to return and face the charge of heresy, in their foolish hopes of finding mercy before Father Abbot Markwart. Or perhaps I will slaughter them, every one, and tear off their heads. Those trophies alone would satisfy my master."

Nightbird stopped his circling; De'Unnero did likewise.

"Do you have a God that you must pray to?" De'Unnero asked.

"My dance was my prayer," the ranger replied. "A prayer that God will have mercy on the souls of those I am forced to kill."

With a howl, the Bishop came on in a fury, knowing that his advantage lay in getting inside the long, deadly reach of the ranger's sword.

Nightbird knew it, too, and though he was surprised by the agility and speed of the other man, he spun away, leaving Tempest's tip in line, forcing the Bishop to twist aside or impale himself.

But, as soon as he passed beside that tip, De'Unnero quickly slid low, then leaped high above the stabbing blade, kicking with one foot, connecting glancingly on the ranger's shoulder.

Again they faced off, but without words this time, just the intense stares of the purest and most hated rivals.

The ranger silently debated whether he should give the deceptively quick man the offensive, or try to back him off with sudden and powerful straightforward attacks. The point became moot in the blink of an eye, for De'Unnero leaped straight ahead, then landed with his legs in perfect order to propel him suddenly to the right. He spun in a circle, coming out of it with that deadly tiger's paw swiping for the ranger's head.

Tempest missed on the thrust, but the ranger swung the blade about in time to partially deflect the sweeping arm, inflicting a nasty gash on the side of the tiger wrist, but taking a deep cut across his own left shoulder. The Bishop ignored the pain and continued forward, demanding a desperate and off-balance retreat from the ranger.

Nightbird went ahead, dropping Tempest to the ground and leading with a heavy punch that caught the surprised De'Unnero on the chin and buckled his knees. More for support than to attack, the Bishop wrapped his tiger's paw arm around the ranger and dug his claws in, trying to bring his other arm up to block the sudden flurry of left and right blows.

Nightbird felt the burning pain just to the side of his spine. He knew that if he gave De'Unnero any room, the man would tear half his back off. So he bore in harder, launching a short, heavy right punch to the man's ribs, then a sudden left hook to the chin that snapped De'Unnero's head to the side. He felt the pull on his back as the stubborn Bishop started to turn away, so he hooked his right arm over the tiger limb, holding the man fast, more than willing to trade bare-fisted blows.

Or so he thought. Marcalo De'Unnero was the finest fighter ever to walk through the doors of St.-Mere-Abelle, the man who trained brothers justice, none of whom had ever been more than a shadow of his martial arts brilliance. Nightbird had surprised him, had landed some stunningly powerful blows, but now De'Unnero went to work, sending a series of short, sharp jabs to the ranger's chin—and to the chin only because Nightbird was smart enough to understand that the man was trying for his throat and that if De'Unnero ever connected solidly there, the fight would be over.

Even with the successful dodge, the ranger tasted blood. He traded another series of hits, then changed tactics, clamping his large hand over the Bishop's face and squeezing with all his strength. Immediately, the Bishop groaned and stopped punching, grasping desperately instead for the too-powerful arm.

Nightbird thought the fight at its end, saw welcome victory before him. He continued the bear hug, keeping that deadly tiger paw in place as the muscles on his right arm flexed tighter, iron cords taut, driving his fingers into the man's flesh with such power that both of them thought the Bishop's head would explode under the pressure.

De'Unnero grabbed and pulled, but he was no match in strength for the powerful ranger.

Nightbird growled in victory.

But then he felt a sudden sharp pain in the center of his wrist, just under his palm, as De'Unnero worked the tip of his thumb perfectly into the pressure point. To the ranger's amazement, his index and little fingers weakened; to his horror, De'Unnero wrenched his head away from the ranger's grasp and yanked the ranger's arm away.

Instinct sent Nightbird's head forward, as De'Unnero snapped his head forward; only luck brought the ranger's forehead lower than the Bishop's, the two heads connecting with devastating force. Both men staggered, but De'Unnero had taken the brunt of the blow. Clearly dazed, the Bishop lifted his knee quickly, aiming for the ranger's groin, but Nightbird turned his leg, accepting the hit on the thigh. The movement cost the ranger some measure of balance, and he had no choice but to go along when De'Unnero suddenly launched himself backward and to the ground, the pair landing and rolling down the short slope right into the cold lake. They rested for just an instant on the ice, but then broke through into the icy water.

Water churned and reddened about them, and both were too stunned by the sudden icy grip and lack of air to continue their fight.

Nightbird came up gasping and splashing, expecting De'Unnero to surface right beside him. What he got instead was a view of Bradwarden and Roger, the two moving across the clearing. When they spotted their friend, they came ahead fast.

"When did yer dance take to the water?" Bradwarden asked, galloping over to help his hurt and dazed friend from the dangerously frigid water. Elbryan came up shivering and bleeding, and one look at the lines across his back, a wound so similar in appearance to that of Tiel'marawee, told the other two what had transpired. Out came the great bow, Bradwarden stringing it and then setting an arrow in one fluid motion.

"H-he is in the w-water," Elbryan said through chattering teeth.

Roger pulled the cloak from his back and wrapped it about his friend, his expression incredulous. "Bishop De'Unnero did this to you?" he asked.

"Where is the fool?" the centaur asked. "Did ye kill him? Or hurt him enough to drown the rat?"

Elbryan shrugged and turned to scan the lake, not certain.

Then they had their answer, as De'Unnero's head bobbed out of the water near the center of the lake, moving away from them for just an instant, then disappearing under the surface. Bradwarden let fly anyway, his arrow skimming harmlessly across the surface.

"Well, he's havin' to come out," the centaur said, setting another missile. "And then I'll be gettin' me chance!"

Even as he finished, the Bishop emerged as a great cat, coming out of the lake and into the forest in such a rush that Bradwarden didn't even have the chance to let the arrow fly.

"At least he is running," said Roger.

Elbryan shook his head, not believing that for a moment. This man would not run; this man, dangerous enough to win out against them all, was far from finished.

"We can catch him then," Roger offered.

"But the elf's up for no run," Bradwarden reminded, "barely a walk, by me thinkin'."

"Whatever course we choose, we are better by far if we are all together," the ranger reminded, moving to his clothes and dressing quickly. The three set off for the camp then, and found Symphony on their way, the ranger having telepathically instructed the stallion to keep close.

Tiel'marawee was in better shape this day, but still far from being able to travel on her own. They felt that they could move her, though at a very slow pace. With De'Unnero near, Elbryan did not want to stay in one place. The man would likely find a way to strike hard at them. So they went on slowly and covered no more than three miles all through the day. Symphony and his rider ran a perimeter all the way, the ranger searching, hoping that he would find De'Unnero again. Whenever he got far enough from watchful Bradwarden, he shouted out challenges to the dark forest, hoping to lure the man, or tiger, out.

But he saw no sign of the Bishop that day nor the next, nor the next after that. And then they had to rest again, for Tiel'marawee could not continue. She begged them to leave her, asking only for supplies to see her through the week and assuring them that she would be able to survive on her own by that time.

Of course, not a one of them, not the ranger or centaur, not Roger Lockless or any of the five monks, paid the babbling elf any heed whatsoever. They set camp and they waited, as the next day slipped past and the next after that, and then, on the morning of the third day, Bradwarden galloped into the camp. "We got soldiers coming fast from the south," he explained. "And I'm bettin' that our friend the Bishop's ridin' with them."

Elbryan was up on Symphony in seconds, turning the stallion to follow Bradwarden's lead. "Secure the camp!" he called to Roger and Braumin. "Hold a tight group, with every back covered. The soldiers might have come against us, but even if that is not the case, the Bishop may well use this time to strike."

He gave the horse a telepathic call, and Symphony leaped away, easily pacing the centaur. By the time they reached the high bluff, the vantage point from which Bradwarden had spied the approaching troop, the soldiers were close enough to identify.

"Shamus Kilronney," the ranger muttered.

"And De'Unnero ridin' beside him," the centaur remarked. "And we're not for runnin', unless ye're thinkin' o' lettin' Tiel'marawee fend for herself."

"No running," Elbryan said firmly.

"More than a score o' them," the centaur pointed out. "Runnin's seemin' a good idea to me."

"We are not running," the ranger declared.

"I was talkin' about them," Bradwarden said dryly.

The ranger gave him an appreciative, sidelong glance.

"Should we be tellin' the others?" Bradwarden asked.

Elbryan considered that for a long while. "The monks have no offensive magic," he explained. "No magic at all, in fact. I do not know how they will fare against the likes of an armored horseman."

"Bah, ye're just lookin' to keep all the fun to yerself," the centaur replied.

"We'll send our companions into hiding," the ranger reasoned, "and then go to face Shamus and his men. If it comes to blows . . ."

"Ye're thinkin' it won't?" Bradwarden asked incredulously. "De'Unnero's with them, and I'm not believin' for a blinkin' eye that he came all the way out here for talkin'!"

"Then we hit them from afar, and scatter into the forest," the ranger explained.

"Two ain't scatterin'," Bradwarden explained. "Two's just runnin'."

"Same thing," Elbryan replied. "We show them a mighty chase, firing back at them all the while, thinning their numbers until we think we can rush in and defeat those remaining."

"We could be doin' that now," the centaur insisted.

"Lead on, then," the ranger answered, calling his bluff.

Of course, they did it Elbryan's way, going back to the others and charging Roger and Brother Castinagis with hiding and securing the group.

Back on the main trail soon after, the pair had no trouble locating Shamus and the soldiers, the group coming straight up the one clear trail. The riders pulled up short some thirty yards from the ranger and the centaur, Shamus in the middle of the front line of three and De'Unnero, astride a horse—an uncommon seat for the monk—flanking him on the right.

"Pleased I am to see Shamus Kilronney again," the ranger called out, "or would be, if you had come to me in better company."

De'Unnero whispered something to the captain, and Shamus called out, "We have come to take you, Nightbird, and to take the centaur and your monk friends. You keep company with outlaws of the Abellican Church. Gather them; you will be treated fairly, I promise."

"Go kiss a—" Bradwarden started, but Elbryan cut him short.

"*I* will be treated fairly?" the ranger asked, emphasizing the personal pronoun. "Would such treatment include the pleasure of watching my friends be hanged? Or burned at the stake, perhaps—I am told that is a favorite game for Abellican monks."

"We do not wish to fight you," Shamus explained.

"Ye're smarter than ye look, then," Bradwarden replied.

The captain glanced nervously at De'Unnero again. Shamus held a healthy respect for Nightbird, but he had no doubt that he and his soldiers could easily overpower the man and his few companions. That wasn't the problem, however.

A long, tense moment passed.

"Take them," De'Unnero said to Shamus. Then, when the captain made no move, he repeated the order to the soldiers. Several of the men started forward, but Shamus held up his arm, and they obediently stopped.

It was, perhaps, the most terrible moment in the life of Shamus Kilronney. Nightbird and he had sealed a friendship in short weeks, because they had found the trust necessary to battle as close allies. He knew this man, knew his heart, and did not believe for a moment that Nightbird had committed any real crimes against the Church, and certainly not against the state. And yet Shamus could not ignore the presence of the centaur, taken from the dungeons of St.-Mere-Abelle by Nightbird's own admission, nor the rogue monks, who would be tried and likely convicted of heresy and treason.

He looked down the path to Nightbird, locked the man's green eyes with his own stern gaze.

"Take them!" De'Unnero ordered. "And I shall lead!" With that, the Bishop lifted his arm, his great and deadly tiger's paw, and swept it forward in a powerful motion, leaping his horse ahead.

"Stop!" Shamus cried before soldiers began to follow. De'Unnero understood completely that he would be no match for the combined power of Elbryan and the mighty centaur.

De'Unnero tugged his horse around and sat staring at the captain in disbelief.

And Shamus was staring back—or more pointedly, he was staring at that tiger arm and remembering the fate of Baron Bildeborough.

"Now, Captain," De'Unnero growled at him, "I am the Bishop of Palmaris and I order you to arrest that man and that filthy creature beside him!"

Elbryan and Bradwarden exchanged knowing looks and smiles; Shamus Kilronney's expression spoke volumes.

Predictably, the captain shook his head. "I'll not go against Nightbird," he explained. "Nor will my men."

"Outlaws, then!" De'Unnero screamed. "All of you!" He waved his paw to encompass them all. "Any who do not follow me mark themselves as outlaws of the Abellican Church; and that, I promise you, is no enviable position!" He turned as if to charge at the ranger and the centaur then, and there came some uneasy movements from the soldiers behind him, but none would follow—none would ride past Shamus Kilronney, their trusted leader.

"Come on then yerself," Bradwarden bade the Bishop. "Ain't never ate a human, but for yerself, I might be makin' an exception."

"This is not settled," De'Unnero said to Nightbird. "You will not escape me this time."

"I am not even trying to run," the ranger said grimly.

De'Unnero stared at him hard, and at his mighty companion, then turned to study Shamus Kilronney and his foolish soldiers.

Elbryan understood what would happen then, and so he propelled his great horse ahead at a charge.

De'Unnero reacted quickly, turning his own horse and driving his heels into the creature's flanks, rushing past Shamus and the soldiers, down the southern road.

Bradwarden moved next, lifting his great bow and shooting a huge arrow, but the Bishop, anticipating such an attack, veered his horse left and then right, and the arrow whizzed past him harmlessly.

Up came Hawkwing, but before the ranger could let fly, Symphony gaining on the lesser horse with every tremendous stride, the Bishop surprised him by leaping from his mount, transforming immediately, robes and all, into the sleek form of the great tiger, and then darting to the side of the trail into the brush.

In charged Symphony, Nightbird slinging Hawkwing over his back, for he knew that he'd find no shot in here, then bending low and drawing out Tempest. He urged Symphony on, and the great horse thundered ahead at all possible speed.

But the horse was no match for the sleek, swift tiger in the thick brush, and when Nightbird broke out of the tangle in a clearing, he saw De'Unnero already bounding into the brush at the other side, in full flight to the south.

The ranger pulled Symphony up to a trot, realizing that he would not catch the man. He turned the horse, coming back to the others, to see the soldiers still shaking their heads and chattering in disbelief, for they had never seen such a thing as a man transforming into a great cat!

"And so we are outlaws," the ranger said to Shamus as he walked his mount back to the group, "declared so by the murderer of Baron Rochefort Bildeborough."

CHAPTER

❖ 30 ❖

Darkness and Light

"Truly a miracle," Brother Francis mumbled in disbelief when he saw Father Abbot Markwart exiting his room at St. Precious, seemingly as fit and strong as he had been before the attempt on his life, walking with that same eager bounce that had so recently returned to his step. At the very least, Francis had expected some bitterness from the old man: outrage and uncertainty, and fear. But Markwart, from the first moment he had regained consciousness after being so brutally struck, had exhibited none of those negative attitudes. He had very publicly thanked God for saving his life—with a jaw that was working well, a jaw that had seemed all but gone only hours before!—and then had explained his sudden inspiration that this might provide an even deeper benefit. The recall Bishop De'Unnero had begun of the gemstones would be more welcomed by the doubting and tentative King Danube. To hear Markwart express it, the potential growth of power for the Abellican Church seemed perfectly astonishing.

And for Brother Francis, confused and still trying to shed that unbearable guilt, it rang out as proof that he had chosen right in believing in the Father Abbot.

He had to hustle to catch up to his mentor, and then had to continue a swift stride to pace the man. Danube Brock Ursal had come into St. Precious, surrounded by a host of guards, to offer comfort to the wounded Father Abbot. How surprised he was when Markwart strode confidently into the audience chamber, a wide, though somewhat crooked smile splayed on his old, leathery face. He took his seat opposite King Danube, while his escort scurried to place chairs respectfully behind him.

"Greetings, Father Abbot," Danube managed to say after the shock of Markwart's obvious health wore off. "I had heard that you were more seriously injured—some of your monks expressed their fears that you would not survive, even with their magical healing."

"And so I would not have," Markwart replied with a slight lisp, "had not God chosen to keep me in this place."

Duke Kalas, sitting behind the King, snorted, then tried, not so hard, to disguise it as a cough.

Markwart's glare cut off those impertinent sounds, the Father Abbot's dark eyes narrowing dangerously, the tension suddenly palpable. Kalas, normally so cocksure and determined, blanched at the sight, and so did King Danube, who had seen this old man before, during that terrible night-time visit.

"He knows that I still have much to achieve," Markwart went on, letting it end at that.

"He?" Danube asked, losing track of the conversation, noticeably shaken by that imposing glare.

"God," Markwart explained.

"How often have men justified their actions by proclaiming the name of God," Kalas dared to utter.

"Not as often as doubters have come to know the truth too late in their miserable lives," Markwart replied. "Too many have prayed for forgiveness on their deathbeds, realizing at long last that, despite their doubts, God holds the only true meaning; for the only future that really matters is the future we find when we shake off this fragile and imperfect mortal coil."

Brother Francis locked stares with Constance Pemblebury then, the two of them sharing the same incredulous feelings about the less-than-civil undercurrent of the exchange. At that moment, it was not hard for either of them to understand who would walk out as victor should Kalas continue this fight with the Father Abbot.

Markwart would utterly destroy him.

King Danube saw it, too.

"Now you understand the recall of the gemstones," Markwart said to him. "These are tools not meant for the common man."

"I would hardly call the nobility of Honce-the-Bear 'common,'" Duke Kalas argued.

"Nor would I label them 'holy,'" Markwart replied calmly. "And that is the distinction I draw. The stones are the gifts of God, meant for the chosen of God."

"You and yours," Kalas said dryly.

"If you wish to join the Order, then prove yourself worthy of it and I will personally see to your admission," Markwart answered.

Kalas glared at him. "Why would I want to do such a thing?" he asked.

"Perhaps that question perfectly illustrates my point concerning the gemstones," said Markwart. "We of the Abellican Order preach emotional control before granting such power as is afforded by the gemstones.

Without that safeguard, the potential for destruction is simply too great. Thus, the stones are to be recalled. Every one of them."

It came as a startling proclamation, one that had even Abbot Je'howith, who was standing dutifully behind Markwart, reeling. For Je'howith had assured King Danube that the program of recalling stones was confined to Palmaris and would not affect him and his court. Now Je'howith held his breath, expecting the King to explode with outrage.

But Markwart riveted him with his stare, reminding him silently of the nocturnal visit and of the power he should not oppose.

"I will need assurances that the power of the gemstones, when all are placed under Church control, will continue to be used in concert with the desires of the throne," King Danube replied, to the utter amazement of his secular advisers, even of Je'howith.

"The details will be negotiated," Markwart said, shifting his threatening stare to Kalas, for the man was obviously ready to cry out in protest.

The Father Abbot stood up then, signaling the end of the meeting without so much as an acknowledgment from the King. "I do hope you will find your stay in our accommodating quarters at the house of merchant Crump acceptable, King Danube," he said. Constance and Kalas both gasped, for from the tone of his voice it came clear that Markwart was not offering the words as a groveling kindness toward a superior, but rather as a condescending gesture toward one he would tolerate.

And even more startling came Danube's accepting nod.

Brother Francis was the last of the monks out of the room, glancing back once to see the ruffled King and his court still sitting in their assigned chairs, their impotence affirming yet again that Francis had thrown his loyalty behind the right faction.

Markwart's cheerful mood after the meeting with King Danube did not last the day. He had called for a second meeting that morning, one with the commanders of the soldiers and the higher-ranking brothers of St. Precious to determine the progress of the search for his attacker. Not one of them offered a plausible direction for the search or a hint of who might have been behind the attack. Most suspected the Behrenese, but Markwart didn't believe that for a moment: he knew the yatol religion's disdain of gemstone use and had never heard a single report of a Behrenese man or woman showing any proficiency with the magic. And whoever had attacked him, he knew without doubt, was proficient with the magic, was very powerful. The soldiers had located three suspected attack positions, all on rooftops far from the parade route. For someone to drive a lodestone such a distance with such force indicated a level of mastery and power that would outdo many, perhaps all, the masters of St.-Mere-Abelle—that would rival the power of Markwart himself!

That, along with the fact that a lodestone had been among the stones stolen by Avelyn Desbris, told the Father Abbot much about his attacker. The name "Jill" came to his mind often during the meeting.

One other clue struck him. One of the soldiers, a bristling red-haired woman named Colleen Kilronney, kept insisting that the attacker must have been a rogue merchant, or an assassin hired by a merchant. As Francis and the others questioned her more deeply, they found little practical basis for the claim, but still, Colleen Kilronney held stubbornly to it.

Too stubbornly, perhaps?

That was only one of many things on Markwart's mind when he walked from the meeting to his private chambers. He had no pentagram inscribed on the floor here, of course, but he cleared a place in one corner of the room and sat down facing the corner, washing his mind to find a deep state of meditation. That now-familiar voice followed him into the emptiness.

He tried to sort through the many differing opinions he had heard, bounced the notion of a Behrenese plot against the anger of a rogue merchant, perhaps one who had managed to hide a lodestone from the searches of Bishop De'Unnero. But while the attacker might have been a merchant, or an assassin hired by merchants, that possibility did not stand up against Markwart's suspicions that his attacker really was Jill or some other disciple of Avelyn Desbris.

Through it all, the voice kept whispering about the red-haired soldier woman. Markwart argued, thinking the voice was trying to convince him of the plausibility of the woman's theory concerning merchants; but soon he realized that it was telling him something completely different, something about the source and not the information.

"A distraction," the Father Abbot whispered, and as he considered any possible reason the warrior woman might have for putting forth such a theory, he knew the direction of his personal search.

He stormed out of his quarters, ordering Brother Francis to bring Colleen Kilronney to him at once.

And then he waited, a spider at the center of its web.

Colleen came tentatively into the room, and Markwart recognized that she was on her guard—yet another sign that the voice had steered him correctly.

"You were adamant that the attacker was a merchant, or one hired by merchants," he said, getting right to the point and motioning for Colleen to take a seat opposite his desk, and then motioning for Brother Francis to leave them.

"Seemin' the obvious direction," she said.

"Is it?" The simplicity of the question made suspicious Colleen tilt her head to better study the old man, another movement that was not lost on perceptive Markwart.

"Yer Bishop's made a few enemies among them," Colleen explained, "mostly with the friends o' Aloysius Crump. Murdered him, ye know, and in a horrible way and in a public place."

Markwart held up his hand, not the least interested in pursuing any discussion with this inconsequential woman about Palmaris policy or De'Unnero's shortcomings.

"Might it not have been a friend of Avelyn Desbris?" he asked innocently.

"I'm not knowin' the name," Colleen insisted at once, but her body language told a different story altogether.

"Ah," Markwart said, nodding. "That would explain your insistence on the merchant theory." He stopped and tapped his lips with one finger, dismissively waving Colleen out of the room with his other hand. He called out to her as she opened the door, telling her to send Brother Francis back in immediately, and the confused woman merely nodded and grunted.

"Find me those who know her movements," Markwart ordered Francis a moment later, for he knew, and the voice was in full agreement, that Colleen Kilronney not only had recognized the name of Avelyn Desbris but also had been in recent contact—and knew it!—with one of the heretic's disciples.

Before the day was out, Father Abbot Markwart had discerned another spot for his personal search: Fellowship Way. His spirit walked out of St. Precious that stormy night.

With the rain and the wind and the brilliant strokes of lightning, few soldiers were out that night, and so the company-starved folk of Palmaris dared to slip out of their homes. Fellowship Way bustled with patrons, all talking excitedly, trying to catch up on the momentous events since their last meeting, before the attack on Father Abbot Markwart. Some chatted about seeing the King; others hoped that King Danube would put the city in proper order and lessen Church influence.

More than one patron argued against that, saying that the brutal assassination attempt on Markwart had sealed his position within the city, and that the King would never go against the Father Abbot so soon after the attack.

That line of reasoning, of course, hit Pony painfully hard as she moved from table to table. She still could hardly believe that the old man had survived, but now that it was obvious that Markwart was alive, even well, she thought herself incredibly foolish. She still wished that she had found a way to kill him, but having failed to eliminate the old wretch, she had, in fact, only strengthened his position!

Many times did she sigh helplessly during that long night.

While the human folk of Palmaris who dared the night storm hustled to their destinations, eager to get to shelter, the Touel'alfar didn't mind the rain in the least. So attuned to nature, the elves accepted whatever she gave them. Blizzards were a time for quiet respite near a cozy fire, but as soon as the dangerous wind and blinding snow died down, they would be out in force, frolicking about the drifts, engaging in snowball fights or tunnel digging. And so this late-winter rainstorm brought them little discomfort and only made easier their business of moving about Palmaris' streets.

Lady Dasslerond and Belli'mar Juraviel sat on the roof of Fellowship Way under an overhang, chatting calmly about recent events and their hoped-for course. Other elves moved about the house of Crump, seeking some way—a connection with an important soldier or noble, or even a secret passage into the King's private quarters—to find an audience for their lady with the King of Honce-the-Bear.

"Glad I will be when our business here is finished and we can return to the quiet meadows of Andur'Blough Inninness," Lady Dasslerond said.

Juraviel didn't disagree. "I left Nightbird so that I could again walk those meadows," he explained. "I had hoped to spend the entirety of the spring in our valley."

"Just the spring?"

"And all the seasons after that," Juraviel clarified. "I have seen enough of human problems. Too much, I fear."

To Dasslerond, Juraviel's words came as a welcome admission. She feared for him and his deep love for Nightbird and Pony. She considered Nightbird, as she did all the rangers, as almost her child; and from all she had heard, she believed that she could come to love the woman, Pony, too. But she was Touel'alfar, and they were not—no small matter to the clannish elves. And she was the leader of Andur'Blough Inninness, with responsibilities to no human, but only to her elvish people.

"I do look forward to my future meetings with Nightbird and Pony," Juraviel admitted. "And with their child, who may be heir to a greatness not seen, and sorely needed, among the humans."

"Perhaps I will accompany you on that future date," Dasslerond said, and Juraviel did not miss the honor she had just bestowed upon him, and upon his friends, with those kind words. "As the years pass and the human world calms, we might do well to venture out again, if for no other reason than personal enjoyment. Or perhaps we will lift the blocking veil over Andur'Blough Inninness and invite Nightbird and his wife and child to come and visit us."

Juraviel stared at her long and hard, thrilled by her softening tone and words. He knew that Dasslerond remained disappointed in Nightbird for showing Pony *bi'nelle dasada*, and outraged at Pony for acting so rashly against Father Abbot Markwart, but the lady was trying to look past that, was hoping for a better future relationship with the ranger and his loved ones. So while the night seemed dark and stormy, Belli'mar Juraviel had reason to hope that the dawn would yet come.

But then he felt the presence, an absolute darkness and coldness, as he had one night in the forest with a band of human refugees.

Dasslerond felt it, too, and was up in an instant, one hand to her sword hilt, the other to a pouch at her side, a pouch that held her single gemstone, a mighty green emerald, a gift from Terranen Dinoniel to the elves centuries before, during the previous war with the dactyl Bestesbulzibar—easily the most powerful stone possessed by the Touel'alfar.

"Jilseponie," Lady Dasslerond breathed, and she and Juraviel rushed to the edge of the building, signaling another nearby elf to rally the forces.

Pony moved back to the bar to collect a tray of mugs from Belster. She stopped, though, feeling suddenly strange, and glanced all about, wondering who might be calling her.

"You will have to move faster than that if you mean to keep them all happy," Belster said with a laugh.

Pony took a step closer, but stopped and glanced nervously about again, the hairs on the back of her neck tingling as her warrior instincts put her on her guard.

"Caralee?" Belster asked, taking care not to use her real name publicly.

Pony turned to him and gave a slight shrug, thoroughly confused. She came by swiftly then, pulling her apron from about her waist and setting it on the bar. "I will return soon," she promised, scurrying past Belster and through the door to the private rooms.

Before she even reached her room, she stopped again. She was not alone; she knew that beyond doubt. And then the truth of it, at least a small part of that truth, hit her hard: she was being monitored by a spirit-walking monk!

Pony rushed to her room, not knowing where to turn next. Should she find a stone to counter the spiritual intrusion? Should she go about her business calmly, as though nothing was amiss, playing the part of Belster's wife?

Jill, came a call in her head. The woman stopped and concentrated, trying to identify the source.

You are Jill, came the voice, and she realized by that question that this was no friend! She spun about, thinking to rush back in the common room and blend into the crowd, but then she froze in place.

The specter of Father Abbot Markwart stared at her, hovering visibly in the doorway.

"Jill, friend of Nightbird, friend of Avelyn Desbris," came the Father Abbot's voice—aloud!

Pony didn't know how to respond. She had never witnessed this type of magical communication before, had no idea that spirit-walking could be taken to such a level!

"Jill the assassin," said the Father Abbot. "You hit me hard, my dear."

He gave a laugh as he finished, an awful, wicked laugh that sent a shudder through her.

"I believe you have something that belongs to me, Jill, friend of Avelyn," he went on, "something that Avelyn took from me."

"Be gone from this place," the woman replied in as strong a tone as she could muster. "You are not welcome here."

The spirit laughed at her more loudly. "I will have my gemstones back," Markwart said, "this very night. I know you, Jilseponie Chilichunk."

That name hurt—and moved a wall of anger against Pony's very real fears. This was the man who had killed her parents, the man she wanted to destroy; and yet she could not ignore the power of his presence, a strength she had never felt. . . .

No, not never, she realized to her horror.

"Do you see what you have done to me?" the spirit asked, and it changed form then, its lower jaw all but disappearing, flaps of torn tongue hanging low from its blasted mouth. "You, I say! And only by the power of the gemstones am I able to paint an image of my face as it was, and only by the telepathic power of the soul stone am I able to communicate so that those around me think that I am speaking to them."

Pony's own jaw went slack as she considered the implications of the man's words—for she did not disbelieve him. The man's face was destroyed—she had destroyed it—and yet, using gemstones, he was maintaining an illusion of wholeness: using gemstones, he was creating an illusion of speaking audibly! Pony could hardly conceive of the power implied by such an illusion, the maintenance of gemstone magic for so long!

"I know you, and I am coming for you," the spirit promised.

The woman exploded into motion, pulling her disguise off and collecting Defender and the gemstones. "I deny you!" she growled at the hovering specter, and she ran right through the image—a most unsettled experience! She thought to go to Belster, but realized that the best course she could take for her friends was to simply run away from them.

Dainsey Aucomb found her before she reached the back door.

"Ah, Miss Pony, are ye all right then?" the woman asked. "Belster said ye'd run out without—"

"Hear me well, Dainsey," Pony said, after a nervous glance around told her that the specter had not followed. "I am leaving now, and likely forever."

"But yer child—"

Pony cut that thought short, terrified that Markwart might hear. "You do not know the truth of me," Pony said, rather loudly, hoping to take some of the blame from her vulnerable friends. "Take Belster and run and hide. Better that you two are not involved."

"M-miss Pony," Dainsey stuttered.

"That is all I have time to explain," Pony insisted, grabbing the woman by the shoulders and giving her a good shake to focus her. "Good-bye, Dainsey. Know that you have been a dear friend." She kissed the woman on the cheek. "Kiss Belster for me, and run and be safe."

Dainsey just stood there, stunned.

"Promise me!" Pony insisted. "Go now. Right now! Promise me!"

The dumfounded woman nodded, and then Pony ran out into the stormy night, her thoughts whirling. She had been discovered, and more of her loved ones might pay dearly for her errors, but she knew then that the best thing she could do for Belster and for Dainsey and all the others was to get as far away from them as possible. Understanding just how far she might have to run, recognizing the only real destination open to her, she went not for the alleys of the city but for the northern gate and the stable near it, where she boarded Greystone.

Belli'mar Juraviel and Lady Dasslerond watched her run out into the storm.

"It was him," Juraviel breathed. "He knows."

Another elf rushed to join them. "Gather all," Lady Dasslerond explained quickly. "To the north gate and beyond."

"We must help her," Juraviel declared, and he looked up at his lady, at the elven queen who had, just moments ago, talked of future meetings with Pony and Nightbird and the child, and he recognized the uncertainty on her fair face.

At least they were moving in the right direction, shadowing Pony to the north.

She was relieved to find Greystone's stable quiet and with no soldiers about. All the way to the place, Pony had feared that Markwart had found out all her secrets and that all escape routes would be cut off. But the stable boy helped her ready the horse, even offered her some old saddlebags and some supplies to put in them.

And then she went out onto the streets again, wincing at every loud clip-clop of freshly shod hooves. She tried to formulate some plan that might get her quietly through the northern gate—in the guise of a farmer's wife, perhaps—but she dismissed that. She might be recognized by soldiers put on the alert, and few folk would dare this storm except in an emergency.

She took a different route instead, moving far to the side of the guarded gate, to a quiet and dark place along the city wall. She brought Greystone into a short run, then, well before the base of the wall, fell into the malachite gemstone, extending its magic not only to herself but to her horse as well. The two lifted weightlessly from the ground, their momentum carrying them toward the wall.

Greystone kicked and whinnied in terror, but Pony held him steady and sent more energy into the stone, lifting them higher, lifting them right over the wall, to touch down on the grassy fields beyond. She heard the commotion back at the wall, as guards rushed around, trying to find out what, if anything, had just happened. She hardly cared, urging Greystone into a swift canter across the darkened fields.

By the time the physical Markwart and his entourage arrived at the Fellowship Way, she would be far to the north, she hoped; and she could only pray that Dainsey would not fail her, that she and Belster would also be long gone—perhaps with Captain Al'u'met, perhaps into the secret caves of the Behrenese.

She couldn't bear the thought of yet another loved one being killed for her crimes, and thought for a moment that she should go back and surrender herself to Markwart so that all her friends in Palmaris would not be persecuted, tortured for information about her.

But then she thought of her unborn child, of Elbryan's child, and she knew that she had to trust Belster and Dainsey and all the others. Oh, what a fool she thought herself for attacking Markwart! For putting them all in danger!

Tears mingled with the driving rain on her cheeks.

But she would run on, she determined, all the way to Caer Tinella, all the way to Dundalis and into Elbryan's loving arms. Together they would face Markwart.

Together.

Greystone shuddered and skidded suddenly, neighing wildly and rearing up; and Pony was thrown to the muddy field.

She rolled and groaned, and started to move her hands instinctively to her belly, fearing for her child. The shooting pain in one shoulder stopped her, though, and then so did something else, a feeling of dread beyond anything she had ever known. Growling away the stinging pain, she rolled over, looking for her horse. Greystone stood very still, head down.

Pony struggled to her feet and moved her good arm to her pouch of stones.

And then he was there—not in physical form but in spectral—so clearly that Pony could make out every detail of his features. "Running away?" Markwart said to her. "Coward. From all that I had heard concerning the mighty Jilseponie, I would have thought you would have welcomed the chance to test your strength against me."

"No coward, Markwart the murderer," Pony answered with as much courage as she could muster. Indeed, in another time and place, she would have welcomed this fight. Now she could not forget the promise she had made to Juraviel before she had left the northland—the promise she had made, in effect, to her unborn child.

"How your names do hurt me," the Father Abbot teased.

To Pony's amazement, the image strengthened then, seemed to grow solid, as if Markwart had just stepped through the connection between body and spirit!

"If you surrender to me, I promise you a quick death," the Father Abbot remarked, "a merciful one, so long as you publicly disavow the heretic Avelyn."

Pony laughed.

"Otherwise, I promise only that I will torture you until you disavow Avelyn," the Father Abbot added, "and then I will kill you slowly, savoring every moment. But you will accept even that, do not doubt, for any course leading to death will seem preferable to the life I offer you."

"The life you offer all your subjects," Pony retorted. "How far from God you have fallen! You cannot begin to understand the truth of Avelyn, the light that shone about him. You cannot—"

The words caught in her throat as Markwart grabbed her—not physically but with some mental connection that choked her as surely as his hands might have. Pony clutched her hematite, not leaving her body, but focusing her thoughts into the spirit realm. There she saw the shadow of Markwart's spirit, a tangible thing, standing right before her, hands out and about her throat. Black shadow arms came up from Pony's side as well, grabbing at Markwart's spirit image, and she pushed with all her strength, backing Markwart until their two battling spirit images stood halfway between their bodies.

"You are strong!" she heard Markwart say, surprisingly with glee in his voice. "Too long have I waited for this challenge!"

Pony growled again and grabbed harder, driving his shadow back a bit more and rising over it, pushing it down. Her spirit seemed to thicken, to grow darker and stronger, while Markwart's diminished, fading to gray.

Then Markwart came back at her, tenfold in strength, pushing her, then forcing her spirit back, back toward her waiting form. And somehow she knew that if he got her spirit back into her physical body, with his spirit still clenching and pushing, she would be destroyed.

She fought back with all her strength, and her spirit held her ground. But she could make no progress, could push Markwart back not another step.

And the Father Abbot was laughing at her.

When the elves arrived at the point along the wall where Pony had crossed, they found several town guards searching that area.

But Dasslerond wouldn't be slowed, not now. She motioned to her elves, and over they went, quickly, their wings fluttering. Soldiers yelled and scrambled, trying to get at the rushing creatures, but the elves were over and out into the night before the guards ever came close, leaving them confused and whispering.

Dasslerond and her band rejoined in the field on the other side and started north immediately, but then the lady stopped suddenly, turning to stare curiously at her companions.

"What is it?" Belli'mar Juraviel prompted.

The lady of Andur'Blough Inninness wasn't sure. Something magical had passed them by, some disturbance in the very fabric of space. The elves possessed three separate forms of magic. First was their song that could lull a man to sleep and could part the perpetual mists that covered Andur'Blough Inninness each night and coax them back with the rise of the sun. Then—most crucial to the Touel'alfar—came the second magic, that of the plants. The elves knew every medicinal, nutritional, or other use of every plant. They could make healing salves, or even concoctions that could allow one to live without air to breathe for a long, long while. They could speak with the plants to learn of the passage of friend or enemy, or to learn the recent history of any place.

And the third magic had been given to them from a human, from a great hero, a man possessed of elvish and human blood—a rare combination indeed! Terranen Dinoniel was his name, and in the first great battle of the elves and humans against the minions of Bestesbulzibar, Dinoniel had given the emerald gemstone, among the most powerful magical stones in all the world, to the Touel'alfar. This was the stone of the earth, the gem that heightened Lady Dasslerond's awareness of the living things about her and her connection to them. This was the stone that helped support Andur'Blough Inninness in its preternatural beauty and brought security to the elven valley; for with it, Dasslerond could alter the trails surrounding the valley, could shift the directions of paths so that any would-be intruders would find themselves walking in circles.

Now that stone told her that some creature had magically walked right by her band.

She knew the source, and so when she came out of her meditation, she prodded her companions on even faster.

They held in a state of balance, fighting hard. Pony tried to conjure all her rage, her memories of Dundalis destroyed and, more particularly, of her murdered parents, of the demon-filled corpses that had arisen against her in the bowels of this wicked man's home. That rage seemed to be working for a moment, as her shadow grew darker and stronger, forcing Markwart's back another step.

But then came the waves of despair, the fear for the child in her womb, the desperation that she had stolen from Elbryan the most precious thing of all: his son.

Pony tried to focus, fought with all her will to quickly build a wall of rage, but it was too late. The spirit of Markwart came powerfully—and it seemed to Pony as if the shadow had grown huge, batlike wings!

Now she was back in her body and she felt the presence of those hands around her throat—icy cold and choking the life from her.

Darkness crept around the edges of her vision.

Markwart had her! He would defeat her, he decided, but not destroy her. Not yet. How sweet this would be!

The spirit drove Pony down to her knees, and Markwart watched with glee as the woman's physical hands came up to her throat, clawing and scratching—with no effect whatsoever on his shadow arms. No, he couldn't hold back, the Father Abbot realized. This moment was too powerful, filled with ecstasy as he destroyed his greatest enemy in all the world!

He saw the blood dripping from Pony's throat, heard her dying gasp.

But then he felt something else, another presence. At first he glanced about, thinking that some third party had joined against him.

A jumble of confusion, and then glee, overwhelmed him as he recognized the source of that little spirit, that infant spirit, as he looked down more carefully at the woman's swollen belly.

The darkness closed in about her, leaving her looking at the world as if through a long and dark tunnel. She could not draw breath, could not feel her fingers clawing into her throat, though she knew somewhere deep in her mind that she was digging deep lines there. But, even consciously knowing that her physical hands were having no effect on the shadowy arms, she could not stop, could not overcome her instincts for survival.

The shadow's grip suddenly lessened, and Pony felt a stab in her belly.

Horrified as she recognized the sudden danger to her baby, she released all her magical energy in one sudden, brutal burst, one spiritual scream that flung the Father Abbot away from her.

And then the ground rushed up as if to swallow her, and she lay on her back, completely exhausted, panting, dying. And he was there standing above her, looking down at her. The victor.

He reached down as if to scoop her broken body into his arms.

She could not resist.

But then there came a tremendous shaking of the ground and the spirit of Markwart glanced around in surprise. "Wretched elf!" Pony heard him shout—and even as he finished, his voice and form faded away.

But Pony was falling into a blackness more profound than anything she had ever felt before.

Lady Dasslerond had little energy left to give to the mortally wounded woman, for it had taken every ounce of her power to force the spirit of Markwart back into his physical body. Every ounce of her considerable power and every bit of power the mighty emerald could offer had barely been enough—and she had caught him by surprise! The implications of the Father Abbot's surprising strength horrified her.

And now the elves flocked about Pony, Belli'mar Juraviel leading the effort to minister to her wounds using the second elven magic, the healing salves of plants. Some of the wounds, like the scratches on the neck, were easily tended, but others went very deep, wounds to the soul. Despite all their efforts, when Belli'mar Juraviel reported to Lady Dasslerond, he had to shake his head.

"What of the child?" Dasslerond asked him.

Juraviel shrugged, for he did not know. "It may be the child that is killing her," he reasoned. "Perhaps Jilseponie hasn't the strength for both of them."

Another elf rushed over to inform the lady that the northern gates of Palmaris were open, soldiers and monks streaming through.

Lady Dasslerond knew then what they had to do.

❖ 31 ❖

The House of the Holy

"Ah, but ye'd be the fool to go back," Bradwarden said to Shamus some hours later, after the group had returned to the camp to find Tiel'marawee resting easily. The captain had insisted that he and his men were going to return to Palmaris and openly oppose Bishop De'Unnero in a court convened by the King. "He'll not let ye even get word to the King afore he has ye killed in the public square."

"The Church does not rule in Honce-the-Bear," Shamus Kilronney asserted with as much determination as he could muster. But even that pitiful attempt showed that the man was losing this battle, was losing the foundation upon which his entire world had been built.

"Bradwarden speaks the truth," Elbryan added. "We'll not catch De'Unnero before he returns to Palmaris. Once he is there, he will surround himself with too great a force. We cannot fight him—not there."

"Then how?" Shamus asked. "The King must learn of these events!"

"The same King that made the man bishop?" Bradwarden asked dryly.

"He did not know . . ." Shamus started to argue, but he stopped, shook his head, and gave a frustrated growl. Shamus now had to face the obvious facts. The Bishop of Palmaris, appointed by both the King and the Father Abbot, held all the power in Palmaris, and thus, in all the northern reaches of Honce-the-Bear.

"King Danube might not understand the truth of the man," Elbryan replied calmly, trying to ease his friend's pain. "And when he learns that truth, perhaps we can return to Palmaris and throw ourselves on the mercy of an open and just court. But that day has not yet arrived—far from it!"

"Then we must tell the King," Shamus reasoned.

"Ye've got to get through De'Unnero to do that," Bradwarden reminded him.

Elbryan was shaking his head even as the centaur spoke. "We have an ally who means to do just that," he explained. "Though I am not certain

King Danube would listen to her words. The easier course for him might be to go along with the Father Abbot and his lackey the Bishop."

"And then?" Shamus asked.

"And then we are outlaws forever more," Elbryan replied. "And then we shall spend our days in the northland, in the deep forests of the Timberlands, perhaps, and oppose any who come in the name of Church or state."

"Not a promising position," Brother Braumin piped in, but he was smiling, for Braumin and his monk companions had already come to the same conclusions as the ranger.

"What ally?" Shamus asked.

"Pony," the ranger replied immediately. "She is in Palmaris, working secretly with those who oppose De'Unnero. Do not underestimate her!" he added when he saw Shamus and several others frown.

"And are we to hide and wait, then?" one of the other soldiers remarked.

"We are going north, to the Barbacan," Elbryan explained. That brought gasps of astonishment.

"It was my wish," Brother Braumin explained. "For there, at the grave of Brother Avelyn, we will find our peace and our purpose. I know this from a vision, Captain Kilronney. My place is there, and glory to those who accompany me!"

The grand proclamation brought wide smiles, even cheers, from the four other monks. But while Elbryan, Roger, and Bradwarden all managed meager smiles, it seemed obvious to them that the soldiers did not hold hopes quite so high.

A moment later, Shamus motioned his men to mount up. "We will go and talk privately about these events," he informed the others. "This is too big a decision to be made without the consent of all involved." He climbed on his own horse then, and walked past his soldiers, leading them away.

"Suren that there's some tellin' yer captain friend to come and get us," Bradwarden reasoned after several minutes of heated debate within the group of soldiers—though they were too far away for the ranger or the centaur to make out more than a few words. "Now that they're knowin' the truth o' their plight, De'Unnero's offer's likely seemin' the better course."

"I trust Shamus," the ranger replied. "Some may choose to leave, but the captain will not go against us, nor will he allow any of the others to do so."

"And I'm trustin' yerself," the centaur agreed. "But be knowin', me friend, that if yer captain friend turns on us, I'll take him down afore he yells out for the charge."

Elbryan saw that Bradwarden had set another arrow to his great bow, and, given the size and tremendous poundage of that weapon, the ranger had little doubt that a single shot would be more than enough.

It didn't come to that, for Shamus Kilronney trotted his mount over to them a few moments later and dismounted to stand before the ranger and the centaur. "A few do not wish to make the journey, I admit," he said, "but the rest are going. Even those doubters have decided to follow, seeing few options."

Elbryan gave a grim nod, too understanding of the road ahead to be thrilled by the captain's decision. "Tiel'marawee will be able to travel in the morning, perhaps," he replied. "Until then, let us be extra vigilant. We do not know if De'Unnero has decided to turn about, looking to strike at us once again."

The rest of the day, and that night, passed uneventfully. Tiel'marawee was feeling stronger the next day, and Brother Braumin determined that she could travel, as long as the pace was not too fast.

They set off, hoping that no late winter storms would arise before them.

"You know," the melodic voice said calmly, the slender figure moving into full view.

King Danube gasped and, clutching the candlestick he had picked up as an impromptu weapon, took a step back.

"You are of the noble line," Lady Dasslerond scolded, "from your father, to his before him, to his before him. You were told the truth of the Touel'alfar from your childhood days, unless your family has become greater fools than I believe."

"Fairy tales," King Danube said weakly.

"And you know the truth of *Questel ni'touel*, which you call boggle," Dasslerond went on, advancing calmly. "You know, King Danube, so find your heart and your composure. My time grows short in this place and there are things I must tell you."

He was the King of Honce-the-Bear, greatest kingdom in the known world, and he was descended from a long line of royalty. Now he was unnerved by this tiny winged creature, a fairy tale come to life. But Dasslerond had spoken truly—he had indeed been told stories of the Touel'alfar many times during his childhood—and Danube managed to regain his composure.

She left him some time later, via the secret entry her scouts had created by cleaning out an unused chimney in the mansion.

Danube had learned the elves' opinion of the overwhelming events that had occurred in Palmaris, a judgment that did not favor Father Abbot Markwart and the Abellican Church. But Danube still saw clearly the specter of Markwart, the nighttime visitor, a vision that all his years of training and all his years of ruling could not overcome.

Lady Dasslerond motioned to Belli'mar Juraviel and he handed the gemstone pouch, holding every one of Pony's stones, to Belster O'Comely.

That innkeeper held them in trembling hands. "What if she does not recover?" he asked, looking at Pony, who lay, looking fragile, on a padded cot next to the side wall of the basement.

"That is for you to decide," Lady Dasslerond replied. "We have entrusted Jilseponie to your care, and the responsibility for the gemstones rests with her. It is not a matter for the Touel'alfar, nor is she."

Belli'mar Juraviel winced when he heard those words. He could not come to terms with Dasslerond's brutal decision out on the field when Pony lay near death, but he knew that he had to accept that decision.

"W-we have friends," Belster stuttered. "The Behrenese sailor—"

"I care not," Lady Dasslerond said coldly, stopping him short. "You humans have chosen this fight amongst yourselves, so fight well, I offer—and know that my goodwill is more than any of you deserve. Do what you will with the woman. By bringing the fight at this time to Father Abbot Markwart, she chose her course—and chose wrongly, I say, though I wish her no ill."

Belster started to reply, but Dasslerond turned away and, gathering up her elven companions, left the cellar of the Fellowship Way. Belster followed them up the stairs, nodding to the frightened Dainsey and handing her the gemstones as they passed on the top landing. The woman glanced nervously at the unexpected nonhuman guests, then rushed down to be at Pony's side.

"There is nothing I can say to change your mind?" Belster tried one last time as Dasselrond and several of the elves paused—only long enough for one of them to go to the open window and look out to a companion scouting the alley, to make sure that the area was clear of soldiers.

"You should take her from this place," Dasselrond replied. "The Father Abbot found her here, and here he will look again. Take her, and be gone yourself. That is my counsel."

And then they were gone, leaving Belster standing at the open window, frightened and uncertain. He had sent Mallory and Prim O'Bryen out already to secure an escape route. He could only hope that Captain Al'u'met and the other Behrenese would accept Pony—and the rest of them.

He stood at the window for a long while, staring and thinking.

"She woke up," came Dainsey's voice behind him. He started immediately for the stairs, but Dainsey grabbed him by the arm to stop him.

"Just for a moment," the woman replied. "Just long enough to know that her belly was empty o' the child."

Belster winced, his heart breaking for Pony, this woman who had seen far too much tragedy in her short life.

"She said that Markwart killed him," Dainsey went on. "Says she felt the sting on the field, and knew even then that the foul creature had struck. Now she's vowin' to kill the monster."

Belster shook his head and sighed, and wiped the tears from his eyes. Poor Pony, so full of rage and hate, so torn apart.

"And then she started cryin' and shakin', but she couldn't stay awake with all the pain," Dainsey explained. "She tried using the gray stone, and using me for strength, but I'm thinkin' that her pain's too deep, and not just of the body."

"It is good that she woke up," Belster said, trying to sound hopeful.

Dainsey put a comforting hand on his arm. "She might not live," the woman said bluntly. "She's hurt, Belster, and ye should keep remindin' yerself just how bad."

Belster gave another great sigh.

A very distressed Heathcomb Mallory entered the Way.

"Too many," Bradwarden said, the centaur obviously distressed—and it was one of the few times Elbryan had ever seen him concerned. "I'd've thought that the damned creatures would've run far from this place after the explosion killed all o' them that was in here."

"They have wandered back in desperate hopes that their leader might still be with them," the ranger reasoned.

"Wandered back and plannin' to stay," said the centaur.

Elbryan's gaze subconsciously turned back to the south.

"We came too far to surrender now," Brother Braumin said determinedly, and he started back for the ridge overlooking the Barbacan bowl. "Bishop De'Unnero could not stop us; his soldiers joined us!"

True enough, the ranger knew. Over the last few days, they had braved the cold winds and blowing snow to work their way through the mountains, and now they had stopped near the exit of the mountain pass, the same trail Elbryan and the others had taken on their first trip to Mount Aida. Within a couple hundred yards of their present position began the sloping descent into the blasted, bowl-shaped valley that had once housed the demon dactyl's great army. The group had already glanced at the place—and had been overwhelmed, and even saddened, by the barrenness of it. Even the white snow could not hide the desolate grayness and emptiness, could not bury the widespread signs of Aida's eruption. When they paused to consider the sight, though, Braumin Herde had called it a blessing, for such emptiness would likely keep the monsters away permanently. Only then could his hopes for Avelyn's grave be realized: turning the place into a shrine, a new symbol for a new Order.

But then, that first night on the mountain ridge, they had spotted distant campfires, and now Bradwarden's scouting had shown them the terrible truth.

The ranger looked to the centaur now for help in making this decision. A large part of Elbryan wanted to turn around and rush to Palmaris, for he feared De'Unnero was there and was not certain if the man had learned that Pony was there.

Pony and his unborn child.

And yet, he had come to this place for a specific purpose, one shown to him by the desperate desires of the five monks and through Oracle. The image of Avelyn's extended arm had been burned into his consciousness during that one session with his uncle Mather, and reinforced in subsequent sessions. As much as he wanted to go to Pony, Elbryan wanted to see that grave site again, to learn what Oracle was trying to teach him.

"We might be gettin' there without a fight," the centaur offered. "Not many of the ugly goblins on this side o' the mountain."

"Just goblins?" the ranger asked.

Bradwarden nodded. "All that I seen, but hunnerds o' the damned things, all set up in caves and shelters along the northern and western walls o' the Barbacan."

The ranger scanned the ring of mountains, his gaze moving from east, around the northern ridge and then back to the west. Then he looked at flat-topped Aida again, the lone mountain in the south-central region of the natural ring, several miles away. He could tell from the outlines of the mountain's highest sections the approximate region where Avelyn was entombed, almost felt as if he might spot that arm, even from this distance, so clear was the image in his mind.

"Did see footprints of a giant," the centaur admitted, "but not many o' them about, to be sure—and not a damned sign that any powries remain."

"Good," the ranger added. He, like all the others who had battled the cunning and tough dwarves during the war, had little desire ever to see one again.

"We can get there," Brother Braumin echoed, his face brightening.

"But what do we do *when* we get there?" the ranger asked. "We shall need a fire if we mean to spend the night on the exposed top of Aida, and that will surely be seen by our unfriendly neighbors, no matter how hard we try to conceal it."

"The place has caves," Braumin reasoned, obviously not willing to give up this close to his goal.

"And thank ye for remindin' me," the centaur replied dryly.

"Still . . ." Brother Braumin pressed.

"If the place has caves, then it is possible that those caves are full of goblins," Elbryan interrupted, "or worse things."

Brother Braumin gave a great sigh and turned away.

"We have come too far to turn back," Brother Castinagis put in.

"I am going to Aida, to see Brother Avelyn's grave, even if I must make the journey alone," added the usually timid Brother Mullahy. "I have given my life to the principles of Master Jojonah, and of Avelyn Desbris, and I will see that special place now, even if it means that there I shall die."

The assertion caught them all off guard and pleased the other monks— except perhaps for poor Marlboro Viscenti, who was so nervous that he had been trembling since Bradwarden's return.

"And we will go," Shamus Kilronney put in, "some of us, at least, while the rest will stay with the horses back here."

Elbryan looked to Bradwarden for counsel, knowing that his decision would be vital, but the centaur only shrugged, apparently willing to go along with whatever decision they all made.

"I do not know if we, I at least, can remain there for long," the ranger said. "But if Bradwarden says that we might be able to get there without a fight, then I am willing to take the chance. We have come too far. Brother Castinagis, and I, too, wish to visit the grave of my dear friend."

At that moment, Roger Lockless appeared on a trail immediately below them, returning from his own scouting mission. "No goblins on the lower slopes," he called up. "The way is clear to the valley."

They set out at once, Bradwarden and Elbryan, Roger and the five monks, Shamus Kilronney and a dozen soldiers—half the contingent that had continued north with Elbryan's band after the unpleasant meeting with Bishop De'Unnero. They left a still-weak Tiel'marawee in the care of the remaining soldiers, along with Symphony and all the other horses.

The journey down was easy, the windblown trails relatively clear of any snow, except on one or two icy and treacherous descents. By early afternoon, they were in the valley, making their way along the same long arm— and even longer now, since the eruption had added tremendous width to the base of the mountain—that Elbryan and the others had followed on their first trip into the dactyl's home. It was much warmer down here, even comfortably so—perhaps from the residual heat of the cooling stone, though the eruption had occurred many months before. Or, Elbryan mused with some concern, perhaps the mountain had remained alive with bubbling, molten lava.

"We should camp on the southern side of the mountain," the ranger decided as they neared the huge mound. "There will be little trouble in finding an alcove sheltered from both the wind and any goblin eyes."

They found such a spot soon after, set a fire, and spent a peaceful, uneventful night, waking early, full of anticipation for what the new day would bring. They had barely gotten out of their alcove and were picking their way along the broken and jagged mountain face, when hope turned to dread. Goblins—a horde of goblins!—poured out of a cave far below them, pointed up at them, and howled. Within moments, the whole base of the southern wall crawled with the ugly creatures, cutting off any escape.

"Too many to fight," the ranger told Kilronney, as Shamus started to put his men in defensive positions. "Keep going, all of you. Bradwarden and I will hold the trail!"

"And thanks to ye for volunteerin' me," Bradwarden remarked after Shamus and the others had climbed out of sight, and the swarms of goblins had climbed considerably nearer the two friends.

"If I decide to charge down through the creatures, I will need something to ride," Elbryan replied lightheartedly. They had made their choice to come to the mountain, knowing the risks; and now, it seemed, they had lost, or soon would lose, everything. But Elbryan had lived on the edge of disaster since the day he had walked out of Andur'Blough Inninness. Such was the life of a ranger, an existence he had accepted fully. He lamented then that he would never see Pony again, or their child, but he deliberately pushed those thoughts from his mind. He was a warrior, trained in body and mind. Elbryan—no, Nightbird—determined that he would go down with such a fight that the goblins of all the world would not soon forget!

The closest creatures were barely fifty yards away then, coming on strong. Nightbird lifted Hawkwing and blew one wretch from its place on the mountainside. That slowed the others down—but only somewhat. Nightbird knew, and Bradwarden knew—and the goblins surely knew—that this time the ranger and his friends, however gallant, could not hope to win.

More arrows flew from Nightbird's and Bradwarden's bows; and many goblins died. But many more continued to move in, and soon the ranger and the centaur had to find a narrow spot on the trail, one where they could not be flanked; and they had to change from bows to sword and club.

And many goblin bodies soon piled at their feet.

For a short time, the pair almost thought that they might hold the pass and save the day, thought that they might kill enough of the creatures so that the rest would give up and run away. But then a rock crashed down beside the pair, narrowly missing Nightbird's head.

Some goblin had found a tunnel that exited higher up on the side of the mountain. The day, and the pass, were lost.

"Get ye runnin'!" Bradwarden cried, and he broke in to a sudden, devastating charge that chased back the closest creatures.

Nightbird turned and rushed up the path, leaping over stones and scrambling over rocky outcroppings—always with Hawkwing ready. Whenever he caught sight of those goblins dropping rocks from up above, he sent an arrow flying at them. One creature plummeted from the ledge down to crash where he and Bradwarden had made their stand, rebounded off that ledge with a sickening crack of bone, and fell the rest of the way to the valley floor.

Then the ranger ran around a sharp bend in the trail—to find a handful of goblins waiting for him.

Braumin Herde, appropriately, was the first to gaze upon the grave site of Avelyn Desbris. And though he knew that the monsters were closing in and that he would not likely live out the day, he was thrilled, overwhelmed even, by the spectacle of that upraised arm.

All nineteen men gathered silently about that upraised mummified arm, and even Roger and the soldiers offered not a word of complaint. All seemed at ease though they could hear the sounds of fighting below and knew that soon, all too soon, the monsters would find them.

Bradwarden realized that though his sudden, brutal charge had certainly taken a toll on the goblin mob—a couple were dead, several more injured, and many more running away—the moment was over, the goblins were coming at him hard, and he couldn't possibly hold them back.

In desperation, he leaped and kicked with his hind legs, hitting nothing and taking a vicious cut from a rusty goblin sword on one of his hind legs. Still, he ran on—and was struck by a spear in the rump and another grazed his back. Even worse, a stone from above clipped the side of his head and his shoulder. With one eye closed and covered in blood and screaming goblins right behind, the centaur ran, thinking it ironic that he would die in this forlorn place, where he thought he had died before.

They believed that they had him by surprise, and so the closest two goblins came at Nightbird with wild, hungry abandon.

But Nightbird was a ranger, and rangers were rarely, if ever, caught by surprise. With a flick of his wrist, he unstrung Hawkwing, and quickly brought the tip of the weapon, now a sturdy staff, straight before him.

The goblins came in, one on either side. Both thought—it seemed the most obvious move—the ranger would try to sweep the one on his right, the one nearest the sheer drop, over the edge. Expecting that, the goblin ducked.

Nightbird would not settle for just one. Faster than the goblins could contemplate the move, the ranger swung Hawkwing around, accepting a hit from the club of the creature on his left in exchange for getting the staff flat across its side. The goblin grabbed him, but the ranger, with the strength of a giant, roared and heaved the goblin back, tearing its hands from him. It hit its stooping companion and somersaulted over the edge, flying free down the side of the mountain.

Then the ranger brought Hawkwing around and landed a terrific blow to the remaining goblin, knocking it, dazed, to the ground.

Nightbird strode past, pausing only long enough to swap Hawkwing for Tempest and to kick the stunned goblin over the edge.

The four remaining goblins came on, stupidly, one goblin far ahead of its companions.

Tempest flashed; then there were three.

They pressed the attack—a club, a spear, and a sword thrusting and jabbing, swishing in from every conceivable angle. But Nightbird was now fully immersed in *bi'nelle dasada*. He dodged a spear thrust from the goblin standing right before him, then ducked a swishing sword from the one on the left, then accepted another stinging, wicked hit from the club wielder.

Tempest dove ahead, and the goblin with the spear shrieked and fell back. The ranger tricked them; he pulled the blade up, twisting his wrist so that Tempest's tip shot out suddenly ahead and to the right just as the sword-wielding goblin moved for what it thought was an opening. Tempest bore into its chest just below the shoulder.

Nightbird now leaped out to the right, slamming his shoulder into the chest of the goblin with the club. The creature went flying back, teetered on the edge, and finally caught its desperate and precarious balance. When it managed to look back, it saw Nightbird standing before it. The goblin brought its club across, frantically trying to block the ranger's deadly sword. To its credit, it would have parried, but instead the ranger struck with his free hand, a mighty punch to the face that launched the flailing goblin away.

Then Nightbird, standing with his back to the remaining goblins, instinctively stepped to the side with his right foot. Bending his right knee, he leaned sideways but his left leg blocked the path.

The goblin he had stabbed went over that leg, pitching headlong into the open air.

The ranger spun, Tempest deflecting the spear the last goblin threw at him. The creature turned and ran for the nearly sheer wall, scrambling to get a handhold.

Nightbird rushed after him, leaping up and catching the fleeing goblin by one foot, pulling it down. He grabbed its other foot and with one pull sent the creature smashing down to the stone. It didn't stay down, for the ranger, still holding its ankles, took it up and hurled it out over the edge.

"Good technique," Bradwarden congratulated, coming around the bend just as Nightbird launched the creature. Their smiles were fleeting in the face of the many wounds on the centaur and the sound of the goblin horde closing in.

On the man and centaur ran, coming at last to the final ascent. That climb of ten feet was sheer, and without enough distance to get a running start, the centaur saw no way of getting up there. "Just as well that I do me stand right here," he said, but the ranger would hear none of it.

"Get your hands up on that ledge and pull with all your might,"he instructed, "and I will push from behind."

Doubting, Bradwarden did as instructed, lifting his forelegs high, gaining a tentative hold with his human hands, and struggling.

He heard a growl behind him, felt Nightbird grabbing hard at his flanks.

And then all thousand pounds of him was in the air, up, up, but against the wall and unable to get high enough to scramble over.

Then Roger and Shamus Kilronney were there above him, grabbing his arms; then the others joined and together, all together, they managed somehow to get the great equine body over the edge and onto the plateau where rested Avelyn's body.

Nightbird came up behind, and he, too, glanced upon the beauty of Avelyn's would-be shrine, and he, too, was at ease.

Then goblin hands appeared on the ledge, and the fighting began anew, all twenty-one defenders fanning out and fighting for all their lives. Many goblins died, many were beaten back, but more and more the defenders had to turn their attention from the next climbing creature to battle one that had slipped up from another position—and that, of course, only allowed more to scramble up on the plateau. One soldier went down, screaming in pain, a spear in his belly. Brother Dellman soon followed, knocked out by a blow to his head.

Dragging their fallen, the defenders were driven inexorably back, until they were clustered about the protruding arm of Avelyn Desbris.

The battle paused there as the goblins regrouped around the perimeter of the circular bowl, more and more climbing up to join their kin, a hundred, then two hundred.

Lady Dasslerond and her elves were out of Palmaris long before the night had passed its midpoint, moving north, back toward Caer Tinella, where they would try to learn news of Nightbird before turning west for their homeland.

Their role in this human war, by Dasslerond's estimation, was at its end. The lady meant to speak with Nightbird one last time, to inform him of Jilseponie's condition and to scold him for ever teaching the woman *bi'nelle dasada*. The lady of Caer'alfar would not back down, nor would she relinquish her anger. Nightbird had chosen the wrong person, for Jilseponie's actions against Markwart had been foolhardy, and anyone who would choose such a foolish course was not deserving to know the elven dance.

Belli'mar Juraviel, despondent, lingered behind the group, turning his eyes back toward Palmaris often. "Farewell, my friends, he said to the evening wind.

But they would not fare well, he knew in his heart.

"You are my brother, Nightbird, and I do not judge you harshly," he said. "For Jilseponie is my sister now, and to her, I can only make one silent promise. And to you, Nightbird, I only pray our paths will cross once more, that we will find a time of mirth again, of friendship on a hillock with Jilseponie and Bradwarden, in a place far removed from the foolishness of human political struggles."

How Juraviel wanted that to come true! Tears rolled from his golden eyes, the first time the elf had ever cried for any human. Sadness nearly overwhelmed him when he considered poor Pony, should she survive, would awaken to yet another brutal loss.

And so he could only hope that someday far in the future, he would meet his friends. But Juraviel, who with his kin had learned so much of the true nature of this enemy, understood that his hopes were a distant possibility.

Juraviel knew what Nightbird and Pony would face, and did not believe that they would win, not now that Lady Dasslerond had decided to abandon the humans.

He lingered for a long while behind his kinfolk, staring forlornly back at Palmaris, at the place that had become so dangerous for Pony, and, soon enough, he suspected, for Nightbird, as well.

Up ahead, Lady Dasslerond led the others in *tiest-tiel*, the star song, the highest pleasure that any elf might know.

But Belli'mar Juraviel did not feel like joining in tonight, for there was no song in his heavy heart.

"Perhaps it is fitting that we die here," the ranger grimly remarked.

"Just wishin' it was a hunnerd years hence," Bradwarden replied.

Marlboro Viscenti started crying; Roger Lockless tried to comfort him, but his shoulders, too, shook with sobs.

"To the legacy of Avelyn Desbris," Brother Braumin began, holding the last syllable melodically, using the half-singing, half-chanting tones of a monk ministering to the flock. "And so we have failed, but have not," he went on. "We were the first, but shall not be the last, to follow our hearts to this place. And so we have found him, our inspiration, our path to God, and so we die blessed."

He bent low as he continued his prayer so that the wounded man, obviously near death, could hear him clearly and take comfort. And the man did stop his thrashing and crying, and Viscenti and Roger stopped crying, too, all listening to the prayer, the last earthly hope, of Brother Braumin Herde.

It went on for a few moments, then was halted by Shamus Kilronney's declaration. "Here they come," he said.

"Pray," cried Brother Braumin.

"Fight," Nightbird grimly corrected, but when he looked at the kneeling monk, he could not hold his edge. "Fight and pray," he conceded with a smile.

And so they prayed, and so they sang, and the goblins, hundreds of goblins, slowly closed. And then their song faded, for they each in turn noticed a humming, a deep resonating sound.

"She's pickin' a fine time to blow up again," Bradwarden remarked, staring down at the dangerous mountain.

All thoughts of anything but the goblins faded at once, for the creatures suddenly howled and charged, barely two running strides away.

Then a low moan, a loud, rolling pulse, emanated from Avelyn's hand, and all—men, centaur and goblins—froze as a purplish ring of energy rolled out through the defenders.

Through the defenders and into the goblins, permeating their bodies. Another pulse came forth, then another, each striking the now-stationary ring of monsters like the waves of an incoming tide.

Goblins opened their mouths as if to scream, but no sound came forth above the low humming of the arm. Goblins tried to turn and run, but could only twist their upper torsos, as if their feet were rooted to the stone.

The men and the centaur winced as they saw the goblin bones, as if their flesh had become translucent.

And then there were just bones, skeletons where the horde of goblins had been.

The humming stopped; the purple glow disappeared.

Hundreds of goblin skeletons crumbled with a great rattling sound.

Brother Braumin prostrated himself before the upraised arm, weeping and crying, "A miracle."

Not even Elbryan the skeptic nor Bradwarden, who had little use for human religions, could find a word to dissuade him, could find any word at all to speak at that moment.

PART FIVE

▾

MIRROR IMAGE

Even hope can be deceived. I never thought about the seemingly eternal struggle between good and evil in those terms before, Uncle Mather, and quite honestly the notion frightens me. But now I know it to be true, and that, I fear, is the real danger to the world of man.

The demon dactyl was a terrifying creature, horrible almost beyond comprehension. When I faced the beast in the bowels of Mount Aida, it took all of my willpower to struggle forward even a step toward Bestesbulzibar. Overwhelmingly malicious, Uncle Mather, evil personified.

But I have said before, and know now, having faced the fiend, that the demon dactyl could never win in the end. Such a force of true, recognizable evil would forever find foes among the men of Corona; someone would always take up the sword and fight. Only by sweeping every man and woman from the world of the living could Bestesbulzibar assure uncontested victory, and what a hollow victory that would be to a creature bent on domination. Its minions, the goblins and giants and powries, might have eradicated the human race, but never could they, never could Bestesbulzibar, capture the real prize: the human soul.

Might subtlety win out where brute force failed?

That is my fear, for far more dangerous than the demons and their monstrous minions are the deceivers, and I believe Father Abbot Markwart to be one, perhaps the foremost one in all the world. He and his Church seem to have perfected the art of coercion, and it horrifies me, and saddens me, to think that they might claim the prize that eluded Bestesbulzibar. How cunning and sly! They publicly say just enough of the right things, and draw just enough logical conclusions, to lend credence to other philosophies which, if examined separately and carefully, would not hold up. They mask untruth with a covering web of truth, and excuse immorality by claiming urgency or hiding behind convenient traditions that hold no logical purpose in the present world.

Why not train a ship's crew of monks for the voyage to collect the sacred gemstones? Why not use those stones to better the lives of the common folk?

They have answers, Uncle Mather. Always there are answers.

But when a sickly mother appears at the gates of St.-Mere-Abelle, begging for healing that her children would not be orphaned . . .

Then there are no excuses. At that moment, all the justifications called forth by tradition or some supposed "greater good" melt away, revealed for the lies they are.

But they are masters, these deceivers, and they frighten me. They speak enough truths to calm the populace, and offer just enough meager morsels to keep the common folk in line, to make those scrambling daily to find food believe that their world will continue to improve, or at least that their children will find a better life. For that, Uncle Mather, in the end, is the most common desire of humanity.

Father Abbot Markwart knows that.

I alluded, half jokingly, that the spirit of Bestesbulzibar might remain, and in an even more dangerous host. I was speaking metaphorically, of course, or so I thought. For now, as this fight between me, Pony, and all the other followers of Avelyn, has intensified against the Abellican Church—Father Abbot Markwart's Church—I have come to wonder if the spirit of Bestesbulzibar does not actually find the hearts of some men, and root there. Are there those among us tainted by the diabolical fiend? And if that is the case, will goodly men, godly men, win out in the end, or will the tide of humanity follow the current of calming words, thickened with truth, but baked, in essence, with lies?

Perhaps even hope can be deceived.

—ELBRYAN WYNDON

CHAPTER

❖ 32 ❖

The Blessed Upper Hand

As he approached the northern gate of Palmaris only his anger prevented Marcalo De'Unnero from fearing Father Abbot Markwart's reaction when he learned of the Bishop's failure to capture Nightbird. Stopped at the gate by questioning guardsmen who did not recognize him, the monk glared at them and they faltered. Finally a soldier who knew the Bishop came upon them and, terrified, led the ruffled and angry De'Unnero away. During that fast walk to Chasewind Manor, De'Unnero heard all the news: the attempted assassination of Father Abbot Markwart, the rumors of continuing struggle between King Danube—who was staying at the manor house of Aloysius Crump—and the Father Abbot, who had taken the more luxurious Chasewind Manor as his own, and, not to De'Unnero's liking, of the outpouring of support from the common folk for the new Bishop, Francis Dellacourt.

De'Unnero swept into Chasewind Manor and didn't even wait for a proper announcement to storm into the glass-enclosed garden where Father Abbot Markwart was partaking of his morning meal, Brother—or was it Master, Abbot, or Bishop?—Francis at his side.

"Your expression alone tells me that the one named Nightbird remains ever elusive," the Father Abbot remarked, more than a bit of sarcasm in his tone. The Father Abbot had settled in quite comfortably. He had come to Chasewind Manor the day after his unexpected meeting with King Danube at St. Precious, the morning after he battered Jill on the field outside of Palmaris, realizing that if he did not take the house as his residence, the King surely would.

"I had him," De'Unnero returned angrily, "up in the Wilderlands, far north of the Timberlands and approaching the Barbacan."

"The Barbacan?" Francis echoed incredulously, reflecting Markwart's feelings exactly, though the old Father Abbot kept a calm and impassive expression.

"But for his friends, Nightbird was mine," De'Unnero went on. "I have met him in open combat and am the stronger."

"And yet he remains at large," Markwart said dryly.

De'Unnero calmed a bit and nodded, having no practical reply.

"And what of the woman Jill?" the Father Abbot asked a moment later.

"She may have been among those who drove me away before I could secure my victory," De'Unnero lied.

"Indeed, then she has long arms, my friend, to reach all the way from Palmaris to the Wilderlands," Markwart said.

De'Unnero spent a long moment digesting that statement, then widened his eyes as he figured out the implications. "You have found her?"

The Father Abbot smiled and nodded.

"Where is she?" a frantic De'Unnero went on. "I will extract whatever information you desire, Father Abbot. I promise—"

"We do not have her," Markwart admitted, "but she has been neutralized. Though she holds the gemstones, I do not believe she will be a danger to us anymore. More likely, her attention will be toward self-preservation. Our attention now must be to the city, placating the King, of course, who is at this very moment eating his morning meal in the house of the merchant you executed. But while placating Danube, we must work quickly to strengthen our grip over Palmaris." He motioned for De'Unnero to sit, then waved a hand at the monk waiting on them, that the newcomer might get a morning meal.

"The situation in Palmaris has changed," Markwart went on.

"A guard at the city gate told me that you had been grievously injured," DeUnnero remarked, trying hard to avoid staring at the garish scar that ran along the side of Markwart's withered face. "A magical attack, so said the guard, and thus, I am led to believe that the woman was involved."

"She has been repaid for her deed," Markwart replied. "I found her and left her broken, and as with your enemy in the northland, only her friends managed to keep us from the complete capture. But that situation will soon be remedied, do not doubt. The soldiers and monks are out and about the city. She'll not escape us this time."

"And then we shall have the stones," Francis put in, somewhat sheepishly. He was obviously uncomfortable with De'Unnero, the Bishop he had replaced, sitting right beside him.

"It is good that you have returned to me," the Father Abbot stated, as if the thought had just come to him. "Though I wish that you had the traitor in tow—how powerful a symbol the one called Nightbird might now be."

"That symbol might be interpreted in two different ways," Francis dared to remark.

"Ah, yes, perception is all the truth," Markwart agreed. "But if we had the man, or the man's head, we would control the images for the peasants, and they would come to understand the true threat to their lives, the true evil of Avelyn and his followers. But no matter. King Danube will not oppose us now, not after the manner in which the woman attacked me, and not after your work, Bishop Francis, in placating the masses. I tested him when he came to visit me, declaring that all the gemstones in the kingdom are to be confiscated by the Church, and he did not deny my claim. Palmaris is ours to rule, wisely and with generosity."

De'Unnero's dark eyes widened. Bishop Francis? Placating the masses? De'Unnero's last official act before running out of the city had been the execution of Aloysius Crump!

"The situation has changed," Markwart said again. "The Church has become the generous benefactor under the guidance of Bishop Francis." He held his hand up to silence De'Unnero before the stream of expected complaints could even begin. "The title I bestowed upon our young brother here was intended to be temporary, though now I have come to the conclusion that I will make it permanent. I have already spoken with Abbot Je'howith, who is also in Palmaris, on this matter and he will not oppose me."

The dangerous De'Unnero glared at Francis.

"You believe yourself deserving of the title?" Markwart asked bluntly.

"I performed as I was instructed," De'Unnero replied. Only then did he begin to understand that Markwart's explicit instructions, including the public execution of Crump, had assured that his tenure as bishop would be temporary. Markwart had set him up, had used him in such a dark way that Francis would shine favorably against that shadow.

"Admirably," Markwart agreed with a broad smile. "I do not, in any way, criticize the reign of Bishop De'Unnero. You were exactly what Palmaris needed in that dark and uncertain time, but the situation has changed. It is time for a gentler hand, one that the King cannot slap aside."

"As it was planned all along?" De'Unnero asked.

Francis shifted uncomfortably, sliding back his chair a bit, expecting an explosion.

But Markwart only nodded. "As it had to be."

"And now I am to be punished?" De'Unnero asked, a growl accompanying each word.

"How so?"

The former bishop held up his hands incredulously and looked all around, as if to exclaim that he had lost all of this—this place, this title, this city.

But Markwart remained unshakably calm. "Do you believe that I would not reward your loyalty and diligence?" he asked with a laugh. "My friend, there are many roles left to fill, and I have plans for you, do not doubt, plans that will bring you all that you desire. As the Church makes its way into the world of secular politics, I expect to make many enemies. Powerful men like Targon Bree Kalas, Duke of Wester-Honce, who is not pleased that the largest city of his duchy has fallen under Church rule. I am old and tired; it may well be that I will need a champion. Who better than Marcalo De'Unnero?"

"Master De'Unnero?" the man asked, still on the edge of anger. "Or merely Brother De'Unnero?"

Markwart laughed loudly. "Abbot of St. Precious," he decided then and there. "Bishop Francis has too many issues to be concerned with already. He will be the hand of state, and you the hand of Church in Palmaris, though I shan't limit your influence and duties to this one city, I promise."

"And who answers to whom?" De'Unnero asked, his glare focused on Francis as he spat out every word.

"Hand of state, hand of Church," Markwart reiterated, "both answer to me. Now, enough of this divisive talk. We have a common opponent here: King Danube Brock Ursal. Our attention must remain with him and his secular advisers, particularly Kalas, who, according to Abbot Je'howith, will prove no easy foe. Kalas once led the Allheart Brigade, and earned two great plumes in his helmet. Indeed, a large contingent of that elite fighting unit accompanied the King to Palmaris. So while our hold appears strong at the moment, one mistake could give the upstart Duke all the room he needs to sweep into power."

Markwart looked at each of the men in turn, his cold stare sending shivers through Francis and igniting eager fires in De'Unnero. "We must plan for every possibility," the Father Abbot said grimly.

"He plays you as he would a lute!" Duke Targon Bree Kalas roared, the loudest and angriest tone he had ever used in speaking to his King.

Danube's glare set the excitable man back on his heels, reminded him of his place. "And which string do *you* intend to pluck?" he replied sarcastically.

"Your pardon, my King," Constance Pemblebury interrupted, moving between the men. "I believe Duke Kalas is concerned about the potential troubles for the Crown." She glared at Kalas as she finished. "Surely he means no insult to the Crown."

Danube chuckled then, alleviating the tension. All of them understood the mood of the city. Father Abbot Markwart had become a sort of hero to the common folk. That, combined with the work of Bishop Francis, who was proving a generous and worthy leader, had weakened the King's position should Danube decide to revoke the title of bishop.

"You allowed him to proclaim his intension to take back every magical stone," Duke Kalas dared to press. "How powerful will the Church then be, and how crippled the Crown?"

"I let the Father Abbot have his way in the meeting out of deference to his delicate condition," the King replied, and he didn't seem the least bit angry, to Constance Pemblebury's relief. "His words at that unofficial meeting carry no legal weight. And even should he openly and publicly proclaim that all gemstones are to be returned to the Church, how will he ever enforce such a position in Ursal? Or in Entel, or in any of the other cities of the south, where the Church is not nearly as influential as up in these forbidding places."

"But here, in Palmaris, in the place where he was attacked and miraculously survived, he is a formidable foe," Constance remarked.

Even Duke Kalas, so obviously frustrated, understood that.

"True enough," King Danube replied, and more true than Constance or Kalas understood, he realized, for he alone knew of the terrifying visit Markwart's spirit had made to his private rooms in Ursal.

"Your carriage, my King," came the announcement of Danube's favored bodyguard.

"He should come to us," Kalas growled, "and we should be at Chasewind Manor, not here." Danube and Constance ignored him, gathering up their traveling cloaks and heading for the door.

They were met at the door of Chasewind Manor by Abbot Je'howith, the old man seeming at ease and welcoming the King with a wide smile and a gentle pat on the shoulder. "Bishop De'Unnero returned to Palmaris this day," he informed the King. "He is at the table with Father Abbot Markwart and Brother—Master Francis Dellacourt, whom the Father Abbot has decided will play a large role in the continuing work to better formulate Palmaris."

"De'Unnero," Duke Kalas spat. "I should cut off his head."

Abbot Je'howith only smiled and nodded, not wishing to start that argument, and also confident that if Duke Kalas, no meager fighter to be sure, ever tried to do so, the dangerous monk would break him into pieces. The warriors of the King's army couldn't understand the truth of the matter, the old abbot mused as he led the King and his entourage to the meeting room. A man might rise to the highest level within the army, might become a leader of the Allheart Brigade, but that man would be far from attaining the skill of a brother justice and certainly could not hope to match one such as De'Unnero, who trained the brothers justice!

Markwart, De'Unnero, and Francis were seated at one end of a long oaken table when Abbot Je'howith led the procession in. The Father Abbot had organized this seating cunningly, Je'howith immediately noted. He had left one end seat vacant, of course, for King Danube, but it faced the eastern window—the King would have the misfortune of looking into the morning sun. Six empty chairs, three on either side of the King's, ran along the table, and Constance Pemblebury and Duke Kalas were quick to take those immediately to the King's right and left.

Abbot Je'howith stared at the four empty chairs, surprised that Markwart had ordered so many put about the table, since he knew that King Danube would come in with only the two advisers. But then Je'howith figured it out, and he looked at the Father Abbot with even more respect. This was a test: which seat would Je'howith choose, one next to a King's adviser or one beside Markwart's advisers?

With a nervous glance at King Danube, the old abbot took a seat—right beside Abbot De'Unnero.

Kalas gave a snort; the battle lines had been drawn.

"I will not shuffle about the issue," King Danube began, interrupting the Father Abbot as the older man started formal greetings. "I have come here to see that the citizens of Palmaris—my citizens—are being treated accordingly, and that the city is under proper control and proper care."

Markwart glared at the man, presenting an even more imposing image with the sun back-lighting him so. "You know Bishop De'Unnero?" he asked, moving his right hand to indicate the powerful monk.

Kalas and De'Unnero immediately locked stares, the two sensing that they shared similar position and purpose for their respective leaders, that fact making them immediate rivals.

"And this is Francis Dellacourt," Markwart went on, extending his left hand. "Until this morning, Brother Francis served as headmaster of St. Precious, but now I intend to promote him to bishop of Palmaris."

That brought curious stares from everyone at Danube's end of the table, even from Je'howith, who had not been informed of just how high Markwart meant to promote young Brother Francis.

"The Bishop sits on your right, by your own introduction," King Danube asserted.

"Former Bishop," Father Abbot Markwart explained. "Master De'Unnero served Palmaris well in his tenure—"

Another loud snort from Duke Kalas.

"For the city was in complete disarray," Markwart finished, ignoring the impertinent Duke. "Now that time has passed, and so has his reign. He will become abbot of St. Precious."

Constance Pemblebury got the King's attention, and Danube gave a slight nod, allowing her to speak for him. "Is not the Bishop of Palmaris also the abbot of St. Precious?" she asked, the question that was on the minds of all of the four from Ursal. There was more than a little concern in the woman's voice, an indication that she, and likely the others, as well, would worry about that proclamation. Did Markwart mean to keep two powerful Church leaders in Palmaris?

"I have plans for St. Precious at this time," Markwart explained. "The reopening of the northern villages and the Timberlands will require much attention from the Church. Bishop Francis will not have the time to turn his eyes to the north, with so many issues yet to be settled in Palmaris."

King Danube sat back to digest the surprising, and somewhat disturbing, information. "Perhaps, then, the time has come again for an abbot and a baron," he said, and Kalas grinned widely at the words he had so desperately wanted to hear.

"Perhaps not," Father Abbot Markwart replied immediately, not even blinking.

That brought a few uneasy shuffles from the King's end of the table. The Father Abbot had openly opposed King Danube!

"Father Abbot," the King began firmly but calmly, "I agreed to a bishop on a trial basis, one that, from the reports I have seen, has failed miserably."

"You have not witnessed enough, then," Markwart replied. "Are you to judge the arrangement based on the first few weeks, when the city was in turmoil and in dire peril?"

"You exaggerate," the King remarked.

Markwart came out of his seat, leaning forward over the table and turning his face so that his garish scar was visible. "Do I?" he yelled.

Kalas, too, jumped to his feet, looking at De'Unnero, but the former Bishop remained calmly seated.

"This alone is proof enough that the sacred gemstones do not belong in the possession of secular fools," the Father Abbot intoned.

The King sat back, holding fast to his calm demeanor. "And has not Father Abbot Markwart himself sold such stones to 'secular fools'?" he asked. "Your words match not your actions, Father Abbot, and so we are left with a difficult situation here. I cannot have the entire merchant class angry with me."

Markwart glared at him, the same imposing look the spirit of the Father Abbot had bestowed on the King when he had visited him in Ursal. And the King internally withered under that gaze. But he was the King, after all, and so he pressed on. "My good Father Abbot," he stated, working hard to keep the tremor out of his voice, "I cannot conduct proper relations with Behren, nor can I satisfy the needs of those important merchant families— the ones who supply Honce-the-Bear with so many vital goods—while you are persecuting such men in this city. I will not tolerate it, Father Abbot. I cannot tolerate it!"

"The greatest threat to the Crown comes now from some who have gemstones in their possession," De'Unnero put in, "secular men, who do not deserve such sacred gifts of God and who do not understand the power and responsibility of such stones."

Father Abbot Markwart, who was about to respond to the King, bit back his words and turned an angry glare on De'Unnero, for it was not De'Unnero's place to speak. Not at all. But not wanting to show any discord within his own ranks, he let him continue.

"They are the disciples of Avelyn Desbris the heretic, and do not doubt their power or their intent to destroy both Church and state," De'Unnero went on. "It was one of them who attacked Father Abbot Markwart—and desires to make a similar attempt upon the life of King Danube, do not doubt."

"The King is well protected," Duke Kalas put in as he resumed his seat. This time, it was King Danube's turn to glare angrily at one of his subordinates. But then the King put his chin in his hands, and Markwart settled back into his chair, both of them seeming more amused than distressed.

"Pray continue, Duke Kalas," Danube said.

"And you, Abbot De'Unnero," Markwart added.

"You do not appreciate the power of these disciples of the heretic, and that may well bring about your downfall," De'Unnero stated before Kalas could cut him off.

Duke Kalas came out of his chair again, leaning threateningly across the table toward the former Bishop, but Constance grabbed his arm and held him back.

"Do tell," the King prompted.

Markwart caught De'Unnero's gaze, reminding the man to tread lightly here. He was speaking, after all, of the death of the King and the monarchy, no light subject!

"The leader of the band, a very dangerous warrior named Nightbird, is operating in the northland, and is even now in the region of the Barbacan, I believe, no doubt rousing monsters to his call this time," the new abbot of St. Precious explained. "And yet, it all could have been averted, for I had him in my grasp—him and all his fellow conspirators. They were mine to take, to kill then and there or to bring back to Palmaris for public trial, one over which both King Danube and Father Abbot Markwart might have presided, that their alliance, the glory of that joining, be revealed to the beleaguered populace of Palmaris."

"Beleaguered," Duke Kalas echoed, snorting to show how ironic he thought it that the former tyrannical Bishop should speak of the folk of Palmaris that way. "There is a fine word."

But King Danube was in no mood for Kalas' antics, for he sensed that De'Unnero would be a formidable foe. "You say that you had them within your grasp," he said to De'Unnero, "and yet you could not take them?"

"No," De'Unnero admitted. "The one called Nightbird and his fellow conspirators run free in the northland—and all because of the actions of soldiers of the Crown."

"If one of my soldiers erred—" the King began.

"Erred?" De'Unnero echoed incredulously, drawing a narrow-eyed gaze from the King, who was not accustomed to being interrupted, and another glare from Markwart, warning him once again to tread lightly. "The leader and his soldiers did not *err*, my King," De'Unnero explained. "At that most critical moment, when the rebellion might have been put down, they turned against the Crown."

That proclamation brought the King's head up, and calmed Duke Kalas considerably, for what had seemed to be the rambling boast of an unimportant man suddenly carried the potential of great weight.

"It is true," De'Unnero went on, glowering at Duke Kalas as he spoke. "In the northland, far north of the Timberlands, I had Nightbird trapped, but an officer of the Kingsmen and his foolish soldiers would not support me. Aye, they turned against me, supporting the rebel Nightbird over their rightful leader, the Bishop of Palmaris, appointed by King and Father Abbot."

"A title you no longer hold," Kalas pointedly reminded him.

"At that time, to Captain Kilronney and his soldiers, I was the Bishop," De'Unnero retorted, not backing down an inch. He knew the King was vulnerable on this point. "And yet, this captain of the Kingsmen, officer of the Crown, went against me, and thus left the most dangerous criminal in the world at large in the wild northland."

"A man whose co-conspirators thrive in Palmaris," Markwart cut in. He nodded at the former Bishop, relaying to De'Unnero his approval of his performance. De'Unnero had played his part perfectly and had turned this meeting greatly in the favor of Father Abbot Markwart.

And so it went for the rest of the morning. Father Abbot Markwart detailed the dangers within Palmaris: the real danger of the Behrenese underground; and the would-be assassin Jill, companion of Nightbird, the other disciple of Avelyn Desbris, who remained at large.

The King sat and listened, impatiently waving for Kalas to sit down and shut his mouth whenever the Duke tried to interrupt.

Afterward, during the carriage ride back to the house of Crump, the King, Kalas, and Constance were quiet. They all knew Markwart had carried the day. De'Unnero's claim that an officer of the Crown had helped an associate of the one who had tried to assassinate the Father Abbot had given the advantage to Markwart, one he had not relinquished for the remainder of the discussion.

In Chasewind Manor, Abbot Je'howith listened carefully as Markwart congratulated De'Unnero.

"You have shown your value in a manner I would not have expected," the Father Abbot remarked, nodding at the man, even patting him on the shoulder.

"Enough so that you would restore me as bishop of Palmaris?" De'Unnero asked, turning his always-dangerous gaze on Francis as he spoke.

"No," Markwart said immediately. "The importance of that position is greatly diminished now. The duty of the Bishop will be no more than to placate the masses and the impertinent merchants. A most distasteful job—and one in which the talents of Marcalo De'Unnero would be wasted."

That brought a smile to De'Unnero and made Francis wince.

"No, my friend, my champion," Markwart purred, "we have other plans to formulate and other regions to conquer."

The confidence was not without merit, Abbot Je'howith believed—and feared, since he was being surprisingly ignored in this conversation, an onlooker to the victory celebration and nothing more.

But the wise old man swallowed his anger and reminded himself that he was better off here than with the pouting Kalas and the nervous King. Je'howith understood that Markwart had won the day, that Church had prevailed over state today and the position of bishop as leader of Palmaris seemed quite secure.

They parted soon after, Je'howith going to the private room Francis had provided for him in St. Precious to reconsider his position. He wanted to be on the winning side, whichever side that might be. He had planned to sit on the fence and anger neither Father Abbot nor King. Now he leaned Markwart's way, for it seemed painfully clear to him that the Father Abbot was the more formidable.

CHAPTER

❖ 33 ❖

Miles Apart

She had come awake enough to realize that her child was gone. Though she should have gone back to sleep, for her body had been battered terribly, she could not. She sat in the quiet darkness of the *Saudi Jacintha*'s hold.

Colleen Kilronney entered the small room a short while later, but Pony didn't acknowledge her, just sat, swaying, staring into the darkness.

"It's good that ye're awake," Colleen said.

No response.

"Ah, but the devil he is," the warrior woman spat. "Father Abbot? Bah! He's a devil, and I'll be payin' him back for ye, don't ye doubt!"

No response.

"And me own cousin," Colleen went on, "captain o' the King's soldiers, all bright and shiny on the outside, and with a heart that's as dark as the wretched Bishop's on the inside. Oh, but I'll be payin' that one back, too!"

No response—Pony didn't even look her way, and Colleen surrendered, moving out of the room.

"Suren that she's in a bad way," the red-haired woman said to Belster and Captain Al'u'met as she joined them in the the captain's stateroom. "He took it from her, the devil, and left a hole that'll be a long time in mendin'."

"I tried to tell her not to fight him," Belster interjected.

"Her cause was just," Al'u'met insisted.

"Indeed, and no arguing from me," the innkeeper replied. "But you cannot wage war without a chance of winning. He is too strong, is Markwart; as is the Bishop."

"That does not mean that she was wrong to try," Al'u'met argued.

"Not wrong, perhaps, but surely foolish," Belster remarked, turning away. He knew that he would not convince the Behrenese sailor, but neither did he have any intention of changing his mind.

"Perhaps you merely believe that her cause was not worth the risk," Al'u'met remarked bluntly.

Belster winced, knowing that he was vulnerable here against the likes of a black-skinned Behrenese. Indeed, he had to admit he might have been more anxious to wage war against the Church if the people it persecuted had been friends of his: Bearmen, as citizens of Honce-the-Bear were sometimes called; and with lineage to match Belster's own. He thought to simply ignore the captain, but, in thinking of Pony, he realized that the time had come to face the truth.

He looked Al'u'met in the eye. "Perhaps your reasoning is sound," he said. "I, like so many of the folk of Palmaris, have never been fond of your kind, Captain Al'u'met."

"Wouldn't it be doin' Pony's heart good to hear us fightin' each other," Colleen remarked dryly.

Neither man paid her any heed; they just continued staring at each other. It was no contest of wills, but rather the two taking an honest measure of each other.

Al'u'met broke the stare first, giving a chuckle. "Well then, Master O'Comely, we will have to show you the truth of us, that you might learn better."

Belster smiled and nodded; perhaps it was time for him to take a clearer and more honest look at the folks from the southern kingdom.

That would be a lesson for another day, though, as they were both reminded when the door unexpectedly swung open, and a haggard-looking Pony stood in the doorway. "I need to go to Elbryan," she whispered.

"He is far to the north," Belster replied, moving to her side and putting an arm about her to support her—and she looked as if she needed the support.

Pony shook her head. "I need to go to Elbryan," she repeated matter-of-factly, as if no amount of distance mattered, "now."

Belster looked from her to Colleen and Al'u'met.

"Ye get yer strength, girl," Colleen said determinedly. "Ye get yer strength and I'll take ye to the north to find yer lover."

"Colleen—" Belster started to protest, but Al'u'met cut him short.

"I can get them north of the city by sea," he said.

"What nonsense are we talking?" Belster demanded. "She was almost killed, and now you are planning to send her on a long journey, and with winter not even past?"

"Ye think her safer in Palmaris?" Colleen replied. "Better that she's runnin' to her lover, I say, than stayin' here where the devil Markwart's sure to find her."

"I can speak for myself," Pony said coldly, "and choose my own road. I will rest for another day or two, no more. And then I will go to Elbryan, whatever course you three might decide for me." And with that, she turned and left.

"Oh, but I'll go with her," Colleen said, her anger simmering near to a boil. "I've a visit to pay me dear cousin Shamus. One he's not wantin', to be sure!"

Belster and Al'u'met exchanged glances, both of them understanding the danger of the present situation in Palmaris, and both of them fearing that things might soon get much worse.

It wasn't much of a shelter, just piles of stones with bundles of brush slapped over the top. But though another storm had buried the Barbacan in several feet of snow, and though the mountain passes to the south were practically impassable, the shelter on the sacred plateau near Avelyn's grave did not need to be strong or warm. Winter's hand, like the goblins', could not seem to touch this place, and all the creatures here—man and elf, centaur and horse alike—were not only comfortable, but were thriving. The men who were badly wounded during the fight with the goblins—even the soldier who had seemed so near to death and Bradwarden, so torn and battered—were fast on the mend, and Tiel'marawee had healed completely.

Elbryan had no explanation; none of them did—other than to declare it a miracle and be glad for it.

And though he was glad that they had survived, Elbryan spent many hours staring forlornly to the blocked southern trails, his thoughts flying to Pony and their unborn child. "Soon after the turn of spring, I would guess," he had informed Bradwarden when the centaur inquired about when the child would be born.

"But we'll get ye there afore it happens," the centaur insisted; though if they could not get out of the Barbacan within the next two weeks—and neither believed that they could—they would hardly be able to cover the six hundred miles back to Palmaris in time.

Elbryan could only stand and stare, hoping that his dear Pony was all right, and that the child would be born healthy.

He could not know that the child was already gone.

"I take my leave," Tiel'marawee announced, moving by the pair.

"Lots of snow, deeper than a tall elf," Bradwarden replied.

Tiel'marawee screwed up her face skeptically; never had the snow been a hindrance to the light-footed Touel'alfar!

"Where is your course?" the ranger asked with sincere interest. "Palmaris?"

"Lady Dasslerond must be told of Bishop De'Unnero and the threat to the Touel'alfar," the elf explained. "I will likely find her in Palmaris."

"I will go with you," the ranger said suddenly.

The elf scoffed at the thought. "You cannot get your horse through the passes now," she said. "You could not even get him down from this plateau to the valley."

"I will walk."

"But I've not the time to wait for you, ranger," Tiel'marawee replied sternly. With that, she leaped from the plateau, wings flapping to bring her to a ledge thirty feet below the pair, a spot it would take Elbryan about a half hour to get to.

She didn't bother to look back.

"Ye'll get back to her," Bradwarden said comfortingly as the elf skipped away, disappearing against the backdrop of the great blasted mountain.

"Not soon enough," Elbryan replied.

"And what o' them?" the centaur asked, nodding in the direction of the soldiers and the monks.

"I think that Brother Braumin and the other monk have decided to live out their lives up here," the ranger replied. "Roger will accompany me, I am sure."

"Warm enough, and safe enough from monsters," said the centaur, "though they'll be hard-pressed to find food close by."

"I am not certain what Shamus and the soldiers think to do," the ranger admitted. "I doubt that they'll try to return to Palmaris—at least until there has been some contact with another emissary from the King or Father Abbot, that they might better understand their situation."

"Not much to understand," said the centaur. "They go back, they get hung. Or burned. Seems them monks are partial to burnin'."

"Shamus will have to decide his own course," the ranger said with a shrug. "My road leads to Pony."

"And she'll be glad to see ye," said Bradwarden.

"Will she?"

The question caught the centaur off guard—until he considered all that Tiel'marawee had told him of Elbryan's feelings about Pony's departure, his fears that she had left him knowing that she was with his child, had chosen not to tell him.

"She's the bravest woman ever me eyes've seen," the centaur remarked. "And braver still if yer fears about her leavin' ye knowingly with child be true."

That brought a perplexed look from Elbryan.

"She knew that ye had a different road ahead of ye, boy," Bradwarden explained. "Knew ye had to go, and knew she could not."

"You act as if she told you as well," the ranger accused.

"And are ye thinkin' so little o' her to believe that?" the centaur answered. "Ye know her better, and know that, whatever she's done, she's done it with yer own best interest in mind and heart."

Elbryan had no argument; and indeed, much of his anger went away at that moment, as he reminded himself of all that Pony had gone through over the last few months. He remained eager, desperate almost, to be out of the Barbacan and on the road south, but now it was an emotional tumult wrought of fear for Pony.

*   *   *

True to his word, Captain Al'u'met put the *Saudi Jacintha* out of Palmaris the next day, despite strong winds and rough waters.

Pony and Colleen Kilronney came up on the deck soon after the ship had left port, soon enough to make out the solitary figure of Belster O'Comely standing on the wharf, staring out at the departing vessel.

"I think ye broke his heart," Colleen remarked to Pony. "Might it be that he took yer impersonation of his wife a bit too far."

Her attempt at levity did little to comfort the beleaguered Pony. She didn't reply, just stood at the rail, looking back at Palmaris, unsure if she would ever return—or if she would ever want to return. She still wanted revenge on Markwart, more so than ever, but felt powerless. He had beaten her, and now all she wanted was to be in Elbryan's arms again, and far, far away from wretched Palmaris.

"Master O'Comely only fears for you," Captain Al'u'met remarked, moving to join the two. "He does not disagree with your decision to leave Palmaris, but fears that you are not yet fit to travel, especially since the possibility remains of more wintry weather."

"He fears too much," Pony replied somewhat coldly. "I have lived on the very borderlands of civilization for many years. Am I to fear winter more than I fear the Abellican Church?"

"A healthy respect for both would suit you well," the captain remarked. "But place no blame on the shoulders of Belster O'Comely. A fine friend, by my estimation."

"Indeed he is," Pony admitted. "And do not doubt my concern for him. He remains in Palmaris, and that place, I fear, is many times more dangerous than the wildest reaches of the Wilderlands."

No one argued that point.

Captain Al'u'met put Pony, Colleen, and their horses down on the coast north of the city, wishing them well and pledging that he would look after Belster and the others.

"What he really prays for is peace," Pony remarked as the two started away along a muddy trail.

"A fine prayer, by me own guess," Colleen replied.

"A peace that will leave De'Unnero and Markwart in power," Pony said.

Colleen let it go at that, knowing that they would only make themselves angrier than ever with such talk. The warrior woman hated the Church leaders, the men responsible for the death of her beloved Baron, every bit as much as did Pony. And how she wished that Pony's attack on the wretch Markwart had been successful!

But that was not the reality, she knew, and hoped that Pony would come to understand. If it came to a fight, then Colleen would fight hard and would hope for the chance to take down her pompous cousin before she, along with all her allies, inevitably lost. But unlike Pony, the warrior woman

wasn't so sure that she wanted that fight—not now, not after seeing the
power of Markwart, who, by all reports of those soldiers close to Chasewind Manor and the house of Aloysius Crump, held the upper hand in the
dealings with King Danube. No, Colleen recognized—if Pony did not—
that no peasant revolt in Palmaris now had any chance of success.

They rode on through the rest of the day, accepting an invitation from a
farmer for an evening meal and a warm and dry place to sleep.

They did not know that another party was even then formulating plans
for leaving Palmaris, that Father Abbot Markwart was working with his
underlings to organize the journey north that would bring the infamous
Nightbird to the Church's version of justice.

CHAPTER

❖ 34 ❖

One-upmanship

King Danube stared out the window of his temporary residence in Palmaris, the fact that this house was so much less spectacular than Chasewind Manor serving as a reminder that his rule here was in jeopardy. Indeed, for the King—who had ruled Honce-the-Bear for more than a quarter of a century, for more than half his life—the conflict with Markwart seemed the most threatening yet, even more than the war against the minions of the demon dactyl.

Only now, after having faced Markwart and his advisers, did Danube begin to appreciate the depth of this threat. The Abellican Church had always been a strong influence in the kingdom, oftentimes stronger than the Crown. During the beginning of his reign, when he was but a teenager, the Church had held great power; in fact, Abbot Je'howith of St. Honce had played a greater role in ruling Ursal than had Danube. That had been only temporary, Danube and his advisers had understood, a necessary aid given to the man who had been thrust into the role of monarch before he had been properly prepared. And when Danube had grown after he had learned the subtleties of gently bribing the populace into grateful submission, or working with the ambassador from Behren, privately granting the man personal gains in exchange for policies that would favor Honce-the-Bear, the Church had backed away, Abbot Je'howith seeming satisfied with his comfortable role behind the scenes.

Now Danube understood that the situation had dramatically changed. This was no temporary power play by Father Abbot Markwart—and by his old friend Je'howith, he constantly reminded himself—for it had been Je'howith who had persuaded him to install a bishop instead of a baron to rule Palmaris. He had given the Church a firm foothold, and dislodging it would prove no easy task.

He should revoke the title immediately, he knew, should privately warn Markwart to remember his place and remain there, or else risk a war that would bring the power of the kingdom against the Abellican Church.

Danube would win such a war, he believed. He might not be able to conquer St.-Mere-Abelle, that vast and mighty fortress, but his armies—twenty thousand strong, including the powerful Allheart Brigade—could certainly pen the monks in their monasteries and keep them there.

It would never come to that, Danube could tell himself, for the Father Abbot, no fool, would certainly see the folly of his ways and back down.

But there was another factor, the King knew. Markwart had come into his private bedchamber in Ursal, walking by all the guards, unhindered by all the locks and stone walls. The kingdom could win, or at least force a favorable stalemate, against the Abellican Church, King Danube did not doubt; but that war might become a personal battle between him and Markwart, and that, he admitted to himself now, he could not win.

And so he stared out the window, more afraid than he had ever been, feeling helpless for the first time in his adult life.

"You summoned me, my King," came the gentle voice of Constance Pemblebury behind him.

Danube turned to regard the woman. Constance was still quite attractive, he realized. Some of the color had faded from her strawberry blond hair, but thirty-five winters had not taken the luster from her sparkling blue eyes or the softness from her dimpled cheeks. She had been Danube's lover many years ago—that was no secret to the Ursulan court—and many assumed that the liaison was the sole reason Constance had been catapulted to a high position as personal adviser, in line, perhaps, for a duchy of her own. But their personal relationship had played no role in her rise. The King respected her for her intelligence and insights. Constance was the best judge of character King Danube had ever met—better than Kalas, certainly.

"I am to go to the north with Duke Kalas," Danube explained.

Constance narrowed her eyes at her obvious exclusion.

"Father Abbot Markwart knows where this man Nightbird is hiding, and so he has decided to go out after the man personally with a contingent of a hundred Abellican monks, the former Bishop among them," Danube explained.

"And of course, you cannot remain behind," Constance agreed. "If the Father Abbot returned to Palmaris with the fugitive in tow, then his popularity would dramatically rise, to the detriment of King Danube."

"So it would seem," the King admitted.

"You bring Kalas as a counterweight to De'Unnero," the perceptive Constance went on. "Your champion against Markwart's?"

The King winced.

"Take care that such a competition does not arise," Constance warned. "I respect Duke Kalas and all that he has accomplished, as a warrior and a nobleman, but De'Unnero is far his superior, I believe, and Kalas' pride will never allow him to admit that. If Kalas is to fight against De'Unnero, then the Crown shall lose."

Good advice, King Danube understood, and that only reaffirmed his decisions concerning her. He crossed the floor then, moving to stand right before her, and he raised his hand to gently stroke her cheek. "I need you now," he explained, "perhaps more than ever before."

Unexpectedly, she kissed him, but it wasn't a kiss filled with passion. Then she backed off, nodding. "You do," she explained. "Abbot Je'howith is no friend of the Crown. He will stand beside you only if he believes you have the upper hand against Markwart. You saw where he chose to sit at the table."

"What am I to do?" Danube asked.

"Dissolve the office of bishop," she advised, "evict Markwart from Chasewind Manor, and appoint Duke Kalas as interim Baron until a suitable replacement for Bildeborough can be found."

Fine words, Danube knew, but impractical given his private meeting with Markwart's specter.

"Father Abbot Markwart has already determined that St. Precious will have a formal abbot again," Constance went on. "That is enough power for the Abellican Church in Palmaris."

"I do not disagree, but it is not as easy as that," Danube replied, turning away. He almost told her the truth then, but he found that he could not admit his fear.

"How so?" Constance pressed.

Danube turned back to her suddenly and waved his hand to dismiss the subject. "We will discuss the disposition of Palmaris' ruling structure upon my return from the north," he explained. "For now, I need you in the city as my eyes and my ears. My strength in this northern crusade must be no less than that of the Father Abbot, I understand. Kalas and the Allheart Brigade will accompany me, a splendid display of power. You will be left with a strong contingent of King's soldiers and sailors to serve as your base of power from which to build an even stronger hold. Publicly you are to be my eyes and my ears, seeing and listening to the edicts of Bishop Francis, who, as I understand, will be left behind at St. Precious."

"Not Chasewind Manor?" Constance asked, wondering if there might be any significance to that.

"St. Precious, from what I have been told," the King replied. "Perhaps Markwart is not ready to entrust Bishop Francis with as much responsibility as he outwardly proclaims."

"Then it is likely that the new Bishop will do little in the Father Abbot's absence," Constance reasoned.

"That is my hope," the King replied. "And in the absence of Markwart and De'Unnero, of King Danube and Duke Kalas, the strongest voice in Palmaris may be that of Constance Pemblebury."

"And yet you have not declared me your mouth," the woman reasoned.

"Not publicly," the King explained. "Our profile shall remain low. I ask you to keep a check on Bishop Francis, to ensure that he makes no overt moves to enlarge Church power. I give you great discretion in this matter. Turn your garrison against St. Precious if you decide you must."

Constance stepped back, her jaw hanging open in disbelief. "You ask me to start a war with the Abellican Church?"

"No, I do not ask any such thing," the King replied. "But I trust your judgment. If the Church makes a grab for power in my absence, then Constance Pemblebury must stop them."

The woman nodded.

"I need you, Constance," Danube said sincerely, moving closer and taking her by the shoulders. "If you fail me in this, then know that the Crown will suffer greatly—know that we may live out the rest of our lives in the shadow of the Abellican Church."

The weight of his words stole her breath. Then King Danube moved in even closer, pressing his lips against hers in a passionate kiss. He moved to take it further, but Constance stopped him, moving back.

"When I return from the northlands, you and I will have much to discuss," King Danube said quietly.

"I am too old to be a mistress," the woman insisted.

The King nodded, letting her understand that he had much more in mind.

He left her, then, with only a small peck on the cheek and a promise to return before the turn of summer.

Constance stood quietly in the empty chamber for a long while. She remembered the first time that she and Danube had made love, when he was just over twenty years old and she a girl of seventeen. The same age as Vivian, whom Danube had married the next morning.

Their affair had continued for several months, nearly a year of passion and excitement. Vivian knew about it—she had to know!—but she had never once confronted Constance. Of course, if Vivian had meant to confront all her husband's lovers, she would have found little time for her own lover.

Several years later, long after Vivian's death, Danube had come to Constance again, and she had allowed him into her bed. The King's passions had calmed by that point; Constance was fairly certain that she was his only lover for all the months of their affair. But he wouldn't marry her, explaining that he could not, that her bloodline was not pure enough to satisfy the nobles. Constance knew this was true. Only great personal accomplishments could make her a suitable queen of Honce-the-Bear. Now, all these years later, with pressure strong on the aging King to produce an heir—a legitimate one, for Danube was rumored to have sired at least two illegitimate children—Constance had achieved those personal accomplishments and would be considered suitable.

But she was as close to forty as to thirty, nearing the end of her child-bearing years, and the King's main reason for marrying anyone must be to produce an heir.

Constance considered the reality of the situation, thought of the potential risks and the heartbreak that would come if she could not become with child. Then King Danube would quickly annul their marriage—if she was lucky—or, if the Church would not grant an annulment, perhaps he'd even be forced to have her murdered!

But the possible gains were too tempting for Constance Pemblebury to dismiss. She liked the thought of being queen, though she held no illusions of any real power coming with the title. Ursulan law was very explicit: Danube's wife would be queen as long as Danube was king, but if he died without children, then his brother, Midalis Brock Ursal, Prince of Vanguard, would assume the throne. And Constance also understood that even while the King lived, no queen would hold much power over the forceful Danube Brock Ursal. But still, the possibilities . . .

Constance liked the idea of having the King's ear on every matter, an influence above the troublesome Kalas and all the others; but more than that, she loved the idea of being the mother of the future King, of being able to mold the child into her image, to prepare him to rule the way she would have ruled had fate granted her the appropriate bloodline.

So, yes, she mused, she would indeed handle Palmaris wisely. Her actions here would please Danube greatly upon his return, she decided; then, when he came to her, she would press the issue, would force him to elaborate on that which he had hinted at before leaving her that morning.

From the window Constance watched the grand entourage, King Danube and Duke Kalas at its head, thunder out of the manor gates, a hundred splendid Allheart soldiers, their plate mail, spear tips, and great helms shining in the morning light. They were, perhaps, the most powerful brigade in the world, the personal guard of the King of Honce-the-Bear.

And, Constance mused, the personal guard of the queen of Honce-the-Bear.

"I leave you with tremendous resources," Father Abbot Markwart told Bishop Francis, handing over a satchel of gemstones—mostly graphite and other potent offensive stones, Francis noted. "Your duty here will be critical in the weeks that I and Abbot De'Unnero are away."

"Tell me your will, and I shall execute it," Francis dutifully replied.

"In the best case, you are to do nothing," Markwart replied. "Maintain the present situation, with no overt actions to ruffle either the populace or whomever King Danube leaves behind as his voice in the city. That will be Constance Pemblebury, likely, and do not underestimate her; Abbot Je'howith regards her highly. Also, it is quite possible that other Dukes, perhaps the Duke of the Mirianic, will make their way to Palmaris, given the gravity of the situation here.

"Master Engress will be your second," Markwart went on. "Expect little from him. He is old and weary of it all, it seems, and he would rather have stayed in St.-Mere-Abelle—where, in retrospect, I should have left him, bringing a younger and stronger man with me. He remains the ranking master, though; and since he is here, we must take care to treat him with respect. But not to fear, for the situation shall be remedied, our ranks strengthened at the lower levels. A contingent of six score brothers is already on its way from our abbey to reinforce your ranks."

"But I am to do nothing," Francis dared to remark.

"In the best case," Markwart reminded. "I desire to find the balance of power in Palmaris as it is now upon my return. If I return and find Palmaris as I left it, then know that you will have done me a great service. Yet I fear that such a task will not prove easy. It might be that King Danube will use my absence to further his own gains within the city, and that, you must not allow."

"How so?" Francis asked. "He will have little official voice, since he will be gone and there is no Baron in place."

"The battleground will be the hearts of the city soldiers," Markwart replied, "many of whom are already in the court of the King. You must hold fast those loyal to the Church."

"I will not fail you, Father Abbot," Francis said, his duty clear.

Markwart nodded and started away, but stopped; almost as an afterthought, he added, "And move your lodging to Chasewind Manor. Let Master Engress preside over St. Precious in Abbot De'Unnero's absence, along with Brother Talumus, who will placate the Palmaris monks. I do not wish to break the tradition of housing the Bishop in the great house."

Francis did not reply, but he could not hide his surprise at the use of the word *tradition*.

"Every tradition must begin somewhere and at some time," the Father Abbot said slyly. "You will live there, from this day forward, and take those monks who arrive from St.-Mere-Abelle into the manor house instead of the abbey, as well. Also, retain many of the city guardsmen. Treat them well, build their confidence and their loyalty, but do not, under any circumstances, entrust them with anything important."

As Father Abbot Markwart left the room, and Francis stared out the window with the same determined expression Constance Pemblebury had worn that morning, his determination was no less than that of the ambitious woman.

They thundered out of the city's northern gate, King Danube and Duke Kalas and a hundred Allheart soldiers.

Flanking them came the Abellican entourage. In their middle was Father Abbot Markwart, riding in the horse-drawn carriage that still bore the hole where the gemstone had embedded itself, still, despite the best efforts of the brothers of St. Precious, stained by Markwart's dried blood. Abbot De'Unnero and a hundred monks, some from St.-Mere-Abelle, but the majority from St. Precious, walked beside the carriage, looking rather unremarkable in their brown robes.

Just outside the city gates, Duke Kalas stopped the brigade while the King moved to speak with Markwart.

"You had indicated that we would move with all speed," Danube remarked, giving a solid tug on the reins of his feisty To-gai-ru stallion, the eager horse obviously ready to gallop away.

"Indeed," replied the Father Abbot, shrugging as if to say that he did not understand why Danube would question him so.

The King looked around at the monks, replying with a shrug of his own. "They intend to keep pace with horses?" he asked.

"Only if my brethren choose an easy pace," Markwart replied.

King Danube cantered back to Kalas. "They think to pace us," he said to the Duke, smiling wryly. "Let us see about that."

Duke Kalas was more than happy to oblige, and away went the Allheart soldiers at a swift trot.

And away went the Abellican monks, superbly trained and conditioned, jogging easily. Amazingly, they did not fall behind after half an hour had passed. Amazingly, they kept up with impossibly long, loping strides.

The King turned an angry eye upon the Duke, but Kalas could only shrug helplessly. No man should have been able to maintain so swift a pace for so long a time! Duke Kalas figured that they would do more than thirty miles that day at their current rate, a brutal trek for a horse, a nearly impossible one for a man—and certainly one that could not be repeated by any man a second or third day in a row.

They broke for a midday meal, then trotted on; the monks, seeming hardly tired, easily kept up with the mounted Allheart soldiers.

When they camped that night, they had put more than thirty miles behind them, but it seemed to Kalas and Danube as if their soldiers and horses showed more wear than the monks.

"Not possible," the Duke remarked to the King. Though he wanted to argue that it was indeed, obviously so, King Danube could only sit and shake his head in disbelief.

For neither man understood the truth: Father Abbot Markwart, aided by his inner voice, had discovered a new use for malachite, the stone of levitation. Sitting comfortably in his carriage, the Father Abbot used a soul stone to make a mental connection with all his brethren. Then he, joined by several other monks, used the stone so that the monks ran almost without weight. Their feet, when they stopped to camp for the night, showed no blisters, their muscles no more weary than if they had merely taken a long walk.

The Father Abbot and De'Unnero sat together at the side of the encampment, both enjoying the obvious distress of the King and his men. Originally, Markwart had planned for his monks to ride, but Abellican monks, never known as horsemen, kept no stables. Markwart realized his group would never be able to keep up with the To-gai-ru horses and the superbly skilled riders of the Allheart Brigade. It had brought great distress to both Markwart and De'Unnero to think that the journey north would show the King's men as superior to their own.

But then came that inner voice, showing Markwart a new use for an old stone.

Now it was Danube and Kalas who were distressed. Though their men seemed so splendid and grand in their shining armor and atop their mighty steeds, the monks on foot had certainly humbled them.

❖ 35 ❖

The Smell of Prey

"They are not so far behind," Pony remarked doubtfully, for she and Colleen had spotted the northward-bound forces of Markwart and King Danube two days before, many miles back at that time, but closer, it seemed, each day. The two women didn't know the disposition of the force, of course, but the mere fact that so large a contingent was outpacing them told them both that these were not ordinary folk, or even common Kingsmen.

"No choice for us," Colleen replied. "Ye've got that fine horse o' Connor's under ye, but me own poor nag's not for runnin' much longer. Besides, it might well be that yer Nightbird's in Caer Tinella."

Pony shook her head. Elbryan was long gone from the place, she knew, in Dundalis, at least, and probably even farther north. The blond woman glanced back over her shoulder, down the southern road. They were a few hours ahead of the moving force, no more, and the thought of stopping for Colleen to get a fresh horse, and of conversing with villagers, who would likely be interrogated afterward, bothered her. But seeing her companion's mount, the mare lathered in sweat and walking awkwardly, for she had thrown a shoe, Pony found that she could hardly disagree. They would get a new horse here, or Colleen would be walking very soon.

"Perhaps we can find someone on the outskirts," Pony suggested, "a farmer out readying fields or gathering firewood, who can help us."

Colleen nodded and Pony led on, circling the village of Landsdown, and then Caer Tinella, to the east. They did spot a couple of men out cutting wood, and spent some time watching the pair from the shadows of the forest's edge. But then they heard the rumble of a wagon and the neighing of a horse.

Moving through the trees, the women soon came to a hillock overlooking a trail heading east, and there, rumbling down the road, two horses drawing his wagon and another pair tied behind, came an enormous man with black, bushy hair, singing and laughing.

And wearing the robes of an Abellican monk.

"Don't ye even think o' killin' the man," Colleen whispered.

Pony turned an astonished glare at her. "Kill him?" she echoed. "I do not even know him!"

"Ye know his robes," Colleen said quietly.

Pony winced and lowered her gaze, sighing. She was no murderer; never would she strike one who did not deserve it. She wondered then if that was a distinction that she could morally make. Who was she, after all, to decide who deserved to live and who did not? Though her hatred for Markwart had not abated, though she believed that if he was in front of her, vulnerable, she would try to strike him down again, Pony worried that she was a lost soul.

She shook the troubling thoughts away. Now she had to get one of those horses, preferably without letting the monk know about it. But how? Pony considered her gemstones. She could use diamond, perhaps to bring a spot of darkness into the monk's eyes, blinding him, and then malachite to lift him high into the air. He might be oblivious of the theft until Pony let him back down and removed the blackness—perhaps even longer if he didn't immediately notice that a different horse had been tethered behind his wagon.

He would know that magic had been used against him, though, gemstone magic. He might even be able to identify the stones used, and wouldn't that be an easy trail for the minions of Markwart to follow?

No, she needed to be subtle. "Go down to the road a hundred yards ahead of him," she instructed Colleen. "Dismount and unsaddle your horse. When he passes, and becomes distracted, be quick and quiet in changing horses with one of those tethered to the back of his wagon."

"I'd rather have one from the front," the warrior woman replied, but when Pony turned to glare at her, she saw that Colleen was smiling.

"Just go," she said dryly.

Despite her mood, Pony did manage a slight smile as Colleen walked her mount away. The woman had become a true friend, a pleasure to be around, one who could read Pony's moods and say just the right things to bring her from darkness or to keep her focused on the present. Pony reached into her pouch and took out her soul stone, then reached into her mind and conjured an image, a reflection of herself standing by a lake after *bi'nelle dasada*. She burned that image into her mind, changing it so that she wouldn't be recognizable, and covering parts of her naked form with diaphanous veils.

Pony clutched the hematite tightly, wondering if she could really pull this off. She would have to be perfect, she realized. One slip would show the monk the truth of the contact, and then all would be lost.

She fell into the stone, again summoning that image and sending it into the mind of the monk.

* * *

Friar Pembleton whistled and sang, enjoying the fine weather, thinking that spring should begin any day.

"Any day!" he cried aloud. "Ha-ha!" He gave a click and shook the reins, urging his team faster. He wanted to make Caer Tinella before midmorning; Janine o' the Lake had promised him a fine meal if he arrived before she had cleaned her table. He wanted . . .

It came to him suddenly, out of nowhere, it seemed, an image alluring and amazing. The friar let up on urging the horses. The wagon slowed, nearly to a stop, but the befuddled man hardly noticed. He sat very still and closed his eyes, trying to make sense of this overwhelming image of a beautiful, tempting woman that had so unexpectedly flooded his thoughts.

He tried to wash it away, even mumbled the beginnings of a prayer.

But it was no use. There she was, so beautiful, and he couldn't dismiss her, and surely couldn't ignore her!

The wagon was hardly moving.

Colleen Kilronney came out of the brush behind it, leading her horse. She made the change, amazed and confused, wondering what Pony had done to the man!

When she rejoined Pony with her fresh horse a few minutes later, she found the woman still deep in concentration, still holding the soul stone in her hand. Colleen looked down the road and saw the wagon crawling along, the friar swaying.

"What did ye do to him, then?" the red-haired woman asked, drawing Pony from the stone magic.

"I gave him something better to watch," Pony replied cryptically.

Colleen looked at her, confused for just a moment, but then a wry smile spread over her face. "Ah, but ye're a wicked one!" she said with a laugh.

The two set off at once, moving down to the trail, then following it east, away from the still very distracted monk.

Friar Pembleton continued slowly on his way, trying to recapture the image all the way to Janine o' the Lake's farm. He never even noticed that one of the horses tied to the back of his wagon—one of the two he was planning to sell in the village—had changed until he moved to untie the beasts outside Janine's door.

They came through Caer Tinella and Landsdown with little fanfare, but surely the two hundred people who had resettled in the region were amazed by the splendor of the procession, by the fabulous Allheart Brigade, riding their famous To-gai-ru pintos.

The force put in at Caer Tinella that the soldiers could rest their horses, checking shoes and saddles, and could oil armor and weapons. Markwart and Danube agreed that they would not remain stationary for more than an hour, though they would only find another two hours on the road after that before sunset forced them to camp.

"Brother Simple!" Janine o' the Lake remarked, seeing De'Unnero among those leaders gathered in the common house of Caer Tinella. "Ye back in the south so soon? I'd thought ye going to Dundalis, to bring yer God to the Timberlands."

De'Unnero merely turned away, having no desire to speak with the peasant woman.

"Seems that many're heading north this season," Janine remarked, heading for the door.

Markwart caught the words, and promptly intercepted her. "What do you mean?" he asked. "Of whom do you speak?"

The woman shrugged. "A friend says he saw a pair riding north just this morning, not six hours before ye came into Caer Tinella, is all," she replied. "That and yer Brother Simple there, who came through a pair o' weeks ago."

"Two riders?" Markwart asked. "And was one of them, or both, perhaps, a woman?"

Again the shrug. "He just says he saw a pair. A long way off, so he's not for knowing. Been a curious day, is all. Friar Pembleton o' yer own came in this morning with horses to sell, and now he's spouting craziness that one of them he brought to sell wasn't his own, that the beast changed form during the trip, and was nearly lame, and missing a shoe—one he insists was on the beast that morning!"

"There is an Abellican friar in town?" Markwart asked. His inner voice prodded him that there might be something significant here.

"Just said there was," Janine replied. "He's all flustered, to be sure, at yer arrival. He's cleaning up and will be along presently, I'd be guessing."

Even as she spoke, Friar Pembleton bounded in, glancing about nervously and wringing his hands. He spotted the Father Abbot standing with Janine, De'Unnero not far away, and shuffled over, bowing with every step.

"I did not know ye were coming, Father Abbot," he sputtered. "Had I known . . ."

Markwart raised a hand to calm the man. "You had problems with a horse, I am told," he said.

Friar Pembleton's eyes widened and he looked over at Janine, seeming horrified that the Father Abbot knew the tale. Would the great man think him crazy? "I—I was confused—am confused, I am sure," he stammered. "Surely it does not look like my horse, but I get so many—I traded many with the caravan you sent north from St.-Mere-Abelle just last year, Father Abbot."

Again Markwart patted his hand in the air to calm the man. "The horse has gone lame?"

Pembleton shrugged. "I know not how to even answer," he said. "I have no recollection. . . ."

"Are you trying to cheat these people, good friar?" Markwart asked. De'Unnero walked over and stood by the man, and though Pembleton outweighed him by fifty pounds, the friar was unnerved by his powerful presence.

"No, Father Abbot, never that!" he cried. "I have been dealing with Caer Tinella for many years, and would never cheat—"

"A good man with honest prices for honest goods," Janine interjected.

"What is it, Pembleton?" Markwart asked calmly. "Is the horse the same one you left your chapel with?"

The friar seemed at a loss, and glanced around repeatedly. "Has to be," he mumbled. "Has to be. One cannot change a horse on the back of a wagon without the driver knowing it, after all! I just do not recognize . . ."

"Is it the same horse?" Markwart pressed.

Pembleton glanced nervously around.

"Look at me!" Markwart demanded, locking the man's gaze with his own, "and answer honestly."

"It's not my horse," Pembleton replied.

Janine snorted and rolled her eyes.

"Truthfully, Father Abbot," the friar said frantically, "I have had every horse in my stable for months—since the caravan from St.-Mere-Abelle came through—and I know every one, and this is not one of them. I have shoed every horse in my care, yet this one wears shoes that I do not know."

Markwart looked at De'Unnero. "Take some of the St. Precious monks and go to this horse," he instructed. "See if they recognize the shoes." Then he turned back to Pembleton and took great care to calm the man, asking him to detail every part of the journey from his chapel to the town. Pembleton did just that, but stuttered at one point; again, Markwart's inner voice told him that might be significant.

He led the friar aside, and the man confessed his sin of the mind.

It was much more than that, Father Abbot Markwart realized, and that was confirmed when De'Unnero returned with news that one of the monks had recognized the shoes as the work of the former baron's own blacksmith, who marked all the shoes he made with a special brand, a combination of his initials.

The horse, who had so mysteriously replaced the one Friar Pembleton had hitched to the back of his wagon—a wagon he had not left, he insisted, all the way to Caer Tinella—had come from Palmaris, and, by De'Unnero's estimate, had been ridden hard recently.

Intrigued, Markwart said no more about it. Later, after the group camped two hours north of Caer Tinella, the Father Abbot returned to his tent and eagerly took up his soul stone. He went quickly north, scouring the region—and he found his quarry, camped beneath the drooping boughs of an ancient pine, their horses tethered nearby. Markwart recognized one of those horses—had seen it on the field outside Palmaris—and so he was not surprised when his spirit slipped through the pine boughs and found his archenemy resting with her back against the tree, with another woman, larger, and wearing the uniform of a Palmaris city guard, lying nearby.

Markwart considered moving right in. But she might be more prepared for him this time, he realized, and he did not have her unborn child this time to use against her undeniably strong will. And he could not be sure if Dasslerond was in the area.

His spirit rushed back to his waiting form. He went out of his tent, calling for Marcalo De'Unnero.

The tiger set off soon after, running straight for the drooping pine.

Or so De'Unnero thought. He encountered many obstacles that Markwart's spirit had bypassed, and by the time he reached the place, dawn had broken and the women were gone. De'Unnero's frustration lasted only as long as it took him to realize he was not alone, that the spirit of the Father Abbot was with him.

"Hear me through the soul stone ring you wear," the Father Abbot instructed. "Attune your thoughts to my spirit and I will guide you."

Away rushed Markwart, faster than the north wind.

He sensed the women's position, then called back to De'Unnero; the chase, though Pony and Colleen didn't know it, was on.

By mid-morning, the tireless De'Unnero had them in sight, while Markwart, his physical form still being comfortably borne on a litter by running monks, hovered nearby. Markwart understood Pony's power, and feared that De'Unnero might be overmatched if she was ready for him, if she had her gemstones in hand.

So he went first, telepathically, screaming into her horse's mind.

Greystone reared and bucked, and Pony barely kept her seat. The horse spun, kicking at the air. Colleen yelled out, trying to make some sense of it all.

Pony flew out of the saddle, the breath blasted from her as she landed on her back. She had the presence of mind to roll out of the way of Greystone's pounding hooves.

"What'd ye do to the thing?" Colleen called, and her words ended abruptly as something large crashed into her, driving her from her saddle. It took her a long while to recover, gathering her wits and wiping the blood and mud from her eyes. Then she saw a monstrous form standing over Pony. She tried to scream but could not, for she could hardly believe the sight before her. From the waist up the creature was a strong man, its face half human, a strange blend of man and cat. It stood in a crouch over Pony, on the legs of a cat, a striped tail swishing, staring down at the woman. Pony tried to get her arms in line to block, but De'Unnero's hand punched into the center of her chest, stealing her breath. Pony jerked up, swung her arms about to try to fend him off, but she was dazed, all strength stolen from her.

Colleen forced herself to her feet and started to draw her sword.

The creature leaped away from Pony, turning to face her.

"I'll be payin' ye back for that one!" Colleen screamed, rushing ahead, her sword slashing viciously.

Up went De'Unnero, springing straight into the air above her slashing sword, and then down hard, putting his full weight behind a tremendous punch that smashed into Colleen's breastbone, driving her down, staggering backward.

She gave a weak swipe with the sword and stared helplessly as her opponent's hand evaded the blade, moving much too fast for her to adjust her swing. The hand grabbed her blade and shoved it farther away. Then De'-Unnero spun, rolling toward Colleen, his hand slapping her face, knocking her back several more steps.

And still he was right in front of her, twisting her sword arm up, then bending her wrist, easily disarming her.

He leaped, rolling over her as he went, never letting go, coming down and twisting Colleen, then using his leverage to throw her under the legs of her nervous horse.

"Run!" she heard Pony call, and she saw the tiger turn to regard her friend, then saw him stagger back, blasted by a lightning bolt.

But the powerful creature growled and rushed right back at Pony, falling upon her before she could loose another bit of magic.

Colleen scrambled to her feet, coming up on the other side of her horse. She had the beast in a run before she was fully in the saddle, for the tiger came on in fast pursuit.

Her horse crashed through the forest, branches banging into poor Colleen, nearly knocking her senseless. She heard the creature behind, and realized then the truth about the death of her beloved Baron.

Her horse took a sharp turn, and she could not hold on, falling down through some evergreen bushes, then sliding through snow and mud down the steep side of a ravine. Bouncing and tumbling, she lost consciousness long before she slammed into a tree stump far below.

She did hear the dying screams of her horse as the tiger fell upon it.

Only the angry specter of Father Abbot Markwart brought De'Unnero from his feast of horseflesh. He came fully out of his tiger state then—to call it coming from his gemstone any longer made no sense, for he wasn't even certain of where the magical tiger's paw might be. He didn't have it in hand nor in his pouch, but he didn't need it any longer, as if somehow he and the gemstone had merged.

But he let go of his feline side completely now, understanding Markwart's ire and fearing it more than he lusted for the sensation of the kill. Nearly drunk on the life energies of the horse, he came back to Pony, reaching down to check that she was still alive, hoping he had not hit her too hard after she had struck him with the lightning bolt. Markwart's instructions had been very clear: De'Unnero was to bring Pony back alive, along with the stolen gemstones. Markwart didn't care at all about the other woman.

Pony came back to consciousness a long time later, to find herself standing, her back against a tree, her hands tied painfully around the trunk.

And there stood Marcalo De'Unnero, eyes narrowed and boring into hers.

"Do you not understand the power of your enemies?" he asked, moving up to her, his face barely an inch from hers.

Pony turned away, unable to look him in the eye. He caught her by the chin and roughly turned her back to face him. For a moment, she thought he would choke the life from her or smash her face to a pulp, but then a wry smile widened across his hard face.

Pony nearly swooned; she was helpless against him. He could do anything to her, could take her then and there.

"So beautiful," De'Unnero remarked, suddenly stroking her cheek, his demeanor changing completely. Pony would rather that he kill her!

She turned away again, but his hand had her by the chin immediately, jerking her head back.

"Beautiful and powerful," De'Unnero said, "skilled with the stones and with the blade, so I am told, and so strong of will."

Pony set her jaw and narrowed her blue eyes.

"You fear that I will take you?" De'Unnero remarked, smiling wide. He grabbed the front of her shirt. "You fear that I will tear off your clothes and leave you naked before me."

Pony eyed him stubbornly, and did not reply.

"You do not even begin to understand me," De'Unnero said, his face so close to her own. But then he backed away and let go of her shirt. "I would fight you on an open field, and willingly kill you if you opposed me—as I shall kill your lover, the one called Nightbird," he explained. "But I take no carnal pleasures with an unwilling woman. I am a man of God."

Pony snorted and looked away. She expected De'Unnero to grab her chin again and jerk her head back.

"Foolish child," she heard De'Unnero say, the man walking away. "You do not begin to understand those you have named your enemies."

Pony had no answers.

She heard horses then, an approaching cavalry, and soon they were all about her, Markwart and the monks, the soldiers in their shining mail, and the King of Honce-the-Bear!

❖ 36 ❖

Unwelcome Homecoming

Greystone found her battered and bloody and too dazed even to think about trying to climb back up to her friend.

Her friend! Colleen ached in heart more than body when she looked up that slope, to where Pony lay at the mercy of that strange beast. But she couldn't get to her friend, and even if she could have managed the climb, the tiger would merely beat her down again.

It was a moot point, though, and Colleen knew it. She could hardly get up on Greystone's back, and once there, she only managed to turn the horse north and urge him on. She slipped in and out of consciousness many times over the next hour, but had had the presence of mind to tie herself to the saddle.

And so she went on alone, knowing that the terrible man-tiger was not far behind.

She didn't camp that night. She couldn't even find the strength to climb down from the horse. Greystone walked on, eating as he went, pausing every now and then, sleeping as the woman slept on his back.

If Pony held any thoughts of speaking with King Danube, they were dashed immediately. On orders from Father Abbot Markwart—and with not a word of complaint from Danube or his entourage—a host of monks surrounded Pony, cut her loose from the tree, and shuffled her away. She saw Markwart showing her gems to the King and heard him remark about some "missing lodestone." King Danube looked over at her, his expression a mixture of pity and disgust.

And then he turned away, and Pony knew that she was doomed.

A few moments later, De'Unnero joined those escorting her, moving right beside her. "You are to run on," he explained. "The brothers will support you, will carry you when your legs give out." Two strong monks moved next to her as he spoke, pulling her arms across their shoulders, hoisting her so that her feet were barely touching the ground.

"You should reconsider your position before we return to Palmaris," De'Unnero said to her. "What a pity that one as strong of mind and body as you will be so horribly and publicly executed." He spun away as he finished, his step light and fast.

Pony didn't know how to interpret his words. Was he showing sincere concern? Or was he playing with her, taunting her within the guise of concern? Or was it, perhaps, something more sinister? Was De'Unnero pretending to be her friend, playing off against the Father Abbot, to keep her off guard?

Whatever it might be, Pony determined that she would not play along. They had beaten her, so it seemed, had taken everything from her, but she would face death with one thing intact: her convictions.

And she was glad to see De'Unnero, she decided. If the dangerous man was here, then he was not out hunting Colleen; though Pony couldn't even be certain whether her friend was alive, or if De'Unnero had killed her before he had come back.

"I will hold my convictions and my hope," she whispered, needing to hear the words, although as soon as she said them, she feared that she might elicit some taunting response from the monks holding her. Neither replied, though one did turn to regard her, eyeing her with some respect.

Pony met that gaze, drawing strength from it. Even if dying bravely was no great accomplishment, it was all she had left.

The pain wasn't so bad the next day, replaced by a grim determination in Colleen that she would get to Nightbird, whatever it took, and tell him of the fate of his lover. She knew that her wounds were serious. One arm was broken and one ankle so swollen that she had to remove her boot. And she had lost blood, and was so very cold.

But Colleen focused only on the road ahead and urged Greystone, wonderful Greystone, ahead, step after step.

Day and night blended together, one long, rolling agony. A rain fell the third day after De'Unnero's attack, but Colleen, delirious, didn't even notice. The soldiers and monks gained on her daily, though she rode long into the night, but again, she didn't, couldn't, notice.

All she knew was the road ahead, the road to Dundalis, the road to the place where she would at last allow herself some rest.

She collapsed on the side of the trail the afternoon of the fourth day, sliding from Greystone, hanging down at the end of the tether, her shoulders and head brushing the ground. The horse knew enough to stop, but there was little else that Greystone, or Colleen, could do. The woman made one attempt to right herself, but only fell back, scraping the side of her face against some crusted snow.

The sun rode low in the western sky. The darkness took her.

* * *

Tiel'marawee moved with the grace and speed that no race other than Touel'alfar could match, skipping over mounds of drifted snow immediately south of the Barbacan, and then running lightly, half flying, over stretches of open ground in the south. She took no meandering course this time, despite her elven love of song and dance, for her heart remained heavy with the loss of Ni'estiel.

Lady Dasslerond had to know: about the dead elf, about the murderous Bishop, and most of all, about the strange magic that had saved Nightbird—and Tiel'marawee—on the plateau of Mount Aida.

With hardly a thought, the elf rushed past Dundalis, passing under the tower on the north slope without disturbing the two sentries. She knew that she should turn west soon, if her destination was Andur'Blough Inninness, but she suspected that her lady might still be in Palmaris, or that Dasslerond would come north first before turning for home.

She listened intently for *tiest-tiel*, the star song.

What she heard instead was the soft nicker of a horse and the groans of a woman.

Tiel'marawee didn't know Colleen Kilronney, nor did she recognize the horse that had served as mount for Jilseponie. But though her business was urgent, the elf couldn't leave the woman like this, hanging upside down under the belly of a horse. With her fine elvish blade, she cut Colleen down, doing her best to pad the woman's fall to the ground. At the very least, she decided to unsaddle the poor horse, for festering sores were showing around the edges of the leather, and perhaps wrap the woman in the blanket, that she might die comfortably.

Colleen managed to open one eye, though the other remained closed, caked with dried blood. "Nightbird," she whispered through parched, cracked lips. "Pony caught."

Tiel'marawee's eyes widened as the meaning of the words came clear to her. "Pony?" she asked, lightly slapping the sides of the woman's face. "Jilseponie? Caught by whom? By the Abellican Church?"

But thinking her message delivered, the delirious Colleen had slipped far away.

Tiel'marawee didn't know where to turn. She hated the thought of slowing her progress to the south, but understood that this might be something significant. She ran back to the north and again passed Dundalis, moving to the bottom of the sentry tower. "A woman on the road," she called up.

The guards scrambled; Tiel'marawee heard their boots and the tumult as they reached for weapons.

"A woman on the road," she called again, "gravely injured. To the south!"

"Who is there?" one guard called back.

But Tiel'marawee was already gone.

Soon after, the elf watched with relief as a group of men rushed down one of the southern trails. They would not have found Colleen, but the elf called out to them, imitating the sounds of a woman in distress, guiding them.

"Palmaris guard," one man remarked, rushing to Colleen's side and gently turning her to her back, while a companion grabbed Greystone's reins and led the horse aside.

"Cousin of Shamus Kilronney," another man, a large man with dark black hair, replied. "Colleen, by name. She came to us in Caer Tinella, with news of the dead Baron."

"She may be soon to join him," a third man remarked. The first, inspecting her wounds, shook his head.

"Not so bad," he said. "Nothing a bit of food and a warm bed won't help. She's been on the road, and injured, for several days, at least, probably tied to the saddle the whole time."

"Good horse," the third man remarked, and only then did the large black-haired man take a moment to regard the animal, haggard-looking and with open sores. How the man's eyes widened!

"But who unsaddled the mount?" the man bending over Colleen asked.

"And who told us about the fallen woman?" the third added.

Tomas Gingerwart could hardly reply for the lump in his throat. He knew that animal, weary and haggard though it was. That was Greystone, Pony's mount! "Get her into town quickly," he bade his companions. "Get her warm and get her fed, and get her, by all means, ready to speak! Now go!"

The other two jumped at the command, gently lifting Colleen and laying her across Greystone's back, then leading the horse away.

Tomas lingered behind, looking around at the forest and the trail, appearing distressed.

Tiel'marawee took a chance, slipping out of the foliage.

Immediately the big man's hands came up, palms outward, showing that he held no weapon and would make no threatening moves. "I am no enemy of the elves," he said, not showing his amazement at seeing one of the diminutive folk.

"You know of us, and know something of the fallen woman," Tiel'marawee reasoned.

"I am Tomas Gingerwart," he explained, "friend of Nightbird, friend of Jilseponie, whose horse carried the stricken woman."

Tiel'marawee did well to hide her concern; if this was Pony's horse, then what had happened to Lady Dasslerond?

"Friend of Belli'mar Juraviel," Tomas finished, "or companion, at least—for he accompanied us to this place before turning for home."

"I am Tiel'marawee," the elf replied, bending low. "The woman has information concerning Jilseponie, I am sure."

"Pray join me, then," Tomas offered, turning for Dundalis.

The elf considered the invitation, then nodded and followed.

Many stares followed her, but none of them threatening, as she and Tomas rushed through the town to Colleen's bedside.

They found poor Colleen half conscious, still mumbling about Pony's being captured, and about the need to inform Nightbird.

"I left Nightbird at the Barbacan," Tiel'marawee explained, "locked in by a winter storm. There he must stay for several more days, at least, and many more than that if winter strikes the northland again."

"But you came through it," Tomas reasoned. "And you can get back."

The elf looked at him long and hard.

"If Pony is in trouble, then Nightbird has to know," the big man said.

"Then go tell him," Tiel'marawee said coldly, her tone leaving no doubt that, by her thinking, her role in this had come to an end.

Tomas looked at her. "You just said that Nightbird could not get through," he replied. "If that is so, then how are any of us to get to him?"

Before Tiel'marawee could answer, the door burst open and a flustered woman staggered into the room. "Soldiers coming," she said breathlessly, "and monks besides. Many monks."

Tomas turned back to Tiel'marawee—and saw the elf scrambling through a side window.

"By the gods," the big man muttered grimly. "Keep her hidden," he instructed those in the room. "By our word of friendship to Nightbird, we know nothing about her." He rushed out of the house, moving fast to join some other folk gathered at the southern end of town, awaiting the arrival of the soldiers. He looked around many times, hoping to catch sight of the elf, though he suspected, correctly, that Tiel'marawee was already far away.

"Now what are ye supposin' soldiers'll be wantin' with us?" one man asked.

"Or monks?" another added with obvious disdain, for he had been out in the forest with Tomas when the dangerous, vicious monk with the tiger's paw had come through, had been the companion of the man whose tunic the monk had shredded with a single swipe.

"Allheart," one of the others whispered to Tomas when the unit came into clear view, the strong, muscled horses churning the turf. "And several with plumed helmets."

"The ornament of a champion," another finished grimly. "The King's own."

"And a far way from Ursal," another man remarked.

They were a spectacular sight, but Tomas looked more to the group wearing the brown robes of Abellican monks running beside the mounted soldiers. One in particular caught his attention, the monk he had encountered in the forest outside of town a couple of weeks before, the monk who had named Tomas and his companions as friends of Nightbird, and thus, as enemies of the Church.

The carriage bearing Markwart came into sight, and a chorus of gasps erupted about Tomas.

Tomas had never seen the Father Abbot of the Abellican Church before, but this man's rank was obvious even before one of the others, one who had seen Markwart, named the old monk as the Church's supreme leader.

"What've we done to bring such attention?" someone asked.

"More likely Nightbird than us," another answered.

Tomas didn't disagree, nor did he bother to comment, so intense was his focus on the approaching procession. And then he saw Pony, bedraggled, propped between two monks, and his heart fell. He thought of all the months that woman and her lover had kept him and his friends alive, remembered the fight with the great giant leader, when the behemoth made the error of following Nightbird into the forest. Only then, seeing Pony so helpless, did Tomas realize how much he loved her and Nightbird, how much they had become heroes to him.

The procession pulled up some twenty feet away from the Dundalis folk. The soldiers formed two rows, their horses side by side, so close together that Tomas and the others couldn't make out the forms of those in the second row.

"Allheart," the other man whispered again, obviously awed, "best in all the world."

Given the soldiers' companions this day, Tomas was not so sure.

A man of about forty years, handsome and strong and quite at ease on his spirited horse, trotted out from the group. On cue, one of the monks rushed out to accompany him, and Tomas gritted his teeth as he recognized the robed man.

"I am Duke Targon Bree Kalas," the rider said.

"And I am Abbot De'Unnero of St. Precious," the monk added. "Do you still call yourself the leader of the folk of Dundalis, Tomas Gingerwart?"

De'Unnero's familiarity with the man obviously caught the Duke off guard, the man glaring down at the monk from his saddle.

"We would have prepared a better reception had we known that such important men were on their way," Tomas replied, dipping a low bow.

"I am well acquainted with your receptions," the abbot said.

Tomas held out his hands. "A stranger approached us unannounced in the forest," he replied. "These are not tame lands, good abbot."

"Good?" De'Unnero echoed skeptically.

"Enough of this banter," the Duke said, jumping down to stand between Tomas and the monk. De'Unnero quickly moved around the Duke as Kalas removed his two-plumed helm. "We have ridden north from Palmaris in search of the one called Nightbird," Kalas explained. "Do you know him?"

"He knows the man well," De'Unnero replied before Tomas could begin to speak, "an ally of the man, and of our guest, Jilseponie, disciple of Avelyn, would-be assassin of Father Abbot Markwart."

Kalas glared at the monk, but De'Unnero did not back down. "I warn you, Tomas Gingerwart," he said in a low and threatening tone, "but only one last time."

"I know of the man called Nightbird," Tomas admitted. "A great hero."

De'Unnero sneered.

"Nightbird," Tomas went on stubbornly, "who, along with Pony—the woman you hold now, beaten and captive—saved us all before the minions of the demon dactyl were driven from the region. And now you claim that you seek him. Hunt him, you mean! And I—and the others who owe their lives to him—are to open our arms and our doors, lending aid to an enemy of our friend?"

"You are to do as you are told," De'Unnero remarked, stepping up to Tomas as if he meant to strike him.

"Good Master Gingerwart," Duke Kalas intervened, "I speak for King Danube himself. Nightbird and the woman have been declared outlaws for their crimes against the Church and the state. We will find him and bring him to Palmaris for trial, with or without the help of the folk of Dundalis."

"These are the Timberlands, not the realm of Honce-the-Bear," a man standing to the side of Tomas remarked.

"I could have your tongue for that," Duke Kalas assured him.

"This is not the domain of our King," Tomas dared to say.

"As you insist that it is not the domain of the Church," De'Unnero put in. "You should be more careful of the enemies you make, Master Gingerwart."

"I desire no enemies," Tomas replied calmly.

"Then know this," Kalas answered forcefully, cutting short De'Unnero, who had started to speak once more. "Those who do not aid us, aid Nightbird, and if he is found guilty of the crimes with which he is charged, then those who aided him will not find Danube to be a merciful King."

He let the words hang in the air for a moment, locking Tomas' eyes with his own, showing the man that there would be no compromise here, that he was of one mind with Abbot De'Unnero.

"Is he here?" Kalas asked calmly.

"No," Tomas replied. "He left many days ago. I know not where."

"You know indeed," De'Unnero remarked. "He went north to the Barbacan, but may have returned by now."

"He is not here," Tomas insisted.

"Search the town!" De'Unnero called out, spinning about and waving his monks to action.

Not to be outdone, Duke Kalas did the same. The Allheart Brigade leaped their horses forward, filtering between the buildings.

"Any who resist will be cut down," Kalas informed Tomas. The big man didn't have to hear a similar promise from the vicious De'Unnero to realize that the monks would be even less forgiving.

The folk had done a fine job of hiding Colleen Kilronney. So fine, in fact, that she would not have been found, except for Greystone. De'Unnero spotted the weary horse, pointed it out, and laughed. "So you have found Jilseponie's horse," he cried. "Good. And pray tell me, good Master Ginger-wart, where is the rider who brought the beast in?"

"He walked in of his own accord," Tomas answered, stiffening his jaw.

"Indeed!" De'Unnero exclaimed dramatically. "All the way from Caer Tinella! What a wise creature he is!" The man's eyes narrowed dangerously and he came up suddenly, putting his face right in front of Tomas'. "She is here," he said. "I can smell her.

"Find the red-haired woman!" De'Unnero called to his monks. "A Palmaris soldier, and wounded, I am sure.

Not to be outdone, Duke Kalas similarly ordered his men. Monks and soldiers shoved into every house, beating down any who opposed them.

Tomas Gingerwart, the leader, the one the folk looked to for answers, had seen enough. He started yelling at De'Unnero, but the monk pushed him aside and started searching the town on his own. Tomas then turned his ire on Duke Kalas, but his protest was short-lived, falling away into stunned silence when another man came out from the Allheart ranks.

"Tomas Gingerwart," King Danube said sternly, moving to stand before the man. "You will interfere no more and speak not another word. I would not have come out here if this matter was not of the utmost urgency. Stand aside, and instruct the folk to do likewise."

"M-my King," Tomas stammered, bowing low.

"Even in the Timberlands," Danube remarked slyly, gazing at the man who had claimed that the Timberlands were not the King's domain. Tomas trembled before the power of the King, then fell to his knees, begging for mercy.

But then Abbot De'Unnero came back, two monks behind him dragging Colleen Kilronney.

Tomas Gingerwart closed his eyes and felt as if he was falling far away. He hardly heard the pronouncements of Abbot De'Unnero or the voice of Markwart, proclaiming him a criminal, a conspirator in a plot against Church and state.

"Not state!" another Dundalis man dared to reply—or started to reply, for his words were cut off abruptly by a smacking sound. Tomas opened his eyes to see the man facedown beside him, Abbot De'Unnero standing behind him.

Tomas looked to King Danube for leniency, but the King walked away.

By the time De'Unnero completed his inquisition, Tomas, five other men, and two women had been taken prisoner. Nine horses were confiscated by the Father Abbot, and the new prisoners and Pony were unceremoniously strapped sideways across their backs, wrists and ankles tied below the horses' bellies.

On the procession rolled through Dundalis, along the road to the north, the same trail Nightbird and his companions had taken.

Both the wounded soldier woman and the leader of Dundalis had charged Tiel'marawee with going to the Barbacan to tell Nightbird of Pony's dilemma. Had the ranger been of the Touel'alfar, the elf would have been long on her way to the north by the time the soldiers and monks had crossed through the small Timberlands town.

But he was *n'Touel'alfar*, as was Pony, and Tiel'marawee's path led to the south, her choice of direction further affirmed that same night, when she heard *tiest-tiel* drifting on the evening breeze.

By the end of the second day, the elf had found Dasslerond and the others. Predictably, her tale of Pony's woe and the impending danger to Nightbird weighed heavily on the shoulders of her kin, particularly on Belli'mar Juraviel.

"We cannot allow this," he said to the lady of Andur'Blough Inninness.

"Both the King of Honce-the-Bear and the Father Abbot of the Abellican Church lead the procession," Lady Dasslerond reminded him. "Are we to start a war with all the humans of the world?"

Juraviel recognized that she spoke the truth, and he bowed his head. "But these events are not distanced from us," he reminded her. "The disposition of Nightbird may well hold implications for the Touel'alfar."

Lady Dasslerond—so tired of it all, wanting only to go back to Andur'-Blough Inninness—could not deny Juraviel's words. She looked around at her kin, all the elves moving closer to hear her every word.

"It is time for the Touel'alfar to return to their home," Dasslerond proclaimed. Every elven head, even Juraviel's, bobbed in agreement. "The situation has become too complicated and too dangerous. Thus, we go home and shut our valley and our eyes to the affairs of the humans."

"But not our ears," Dasslerond continued after a long, pondering pause. "We go home, except for you, Belli'mar Juraviel."

Juraviel turned a surprised eye on his lady.

"You have named yourself as a friend of Nightbird and the woman," Dasslerond explained.

"We have all named Nightbird as our friend," Juraviel replied.

"But not as intimately as Belli'mar Juraviel," Dasslerond went on. "You who fought beside Nightbird and the woman for so long must bear witness to their fate now."

"I thank you, my lady," Juraviel replied.

"Bear witness," Lady Dasslerond repeated firmly. "We are not a part of this, Belli'mar Juraviel. Nightbird and Pony must see their own way, or they will fall. Bear witness and return to us."

Belli'mar Juraviel did not for a moment discount the great honor and trust Lady Dasslerond had just afforded him. She knew his heart concerning Nightbird and Pony, and knew that his love for the two would tempt him to intervene, for Belli'mar Juraviel was their friend.

But more important, Belli'mar Juraviel was Touel'alfar.

CHAPTER

❖ 37 ❖

A Miracle in the Waiting?

I t hadn't snowed in several days and the air had been relatively warm, even away from Avelyn's arm, even in the higher elevations along the mountains ringing the Barbacan. Elbryan, Roger, and several of Shamus' men had gone down to the valley floor and even into the foothills on several occasions, hunting game, the ranger searching for a clear trail south. They hadn't found much, but each time they returned, the ranger's mood had been a bit brighter, for every trip had taken them deeper into the mountains and Elbryan believed that the time of departure was growing near.

"This will be the day," Elbryan had said earlier that morning, as he set out to inspect the trails. But Bradwarden knew from the expression on the ranger's face as he climbed back up to the plateau that he had not yet found a clear trail out of the Barbacan. The ranger wanted to ride Symphony hard to the south, to Pony; but while he, with his elven training, could possibly get through the snowy mountain passes, the horse could not.

"Too thick on the top?" Bradwarden asked.

"I never got near the top," Elbryan replied glumly. "Every steep ascent is clogged with falling drifts."

"Well, but she's meltin' then," Bradwarden said hopefully.

"Not fast enough," the ranger replied, staring back at the southern mountains. "And if we see a freeze, then all will ice over and I shall be trapped in this place for another month."

"No freeze and no more snow," Bradwarden insisted. "And if we do see one, or a snowfall, it'll be gone with the mornin' sun."

"The worst thing of all is that I am sure that the ground is clear south of the mountains," Elbryan said. "If I could just break through, the run to Palmaris would be fast."

"She's fine, boy," the centaur said. "I know ye're worrying for her, and with good cause. But ye got to trust in her. Ye can bet that Pony's got herself surrounded by allies. She'll handle that Markwart—and De'Unnero, too—or she'll be smart enough to keep her head down. Ye need to find yer trust. If the snow's rumblin' down, then ye can expect to be here for a few more days. If we do get another big storm, then ye can expect a few more than that. Symphony's a fine horse, finest I ever seen, but he's not for walkin' mountain trails hidden under snowdrifts. Nor am I—ye ain't seen Bradwarden along for any o' yer huntin' trips, now have ye? No, boy, ye find yer trust and ye find yer patience. We're here until winter decides to let us out."

Elbryan gave a nod, and his smile showed that the centaur's point was well taken.

"At least we got the food for it!" Bradwarden declared.

True enough, Elbryan had to admit. They had plenty of supplies, warmth from Avelyn's arm, and security, as well, for after the slaughter of the goblins, no other monsters had dared approach the place, or had even dared to come anywhere near Elbryan and the others when they went out hunting.

So it could have been worse, much worse; but to Elbryan's thinking, it could have been better. He could be in Pony's arms now, or holding her hand and supporting her as she birthed their child. He knew that she would be getting close to that time by now, and that if he didn't get out of the Barbacan soon, even mighty Symphony would not get him to Palmaris in time.

Markwart, Danube, and their minions found no such obstacles. The trails north of Dundalis were clear, and the procession proceeded at a tremendous pace. During the day they stopped only briefly, to rest and let their horses graze and for a bit of food of their own; they didn't untie the prisoners until they camped for the night.

By that time, Tomas and the others could hardly straighten. Poor Pony, who had just survived the trauma of battling Markwart and losing her child, could not even stand. She curled up on the ground, clutching at her belly.

Tomas begged their captors to allow them, or at least Pony, to ride her horse the next day. Markwart would have none of it, saying that she had created her own prison, and that she would be treated accordingly. But then De'Unnero pointed out to him that if her condition deteriorated, it would slow them down, and also, that a living Jilseponie would aid them greatly when at last they confronted Nightbird.

The next day, Pony rode upright, though she remained dreadfully uncomfortable, the pain in her stomach burning and sharp. She tried to hide it, refusing to give the Father Abbot and the others the pleasure of seeing her distress. She kept her focus on poor Tomas and the other prisoners, strapped over the backs of the horses like corpses or saddlebags, and kept telling herself that they were worse off by far.

Somehow she got through the day, and when they camped for the night, she managed to sit straighter and ignore the continuing pain. She could eat little, though, just enough—she hoped—to keep up her strength.

Sitting on the ground, her eyes were down when a man approached, but she recognized the stiff gait of age and knew that it was Markwart before he spoke to her.

"If you die on the road, I will summon a spirit to inhabit your body," he said. "And then your pretty voice will guide the unsuspecting Nightbird to me."

Pony summoned all her strength and straightened to look up at the old man, matching the hatred in his eyes. "A demon, you mean." She spat. "Call it the pretty word *spirit*, but still it remains a foul beast from hell."

"You do recall the spectacle of a body so inhabited, do you not?" Markwart remarked, unfazed by her accusation.

Pony looked away. She wanted nothing more at that moment than to fight the man again, with his fists or with a soul stone, however he chose. She would beat him, she knew, despite her pain and weakness. She would destroy him this time, and show the truth of him to all. Let King Danube see the black heart of Father Abbot Markwart, and Pony would have a powerful ally in her war against the Abellican Church!

"I went out earlier this evening, scouting the road ahead," Markwart remarked. "I found him, you know." The man spoke truthfully. But he did leave out one disturbing fact about his spiritual journey: something prevented Markwart from going up to the plateau on Mount Aida, though he had seen the ranger and the others from afar.

Despite her better judgment, Pony did look back at him.

"Nightbird, the centaur, and their friends, including the five traitorous monks," the old man continued, obviously enjoying the moment, "perched atop Mount Aida, snowbound within the Barbacan, awaiting our arrival. Three days, dear girl, and your friend Nightbird will join you. How I long to watch him on the road back to Palmaris! Strapped over the back of a horse—what a hero he will seem to the folk when we parade him through the streets."

Pony looked away.

"Oh, but they love an execution, you see," Markwart went on, bending down to come into Pony's line of vision. "The peasants. They love to see a man hanged or crushed under stones or burned—yes, especially burned. Seeing death so real before them reinforces their lives, you see, gives them a sense of immortality.

"Or perhaps they just enjoy witnessing others in agony," the withered old man finished.

"A man of God," Pony muttered sarcastically.

Markwart grabbed her roughly by the chin and jerked her head up. "Yes, a man of God," he sneered, his breath hot in her face. "A merciful God to those deserving mercy, and a vengeful God to those who do not. I have watched your games, Jilseponie. You fancy yourself some hero of the common folk, someone possessing the truth that others cannot see. But you are not a hero. You and your friend bring only misery to those you claim to lead, and your truth is naught but ridiculous pity, with no discipline and no greater designs than the alleviation of temporary suffering."

Pony pulled away from his grasp, but did not look away. For just a moment his words rang with some measure of truth, and she was afraid. But then she considered more carefully the path of her life, reminded herself of the work she and Elbryan had done on behalf of so many during the war, while the monks stayed safely in their fortress abbeys. And she considered the sword dance Elbryan had taught to her, the very pinnacle of discipline.

There was her truth. There was her strength; in light of that, she considered more carefully the words of the old man, tried to glean any helpful information she might, any insights into this dangerous enemy. Most of all, she understood that Elbryan would not be able to escape him and that time grew very short.

She spent the next day in deep meditation, focusing on her pain and on finding the best posture atop her horse to alleviate it. She felt stronger now, as if Markwart's talk had given her a sense of purpose once more. She tried hard not to reveal that, for De'Unnero had become very attentive, jogging along beside her mount most of the time.

She could use that concern, she decided, and as the towering mountains of the southern rim of the Barbacan came into sight, she began to formulate a plan.

That night she appeared very uncomfortable to all who took the moment to notice—though in truth, Pony knew that she was better off than the other prisoners who still had to ride every day strapped over their horses. Her subdued moans increased whenever De'Unnero walked by.

By mid-morning the next day, on which the monks and soldiers expected to reach the southern foothills of the Barbacan, the caravan was moving along steadily, De'Unnero running near Pony's horse. She glanced about to make sure that no other eyes were upon her, then bit hard on the inside of her cheek. When she tasted her own blood, she lurched over suddenly, so violently that she slid along the side of the horse.

De'Unnero moved up beside her, pushing hard to help her, and soon he had her back atop the mount. She wobbled and seemed as if she would fall over again.

"Just let me down and let me die," Pony said in a pitifully weak voice, blood brightening her lips.

The abbot of St. Precious stared up at her, noticing the blood. "Broken already?" he said. "Markwart has not yet even begun with you and already you beg for death."

"No begging," Pony replied groggily, shaking her head and nearly falling once more. "But death is coming, I know. I bleed inside, terribly so, and will not survive the day."

De'Unnero looked up at her, truly concerned. He didn't want her dead, not now, not with Nightbird and the others waiting for them up ahead. If Pony was not with them, he feared the ranger and his friends would fight them. The Allheart soldiers and the monks would slaughter them with ease. But De'Unnero did not want it resolved that way, and certainly neither did Markwart. For then the King could claim credit for bringing down Nightbird and the conspiracy that threatened the Church. More important, the treasonous behavior of Shamus and the Kingsmen would be brushed aside.

No, they needed Pony, alive and well enough to lure Nightbird and the others in. And as much as he wanted to battle the ranger again, one against one, De'Unnero understood a clean and simple capture to be the desired course.

The abbot glanced back at Markwart and saw he was sitting comfortably in his carriage, eyes closed as he concentrated on the gemstones, lending strength and lightness to the other monks. Not wanting to disturb him, De'Unnero acted on instinct, confident in his own decisions, and reached up with his soul-stone ring, touching Pony's belly, then sending his thoughts into the ring to heighten its magic.

Pony felt the connection immediately, felt the inviting depths of the soul stone. Into it went her spirit, flying past De'Unnero's healing hand, out of her body, rushing over the miles to the mountains and beyond.

She saw Aida's flat top and flew to it, saw Elbryan—dear Elbryan!—and came upon him in a rush. *Markwart!* she imparted telepathically, desperately. *Markwart and King Danube approach! Run! Run away for all your lives!*

"What?" the ranger asked Bradwarden, who was standing nearby; but as soon as the centaur turned a quizzical look his way, Elbryan recognized the source of the communication, knew that it was Pony who had come to him! "Pony!" he cried, trying to hold on to something; but she was already gone, already back in her body, though lying on the ground now, Abbot De'Unnero standing over her, one of his fists covered with her blood.

Dazed, Pony looked up at him and smiled, despite the pain and the blood flowing from her nose. A small victory, she knew as the man reached down and smacked her across the face. Then he hoisted her up roughly and threw her across her saddle, instructing the other monks nearby to tie her as they had tied the other prisoners.

Pony accepted the treatment without complaint. She could only hope that Elbryan had heard her, that her lover would run free.

"What is this about?" Markwart asked De'Unnero, rushing to the man's side and glancing back nervously to see if King Danube had taken note of the commotion.

"She tried to possess me," the monk lied. "Sent her spirit into the soul stone even as I used it to heal her wounds—wounds, I discovered, not nearly as grievous as she led me to believe."

Markwart let his glare fall upon Pony. *Not to possess, but to escape,* the voice in his head told him, and then his eyes widened! *To send her spirit to her allies.*

"How long was she within the power of the stone before you noticed?" the Father Abbot asked.

De'Unnero shrugged. "A few moments, no more."

A few moments, Markwart mused; no stranger to spirit-walking, he understood how far Pony might have traveled in those few moments. "She is to have no contact with any stones, even if her life is fast fading away from her," he instructed. Then he rushed back to his carriage and took out his own soul stone. He guessed Pony's course, and now he followed that same path, soaring through the mountains, down past the valley floor and up the side of Mount Aida. They were still there, he knew—Nightbird and the other conspirators. Now he would see them, view their preparations to determine if the woman had gotten to them or not; perhaps he would even possess one of them.

But again his spirit was stopped at the edge of the plateau as surely as if his corporeal body had run into a stone wall.

Markwart tried to break through the barrier, but was blocked by a force more powerful—many times more powerful—than the strength of Dasslerond when she had sent him careening back to his corporeal form in Palmaris.

He didn't understand it, but he knew—and so did the voice within him—that he could not defeat this barrier. He figured that Braumin and the other monks must have come into possession of a very powerful sunstone, but unless it was a stone many times more magnificent than anything the Father Abbot had seen, he could hardly believe that even the five together could so completely deny him access.

Shaken, the Father Abbot returned to his corporeal form in the carriage. Seeing that his monks were lagging behind, he went back to his malachite, lending them strength.

He thought about that mysterious power atop the blasted mountain often during the day, and he was glad he had brought powerful allies with him.

"They are camped on the other side of the pass, though they'll have trouble negotiating the snow with their heavy horses and armor," Roger Lockless dutifully reported that night, returned from a scouting expedition.

Elbryan understood: the Father Abbot and the King had come for him, and likely with De'Unnero along. "Instruct Shamus to keep a vigilant watch this night," the ranger said to Bradwarden. "The Bishop might decide to pay us a visit prematurely."

"Hope he does," the centaur replied. "Might be the only chance we get to hit at that one afore the whole damned army rolls over us."

"Are we to stay up here?" Roger asked in disbelief.

"Where would you have us go?" Elbryan replied. "Goblins still control the ring about the Barbacan other than the southern passes. Markwart, with his gemstones, will find us wherever we run. Up here, with the power of Avelyn backing us, is our best chance."

"Ye should send the monks away, at least," Bradwarden reasoned. "They're not needin' to die up here. If Markwart's just lookin' for Nightbird and Bradwarden, then let them get away."

"I already offered as much," the ranger replied. "Brother Braumin would hear none of it. The man is eager to return to Palmaris as the Father Abbot's prisoner, is eager to speak of the miracle at Mount Aida."

"He'll have a hard time talkin' with his tongue cut from his mouth," the centaur said dryly.

Elbryan didn't doubt it; Markwart would never let Braumin, or any of them, speak the truth. The ranger knew that they would win or lose everything here on Aida, beside the upraised arm of Avelyn. He understood the power of the gemstones, the scouting power of the soul stone, and knew that there was no way they could hope to escape now that Markwart was on their trail.

No, they would win here, with the help from Avelyn, or they would lose everything.

No, the ranger realized as he considered the situation. Not everything.

"You go," he said to Roger. "Now, this very night, on Symphony. Go south to the passes and find a hole to hide in. When Markwart's forces have passed you, then ride south with all speed. Find Pony and tell her the truth—tell her of the miracle and of our final stand. This must not die with us."

"They do not want you dead," Roger reasoned, obviously not happy with the alteration to the plans. "They want you as a prisoner."

"Then all the more important that you escape," the ranger replied. "Take this," he added, almost as an afterthought. He reached up and removed the circlet from around his head, the only gemstone, other than the one set in Tempest's pommel and the turquoise in Symphony's chest, that Pony had left with him when she had departed.

Roger shook his head, looking at the circlet with horror, as if accepting it would mean the end of his relationship with Nightbird, would mean that he might get away while the ranger died. "I came north with you, indeed I urged you north, and so I shall stand beside you. If we are to die, then we are to die together."

"Well spoken," said Elbryan, "but foolish. I am not telling you to run and hide because I fear for you, Roger Lockless. Indeed, your course may prove more perilous than my own! Once Markwart has me, dead or captured, and Bradwarden and the monks—and once the King, if he really is with the Father Abbot, has taken Shamus Kilronney—they will search no further. You alone have the wiles and relative anonymity to get through. I'll not argue the point. When we came north, we agreed that I would lead. Take Symphony and go. Get behind Markwart's forces and get to Pony's side in Palmaris."

Roger looked to Bradwarden for support, but found that the centaur was completely in agreement with the ranger's decision.

"You believe that Avelyn's power will defeat the Father Abbot?" Roger asked, his voice trembling. As he spoke, he reached out and accepted the circlet.

The ranger shrugged. "I had thought us dead up here already," he replied. "Who knows what miracles the spirit of Avelyn has left to bestow?"

Roger and Symphony went out soon after, the man wearing the cat's-eye circlet that enabled him to see in the dark. The trails remained treacherous for a horse, but Symphony managed them, and long before the dawn arrived, Roger was far into the mountains, on a trail near Markwart's expected course, lying low and, like those perched atop Mount Aida, waiting.

They should not have been able to get through the mountains, for the trails at the higher elevations remained thick with snow. But Markwart sent out monks with rubies and lent them some of his own strength. The stones released blasts of fire that disintegrated great drifts into puddles and steam.

Soon after noon, they saw Mount Aida. They would arrive before the sunset.

Ever curious, Roger left Symphony and crept closer, watching the displays of power with amazement. That feeling of awe only heightened as the full troop thundered by, the proud Allheart Brigade leading.

And then Roger's heart dropped, for he saw the prisoners and he could not mistake the thick golden hair of his dearest friend. He glanced around nervously, near panic. He had to get to Elbryan and let him know! He had to tell his friends, or try somehow to rescue Pony.

But the speed of this force daunted him. He could not beat them back to the Barbacan—not without being seen. And if he was seen, he knew that Markwart or some other monk would magically strike him dead on the field.

And any thought of going in to save Pony was ridiculous, he understood. Roger Lockless could only sit and watch helplessly.

"Allheart," Shamus Kilronney groaned as the army made its way across the Barbacan's muddy floor. "We are doomed."

More than one soldier echoed that sentiment.

"Trust in Brother Avelyn," Braumin Herde reminded them all.

"And trust in yer King," Bradwarden added. "Ye said he was a good man, and a good man'll hear yer tale, and not think it the story of a criminal."

Elbryan, looking down at the approaching force, heard the words and considered every implication. If Bradwarden was correct, should they then make a stand here, firing arrows down upon soldiers and monks as they tried to make their way up to the plateau? What might King Danube say to their tale, to any tale, if some of his guards lay dead on Aida's slopes?

The ranger made his decision. Though many of the others, particularly Bradwarden, were not pleased to hear that they would not fight, they accepted the choice when the ranger explained his reasoning.

And so, like Roger Lockless, they sat and they watched. Later that afternoon, the leading edge of the powerful force neared the plateau.

"This is not Honce-the-Bear!" Brother Castinagis called down to them. "You have no authority here!"

In response came a barrage of lightning beyond anything the companions had ever seen, blasting stone into pieces flying all about them, forcing them to fall back until they were in the same helpless position they had been in when the goblins had come.

"Looks like yer King ain't much for talkin'," Bradwarden remarked grimly, stringing his bow.

"Let us see," Elbryan bade him, grabbing the bow to prevent the centaur from firing the first shot as the lead soldiers and monks clambered up the last slope. The soldiers were at the right-hand side—the only place where horses could negotiate the trail—monks at the left, where Elbryan and Bradwarden had first come up when retreating from the goblins.

And leading those monks was Marcalo De'Unnero.

"Oh, but ye got to let me at least kill that one!" Bradwarden cried.

"Thus we meet again, Nightbird," De'Unnero said, unbothered by the centaur.

"I will happily fight you one against one," the ranger replied.

The abbot found the offer tempting, but he remembered his place and his duty. "One day, perhaps," he replied, "before you are executed."

Bradwarden pulled free of the ranger and brought his bow up.

"I have been sent to warn you that if you offer resistance, Nightbird, then your friend Pony, who is now with the Father Abbot on the slopes below us, will be killed most horribly."

The ranger eyed him dangerously, not knowing whether to believe him. The words did stop Bradwarden.

"I am Targon Bree Kalas, Duke of Wester-Honce," one of the soldiers proclaimed, walking his mount forward. "Abbot De'Unnero speaks the truth, Nightbird. You have no fight here, and are fairly caught. Surrender to the Crown, and in exchange, I promise you a fair trial before the King."

The ranger looked at his friends, then slung Hawkwing over one shoulder and motioned for Kilronney's soldiers to put their weapons away. He wasn't quite thinking of surrender, though. He hoped to lure the would-be captors onto the plateau, hoped the power of Avelyn would save them once more. Then he would be quick to Markwart, he decided, and if the King got in his way, then Honce-the-Bear would need to find another king!

"You know me, Captain Kilronney," Duke Kalas went on. "Tell your friend, for I grow impatient. We have come six hundred miles to find you, and many of my soldiers desire a fight after so long and tiresome a journey."

"He is who he claims to be," Shamus said to the ranger.

Elbryan nodded. "Stand calm," he told his companions.

The ring closed about them. Closer, closer.

But no hum came from the mountain, no tingling of power from the arm of Avelyn.

"The magic must be used up," Shamus whispered.

"No," Brother Braumin realized. "These are not monsters, not minions of the demon dactyl."

"Not knowingly, perhaps," Elbryan said dryly. He looked at them all again and realized that they were waiting for his cue. If he drew Tempest and fought, then all of them would willingly join him, would die beside him.

But he could not do that. Not if Pony was the captive of Markwart.

"No!" cried a terrified and outraged Brother Mullahy, the normally quiet man pushed beyond his limits. "No! I'll not go back that my death becomes entertainment for fools who do not understand the truth of wicked Markwart."

"Calm, brother!" Braumin Herde cried out. Brother Castinagis moved to grab his friend and pull him back.

"Silence him," De'Unnero instructed a monk at his side, a monk holding a graphite.

"No!" Mullahy cried again, pulling free of Castinagis and running quickly to the one break in the enemy line, where the side of the plateau dropped away steeply.

"Stop him!" De'Unnero cried. But before the others could react, Brother Romeo Mullahy made his statement, the most profound and stirring statement he had ever made, one that touched the heart and soul of friend and foe alike.

Crying out for Avelyn Desbris, the young monk leaped over the edge, plummeting a hundred feet and more to his death on jagged rocks.

De'Unnero and many others blew a long and disappointed sigh.

Duke Kalas urged his horse and his Allheart soldiers closer; De'Unnero moved up the monks.

"What of it, Nightbird?" the Duke asked. "Have you or your friends any more surprises to offer?"

"You promised a fair trial," Nightbird replied.

Duke Kalas nodded, staring the man directly in the eyes.

The ranger drew out Tempest and threw it at the feet of the Duke's horse.

But Abbot De'Unnero got to the sword first, scooping it up and leading his monks quickly. He let Kalas and the Allheart soldiers take Shamus and the other Kingsmen as their prisoners, but he made sure Bradwarden, the renegade monks, and—most of all—Nightbird were in his care as they left the plateau.

Father Abbot Markwart watched the procession coming down Aida's sides with mixed emotions. Again he had gone up there in spirit, and again he had been prevented.

His confusion and anger increased when he came to understand that the ranger, the monks, and their friends had set up no magical barriers to block his way.

Now that the band of outlaws was taken, Markwart tried again to visit the plateau.

And again he could not.

❖ 38 ❖

A Sacrifice of Conscience

He was not much of a horseman, but, riding Symphony, he did not have to be. Roger turned south as soon as he understood the truth of the disaster at the plateau: the power of Avelyn had not come forth and his friends had all been taken prisoner.

Roger had no idea what he should do.

He thought of trying to sneak into the camp and free Elbryan or Pony. He had executed such maneuvers against the powries in Caer Tinella, after all, had stolen prisoners and food right out from under their sentries. But Roger dismissed the notion. These were not powries. This was the King of Honce-the-Bear and his most elite and powerful fighting unit. Worse, this was Father Abbot Markwart and Bishop De'Unnero and a host of gemstone-armed Abellican monks. Roger might get into the encampment, but he knew without doubt that he would never, ever get away. And even if he did manage to free Elbryan, or Pony, or even both somehow, and get them to their weapons and gemstones, it would do little good. They had been armed, after all, when they had first encountered this force, and it seemed to Roger as if none of the King's or Father Abbot's minions had even been injured!

So he rode, hard and fast, the great stallion easily outpacing the troop. He came into Dundalis and learned, to his continued distress, that Tomas, too, had been taken.

Still he rode, past Caer Tinella and Landsdown, down the road toward Palmaris—though what he might accomplish there, he did not know. Lost and alone, the man spent one night in a pine grove, and only then did he learn that not all his friends were caught or dead. Belli'mar Juraviel found him there, or rather, found Symphony, and came in expecting that Nightbird had somehow eluded the Father Abbot and was even then plotting his counterstrikes.

With a heart that grew heavy as soon as the initial joy and relief at seeing

Juraviel faded, Roger recounted the events at the Barbacan. The elf listened with mounting, profound sadness, for it seemed to him as if all was lost.

"What are we to do?" Roger asked when he had finished, Juraviel making no comment, other than to close his golden eyes.

The elf looked at him and shook his head. "Bear witness," he replied, echoing Lady Dasslerond's instructions.

"Witness?" Roger said incredulously. "Witness to what? A mass execution?"

"Perhaps," Juraviel admitted. "Have they come through Caer Tinella?"

"I know not," Roger admitted. "They came through Dundalis only a day behind me, for I spotted them moving along a lower trail. Yet that was nearly a week ago. Their course was south, to Palmaris, I expect. But they cannot pace Symphony, so I know not how far behind they might be."

"Are Nightbird and Pony still alive?" Juraviel asked. Roger winced, for he, too, had pondered that question often over the last few days.

"It is likely that the King will want them brought to Palmaris for trial," the elf went on.

"So there, we must go," Roger reasoned.

"Outside the gates," Juraviel replied. "I wish to witness their entrance to the city, that we might determine if our friends are still with them, and still alive, and, if we are quick and clever, where they mean to imprison them."

In response, Roger Lockless looked forlornly to the north. The nightmare was in full swing, and the man felt helpless to try and change its course.

Spring was in bloom by the time the grand procession, prisoners in tow, marched through the northern gate of Palmaris. The only concession Danube had won from Markwart on the entire journey south was to allow the prisoners to ride upright, with some measure of dignity until the trial could commence and they were formally condemned.

The upright posture brought little comfort to Elbryan, though. Markwart was careful to keep the dangerous ranger and his equally dangerous wife far apart, both during the day's marches and within the encampment during the nights, affording them no opportunity to speak. They did make eye contact occasionally, and the ranger used the meager opportunity to stare lovingly at Pony, to mouth the words "I love you," to smile—anything at all to make her understand that he was not angry with her, not only that he had forgiven her, but that he understood that there was nothing to forgive.

One thing did perplex him, though, and brought him more than a little worry: Pony was obviously not with child. A multitude of questions assaulted the ranger, all the more frustrating because he knew that he would not soon get the answers. Had the child been born? Had she lost the baby? And if it was alive, then with whom? And if not, then who had killed it?

He could not know, and no one would speak with him. He had been placed in the care of the Allheart line, moved far away from Pony, and Markwart and Danube had been very specific to the soldiers guarding him. They were not to speak with him, not to acknowledge him at all unless an emergency arose. To the ranger's dismay, no emergencies at all confronted them all the way to Palmaris.

He took some comfort, at least, in the fact that Markwart won the argument that ensued once they were inside the city. He, Pony, the five monks, and Bradwarden were to be jailed at St. Precious. Colleen and Shamus Kilronney and the other treasonous Kingsmen, along with Tomas and the folk of Dundalis, fell under the care of Duke Kalas at the house of Aloysius Crump.

During the descent to the dungeons of the abbey, he saw Pony briefly, passing her more closely than at any time.

"I love you," he said quickly, before the nearest monk could force him to be quiet. "We will be together."

And then two monks leaped onto him, forcing him to the floor; one wrapped a gag around his mouth and pulled it tight.

He did hear Pony say, "I love you," and heard, too, her charge that Markwart had murdered their child.

And then he was dragged to his cell and thrown inside, the heavy door slammed in his face.

After a while, the ranger collected himself enough to crawl through the filth to his door and call out for Pony.

To his surprise, a voice answered.

"Pony?" he asked desperately.

"Brother Braumin," came the distant response. "Pony is far down the corridor, the furthest cell from your own. Except for Bradwarden; he is in another corridor, for none of these cells would hold him."

Elbryan sighed and rested his face against the door, thoroughly defeated.

"My brothers and I are all in line between you, my friend," came Braumin's voice. "We will relay your words to her, and hers to you, if you do not mind us hearing them."

Elbryan chuckled at the absurdity of it all, but he did take Braumin up on the offer. He told Pony of all his adventures since she had left him in Caer Tinella, and heard through Braumin Pony's response, most pointedly the tale of the disaster on the field outside Palmaris, when she had lost her—their—baby.

"They will try the monks first," Constance Pemblebury reported to her King the next morning. All Palmaris was alive with gossip; no two people in the city passed by on the street without an exchange of news.

"Those four remaining will be handled quietly and efficiently," King Danube reasoned. "Markwart will surely condemn them, though he will not likely execute them until he secures the sentence of death upon Nightbird and the woman."

"It is all a disgusting and evil affair," Constance dared to say.

King Danube didn't disagree.

"Is there nothing we can do?" she asked.

The King only chuckled helplessly. "We are to hold our own trials," he explained. "And our sentencing will probably be no less harsh than the Father Abbot's. Both the woman Kilronney, soldier of the former Baron, and Shamus of the Kingsmen are surely doomed, rightfully so by their own actions."

"Yet they acted out of conscience, against what they perceived as injustice," Constance remarked.

Again came the chuckle. "Whenever were they granted such permission?" he asked.

"Are we to try them first?" Constance continued. "At the same time as the monks, perhaps, or immediately following?"

King Danube sat back in his chair and spent a long time pondering that question. "Last," he decided, though he was not sure that he would stick with the decision. "Perhaps by that time, the peasants' taste for blood will be sated and some of Shamus Kilronney's soldiers, at least, might be spared."

Constance turned away. She wanted to yell at him, remind him that he was the King, that he could dismiss the charges against all of them, even Nightbird and Pony. Or could he? she suddenly wondered. What would be the price of such an action, in addition to the obvious enmity of the Abellican Church?

"The monk who leaped from Aida," King Danube remarked, shaking his head, "he fell right before me, you know. I saw his face, all the way down, right before he struck the stone."

"I am, sorry, my King," she replied.

"Sorry?" Danube scoffed. "The man was not afraid. He was smiling. Smiling, though he knew that he was but an instant from death. I will never understand these Abellican monks, Constance, so fanatical that they do not even fear death."

"But you must understand them," Constance replied grimly, and that thought settled heavily on both their shoulders. There was little doubt that Markwart now held the upper hand. Markwart, risen from the grave. Markwart, the valiant Father Abbot, so old and yet strong enough to travel all the way to the Barbacan to capture the most dangerous criminals in all the world. Markwart! They were all talking about Markwart, the hero of the common folk. Though Danube had a stronger force within Palmaris, his position seemed weak when compared to that of the Father Abbot.

Duke Kalas entered the room then, obviously outraged.

"The centaur is no criminal," he declared immediately.

"You have interviewed the creature?" Danube asked, eyes wide.

"Bradwarden is his name," Kalas explained. "But, no, the monks would not let me speak with any of the prisoners held in St. Precious."

King Danube banged his fist on the arm of his chair. He had sent Kalas to the abbey to demand an interview with any whose words would be relevant to the trial of Shamus and the other soldiers. He had given the man a personal writ, with the seal of the Crown, demanding an interview.

And Markwart had denied him.

"I did find Abbot Je'howith, making his way from St. Precious to Chasewind Manor," Kalas explained.

"Je'howith," King Danube echoed in a wicked tone, for the King was not pleased with the old abbot.

"He deigned not to speak with me!" the Duke cried. "He would have denied me altogether."

The King looked at him curiously.

"Except that I informed him that he would give me his tongue willingly or I would cut it from his mouth," the volatile Kalas explained. "I had ten Allheart soldiers with me, while Je'howith was accompanied by merely a pair of monks."

"You threatened the abbot of St. Honce?" Constance asked incredulously, though she too, frustrated, didn't seem too upset by the action.

"I would have killed him," Duke Kalas declared flatly, "right there, on the open street, and let Father Abbot Markwart declare me an outlaw and try to bring me to his overused gallows!"

"But you did not," the King prompted.

"He spoke with me," Kalas replied, "as did the other monks. One of them had gone on the first journey to Mount Aida, the one during which Markwart first captured the centaur Bradwarden, and brought him back in chains through Palmaris, taking him all the way to the dungeons of St.-Mere-Abelle."

"And Nightbird and Pony rescued him," Constance reasoned.

Kalas nodded. "Thus sealing their own fates as criminals," he explained. "But that premise is only valid if one considers the centaur a criminal, and from what I have learned, that is far from proven. Bradwarden went to Mount Aida with Nightbird and Pony and several others, including the monk Avelyn Desbris, whom the College of Abbots formally declared heretic last Calember."

"Thus they are criminals by association with the heretic," Danube reasoned.

"They went, so the centaur claims, to destroy the demon dactyl, who raised that army against Honce-the-Bear," Kalas explained. "And, indeed, even the Church admits that the demon dactyl was there destroyed!"

"They saved the country, but are criminals in the eyes of the Church," Constance remarked, shaking her head.

"What are we to do?" Duke Kalas demanded.

King Danube looked away, fixing his gaze on a distant point and then letting that point melt into nothingness as he pondered the situation. He understood Kalas' call for action, for a large part of him wanted to openly declare the Church wrong and demand the release of all prisoners. But Danube understood the truth of the situation, a dire truth that was reinforced by what the lady of Andur'Blough Inninness had secretly told him, and doubly reinforced by his memories of Markwart's powerful specter. He could fight them now, with words if not with soldiers, but if he pushed too hard, Markwart would fight back, viciously.

"I have just informed Constance that we shall delay the trials of Shamus and the others until after the Church completes its inquisition and sentencing," Danube replied at length. "And we shall show mercy to our prisoners. Perhaps we will even find a way to exonerate some of them completely, thus casting a dark shadow on the previous actions of the vengeful Church."

"And what of Nightbird, Pony, and Bradwarden?" Kalas asked. "And what of the captured monks?"

"The monks are not our affair," King Danube was quick to respond. "If Markwart chooses to execute them—and I am certain that he shall—then let the populace judge his actions."

"And the others?" Constance asked.

The King paused for a long moment. "Again, we shall let Markwart do as he sees fit with them," he replied. Constance shook her head, and Duke Kalas growled and banged his fist against the wall.

"If he executes them—" the King began.

"Which he surely shall," said Constance.

The King nodded. "But if the true story of Mount Aida then begins to circulate, if after the executions, the people of Palmaris come to see that Nightbird, Pony, and Bradwarden were not criminals but heroes, then Father Abbot Markwart must surely shoulder the vast amount of blame."

Now both Constance and Kalas were nodding, though their expressions remained grim. Neither liked the idea of sacrificing innocent people, but both understood the pragmatism of King Danube's position.

"In the meantime," the King went on. "I shall appoint Targon Bree Kalas, Duke of Wester-Honce, as baron of Palmaris."

"But there is already a Bishop," Kalas reasoned.

"If Markwart can declare both a bishop and an abbot of St. Precious, then I can justify the appointment of a baron," the King replied. "Markwart cannot oppose me on this, nor can he deny the demand of the new baron that he take residence at Chasewind Manor."

"And the Bishop?" Duke Kalas asked slyly, liking this plan more and more by the second.

"Let us find a powerful merchant who owes us a favor to come north and make a claim that he is a relative of Aloysius Crump. Let us see if we can force the Church from both mansions and put them back in St. Precious where they belong."

That won the approval of both advisers. The King would oppose Markwart, but quietly, and while none liked the idea that several apparently innocent people would be sacrificed for the sake of expediency, all three understood that Markwart's present course might well turn many folk against him.

That position was reinforced later that same day, when Captain Al'u'met arrived at the house of Crump. When the man was granted an immediate audience with the King and his advisers, he begged for royal intervention on behalf of Pony and her friends, declaring they were innocent, indeed were heroes.

None of the folk in the room doubted the man's words, but neither did anyone believe that Al'u'met would find opportunity to make those claims heard during the trial of the supposed conspirators against the Church. Yet, when the seaman left, ultimately frustrated, Danube and his advisers were even more hopeful that Markwart was making a mistake, and that, in the end, the Church would lose favor with the common folk of Palmaris.

But those hopes, even if they came to fruition, would prove of little value to Elbryan, Pony and their friends.

Roger's heart sank even lower at the sight of the Fellowship Way. Once one of the most respected taverns in Palmaris, the place now lay quiet and dark, with no patrons and no staff. Roger had hoped that Belster could provide some information valuable to him and Juraviel, some way perhaps that they might be able to get to their friends.

But there was no Belster to be found. No one at all.

With a shake of his head, the forlorn man moved down the street and into an alley, where he was to meet Belli'mar Juraviel after the elf finished scouting St. Precious.

Prim O'Bryen and Heathcomb Mallory, disguised as incoherent drunks, watched Roger.

"Ye think that's the one?" Mallory asked, for Belster, suspecting and hoping that Roger might show up, had placed them in this very spot. Both men knew Roger from their time in the north before the defeat of the dactyl's army, though they couldn't get a good enough look at the small form now as the man rushed away.

"Worth asking," Prim O'Bryen replied. The two glanced around to make sure that no soldiers or monks were about, then followed the man, stopping at the edge of the alley and carefully peering around. With no one else in sight, the two took a chance and approached.

Roger's face brightened, for he recognized the two men from the north, and they him. Less than an hour later, he came face-to-face with Belster O'Comely in the hold of the *Saudi Jacintha.*

"Markwart's got them both," Roger explained, and the innkeeper was nodding with every word, for his network of spies had provided every detail about the disposition of the prisoners.

"Captain Al'u'met went to the King himself," Belster replied, indicating the tall black man.

Roger regarded Belster's friend, whom he had just met.

"I believe the King to be sympathetic," Al'u'met said, "but he'll not go against the Father Abbot. Our friends will find no help from the Crown."

"They are doomed," Belster added.

"We have to get them out," Roger said determinedly, but his tone did little to bolster the confidence of his companions.

"If we gathered every ally and convinced them of our cause, and went unified against St. Precious, we would all be dead on the street within a matter of moments," Al'u'met answered. "You make the same mistake as Jilseponie, I fear. You believe that we can fight openly against the Church, but that, my friend, will bring nothing but disaster."

"Are we to let them die?" Roger asked, aiming the painful question at Belster.

"If we get ourselves killed trying to help them, then know that they will feel their own deaths far more painfully," the innkeeper replied.

"Their fates are not sealed," Roger growled. "I came into Palmaris beside Belli'mar Juraviel. He'll not stand idly by while his friends are murdered!"

The name of Juraviel did bring a glimmer of hope to Belster's sad eyes. The innkeeper looked to Al'u'met. "Juraviel of the Touel'alfar," he explained, "an elf friend of Nightbird and Pony."

"Elf," Al'u'met echoed, and he, too, managed a slightly hopeful smile. Captain Al'u'met knew Juraviel, or had seen the elf with Elbryan, Pony, and Bradwarden, when he'd ferried them across the Masur Delaval. The captain did not understand the Touel'alfar, knew practically nothing about them other than Juraviel's appearance, but from Roger's determination and Belster's somewhat hopeful smile, he, too, dared to hope that perhaps all was not lost.

At the same time as the meeting in the hold of the *Saudi Jacintha,* Belli'mar Juraviel made his way along the corridors of the house of Crump. Juraviel had taken the same secret route into the place Dasslerond had used to meet with the King; and when he had first entered, the elf had considered going to speak privately with King Danube.

But that he could not do, he realized, for the lady had forbade him to interfere. Still, feeling that he had to do something for his friends, the elf had not left the place, but had slipped down into the bowels of the old house. An elvish trick got him by the half-asleep guards, and his size allowed him to fit through a fireplace and into the chimney network, moving to the musty cellar and large room where Colleen, Shamus, and the other soldiers were being held.

They milled about the cellar unchained, but unarmed, with no chance of escape. A single stairway led to the one heavy door above, and that, Juraviel knew, was heavily barred.

The elf stayed out of sight for some time, listening, taking a measure of the group, particularly of Colleen, whom he had learned had been a companion of Pony. The other soldiers knew of Tiel'marawee, so, trusting their reaction, Juraviel came out of the chimney, announcing his presence quietly.

"I am Belli'mar Juraviel," he explained, "a friend of Nightbird, and," he added, looking Colleen in the eye, "of Pony."

The soldiers scrambled to encircle the elf.

"Have ye seen her?" Colleen asked him. The woman was the most unnerved of the group, for though she had heard much of the Touel'alfar—of Juraviel, in fact—she had never before seen an elf.

"Or Nightbird?" Shamus added. "How fares Nightbird?"

"They are in St. Precious," Juraviel explained. "And there I have not yet dared to venture. I fear the power of the monks and their gemstones."

"There is no one to trust," Shamus said gravely. "For those who believe in us have not the power, nor the courage, to stand with us. I only hope that King Danube will let me speak before passing judgment over me and my men, and I trust that he shall. But for Nightbird and Pony and the others in the clutches of Father Abbot Markwart, alas!"

"Then speak your words as loudly as you are allowed," Juraviel insisted. "For even if they will not help our friends, they will assure that Nightbird and Pony have not died in vain."

"Tell him of the miracle," another soldier prompted, and Shamus Kilronney recounted the tale of the goblin battle atop Mount Aida, the same story Roger had told the elf on their journey to Palmaris.

"Keep well that tale," Juraviel replied, and, hearing some noise outside, he turned back for the fireplace. Colleen Kilronney went with him.

"Brother Talumus," she whispered as the elf slipped into the chimney, "a monk of St. Precious. He is a friend, perhaps."

The conversation ended before she could give a proper description, for the door banged open and a host of Allheart soldiers came down the stairs, bearing trays of food.

*   *   *

By the time Roger found Juraviel in the alley near the Fellowship Way, the elf had already visited St. Precious, though he had not ventured in and had not found Brother Talumus. The two went back to the *Saudi Jacintha*, and Belster O'Comely assured them both that finding the monk would not be difficult. The innkeeper added a stern warning, though, that if this Abellican monk learned too much about them and could not be trusted, he would not be allowed to leave.

The very next night, Roger met with Brother Talumus, with Juraviel joining the conversation from the shadows at the sides of the alley. Again the monk showed his reluctance to take any overt action against the Church, though he admitted his uneasiness with the trial and expected executions, even going so far as to declare the Father Abbot wrong on this issue when prodded hard enough by Juraviel.

"Then make a difference," the elf demanded. "Find a way to help us. If we are caught, then your name will not be uttered, I assure you. If we succeed, or if we do not, Brother Talumus can sleep with conscience clear."

"You speak fine words," the monk replied, peering into the shadows, though he could not get a glimpse of the elusive Juraviel. "Yet you misunderstand me. You think that I am afraid for my own life, but that is not the case. What I fear is doing harm to my Church, for that I cannot tolerate. I am not the only one who believes that this situation has become terrible, and hardly godly. At least one master—" The monk stopped abruptly, and it was obvious that he did not want to break a confidence.

"You do not wish to harm your Church," Juraviel said from the shadows. "Yet, how will aiding innocents bring such harm? If the Church is worth following, then should not such an action strengthen it?"

"You twist my words," Talumus argued, but he was clearly coming to understand that he could not sit back and let these terrible executions happen.

By the time he left the alley, the plan had been formed.

But by the time Brother Talumus walked in through the great doors of St. Precious Abbey, he knew that he would not have the strength to see it through. Wracked with guilt, the confused young man went to the only superior he felt he could trust, seeking the blessing of Penitence, betraying himself, and, at gentle prodding, his friends.

Brother Talumus felt better when he left that meeting, but the master who had bestowed the blessing, Master Theorelle Engress, surely did not. For the second time in a few short months, Engress had heard a story of conspiracy and complicity, a tearing of heart against Markwart-directed precept, of conscience against rank. For many weeks, the gentle master had sat back and watched as the Father Abbot had taken the Church in a new, dominating direction, rolling roughshod over anyone who stood in his way. Now they were approaching the pinnacle of that Church ascent, and that height would be reached on top of the bodies of innocents.

Engress had heard enough. He went back to Brother Talumus that same night, and the younger man was surprised by what the aged master had in mind.

"He offered amnesty to Castinagis, Dellman, and Viscenti if they would speak against you at your trial," Brother Braumin told Elbryan that same night, the monk returned to his cell after the swift and brutal interrogation by Markwart.

"And what of Brother Braumin?" the ranger asked.

"No amnesty," the monk replied, and to Elbryan, his voice did not sound heavy. "I will confess and implicate you, Pony, and Bradwarden, because I will be tortured until I do so. But no matter what I say, I will die right after you three are convicted. Markwart did offer me a quick death if I spoke against you, but nothing more."

The ranger pitied the man, though he understood that his own end would be just as terrible.

"But all three have vowed not to speak against you," Brother Braumin added firmly. "They understand, as do I, as did Jojonah, that to deny our cause and our beliefs is to strengthen Markwart."

"The alternative for those three is death," the ranger reminded. "Yet they can save their lives with a few words."

"We all die, Nightbird," the monk replied calmly, "every man and every woman. Better to die young, with principles intact, than to live out a life that is a lie. What guilt would a man who goes so directly against his heart have to carry through the years? What life worth living might he find? You must understand the process of becoming an Abellican monk, the dedication and the faith. No man who fears death could have ever walked through the gates of St.-Mere-Abelle in the robes of an Abellican initiate."

The ranger took comfort in that. It pained him that these brothers would die, as they were all pained by the glorious death of Brother Mullahy, and yet he, and they, understood that holding fast to their principles was by far the nobler course.

The conversation ended abruptly as footsteps sounded in the hall, followed by a jingling at Elbryan's door, as if someone was fiddling with keys. After several moments, the door finally opened, and the ranger was surprised to see only a single Abellican monk—usually they sent three.

The ranger used the wall for support as he stood up on shaky legs. He considered attacking, but since the monk's cowl was pulled low, hiding his face, he feared that this might be De'Unnero, come, perhaps, to challenge him once again.

And then Elbryan nearly fell over, for Roger Lockless pulled back the cowl, smiling widely. "I know," he apologized. "I should have arrived more quickly. But there were complications."

Elbryan hit him with a bear hug that nearly sent them both to the floor. "How?" the ranger asked.

"I had to wait for these," Roger replied, opening his robe. There, hanging from the man's belt, hung Pony's pouch of gemstones. "Fortunately, they kept much of the evidence together," Roger explained. "Juraviel is outside waiting for us, though he is troubled since we were not yet able to find the elven sword and bow."

Another man entered the corridor then, a high-ranking Abellican master, judging from the golden belt tied about his brown robe. His face was wrinkled and old, his eyes soft.

"Gather your friends and be out quickly," he said to Elbryan. "Run away as far as your horses will carry you, though I fear that even that distance will not prove far enough."

"Who are you?" the ranger replied. "How is this possible?"

"Master Engress," Roger explained as he began sorting through the huge ring of keys before on Braumin's door. "A friend."

"A friend who will run to the north with us," Elbryan decided, but the old man laughed at the notion before the ranger even finished.

"I will be caught, and will not deny my role in your escape," Engress explained. "I am old and near death anyway. To give my life so that seven others, younger and more deserving of their futures than I, might live, is no cause for sadness."

Elbryan still did not understand, but he had no time to question him further, for Roger had Braumin free and moved to the next door. More important, the ranger heard a voice from the end of the corridor that he could not ignore. He sprinted to Pony's door, running his hands over, testing it to see if he could simply pull it from its hinges. Roger saw him and came to that door next. A moment later the lovers were reunited, in each others' arms for the first time in what seemed like years. Elbryan crushed her against him, whispering in her ear for her to be quiet, that everything was now all right.

Of course, that was far from the truth, but soon after, Roger and the others joined Juraviel in the alley outside of St. Precious and ran off into the darkness.

Friends met them in the alleys and separated them, for Bradwarden could not possibly get through the submerged cave openings. Elbryan suggested they go right out then, all of them, to the wilds of the north. That was not possible, the scouts responded, since the Allheart soldiers and a host of monks were guarding the northern wall.

It was too close to dawn to hope for an escape from the city now, and besides, word would spread quickly from St. Precious of their escape. Better to hide the fugitives until a clearer route out of the city could be discerned.

Elbryan, Pony, and the four monks were in the secret caverns along the banks of the Masur Delaval soon after dawn.

By that time, soldiers and monks charged along the city's streets in frantic search, the soldiers led by Duke Kalas, as eager to capture the fugitives as the monks, with Kalas planning that if his soldiers did find them, they would be brought to the house of Crump and not to St. Precious.

"Strike me dead," Master Engress said to Markwart, holding his arms out wide in absolute submission. "I could not allow this, Dalebert Markwart. I watched you burn Jojonah and unjustly proclaim Avelyn a heretic—"

The words caught in the old man's throat as Markwart's spirit surged through the hematite and grabbed him.

Engress went down to his knees but managed somehow to speak once more. "Avelyn destroyed Bestesbulzibar," he gasped. "They are not criminals."

And then he died on the floor of Chasewind Manor, murdered by Markwart as abbots De'Unnero and Je'howith, Bishop Francis, and several other monks—including a very afraid Brother Talumus—looked on.

But Engress had died contented. He had gone straight to the outraged Markwart and admitted his crime, and then had goaded the old man so that Markwart would kill him quickly, before the Father Abbot could learn that Brother Talumus, too, had played a role in the escape.

CHAPTER

❖ 39 ❖

A Clash of Philosophy

The cave was comfortable, with enough ventilation for several small fires, though the only exit large enough for a person was through water. Those fires were needed, to take the chill out of bones and the wetness from clothes soaked in the cold waters of the Masur Delaval.

Elbryan huddled under a blanket with Pony all through the night, holding her, reminding her how much he loved her, and trying with all his heart to make her understand that he held no anger toward her for her decision to leave him, and certainly did not blame her for the loss of their child.

Every time he mentioned that child, he felt Pony stiffen, felt tension surge through her otherwise weary limbs.

None in the cave got much sleep, though they had no way of knowing what time of day or night it was. For light, they remained wholly dependent on the fires—which were burning low since they had not much fuel and had to conserve it. They did not know how long they would have to remain in the cave.

Elbryan woke first and lay still, staring at Pony. She seemed so gentle in slumber, the beautiful young woman he had first kissed on the north slope of Dundalis, on the day the goblins had come, the day that both of them had been orphaned. He remembered the first time he had seen her again after their long separation, when she had gone with Avelyn back to Dundalis.

She seemed no less beautiful to him now, and that amazed him when he considered all the trials and tragedy they had witnessed, all the losses that Pony, in particular, had suffered. He reached to stroke that smooth face, and Pony opened a sleepy eye to regard him. Elbryan rolled toward her, meaning to embrace her, but she sat up suddenly and Elbryan felt her arm muscles tighten.

"Let go of your anger," he bade her softly.

Pony looked at him as if he had just betrayed her.

"The fight is ended for this day," the ranger tried to explain. "We will steal away—"

"No," Pony interrupted, shaking her head.

"We cannot possibly win."

"Perhaps I do not need to win," Pony replied with such coldness as to give the ranger pause. He shook his head and moved to hug her once more, but again she pushed him away.

"I had a child within me," she explained. "Your child, our child. And he took it. Markwart murdered our child, as he murdered my parents."

Brother Braumin crawled over to the couple then, and Elbryan and Pony realized that the others had been listening.

"Come with me," Braumin offered to Pony, holding out his hand. "I will bestow upon you the blessing of Communal Prayer, that you might find contentment."

Pony shrank from that offered hand and stared at the monk incredulously. "Markwart," she said, "the Father Abbot of your Church murdered my baby, my innocent child, within my womb."

"He is not my Father Abbot," Brother Braumin tried to explain, but Pony, so full of venom, wasn't listening.

"You do not understand the depth of his evil," she went on. "I have felt such a presence once before, in the bowels of a mountain far to the north, the same mountain where Markwart took you all as his prisoners."

She looked at Elbryan, who seemed surprised. "Yes," she said, nodding. "He is as strong and as wicked as ever was Bestesbulzibar."

"He is a man," Brother Braumin reasoned.

"Much more than a man!" Pony snapped back. "Much more, I say. And as Avelyn went into the darkness of Aida to battle the demon dactyl, though he believed that he could not win, so shall I battle Markwart once more, to repay him for his crimes against my child and to rid the world of his vile presence."

"But another day," the ranger insisted, "a day when he is not prepared to battle against us. When he is not surrounded by De'Unnero and the host of monks, by the King and the Allheart Brigade."

Pony eyed him unblinking, but did not respond. The group all sat quiet as the morning—if it was morning—passed. Elbryan stayed near Pony, but he did not question her further. He had never seen her this angry, not even after the rescue of Bradwarden at the end of the last summer, when she had tried to turn back and storm into St.-Mere-Abelle. All he could do to help her now was to support and to trust her, and to try, desperately, to keep her as far away as possible from the unbeatable enemies they had made.

That task seemed more difficult when a Behrenese man surfaced in the cave later that morning. "They are tearing the city apart," he gasped, crawling out of the cold water to the stone floor. "The *Saudi Jacintha* fled from port, but a host of warships overtook her and destroyed her sails, then dragged her back in. Captain Al'u'met and many of my people have been taken prisoner."

"By King or Church?" Elbryan asked, and the dark-skinned man stared at him as if he did not understand the significance of the question.

"The warships were of King Danube's fleet," the man replied. "But the monks, too, have dragged many from the streets. And it was a host of monks . . ." The man paused and turned a sympathetic look over Pony, something that the others did not miss.

"Your little friend told us," the man stammered.

"Told you what?" Pony demanded angrily.

"The tavern where you lived," the Behrenese man explained. "It was burned to the ground. Even now they sift through its ashes."

Pony closed her eyes, a low sound—both growl and groan—escaping her lips.

"What of Belster?" Elbryan asked with concern.

"He is in hiding," the man replied, "beside the others from the place. But they fear, we all fear, that they will soon be caught."

"Bring him here," Brother Braumin said, trying hard to help.

"We cannot," the dark-skinned man explained. "It was dangerous even for me to come to you, for the soldiers and monks are everywhere. We must advise you to flee, however you may. They have taken many folk, and it is rumored that the secret of the caves may have already been given to one of the interrogating jailors. Beware of visitors," he added grimly. "And not just visitors in the flesh, for the monks with their evil magic are sending their *chezchus* . . ." He paused, searching for the right translation of the yatol term. "Their spirits?" he asked.

Pony nodded. "They are spirit-walking," she explained.

"Through walls," the Behrenese man explained. "No one is safe!"

"We must get out," Brother Castinagis reasoned.

"But the city is no doubt buttoned down," Brother Dellman replied.

"All the wall is patrolled by monks and soldiers, hundreds of soldiers," the Behrenese man agreed.

"The river then," the ranger remarked. "In the dark of night, we will leave the cave, but stay in the water, floating, swimming, downstream, and hope to climb to a bank far to the south of Palmaris."

"The river, too, is heavily guarded," the Behrenese man warned. "The King's warships are all about."

"They'll not see a head bobbing in the nighttime water," Elbryan replied. "And what of you? Are you to leave us again? Do you have anywhere to run?"

The man bowed, recognizing and appreciating the ranger's offer that he remain with them. "My duty is to my people," he explained. "I came only to warn you. The sun is past its zenith, though not yet halfway to the west. May Chezru go with you."

Even the Abellican monks, men who denied the yatol interpretation of Chezru as God, accepted the spirit of that blessing with gratitude.

"Tell Belster of our plan," Elbryan instructed the man, "and inform our friends, the small man and his smaller companion, if you can get word to them."

The man nodded, and dove back into the water.

If the mood in the cave that morning had been somber, it was worse now, with hope fading fast. Now they had to accept, every one of them, that their defiance of Markwart was costing many other citizens of Palmaris dearly.

Elbryan kept watch over Pony, who would not sit still. She reached for the pouch of gemstones; the ranger moved to intercept, but the glare Pony put over him backed his hand away.

Pony pulled open the pouch and dumped the stones on the blanket in front of her. They were all there, she recognized soon enough—even the magnetite she had fired through Markwart's ugly face. As Roger had said, they had kept all the evidence together.

She scooped the soul stone into her hand, clenching her fist tight as the ranger's hand came over to grab at it. He got her by the wrist instead, holding her firmly and moving around to face her directly.

"Where do you intend to fly?" he asked.

"Where is the dog Markwart?" she replied coldly.

"You would go to him now, with all of us trapped in this place?" the ranger asked. "If he follows you back, then the rest of us will pay for your risk."

Pony unclenched her fist and let the stone fall to the blanket, defeated. "I could go out carefully and scout," she offered as Elbryan began scooping the stones back into the pouch, the ranger shaking his head before she finished.

So they sat quietly. The monks formed a circle and began to pray, and asked if Elbryan and Pony wanted to join. The ranger turned a hopeful look over Pony, thinking that prayer might be just what she needed, but she shook her head and turned away.

Elbryan waited a while, let the rhythmic, soothing chanting fill the small cave, then moved again in front of his wife, drawing her gaze with an unthreatening, disarming, and amazingly peaceful grin. "Have I told you of Avelyn's miracle?" he asked calmly.

The woman nodded; it had been all the talk along their corridor of cells.

"Not just what happened," the ranger explained, "but how it happened. How the spirit of our dear friend came to me on that plateau, bringing comfort and peace."

Pony matched his smile with a wry grin. "Where was he when Markwart came?" she asked sarcastically.

Elbryan let it roll off his strong shoulders, reminding himself of the depth of her pain. He started to recount the story of the goblin fight again, offering insights at every critical point, and hinting that those insights had been inspired by Avelyn. He knew that any reminder of the times before their first journey to Mount Aida, when their lives seemed so much simpler, their common purpose so visible, would help to bring her to a better emotional place.

It seemed to be working, and Pony even managed a smile, but then the water churned and Roger Lockless appeared.

"You should not be here!" the ranger scolded, moving to pull his friend from the water. "I told you to distance yourself—"

"At the price of friendship, I had to come," Roger retorted. "For Juraviel told me that you are found, that Markwart knows of the caves, and even as we speak, a force begins its march to the Masur Delaval!"

Everyone in the cave started scrambling, gathering their belongings, stripping their clothes and tying them in tight bundles.

"Get out! Get out!" Roger cried frantically. "And be quick!"

"The path leads to the north, but that is not our course," Elbryan instructed them all. "Stay low in the water and go the other way, along the bank to the south. Hug the rocks, use them to hide, and be quiet!"

Into the water went Braumin, then, one after another, Viscenti, Castinagis, and Dellman. In went Roger, after grabbing Elbryan's wrist and squeezing tightly.

"I love you," Elbryan said to Pony as she moved by him to the water's edge.

She looked back at him and managed a warm smile. "I know," she replied, and in she went.

Following the guide ropes set by the Behrenese, the seven had no trouble navigating the cave entrance and getting out into the open waters of the Masur Delaval. The first out, Braumin and Viscenti, started south as the ranger had instructed, with the other two monks and Roger following closely.

When Pony surfaced, however, she did not stop at the water's edge, but continued up, moving right out of the water, floating up the side of the cliff face, using her free hand to guide her.

As soon as Elbryan broke the surface, he understood. The woman had called upon her malachite gemstone. The woman was going after Markwart!

"Pony!" he called, but she did not look back.

Elbryan scrambled for the bank and pulled himself from the water, rushing to dress. Roger and the monks came out behind him.

"Go, go!" Elbryan bade them. "Flee to safety and bear witness."

But none of them listened. The ranger had to go after Pony out of love, and the others were similarly bound to both of them.

Pony got to the cliff top, in almost exactly the same spot along the fence where she had battled the Behrenese scouts. She paused long enough to dress, to sort through her gemstones, and to consider the daunting road before her. She knew that Markwart would be at Chasewind Manor— the man hadn't gone to St. Precious in all the time Pony had been in Palmaris—and she knew the way to the Bildeborough house. But it was evident, even from this remote corner of the city, that her path would not be clear. She could hear the commotion in the town, the thunder of hooves, the screams, and she saw plumes of black smoke wafting in the evening air.

Pony looked west across the town, to the sun hanging low in the sky. Dusk was settling over the city, but it was still too light for her to pass unseen. Yet she could not wait for night.

But how? she wondered, looking again to her gemstones. Perhaps she should go after Markwart spiritually, with the hematite.

Pony glanced back down the cliff, to see Elbryan and the others already moving off the riverbank, and knew that she could not leave her corporeal form so vulnerable to friend and foe alike. Her gaze focused on the lodestone, the magnetite, the stone she had used against Markwart, the damning piece of evidence that would surely seal her doom should she ever go to trial.

She remembered what Bradwarden had hinted about that particular gem, about another use for its metal-attracting properties. She considered her diamond, which she could use to bring forth brilliant light, but could also use, she had learned in a battle at Caer Tinella, to create an absence of light.

The woman clenched the lodestone in one hand, ruby, serpentine, graphite, malachite, and hematite in the other and began her determined march, not moving from shadow to shadow, behind the cover of buildings, but walking straight and proud in open defiance.

The path was not straight for Elbryan and the others, for the streets, right down to the wharves, bustled with mounted soldiers, and more than two dozen Ursal warships, fully crewed, were tied to the piers.

They went from shadow to shadow, as swiftly as the ranger could manage. Roger rushed out to the side, motioning to Elbryan that he would scout the flank, and on they ran. They found allies, Prim O'Bryen among them, who bade Elbryan follow him to a safe place, but the ranger ran on, and the monks did not hesitate to follow.

Soon others were running, too, in the same general direction. Belster, and Prim, Heathcomb Mallory and Dainsey Aucomb, and many others, allies of Elbryan and Pony, or allies of Markwart, and even those neutral in the war who were, merely curious about the moving crowd.

As soon as she came into the city, just west of the docks, Pony found Allheart soldiers all about her. She kept her determined course, trying to

appear inconspicuous, for, given the chaos of the day, the burning of buildings and the rousting of innocents from their homes, the streets were fairly
packed with peasants rushing this way and that.

But she was seen and recognized, and the call went up.

Pony found her concentration, found her rage, and launched it furiously
into the lodestone.

She reversed the magic, as she had done with the diamond in Caer
Tinella that night long ago, thus instead of focusing the attraction powers of
the stone upon a single item, as she had done with Markwart's tooth, she
sent out a general repellent power. Though she understood the magnitude
of the energy she was sending into the stone, she had no idea of how strong
the force might be until a pair of Allheart riders charged to block her path.
Twenty feet away, their horses started to skitter and buck, then began
sliding backward! The riders, eyes wide with confusion, jerked weirdly,
grabbing tightly to the reins before they went flying away.

Vendors' carts uprighted, metal-handled doors flew open—flew in, even
if they were hinged to open out—and within the houses she heard the surprised cries of women, their pans flying about wildly.

It became insane, out of control. More soldiers approached, some running, others riding. More soldiers went flying away. More horses skidded
backward, some falling over, then sliding away on their sides.

Pony held to her focus, thought of her dead parents, of her dead child.
She started to run, bowing her head, watching only the clearing path before
her and trying hard to block out the sounds of confusion and destruction
behind.

"Chaos, my King! Chaos!" the soldier cried, stumbling into the room
where Danube and Constance quietly talked.

Duke Kalas rushed in on the messenger's heels.

"It is the woman, Jilseponie," the frantic soldier explained. "She moves
openly through the streets with a power we do not understand, throwing us
away before we can get near her!"

"Through the streets?" the King echoed. "Heading where?"

"Across the city to the west," the man cried. "Toward you, my King!"

Kalas started to cry out, but Danube cut him short, holding up his hand
and shaking his head.

"To Chasewind Manor, more likely," Constance reasoned.

"She is after Markwart," the King agreed. "Prepare my carriage."

Constance tried to tell the King that he should remain protected. But
Danube, like so many others in Palmaris that late afternoon, recognized
that something momentous had begun here, and he would not be denied.

From the high wall encircling St. Precious' roof, Brother Talumus
watched the commotion with mounting horror. He spotted Jilseponie

moving determinedly along a distant street; he saw a pair of soldiers, and then a monk, go flying away from her as if they had stepped into a hurricane.

The level of magic awed him. He wondered what he had done in going to Master Engress, in beginning the course that had led to freedom for this one and her dangerous companions. They were supposed to run away, into hiding in deep mountain holes, never to be seen again.

But Talumus recognized that Jilseponie was not running away now, and knew instinctively where she was going.

Out from the abbey went Talumus and many other monks, running to the side of their Father Abbot.

In a darkened room deep within St. Precious, Belli'mar Juraviel kept his head down and waited for the tumult to subside. He had come in secretly, down an unused chimney, immediately after instructing Roger to go and warn their friends, thinking to rescue Tempest and Hawkwing, the elven weapons that did not belong in the hands of Markwart's Abellican Church.

He had hoped to meet his friends again, on the quiet fields north of the city. But in listening to the words of the scrambling monks that rushed outside the door of the small room, the elf knew that he would find no such enjoyment.

And now, worst of all, Juraviel had to sit quietly and wait until he could make his escape from the fortified abbey.

At an intersection not far from the abbey, Brother Talumus and his group found another band of monks running their way. De'Unnero and some of the monks from St.-Mere-Abelle had gone out to the fields north of Palmaris to search for signs of the escaped prisoners, and they, like everyone else in the city, it seemed, had come to learn of the brewing disaster.

"It is the woman," Talumus explained as the abbot ran to him.

De'Unnero considered the commotion all about him, the pointing fingers, the rushing soldiers and peasants, and turned west, toward the wealthier section of Palmaris, toward Chasewind Manor, and ran off at full speed.

And all the city swirled behind him, behind Pony, moving to converge on the great manor that used to house their beloved Baron and now held the dignitaries of the Abellican Church.

Too many soldiers and too many monks. They had not even reached the merchant section when a cry rang out and a host of monks charged at them. The group split apart on the ranger's orders. Brother Castinagis was caught almost immediately, though he put up a terrific fight and managed to drop two monks to the ground before being pulled down.

Brother Viscenti, surrounded, weapons leveled his way, threw up his hands in surrender, and then Braumin went down, offering no resistance other than begging his fellow monks to bear witness to this, to learn the truth of Markwart.

A monk leaped in front of Nightbird, dropping into a sudden crouch and spinning, leg flying high.

The ranger ducked and hit the foolish monk with a punch in the chest that seemed almost to break the man in half, and sent him shuddering down to the ground.

Another monk leaped in from the side, flying for the ranger's head. Nightbird caught him in midair and used his momentum to throw him far to the side, crashing into a vendor's cart of fish.

On ran the ranger, pained to see his friends pulled down behind him. Only Dellman was still running, and then he, too, was stopped, surrendering at the point of an Allheart soldier's spear.

Nightbird heard the clamor of horses coming down a side street and, fearing a patrol of soldiers, swerved aside down an alley.

But then he heard Roger's cry for him to come back, and he spotted his friend waving to him from a rooftop.

The horses were riderless, a stampede that seemed almost fitting in the wildness of the moment. Nightbird motioned to Roger, then ran to catch a horse.

"Oh, but I'd be a better ride than that old nag!" came a familiar, most-welcomed voice, and Nightbird focused on the sound just as Bradwarden threw the blanket from his telltale human torso, revealing himself.

He thundered by, and the ranger leaped atop his back.

"Chasewind Manor!" the ranger yelled.

"Ye think I'm not knowin'?" the centaur yelled back. "Even the damned horses knew!"

The gates of Chasewind Manor were closed and chained—the great metal gates of Chasewind Manor.

Pony winced, for a monk moved right behind them as she neared, and when her repelling magic blew the gates wide, snapping the chain, the poor man got smashed hard and thrown backward.

He lay on the ground, groaning, as Pony strode by.

Three others came out to face her. The first held a metal-tipped spear, which promptly snapped back into his face, dropping him straight to the ground, and then flying away as if it had been launched by the mightiest of ballistae. The second monk, having the misfortune of wearing a metal ring, assumed a fighting stance, then flailed wildly as he followed the spear.

But the third carried no metal and held his ground—until grim-faced Pony calmly held out her other hand and laid him low with a stroke of lightning.

Inside the great house, Bishop Francis and Abbot Je'howith scrambled to warn the Father Abbot. They found him sitting comfortably in his throne in the great audience hall.

They tried to tell him to flee.

Markwart, who wanted this confrontation as much as Pony wanted it, laughed at them. "Hinder her not," he instructed. "And know that when this day is through, our power will be even greater in Honce-the-Bear. Begone!"

The two monks, confused and frightened, glanced nervously at each other and ran off.

The King's carriage, surrounded by Allheart horsemen, thundered through the blasted gate just as Pony entered the house.

"There!" Duke Kalas cried to his soldiers, pointing to the woman. "Stop her!"

"No!" the King countermanded, and then he motioned for Kalas to sit beside him. "Let us see how this plays out," Danube explained to the surprised Duke. "This has been Markwart's fight from the beginning."

More soldiers, more monks, and even common folk, rushed into the courtyard.

"To the wall!" came the cry of a soldier, and all eyes turned to see the huge centaur crash through the hedge at the top of the eight-foot wall. Bradwarden could not make the leap cleanly, though he managed to get his forelegs and the bulk of his torso over the barrier before crashing. Then he and his rider rolled over, falling to the ground, Nightbird kicking far away from the tumbling centaur.

"Oh, but that hurt," Bradwarden groaned, struggling to rise. Nightbird started for him, but the centaur, seeing soldiers and monks closing fast, waved him away. "Go to her!" he cried.

Nightbird turned to face a soldier charging in with sword raised overhead, meaning to cleave the ranger's head in half.

Up came Nightbird's crossed arms, and he stepped forward, catching the man's hands on the downswing. He let the sword descend a bit lower, then threw it up high, punching the soldier in the face. Then he grabbed the man's arms and pulled the sword down again, knifing his hand between the soldier's hands, taking his sword. In the same devastating, brutally efficient movement, the ranger's free hand smashed the man on the side of the face and launched him sidelong to the ground.

Now Nightbird had a sword, and the door of the great house was in sight. But a dozen soldiers and twice that number of monks moved to block his path.

"Let him pass!" King Danube cried, standing tall in his carriage. Neither monk nor soldier dared to go against the man, their ranks parting as the ranger charged.

"Only him!" Danube called. "Ring the house and let no others enter!"

"You take a great chance," Constance remarked.

The look Danube gave her and Kalas was one of the coldest either of them had ever seen. "Damn Markwart," Danube quietly spat. "May Nightbird and Pony emerge as victors with the Father Abbot's head in hand."

Constance's eyes widened at the bold declaration, but Duke Kalas smiled and had to fight hard to stop himself from wrapping his King in a great hug.

Nightbird reached the door just as Je'howith and Francis came out. Francis moved to grab the ranger—and was promptly launched aside by a mighty punch, one that put him on his back on the grass.

Old Abbot Je'howith put up his hands and stepped aside.

"Ever the diplomat," King Danube remarked dryly.

The crowd converged on Chasewind Manor from every section of Palmaris, wealthy merchants and lowly peasants; a crowd of St. Precious' monks, confused and some crying; even a gathering of Behrenese, chanting loudly for the release of Captain Al'u'met.

Duke Kalas moved his forces, soldiers and monks alike, into defensive formations, holding back the crowd. The Duke understood that this whole situation could explode into a riot. In that case, he informed his soldiers, the safety of the King was paramount, no matter who had to be trampled into the dirt.

For the most part, the crowd stayed back, though the yells intensified. One man, an Abellican monk, did run through the line of soldiers, sprinting for the manor house.

The soldiers stopped him before he reached the doors.

"Do you know who I am?" the monk cried

The nervous soldiers did indeed recognize the former bishop, and they glanced nervously at Kalas, who was far to the side. Despite De'Unnero's insistence and bullying, though, the Duke shook his head and the soldiers held their ground.

De'Unnero turned toward the King's carriage. "I demand—" he began.

"You demand nothing of me," King Danube cut him short. "Hold the house secure!" he cried to the soldiers. "None are to enter!"

De'Unnero broke away, sprinting for the door. When soldiers beat him to the mark, he continued his run around the front of the house, then along the side.

Duke Kalas instructed several men to follow, but he wasn't concerned, for Chasewind Manor had only two doors, the great front entrance and a smaller way in, also heavily guarded, on the side of the house opposite where the former Bishop had run.

Frustrated, De'Unnero ran frantically around to the back. Then he skidded to a stop looking up at the one window large enough to accommodate a man.

But that window was thirty feet off the ground.

In front of the house, Brother Braumin and the other three monk prisoners were dragged through the gates by Allheart soldiers. Kalas ordered the men to take them away to a prison, but Danube overruled him.

"Let them stay," the King decided. "This may well determine their fate. Keep them secure, but allow them to bear witness."

Another man slipped onto the lawn as well, easily blending in with the crowd. Roger spotted Bradwarden immediately, the centaur standing but obviously wounded, held steady between two mounted Allheart soldiers.

Roger felt as trapped as his friend, for there seemed no way in. All he could do was stand and watch.

Once inside the manor house, the ranger had little trouble following Pony, for she had left a trail of devastation: twisted metal, blasted doors, shattered glass, and more than one groaning monk.

He went down the corridor into a great, pillared hall and up a wide, sweeping staircase. Then down another narrow hall and into the most decorated corridor in all the house. And at the far end of the long corridor, he spied a door, carved and decorated, and he knew without doubt that Pony was behind that portal.

And so was Markwart.

The soldiers came around the back corner, calling to the monk to stand his ground.

De'Unnero ignored them, and transformed his lower torso into the shape of the tiger. He glanced at the soldiers and snarled, and the men fell all over one another trying to keep back.

De'Unnero looked to the window. "You cannot escape," he heard one soldier say, and then he was flying, up, up.

On Nightbird ran, along the huge, decorated window overlooking the back gardens, thinking to put his shoulder down and barrel right into the room. But then he fell aside with a surprised cry as the window crashed in, De'Unnero, bursting into the hall.

In the blink of an eye, the two men faced off.

"So I get my wish," the former Bishop purred.

There he sat, so smug in his great chair, the embodiment of everything Pony hated, of everything she considered evil in humankind.

"Clever of you to get out of St. Precious," Markwart congratulated. "Master Engress died for that."

"You intend to kill everybody who opposes you," she replied, "destroy them all."

"If I must," said Markwart, leaning forward suddenly in his chair. "Because I am right, you fool. I speak to God."

"You speak to Bestesbulzibar, none other!" Pony snapped back, advancing undaunted. She lifted her arm, hematite in hand, and went into the stone eagerly, all her hatred leading the way.

But the spirit of Markwart was waiting for her, and though she hit it with all the momentum of her emotions behind her, managed to push the spirit back toward the physical form, it was but a temporary advantage.

Markwart, so powerful, held her at bay, retaliating with the power of a demon.

Nightbird knew the danger of De'Unnero, knew that he had to fight a long and progressive dance, gaining one tiny advantage at a time. From their previous battle, he understood that De'Unnero was his equal, or near it, and that every movement must lead to something stronger, for this was a game of strategy, not a test of speed.

One tiny advantage gained, leading to the next.

And yet, how could the ranger endure such a prolonged, calculating dance when that ornate door at the end of the hall beckoned to him, when he knew Pony was beyond that portal, facing Markwart, a foe who had beaten her before? How could he wait?

He charged powerfully at De'Unnero, closing ground and thrusting ahead with the unbalanced sword he had taken from the guard outside.

De'Unnero leapt above and to the side, and came back at once, forcing the ranger to dodge, throwing himself against the wall for balance and swiping the sword harmlessly across.

"He is torturing her," the monk teased, coming at the ranger, then sliding to the side, keeping between Nightbird and the door.

Nightbird didn't take the bait. He came off the wall calmly, in full balance and control, reminding himself that he would do no good for Pony if he was lying dead out here. He skipped forward and stabbed, then fell back as De'Unnero, one arm now the arm of a tiger, countered with a sudden rush and swipe.

Forward came the ranger, but the monk had measured Nightbird's reach and was retreating cautiously before the sword could get anywhere near the mark.

And so it went, back and forth, with neither making any brazen offensive attacks and neither giving the other any opening.

But then, from within the room, Pony cried out.

De'Unnero's smile was wide as he turned his gaze from the ranger to consider the door.

Nightbird charged, stabbing and slashing.

And De'Unnero charged, feinting a leap then diving to the ground, a more comfortable approach for his tiger legs, skittering under the extended sword and smashing the side of the ranger's knee, claws hooking and tearing and throwing the man to the ground.

Nightbird rolled on his back and brought his sword up, forcing De'Unnero to skid to a sudden stop. The ranger used that break to roll backward, landing lightly on his feet and coming forward with two quick steps and a thrust to De'Unnero's shoulder. Had it been Tempest in the ranger's hand, the blade would have slashed right through, tearing muscle and splitting bone. But this sword nicked away.

Still, the monk reeled with the pain and fell back, clutching at his human arm with his tiger paw.

On came Nightbird, perfectly balanced. But he did not appreciate the true power of those feline legs. De'Unnero stumbled backward, then dug in his claws quickly—and launched himself at the ranger. He caught him between sword thrusts, slapped the blade aside, and drove on, slamming into him, locking Nightbird's arms at his sides in a powerful hug.

And that hug was all the more deadly since one of the monk's hands carried the daggerlike claws of a great cat.

Nightbird felt those claws digging into his back, near his kidney. With a great burst of strength, he believed that he could break the hold, but he recognized that in doing so, De'Unnero's tiger paw would tear half his back away! He dropped his sword and squirmed to get one hand up under the tight hold.

De'Unnero clenched all the tighter, claws extending, stabbing deep holes.

But Nightbird had his right arm under the tiger paw, and worked slowly with his superior strength to throw the monk off balance, to force De'Unnero to exert energy to keep his footing as well as his tight hold.

Now the ranger flexed his shoulders, weakening the monk's grasp. Ironcorded muscles stretched and pushed, the ranger moving himself so that his back followed the monk's tiger paw, while the human hand slipped farther and farther away.

Then he saw a change coming over the man's face, the transformation of his mouth into a great fanged maw.

Nightbird snapped his head forward suddenly, brutally smashing the monk's nose even as it elongated. He hammered his forehead in again, and then, knowing he was out of time, feeling the monk's other hand, too, becoming a clawed paw, he roared and threw his arms wide, accepting the agony as De'Unnero's claws scored deep lines across the side of his lower back, slashing all the way around to the side of Nightbird's rib cage.

The ranger's right hand slapped the changing face, while his other came in hard against De'Unnero's crotch. Grabbing a tight hold with both, screaming with every movement, the ranger spun, lifting De'Unnero from the ground, then slamming him hard against the wall. He pulled the monk back and slammed him again, and then a third time, despite De'Unnero's wildly slashing paws, one swipe of which caught the ranger on the side of the face, digging a line beside his eye.

Nightbird let the monk go with the third slam and launched a flurry of heavy punches, right and left repeatedly, to the monk's face and upper chest. Then he leaped back, paused, and lunged, forehead first, squarely into the middle of the monk's disfigured face.

De'Unnero's legs buckled, but the ranger wouldn't let it end so easily. One of his hands caught the chin, one the crotch, and up went the monk, high into the air. The ranger turned and rushed across the corridor, purposely aiming for a part of the great window the monk had not already broken, then heaved the dazed man through the glass to fall the thirty feet to the ground.

Lurching with pain, feeling his guts spilling out his side, Nightbird looked out the window and was satisfied when he saw that the dangerous creature lay still on the lawn, broken and bloody atop the sharp shards of glass.

Not even bothering to retrieve the sword, for he knew that such a weapon would be useless against Markwart—and knew, too, that his own strength was fast fading—Nightbird went for the door.

Their struggle, greater than on the darkened Palmaris field that terrible night, now became so intense that it transcended the spiritual, spilling over into the physical.

Outside the manor house, the crowd gasped as one and fell back, for the house thrummed with energy, lights flashing black and white, windows blowing out of their casings.

"Pray that Markwart does not emerge victorious," King Danube whispered to his two friends, and to Je'howith, who had moved near the carriage.

Kalas and Constance were already doing just that, and the old abbot, horrified by the spectacle before him, did not chastise the King.

Even Brother Francis, standing on the lawn, the closest man to the house, could only stare helplessly.

The door flew open and a pair of young monks staggered out, falling to the grass and crawling away, crying for mercy from God.

The stunned Francis did not dare to enter the place.

She had no child within her, no vulnerability, and so she fought with all her strength and all her rage.

But she could not win. Pony knew that. The spirit within Markwart was too strong, impossibly strong, and darker than anything she had ever known. She struggled valiantly, hit him with every ounce of energy and willpower she could muster, and held her ground as minute after minute slipped past.

The force of Markwart, surprised by the strength of the woman, came on and on, grew larger to tower over the woman's spirit, to engulf her as if to swallow her. Yet he could not, and so they struggled, and both of them knew that time worked against Pony, that she would tire first, despite her rage.

But then the woman felt a touch on her physical shoulder—and the temporary distraction sent Markwart's spirit driving her backward. It was a gentle touch, though, the stroke of a friend, of a lover, and then, somehow, a third spirit joined the pair, the specter of Nightbird, come to Pony's aid.

Both together then! Markwart telepathically imparted. *Better to be done with both of you, to be rid of the troublesome pair.* On he came, great bat-like wings sprouting from his spiritual shadow, rising up and towering over them.

Elbryan's spirit fell against Pony's, touching her, bonding in an embrace as intimate as any the couple had ever known.

On came Markwart. But now the two were one, linked spiritually as they had often used *bi'nelle dasada* to link physically. Together they stopped the progress of the Father Abbot, together they pushed the dark spirit back toward its host. Each inch of ground cost them dearly, ate at their life forces, drained energy.

They pushed on, the ranger taking the lead, putting his spirit against the strikes of Markwart, accepting the punishment, for Elbryan knew something that Pony did not, knew that his physical form was fast fading, his guts spilling, blood running. If he told her, or even let her know, she would rush from the fight and turn her attention with hematite to his wounds.

But Elbryan had known the sacrifice needed in coming into this battle, and he understood, too, that Pony could not afford such a retreat, that if she went to tend him, Markwart would destroy them both.

They were near Markwart now, and all three knew that to push the spirit back into its host, and then to follow it, meant victory. The Father Abbot dug in, roared at them telepathically and fought back.

Coldness engulfed the ranger's physical form. He felt it and understood what it foretold. This was the test of his faith, he knew, the test of all his training. This, the ultimate sacrifice, was what it meant to be a ranger.

By every instinct within him, he had to stop, had to tell Pony, had to live. He drove on instead.

Markwart screamed, telepathically and physically. Elbryan heard it, but it seemed distant.

All the world seemed distant.

To those outside, it ended as a great burst of black light, a great dark flash, and then the house went quiet. Francis rushed in, as did Danube and his advisers, Roger and Bradwarden, and none moved to stop them. Almost as an afterthought, standing at the entryway, King Danube looked back and called to his soldiers to bring the prisoner monks. "For their lives surely hang in the balance," he explained.

At the back of the house, Belli'mar Juraviel paused only for a moment to consider the broken form of De'Unnero, then flew up to the window and the great hallway.

Pony felt the spirit of Markwart break apart and knew the man was defeated. Her joy became quickly tempered, though, as she felt another spirit diminish, as she watched Elbryan's life force fade fast before her. The woman came from her trance, back to her corporeal form, to see Markwart standing on shaky legs, staring at her in disbelief, to see Elbryan lying next to her, his body very still and very pale, surrounded by blood.

The woman fell over her lover, called to him desperately, tried to reach out for him with the hematite. But as she went down, all of her energy gone, she felt the floor come up after her, swallowing her in a profound blackness.

Markwart watched with horror. They had beaten him—no, not just him, but also that inner voice that had guided him for so long, a voice that he recognized now not as insight, but as a separate being! For now the Father Abbot knew the truth of it, and knew his life to be a lie, his course to be one of darkness and not redemption.

He could have killed them both, but that was the furthest thought from his mind at that terrible moment. He went to them, confused, and when he realized the man to be beyond his help and heard the noise of rushing feet down below in the house, he scooped the woman in his arms and moved, stiff-legged, to the door.

He came through, not even noticing the small form of the elf standing right beside it.

Poor Juraviel didn't know what to make of it. He heard Pony groan and sensed that the old man—and how old and battered Markwart appeared!—would not, could not, harm her further. No, something had happened to Markwart; the elf understood that the man would not live for long, that he had been beaten. He thought to put his sword into the man's back anyway, and refrained only because he realized the terrible consequences such an action might have for his folk. He started to go to Pony, thinking to take her away from the horrid wretch who had brought her so much pain, but then he saw his friend, who had been as his son, lying still on the floor.

Juraviel rushed to Elbryan's side. He tried to tuck the spilling guts back with his bare hands.

But it was too late, he knew.

The ranger opened his green eyes.

"Pony lives," Juraviel said, moving very close to the ranger's ashen face.

"She won," the ranger gasped. "The demon is purged." His eyes rolled back and closed and he drew in a deep breath.

"Your son!" Juraviel said to him, made him hear in the very last instants of his life. "Your son lives, in Andur'Blough Inninness, under the care of Lady Dasslerond!"

Elbryan's eyes opened, his grip tightening on the elf's arm, and he managed a smile.

And then he died.

Bishop Francis, first up the stairs and first into the grand corridor, came upon Markwart, walking stiffly, bearing Pony in his arms. The younger monk grabbed his mentor and took the burden, laying Pony gently on the floor, then catching the falling Markwart and easing his way down.

The others crashed into the hall behind him, Roger yelling out for Pony.

"I chose wrong," Markwart said to Francis, managing a weak smile. "With Jojonah, with Avelyn. Yes, with Avelyn. I should have recognized the truth."

"No, Father," Francis started to say.

Markwart's dark eyes opened wide and he grabbed Francis tightly, with strength beyond his broken frame. "Yes!" he hissed. "Yes! I chose wrong. See to my Church, dear Francis. Become the shepherd of the flock and not the dictator. But beware—" A convulsion hit the man hard, knocking him from Francis' grasp to fall back to the floor. The younger monk moved over him immediately, propping his head up.

"Beware!" Markwart said again. "Beware that in your quest for humanism you do not steal the mystery of spiritualism."

Another convulsion wracked the man, and when it ended, the Abellican Church had no leader.

"She is alive!" Bishop Francis heard Roger cry behind him. He turned to see Roger working furiously over the woman—and to see Roger quietly pocket her gemstones in the process.

Behind the man and the prone woman stood King Danube and his advisers, with soldiers behind them keeping the monks at bay. But not Bradwarden. The centaur, wounded though he was, pushed through the Allheart line and past the King, heading for the room at the end of the hall. Some soldiers moved to pursue, but Danube motioned them back.

"The Father Abbot!" old Je'howith cried, coming through the door.

"Is dead," Bishop Francis answered softly.

"Assassin!" Je'howith shrieked. "The Father Abbot's blood demands justice! Guards!"

"Shut your mouth!" Brother Braumin insisted, pulling free of the soldier holding him—and King Danube motioned for the Allheart knight to step back and let the monk free. "If Dalebert Markwart is dead, it is because of the dark road he chose to walk!" Braumin declared openly.

"Sacrilege!" Je'howith yelled in the man's face, but the next order to shut up came from a most unexpected source.

"You heard the man tell you to be quiet, good abbot," Bishop Francis insisted. "We will discuss this matter at length among are own—at a college that we must quickly convene."

"Brother Francis!" Je'howith started to protest.

"But I warn you," Francis went on, ignoring the man, "if you side with dead Markwart against Brother Braumin and the others, I will go against you."

Je'howith stammered and stuttered, and had no reply. He looked to the King, but Danube offered no support.

Francis turned to Pony, and to Roger, who nodded that he believed the woman would live. "By the Father Abbot's own dying words," said Francis, "the time has come for change in the Church. Look at her, the disciple of Avelyn, named as an outlaw. And yet, I will nominate her as the Mother Abbess of the new Church."

"What foolishness is this?" Je'howith demanded.

"At the same time I nominate Brother Avelyn Desbris as a candidate for canonization," the surprising Bishop Francis added.

"St. Avelyn!" Brother Viscenti cried.

"Impossible!" shouted Je'howith.

"Why do we tolerate them, my King?" asked a disgusted Duke Kalas.

Danube managed a chuckle, for in truth, he had heard enough from the troublesome Abellican Church. "I hereby dismiss the office of bishop of Palmaris," he said, his tone leaving little room for debate. "And I warn you all. Put your house in order, else I shall do it for you. If a monk can assume the role of bishop, then similar precedents can place the King in the role of Father Abbot!"

Francis looked to Braumin and nodded determinedly.

Je'howith, catching the signal, wondered if he would survive with his position of abbot intact.

Bradwarden came out of the room then, bearing the body of Elbryan, and there would be no time of celebration for those who had known the man as friend and companion.

Brother Braumin and the other monks bowed their heads in respect. Roger fell over Pony, sobbing for himself and for her.

Outside the manor house, standing in the glass from the smashed window, Belli'mar Juraviel looked up one last time, his heart broken. He understood that it was time for him to return to Andur'Blough Inninness, time for him to run away from the humans and their foolish battles.

What he could not understand, though, was how the body of Marcalo De'Unnero had disappeared.

Epilogue

She heard them arguing in the house behind her, heard her own name spoken many times, but it was unimportant to Pony that gray and windy summer day. Everything seemed unimportant at that moment, save the two commemorative markers set in the garden of Chasewind Manor. One had been a gift from King Danube, a symbolic gesture as the man had reclaimed Chasewind Manor. The other had come from Brother Braumin and, surprisingly, from Brother Francis, to signify the support of the new Abellican Church.

Or was it still the Abellican Church? During the heated arguments, Brother Braumin had hinted that his group and any who would follow— and his opponent, Abbot Je'howith, had recognized that the list of followers might be long—might splinter from the Abellican Church to begin the Church of Avelyn.

"They love us now," the woman said to the marker. It was only a marker, for Elbryan's body wasn't interred there. Pony would not allow it. Her husband was to be buried in the grove beyond Dundalis, the place where he had found the grave of his uncle Mather and where he had earned Tempest. To that end, Bradwarden and Roger were leaving Palmaris that very day, the centaur pulling a caisson carrying Elbryan's casket.

Pony could hardly believe he was gone. She stood there, very still, trying to replay the events that had brought her to this terrible place. But she could not fathom it all. Half her soul had been torn away, and now she was empty.

They talked of making her the Mother Abbess, the leader of the Church. King Danube had promised her much, perhaps even the barony of Palmaris, in honor of her service to the kingdom—for the defeat of Markwart was now being heralded as a victory for the Crown. At that moment, despite her desire to do good, Pony hoped that none of it would come true, that they would all just leave her alone with her memories and her pain. Perhaps she could be a great leader for the Church, perhaps take it in the direction Avelyn had espoused.

She hardly cared.

For all she knew was emptiness and helplessness, a sense of unreality that this terrible thing could not have happened. When she thought back to the previous fall, pregnant in Caer Tinella, making love with Elbryan on the field, she nearly toppled over with weakness.

A gentle hand touched Pony's shoulder, and she turned to see Kalas, the interim baron of Palmaris, and Constance Pemblebury.

"Are you going with them to the north?" Constance asked.

"Tomorrow, perhaps," Pony answered noncommittally. "Or if this business with the Church is not finished, then perhaps sometime later on." In truth, Pony did not want to go back to Dundalis, could not bear to watch Elbryan's casket be lowered into the ground.

They walked solemnly, staring straight ahead and not at the crowds gathered along the roads, many throwing flowers at the caisson. Elbryan, Nightbird, was fast becoming legend to the folk of Palmaris, something that both Roger and Bradwarden welcomed cautiously. For though they knew their friend was worthy of any honor bestowed him, they wanted to remember the truth of the man, and didn't want that truth, impressive enough of its own accord, blurred by ridiculously exaggerated legend.

This moment, Elbryan's moment, would live on in the memories of all who watched—and that audience included King Danube Brock Ursal himself.

A contingent of Allheart horsemen led the way, and would accompany the caisson all the way to Dundalis.

They came through the northern gate of Palmaris to find many more folk, all the farmers of the northern fields. Then another onlooker reared and cried out; mighty Symphony on a hillock not far away.

"He knows," Bradwarden assured Roger.

As if on cue, the great stallion charged down the hill to join them, cantering past the Allheart soldiers, who sat in silent awe of the magnificent steed, stronger and swifter than even their famed To-gai-ru horses.

Symphony pawed at the caisson, and Bradwarden, ever attuned to the desires of horses, pulled the harness from over his head and strapped it on the stallion.

On they went, quietly to the north.

From far away, Belli'mar Juraviel watched the procession, the last journey of his dear friend, then turned for home.

Unseen by the elf—though not so far away—Marcalo De'Unnero watched, too. His physical wounds were nearly healed by the power of his hematite ring, but his emotional scars ran deeper. The monk—former monk, it would seem—came to question so many things as he watched the outpouring for Nightbird, as he secretly listened to the conversations of farmers, damning Markwart, praising the ranger, and speaking in hopeful terms of a great and miraculous change within the Abellican Church.

De'Unnero could hardly believe the turn of events, but he had too many problems of his own to sit and ponder them. He had no idea of where his favored gemstone might be, had not seen it in weeks, and believed that it had somehow merged with his soul. For now he was man and beast, and though he could often willfully shift from one form to the other, or to something in between, there were other times, times of anger or when he smelled prey, that the urge to fall into the form of the tiger overwhelmed him.

A pall settled over Andur'Blough Inninness later that summer, when Belli'mar Juraviel returned with news that Nightbird had fallen. Though the war had ended favorably, though Juraviel had returned to them, though the child of Nightbird and Pony was growing strong and healthy, the loss of Nightbird and Ni'estiel weighed heavily on the small and intimate family of the Touel'alfar.

The one real bright spot seemed to be the child, so full of smiles.

Juraviel and Lady Dasslerond went to the babe soon after Juraviel's return, standing over it as it lay on the shining green grass, the Lady bending low to stroke his soft cheek.

"He will grow strong and special," Dasslerond remarked, "will come to greatness beyond that of his father and his mother."

"She lives," Juraviel replied.

Dasslerond turned a firm stare on the elf. Of course she already knew about Pony, and knew, too, that Juraviel had only made the remark to hint that he believed that the child belonged with its mother. Lady Dasslerond would hear none of that, her stare reminded Juraviel. They had taken the babe as their protégé, the child of Nightbird and not of Elbryan, the child of Andur'Blough Inninness, and to the elven lady, the issue was settled.

"I aided them in their escape," Juraviel admitted.

Lady Dasslerond gave a little laugh. "Do you believe that I did not know you would do as much when I allowed you to return to them?" she asked, putting her companion at ease. "You chose well on this matter."

"What of Jilseponie?" Juraviel asked. "She knows *bi'nelle dasada*. We cannot take that from her."

Lady Dasslerond didn't seem concerned. "Jilseponie was a fine companion to Nightbird," she replied. "The woman will not betray him by sharing that which he taught her."

Juraviel hoped the lady was right, for he knew that Dasslerond would be watching the humans more closely for a long while, and that if Pony did begin to teach the sword dance, to King's soldiers or to monks, she would be taken prisoner by the Touel'alfar.

If she was lucky, and if Dasslerond was feeling particularly compassionate.

A giggle from below turned their attention to the babe. His crooked little grin resembled that of young Elbryan when he had first come to Andur' Blough Inninness, but the child showed the same bright blue sparkles in his eyes as his mother.

Except when the elves left him alone, for then came a hint of a red fire behind those blue orbs, a trait inherited not from his mother nor his father, but planted within the child, within Pony's womb, by the demon dactyl during her first battle with Dalebert Markwart, the corporeal vessel of Bestesbulzibar.

About the Author

R. A. SALVATORE was born in Massachusetts in 1959. His first published novel was *The Crystal Shard*. He has since published more than two dozen novels, including the *New York Times* bestsellers *The Halfling's Gem, Sojourn, The Legacy*, and *Starless Night*. He makes his home in Massachussetts with his wife, Diane, and their three children.